Nicola Barker's eight previous novels include *Darkmans* (shortlisted for the 2007 Booker and Ondaatje prizes, and winner of the Hawthornden), *Wide Open* (winner of the 2000 IMPAC Dublin Literary Award) and *Clear* (longlisted for The Booker Prize in 2004). She has also written two prize-winning collections of short-stories. Her work has been translated into more than twenty languages. She lives in east London.

From the reviews of *The Yips*:

'This bar-room story of golf, pubic-hair tattoo-artists, Muslim sex therapists and peculiar sporting injuries has a stalk-eyed gravity all its own. No writer gets the darkness, hilarity and irrelevance of modern Britain better'

TIM MARTIN, *Daily Telegraph*, Books of the Year

'A bravura concoction of golf, social comedy and gloriously bonkers invention' JAMES KIDD, *Independent*, Books of the Year

'Barker is a most peculiar writer. This is a good thing. Her dementedly imaginative mind paints modern Britain as a grotesque carnival'

Financial Times, Books of the Year

'Out-Amised Amis with its freewheeling inventive golfing confessional-cum-state-of-the-nation-satire – set in Luton'

BOYD TONKIN, *Independent*, Books of the Year

D0293347

30128 80108 772 6

'Tolstoyan in its heft if not its tone, it's a compendium of unhappy families, being unhappy in often staggeringly unusual ways ... more consistently surprising than *War and Peace*'

STEPHEN ABELL, *Sunday Telegraph*

'There is nothing conventional about *The Yips* ... its originality, its charm or its peculiar beauty ... yet [it is] is full of straightforward reading pleasures. She combines serious intentions with lightness of touch, toughness with compassion, and has a unique imagination'

EDMUND GORDON, *Sunday Times*

'Deliriously funny ... Barker's oeuvre is one of the high points of contemporary English writing; her work dares and dances while her peers plod and preach' STUART KELLY, *Scotsman*

By the same author

Love Your Enemies
Reversed Forecast
Small Holdings
Heading Inland
Wide Open
Five Miles from Outer Hope
Behindlings
Clear
Darkmans
Burley Cross Postbox Theft

THE YIPS
NICOLA BARKER

FOURTH ESTATE · London

Fourth Estate
An imprint of HarperCollins*Publishers*
77–85 Fulham Palace Road
Hammersmith, London W6 8JB

This Fourth Estate paperback edition published 2013
1

First published in Great Britain by Fourth Estate in 2012

A catalogue record for this book is
available from the British Library

ISBN 978-0-00-747666-4

Typeset in Plantin Light by
G&M Designs Limited, Raunds, Northamptonshire
Printed and bound in Great Britain by
Clays Ltd, St Ives plc

In fond remembrance of Owain 'Oz' Wright;
The Man, The Voice

yips (y ps). pl. n. Nervousness or tension that causes an athlete to fail to perform effectively, especially in missing short putts in golf.

The Free Dictionary

1

Stuart Ransom, professional golfer, is drunkenly reeling off an
interminable series of stats about the women's game in Korea
(or the Ladies Game, as he is determined to have it): 'Don't
scowl at me, beautiful …!' – directed, with his trademark
Yorkshire twinkle, at Jen, who lounges, sullenly, behind the
hotel bar. 'They *like* to be called ladies. In fact they *demand* it.
I mean …' Ransom lobs a well-aimed peanut at her – she
ducks – and it strikes a lovely, clear note against a Gordon's
Gin bottle. '… they *are* ladies, for Christsakes!'

It's well past midnight on an oppressively hot and muggy
Sunday in July and Ransom is the only remaining customer
still cheerfully demanding service from the fine vantage point
of his squeaking barstool at the Thistle, a clean but generic
hotel which flies its five, proud flags hard up against the
multi-storey car park and an especially unforgiving slab of
Luton's Arndale.

'But *why* did you change your booking from the Leaside?'
Jen petulantly demands (as she fishes the stray peanut from its
current hidey-hole between the Wild Turkey and the Kahlua).
'The Leaside's pure class.'

'Eh?'

Ransom is momentarily caught off his stride. He was just idly
pondering the wonky pathway of spotless scalp which lies –
like a seductive trickle of tropical-white sand – between Jen's
scruffy, dark-rooted, peroxide-blonde ponytails, and then, as
she spins back around (pinching that errant nut, fastidiously,

between her finger and thumb), he ponders the voluptuous outline of her pert, nineteen-year-old breasts beneath her starchy, cream-coloured work blouse (assessing these other – rather more intimate – physical attributes with the keen yet dispassionate eyes of a man who has oft pitted his talents against the merciless dips and mounds of the Old Course at St Andrews).

'I'd give anything to stay at the Leaside,' Jen persists, gazing dreamily up at the light-fitment (where three stray midges are joyriding, frenetically, around the bulb). 'The Leaside's so quaint – perched on its own little hill, right in the heart of town, but just out of all the hubbub …'

Jen's pierced tongue trips on the word hubbub and she frowns –

Hubbub?

Ransom stares around him – tipsy and slightly bewildered – struggling to assess the aesthetic shortcomings of his current environs, then starts, theatrically, at the nightmarish spectre of earth-shattering mediocrity he suddenly – quite unwittingly – finds himself party to. He runs an unsteady hand through his short, brown, fastidiously managed head of hair and then instinctively reaches towards his shirt pocket (groping for his trusty pack of Bensons), but falters, mid-manoeuvre, as he peers, blearily, through the large, plate-glass window directly to his left. Beyond that window a small cluster of shadowy figures may be seen, consorting together, ominously, in the half-light. He debates what his chances are of sneaking a furtive puff inside.

'Hub-bub,' Gene, the replacement barman, parrots to himself, amused, as he polishes a low, glass table in the adjacent snug.

Ransom glances over at Gene, then turns to inspect Jen again, who has momentarily stopped considering the countless, bizarre ramifications of the word hubbub for just long enough to become horribly aware of the proximity of the front desk (not actually visible from where she's standing). 'Although there's really nothing out there to match our incomparable health and leisure club facilities,' she proclaims loudly, with suitably glassy eyes and a ghoulish smile. Ransom sighs, squints down at his watch, grimaces, clears his throat, takes out his phone, checks his texts, and then quickly goes on to discuss how there are plenty of successful Korean ladies doing extremely well on the American circuit right now. In fact, he says, draining his glass, there are several whose careers he even takes an active interest in (Aree Song for one, Birdie Kim for another, Inbee Park for a third: 'Aren't their names just completely friggin' brilliant?') and not only because he finds Korean ladies pretty damn hot …

He turns and asks Gene (who is now removing his empty glass and replacing his damp, paper coaster with a clean one) if he finds Korean ladies hot, and as he says so he darts a mischievous glance at Jen again, who neglects to look back because she has been obliged to move to the small, transparent hatch – which connects the bar to the overpass – and calmly inform a persistent individual who is banging on the glass there that they are no longer serving (by dint of a sharp, slicing movement across her taut, milky throat). The individual curses, gesticulates (a deft two-finger salute), then scuttles off.

'Thanks,' Jen snarls after him. '*Charmed.*'

Gene – following a brief moment's thought – politely confesses to Ransom that he's never previously given this issue (about the relative hotness – or notness – of female Koreans) much serious consideration. Ransom appraises Gene, at his leisure, and decides that he is an intensely dull yet profoundly dependable kind of fellow who bears a passing resemblance – the short, swept-back, auburn hair, the square jaw, the calm, hazel eyes – to one of his sporting heroes: a young Tom Watson. His own eyes mist up and he blinks, poignantly (although why the perfectly successful and functional Watson might be inclined to inspire Ransom's compassion at this juncture is – and will remain – something of a puzzle).

'All work and no play, eh?' Ransom says, pityingly, indicating towards a neighbouring barstool with a benign and inclusive sweep of his arm. Gene frowns. In truth, he feels scant inclination to get involved in a fatuous discussion with the tipsy Yorkshireman (he's on duty and has a certain number of chores to complete before knocking off at one) but then he detects an odd look – almost of desperation – in Ransom's bloodshot eyes and slowly relents.

Okay, Gene confides (backing into the stool and perching a single, taut buttock on it), so yes, if put on the spot he will admit that he does think Korean woman are quite beautiful. They have a certain measure of ... of poise, a certain ... a certain understated ... uh ... *grace* ...

Ransom scowls when Gene uses the word 'grace'. The word 'grace' has no place – no place at all – in the kind of conversation he was angling for. Gene (as luck would have it) is also scowling now (and rapidly backtracking), saying that, on reflection, he hasn't actually met that many Korean women in his life, apart from a couple who work in local restaurants. He says he therefore supposes that his assessment of the virtues of Korean women – as a unified class – is based entirely on a series of ill-considered – even stereotypical – ideas he has about Eastern women, and he is sure that this is a little stupid – even patronizing – of him because Korean women are doubtless very idiosyncratic, with their own distinct features and dreams and ideas and habits.

'I'll grant you that,' Ransom concurs with a sage nod (informing Jen of his need for another drink with an imperiously raised finger). 'They've got much fuller tits than the Japanese.'

Gene draws back, dismayed, uncertain whether Ransom is joking or not. Ransom collapses forward on to the bar, shaking his head (apparently experiencing this same problem, first-hand). '*Fuuuuck*,' he groans, 'I honestly can't believe I just said that.'

Gene peers over at Jen (who has chosen to ignore Ransom's request and is now cleaning out the coffee machine). He stands up and goes to fetch Ransom the drink himself (thereby symbolically re-emphasizing the wide emotional, intellectual and psychological distance between them by dint of the happy barrier that is the bar).

As Ransom continues to groan (banging his forehead, gently, on the bar top), Gene goes on to say how he once watched a fascinating documentary about a Japanese girl who was kidnapped by the North Korean government – quite randomly – as she walked home from school one day. The girl was called Nagumi … no … no, *Me*-gumi, he corrects himself. Apparently (he continues) the North Koreans kidnapped many such young Japanese during this particular historical timeframe (the mid- to late 1970s) to study their behaviour so that their spies could pretend to be Japanese while undertaking terrorist attacks abroad. It transpires that the cultural differences between the North Koreans and the Japanese are very marked (Gene quickly warms to his theme), the way they wash their faces, for example, is very different (he impersonates the two styles: one a lazy splash, the other a more frenetic rub). The way they excuse themselves after sneezing. The way they say hello. The way they blow their noses or position their napkins. All tiny but vital cultural differences.

'Michelle Wie,' Stuart Ransom suddenly butts in (having taken a long draught of his new drink, straight from the bottle), 'has *massive* feet. Whenever I watch her play I just keep staring at her feet. They're friggin' *huge* …'
Gene frowns.
'But I still find her pretty damn tasty all the same,' Ransom avows, glancing down at his phone again and noticing, as he

does so, that his hand is shaking. He grimaces, clenches his fingers into a tight fist and then shoves his hand, scowling furiously, into his trouser pocket.

'*Merde!* This is useless! My hand just keeps shaking!' her mother grumbles – in her strange, heavily accented English – awkwardly adjusting a toothbrush between her fingers.
'Because you're holding it all wrong,' Valentine explains. 'You're holding it like you'd hold a pen. Why not try and hold it like you'd hold a … a …' – she thinks hard for a second – 'a *hair*brush?'
As she speaks, Valentine lifts a warm, bare foot from the bathroom linoleum (producing a tiny, glutinous, farting sound) and then dreamily inspects the steamy imprint that remains. She imagines her neat heel as the nose (or jaw) of a cartoon reindeer, and her toes as its modest, five-pronged crown of truncated horns.
'I DON'T FUCKING REMEMBER!' her mother suddenly yells, hurling the offending toothbrush into the toilet bowl.
'Bloody hell, Mum!' Valentine retrieves the toothbrush, runs it under the hot tap, squeezes on some more paste and then patiently proffers it back to her.
'I CAN'T USE THAT FILTHY THING NOW!' her mother bellows. 'ARE YOU COMPLETELY INSANE?!'
'*Shhhh!*' Valentine whispers, pointing to the door. 'It's after twelve. You'll wake Nessa.'
'But *how* do I hold a hairbrush?'
Her mother begins hunting around the bathroom for a hairbrush.
'Like this …' Valentine neatly demonstrates exactly how to hold the toothbrush.
'But that's a *tooth*brush and I want a *hair*brush,' her mother snaps. 'I want to know how I'd hold a *hair*brush.'

Valentine opens the bathroom cabinet. 'Here's a comb,' she says, removing an old nit comb from behind a medicated shampoo bottle.

She passes it over.

Her mother takes the comb. She holds it correctly, instinctively. She stares at it for a moment, blinks, and then: 'Why the hell have you given me a fucking nit comb?' she demands.

'For some reason I always thought Michelle Wie was part-Hawaiian,' Gene muses – half to himself – as he polishes a glass.

'Nah-*ah*. You're confusing her with Tiger Woods, mate.' Ransom shrugs.

'Michelle *who*?' Jen suddenly interjects after a five-second hiatus (Jen is generally a bright, engaging conversationalist, but she's just completing an exhausting, twelve-hour shift and also has a small – yet resilient – raft of 'subsidiary' issues to contend with, which Ransom can't possibly have any inkling of, i.e. a) the tail-end of a painful dose of conjunctivitis – caught from her cat, Wookey, a magnificent, pedigree Maine Coon – combined with a prodigious pair of false eyelashes which are so long and audacious that they tickle both her cheeks, distractingly, every time she blinks, b) a ludicrously handsome, lusty and untrustworthy Irish boyfriend – by the name of Sinclair – who is currently living it up for a week on a lads-only break in Tangier, and c) the frightful responsibility of three E grade A-levels to re-sit over the summer. Jen longs to become a vet and is obsessed by Australian marsupials; their fluffy tails, their tiny hands, their huge, saucer-like eyes. Her favourite kind of marsupial is the sugar-glider. She even invented her own cocktail of the same name – a sickly combination of cold espresso, coconut milk and Malibu – which they sell at the bar simply to indulge her).

'Michelle Wie,' Gene says, politely glancing over at Ransom for confirmation, 'is a young, female golfer who ruffled a few feathers a while back by insisting on competing professionally alongside the males –'

'Why can't women play golf?' Ransom jovially interrupts him, with a leer.

Pause.

'I don't know,' Gene answers, cautiously, 'why can't women play golf?'

'Because they're good with an iron ...' Ransom's voice cracks with ill-suppressed hilarity, 'but they can't drive! *Boom Boom!*'

Gene smiles, thinly.

'Sorry,' Ransom apologizes, simulating embarrassment, 'that one's old as the friggin' hills.'

'Michelle *Wee*?!' Jen snorts (totally ignoring Ransom's attempted quip). 'That's brilliant!'

'She's a perfectly good little athlete,' Ransom allows, 'but she's ruined her game by over-swinging. Fact is she *can't* compete with the men. Not possible. She simply hasn't got the power in her upper torso.'

'Although I imagine the huge advances in club technology over the last decade or so –' Gene interjects.

'*Phooey*,' Ransom slaps him down, irritated, 'because when club technology improves, the male players automatically hit that much further themselves.'

'*God*,' Jen groans, rolling her eyes, boredly, 'what *is* this fatal attraction between footballers and bloody golf, eh?'

'Huh?' Ransom's head snaps around. He frowns. He looks a little confused.

'I just don't get it,' Jen persists (ignoring a pointed look that Gene is now darting at her), 'because golf's so unbelievably *dull*. I mean why rattle on endlessly about golf all night when there's so much other great stuff to talk about, like ... I dunno ...' She throws up her hands.

'Basket-weaving,' Gene suggests, wryly.

'Topiary,' Ransom helpfully volunteers.

'The comic novels of Saki,' Gene effortlessly parries.

'UFOs.' Ransom grins.

'The worst services on the M4,' Gene deftly volleys, 'between Reading and Newport.'

'The *best* services on the M1,' Ransom vigorously retaliates, 'between Watford and Leeds.'

'I've never been to the North,' Jen confesses (with cheerful candour), at exactly the same moment as Gene hollers, '*Leicester Forest East!*' (then blushes).

'I favour Shovel myself.' Ransom shrugs.

'Although I *have* been to Norfolk,' Jen concedes.

'Norfolk?' Ransom echoes, bewildered. 'Norfolk isn't *in* the North, you bloomin' half-wit!'

'I *know* that!' Jen snaps.

'Crop circles!' Gene promptly endeavours to divert them.

'The Chinese Horoscope!' (Ransom's easily distracted.)

'The current export price of British beef,' Gene casually raises him.

'Which is the luckier number' – Ransom plucks at his unshaven chin with comedic thoughtfulness – 'three or seven?'

'Stones versus Beatles!' Gene's starting to sweat a little.

'Leeches!' Ransom whoops (slamming down his beer bottle – for extra emphasis – then cursing as it foams up, over and on to the bar top).

Leeches?

'But I *love* leeches!' Jen squeals, baby-clapping delightedly. 'Let's talk about leeches! Let's! Let's! Oh, *do* let's!'

Ransom recoils slightly at the unexpected violence of Jen's reaction.

'Jen's into nature,' Gene explains (with an avuncular smile), 'she's hoping to become a vet when she eventually grows up.'

Jen shoots Gene a *faux*-filthy/*faux*-flirty look.

'Okay ...' Ransom tosses a quick peanut into his mouth and then launches, vaingloriously, into the requisite anecdote.

'So I was playing this shonky tournament in Japan once,' he starts off, 'and I sliced a shot on the fourth which landed just to the right of the green in this really tricky area of rough –' 'Hang on a minute,' Jen interrupts, holding up her hand, exasperated. 'Please, please, *please* tell me we're not back to talking about sodding *golf* again?!'

'Did you hear that?' Valentine asks, cocking her head and listening intently.

'What?' Her mother stops brushing. She's been brushing so diligently that her gums are bleeding and the white foam in her mouth has turned pink.

'A squeak ... this tiny squeak and then a sharp kind of ... of scratching sound.'

Her mother also listens. A cat pads into the bathroom, sits down and commences licking its paws. There are now three cats in the room: one on the windowsill, one in the bath (where it's just squatting to defecate over the plug-hole) and one sitting by the door.

'This house is full of stinking cats,' her mother grumbles. 'How can we have rats in a house full of stinking cats?' Valentine doesn't answer. She closes her eyes. She places a finger to her lips.

Her mother ignores her. 'Bobby's *sur le point de chier énormément*,' she announces.

'Huh?'

Valentine is still listening out, intently, for another squeak.

'Bobby. The stinking cat. He's shitting on the plug.'

Valentine's eyes fly open. She turns. She does a quick double-take.

'No! *Bobby!*' she yells. 'STOP!'

★ ★ ★

'Football's bad enough,' Jen grumbles, attacking the coffee machine with a renewed ferocity, 'but golf? *Urgh!* You just can't get away from it. It's everywhere – like a contagious *disease.*'

'"A good walk, spoiled," I believe the saying goes.'

As he speaks, Gene reaches under the counter and withdraws a small, black notepad (with a broken, red Bic shoved into its metal binder). He opens the book, removes the pen, jots down a quick reminder about the squeaking barstool, then turns to the back page and in large, block letters writes: IT'S STUART RANSOM – THE FAMOUS PRO GOLFER, STUPID!

He then casually leans back and proffers Jen the pad.

'In fact this really lovely friend of mine called Candy Rose, who I first met at jazz/tap classes when I was nine ...' Jen pauses, ruminatively, pointedly ignoring the pad. 'Although – strictly speaking – we already knew each other, by sight, from nursery school ...'

Ransom yawns and glances down at his phone.

'*Anyhow,*' Jen blithely continues, 'Candy works for this animal refuge near Wandon End, and they were desperate to expand their workspace into some adjacent farmland. The farmer seemed perfectly happy to rent it out to them, but for some strange reason the council kept raising all these petty objections to their planning application. Then the next thing we know, this huge, twenty-five-acre plot –'

'The yamabiru.' Ransom suddenly turns, quite deliberately, and addresses himself directly to Gene. 'The Japanese land leech. The mountains are their natural habitat, but over recent years they've taken to hitching a ride down on to the flatlands with packs of roaming boar and deer. They've become a real pest in the towns where they enjoy slithering into people's socks and quietly ingesting a quick takeaway meal ...'

'*Jesus!*' Gene is revolted. 'How big?'

'Small. Around half an inch to begin with, but they can swell to almost ten times that size. I had one gnawing away at my ankle but I didn't have a clue about it till I felt this nasty twinge by the fourth and yanked off my shoe. At first I thought it was just a thorn or a thistle, but then I realized my sock was totally soaked ...' he pauses, dramatically, '... saturated with my own blood.'

'Wow!' Jen is clearly impressed. 'A *land* leech? That's wild!'

'A yamabiru.' Ransom nods. 'I swear I nearly shat myself.'

'Spell that out for me ...' Jen snatches the pad from Gene. 'I'm gonna look it up on the internet.'

'Did it hurt?' Gene wonders.

'*Nah*. It was more the shock of it than anything. I mean the sheer *volume* of ...'

'*Wow!*' Jen repeats. 'So what did you do with it? Did you kill it? Did you stamp on it? *SPLAT!*'
Jen stamps her foot, violently. 'Did it explode like a water-bomb? I *bet* you did. I *bet* you killed it.'

'Damn, fuckin' right I would've!' Ransom exclaims, indignant. 'But I never got the chance. The little swine'd drunk its fill and scarpered.'

'So how ...?' Gene looks mystified.

'The course quack. He identified the wound. Said it was a pretty common problem on golf courses in those parts.'

'*Yik!*' Jen is mesmerized. She is still holding the pad.

'Did you quit the match?' Gene wonders.

'*Quit?*' Ransom looks astounded. 'Whadd'ya take me for?! I poured a small bottle of iced water over my head, smoked a quick fag, downed a quart of Scotch and finished in a perfectly respectable five over par.'

A short silence follows. Ransom takes a long swig of his beer.

'Although the leeches were the least of my problems in Japan.' He hiccups. '*Oops.*' He places his hand over his mouth. 'It turns out the tournament had been arranged by the Yakuza ...'

'The Japanese mafia?' Gene's eyes widen.

'Yep. They were extorting cash from local businessmen by forcing them to take part and then charging them huge entry fees. I kept wondering at the time why all the course officials seemed so jittery ...'

'Bloody *golf*!' Jen exclaims, slapping the pad down, forcefully. 'Even the *word* is ridiculous – like a cat vomiting up a giant hair-ball: *GOLLUFF!*' she huskily intones, rolling her eyes while making an alarming retching motion with her throat. Both men turn to stare at her, alarmed. 'Just name me any game,' Jen challenges them, 'I mean *any* sport on the planet more selfish than golf is.'

Silence.

'Formula One,' Gene finally responds.

'Shooting,' Ransom suggests, cocking and aiming an imaginary gun at her.

'Yeah ...' Jen's plainly not convinced. 'But could you really call that a sport, as such?'

'*KA-BOOM!*'

Ransom fires. It's a clean shot.

'They have an Olympic team,' Gene says, snatching up the pad again, opening it and proffering it to her.

'It's not only golf, though.' Jen waves the pad away. 'I can't stand tennis, either. I *hate* tennis. To my way of thinking it's just a game invented *by* idiots, *for* idiots. Simple as.'

Before Jen can further substantiate this hypothesis, Gene has grabbed her by the arm and spun her around to face the back wall of the bar. 'What's got into you tonight?' he hisses. Jen gazes up at him, wide-eyed. 'I hate tennis, Gene.' She shrugs (raising both hands, limp-wristedly, like a world-weary Jewish dowager). 'Is that suddenly such a crime?'

Gene studies her face for a second, grimaces, releases her arm, then slaps the black notebook shut and tosses it – defeated – back under the counter.

Ransom downs the remainder of his beer in a single gulp, then burps, majestically, from the other side of the bar. Jen snorts, ribaldly. Gene shoots her a warning look.

Her mother swallows the paste and then gently belches.

'You really shouldn't swallow it,' Valentine mutters. She's just flushed the cat mess down the toilet and is now washing her hands, fastidiously, under the hot tap.

'I've always swallowed it,' her mother maintains.

'Well, you taught *me* not to swallow it.' Valentine turns the tap off.

Her mother inspects her teeth, critically, in the bathroom mirror.

'You're not meant to swallow it,' Valentine persists, 'you're meant to spit it out.'

'Really? *Il dit ça sur le tube?*'

'Pardon?'

'Does it say that on the tube?'

Valentine shrugs. 'I don't know.'

'Have a look.'

Her mother grabs the tube and proffers it to Valentine. Valentine shakes the water off her hands, takes the tube and inspects it.

'Does it say you shouldn't swallow?'

Her mother peers at the tube over Valentine's shoulder.

'No.' Valentine frowns. 'But that doesn't necessarily ...'

Her mother recommences brushing again. Valentine places the tube back into the tooth mug. She watches her mother for a while and then: 'I think you've probably been brushing for long enough now,' she says.

'Really?' Her mother stops brushing. 'How long is "enough"?'

Valentine shrugs. 'Two minutes?'

'And how long have I ...?'

'About four.'

Her mother stares at her, blankly.

'Four minutes. One, two, three, *four* ...'
Valentine slowly counts the digits out on to her fingers. 'So you've basically been brushing for almost double the amount of time you need to.'
Valentine illustrates this point, visually, by dividing the four fingers into two.

Her mother stares at Valentine's fingers, intrigued. 'If two twos are double,' she wonders, 'then what about three threes? Are three threes double?'

'Uh ... no.' Valentine shakes her head. 'Three times three is nine. That's triple. Two times three is double.'

'Two threes are six,' her mother says.

'Exactly.' Valentine nods, encouragingly. 'Two times three is six. Well done.'

She holds up six fingers and divides them in half.

'Okay' – her mother is now concentrating extremely hard – 'and twice times fifty-fivety?'

'Two times fifty-five is one hundred and ten.' Valentine nods again. 'Well done. That's double, too.'

'And twice times –'

'You generally say two times,' Valentine interrupts, 'and it's always double. Two of anything is always double. That's the rule.'

She turns to dry her hands on a towel.

'My teeth still feel furry, though,' her mother murmurs, taking a small step forward and staring, fixedly, into the mirror again. 'I want them to feel clean. I want them to feel *toutes lisses*.'

'We've talked about this before.' Valentine gently takes the toothbrush from her. 'You just *think* they aren't clean, but they are. Remember how the dentist ...?'

'You're being unbelievably patronizing,' her mother exclaims, suddenly irritable.

She pauses.

'*Condescendant!* And by the way,' she continues, 'I find it really disgusting that you flushed the cat mess down the loo.'

She goes and peers into the toilet bowl.

'*Je n'ai pas t'élevée comme ça! Ça fait trop commun.*'

Valentine is inspecting her own, clear complexion in the bathroom mirror. The cat sitting closest to the doorway commences scratching itself, vigorously.

'The toilet bowl is filthy! It's disgusting,' her mother grumbles. She turns to inspect the cat. 'And these cats are disgusting, too. So many of them, *et tellement poilus!* In fact this entire room is disgusting. All the fitments are disgusting. The light-fitment, the blind, even the colour is disgusting. *Especially* the colour.'

'You used to adore these tiles,' Valentine tells her. 'The bathroom was one of the main reasons why you and Dad first fell in love with this house.'

'*Please!*' her mother snorts. '*Impossible!* I don't believe you! This shade of pink? Taramasalata pink? Vomit pink? It's vile! Disgusting!'

'You're finding an awful lot to be disgusted about tonight,' Valentine observes, dryly.

Her mother considers this notion for a moment, and then, 'Because there's a lot to be disgusted *by*, I suppose,' she sighs.

'You know it's always struck me as ridiculous,' Gene says, removing a large jar of salted cashews from under the counter, unscrewing the lid and then carefully topping up Ransom's bar-snacks, 'that golf doesn't have the status of an Olympic sport yet.'

'I do quite enjoy the odd match of ping-pong,' Jen quietly ruminates from the rear, 'but then it's a completely different order of game to proper tennis.'

'Well there's the *table* part, for starters,' Gene mutters (although his voice is pretty much obliterated as Jen commences flushing a clean jug of water through the coffee machine).

'Golf,' Ransom is sullenly addressing his beer bottle. '*Goll-oll-llolf.*'

He frowns. 'It isn't stupid,' he protests. 'What's so bloody stupid about it?'

He turns to Gene. 'Do *you* think it's stupid?'

Gene shrugs, helplessly.

'*Goll-lluf,*' Ransom repeats, exploring each individual letter with his tongue and his teeth.

'Although I *do* find snooker quite selfish,' Jen suddenly interjects (as the water finally completes its noisy cycle), 'and snooker's a table sport, so it can't be entirely about the furniture, can it?'

Gene opens his mouth to respond and then closes it again, stumped.

'I don't even understand what you *mean* by selfish,' Ransom grumbles, checking his phone and sending a quick text.

'Well' – Jen carefully adjusts an eyelash (which has briefly become unglued) – 'by selfish I suppose I mean ...' She gnaws on her lower lip, thoughtfully. 'I dunno. Selfish ... Self-centred. Self-obsessed. Self-indulgent. Self-absorbed ...'

'I think we might best summarize Jen's position,' Gene quickly interjects, 'as a borderline-irrational hatred of all so-called "individual" sports.'

'*Ahhh.*' Ransom finally starts to make sense of things.

'Although I do quite like bowling,' Jen demurs.

'People generally bowl in a team.' Gene shrugs.

'And gymnastics. I like gymnastics.'

'*Ditto.*'

17

'And I've always liked the javelin,' Jen presses on. 'In fact I *love* the javelin. There's something really ... really basic and primeval about the javelin.'

To illustrate her point, Jen lobs an imaginary javelin towards Eugene's head.

'Okay. So the theory's not entirely watertight,' Gene concedes, flinching.

'And surfing ...' Jen persists. 'I really, *really* –'

'I USED TO BE A SURFER!' Ransom suddenly yells, tossing down his phone and leaping up from his stool. 'I USED TO BE A BLOODY SURFER! *EVERYBODY KNOWS THAT!*'

'Uh ... Could you just ...?' Jen raises a sardonic hand to her ear.

'I did! I DID!' Ransom is bouncing, hyperactively, from foot to foot. '*Everybody* knows that. Ask anybody! Ask ... Ask *him* ...' Ransom points at Gene. 'Surfing was my *life*. I was a total, surfing freak. I loved it. I *lived* it. I had the tan, the boarding shorts, the flip-flops, the bleached hair ...'

'The hair was pretty extravagant,' Gene concurs.

'All the way down to there, it was ...' Ransom lightly touches his chest with his free hand. 'I kept it that length for years. It was like my talisman, my trademark, my *signature* ...'

'Didn't you insure it at one point for some inordinately huge amount?' Gene asks.

'Half a million squid.' Ransom nods. 'Although it was just some cheap publicity stunt dreamed up by my ex-manager.'

'Ah ...' Gene affects nonchalance.

'But I was in all the fashion mags,' Ransom persists. 'Started my own clothing line. Had lucrative contracts with two types of styling gels. Modelled for Westwood in London, McQueen in New York, Gaultier in Paris – which is where I first met Karma ...'

He stares at Jen, expectantly.

'Karma,' he repeats, 'Karma Dean? The model? The muse? Come *on*! You *must've* heard of Karma Dean!'
'*Hmmn?*'
Jen just gazes back at him, blankly.

Her mother is perched on the edge of the bed, her slight but curvaceous frame encased in a delicate, apricot-coloured silk nightdress. She is staring at Valentine, expectantly. Valentine is standing close by, looking puzzled. She is holding a small, black vibrator in her hand.

'I'm really sorry, Mum,' she eventually murmurs, 'but the battery's completely dead.'
Her mother's mouth starts to quiver. Her eyes fill with tears.
'I'm really, really sorry, Mum,' Valentine repeats.
'Can't we just take one from the video?' her mother wheedles. 'We've done that before, remember? Just take one from the remote control!'
'I don't think that would work.' Valentine speaks softly and in measured tones. 'It's a different size battery.'
'No! No it's *not*!' Her mother stamps her foot. 'You're lying! You're just fobbing me off again, same as always!'
'I'm not lying, Mum. In fact I'm pretty certain –'
'Stop calling me that!' her mother snaps.
'Sorry?'
'I'm not your "mum". How many times do I have to tell you? I'm a person! I have a name! My name is *Frédérique*!'
'Like I was saying,' Valentine persists, ignoring this last interjection, 'I'm pretty certain that the ones in the remote are several sizes smaller ...'
Her mother hurls herself on to her back. 'JESUS CHRIST!' she hollers. 'IS THIS WHAT I'M TO BE REDUCED TO?'
'*Shhh!*'

Valentine glances over towards the door. Her mother clenches both hands into fists and *boffs* them, repeatedly, against the counterpane.

'I'd go to the shops, Mum,' Valentine struggles to mollify her, 'but Nessa's in bed and –'

'THEN ASK A FUCKING NEIGHBOUR!' her mother bellows.

Valentine closes her eyes and draws a deep breath. 'Why don't we try some of those breathing exercises you learned at the day centre the other day?' she suggests, her voice artificially bright. 'Or I can fetch you your crochet ...'

Hostile silence.

'I can't ask a neighbour, Mum. It's way after twelve ...' She pauses, grimacing. 'And anyway, the doctor –'

'Ah-*ha!*'

Her mother sits bolt upright again. She has a victorious look on her face.

'*Maintenant nous arrivons au coeur de la question!*'

'He just thinks it's advisable for you to try and lay off ...'

'Number one' – her mother lifts a single, accusing digit – 'you're too damn *scared* to go out on your own, Nessa or *no* Nessa. Number blue' – she lifts a second finger – 'you've swapped the live batteries with dead ones – on the doctor's instructions – simply to spite me and stop me from having a bit of fun. Number tree' – she lifts a third finger – 'I'm a gorgeous, healthy –'

'... because this thing is much too hard,' Valentine interrupts her, 'and you're rubbing yourself *raw* with it.'

Her mother lifts her nightie, opens her legs and shows Valentine her vagina.

'*C'est belle!* And you should know! You've seen enough of the damn things over the years!'

'*Mum ...*'

Valentine is upset.

'What?'

Her mother is unrepentant.

'Will you just ...?'

'What?'

'That's not really ...'

'*WHAT?!*'

'That's just not really *acceptable*, Mum.'

Her mother drops the nightie. 'But it's acceptable to interfere with my toy and then stand there, bold as brass, and lie to my face about it?'

'I didn't ...' Valentine begins.

'God!' Her mother collapses back on to her bed again. 'You *bore* me! This is so *boring*! I'm so fucking *bored*!'

Valentine turns to leave.

'*Menteuse!*' her mother mewls. 'Imbecile! Prude!'

'But of course I've heard of Karma Dean!' Jen scoffs. 'Are you crazy?! I mean who *hasn't* heard of Karma Dean? She's huge!'

'Well we were an item for about eighteen months.' Ransom shrugs, nonchalant. 'She was still married at the time – to some pig-ugly old French actor ... I forget his name. The tabloids had a fuckin' *field*-day. It was totally insane.'

Ransom takes a long swig of his beer. He seems understandably smug at the sheer magnitude of this revelation. *Silence.*

'But Karma Dean's really famous,' Jen eventually murmurs.

'Yeah. I know.' Ransom scowls.

'I'm serious!'

Jen pulls her 'serious' face.

'Yes, I *know*.' Ransom struggles to hide his irritation.

'But I don't think you *do*,' Jen enunciates slowly and clearly (as if describing something new-fangled to a deaf octogenarian), 'Karma Dean's really, *really* ...'

'FAMOUS! YES! I *KNOW*!' Ransom barks.

'Here.' Gene chucks Jen her cleaning cloth. She catches it. He points at the machine, and then (when she shows no inclination to get on with the job) he gently but firmly angles her towards it. Jen finally gives in to him (with a cheeky, half-smile) and commences cleaning again.

'I remember how you always used to wear it in those two, scruffy plaits ...' Gene gamely returns to their former subject. 'Hiawatha-style.'

'*Huh?*'

Ransom's still gazing over at Jen, scowling.

'Your hair?'

'My ...? Oh, *yeah* ...' Ransom finally catches up. 'I was the original golf punk. *Man.* D'you remember all the fuckin' stick I got for that?'

'Absolutely.' Gene nods.

'An' Ian Poulter suddenly thinks *he's* the latest wrinkle just 'cos he's got himself a couple of measly highlights!' Ransom snorts.

'The latest *wrinkle*?!' Jen sniggers.

'I still miss the old goatee, though.' Ransom fondly strokes his chin (doing his utmost to ignore her).

'It was pretty demonic,' Gene agrees. 'I believe you grew that around about the time the tabloids first coined ...'

'"The Devil's Ransom." Yeah ...' Ransom grimaces. 'But I loved that goatee. Shaved it off for charity just before my big comeback in 2004 – my new manager's idea. That twatty comedian did it, live, during *Children in Need.*' Ransom scowls. 'The bald one with the fat collars and all the –'

'D'you remember that brilliant campaign she did for Burberry?' Jen turns from the coffee machine.

'Huh?' Ransom looks blank.

'Karma. Karma Dean. That amazing ...?'

'*Urgh.* Don't tell me ...' He rolls his eyes, bored. 'Nude, on a beach, with the teacup chihuahua slung over her shoulder inside a Burberry rucksack? I was there when they took that shot. The dead of winter in San Tropez. She got a mild case of hypothermia – lost all sensation in her feet. Believe it or not, journos still pester me about it now, a whole seven years later ...'

'What a drag,' Jen smirks, tipping a pile of damp coffee grounds into a brown, paper bag.

'Yeah,' Ransom sighs, glancing down at his phone (seemingly oblivious to the irony in Jen's tone). 'It's dog eat dog out there, kid.'

'Weren't you banned from the Spanish Open or something?' Gene quickly interjects.

'Huh?'

Ransom looks up, confused.

'The Spanish Open. Weren't you banned from that at one stage?'

'*Bingo!*' Ransom snaps his fingers. 'The German Open. They tried to ban me! It was all over the papers. Because of the plaits. They couldn't accept the plaits. Everybody remembers the friggin' plaits! *C'mon!* Who doesn't remember the plaits?! The plaits are *legendary* ...'

As Ransom holds forth, Jen passes Gene the bag of grounds to dispose of. Gene takes the bag and then curses as it drips cold coffee on to his loafers.

'Although the point I'm actually trying to make here' – Ransom ignores Gene's muted oaths – 'is that I was a professional surfer – a *successful* surfer – on the international circuit for two, solid years before I was wiped out in South Africa, so I'm in the perfect position to know, first-hand, how unbelievably *selfish* surfing is ...'

'Are they real suede?' Jen crouches down and dabs at Gene's shoes with a used napkin.

'Yeah,' Gene mutters. 'My wife got me them for Christmas.'

'Oops.'

Jen grimaces, apologetically.

'... *way* more selfish than golf,' Ransom stubbornly persists, '*infinitely* more selfish.'

'Well, I can't pretend to be much of an expert on the matter,' Jen avers, screwing the damp napkin into a ball and rising to her feet again, 'but I generally find the most efficient way to delineate between a so-called "normal" sport and a "selfish" one' – she paints four, ironic speech marks into the air with her fingers – 'is by employing the handy axiom of sex *versus* masturbation' – she flings the ball, carelessly, towards the bin – 'and then sorting them into categories under similar lines.'

On 'axiom' Gene's jaw slackens. On 'sex' his eyes bulge. On 'masturbation' his grip involuntarily loosens and he almost drops the grounds. Stuart Ransom is struck dumb for a second and then, 'MASTURBATION *IS* SEX!' he explodes. '*Exactly*,' Jen confirms, with a broad grin (like a seasoned fisherman reeling in a prize-winning carp), 'but selfish sex.'

'Mum?'
Valentine tentatively pushes open the bedroom door and peers inside. The room is dark. Her mother appears to be asleep in bed with the coverlet pulled over her head.

'Mum?' Valentine repeats.
Her mother begins to stir.
'Mum?'
'*Huh?*' Her mother slowly pushes back the coverlet and yawns.

Valentine slowly moves her hand towards the light.
'NOT THE LIGHT!' her mother yells.

'*Shhh!*' Valentine frantically tries to quieten her. 'Nessa's asleep next door, remember?'
Her mother sits up.
'What is it?' she demands.

'Did you take the remote by any chance?' Valentine enquires.

'The what?!'

'The remote. The video remote. It's gone missing.'

'You think *I* took the remote?' Her mother looks astonished. *Pause.*

'Yes.'

'You woke me up when I was fast asleep to find out if *I* took the remote?!'

'Yes.'

'*Vraiment?!*'

'Pardon?'

'*Seriously?*'

'Yes.'

Longer pause.

'Oh. *Fine.*' Her mother crosses her arms, defiant. 'Well I didn't.'

'I see …'

Valentine nervously pushes her fringe from her eyes. 'Then I guess you wouldn't mind if I just …?'

She slowly inches her way into the room.

'Good *Christ!*' her mother exclaims, drawing the coverlet up to her chin like an imperilled starlet in an exploitation movie. 'What *is* this?! Who the hell *are* you?! The fucking *remote* Gestapo?!'

'I hardly think it's fair to compare –' Gene slowly starts off, shaking his head, evidently bewildered.

'But what about match-play?' Ransom interrupts him. 'What about the Ryder Cup? That's *team* golf, right there!'

Pause.

'Good point,' Jen concedes, then returns her full attention back to the coffee machine.

Ransom is initially gratified, then oddly deflated, by Jen's sudden *volte face.*

'I was selected for Sam Torrance's team in 2002,' he blusters, 'and we fuckin' *stormed* it. Pretty much left the Yanks for dead that year ...'

'That must've been an incredible feeling ...' Gene tries his best to buoy him up.

'It was,' Ransom confirms.

'To be perfectly honest with you' – Jen peers over her shoulder – 'I don't even know what the Ryder Cup *is* ...' She pauses for a moment, thoughtfully. 'Although when Andy Murray exaggerated the severity of his piddling *knee* injury to pike out of playing in the Davis Cup the other year ... *Urgh!*' She shakes her head, appalled.

Ransom gazes at Gene, befuddled. 'Is she always like this?' he demands, hoarsely.

'We had Jon Snow in here the other week,' Gene confirms, 'and Jen spent the whole night labouring under the misapprehension that he was her old science teacher from Middle School ...'

'Mr Spencer,' Jen interjects, helpfully, 'from Mill Vale.'

'... which was pretty embarrassing in itself,' Gene continues, 'but then she swans off to the kitchens ...'

'I just kept asking if he'd kept in contact with Miss Bartholomew – my Year Seven form teacher,' Jen butts in, 'and he was *totally* polite about it, bless him. He kept saying, "I'm not really sure that I have." Which I thought at the time was kinda *weird* ... I mean you either keep up with someone or you don't.'

'So she heads over to the kitchens,' Gene repeats, 'and one of the waitresses mentions having served Mr Snow for dinner. Jen puts two and two together, makes five, and then sprints back to the bar to apologize: "I thought you were my old science teacher," she says, "I had no idea you were a famous weatherman."'

'*SHIIIT!*' Ransom covers his face with his hands.

'That was Lenny's fault!' Jen shrieks. 'It was Len who said –'

'Lenny's still struggling to come to terms with the trauma of decimalization,' Gene snorts. 'Is he really the best person to be taking direction from on these matters?'

'Jon Snow's a fuckin' *news*reader, you *dick!*' Ransom gloats. '*Everybody* knows that.'

'I never watch the news' – Jen shrugs, unabashed – 'although when Carol Smillie came in just before Christmas,' she sighs, dreamily, 'I was totally star-struck ...'

'If I remember correctly,' Gene takes up the story, 'you served her with a chilled glass of Pinot Grigio and then said, "I think you're amazing, Carol. I'm addicted to *Countdown*. I've never missed a single show."'

'And?!' Jen demands, haughtily.

'Carol *Vorderman* presented *Countdown*, you friggin' dildo!' Ransom crows.

'Oh.' Jen scowls as Ransom exchanges a celebratory high-five with her benighted co-worker before he turns on his heel (with an apologetic shrug) and departs for the kitchens. Ransom – brimming with a sudden, almost overwhelming exuberance – taps out a gleeful tattoo with his index fingers on to the bar top.

'She was a real class act,' Jen mutters, distractedly (her eyes still fixed on the retreating Gene), 'beautiful skin, immaculate teeth, and perfectly happy to sign an autograph for my dad ...'

As soon as Gene's safely out of earshot, however, she abruptly interrupts her eulogy, places both hands flat on to the bar top, leans forward, conspiratorially, and whispers, 'I know *exactly* who you are, by the way.'

★   ★   ★

Valentine is crawling around the room on her hands and knees, feeling along the carpet in the semi-darkness.

'I know the sudden change from dark to light upsets you,' she's muttering, 'that it *jolts* you – but if we could just …' She slowly reaches towards the light on the bedside table.

'A CAT'S COME IN!' her mother screeches. 'YOU'VE GONE AND LET ONE OF THOSE FILTHY *CATS* IN!' She leaps from her bed. 'OUT, YOU DIRTY, LITTLE SWINE! OUT! OUT! *OUT!*'

As her mother chases the cat from the room, Valentine takes the opportunity to dive under the coverlet and sweep her arm across the bed-sheet.

'*LA VICTOIRE!*' her mother yells, ejecting the offending feline with a swift prod of her foot, and then – before Valentine can throw off the coverlet, draw breath, and commence a heartfelt plea to persuade her to do otherwise: '*GOOD RIDDANCE!*' she bellows, smashing the door shut, triumphantly, behind it.

The door reverberates so violently inside its wooden frame that a small ornament (a cheap, plastic model of St Jude) falls off the windowsill on the opposite wall, and a young child starts wailing in a neighbouring room.

'*Jesus*, Mum …!' Valentine hoarsely chastises her, starting to withdraw her head from under the coverlet, but before she can manage it, her mother – possibly alerted to her daughter's clandestine activities by the sound of the falling saint – has turned and propelled herself – '*NOOOOOOOOO!*' – (a howling, rotating, silken-apricot swastika), back on to the bed again.

Valentine gasps as her mother's knee crashes into her cheek (although this sharp expostulation is pretty much obliterated by:

a) the cotton coverlet
b) the extraordinary racket her mother is making

---

c) the traumatized squeal of the bedsprings).

She eventually manages to extract herself and collapses, backwards, on to the carpet.

'*Ow!*' she groans, feeling blindly for her nose. 'I think you might've ... *Woah!*'

Her normal vision is briefly punctuated by a smattering of flashing, day-glo asterisks.

'*NO BLOOD ON MY NEW CARPET!*' her mother bellows.

'*Eh?!*'

Valentine feels a sudden, inexplicable surfeit of warm liquid on her upper lip. She throws back her head, pinches the bridge of her nose and gesticulates, wildly, towards a nearby box of tissues. Her mother (unusually obliging) grabs a clumsy handful and shoves them, wordlessly, into her outstretched palm.

'Didn't you see me?' Valentine demands, applying all the tissues to her face, *en masse*.

'See you?' her mother clucks. 'Where?'

'Where?!' Valentine honks at the ceiling, through a mouthful of paper. 'Under the coverlet! In the bed!'

Shocked pause.

'You were in the bed?'

Her mother affects surprise.

'Of *course* I was in the bed!' Valentine squawks (through her mask of tissue). 'You just *jumped* on me! You just *landed* on me! You just kicked me square in the face!'

'Did I?'

Her mother seems astonished by this news.

'Yes!'

Valentine straightens her head and stares at her, indignant.

'Yes!' she repeats, removing the tissues. 'You did!'

'Oh.'

Pause.

'Well what the hell did you *expect*?' her mother rapidly changes tack. 'You were crawling around under there like some huge maggot! I panicked! I was terrified!'

'But that's hardly –' Valentine starts off.

'I mean you wake me up in the middle of the night,' her mother interrupts her, counting off Valentine's offences on to her fingers, 'yell at me, accuse me of stealing the stupid *remote* …'

'I never yelled at you!' Valentine's deeply offended. 'I would never –'

'Then you lure one of your stinking *cats* into the room.' Her mother points to the door, dramatically.

'I didn't *lure* the cat anywhere!' Valentine is gently feeling her nose for any evidence of a bump. 'The cat simply …' She shakes her head, frustrated. 'The *point* is …'

'You *know* I don't like those cats in my room!' her mother hollers, almost hysterical. 'You *know* how much I loathe them! *Petits cons! Les chats sont venus du diable pour me tourmenter! Tu es venue du diable pour me tourmenter! Vraiment!*'

Valentine reapplies the tissues to her face again. After a few seconds she removes them and subjects them to a close inspection. The sudden flow of blood appears to have abated. She wiggles her nose and then sniffs, experimentally.

'I'm very sorry about the cat,' she finally volunteers, glancing up, 'it just followed me in here out of habit, I suppose.'

'You *know* how much I hate them!' her mother hisses.

'Of course,' Valentine acknowledges, 'it's just …' She hesitates, plainly conflicted. 'D'you remember that conversation we had the other day about all the various *adjustments* we've been making ever since …' She pauses, delicately. Her mother simply grimaces.

'Well, one of the adjustments *I* obviously need to make,' Valentine doggedly continues, 'is to understand that your feelings have changed about the cats, that you're not –'

'*I HATE THOSE BLESSED CATS!*' her mother yells.

'I hear you.'

Valentine dabs at her nose again. 'Although there was a time,' she murmurs, smiling nostalgically, 'when you used to actively encourage them into this room. You used to *love* having them in bed. You used to lie there with them draped all over you. In fact you and Dad were constantly at loggerheads about it …'

'I don't *care!*' her mother growls. 'That was *her*. *C'est hors de propos à ce moment!*'

'Yes,' Valentine sighs, standing up. She glances around the room and spots the fallen saint lying in a muddy patch of moonlight on the carpet. She grabs it and returns it to its original place on the windowsill, then cautiously picks her way around the foot of the bed, preparing to make her exit.

On her way out, she bumps into a wastepaper basket and almost upends it. She tuts, catches it before it tips, sets it straight, then impulsively pushes an exploratory hand inside it. Her idly swirling fingers soon make contact with something small, rectangular and plastic.

She calmly retrieves this mysterious object and holds it aloft, balefully, like a down-at-heel court official tiredly displaying an especially incriminating piece of criminal evidence to judge and jury.

'*Huh?*'

Ransom's virile tattoo slows down to a gentle pitter-pat.

'I know who you are,' Jen repeats (struggling to repress a grin), 'I'm just pretending that I don't to wind Eugene up.'

'Eugene?'

Ransom's tattoo stops.

'Eugene. *Gene*. The barman. I love taking the mick out of him when someone famous comes in. It's just this sick little game we like to play …' She pauses, thoughtfully. 'Or this sick, little game I like to play' – she chuckles, naughtily – 'kind of at Gene's expense.'

Ransom stares at Jen, blankly, and then the penny suddenly drops. 'Oh wow …' he murmurs, instinctively withdrawing his fingers into his fists. 'Oh *shit*.'

'I mean don't get me wrong,' Jen chunters on, oblivious, 'I love Eugene to bits, but he's just so infuriatingly laid back' – she rolls her eyes, riled – 'and gentle and polite and *decent*, that I can never quite resist …'

She glances over at the golfer as she speaks, registers his stricken expression and then pulls herself up short. 'Oh *heck*,' she mutters, shocked. 'Didn't you realize? But I made it so obvious! I mean all the stuff about … about tennis and leeches and … and *Norfolk*. God. I thought I was telegraphing it from the rooftops!'

Long pause.

'Oh, yeah. *Yeah*.' Ransom flaps his hand at her, airily (although both cheeks – by sharp contrast – are now flushing a deep crimson). 'Of course I realized! Don't be ridiculous!'

'Really?'

Jen isn't convinced.

'Of *course* I fuckin' realized!' Ransom snaps, almost belligerent.

Jen grabs his empty beer bottle, tosses it into a crate behind the counter and then fetches him a replacement (flipping off the lid by hitting it, flamboyantly, against the edge of the bar top).

'*Jesus!*' Ransom is leaning back on his stool, meanwhile, a light patina of moisture forming on his upper lip. '*Jesus!*' he repeats, glancing anxiously over his shoulder, towards the kitchens.

'Here.'

Jen hands him the fresh beer.

'Cheers.' The golfer snatches it from her and affixes it, hungrily, to his lips. Jen watches him, speculatively, as he drinks.

'*FUUUCK!*' he gasps, finally slamming down the empty bottle, with an exaggerated flourish. 'What a *gull*, eh?'

'Pardon?'

'What a sucker!'

Jen looks baffled.

'A gull – a *stooge* – a patsy!' Ransom expands.

Jen still looks baffled.

'Eugenc. *Gene.* Your barman. What a gull! What a royal fuckin' *doofus!*'

Ransom wipes his mouth with the palm of his hand and then burps, majestically. 'That poor fucker was *totally* duped back there!'

'You reckon?' Jen's understandably sceptical.

'Yeah. *Yeah.* Absolutely ...' Ransom chuckles, vindictively. 'He didn't have the first friggin' *clue.*'

'I dunno.' Jen's still not buying it. 'Gene's a whole lot smarter than you think. Could just be one of those double-bluff scenarios ...'

But Ransom's not listening. His eyes de-focus for a second, and then, 'My *God!*' he erupts. 'What a *performance!* You were completely friggin' nuts back there! You were truly demented!'

Jen merely smiles.

'And the stuff about selfish sports was a fuckin' *master* stroke!' Ransom continues. 'It was brilliant! Insane! How the hell'd you just spontaneously come up with all that shit?'

'I'm a genius.' Jen shrugs.

'*Ha!*' Ransom grins at her, grotesquely, like an overheating bull terrier in dire need of water.

'No joke,' Jen says, firmly, 'I *am* a genius. I have an IQ of 210 ...'

'Pull the other one!'

Ransom kicks out his foot. 'It's got bells on!'

'... which is apparently the exact-same score as that scientist guy,' Jen elaborates.

'Who? *Einstein?*' Ransom quips.

Jen thinks hard for a moment. 'Stephen Hoskins ...? Hokings? Hawkwing?'

Pause.

'Hawking?' Ransom suggests.

'The one who wrote that book about ... *uh* ...'

'Time travel. *A Brief History of Time.* Stephen Hawking.'

'Yeah. *Yeah.* Stephen Hawkwing. We have the same –'

'Haw-*king*,' Ransom interrupts.

'Pardon?'

'Haw-*king*. You keep saying Hawk-*wing*, but it's actually ...'

'I'm crap with names,' Jen sighs. 'People automatically assume that I'll have this amazing memory just because I'm super-brainy, but I don't. My short-term memory is completely shot. I'm not "clever" at all – at least not in any practical sense of the word. I'm *intellectual*, yes – *hyper*-intellectual, even – but I'm definitely not clever. The embarrassing truth about intellectuals is that we can be amazingly *dense* sometimes. And clumsy. And insensitive. And really, really tactless. And *incredibly* forgetful,' she sighs. 'It just goes with the territory. Remember Russell Crowe in *A Beautiful Mind?*'

'I saw it on a plane,' the golfer murmurs, eyeing her, suspiciously, '*twice*. But I fell asleep both times.'

'Because our brains are generally operating at such a high level,' Jen expands, 'that we simply don't have the space up there for all these reams and reams of more *conventional* data ...'

The golfer gazes at her, perplexed, noting, as he does so, a slight, pinkened area – almost a gentle chapping – on her upper lip. This idle observation sends a frisson of excitement from his inside knee to his thigh.

'... data relating to, say – I dunno – *table* manners,' Jen rambles on, 'or road safety, or basic personal hygiene. Take me, for example,' she expands, 'I actually started reading Aristotle when I was five – in the original Greek. By seven I'd discovered that a particular chemical component in bananas advances the ripening processes in other fruits. A tiny fact, something people just take for granted nowadays. But it was a huge revelation at the time – had a *massive* impact on the wine and fruit export industries ...' She shrugs. 'I got my English language GCSE when I was eight, maths A-level when I was nine. But I was actually twelve years of age before I was successfully toilet-trained.'

'*Wuh?!*'

Ransom's horrified.

'And I never learned to tell the time.' She points to her wrist. 'Couldn't ever really *master* it, somehow. I just thank God the world had the good sense to go digital ...' She fondly inspects her watch, notices a tiny smear on its face and then casually buffs it clean on her breast (Ransom observes these proceedings with copious levels of interest).

'Even tying my own shoelaces was a nightmare,' Jen continues. 'At school I always wore trainers with Velcro flaps ...'

She illustrates this poignant detail with a little mime. Halfway through, though, Ransom clambers to his feet, reaches over the counter, grabs her arm and yanks her, unceremoniously, towards him.

She squeals, half-resisting. He ignores her protests, roughly twists her wrist and pulls the newly buffed timepiece right up close to his face. He inspects it for several seconds, his breathing laboured.

'You manipulative little *cow*,' he eventually mutters.

Much as he'd surmised, her watch has a leather strap, a gold surround, a traditional dial and two hands.

⋆   ⋆   ⋆

'So you just took out the batteries and then tossed the casing into the bin,' Valentine murmurs (more rueful now than accusing).

Her mother gazes at Valentine in much the same way a slightly tipsy shepherd might gaze at the eviscerated corpse of a stray sheep on a neighbouring farmer's land (a gentle, watercolour wash of concern, querulousness and supreme indifference).

'Well it's *my* remote,' she eventually sniffs, 'so I can do what the hell I like with it!'

As if to prove this point, categorically, she marches over to her daughter, snatches the remote from her hand and returns to her bed again.

Valentine remains where she stands. 'It's not really a question of *ownership*, Mum –'

'Frédérique,' her mother interrupts.

'Sorry?'

'Frédérique,' her mother repeats.

Valentine struggles to maintain her composure.

'It's not really a question of ownership, Frédérique ...' (she pronounces the name with a measure of emotional resistance), 'no one's denying that the remote is *yours*. It's more a question of ...'

She is about to say trust.

'Piffle!' her mother snorts (before she gets a chance to). 'Absolute, bloody piffle!'

Valentine freezes.

'I do find it odd how it's never a question of ownership,' her mother grumbles on, oblivious, 'whenever *I* happen to own something.'

Valentine doesn't respond.

'I mean don't you find that just a *tad* hypocritical?' her mother persists.

Still nothing from Valentine.

'Well *don't* you, though?'

Her mother squints over at her daughter through the gloom.

Valentine is silent for a few seconds longer and then, '*Piffle!*' she whispers, awed.

'What?'

Her mother stiffens.

'*Piffle!*' Valentine repeats, raising a shaky hand to her throat, her voice starting to quiver. 'You just said ... you just said ...' She can't bring herself to utter it again. 'That was one of *Mum's* favourite ...'

'I'M FRÉDÉRIQUE!' her mother snarls, pointing the remote at her (as if hoping to turn her off with it – or, at the very least, to change the channel). 'Don't you *dare* start all that nonsense again!'

Valentine promptly bursts into tears.

'STOP IT!' her mother yells.

'I *can't* stop it!' Valentine sobs, the grip of her hand on her throat growing tighter. 'That was one of *Mum's* favourite words, don't you see? She used to say it all the time! Not in a nasty way. Not in a mean way. But when there was some ... something she didn't like on the TV or the ra ... radio. "Piffle!" she'd say. "Absolute, bloody p ... piffle!" And then she'd reach for the –'

'*FRÉDÉRIQUE!*' her mother screams, covering her ears. Valentine's suddenly bent over double, her chest heaving, her face convulsing. She can't breathe.

'GET OUT! GET OUT! I *HATE* YOU!' her mother yells, then hurls the remote at her. The remote flies over Valentine's shoulder and hits the wall behind her. Valentine turns, feels blindly for it in the half-light, locates it, grabs it and then darts for the door. She staggers out into the hallway.

'I feel dizzy, Mum,' she pants, clutching at her throat again. 'I can't breathe. I think I might be going to ... I think I might be ...'

Her voice slowly fades down the stairwell. In a neighbouring room a child is crying. Valentine's mother cocks

---

37

her head and listens intently for a while, then, '*VALENTINE!*' she yells.
Pause.
   'What?' Valentine finally answers, hoarsely, from some distance off.
'How about twice of thirty-one?' her mother demands.
'*What?*' Valentine repeats, incredulous.
'Twice of thirty-one. Twice of ... *Merde!*' her mother curses.
'*Tu es sourde ou seulement –*'
'SIXTY-TWO!' Valentine howls. 'SIXTY-*TWO*! DOUBLE! DOUBLE! *DOUBLE!*'

Jen snatches her wrist from him, clamps her hand over her mouth and staggers backwards, her eyes bulging, bent double, convulsing, like she's choking on something.
   Ransom gawps at her, in alarm, then realizes (with a sudden, sinking feeling) that she's not actually choking, but laughing – at *him*.
   'Oh God!' she wails. 'I'm so sorry! I just couldn't *resist* ...' And then, '*Urgh!* Look! How disgusting! I've snotted on my hand!'
She holds up the offending digits and then goes to grab a napkin.
   To mask his confusion, Ransom lunges for the beer bottle and tries to take a swig from it, but the bottle is empty.
   'My dad always says if there was an A-level in bullshit then I'd get top marks ...' Jen chatters away, amiably, 'but, as luck would have it, I'm compelled to operate within the tedious constraints of a regular school syllabus.'
   She gently blots the tears from the corners of her eyes. 'I got such a low score for my maths GCSE that my teacher took me aside and congratulated me for it. She said it took a certain measure of *creativity* to get a mark that bad.' Jen blinks

a couple of times as she speaks. 'Are my eyes still all red and puffy?'

She leans towards him, over the bar top.

Ransom puts down the bottle and gazes into her eyes, noticing – as she draws in still closer – that she has a tiny tuft of tissue caught on the side of one nostril and that she smells of raisins, industrial-strength detergent and baby sick.

'You've smudged your make-up,' he mutters (there's a thin streak of black eye-liner on her cheekbone). He takes the napkin from her and gently dabs at her cheek.

'Thanks,' she says, surprised.

After he's finished dabbing he doesn't immediately pull back. Three, long seconds pass between them in a silence so deafening it's as if the bottles of spirits behind the bar have just thundered out the last, climactic notes of a rousing concerto. This hiatus is only broken by the quiet beep of Ransom's phone.

'So you'd do *anything* to stay at the Leaside?' he murmurs, ignoring the phone and focusing in on the nostril again, his tone ruthlessly casual.

'Pardon?'

Jen blinks.

'Earlier' – he grins – 'I thought you said ...'

As he speaks, he notices how the milky-white flesh of her inner arm is now stained by an angry, red handprint. His grin falters.

'I have a boyfriend,' Jen says, stiffly.

'*God*,' Ransom mutters, withdrawing slightly, his mind turning – briefly – to Fleur, his deeply suspicious (and litigious) American wife. 'I feel really, really *pissed*.'

He glances down at his phone and then back over his shoulder again, as though willing Gene to reappear, but Gene's nowhere to be seen, so he lifts his hands and rubs his face with them (as if trying to revive himself, or excoriate something, perhaps). Jen, meanwhile, has tossed the used napkin into the bin and strolled over to the till, where she starts to cash up.

'You know we had a kid like that at school,' Ransom mumbles, dropping his hands. 'Percy McCord. Played cymbals in the band. Wore lace-up boots, knee-high green socks an' a pair of burgundy, corduroy knickerbockers. Total mooncalf, he was.'

'Talking of performances' – Jen smirks at him over her shoulder – 'you put on a pretty impressive show back there yourself if you don't mind my saying so.'

'Huh?'

'I mean all the crazy stuff about your *plaits* ...'
Jen twirls her two ponytails at him, teasingly.

'My ...? Oh. Yeah ...' Ransom winces, pained.
'*EVERYBODY REMEMBERS THE PLAITS!*' Jen bellows (in a surprisingly passable northern accent). '*THE PLAITS ARE BLOOMIN' LEGENDARY!*'

'*Hah.*' Ransom smiles weakly as he reaches for the pocket containing his cigarettes, but his hand is shaking so violently that he quickly withdraws it again.

'I was really getting into character at that point,' he mutters.

'Well you deserved a bloody BAFTA!' Jen heartily commends him. 'Not that those things are worth diddly-squat, quite frankly,' she adds.

'I did a guest appearance on *Neighbours* once,' Ransom recalls, almost poignantly, 'and the director said I put in one of the most gutsy performances she'd ever –'

'*I MODELLED IN PARIS FOR JEAN PAUL GAULTIER!*'
Jen strikes a gruesome array of camp poses in rapid succession.

Ransom grimaces. A tiny pulse starts to throb in his lower cheek. His phone beeps.

'So will we let him in on the whole thing when he eventually gets back?' he wonders, glancing down at his phone and casually scanning through his messages.

'Who?'

Jen coldly inspects Ransom's hairline as she speaks (it's slightly receding), and the way his golfer's tan kicks in halfway down his forehead.

'Who?' Ransom snorts, looking up from his phone and focusing in on Jen's lips. 'Your idiot barman, who else?'

'I keep telling you' – Jen's lips tighten – 'Gene's not an idiot. He's really wise, really funny, really emotionally intelligent –'

'*Emotionally* intelligent?' Ransom butts in, sniggering. 'Next you'll be calling him "one of the good guys"!'

Jen lets this pass.

'Emotionally intelligent?!' Ransom repeats, a single brow raised, tauntingly.

'He runs marathons,' Jen attempts to elaborate, evidently discomforted.

'*Marathons?!*' Ransom gasps. 'No! *Seriously?!*'

'Sponsored marathons,' Jen snaps. 'He organizes them.'

'*Sponsored* marathons?' Ransom clutches on to the counter, for support.

'And triathalons.'

'*And* triathalons?! Wow-wee!'

Ransom swoons across the bar top, overwhelmed.

'Last year he raised almost fifteen thousand –'

'I once raised *double* that amount in a single afternoon,' Ransom interrupts her, straightening up, 'for a land-mine charity. Just after Diana died, it was. My rookie year. I had this little, pre-match wager with Jim Furyk's caddie ...'

'That's very impressive,' Jen concedes, 'but have you ever been diagnosed with terminal cancer?'

'Sorry?'

Ransom's temporarily thrown off his stride.

'Cancer. Gene's had it, almost constantly, ever since he was a kid. In pretty much every region of his body. Twice it was pronounced terminal. But he's fought it and he's beaten it – eight or nine times. He's a miracle of science. In fact he was awarded an OBE or a CBE or something,' she adds, nonchalantly, 'for his voluntary educational work in local schools and colleges.'

Ransom receives this mass of information with a completely blank expression.

'And he does all these fundraising activities for armed forces charities,' Jen persists (with a redoubled enthusiasm). 'His grandad was a war veteran. Gene always dreamed of becoming a soldier himself, but his health got in the way of it. His parents were both Carneys: – his dad worked as a mechanic and his mum was a palm-reader. She came from a long, long line of palmists. Her great-uncle was Cheiro ...'

She glances at Ransom for some visible sign of recognition. 'He's really famous.' She shrugs (having received none). 'Anyhow, Gene's family toured all over Europe with loads of the big fairs, but when Gene started getting sick, he couldn't stay on the road. So they dumped him here, in Luton, with his paternal grandparents. His dad's dad suffered from severe shell-shock. He was a lovely guy, heavily decorated – amazing brass player. He actually lived on the same street as my mum: Havelock Rise, near the People's Park. All the local kids were scared of him. He'd be sitting quietly on a bench one minute, then the next he'd just go nuts. Start screaming and yelling ...'

'Hang on a second' – Ransom's overwhelmed – 'his mother was a famous ...?'

'No,' Jen tuts, 'his mother's great-*uncle* was Cheiro. He was the really famous one – wrote loads of bestselling books and stuff. Although his mother was pretty talented herself, by all accounts, and so was Gene. Had a real gift for it, apparently. Like I said, he toured with the family before he got sick. His sister did this amazing contortionist act ...'

She pauses to adjust a false eyelash, blinking a couple of times, experimentally. 'And another thing,' she adds (unwittingly knocking the fleck of lint from her nostril with her cuff), 'about three or four years ago, just when he was really starting to turn things around, his sister and her husband were involved in this awful car crash. They were both killed. Gene was sitting in the back with his stepson and their daughter. His stepson was unharmed. Gene's legs were completely smashed up. They're held together by these massive metal pins now, but he still ran the London Marathon last year in under three hours ...' She pauses, thoughtfully. 'Oh yeah, and they adopted his niece – Mallory – which is French for unlucky, and then his wife became a hardcore Christian – a Pentecostal minister ...' She pauses again, frowning. 'Or – I forget – is she with the C of E?'

Ransom's gawping at her, incredulous.

'*Psycho*, huh?' She chuckles. 'She's about nine years old – Mallory – but the whole lower half of her face was totally destroyed in the crash. Her teeth are a disaster. Two-thirds of her tongue was bitten off. Her jaw's been completely rebuilt. She still can't eat solids. Gene works three jobs to try and raise enough cash to afford private dental and cosmetic surgery for her in America. They've got the world's most advanced specialists in the field in California – brilliant cosmetic dentists and what-not. So he works all the hours reading people's electricity meters, collecting charity boxes and running the men's toilets in the Arndale ... Hi.' Jen glances over Ransom's shoulder. 'Can I help you with something, there?'

Ransom turns – slightly dazed – to see a very tall, very lean young man standing directly behind him. The man is dripping with sweat and his chest is heaving, as if he's been running.

'Noel!' Ransom exclaims, clambering to his feet.

'You're a real piece of work, Ransom,' Noel hisses, shoving him straight back down again. 'Anyone ever tell you that?'

*   *   *

Valentine – still gasping for breath – strikes a match and crouches down to light a candle and a bright cone of incense. Her hand is shaking so violently that she's obliged to strike a second match, then a third. Once the candle and cone are finally lit, she places them on to a small, battered yellow shrine and sits, cross-legged, in front of it.

'Calm down, you idiot!' she chides herself, then closes her eyes and gently starts to rock. Five seconds later, her eyes fly open and the rocking stops. 'No! Don't calm down!' she growls. 'Don't! Be angry! Feel something for once in your miserable life!'

She starts rocking again, more violently, now.

'I hate her!' she confides to a small, primitive portrait of the goddess Kali which rests, in pride of place, at the centre of the shrine. Kali is a terrifying, cartoon-like figure with a pitch-black face and wild, coarse, flying hair. She stands astride the prostrate body of a man (her husband, the god Shiva, whom she's accidentally slain in an orgy of bloodlust) surrounded by mounds of corpses (her victims), wearing a necklace of baby heads while screaming, demonically.

Valentine stops rocking. Her eyes shift off, guiltily, to the left. On a nearby bookshelf is a statue of the Virgin Mary. Mary stands there, uncontentiously, smiling, benignly, in her azure-blue cloak, gently cosseting a prim, bleeding heart between her two, soft, white hands.

'Nope. Not angry,' Valentine murmurs, 'that's stupid – counter-productive. Be calm. Calm. Renunciation. Equanimity. Focus. Renunciation. Equanimity ... Urgh!' She shakes her head, frustratedly. 'Don't give in to her! Why do you always give in to her? Why?'

Her eyes well up with tears.

'Stop crying, you pathetic fool!' she hisses.

Her hand moves to her throat. 'No!' She wrenches the hand away again. 'Ignore the cruel voice. Ignore it! Say whatever you want! Feel whatever you like!'

She pauses, frowning.

'What *am* I feeling?'

She looks panicked and quickly hones in on the image of Kali. After a couple of seconds she raises her eyes to the ceiling, focusing intently, twisting her hands together on her lap.

'*Can mercy be found in the heart of her who was born of stone?*' she recites, haltingly.

'*Were she not merciless, would she kick the breast of her Lord?*'

She lowers her eyes, shakes her head, forlornly, and then focuses in on the picture again.

'*Men call you merciful,*' she whispers, awed, '*but there is no mercy in you, Mother.*'

She bites her lower lip, grimacing. '*You have cut off the heads of the children of others, and these you wear as garlands around your neck ...*'

She reaches out and picks up a long string of sandalwood beads, looking almost afraid. '*It matters not how much I call you "Mother", Mother,*' she concludes, shrugging. '*You hear me but you will not listen.*'

Valentine raises the beads to her lips and kisses them, then closes her eyes again.

'*Om krimkalyai nama,*' she intones, hardly audible.

'*Om kapalnaye Namah.*' Her voice grows louder.

'*Om hrim shrim krim –*

Parameshvari kalike svaha!'

She repeats this phrase in a flat monotone, and each time she repeats it she moves one bead on the necklace forward with her middle finger. As she incants, a small child can be seen, through the open door into the hallway, gradually making her way down the stairs. When she reaches the bottom stair, she pushes open the gate and toddles through into the living room. She stands and watches Valentine for a while, then takes off her nightdress, drops it on to the floor and wanders, naked, around the room, touching various objects with her hand. She finally sits down (with a bump) on the rug directly behind Valentine and gazes at her, fascinated, rocking along in time.

Valentine eventually stops chanting. Approximately ten or so minutes have now passed. She slowly opens her eyes. She stares at the picture of Kali again, raptly, pulling her face in close to it.

'Monster!' she murmurs, smiling.

She seems calmer.

'Where's Daddy?' a little voice suddenly demands.

Valentine turns, surprised. She gazes at the small child.

'Where's your nightie, Nessa?' she asks.

'What's rehob?'

'Rehob?' Valentine echoes.

'Is Grandad gone to rehob?' the little girl wonders.

'How did you get down here?' Valentine tuts, gazing out into the hallway. 'You should be in bed.'

The little girl just stares at her.

'No,' Valentine eventually answers, 'Grandad is in heaven. Mummy is in … in rehab.'

She pauses. 'Mummy will come home soon, but Grandad …' She frowns.

The little girl stares at her, blankly. Valentine takes the sandalwood beads and hangs them around the child's neck. 'Beautiful!' She smiles, then claps the child's hands together. '*Hurray!*'

The little girl peers down at the beads.

'So who told you about rehab?' Valentine wonders.

The little girl continues to inspect the beads.

'Was it one of the big boys at Aunty Sasha's?'

The little girl doesn't answer.

Valentine sighs then turns, picks up the candle from the shrine and offers it to her.

'Would you like to blow the candle out?'

The little girl nods.

'Okay, then. Deep breath,' Valentine instructs her. '*Deep*, deep breath.'

The child leans forward and exhales, as hard as she possibly can, but the flame just flattens – like a canny boxer avoiding a serious body blow – then gamely straightens up again.

Although plainly startled – and not a little annoyed – by Noel's boorish behaviour, Ransom tries his best to disguise his irritation. 'You've lost weight,' he mutters, appraising him, almost tenderly.

Noel has long, curly black hair, pale green eyes and an intelligent face, but his youthful bloom (he's only twenty-one) has all but evaporated. There is a weariness about him, a sallowness to the skin, a sunkenness under the eyes and cheeks. He looks hollowed-out, withered, shop-soiled. He reeks of skunk and cigarettes. One of his front teeth is badly chipped and prematurely yellowed. He is heavily tattooed. The left hand has, among other things, LTFC printed – in a somewhat amateurish script – across the knuckles. The right hand and arm – by absolute contrast – have been expertly fashioned into the eerily lifelike head, neck and torso of a snake. Only his fingers remain un-inked and protrude, somewhat alarmingly, from the serpent's gaping mouth.

'Can I get you a drink?' Ransom asks (gazing, mesmerized, at the reptilian tattoo), and then (when this question garners no audible response), 'You seem a little tense.'

'My mother used to work in this place,' Noel growls, glancing around him, angrily. 'Head of Housekeeping. But I guess you already knew that.'

'Sorry?' Ransom stares up at him, confused.

'My mother,' Noel repeats, more slowly this time, more ominously, his nostrils flaring. 'My mother used to work at this hotel.'

'What?! *Here?!* At this hotel?' Ransom echoes, visibly
stricken. 'You're kidding me!'

'Kidding you?' Noel scoffs. 'You actually think I'd joke about
a thing like that?'

While this short exchange takes place, Jen casually strolls to
the far end of the counter and peers over towards the front
desk. The desk has been temporarily vacated. A small,
conservatively dressed, middle-aged Japanese woman is
standing in front of it, her finger delicately poised over the
bell.

Jen cocks her head for a moment and listens, carefully. She
thinks she hears a commotion near the hotel's front entrance
and wonders if the receptionist might be offering back-up to
Gerwyn from Security (who's currently on door duty). She
scowls, checks the time, then returns her full attention back to
the bar again.

'*Man!* You're just incredible!' Noel's laughing, hollowly. 'I
mean the levels you'll sink to for a little bit of press.'
He shakes his head in disbelief. 'It's scary, Ransom. It's
fucked-up. It's *sick.*'

'Now hold on a second ...'
The golfer frowns as his drink-addled brain slowly puts two
and two together, then his expression rapidly transmogrifies
from one of vague bemusement, to one of deep mortification.
'Aw come *on*, Noel!' he wheedles. 'You can't *seriously*
think ...?'

Noel delivers him a straight look.
'But that's *crazy*!' Ransom squawks. 'I didn't have the first
idea – I *swear*. I just got a message from Esther. You know
Esther? My PR?'

Noel looks blank.

'Esther. Remember? Jamaican? Bad attitude? I was booked in
at the Leaside. She texted and said you'd switched the venue,
so I –'

'So you thought you'd set up a lovely, little photo opportunity at the Thistle, *eh?*' Noel sneers, pointing. 'Slap bang in front of the giant, plate-glass window.'

Ransom turns and gazes over at the window. Three photographers are now standing behind the glass, two of them busily snapping. The third starts banging, aggressively, at the service hatch.

'FUCK *OFF*!'

The golfer grabs a handful of nuts and hurls them towards the glass.

'*Oi!*' Jen yells (in conjunction with the golfer – recognizing this malefactor from their previous encounter). 'I thought I told you earlier ...'

She stands there for a second, momentarily flummoxed, then reaches under the counter, grabs the first aerosol that comes to hand, and steams around the bar.

'I don't understand ...' Ransom pulls out his phone. 'This doesn't make any kind of sense ... I was booked in at the Leaside and then I got a text ...'

He begins paging through his messages while Jen dances around in front of the window, chuckling vengefully and spraying voluminous clouds of furniture polish all over the glass. The photographers curse and bellow as their view is initially compromised and then entirely obfuscated (Jen only adds insult to injury by sketching a dainty, girlish heart in the centre of the goo and then – after a brief pause – neatly autographing it).

Ransom finally locates the message and shows it to Noel. 'There. See?' He passes Noel his phone. Noel takes it, inspects it for a few seconds and then tosses it over his shoulder. The phone slides across the parquet and comes to rest, with a clatter, under a nearby table. Jen – like a well-trained blonde labrador – promptly charges off to retrieve it.

'Just tell me what you want,' Noel growls, 'so I can get the hell out of here. This place gives me the creeps.'

'*Jesus.*' Ransom shakes his head, depressed. 'You really must think I'm some kind of a monster ...'

'You destroyed my family.' Noel shrugs.

'And I'm really, really sorry about that, Noel' – Ransom's plaintive, almost resentful – 'but it was a fuckin' *accident*, remember? And like I've said countless times before ...'

'It's not the accident I'm talking about,' Noel snarls, 'as well you know. It's all the crap that came with it.'

'But that's hardly –'

'Save it!' Noel snaps.

'Here.' Jen hands Ransom his phone back, then turns to Noel. 'I'm about to close the bar, so if you're wanting a snack or a drink ...'

She pauses, mid-sentence, peering up into his face, quizzically. 'I recognize you. We met before somewhere ...'

Noel ignores her. His eyes remain locked on the golfer's.

'*Pizza Hut!*' Jen exclaims. 'Didn't you temp there for a while on the delivery truck?'

'Two beers.' Ransom valiantly attempts to dispatch her.

'Or ... Hang on a sec ... Weren't you the guy roadying for that crappy DJ at Amigos last Thursday when the big fight broke out with those lippy, Sikh kids and you went and got my friend Sinead her bag back?'

'What's wrong with you people?' Noel hisses, his face suddenly reddening. 'I don't want a stupid *drink* and I don't want a stupid *chat*, all I want is to find out why the hell it was you called me here!'

He glowers down at the golfer, his fists clenching and unclenching. 'So for the last fucking *time* –'

'I'm really sorry, Noel,' Ransom interrupts him, 'but there's been some kind of a mix-up. I honestly thought *you* organized this meeting tonight.'

Noel looks astonished, then livid.

'WHAT *IS* THIS?!' he yells, finally losing his rag. 'Are you *DEAF*?! Are you STUPID?! Do we need a fucking INTERPRETER here?'

'I got a call from Esther, my PR, like I said –'
Before Ransom can complete his sentence Noel has grabbed the empty beer bottle on the bar top and has slammed it, violently, against the edge of the counter. Jen shies away as shards of glass cascade through the air. Ransom doesn't move. He doesn't flinch. He barely even blinks.

'You want *drama*?!' Noel menaces the golfer with the bottle's jagged edge. 'A little *excitement*?! Is *that* the deal?!'
Ransom slowly shakes his head.

'Or how about *this*?' Noel calmly pushes the bottle against his own throat. 'Is *this* more like it? Is *this* the kind of thing you had in mind, eh?'

'Fabulous tattoo,' Jen mutters, inspecting Noel's forearm as she straightens up and shakes out her hair. 'What is it? A swan? A goose?'
Noel ignores her.

'I swear on my life I didn't set this thing up,' Ransom persists. 'I swear on my daughter's life –'
'Fuck *off*!' Noel snaps, stepping back, jabbing harder. A small rivulet of blood begins trickling down his neck.

'Or a big duck,' Jen speculates. 'A big, ugly old duck ...'
As she speaks Jen sees the Japanese woman from the front desk entering the bar and peering around her. Jen makes a small gesture with her hand to warn her off. The woman stands her ground. Jen repeats the gesture.

'This is crazy, Noel,' Ransom is murmuring. 'I'm sure if we just ...'
'A really big, ugly, old duck,' Jen repeats. 'A really nasty, *mean* old duck. Like a ... a ...'
She struggles to think of a specific breed of duck. '... a Muscovy or a ...'
Noel's eyes flit towards her.

51

'It's not a fucking *duck*,' he growls, insulted.

'Sorry?'

Jen takes a small step forward.

'It's not a *duck*,' he hisses, lifting the arm, 'it's a *snake*, you fucking bubble-head.'

'Really?' Jen draws in still closer, taking hold of the arm and perusing it at her leisure. 'A snake you say? Lemme just ... Oh ... yeah ... *yeah!* Look at that! I can see all the scales now. The detailing's incredible!'

Noel says nothing.

'So what kind of a snake?' Jen persists. 'Is it indigenous or tropical?'

Noel ignores her. He's focusing in on the golfer again.

'An asp?' Jen suggests.

Still nothing.

'A viper?'

'It's a fucking *adder*.'

On 'adder' Noel pushes the bottle even harder into his throat.

'Oh *God*, yes,' Jen exclaims, 'of course it is. An adder. I can see that now. If you look really closely you can make out the intricate diamond design on the ...'

Behind them – and over the continuing commotion from beyond the window – another conversation suddenly becomes audible.

'Ricker,' a woman is saying, 'Mr Ricker.'

'Did you enquire at the front desk?'

(Gene's voice, getting louder.)

'I went to desk,' the woman replies, in halting English, 'but there is nobody ...'

'Did you ring the bell?'

'She say he will meet in bar. Mr Ricker.'

'Well, the bar's almost shut now. It's very late ...'

(They enter the bar.)

'I know. Yes. My flight also late. My plane also late.'

'It's been pretty much empty since ...'

Gene slams to a halt as he apprehends the scene.

'What on earth's happened to the window?' he demands, indignant.

'If you don't mind' – Jen raises a peremptory hand – 'we're actually just in the middle of something here ...'

Gene focuses in on Noel, who currently has his back to them (and Ransom, who's all but obscured by Noel). He starts to look a little wary.

'Mr Ricker?'

The Japanese woman steps forward. Noel half turns his head.

'Is everything all right?' Gene asks.

'Everything's fine,' Jen says, nodding emphatically.

'No problem,' Ransom echoes, shifting into view and smiling, jovially.

Noel slowly lowers the bottle from his throat.

'What's happened to your cheek?' Gene wonders.

(There is blood on Ransom's cheek where a tiny splinter of glass from the beer bottle has lightly nicked his skin.) Ransom lifts a hand to the cheek and pats at it, cautiously. 'It's fine.' He winces. 'It's nothing.'

As Ransom speaks, Noel gently places the broken bottle on to the bar and then casually lifts his shirt to show Jen his chest. His chest is painfully emaciated but exquisitely decorated. The tail of the adder curls over his shoulder and finishes – in a neat twirl – around his nipple. All the remaining skin on his belly, waist and diaphragm has been intricately inked into a crazily lifelike, rough, wicker corset.

'Oh God!' Jen gasps, suddenly remembering. 'Wickers!' Noel grins.

'But of *course* – my dad coached you in five-a-side for years ...'

She squints at the tattoo work, amazed, as bright trickles of blood drip down on to the design.

'Mr Ricker?' The Japanese woman takes another cautious step forward.

Noel half turns, dropping the T-shirt. 'Mrs Kawamura?'

Mrs Kawamura bows her head as Noel tramps his way, carelessly, through shards of glass and goes over to formally introduce himself. They shake hands, then Noel politely indicates the way and they leave the foyer together. Gene gazes after Noel, bemused.

'His mum was Head of Housekeeping,' Jen says, matter-of-factly. 'Mrs Wickers. D'you remember her?'

'Uh … no.' Gene shakes his head.

Jen squats down and starts picking up the larger pieces of glass. Ransom is still sitting on his stool, looking pale and disorientated.

'Should I fetch the first aid box?' Gene wonders.

'Hang on a second …' Ransom lifts a hand. 'You didn't …' He blinks a couple of times then frowns. 'That story you were telling earlier. About the Jap kid. The one who was kidnapped by the North Koreans …'

'Sorry?'

It takes Gene a few moments to make the connection. 'You mean Megumi? The girl who –'

'Did they ever find her?' Ransom interrupts.

'Find her?' Gene echoes, frowning. 'Uh, no. No. I don't believe they did.'

'Oh. Great.' Ransom looks depressed.

'Although, in the final reckoning, Megumi's disappearance was actually just the start of something way bigger – something almost revolutionary –'

'How d'you mean?' Ransom interrupts again, somewhat irascibly.

'Well, her case ended up having all these really widespread social and political repercussions throughout pretty much all of Japanese culture,' Gene continues (somewhat haltingly to begin with). 'I mean it's fairly complicated' – he shrugs – 'but what basically happened was that quite a few years after Megumi first disappeared her parents were approached – out of the blue – by this North Korean spy who claimed to have been involved in the initial kidnap plot. He was seeking asylum in Japan and told them exactly what had happened to their daughter and why ...'

'They believed him?' Ransom's sceptical.

'It seems he was fairly convincing' – Gene nods – 'so they promptly informed the Japanese authorities of what they knew, but the Japanese government refused to do anything about it.'

'Why not?' Jen looks up, outraged, from her position on the floor.

'Because they didn't want to risk antagonizing the North Koreans,' Gene explains. 'Relations between the two countries were especially volatile during that period ...'

'How many people are we talking about, here?' Jen wonders. 'Kidnap victims, I mean. In total?'

'I don't actually remember,' Gene confesses. 'Quite a number. Definitely in double figures. Fifteen? Nineteen?'

Jen receives this information without further comment.

'Anyhow, instead of just putting up and shutting up – like the government wanted – Megumi's parents decided to take matters into their own hands. They virtually bankrupted themselves spearheading this massive, public campaign, transforming Megumi and her plight into a huge, *cause célèbre.*'

He clears his throat. 'It's important to bear in mind that what they did – how they behaved – was considered completely shocking and outrageous in the Japan of that era. In general people weren't encouraged to make a public fuss about personal dramas. It flew in the face of Japanese etiquette which prefers, as you'll probably know from your own extensive experience,' Gene addresses Ransom, respectfully, 'to do things quietly, surreptitiously, behind the scenes, so that people in positions of authority don't ever risk feeling compromised.'

The golfer takes out his phone and starts checking his texts, so Gene focuses his attention back on Jen again.

'But Megumi's parents flew in the face of all that, marching, picketing, leafleting, protesting for year after year after year. Megumi became a household name throughout all of Japan – a celebrity. And in the end the Japanese government were pressurized into making some kind of a deal with the North Koreans whose rice crop had just failed so they were desperate for Japanese aid. This was ten or more years later – even longer – maybe fifteen ...'

Ransom finally puts his phone away.

'Up until then the North Koreans had always hotly denied any knowledge of Megumi and the other kidnap victims,' Gene continues. 'They were obliged to perform a complete about-turn – it was deeply humiliating for them – and quite a few of the victims were eventually returned to Japan, to this huge, public fanfare.'

'But not her.' Ransom's poignant.

'Nope. Megumi never made it back. They claimed she was dead. They said she'd hung herself during a short stay in a mental hospital when she was around twenty-six or twenty-seven, although there was scant formal evidence to back this up. What they did admit, though – and I suppose this is one of the few, really positive aspects to the story – was that she'd given birth to a child during her captivity, this beautiful little –'

'*Christ*. I gotta get out of here!'

Ransom turns and dry retches on to the bar top.

'Oh great,' Jen murmurs. 'Oh bloody wonderful.'

2

Ransom rolls on to his back, yawns, stretches out his legs and farts, luxuriously. He feels good. No. *No.* Scratch that. He feels *great*. And he smells coffee. The golfer flares his nostrils and inhales deeply. Coffee! He *loves* coffee! He wiggles his toes, excitedly, then frowns. His feet appear to be protruding – Alice in Wonderland-style – from the end of his bed. He puts a hand above his head (thinking he might've inadvertently slipped down) and his hand smacks into a wooden headboard.

Ow!

He opens a furtive eye and gazes up at the ceiling. He double-blinks. He is in a tiny room. It is a pink room, and it is a smaller room than any room he can ever remember inhabiting previously. A broom cupboard with a window. Yes. And it is pink. And the bed is very small. He is covered with a duvet, a pink duvet, and the duvet has – his sleep-addled eyes struggle to focus – pink ponies on it! Little pink ponies, dancing around! The duvet is tiny – ludicrously small, like a joke. A laughably tiny duvet. A trick duvet. A miniature duvet. He tries to adjust it but he feels like he's adjusting some kind of baby throw. A dog blanket. When he moves it one way, a different part of his body protrudes on the other side. His body (he is forced to observe) is not looking at its best. His body looks very big. His body looks coarse and capacious in this tiny, dainty, girly, pink room. His body looks hairy. It feels voluminous.

He shuts his eyes again. He suddenly has a headache. He thinks about the coffee. He can definitely smell coffee. He needs a coffee. He opens his eyes, turns his head and peers off to his right. (Might there be a door to this room so that he can eventually get –)

WHAH!

Ransom yelps, startled, snatching at the duvet. Two women – *complete strangers!* – are standing by the bed and staring down at him, inquisitively. Not two women. No. *Not …*

A woman and a girl. Yes. But the woman isn't a woman, she is a priest (in her black shirt and dog collar), and the girl isn't a girl, she's … What *is* she? He inspects the girl, horrified. She's half a girl. The lower section of her face is … It's missing. A catastrophe. It's gone walkabout. Or if not quite missing, exactly, then … *uh* … a work in progress. A mess of wire and scar and scaffolding.

The girl registers his disquiet and quickly covers her jaw with her hand. Ransom immediately switches his gaze back to the priest again, embarrassed.

'Thank goodness he's finally awake,' the priest murmurs, relieved.

The half-faced girl nods, emphatically. She is wearing a school uniform. Her hair is in two, neat plaits.

'I don't recognize him,' she whispers, from behind her hand. 'Dad said he was really famous, but I don't recognize him *at all.*'

It takes a while for Ransom to fully decipher her jumbled speech, and when he finally succeeds he feels an odd combination of satisfaction and disgruntlement.

'*Ssshh!*' the priest cautions her.

'Where am I?' Ransom croaks, trying to lift his head.

'You're in my bedroom,' the girl promptly answers.

'I left you to lie in for as long as I could,' the priest tells him (rather brusquely, Ransom feels). 'Gene left for work several hours ago. But Mallory needs to go to school and I'm scheduled to meet the bishop in Northampton at ten ...' She checks the time. 'I don't have the slightest *clue* where Stan is right now, so ...'

She shrugs.

'Oh.'

Ransom feels overwhelmed by an excess of information.

'I like your feet.' The girl chuckles, pointing.

After a short period of deciphering, Ransom peers down at his feet. He can see nothing particularly remarkable or amusing about them.

'Thanks,' he says, just the same, and then slips a hand under the duvet to check he's still decent (he is – just about).

'Your clothes are folded up on the stool,' the priest says, pointing to a pile of clothes folded up on a pink stool.

'*I* folded them,' the girl says.

Ransom lightly touches his head. He suddenly feels a little dizzy. And he feels huge. It's a strange feeling. Because it's not just his actual, physical *size*, it's also his ... it's ... it's ...

'I suddenly feel a bit ...'

'Nauseous?' the priest fills in, anxiously. 'There's a bucket next to the bed if you're ...'

'If he's sick in my bed I'll just *die!*' the girl exclaims.

'... big,' Ransom finally concludes. 'I suddenly feel very ... very *big*. Very *large*.'

He pauses. 'And conspicuous,' he adds, 'and vulnerable.' He shudders (impressing himself inordinately with how frank and brave and articulate he's being).

Nobody says anything. They just stare down at him again, silently.

'I've brought you some coffee,' the woman eventually mutters. She proffers him a cup.

'If he's sick in my bed I'll just *die!*' the girl repeats, still more emphatically.

'I feel like I'm trapped inside this weird, fish-eye lens,' Ransom continues, holding out his hands in front of his face and wiggling his fingers, 'like I'm –'

'There should be a little water left in the boiler,' the priest interrupts him, 'enough for a quick shower. You can use the pink towel. It's clean. And you can help yourself to some cereal, but I'm afraid we're all out of –'

'Not the pink towel, Mum!' Mallory whispers, imploringly. 'Not *my* towel!'

'It's the only clean towel we've got,' the priest explains. 'I haven't had time to do the –'

'But it's –'

'*Enough*, Mallory!' the priest reprimands her, pushing the coffee cup into Ransom's outstretched hands. 'You're already late for school. Did you pack up your lunch yet?'

The girl slowly shakes her head.

'Well hadn't you better go and do it, then?'

They turn for the door.

'I won't use the pink towel,' Ransom pipes up.

The priest glances over her shoulder at him, irritably.

'I won't have a shower,' Ransom says, intimidated (she *is* intimidating). 'I can always have one when I get back to the hotel.'

'Fine.' She shrugs. 'But if you *do* decide to …'

'I won't,' he insists. 'So don't fret,' he yells after the girl. 'Your towel is safe.'

He carefully props himself up on to his elbow and takes a quick sip of his coffee, then winces (it's instant – *bad* instant).

'Where am I, exactly?' he asks, but nobody's listening. They've already left him.

'Where am I, exactly?' he asks again, more ruminatively this time, pretending – as a matter of pride – that he was only ever really posing this question – and in a purely *metaphysical* sense, of course – to himself.

★   ★   ★

Gene knocks on the door and then waits. After a few seconds he inspects his watch, grimaces, knocks again, then stares, blankly, at the decorative panes of stained glass inside the door's three, main panels. In his hands he holds the essential tools of his trade: a small mirror (hidden within a slightly dented metal powder compact, long denuded of its powder), a miniature torch (bottle green in colour, the type a film critic might use) and a clipboard (with his plastic, identification badge pinned on to the front of it).

No answer.

He studies his watch again, frowning. He knocks at the door for a third time, slightly harder, and realizes, as he does so, that the door isn't actually shut, just loosely pulled to.

He scowls, cocks his head and listens. He thinks he can hear the buzz of an electric razor emerging from inside. He pushes the door ajar and pops his head through the gap. '*Hello?*' he calls.

No answer. Still the hum of the razor.

'HELLO?' Gene repeats, even louder. 'Is anybody home?'

The razor is turned off for a moment.

'*Upstairs!*' a voice yells back (a female voice, an emphatic voice). 'In the bathroom!'

Gene frowns. He pushes the door wider. The razor starts up again.

'*HELLO?*'

The razor is turned off again (with a sharp tut).

'The *bath*room!' the voice repeats, even more emphatically. '*Upstairs!*'

The razor is turned on again.

Gene gingerly steps into the hallway. He closes the door behind him. The hallway is long and thin with the original – heavily cracked – blue and brown ceramic tiles on the floor. There are two doors leading off from it (one directly to his left and one at the far end of the corridor, beyond the stairway. Both are currently closed, although the buzz of the razor appears to be emerging from the door that's further off).

The stairs lie directly ahead of him. Gene hesitates for a moment and then moves towards them. At the foot of the stairs is a small cupboard. He has already visited seven similar properties on this particular road and he knows for a fact that in all seven of the aforementioned properties the electricity meter is comfortably stored inside this neat, custom-made aperture. Gene pauses, stares at the cupboard, then reaches out a tentative hand towards it.

His fingers are just about to grip the handle when –
'*UPSTAIRS!*'
The woman yells.

Gene quickly withdraws his hand. He sighs. He shakes his head. He gazes up the stairs, with a measure of foreboding. 'THE *BATH*ROOM!' the voice re-emphasizes, quite urgently. '*QUICK!*'

Gene starts climbing the stairs. Sitting on the landing at the top of the stairs is a large, long-haired tabby cat which coolly appraises his grudging ascent. When he reaches the landing it turns and darts off, ears pricked, tail high, jinking a sharp left into an adjacent room which – from the particular quality of the light flowing from it – Gene takes to be the bathroom. Gene follows the cat into this room and then draws to a sharp halt.

The bathroom (his hunch proved correct) is crammed full of cats. Five cats, to be exact. One cat is perched on the windowsill (the window is slightly ajar) and it takes fright on his entering (leaping to its feet, hackles rising, hissing), then squeezes through the gap and promptly disappears. Three others – with rather more sanguine dispositions – are arranged on the worn linoleum in a polite semicircle around the edge of the bath. The fifth cat – and the boldest – is sitting on the corner of the bath itself, closest to the taps.

The bath – an old bath, long and narrow, with heavily chipped enamel – is currently full of water. Next to the bath (and the cats) is an old, metal watering can which Gene inadvertently kicks on first entering. He exclaims as his toe makes contact, but it isn't so much the can (or his clumsiness) that he's exclaiming at. He is exclaiming – with a mixture of surprise and consternation – at the rat.

There is a rat in the bath – a large, brown rat – doggy-paddling aimlessly around. Gene bends down and slowly adjusts the watering can, his eyes glued to the rodent.

It is huge – at least twelve inches in length (excluding the tail) – and it is plainly exhausted. As Gene quietly watches, it suddenly stops swimming and tries to stand up, but the water is too deep. It goes under for a second, panics, and then returns to the surface again, spluttering.

Gene is no great fan of rats – or of rodents, in general – yet he can't help but feel moved by this particular one's predicament.

'I suppose I'd better get you out of there, eh?' he mutters, popping the torch between his teeth, transferring the powder compact into the hand with the clipboard, reaching down and calmly grabbing its tail.

The rat is heavier than he anticipated as it exits the water. He observes (from its prodigious testicles) that it is male. 'How long've you been in there, huh?' Gene chuckles, through clenched teeth, as it jerks and swings through the air, legs scrabbling, frantic to escape.

The cats all commence padding around below it. Two rise on to their back haunches, paws tentatively raised.

'Sod off!' Gene knees a cat out of the way and lifts the rat higher, suddenly rather protective of it. The rat gives up its struggle, relaxes and just hangs there, limply.

'Very sensible,' Gene commends it. He peers around the bathroom (to check there's nothing left in there to detain him), then slowly processes downstairs carrying the rat, gingerly, ahead of him (followed by a furry, feline train).

He pauses for a second in the hallway, unsure of what to do next. He decides (spurred on by the sound of voices) to consult with the opinionated female on this issue – presumably the home-owner – and so pads down the corridor.

It is difficult for him to knock (or to speak, for that matter, with the torch still gripped between his teeth) so he simply bangs on the door with his elbow and shoves it open with his shoulder.

He is not entirely prepared for the sight that greets him. He blinks. The room is cream-coloured – cream walls, cream blinds, imbued with an almost surgical atmosphere – and flooded with artificial light. A crouching woman with red lips and quiffed, auburn hair (tied up, forces' sweetheart-style, in a neatly knotted, polka-dotted scarf), gasps as he enters. Another woman – dark-haired, semi-naked, her back to him (thank heaven for small mercies!) – propped up on a special, padded bench, is inspecting her own genitals in a small, hand-held mirror, as the first woman (the gasping woman) shines a tiny torch into the requisite area. The rat begins to struggle.

Gene immediately backs out of the room, horrified. The door swings shut on its hinges. He retreats down the corridor, hearing an excitable discussion taking place inside (crowned by several, muttered apologies, then rapid footsteps). The door opens. The auburn-haired woman stands before him. She is wearing a white, plastic, disposable apron and matching disposable gloves. She is still holding the torch. She seems furious, then terrified (on seeing the rat, close at hand) then furious again.

He notices that her auburn hair is quaintly pin-curled underneath the scarf (which reminds him – with a sudden, painful stab of emotion – of his beloved late grandmother, who once used to curl her hair in exactly this manner). The woman is slight but curvaceous (the kind of girl who at one time might've been lovingly etched on to the nose of a spitfire) with a sweet, heart-shaped face (he sees a sprinkling of light freckles under her make-up), two perfectly angular, black eyebrows and a pair of wide, dark blue eyes, the top lids of which are painstakingly liquid-lined. Her lips are a deep, poppy red, although her lipstick – he notes, fascinated – is slightly smudged at one corner.

'Who are you?' she demands, flapping her hands at him to move him further on down the hallway. 'What on earth d'you think you're doing?'

'I've come to read the …'

Gene lifts the clipboard, trying not to trip up over the cats, his speech (through the torch) somewhat slurred. Both parties notice, at the same moment, that their torches are identical.

'I should probably …' He lifts the struggling rat.

The woman darts past him (he registers the solid sound of her heels on the tiles), yanks the door open and shoves him outside. Gene drops the rat into the tiny, paved, front garden and it immediately seeks shelter behind a group of bins.

'I thought you were my brother!' the woman exclaims. Gene spits out his torch. 'I came to read your meter,' he stutters, 'but the door was ajar and when I …'

A phone commences ringing in the hallway behind her. It has an old-fashioned ring. It is an old-fashioned phone: black, square, Bakelite, perched on a tall, walnut table, just along from a large aspidistra in a jardinière. Gene frowns. He has no recollection of noticing either the phone or the plant on first entering the hallway a short while earlier.

The woman turns to inspect the phone, then turns back to face him again.

'Stay there,' she mutters, glowering. 'I should answer that.' She slams the door shut.

Gene waits on the step as a brief conversation takes place inside. He glances around him, looking for the rat. He inspects his watch again. He dries his torch on his shirt-front. The door opens.

'It was just a bit of a shock ...' the woman explains, calmer now.

'Of course.' Gene grimaces. 'I really should have knocked. I just –'

'We have the same torch,' she interrupts him, pointing.

'Yes.' Gene nods.

'Mine's a little unreliable,' the woman confides, flipping it on and then off again.

'There's this tiny spring inside the top.' Gene points to the top of her torch, where the spring is situated. 'I actually ended up replacing the one in mine.'

The woman studies the torch for a moment and then peers up at him, speculatively. 'I suppose I should thank you for getting rid of the rat ...' She indicates, somewhat querulously, towards the bins. 'I ran a bath a couple of hours ago, popped downstairs to fetch the watering can ...' She pauses (as if some kind of explanation might be in order, but then fails to provide one). 'And when I came back ...'
She shudders.

Gene struggles to expel a sudden vision in his mind of her reclining, soapily, in the tub. He clears his throat. 'It was nothing,' he mutters, then stares at the corner of her lip, fixedly, where her lipstick is smudged.

'Well thanks for that, anyway,' she says, her mouth tightening, self-consciously. He quickly adjusts his gaze and notices a light glow of perspiration on her forehead, then a subtle glint of moisture on her upper lip, a touch of shine on her chin, a further, gentle glimmer on her breastbone ...
He quickly averts his gaze again.

'I'm actually ...' She glances over her shoulder, frowning. 'I'm actually in a bit of a fix' – she leans forward and gently tips his clipboard towards her so that she can read the name on his identification badge – 'Eugene,' she clumsily finishes off.

Gene can't help noticing her bare arms as she leans towards him. Her arms are very smooth. Utterly hairless. Slightly freckled. Her skin has a strange kind of … of *texture* to it and exudes – his nose twitches – a slight aroma of incense (Cedarwood? Sandalwood? Frankincense? Musk?).

Under her semi-transparent plastic apron, she's wearing a strangely old-fashioned, tight, cap-sleeved khaki shirt (in the military style), unfastened to the breastbone with a jaunty, cotton turquoise bra (frilled in shocking red nylon) peeking out from between the buttons.

Gene blinks and looks lower. On her bottom half he can make out a pair of dark, wide-cut denims, rolled up to the knee. On her feet, some round-toed, turquoise shoes with neat ankle straps and high, straight heels.

'… I mean I know it's a little cheeky of me,' she's saying, 'but it's only eight doors down. The other side of the road – number nineteen …'

'Pardon?'

Gene tries to re-focus.

'My niece. I have to go and fetch her. It's just …' – she indicates over her shoulder – 'I really should get back to my client. She wasn't very happy about …'

She winces.

Gene stares at her for a moment, confused.

'And if you're headed in that direction anyway …'

He finally realizes what she's getting at. 'Oh. Wow. You mean you want *me* to go and …?'

'Would you mind?' She bites down on her lower lip.

'Uh, no. *No*. Of course not. It's fine,' Gene insists. He glances up the road, appalled.

'I'd go myself' – she indicates over her shoulder again – 'it's just that I really should …'

'Of course.'

Gene nods, emphatically. They stare at each other, wordlessly, in a strange kind of agony, like two distant acquaintances who've just met up, arbitrarily, in the waiting room of a VD clinic.

'So what's her name?' Gene finally enquires.

'Her name? *Uh* ...' She puts a tentative hand to her headscarf. 'You know I honestly can't remember ...' She frowns. 'Isn't that terrible? Something unpronounceable, like ... like Hokakushi ...' Her frown deepens. 'Or Hokusha. It's Japanese.'

'Your niece is Japanese?' Gene deadpans.

'My niece?' The woman looks mystified, then mortified. 'Oh God! *Sorry* ...' She shakes her head. 'I've been up all night. I'm not firing on all cylinders, obviously. My niece ... My *niece*. My niece is called Nessie. Nessa. And the woman who's minding her is called Sasha ...' She pauses, sheepishly. 'And I'm Valentine.'

She holds out a gloved hand. Gene reaches out his own, in automatic response, but before their fingers can touch, she quickly withdraws hers, apologizing, and starts trying to remove the plastic glove, muttering something about 'needing to maintain hygiene'.

'Don't worry.' Gene smiles, taking a small step back. 'I should probably ...'

'Yes ...' Valentine's eyes are now lingering on his wedding ring. 'Well I suppose I'd better ...' She thumbs over her shoulder. 'My poor client ...'

'Absolutely.' Gene takes another step. He inspects his watch. She remains where she is, though, still gazing at him. He isn't sure why, exactly.

'You have the original glass,' he mumbles, pointing, somewhat uneasily.

'Pardon?'

'The original glass panels, in the door ...' He can gradually feel his colour rising. 'You're one of the only houses left on the street.'

'Oh. Yeah. *Yeah.* The glass ...' Valentine peers across at it, fondly. 'My dad always loved it. He was completely obsessed by this period of design. I guess you could say it was his ...'

Gene suddenly turns – while she's still talking – and hurries down the short path, then out of the garden (the gate swings gently behind him). He knows it's a little strange. He knows it's a little rude. And even as he's walking – just as soon as he starts walking – he's reproaching himself for it ('What is this? What are you playing at? Are you crazy?!').

Valentine watches him go, surprised. He senses her blue eyes upon him, and feels – possibly for the first time in his adult life – an excruciating awareness of all his physical shortcomings. He automatically lifts his chin and pushes back his shoulders. He tightens his stomach. But even as he does so he's haranguing himself for it, lambasting himself for it ('You bloody fool. This is ridiculous. This is *laughable*'). His body feels leaden and yet light, all at once. His chest feels too small to contain his breath. He longs – above everything – to escape, to bolt, to flee. It's as much as he can do not to break into a sprint.

'They're Gene's,' a sullen voice announces. 'All of them.'

'*Huh?*'

Ransom glances up, startled. He's just been idly rifling through a deep drawer in a heavy, dark (and profoundly unfashionable) Victorian sideboard in a somewhat cramped and boxy sitting room. In one hand he holds a bowl of cereal (mini shredded-wheat, drenched in milk, which he's eating with a fork), in the other he holds a medal. The person sullenly addressing him is a boy – a short, thick-set teenager with a dense mop of black hair (carefully arranged to hang, with a fastidious lopsidedness, over one eye) and a copy of Bruce Lee's *Artist of Life* propped under his elbow.

'I don't know why he keeps them there,' the boy continues, stolidly. 'He's got dozens of the stupid things. Mum's always nagging at him to display them properly.'

'I was looking for a spoon.' Ransom quickly drops the medal back into the drawer, adjusts the towel he's wearing (a pink towel) and turns to engage with the boy directly.

'You finished the milk,' the boy mutters, darting Ransom's cereal bowl a petulant look before silently retreating.

Ransom glances down at his bowl, shrugs, devours another forkful, saunters over to a nearby bookshelf and casually scans the books on display there. After a brief inspection he soon deduces that the books are divided – by and large – into two main categories: the military and the spiritual. Ransom instinctively shrinks from the religious side and focuses his attention on the military end instead. Here, his eyes run over Clausewitz's *On War*, Conrad Lorenz's *On Aggression*, Richard Holmes's *Acts of War*, then rest – for a brief interlude – on Wendy Holden's *Shell Shock*. He carefully places down his bowl and pulls it out, opening it, randomly: 'Too many people are jumping on the trauma bandwagon,' he reads, 'in a society where to be a victim confers on people a state of innocence.'

He scowls, tips the book over and inspects the cover, then slaps it shut and shoves it, carelessly, back into the shelves again. Next he removes the Clausewitz. 'The element of chance, only, is wanting to make of war a game,' he reads, 'there is no human affair which stands so constantly and so generally in close connection with chance as war ...' He scratches his head, intrigued. 'War is a game both objectively and subjectively ...' he continues, and then, 'Every activity in war necessarily relates to the combat, either directly or indirectly. The soldier is levied, clothed, armed, exercised, he sleeps, eats, drinks and marches all merely to fight at the right time and place.'

Ransom ponders this for a moment and then places the book under his arm, grabs Richard Holmes's *Acts of War*, and quickly flips through it, pausing for a moment, beguiled, at a section that discusses how man's aggressive drive is inherited from his anthropoid ancestors. This genetic legacy apparently inclines him to fight members of his own species. Most other creatures, he discovers, avoid lethal combat with their own kind by employing a series of simple mechanisms like a pecking order, the ritualization of combat etc. Piranhas generally prefer to attack other piranhas with their tails rather than their teeth. Rattlesnakes air their grievances not by biting other rattlers but through bouts of wrestling ...

'*Brilliant!*'

Ransom chuckles to himself as he carefully turns over the corner of the page (for future reference), closes the book and shoves it under his elbow along with the Clausewitz.

His eye now settles on a tiny copy of Sun Tzu's *Art of War*, which has been secreted, sideways, on top of a row. He pulls it out with a small, wry smile of recognition. It's a miniature hardback – under three inches in width – wrapped, like an expensive chocolate, in shiny black, red and silver foil-effect paper. He enjoys the sumptuous feel of it in his hand. He opens it up.

'Simulated chaos is given birth from control,' he reads. 'The illusion of fear is given birth from courage; feigned weakness is given birth from strength.'

He muses on this for a moment, his attention briefly distracted by the sound of a phone ringing in a far corner of the house. He can tell from the distinctive ringtone (Queen's 'We Are The Champions') that it is his phone. He scowls. The ringing stops. His eye returns to the Sun Tzu and he slowly re-reads the previous sentence: 'Simulated chaos is given birth from control; the illusion of fear is given birth from courage; feigned weakness is given birth from strength.'

Ransom considers this for a while, then he smiles, almost sentimentally, closes the book, carefully slots it under his elbow (alongside the other two) and is about to grab his cereal and move away when his eye alights on a distinctive-looking beige and black hardback with an old-fashioned drawing of an open palm on its spine. He pauses. His mind turns – very briefly – to the previous evening and to Jen.

Ah yes, *Jen*. Jen with her pale arms, her chapped upper lip and her infinite lashes. Jen with her ponytails and her pierced – and piercing – tongue. *Jen*. He winces. He draws in closer. Written above the illustrated hand he reads: *Cheiro's Palmistry for All; 2/6 NET*.

'Cheiro?' He pronounces the name out loud, as if trying it on for size.

'*Cheiro*.'

He pauses. Then, 'Goll-*uff*,' he murmurs, quizzically. '*Gol-ol-ol-ol* ...'

He shakes his head. 'Cheiro! Cheiro! Cheiro!'

He tweets the name like a canary, then snorts, pulls the book out and opens it up, randomly, to 'an autographed impression of Lord Kitchener's hand given to "Cheiro"' –

'*Eh?*'

– 'on the 21st of July, 1894 (hitherto unpublished).'

As he gazes down at the photograph, two important things happen. The first is that the boy – the stroppy, dark-haired teenager – enters the room, holding out a dripping mobile. 'I just found this in the toilet bowl,' he's saying. 'Is it yours by any chance?'

The second is that a loose wad of papers falls down from within the pages of the palmistry book – an old letter, a dried flower, a couple of photos, the order of service for a funeral ...

Ransom curses, loudly, as the order of service and the photo slide down on to the floor, but the dried flower and the letter plop into his cereal bowl. He instinctively snatches for the letter – keen to preserve it – but, in his panic, he clumsily knocks his knuckle into the fork and tips up the bowl, sending it (and all its contents) cascading down on to the carpet. Ransom stares at the milky, wheaten mess, agog.

'Wow!' The boy is impressed (and Ransom can instantly deduce that it takes a fair amount to impress this kid): 'You really fucked up,' he announces, delighted (like all teenagers, immeasurably enlivened by the prospect of a catastrophe), 'that stuff belonged to Mallory's dead mum.'

Ransom's already on his knees, yelping plaintively, plucking photos and dried flowers from the goo.

'Kitchen roll,' the boy announces, sagely, and then promptly abandons him.

'I don't understand,' the woman mutters, peering over Gene's shoulder. 'You've come to collect Nessa, but now that you're here you've decided to ...'

'Read the meter. Yeah.' Gene tries to sound nonchalant as he straightens up, switches off his torch and scribbles the relevant digits on to his clipboard. 'It'll save me from bothering you twice, that's all.'

'I see.'

The woman gives this some thought, and then, 'But you *are* actually friends with Valentine?' she demands (she is short and heavy-hipped, with long, wavy, black hair, down to her waist, and a piercing, brown gaze). 'I mean you do actually know each other?'

'Uh ...' Gene frowns. He senses trouble. 'Uh ... Yes. *Yes*. Of course I know Valentine,' he insists. 'Of course I do.'

'Of course you do.' The woman laughs, nervously, then smiles up at him, somewhat ruefully. '*God* – I'm getting so cynical in my old age! I mean it's hardly as if you just turned up at her house to read her meter and then the next thing you know she's railroading you into ...'

Gene clears his throat and glances off, sideways.

The woman pauses, alarmed. 'I mean she wouldn't ...?'

'Good gracious, no!' Gene exclaims. 'That would be ...' He struggles to find the right word, but can't; 'pathetic,' he eventually manages.

Pathetic?

'Yes.' The woman's keen, dark eyes search his face. 'Sorry,' she eventually apologizes (plainly mollified by whatever it is that she finds there), 'you must think I'm completely paranoid.' She shakes her head, exasperated, then turns and guides him down the corridor. 'It's just that I've known Vee since she was a teenager' – she glances over her shoulder, raising a single, deeply expressive, black brow – 'and she's always had this incredible gift – this ... this *knack* – for making people feel ...'

She suddenly checks herself. 'Have you been friends with Vee for long, then?'

'Long?' Gene parrots, like the word is somehow incomprehensible to him.

'Yeah. Long. *Long* ...' She rolls her eyes, sardonically. 'As in how'd the two of you first become acquainted?'

'Uh ...' Gene tries to think on his feet. 'I work in a bar. At the Thistle. In town.'

'Okay ...'

The woman nods, as if expecting something more.

'It's not full-time,' he elects, 'I just fill in when they're short-staffed, sometimes.'

'Right.' The woman sniffs, nonplussed. She is silent for a moment and then, 'Well it really has been incredibly tough on her,' she confides (determined – in spite of Gene's best efforts – to broaden the level of their interaction). 'I mean what happened to her mother ...' She shudders. 'And to lose her dad like that. Then all the problems with her brother. Then her sister-in-law being carted off into ...'

She points her finger to her temple and rotates it.

'Awful,' Gene confirms, in studied tones.

'Devastating,' the woman persists. 'And I do think she's coped extremely well ...' she concedes (perhaps a little grudgingly), 'I mean under the circumstances. Although in some respects she barely copes at all – just doesn't have the emotional ...' She rotates her hands, struggling to find the correct adjective. '*Chutzpah!*' she eventually finishes off.

They arrive at the kitchen door. She pushes it open and waves him through.

'I blame the parents, obviously ...'

She grimaces, self-deprecatingly, after delivering this cliché. 'D'you have kids of your own?'

'A couple.' Gene nods. 'A boy and a girl ...' He pauses. 'Both adopted,' he qualifies.

'I mean I love Vee,' she insists (barely acknowledging his answer). 'Who doesn't love Vee? She's a wonderful girl. Very sweet. Very creative. Very genuine. Just a bit of a lame duck, really ...' She pauses, thoughtfully. 'Reggie's at the root of it all.' She sighs. 'Did you ever have the honour of meeting Vee's dad?'

'Vee's dad?' Gene frowns. 'No. *No*. I don't believe we ever ...'

He passes through the door and then waits, politely, at the other side. Directly ahead of him is a large, kitchen table (currently covered in piles of washing), and beyond that, an open door which leads out into a long, lush and meandering back garden where a gang of children – mainly boys – can be seen playing together on a trampoline.

'So you work two jobs?'

'Pardon?'

Gene drags his eyes away from the carefree scene outside. The woman has grabbed a pair of matching socks from a prodigious, cotton-mix hillock and is now deftly rolling them into a single ball.

'Two jobs?' she repeats, inclining her head towards his clipboard.

'Uh –'

'Of course Reg adored Vee,' she interrupts him, identifying a second pair and grabbing them. 'She was the apple of his eye. Reg doted on the girl. Although he could be very strict with her – quite domineering – overbearing, even, on occasion. In fact I read this excellent article recently about how people with Vee's …' she pauses, delicately, '… problem …' She pauses again. 'I mean I suppose you should call it an illness, really …' She looks to Gene for confirmation. Gene just gazes – pointedly – back out into the garden.

'Well they normally have an overbearing father-figure,' she persists, 'a controlling dad. That's apparently very common …'

While she's speaking the woman is rolling up her shirtsleeve: 'Here – take a look …'

She shows Gene a large, black and grey tattoo on her forearm which depicts a coffin lying on a bed of roses, inscribed with the words: MUM, RIP, 1946–1998.

Gene inspects the tattoo.

'It's a Reggie T original.'

She smiles up at him, proudly.

Gene re-examines the tattoo more closely. It's certainly a fine piece of work: delicately inked, distinctive, very traditional.

'D'you like it?' she demands (possibly irritated by his protracted silence).

'It's great,' he answers, a little awkwardly. 'I mean it's extremely' – he frowns – 'accomplished.'

She gazes down at the tattoo herself, somewhat mollified. 'He was a filthy old bigot,' she grumbles, unrolling her sleeve again. 'A neighbour once told me how he developed his hatred of all foreigners after his mum had an affair with an

American serviceman during the war. His dad went crazy when he found out. Did a hike. Reg was only a toddler at the time, but he never got over it.'

'That's tough,' Gene volunteers, blandly.

'Although – to Reggie's credit – he'd never be rude to your face. Not directly. He was very charming in person. Very amiable. Always campaigned for the NF or the BNP at election time. Stood as the borough candidate every opportunity he got. Made no secret of his views, but was never nasty about it, never rude. I mean I'm half Filipino. My dad was from the Philippines. They'd play darts together down the –'

Her monologue is briefly interrupted by a sharp, girlish scream from the garden. She moves over towards the open doorway and blinks out into the bright sunlight.

'Got any yourself?' she wonders, after a short pause.

'Sorry?'

'Her last man was covered in them.' She turns, patting her forearm, by way of explanation, 'Hands, legs, feet. Had this massive, tangerine-coloured carp swimming across his neck – its eye just' – she points to her throat – 'just there. On his Adam's apple. It'd bob up and down whenever he spoke.' She grins. 'Russian, he was. Size of a house. But wouldn't say boo to a goose. Gentle as a mouse. Lovely boy. Ran off to live on an Indian commune with this woman they call "The Hugging Saint". Very weird. *Very* weird. Did Vee ever tell you about all that?'

'Uh, no. No she didn't.'

Gene frowns, uneasily, his cheeks reddening. 'And just for the record …'

As he speaks, another sharp, girlish scream resounds around the garden. The woman turns and peers outside again, shading her eyes with her hand this time.

'Would you believe it?' she mutters. 'The little devil's climbed straight back on again after I clearly told her …'

Gene glances outside himself. In the garden he sees a small girl bouncing up and down on a trampoline wearing a short, white, cotton dress and no underwear. As she bounces, a group of older boys stand nearby in a furtive huddle, watching on.

'Awful, isn't it?' The woman turns and observes Gene's slightly queasy look. Then, before he can answer, 'In fact I'm glad you're here to see it for yourself, because now you can have a word with Vee about it. I've tried to raise it with her before, but she always just fobs me off.'

Gene watches, transfixed, as the small girl bounces higher and higher, kicking out her legs with joyous abandon, each time providing the assembled company with an exemplary view of her dimpled buttocks and tiny vagina.

'I mean they're good boys – all of them,' the woman insists. 'It's just that she's way too young to be playing with this crowd, but she tags along with little Natalie, there ...'
She points to another child, an older girl, who is sitting in a deck chair picking out pebbles from between the tread in her sandals.
'Natalie's at that age where she enjoys playing the "older sister" ...'

'Perhaps we should think about calling her in,' Gene prompts.
'Good idea.'
The woman pops her head through the open doorway.
'Nessie? Nessa!' she yells. 'Get down off there and come inside, *pronto!*'
Pause.
'*NESSA!*'
Pause.
'*NOW!*'
The child finally stops bouncing.

'She's such a wilful little creature' – the woman tuts – 'a terrible exhibitionist. Was your own daughter ever that way inclined?'

'Sorry?'

'Did your own daughter ...?'

'Absolutely not!'

Gene's almost aggrieved at the mere suggestion.

'So you'll speak to Vee about it, then?'

'Uh ...'

Before he can fashion a suitable answer, Gene's phone starts to ring. He jumps, startled, reaches into his jacket pocket and pulls it out.

'Hello?'

He turns to face the opposite wall (profoundly grateful for the temporary distraction).

'Gene?'

'Sorry ...?'

It takes him a second to register the voice.

'*Jen?*'

'Yeah, you goof! Don't sound so surprised. I bribed your number out of Nihal on reception.'

(Gene makes a quick mental note to have a quiet word with Nihal.)

'I just wanted to check if you got home all right. Things got pretty crazy last night after you left.'

'Oh. Yeah.'

Gene hunches his shoulders, defensively.

'So did you manage to bundle him into the cab or what?' she prompts him.

'No. Uh ...'

Gene switches the phone to his other ear. 'I'm actually in the middle of something right now, Jen, could I possibly –'

'There's this terrible photo in the *Daily Star* website ...'

'Is there?'

'And one in the *Mirror*'s. He's sprawled over a car bonnet. It's taken from the back, but it's gruesome. In fact if you look really closely you can make out part of your arm – you've got him in some weird kind of head-lock ...'

'I was simply trying to hold him up.' Gene scowls, exasperated.

'He'd had a good skinful.' Jen sniggers.

'He had his cap pulled down over his face. Didn't have a clue where he was going. Then someone knocked the thing askew in the scramble – probably a photographer – and he completely lost the plot. Started throwing punches, spitting, swearing – ended up vomiting all over the bonnet of the cab. The cabbie was livid and promptly drove off ...'

'Oh my God.'

'... so I ended up just piling him into the Megane and driving him myself.'

As Gene speaks, the small girl enters the kitchen. He turns to look at her.

'Where to? Back to the Leaside?'

The child peers up at him and smiles. She's a beautiful little thing with angelic blue eyes and short, white-blonde curls.

'Back to the Leaside?' Jen repeats.

'Uh ...' Gene frowns, struggling to focus. 'No. *No.*'

He turns to face the wall again. 'When we got back to the Leaside he became convinced that he wouldn't be safe there, that we'd been followed. He got all tearful and melodramatic ...'

He rolls his eyes. 'It was quite a performance.'

'So what did you do?'

'What could I do? I just took him home and stuck him in Mallory's bed for the night.'

'Bloody hell!' Jen chortles. 'Back to the rectory?!'

'It was fine. Mallory came in with Sheila and me. He'd virtually passed out by that point, anyhow –'

'So where's he now?' Jen interrupts.

'I haven't a clue.'

'Won't he still be at your place?'

'I doubt it.' Gene frowns, peering down at his watch.

'Well give me your home phone number and I'll check,' Jen suggests.

'Sorry?'

Gene's patently not sold on the idea.

'Your home phone number. So I can check.'

'But I'm pretty sure –'

'Just give it to me, Gene!' Jen snaps.

Gene gives her the phone number.

'Brilliant! You're a star!'

Jen hangs up.

Gene removes his phone from his ear and stares down at it for a second, scowling, then shoves it back into his pocket, draws a deep breath, carefully fixes his expression and turns.

'So let's get this show on the road, shall we?' he exclaims, holding out his hand to the child with what he hopes is an air of confident jocularity.

'Is it salvageable?'

They are hunched over the cracked and fissured lemon-coloured laminate of the breakfast bar in the rectory's rickety, L-shaped kitchen, inspecting the sodden letter.

'I don't know.' Stan scowls. 'I mean I've done my best with the first page ...'

He holds it up to the light, squinting. 'But it's very blurred in places ...'

A bare-chested Ransom snatches it from him, impatiently.

'It's *perfectly* legible!' he exclaims.

'Yeah, well ...'

Stan isn't convinced.

'You've done a brilliant job!' Ransom enthuses, picking up the pressed flower. 'And the flower's still basically intact, which is great ...'

'It's a flowering clover,' Stan mutters. 'A *lucky* clover. It had four leaves originally.'

'*So?*'

Ransom refuses to be dispirited.

'So one of the leaves is now completely ...'

Stan grimaces as he points to it. 'That's just mangled.'

Even Ransom can't deny the harsh truth of this statement. 'Yeah. *Yeah*. But ...' He blows softly on the clover (hoping to bulk it out with his breath, perhaps). 'But you still get the general *idea* ...'

Stan picks up the damaged photo. It's an old, black and white publicity shot of a young, dark-haired, female contortionist in a harlequin-style leotard (with the obligatory white, frilled ruff) performing an exaggerated backbend. Her face smiles out from between her ankles (her chin resting, jauntily, on her hands). A quantity of the shredded wheat obscures one leg, knee and foot.

'Her face is fine,' Ransom mutters, peering, intrigued, at her sharply jutting pubic bone. 'If we could maybe just ...' He leans over and starts prodding, clumsily, at a damp strand of the wheat with his forefinger.

'Careful!' Stan yelps, snatching it away. 'The photographic ink's still really unstable.'

Ransom withdraws his hand, jarred.

'Perhaps we should use a hairdryer?' he volunteers. 'See if it peels off more easily once the liquid's all evaporated?'

'Yeah.'

The kid doesn't seem especially enthused by this notion. He places down the photo (beyond the golfer's reach) and picks up the Order of Service.

'How's that thing coming on?' Ransom reaches over and grabs a hold of it. The paper on the bottom half has bubbled up and the print has become furry in several places. He gives it a tentative sniff.

'Not too bad,' he murmurs (wincing at the sour smell of the milk), 'I mean we're definitely making progress here ...'

As Ransom appraises all the artefacts, *en masse*, he suddenly feels curiously distended again. Swollen. Like a sheep bloated with methane. He puffs out his cheeks (as a physical expression of this odd, internal sensation) and then expels the air, violently (producing a loud, hollow, farting sound).

Stan glances up, startled. The golfer tosses down the Order of Service and picks up Stan's copy of Bruce Lee's *Artist of Life*. 'This thing any good?' he asks, idly flipping through it.

'Depends on your definition of "good",' Stan answers, somewhat inscrutably.

Ransom thinks for a few seconds. 'Gisele Bundchen's baps,' he eventually volunteers.

Stan carefully considers this suggestion. 'I'm not sure if that's an appropriate frame of reference,' he eventually concludes.

Ransom places down the book again. 'I actually had a brief correspondence with Linda Lee Cadwell ...'

'Lee's wife?'

Stan's impressed. 'What about?'

'I dunno. Bruce. Fame. Mysticism. Sport. Competition. Life ...'

Ransom commences picking, distractedly, at an ingrown hair on his forearm.

'So once we've dried all this stuff off,' he eventually mutters, abandoning the ingrown hair, gazing down at his naked torso, tensing his chest muscles and watching his generous, brown nipples jerk skyward, 'then what?'

Stan frowns, focusing on the nipples himself (his dark brows automatically arching, in sync). 'How d'you mean?'

'Well d'you reckon it might be possible to just stick it all back into the book and ... uh ...' Ransom shrugs.

'What?' Stan looks scandalized. 'Bang it back on to the shelf again like nothing's happened?'

Ransom shifts in his seat, quickly diverting his attention from Stan's accusing gaze to a small window cut into the tiling above the stainless-steel sink. Beyond this window stands a large vehicle covered in tarpaulin.

'What *is* that out there?' he demands, rising slightly. 'A truck of some kind? A jeep?'

'But wouldn't that just be *wrong*?' Stan interrupts, refusing to be diverted.

Ransom flinches at the word 'wrong'. He abhors moral imperatives. The word 'wrong' hangs in the air between them, buzzing, self-righteously, like an angry black hornet.

'Absolutely,' Ransom finally concedes, smiling brightly as he sits back down again, 'of course it would be wrong. Of *course* it would be. I was just thinking out loud – just trying the idea on for size – *brain*storming, if you like … Although …' He pauses, thoughtfully. 'Although in my experience, which is – as I'm sure you can imagine – pretty extensive …' (He pauses again, portentously.) 'Golf *is* principally a game of the mind, a game of strategy, after all … I've generally found that actually telling people about something like this – a serious problem or a terrible catastrophe – *confronting* them with it, unhelpfully, at an inappropriate moment, can often end up generating more hurt and distress than simply letting the whole thing unfold in a more gradual, a more natural, a more … uh … how to put this? A more *organic* way.'

'But if we just stick the book back on to the shelf again and say nothing,' Stan interrupts, scowling, 'what happens when they *do* eventually find out? Won't I just cop all the flack for something that wasn't even my fault?'

'*You?*' Ransom appears stunned by this humble teenager's fundamental grasp of basic, deductive logic. 'But why on earth would they blame you? That's totally illogical! Like you say, it wasn't your fault …' He pauses, thoughtfully. 'Although if you hadn't come charging into the room, at the worst possible moment, like a bull in a bloody china shop ...'

As Ransom speaks he darts a malevolent look towards his phone (where it currently sits, moistly – but still disturbingly functional – on the countertop).

'Well who else are they going to blame?' Stan snorts.

'They might not blame anyone!' Ransom declaims, indignant. 'They might not even notice anything's wrong. They might just put the staining down to a little natural wear and tear, or think that there's a touch of damp behind the bookshelf, or ...' He pauses. 'Or an infestation of silverfish. It's a common enough problem, uh ...'

He peers at Stan, enquiringly. 'What was your name again?'

'Stanislav,' Stan enlightens him.

'Polish?'

Stan nods. 'On my dad's side.'

'Really? Gene's a Pole?' Ransom's surprised.

'Not Gene. I mean my real dad. Gene's my stepdad.'

'Oh. Okay.' Ransom accepts this information, impassively. 'Well, for all we know, Stanislav,' (he promptly returns to the issue at hand), 'it's entirely possible that nobody will get around to picking up this book and looking inside it for weeks – months – *years*, even. In fact it's not beyond reason that we might actually be the last two people on the planet ever to handle this thing.'

He holds up the palmistry book with a suitably portentous expression.

'I seriously doubt that,' Stan quickly (and firmly) debunks his theory. 'It's a precious, family heirloom, not just some crummy, old book that nobody cares about.'

'But that's the very *nature* of an heirloom, don't you see?' Ransom exclaims, frustrated. 'They're not especially important – not in themselves. They're just old things from the past that "represent" stuff ...' – he rolls his eyes, boredly – 'stuff about, *urgh* ... I dunno ... ideas and memories and feelings and shit, but they don't actually *mean* anything. They're not actually *worth* anything ...'

'Well you were interested enough to take a look at it,' Stan mutters.

'This house could suddenly go up in flames!' Ransom leaps to his feet, dramatically. 'Tonight! Next weekend! An electrical fault! It could be razed to the ground! Then all this worrying and heart-searching will've been a complete waste of bloody energy.'

Stan indicates, mutely, to a small, flashing smoke alarm which is situated on the ceiling directly above their heads.

'A flood, then,' Ransom improvises, irritated. 'A flash-flood – and you barely have time to evacuate the place ...'

'In *Luton*?!' Stan snorts.

'Yeah. Why not?'

'No big rivers.'

'None at all?'

'The Lee, but that hardly counts.'

'No canals? No lakes?'

Stan gives this some thought. 'I suppose there's always the lake over in Wardown Park, but that's –'

'A burst water main! *Hah!*' Ransom slaps the worktop, victorious. 'I rest my case!'

'These are Mallory's things, anyway,' Stan persists (instinctively shielding the vulnerable clover from Ransom's violent show of exuberance). 'They're her dead mum's things. They belonged to her dead mother,' he reiterates (just in case Ransom was in any, remaining doubt about the objects' sacred provenance). 'Mallory's the one you've got to be seriously worried about here.'

'Mallory's just a kid!' Ransom swiftly pooh-poohs him. 'She probably won't even notice ...'

'Oh really?!' Stan guffaws. 'You obviously don't know Mallory very well. Mallory's officially the world's most uptight kid. She's a neat-freak – a lunatic. She pretty much has a heart attack if she steps in a puddle on her way to school. Top of her Christmas list last year was a shoe store and a *lint* roller.'

'Well I bet Mallory has loads of knick-knacks knocking about the place from when her mum was still alive,' Ransom contends.

'There was her mum's old teddy bear ...' Stan willingly concedes.

'A teddy bear!' Ransom throws up his hands. 'Perfect! What better memento of a loved one than a teddy bear?'

'... but it was destroyed by moths,' Stan finishes off.

'Oh.'

'And there was her mum's gold, heart-shaped locket with a tuft of her dad's hair hidden inside ...'

'Bingo!' Ransom snaps his fingers. 'Top that! Precious, wearable *and* sentimental.'

'... but it was stolen from her locker at the swimming pool last year.'

A lengthy silence follows in which Ransom stares, inscrutably, into the middle distance (pulling rhythmically – and not a little repulsively – at the hair under his armpit), until, 'So what the heck *is* that thing?' he finally demands, pointing. 'A jeep, a van, a truck ...?'

'Cheiro,' Gene says, 'was this well-known –'

'Palm-reader,' she interrupts, 'and a clairvoyant. Yeah. I know all about him.'

Valentine holds out her hand. 'Can I take a proper look?' Gene removes the ring from his little finger and passes it over. They are standing in the hallway together.

'Although the story's probably just apocryphal.' He shrugs, noticing how her make-up is perfect now (the bright, red lipstick no longer smudged at one corner but adhering – neatly and faithfully – to the smooth line of her lips).

'Apocry-what?' She grins up at him.

'Apocryphal. Not genuine. My mother was a professional palmist. I suppose it was a rather convenient piece of lineage to have.'

Valentine inspects the ring closely.

'It's incredibly pretty,' she murmurs. 'Is that a ruby?'

As she pores over the ring, Gene's eyes are drawn to the short, delicate fronds of auburn hair at the nape of her neck which protrude – in irresistible wisps – from below her scarf.

'Is that a ruby?' she repeats, glancing up.

'A ruby?' Gene starts. 'No. No, it's actually a garnet. I believe it's Persian. He apparently wore it on the little finger of his right hand to ward off evil spirits.'

He smiles, drolly.

'And the cigarette case? Do you have that, too?' Valentine wonders (ignoring the drollery).

'Pardon?'

'The cigarette case. Wasn't it the silver cigarette case that saved his life when he was stabbed by a disgruntled client in his New York apartment?'

Gene looks bewildered.

'There's no official biography' – Valentine shrugs – 'but you can find out all about him on the internet. His books still sell in bucket-loads – they're considered classics in the field. From what I can recollect, I'm pretty sure he was raised in Ireland, although he finished up in California, working as a screenwriter ...'

'I get the general impression,' Gene interjects (somewhat dryly), 'that his personal history probably always owed a certain debt to the screenwriter's art.'

'So there's a powerful emotional connection with your mother, at the very least,' Valentine ruminates.

Gene frowns, not following her logic.

'They both enjoyed spinning the odd yarn.' She grins.

He considers this for a second and then smiles himself.

'Although if your mother's story *is* to be considered credible,' she reasons, 'if the connection *is* biological, then you'd actually be his great-great-nephew or something ...' She raises a mildly satirical brow. 'I never got the impression that Cheiro was "the marrying kind".'

'There was a sister,' Gene muses, 'a Mary Louise Warner, but I suspect our connection might've been by marriage alone.'

Valentine continues to inspect the ring.

'Anyhow ...' Gene draws a deep breath, struggling to re-focus. 'I just didn't feel it would be right to let the incident pass without at least drawing your attention to it in some way.' He glances down the corridor and indicates (somewhat limply) towards the child.

Valentine slips the ring on to her index finger, straightens out her arm and holds it at a distance (to admire it, *in situ*). 'I'm really interested in palms,' she murmurs, turning her hand over and inspecting her own, 'I'm obsessed by the skin, in general, same as my dad was. Just how strong it is – how tough and soft and durable. The skin's actually the largest organ of the body. Did you know that?'

Gene doesn't respond. He's still peering over at Nessa who is currently having a loud, imaginary conversation on the heavy, black, Bakelite phone.

'Just forget about the other thing.' Valentine smiles (glancing over towards the child herself). 'Sasha's so uptight about that kind of stuff. Nessa's still a baby. She's a free spirit. She hates to feel confined – hemmed in – by clothes, walls, *rules* ... And she's the world's worst exhibitionist. I've got no idea where ...'

Valentine pauses for a second, mid-sentence, then frowns. 'I mean I'm sure she'll grow out of it. It's just this silly phase she's going through.'

'She's certainly quite a character,' Gene murmurs as Nessa lifts up the back of her dress, pulls the hem over her forehead and commences wearing it as a kind of half-veil, beaming all the while.

'She's completely brazen!' Valentine chuckles. 'Brimming with confidence! Life has a nasty habit of knocking the stuffing out of people ...' She gazes up at him, appealingly.

'I take your point,' Gene concedes, 'although I do think that when girls reach a certain age ...' He pauses, cautiously. 'And I have a daughter of my own, so I'm speaking from painful experience here ... These things can occasionally start to develop – if you're not extremely careful – into something rather more ... uh ... something rather more ...'

'But she's still just a baby!' Valentine repeats.

'Yes. She is. Absolutely ...' Gene clears his throat. 'It's simply that the other children in the group – the boys, in particular ...'

Gene focuses, intently, on the aspidistra. He can't quite believe he's having this conversation.

'The boys?' Valentine's brows rise.

'Yeah. *Yeah*. The older boys,' Gene murmurs. 'It's nothing explicit, nothing ... just a ... a particular kind of ... well ... a certain kind of ... of atmosphere ...'

'An atmosphere?' Valentine looks shocked. 'An *atmosphere*?' she repeats, lifting a tentative hand to the back of her head.

'Yeah ...' Gene follows the progress of the hand from the corner of his eye (it's an attractive hand – soft and graceful, with lean, tapering fingers. An artistic hand, he suddenly thinks, switching, automatically, into palm-reading mode, a conic hand ...). 'Yeah ...' he repeats, blinking. 'I mean they're certainly not doing anything ... anything inappropriate, they're just naturally ... uh ... inquisitive. Just registering an ... an idle *interest*, so to speak. There's nothing ... nothing specifically wrong about it – not exactly ... yet it still feels slightly ... well ...' – he winces – 'slightly ... what's the word? I don't know ... slightly, uh, well, *unsavoury* ...'

'*Unsavoury?*' Valentine snorts, incredulous. 'Bloody hell! They're only kids, for heaven's sake!'

'Absolutely!' Gene insists. 'Completely!' he reaffirms. 'I mean it would be ridiculous – stupid, *ludicrous* – to blow this thing all out of –'

'Wouldn't it, though?' Valentine interrupts, tartly.

Gene winces, stung.

'I'm sorry,' she immediately apologizes.

'No.' Gene shakes his head. 'It's fine. I probably deserved that. I've overstepped the mark.'

A strange pulse passes between them.

'It just seems like a sad reflection of the modern world,' Valentine finally volunteers, 'if an innocent, little girl, a child, can't just –'

'If you'll forgive me for saying so,' Gene promptly interrupts her (his confidence burgeoning, exponentially, as the discussion moves from the personal to the generic), 'this isn't really about the relative goodness or badness of the world. It's not a complex social or philosophical issue, it's purely a pragmatic one – a practical one. It's essentially about accepting our responsibility as adults. Children need protecting – as much from themselves as from other people – protecting from their own innocence, even ...'

As Gene speaks, a commotion becomes audible in the street outside. A vehicle pulls up at the kerb, the engine cuts out, car doors slam, the gate creaks, footsteps can be heard tramping up the garden path (and voices, engaged in lively conversation).

Valentine gives no indication of having noticed, though. She continues to stare up at him, totally engrossed in what he's saying, her lips moving as his lips move, her hands knitted together so tightly that the knuckles are whitening. On noticing her hands – the stress in them – Gene suddenly loses the strand of what he's saying. He glances over towards the door. 'I should probably ... uh ...' he mutters, gesticulating.

Valentine says nothing for a few seconds and then, 'Yes,' she murmurs, her voice unexpectedly flat and colourless. Gene turns and takes a small step forward.

'Wait …!'

Valentine reaches out her arm and touches his shoulder. He spins around, as if stung. She pulls his ring off her finger and offers it to him. He takes it from her. He starts to say something – something off the cuff, something low and intense and curiously heartfelt – then the door flies open and his words are swiftly obliterated in the ensuing commotion.

'Shouldn't you be at school or something?'

They are standing in the garden together inspecting a large, tarpaulin-covered vehicle. Ransom has thrown on his jeans again (in haste – one of the pockets is hanging out) along with an antique, military cap and matching jacket (he's still resolutely bare-chested underneath it). The uniform he unearthed (mere moments earlier) in the hallway cupboard as Stan hastily disposed of the mop and bucket.

The cap's a perfect fit, but the jacket's strong, sepia-coloured fabric forms two taut ridges between his shoulder blades and creaks a fusty protest from beneath his armpits.

'I've got the day off, actually,' Stanislav swanks.

'Really?' Ransom starts grappling, ham-fistedly, with the tarpaulin. 'How'd you manage to wrangle that, then?'

'School Exchange Programme.' The teenager tries (and fails) to look nonchalant. 'I'm flying to Krakow this afternoon. For a month.'

'Ah, Krakow.' Ransom smiles, dreamily. 'There's a fabulous Ronald Fream course in Krakow. The Krakow Valley Golf and Country Club. Ever played there?'

Stan shakes his head.

'Well you should definitely check it out if you get the opportunity. It's fuckin' amazing. There's this crazy –

almost ... I dunno ... *Jurassic* – feel to the landscape. The tee distance is incredible – something like six and a half thousand –'

'I'm actually more into basketball myself,' Stan interrupts, pushing aside a couple of the tarpaulin's supporting bricks with a pristine-trainered toe.

'Basketball?' Ransom is nonplussed. 'D'you play at all?' As he speaks he instinctively starts feeling around inside the pocket of the jacket for his cigarettes, but ends up gingerly withdrawing an old, red tassel – heavily faded – of the kind that might be attached to a trumpet or bugle. He stares at it for a moment, perplexed, then shoves it away again, frowning.

'I started the school team,' Stan volunteers.

'Really?' Ransom appraises him, quizzically. 'But surely you're way too short to take it seriously? I mean how tall are you?' He quickly sizes him up: 'Five foot four? Five foot five?'

'Basketball's huge in Europe right now,' Stan mutters (as if his chosen sport's burgeoning size on the international scene must, inevitably, have some significant bearing on his own – admittedly diminutive – status), 'and it's really massive in the old Eastern Bloc: the Russians just can't get enough of it.'

'They friggin' *love* it in China,' Ransom volunteers, 'and let's face it' – he shrugs, obligingly – 'they're pretty much *all* short-arses over there.'

Stan gazes at the golfer, balefully, as if awaiting a punchline (or – better still – a sheepish retraction of some kind). None is forthcoming.

'I used to love shooting hoops as a kid,' Ransom reminisces, 'but golf was always destined to be my game of choice. I suppose you could say it was written in the stars ...' He waves a lordly hand, heavenward. 'I mean I was sporting mad, in general; played footie, rugby, had a stunt-bike, skated, skateboarded. We lived alongside this small, public course in Ilkley. I started caddying for my dad just about as soon as I could toddle. Then, after inheriting my grandad's old clubs when I was around four or five, I started taking a serious interest in the game myself ...'

'Four or five?' Stan echoes, almost disbelieving.

'You betcha!' Ransom nods. 'Dad wanted to cut the clubs short but I wouldn't hear of it. Had quite a tantrum about it as I recall. Because I always *enjoyed* playing with them at full stretch.' He lifts his chin, proudly. 'I relished the challenge. I suppose you could say I'm from the "Grip it and rip it" school. A feel player. My swing's always been pretty powerful, pretty distinctive, pretty ... uh ... *loose.*'

Ransom performs a basic simulacrum of his swing (although its grand scope is somewhat retarded by his beleaguered armpits). 'Pundits like to call it "unorthodox", or ... or "maverick"' – he grimaces, sourly – 'or *"singular"*. Peter Alliss – the commentator? On the BBC? – he once called it "grotesque". *Grotesque?!*'

The golfer gazes at Stan, horrified. 'Unbelievable!'

Stan opens his mouth to comment.

'But what Alliss simply doesn't get,' Ransom canters on, oblivious, 'what he *never* got, is that I'm an instinctive player, a *gut* player. I play straight from here ...' He pats his breast-pocket, feelingly. 'The heart,' he adds (no hint of irony), 'and that's something you're born with. It can't be taught. I learned my game from the floor up. I developed it as a kid, inch by inch, through trial and error. Adapting my stroke – experimenting – making judgements – taking risks. I was relentless. Never took a lesson. Never needed to. Just used these ...'

Ransom points at his two eyes: 'Drank everything in, like a sponge. And it bore fruit. By ten I was playing off a handicap of seven ...'

(Stan's grudgingly impressed.)

'By thirteen I was playing off scratch. Although my game went to shit for a while after my parents split up ...' Ransom begins searching the pockets of the military jacket for his cigarettes (then realizes – with a start – that the jacket isn't actually his). 'Got a fag on you by any chance?'

Stan shakes his head.

'Messy, messy divorce.' The golfer sighs. 'My handicap shot up to five after Mam moved to St Ives with Roderick, her new partner. Although – on a purely selfish tip – I'd've never got to spend my summers down on the coast if the old folks'd stayed together. As it was I just had a blast, basically; staying out all hours, running wild, ripping it up in the surf ... And whenever I got myself into a tight spot' – he grins, mischievously – 'exploiting that trusty, parental guilt mechanism for all it was worth ...'

'Jammy bastard,' Stan mutters, jealous.

'Don't get me wrong,' Ransom rapidly backtracks (keen to maintain his hard-bitten, northern lustre), 'first and foremost I was always a hustler. Had to be. My folks weren't made of money. Dad sold car insurance for a living. Mam worked in the school canteen. I raised the funds to surf by playing golf for cash. And while I was never what you might call an ambitious player, at least not in the formal sense of the word – never gave a toss about trophies and prizes and all that crap – I was competitive as all hell. Still am, to a fault. It's like ...' He frowns. 'It's like I don't care if I win the tournament, but I do care if I get thrashed by some smarmy, tight-arsed, Norwegian *dick*, dressed head to toe in fuckin' ...'

Ransom throws out an irritated hand. '... fuckin' *Galvin Green*, who spends his entire life nibbling on energy bars and doing bench presses in the fuckin' gym. It's personal with me. Always has been. A pride thing. I need to be the big dog – the biggest dog – win or lose. And if I'm gonna lose, then I'll piss all over the fairways. I'll leave divots a foot fuckin' deep. I'll give the groundsman a fuckin' coronary. I'll be filthy. I'll lose like a fucking pig. I'll lose worse than anyone ever lost before. I'll make an *art* out of it. I'll hit the ball through the clubhouse window. I'll play five shots from the car park. Because I'm a wild-card, Stan, a headcase: *"Better to burn out than to fade away."* That's always been my motto.'

Stan gazes at him, blankly.

'Neil Young, dipstick! It's the lyric Kurt Cobain quoted in his suicide note. You're a teenager – you should *know* that. I quoted it at my coach the other day and he just stared at me, like – *duh?* I go, "It's Neil fuckin' *Young*, Roger." He goes, "Neil Young? Of course it's Neil Young! I *love* Neil Young! Are you kidding me?! *The Jazz Singer*'s my favourite film of all time!" I just looked down at myself and I thought, Ransom, you're on a hiding to friggin' nowhere here. So I sacked the little turd, on the spot.'

'Seriously?' Stan's impressed.

'Yeah.' Ransom bridles. 'Of course I'm fuckin' serious. Although now the greedy twat's suing me for unfair dismissal.'

'Ouch.'

Stan looks pained.

'The more I think about it, though,' Ransom muses, adjusting his cap to a less rakish angle, 'the more I feel like I'm ... I dunno ... like I'm a man out of time ...' He pauses, wistfully. 'Nah-*ah*,' he promptly corrects himself, 'it's *worse* than that. Sometimes when I walk into the locker room at the start of a tournament I feel like I've just landed from another planet. Like I'm extraterrestrial. An alien! And it's not just that I'm Old School, that I'm Hardcore ... It's much more ... I dunno ... much more fundamental. There's something different about me. A uniqueness. I have this ... this natural ... this basic ... this essential *quality* about me which marks me out from ninety-nine per cent of players in the professional game right now ...' Ransom fixes Stanislav with an implacable stare. 'D'you know what that quality is, Stan?'

Stan shakes his head.

'Shall I enlighten you?'

Stan shrugs.

'Personality!' Ransom grins. 'It's *personality*, kiddo! I have *character*. Gallons of the stuff. And I'm just too damn *creative* – too much of a fuckin' *individual* – to turn myself into one of those gormless, brainwashed, Ledbetter-style automatons who only ever plays the next hole, the next shot, while spouting endless, turgid platitudes about their "mental game" and the arc of their fucking "*swing* plane". D'you know what I mean?' Stan just gazes at him, blankly (he has no idea).

'Lemme put it this way.' Ransom gamely attempts to re-state his position: 'I remember this shit-for-brains journo cornering John Daly outside the clubhouse at the start of a major tournament one time – I forget which tournament it was, off-hand – getting right up in his face and demanding to know what his "golfing strategy" was for the week's play ahead. Daly's obviously really unimpressed by this half-wit's attitude, not to say bored and pissed off by the question itself, but, as always, he's very friendly and courteous and listens to the journalist really politely before considering his reply. "My strategy?" he finally murmurs, plucking at his chin for a moment as if he's going to say something really deep, really significant. "*Yeah* ... Well I guess that would probably be ..."' Ransom clears his throat and then attempts a (perfectly passable) impersonation of Daly's slow American drawl: "*Hit* the ball, *find* the ball, then *hit* the ball again."'

Ransom smiles at Stan, beatifically. Stan looks puzzled.

'"*Hit* the ball, *find* the ball ..."' Ransom repeats, slapping his hand against his thigh, snorting, 'like this is the most incredibly *profound*, fuckin' insight: "*Hit* the ball, *find* the ball ..." Like this is the hugest fuckin' revelation! *Man!* It was pure, undiluted *genius*! A defining moment in the history of the game! A two-finger salute to all the vultures and the bullshitters and the mind-wizards and the ... the ...' (Ransom momentarily runs out of suitable targets for his mirthful ire, and flounders. His eyes fill with sudden, hot tears.) 'It was absolutely fuckin' *brilliant*,' he huffs, then turns – blinking, self-consciously – and gazes, impatiently, past the modern, slightly shabby rectory building, to the large, somewhat static and forbidding, Victorian, red-brick church beyond.

'What was that phrase Dad always liked to use?' Valentine wonders, indicating, somewhat wryly, towards her mother. 'Full of piss and vinegar?'

Her mother – who seems in unusually high spirits – is singing 'Frère Jacques' at the top of her lungs to a slightly bedraggled cat which is crouching, terrified, halfway up the stairs.

'So what're they trying to pin on me this time?' Noel demands, slowly unwinding a grubby-looking keffiyeh scarf, while carefully ensuring that the sterile gauze dressings (which have been neatly applied to his neck beneath it) remain intact.

'Pin on you?' Valentine's down on her knees, unfastening Nessa's shoes. 'Who d'you mean?'

'Who?!' Noel exclaims, thumbing over his shoulder, towards the front door. 'Who the fuck *else*, stupid?!'

'Watch your *mouth*, stupid!'
Valentine glances up at him, indignant, as she removes the first shoe. 'And don't call me stupid,' she adds (as a guilty afterthought), inclining her head, warningly, towards the child.

'Yeah, *stupid!*' Nessa immediately echoes, snatching her other foot from her aunt's grip, jutting out her chin and boldly squaring up to him.

'Oh great.' Valentine rolls her eyes.
'Yeah, *stupid!*' Nessa repeats, grabbing a handful of the baggy fabric of her father's jeans and yanking at it, hard.

'Get the fuck off!' Noel screeches, snatching for the belt on his trousers (which are already alarmingly low-slung), but his response is too slow, and the trousers slip down, with virtually no resistance, from his hip-bones to his knees.

Nessa clings on to the concertinaed fabric, giggling, delighted. Valentine struggles to contain a wan smile.

'*Enough!*' Noel hisses, raising the back of a warning hand to the child. Nessa promptly lets go and Noel yanks the trousers up again, cursing. Valentine pulls the toddler back towards her and embraces her, protectively.

'*MUM!*' Noel bellows – effortlessly displacing his irritation (principally, admittedly, with himself). 'Could you put a bloody sock in it, please?'

His mother sings – if possible – still louder.

'I said could you put a *sock* in it?' Noel repeats (an added edge of menace in his voice this time).

'She'll carry on for hours at this rate,' Valentine mutters (with a strong element of 'and I can't say I'd blame her if she did …').

'She's been singing that damn thing, non-stop, since we left the day centre,' Noel gripes. 'It's driving me round the twist.'

'Let it go, Bro',' Valentine advises him, stifling a yawn.

'I had to remove her filthy hand from my thigh, *twice*, in the car on the drive home,' Noel hisses. 'She's absolutely, bloody disgusting!'

'I'll have a word with her about it, later,' Valentine promises, untangling one of Nessa's bright, blonde curls with a distracted finger.

'So where's your client?' Noel demands, suddenly glancing around him.

'Gone.' Valentine shrugs. 'I called her a cab.'

'Jeez. That was one hell of a turnaround,' Noel murmurs (cheerfully ignoring the fact that he'd promised, faithfully, to transport her himself). 'Was she happy with the end result?'

'I dunno … Yeah' – Valentine nods – 'so far as I could tell. She was shy. Her English wasn't great, but she cried when she saw it in the mirror.'

Pause.

'Did she pay in cash?'

Her brother tries to appear disinterested.
'By cheque ...'
Valentine starts to remove Nessa's other shoe.
  'I thought we had a strict rule about that,' Noel grumbles.
'We do ...'
Longer pause.
'... but she needed some of the cash she'd put aside to pay for
her ride to the airport.'
  Noel turns to glower at his mother again (who is now
banging along in time to her ditty on the wooden banister).
  'So how'd it look?' he demands, turning back to face her.
'Fine. Nice. *Good.* Although I was so knackered by the end of
it that I could hardly ...'
  'But she was happy?' he repeats.
'Yeah. So far as I could tell. The skin was incredibly delicate –
unusually delicate. I really had to hammer away at it.'
  'Did you get a photo?' Noel demands.
'For my portfolio?' Valentine asks, fixing him with a dry look.
'Why else?' He shrugs, grinning.
'Why else,' she echoes, smiling back.
'So did you?' he persists.
  'Nope.' Valentine shakes her head. 'It was difficult to get
her to trust me and relax. I mean after all the fuss at the
hotel ...'
Noel raises a tentative hand to his throat.
  'And – like I said – her English wasn't all that great. She
was really stressing out about making her flight in time. She'd
lied to her husband about taking the trip. She'd told him she
was visiting her sister in Osaka. She didn't want him getting
suspicious. She was planning to surprise him for their
anniversary ...' Valentine pauses for a second, cradling
Nessa's tiny shoe in her hand. 'Then, just when I was about
to take the plunge and ask her, this guy turned up to read the
meter and walked in on us by mistake –'

'Hang on a second,' Noel interrupts, alarmed. 'Which guy? Not the hotel guy?'

'Hotel guy?' Valentine echoes, confused.

'He said he'd come to read the meter?!' Noel snorts, derisively.

'The hotel guy?' Valentine repeats. 'Which hotel guy?'

'To read the meter?!' Noel rolls his eyes. 'Are you having me on?'

'No.' Valentine shakes her head, defensively, then she pauses. 'Although ...'

She glances over towards the meter, frowning. 'I'm not sure if he actually got around to ...'

'And you thought he was credible?' Noel demands.

'Credible?' Valentine's starting to look paranoid. 'What's that supposed to mean?'

'Did he have all the official documentation and shit?'

'Documentation?!' Valentine exclaims, almost irritated. 'He came to read the meter, Noel. He was perfectly nice and polite and professional ...'

'So you saw his badge?' Noel jumps in.

'His badge?'

'You checked his badge?'

'Yes. *Yes.* I saw his badge.' She flaps a hand at him, dismissively. 'I checked his badge. Of course I did. I'm not a complete idiot. He had a clipboard and this tiny –'

'Although an impostor could forge a badge, easily enough,' Noel reasons.

'You think an impostor would have a tiny torch?!' Valentine's almost deriding him, now. 'And a special, little mirror inside an old powder compact?'

'Yeah. Sure. Why not?' Noel bristles.

'Well he wasn't an impostor, Noel.' She scowls. 'He was just some guy. And if you'd come home on time, like you promised ...'

Noel glares at her, balefully.

She rubs at her eyes, exhausted, as the child coyly whispers something into her ear.

'Nessa needs the toilet,' she murmurs. 'Would you mind taking her up while I get started on some sandwiches?'

'Can't she use the potty down here?' Noel groans.

'Absolutely not!'

Her voice is suddenly implacable. 'We're trying to encourage her into a set routine, remember?'

Noel gazes down at the child, malevolently. Nessa grips on to her genitals, twists her legs together and grimaces.

'I've got a headache,' he mutters, thickly, 'and I feel like shit.'

'You've got a hangover, Noel,' Valentine corrects him, almost tenderly, 'and an extremely beautiful and brilliant two-year-old daughter' – she pushes the child forward, very gently – 'who really, really needs to do a wee.'

'John Daly?'

Stanislav battles to place him, mentally: 'Isn't he that fat, alcoholic red-neck with the weird, pudding-bowl haircut?'

Ransom turns and inspects the boy with a haughty, almost pitying eye. 'When I was a kid your age,' he tells him, 'there was only one golfer I ever gave a damn about. No one else even came close. The others weren't fit to lick his shoes. He was a god in human form – a golfing deity. He single-handedly re-wrote the game's rule book. D'you know who I'm talking about?'

Stan shrugs. 'Faldo?'

'Faldo? *Faldo?!*' Ransom's horrorstruck. 'Are you swinging on my *dick*?! It was *Seve*, you fuckin' *dip*stick! Seve! Seve Ballesteros! It's like …' Ransom frowns. 'One of the defining moments in my life was the birth of my daughter, Chelsea – four years ago, in Santa Barbara – but I can honestly say – with no word of a lie – that *the* defining moment – and I mean *the* defining moment – was watching Seve sink that final putt in the 1984 Open Championship at St Andrews. I must've been around ...' Ransom ponders. 'I dunno, ten, eleven years old at the time. *Man* ...' – he shakes his head, almost forlornly – 'I fuckin' idolized Seve as a kid. I wanted to be his double. Seve was my hero, my role model. I wanted to be an *artist*, just like Seve was. Because Seve was the real deal. He was the Big Cheese. He was the golfing gorgonzola and I wanted to play *exactly* like he did – you know? All that amazing spunk and fire and recklessness? I dreamed about painting on the greens with my putter, the way Seve could. Because at his best, Seve was – without doubt – the most brilliant, the most explosive, the most *creative* player that gololf has ever ...'

Ransom pauses for a second. 'Gololf,' he backtracks, cautiously, 'glol-ol-o-ol ...'

Then he sneezes.

Stan stares at him, perplexed.

'And a real *dude*, to boot,' Ransom continues (pulling at his nose and sniffing). 'Totally sharp. I mean *totally* sharp – an absolute Geezer, a Face. Seve was like the Sean Connery of golf ...'

He sneezes again. '... the Salvador fuckin' *Dali* of golf ...'

He sneezes for a third time. 'Bollocks!' He shakes his head, blinking.

'Is he still playing today?' Stan wonders.

'Seve was wild to the fuckin' core.' Ransom grins (ignoring the question). 'Unruly – *tempestuous*. He redefined the game's parameters. He broke the mould. And I loved him for it, man, I *worshipped* him for it, because I've always been a lawless, little bastard myself. A firebrand. I guess I'm just anarchic by nature ...' Ransom shrugs, then inspects Stan for a second, speculatively. 'How about you, Poland?'

'Pardon?'

(Stan is momentarily thrown by his new moniker.)

'Are you anarchic?'

'Me? Uh. Oh. Yeah. Of course I am.' Stan nods, emphatically.

'Too fuckin' right, you are!'

Ransom ebulliently high-fives him. The high-five is accompanied by a sharp tearing sound (as one of the jacket's armpits finally gives way). The golfer's brows rise (his expression a combination of admiration and surprise – as if he thinks the teen has just discharged a loud fart). Stan returns his gaze – slightly bemused (plainly thinking the same thing about the golfer).

'I mean I'll make no bones about it,' Ransom returns (with enviable focus) to the subject at hand, 'I was almost *too* anarchic back then. I was pretty much completely, fuckin' *feral*. I just flew by the seat of my pants. And if my pants had holes in 'em – which they generally did – then I flew by the hair on my fuckin' *balls*.'

Stan winces, fastidiously.

'One thing's for sure' – Ransom starts ransacking his pockets for cigarettes again – 'while I was always pretty obsessed by the game of golf ...' – he twitches his nose but doesn't sneeze this time – 'it certainly wasn't ...' – now he sneezes – 'the be-all and end-all for me back then. Not like it is today. It was definitely more of a means to an end than anything else. Surfing was my true passion. I was deadly serious about it – spent the best part of '90, '91 bumming my way around the planet, catching waves in all the world's top, surfing hotspots: Morocco, Australia, the Indian Ocean ... In fact I was just starting to garner some serious recognition on the amateur circuit when I fractured this' – Ransom cuffs his hip, irritably – 'in a motorcycle accident: Kommertjie, South Africa. February 5th, 1992.' He shakes his head, forlornly. 'I'll never forget that date, long as I live. A yellow Kawasaki 200cc scrambler. Borrowed it off a mate. No mudguards, no mufflers. Pair of cut-off jeans, no shoes, no gloves. Popped a wheelie – just showing off to some beach babe – then hit a fuckin' pothole and flipped the damn thing. I'm still carrying the red dirt from that road under the skin of both elbows ...' Ransom shoves up the sleeves of the military jacket (with some effort).

'So your surfing career was over?' Stan asks, neglecting to acknowledge the (fairly impressive) scars Ransom has just revealed.

'*Nah-ah*. The injury wasn't serious enough to ground me for good. I almost wish it had been, with hindsight. Life just got in the way there for a while ...' Ransom delivers Stan a warning look. 'It has a nasty, fuckin' habit of doing that.'

Stan – perhaps prompted into action by Ransom's tone of foreboding (and an equally powerful urge not to acknowledge it) – silently recommences uncovering the vehicle.

'I never quit, not officially,' Ransom continues, 'in fact I don't think I would've been mentally capable of quitting at that stage. Surfing was my life. My dream. I just played a few holes in the Cape while I was on the mend, came second in an amateur event there, flew to Jamaica – on a whim – with the prize money, hung out for a while, got stoned, got laid, got dumped, got ripped off, got into a bit of financial strife, then hustled on a couple of courses to raise my fare home. Got into more strife.' He rolls his eyes, exasperated. 'Don't even ask ...' (Stan wasn't intending to), 'and eventually got deported.' He shrugs. 'Then, when I finally arrived back home, the whole thing kinda steamrollered. Two years later, I'm number one on the British amateur circuit. Turned pro in '93 and entered the Big Time, wholescale. Everyone said it was too early, but what the fuck? It was *wild*. It was a blast! I didn't really have the first, bloody clue what'd hit me.'

By the time Ransom's potted biography has concluded, the tarp has been removed and an old, military Hummer with immaculately maintained camouflage paintwork has been revealed in all its glory. They stand and silently appraise the vehicle together. Ransom kicks a wheel.

'She's a beaut'.'

'Yeah.' Stan nods. 'She was my dad's, originally. He ran a war games shop in the centre of town. Used it for publicity. But the business went bust last year, so he flogged it to Gene for a couple of hundred quid before his creditors could get a hold of it. Gene'd helped him to do it up and stuff. Mum hates having it stuck out here. She says there's no room to barbecue, but we never barbecued anyway ...'

Ransom tries the door handle but the Hummer is locked. 'I had this dinky, little military jeep in the early nineties,' he muses. 'Haven't thought about it in years. It was nuts. Looked like something out of *Mad Max*. I totalled it about five times but it just kept on going. People would stand in the street, their mouths hanging open, pointing at it and laughing. It was *completely* fuckin' wrecked. God, I loved that vehicle ... I remember I was driving it around Paris with Karma this one time ...'

'Karma?' Stan's head jerks around. 'Not Karma Dean?'

'Huh?'

Ransom's still thinking about his old jeep.

'Did you check out the huge poster in my room?' Stan demands, excited.

'Poster?'

'In my room. The massive poster. The massive Karma Dean poster.'

'A Karma Dean poster? Uh ... no.' Ransom slowly shakes his head (plainly irritated by the teen's sudden, high levels of engagement).

'Oh.'

Stan looks disappointed.

'I guess what people generally tend to forget,' Ransom mutters (his mind turning back, momentarily, to Jen, and the previous night in the hotel bar), 'is that Karma was basically a nobody when she and I first hooked up. Just another very boring, very ambitious French model in a long line of very boring, very ambitious French models. I was never serious about her. I'd recently split with Suzanne Amour. Karma was essentially just rebound fodder ...'

Ransom pauses to gauge Stan's reaction to the Suzanne Amour revelation (there isn't one).

'Now Suzanne really *was* sensational,' Ransom persists. 'Really crazy. Really wild. Had the weirdest, cutest little vagina you ever saw, kinda like an inside-out flower, like a sea-anemone ...'

Ransom describes the shape of Suzanne Amour's strange vagina in the air with his finger.

'A complete one-off. In all my years of pussy, I've never seen another like it – not even when I fucked her sister.'

Stan looks slightly uneasy.

'She was probably a little before your time ...' Ransom shrugs. 'An exotic dancer – the former girlfriend of Plastic Bertrand.'

Stan now looks utterly bemused.

'The punk singer. "*Ça Plane Pour Moi*"?'

Stan shakes his head, apologetically.

'Yeah. Well the point I'm trying to make here is that Karma was pretty much a nobody back then. She'd done an advert for this second-rate brand of pantyhose. She had a great pair of legs. Amazing legs. In fact she still has great legs – although the tits are a complete fabrication. The tits are just a big, old lie, a *huge* lie, I can promise you that ... Anyhow, the truth was that *I* was the big star at that stage. Aside from Faldo, I was basically the biggest thing to happen in European golf for years ...' He pauses for a second, thoughtfully. 'Though – credit where credit's due – Karma always really believed in herself. It's like – I dunno – people sometimes say that to be a star you have to *think* like a star, and Karma always thought like a star. She always acted "The Star". She was ridiculously, high-maintenance, even back then. My old jeep was the bane of her life. She loathed that jeep. In fact ...' – Ransom scowls as he remembers – '*no* … She actually *loved* the jeep to begin with. Yeah, typical female – she fuckin' *loved* the jeep. And I'm like the wild, crazy, English kid with the jeep. She thinks the jeep is brilliant; it's so funny and cool and eccentric. Then the next thing you know, we've been dating for about a week and she's griping on about her hair getting messed up every time we head out in the damn thing …'

'So you didn't get to check out the poster?' (Stan just wants to make absolutely sure.)

'What?'

Ransom's momentarily thrown off his stride.

'In my room. The huge film poster? It covers an entire wall.'

'Nope.' Ransom shakes his head, then winces. 'I didn't actually see anything. I just dragged myself out of bed and stood shivering under the shower for half an hour …' He massages his temples. 'For the record: the water pressure in your bathroom is completely, fuckin' abysmal.'

'It's from *Lady Spellbound*,' Stan elucidates, 'the Polish version. My dad got it for me on a trip to Warsaw. He has a friend who runs this independent cinema over there.'

Ransom looks blank.

'*Lady Spellbound*?' Stan reiterates. 'The first of *The Vala Chronicles*? The original merchandise from that film is worth a small fortune now. English versions sell for, like, three thousand pounds on eBay …'

'*Lady* …' Ransom frowns for a second and then, 'Oh God – yeah. Now I'm with you. I've actually never seen the thing.'

'Never seen *Lady Spellbound*?!' Stan parrots, astonished.

'Nope.' Ransom shakes his head. 'But isn't it meant to be really terrible?'

'Oh … uh …'

Stan quickly reassesses the situation. 'Yeah … Well I mean it's basically just a kids' film' – he shrugs – 'although Bill Murray's pretty good in it. Has this great cameo …'

'I played a pro-am tournament with Murray once,' Ransom recollects; 'he's actually a very handy player. On the third day he turned up at the clubhouse wearing this long, blonde wig, the hair all ...'

Ransom gesticulates, wildly. '*Man.* I laughed till I bawled.'

'Because he wore a wig?' Stan frowns.

'*Duh!*' Ransom's patently astonished at the kid's ignorance. 'He wore it as a *piss*-take, obviously!'

'A piss-take of what?'

Stan's still frowning.

'Of what?! Are you crazy?! My *hair*, Dumbo! A piss-take of the legendary Stuart Ransom coiffure!'

Stan looks lost for a few seconds and then, suddenly, 'Oh yeah. *Yeah* ...' A slow grin starts to ambush his face. 'Weren't you nearly chucked off a tournament once because it was such an unbelievable bird's nest?'

'Bingo!'

Ransom high-fives him again.

'And then you claimed in all the papers that you couldn't brush it because some loopy fan had ...'

'Stolen my hairbrush! Yeah!' Ransom's beatific. 'And I was deadly, fuckin' serious. She *had* stolen it. But they still refused to let me compete, so as a compromise, I plaited it. Two plaits. The plaits were like this *massive* sensation. Everyone went wild about them. I was front page news in all the papers for about a week. Got a huge spread in *Playgirl*. Ridiculous, really, when you actually come to think about it ...'

'Crazy,' Stan agrees (perhaps too readily).

'Although this was way before Beckham had his mohawk,' Ransom rallies. 'Way before all the drama with the sarong. It was the German Open. I actually won that year.'

'Stealing a hairbrush ...' Stan muses (apparently very taken by the idea). 'That's seriously deluded.'

'Yup. Mandy Pope.' Ransom rolls his eyes. 'Canadian Druid. Total fuckin' nutter. Stalked me for seven years. I had a restraining order out on her. She'd break into my flat while I was off on tour, steal my jockeys and leave these weird, little messages inside my coffee jar ...'

'A Canadian Druid ...?' Stan ruminates. 'That's retarded.'
'Tell me about it!' Ransom clucks. '*Total* fuckin' headcase, she was. But it only gets better,' he continues. 'I saw a list of the hundred most visited sites on the internet a while back and nearly puked when I saw her blog close to the top of it.'

'No way!'
Stan's impressed.
'You'd better believe it, kid. Mandy fuckin' *Pope*. Gets arrested for stealing my jockeys one week, the next she's at the head of an international fuckin' *faith* empire.'
'That's sick!' Stan's deeply amused.

A short silence follows as they both appraise the Hummer again.
'So your dad's a Pole?'
Stan nods.
'You speak any Polish?'
'Some.'

'Can you get me a coffee, please?' Ransom demands.
'Get your own, Monkey-knob,' Stan responds.

'Not bad!' Ransom nods, approvingly.
'Thanks.'
'Are you studying it at school?'
'Nope. At tech. My school doesn't currently have –'

'Brilliant,' Ransom interrupts. 'So shall we take this little beauty out for a quick spin now, or what?'
Stan turns to stare at him, shocked.

Ransom leans forward and tries the handle on the door for a second time. The door is – unsurprisingly – still locked.
'I bet I can get this thing moving without a key,' Ransom brags.

Stan, meanwhile, is reaching into the pocket of his baggy jeans and feeling around for something. He eventually locates what he's looking for and withdraws it.

'You know, basketball's one of the few sports I've never really followed,' Ransom ruminates (sensing imminent defeat on the Hummer front). 'The skill sets are just so different to those in golf. Although I was playing this tournament in the Dominican Republic a while back ...'

He peers over at Stan and then abruptly falls silent. Stan is carefully unfolding a clean, white, cotton handkerchief. Lying in the middle of it is a long, fat, neatly pre-rolled joint.

'It's really good shit,' he confides, proudly, as Ransom reaches out to grab it with a delighted whoop. 'I got it at Christian camp.'

3

'Leave it. It's fine. It doesn't need mending.' Gene tries to grab the jacket from her. 'It's not like I ever wear the thing – it's just a keepsake ...'

'So when were you planning to tell me, exactly?'
His wife refuses to give the jacket up. She plumps it down on to her lap and starts rooting around inside an old biscuit tin for a reel of thread in an appropriate colour. She is still wearing her dog collar, but her hair (usually drawn back into a scruffy bun) has been recently washed and hangs down in loose, damp curls across her shoulders. Her face – generally calm but serious, even solemn – currently looks drawn and stressed. Gene notices dark rings around her brown eyes, which – as always – are utterly devoid of make-up.

'I mean if that girl from your work hadn't phoned ...' She frowns. 'Jess. Jane ...'
'Jen.'

He notices some tinges of grey around her temples. He inspects her eyebrows. They are thick and un-plucked, but their line is still good, still shapely and graceful. She is attractive, he decides, but in a natural way – unadorned – homely.

Homely? No. He frowns. Not homely.
Powerful? Yes.
Charismatic? Certainly.
Austere? *Well* ...

His frown deepens.
Handsome, then?

Handsome?! He almost smiles. Why not? With that strong mouth, that straight nose, that no-nonsense set to her jaw … He inspects her face, fondly.

Handsome? He ponders the word for a moment, perturbed. Isn't handsome the kind of adjective you'd use to describe a brusque but peerlessly efficient ward matron of uncertain vintage? A dashing, Oxbridge undergraduate (male)? An admirably proportioned Arabian stallion?

She is perched on the stool of her dressing table with the reel of cotton clenched tightly in her fist and a needle held – delicately suspended – in the corner of her mouth.

'If Jen hadn't phoned,' she reiterates, 'I wouldn't have had the slightest –'

'I planned to tell you over dinner,' Gene interjects, 'it just didn't seem fair to unload all this stuff on to you directly before Stan headed off on his exchange – you were anxious enough already …'

'You made a deal with him,' she snaps.

'We forged a compromise,' he corrects her.

'I kept thinking how unusually quiet he was on the drive,' she muses, irritated, 'I just put it down to nerves.'

'He was a little subdued,' Gene confirms.

'I could happily strangle him!'

She stares up at the light-fitment, her eyes filling with tears.

'I told him you'd be disappointed,' Gene tries to reassure her. 'I said, "She won't be angry, Stan, she'll just be really disappointed – *really* disappointed." He was devastated. He actually began to sob when I said that.'

Silence.

'Fine.'

She blinks her own tears back. 'So they smoked a huge quantity of pot, and then what?'

On 'then' (possibly pronounced more forcefully than she'd intended) she inadvertently spits the needle out on to the carpet.

'Just one joint,' Gene corrects her, 'not "a huge amount".'

'Oh. Okay. Just one joint,' she echoes, sarcastically, 'just one, measly, *insignificant* little joint.'

She's down on her knees now, searching for the needle.

'I didn't ...' Gene starts off.

'I mean, good gracious!' She rolls her eyes, facetiously. 'What on *earth* am I getting myself so worked up about?!'

Gene suddenly spots the needle, glinting in the half-light, and dives down to retrieve it.

'I'm not saying it wasn't significant,' he murmurs, plucking the needle from the carpet's worn pile and carefully passing it over, 'I'm just trying to keep a lid on things, that's all. It's late ...'

He inspects his watch and realizes – to his dismay – that it's much earlier than he'd imagined. 'You've had a long day,' he quickly runs on, 'and after your disastrous meeting with the bishop ...'

'He's such a stickler for punctuality,' she growls, returning to her stool. 'I was over half an hour –'

'Yes,' Gene interrupts, 'I know. I remember. I believe I've already apologized for that.'

At least twice, he thinks.

'So they smoked the joint,' she repeats, shoving some hair behind her ear, 'this piddling, *insignificant*, little joint of yours – and then what?'

'It wasn't *my* joint,' Gene says, testily.

'Actually, no' – she raises a peremptory hand to silence him – 'let me *guess* ...' She taps a speculative, index finger against the side of her cheek. 'They smoke the joint and then they think, *Hmmn*. What next? Why not steal the Hummer and go out for a quick joyride? Wouldn't *that* be a hoot?!'

'Stan didn't get behind the wheel,' Gene insists. 'He was extremely lucid on that point. He said nothing would've persuaded him to get behind the wheel – *nothing*. Ransom drove. And while I know it wasn't ideal, he does have extensive experience in handling vehicles of that size ...'

'Great!' She laughs, clapping her hands together. 'He has extensive experience! Well that's wonderful, Gene! That's just terrific!'

Gene struggles to maintain his air of infinite calm.

'I'm not saying it's all right, Sheila,' he eventually murmurs, 'I'm just ...'

'Then the dratted thing goes and breaks down on them – *Surprise! Surprise!*'

She glances up at him, almost vengefully.

'They were literally two roads away when it happened. And it didn't break down, it ran out of fuel. I purposely keep the tank –'

'There's definitely a leak,' she snaps, exasperated, 'I've been complaining about it for weeks. There's been diesel seeping out of the damn thing all over the patio ...'

'Yes. You did mention the leak,' Gene concedes, nodding, 'but I think it's probably brake fluid rather than –'

'So the brakes are dodgy?!'

She throws up her hands.

'I didn't ... No. The brakes are fine. They're fine. So far as I am aware, the Hummer is in excellent, working order, which is why I made extra sure that there wasn't a sufficient amount of fuel in the tank to –'

'Because you didn't trust him?' she interrupts. 'You suspected he might do something like this, but you didn't feel it was appropriate to confide in me about it? Perhaps you thought I wouldn't be interested in what my fourteen-year-old son is getting up to?'

She gazes over at him, wounded.

'No. *No.* It wasn't Stan I was worried about so much as ...'

He makes an expansive gesture with his hand, meant to signify 'the broader community – chiefly its youthful contingent'.

116

'That bloody jeep is a magnet for trouble,' she growls, un-mollified, 'I said that from the outset.'

'You did. Although on a slightly more positive note, if the tank hadn't been —'

'Don't you *dare*,' his wife snaps.

'The point is —'

'The *point* is,' she rapidly supersedes him, 'that I warned you when Marek initially approached us with the idea that the whole thing would end in tears. Marek's schemes invariably do.'

'And you were right.' He shrugs. 'I accept that. I accepted it at the time. But my hands were tied, Sheila. I just didn't really feel I could refuse him without —'

'Heaven forbid you should upset Marek!' his wife harrumphs.

'He was desperate. And I knew how much it would mean to Stan —'

'So now, in celebration of that fact,' his wife interrupts, 'as an expression of this "enormous gratitude" he apparently feels, Stan's taking the damn thing out on spontaneous joyrides, stoned out of his tiny, little mind!'

Silence.

'Well he certainly paid a price for it,' Gene eventually avows, 'if that's any kind of comfort.'

'It isn't.'

'He was completely humiliated, Sheila.'

She sits down on her stool again, pops the needle back between her lips and grimly unwinds a length of cotton. 'And he did at least have the foresight – the emotional maturity – to ring me, immediately, once the shit started hitting the fan.'

'Charming turn of phrase!' she commends him.

He shrugs.

'So that girl … I forget her name …'

'Who?'

'*Who?*'

She delivers him a sharp look.

'You mean Jen?'

'Jen. That's right. Jen. She said he was being sick everywhere?'

'She did?' Gene grimaces. 'Well that's a slight
exaggeration ...'

'She said there was vomit everywhere. It was "wall-to-wall",
she said.'

Gene takes off his watch and his rings, and turns to place
them on his bedside table. 'Thanks, Jen,' he mouths.

'Perhaps it wasn't just pot they smoked ...' Sheila muses,
paranoid. 'Are you sure they didn't ...?'
She removes the needle, horrified. 'I mean it could've been
anything! We plainly have *no* idea ...'

'It was definitely just pot.' Gene refuses to be roused. He
pulls off his jumper, then starts to unbutton his shirt. 'A very
powerful variety, that's all. Some kind of – I don't know –
skunk ...'

His wife moistens the tip of the length of cotton on her
tongue, and then holds it – with the needle – up to the light. 'I
find it difficult to understand,' she ruminates, darkly, half to
herself, 'how a supposedly mature and responsible adult, a
public figure, a *sports*man of all people ...'

Gene draws a deep, preparatory breath.
'For the record,' he murmurs, his voice so quiet as to be
virtually inaudible, 'it wasn't actually Ransom's dope.'
Sheila continues to try and thread the needle.
'It wasn't Ransom's dope,' Gene repeats, mechanically, 'it was
Stan's dope.'

The fine piece of khaki-coloured cotton finally enters the
tiny hole. His wife releases the thread and pulls it through.
'Pardon?' she says, once the thread has been carefully secured
and knotted.
Gene doesn't respond. She gazes at him, blankly.

'*Stan's* dope?' she eventually echoes, her voice wavering, affectingly. Gene nods.

'But …?'

She springs to her feet and goes over to close the bedroom door (perhaps afraid that Mallory might overhear them, and be instantly corrupted by the news). 'How? When? *Where?*'

Gene bites his lip.

'School? College? Basketball? *Tell* me!'

'Taizé,' he eventually mutters.

'*What?!*'

She gapes at him, amazed.

'Taizé,' Gene repeats. 'He said he got it at Christian camp.'

'*Christian* camp?' His wife is stunned.

'He said everyone was doing it there.' Gene shrugs. 'He said –'

'And he smuggled it *home*?' she interrupts. 'I mean he actually *smuggled* it home on the Eurostar?'

'Yup' – Gene nods – 'I'm afraid so.'

'How much?'

'Not much. Just one joint. He said he was saving it for a special –'

'Good Lord!'

She crosses herself, and then, 'Look at me!' she exclaims, mortified. 'I'm *crossing* myself!'

'The point is –'

'I mean after everything we've *taught* him! After everything *you've* been through. *And* Mallory! After everything …!'

'I know.' Gene takes a couple of steps towards her. 'I'm as shattered by this as you are. But if it's any kind of compensation, I honestly think he learned a valuable lesson today, and he's not going to be rushing off to do it again any time soon.'

'You already said that.'

She takes a couple of steps away from him. 'And it isn't,' she adds, flatly, almost as an afterthought, 'it isn't "okay", I mean.'

Gene stares at her, morosely, and then returns to the bed. He removes his shirt. He is silently cursing Jen in his head. Sheila has sat back down and is picking up the jacket. 'Why did you say she was here again?' she asks (as though reading his thoughts). 'I'm still a little confused about that part.'

'Your guess is as good as mine.' Gene shrugs, and then, 'D'you need more light?'

He leans over to the lamp on his bedside table and turns it on. As the extra light fills the room, she glances over at him, irritably, then her eyes widen as they settle on a strange, blue-red bruise on his shoulder.

'When she found out that Ransom had stayed here overnight ...'

'Found out?' Sheila echoes, distractedly. 'How did she find out?'

'She rang me at work.'

'She has your mobile number?'

His wife looks mildly surprised.

'She got it off one of the receptionists at the Thistle.'

He sits down on the bed.

'I see.' Sheila nods. She seems to find this answer satisfactory. 'When she found out he'd stayed here overnight, she demanded our home phone number.'

'And you gave it to her?'

His wife's eyes are drawn back to the bruise again as he reaches under his pillow and withdraws a vest and some pyjama bottoms.

'She caught me off guard. I was in the middle of this complicated scenario at work, collecting a little girl from her childminder as a favour to a client. It was ...' He scowls. 'It was complicated,' he repeats. 'The child had been jumping on a trampoline without any underwear, and the neighbour – the childminder – asked me to have a quiet word with the mother – or the aunt ...'

He glances over at his wife as he speaks. She is staring at him, almost speculatively. He struggles to decipher the exact nature of her look.

'It was this ridiculously loaded situation,' he continues, his confidence starting to flag slightly, 'a *stupid* situation, just really embarrassing, and then Jen happens to ring up in the middle of it all.' He grimaces. 'I just gave her the number to get rid of her. She probably tried it a few times, got no answer, so decided to head over to the house on the off-chance –'

'She has our address.'
This is a statement, not a question, and Sheila's voice sounds disturbingly matter-of-fact.

'Well she knows you're the rector of the church.' Gene shrugs. 'It probably didn't take much native ingenuity to work it out.'
Gene starts to take his trousers off.

'You have a huge bruise on your back,' his wife announces.
'Pardon?'
He peers over at her, frowning.
'A huge bruise.'
'Do I?'
Gene puts a clumsy hand to his back.
'Higher. On the shoulder. It's pretty bad, actually.'
Gene tries to peer over at it.

'D'you have any idea how you might've done that?'
'Uh ... No.' Gene scowls. 'Not really.'

Sheila gently places down the jacket. She suddenly looks pale, almost ill.
'I need to clear my head,' she announces, standing up.
'Why? Where are you going?' Gene asks, confused (still feeling around, aimlessly, for the bruise).

She walks to the door, her voice so low when she finally answers him as to be rendered virtually inaudible.

'To pray,' she murmurs, huskily, 'that's all.'

A flat-footed, heavily pregnant Jamaican woman (a veritable hormonal maelstrom, with slightly receding hair, a bad weave, gappy teeth and tired, bloodshot eyes) stands at Ransom's shoulder as he completes his shave in a large, beautifully appointed hotel bathroom.

'Remember what Jimmie always use to say, eh, Stu?'

She tenderly plucks a pale flake of dandruff from the shoulder of his dark grey bathrobe.

No response.

Ransom carefully glides the razor from his chin to his sideburn.

'Jimmie always say: "Good golf – *successful* golf – not about aiming for the star or settin' yourself unreachable goal, it all about acceptin' where you are, consolidatin' what you got, then gently transitioning to the next level."'

Still no response.

'Baby step, eh, Stu?' she persists. 'That all we need from you right now. That all we askin' from you right now. Not huge leap or giant stride or any of that other crazy shit. Just baby step. You know?'

'*We?*'

Ransom leans forward and inspects the small glass cut on his cheek in the mirror.

'*We?*' he repeats, snorting, his eyes flicking towards her. 'I thought I sacked all the others.'

'You sack me too' – she grimaces – 'but I was dumb enough to stick around.'

'Yeah, funny, that ...'

Ransom gently moves his nose to the left and carefully applies the blade to an especially hard-to-reach area below his right nostril.

'Must be some kinda glutton for punishment!'
She tries to make light of it.

'You know what your problem is?' Ransom directs an utterly insincere, saccharin-coated smile her way. 'One might even go so far as to call it your Achilles heel, Esther: *loyalty*. You're just way too loyal. Loyal to a fault. And while it's extremely sweet ...'

He nudges a tiny fleck of foam from the tip of his nose with his knuckle. '... almost touching, on occasion, it sometimes borders on ...' He pauses, pensively. 'It borders on the annoying. You're like one of those irritating, little burrs that gets snagged on my trouser leg when I'm stuck in the rough. Those pesky little fuckers that won't come off no matter how hard I pick away at them.'
He wrinkles up his nose, fastidiously.

'Pick all you wan', darlin',' Esther mutters, falling – still deeper – into her smooth, honey-coated *patois*, ''cos I ain't goin' nowhere wit-out dem nine an' a half mont' outstandin' back pay, ya hear?'

'How much is that in total?' Ransom wonders, idly. 'In old money, I mean: pounds and pence? I don't even know what I'm paying you. I don't even know if you're *worth* that amount. I don't even know what you're doing for me nowadays ...' He glances at her in the mirror. 'What *are* you doing for me? What's your role? What's your official title?'

'Chump,' Esther answers, effortlessly.
'That'd be right ...' Ransom addresses himself in the mirror again: '"Stuart Ransom, Professional Golfer, Chalk-talked by Chump!"'
He rolls his eyes, drolly. 'I mean "transitioning", Esther? Seriously? Is it any fucking wonder my game has gone to shite?'

He returns to his shave again.

'Me not chalk-talkin' ya, Stu,' Esther mutters, wounded, 'just offerin' some tiny scrap of encouragement at the start of a long week ...'
She glances over her shoulder with a significant look. 'I don't see nobody else here clamouring to do it.'

'Is this how low we've sunk?' Ransom addresses himself in the mirror again. 'My idiotic PA catches half of *Happy Gilmore* on Sky Movies Gold and suddenly starts thinking she's Dr Bob fuckin' Rotella?!'

'All I'm sayin" – Esther reaches out and adjusts the angle of the spotlight above the mirror to render the golfer's complexion in a more congenial pallor – 'is Jimmie had a fair point to make about –'

'Yeah. Baby steps. *Ouch.*'
Ransom winces as she inadvertently jogs him with her bump. The razor nicks into the side of his lip. She promptly leans down and grabs a square of toilet paper from the roll, tears off a tiny corner, crumples it up, and applies it to the wound.

'So far as I recollect,' Ransom mutters, 'Jimmie had a lot of fair points to make. If only he'd kept his cock in his pocket he could've still been making them.'

'Jimmie cock never enter into it!' Esther snorts, withdrawing. 'The man a fine coach – a great coach – an' cheap at half the money. Truth is, you just couldn't handle what he was dishin' out.'
'Lucky you were there to handle it, then, eh?' Ransom purrs, eyeing her distended belly, meaningfully.

Esther doesn't react.
'And while we're on the subject,' Ransom continues, 'Jimmie? A great coach? Seriously? *A great coach?!* He wasn't even a *good* coach! He was average, at best. And he was the worst kind of drunk: boring, stupid, charmless ... A *hectoring* drunk. The man was a total, fucking liability, Esther. He was also

twice your age and happily married when he knocked you up. Remember?'

'Change the record, Stu,' Esther mutters, flushing. 'Me not got nothin' to do with it. It was *all* about you an' your precious swing.'

'Oh really?' Ransom half turns to face her.

'Jimmie was a damn fool tryin' a mess with it.' She rolls her eyes, sardonic. 'Nation may rise an' nation may fall,' she sings, 'but the Lord knows: Stuart Ransom swing – that precious swing of his – transcend it all!'

'I know you're not the sharpest knife in the drawer, Est,' Ransom grumbles, 'but don't you find it even a *little* bit ironic that my swing was the thing Jimmie most admired about my game when we first started working together? Jimmie loved my swing! Jimmie said my swing was "at the heart" of who I was as a golfer! He said my swing had – I quote – "a superabundance of character"! I mean what a friggin' wheeze! What a rib-tickler! What a monumental, fuckin' *card* the old boy was, eh?'

'Ha ha,' Esther laughs, hollowly.

'How's that famous saying go?' Ransom wonders. 'The one about people always killing the things they love?'

'Ain't got a clue.'

Esther is implacable.

'It's a famous saying, dick-head! Look it up on Ask Jeeves or something if you don't believe me.'

'I'll be sure an' do that' – Esther nods – 'on my next schedule day off.'

(Esther hasn't been scheduled a day off in the previous thirteen months.)

Ransom digests this sullen observation, without comment, before: 'Where's the latest edition of *Golf World* got to? Did you unpack the rest of my stuff yet? I wanna show you that Butch Harmon piece I told you about in the cab. The one where he says nobody gives a flying fuck about swing knowledge any more. The one where he says swing knowledge is yesterday's chip paper ...'

'Ain't stop him floggin' that Swing Memory device of his all over the golfin' channel every chance he get,' Esther demurs.

'That's just a sop for the punters!' Ransom snorts. 'He's all about "maximizing your ability" nowadays – which means doing more of what you do well, basically ...'

'Baby step.' Esther shrugs.

'Baby steps my arse! It's a completely different psychological approach!' Ransom scoffs. 'Fuck baby steps! Leave baby steps to the babies! Look at Westwood for Christ's sake! He got his game back by just allowing himself to *feel* again ...'

'Feel again?!' Esther echoes, disparagingly. 'Lee rebuild his game from the ground up, an' lost himself three stone while he was at it!'

Esther slaps Ransom's belly with the back of her hand. 'You want his dietician number so you can fire her, too?'

'What *is* it with you and paternity?' Ransom hits back where it hurts most. 'Three kids by different dads, and each time it's like some major, friggin' whodunnit – a bad episode of friggin' *Poirot*! A stupid game of friggin' *Cluedo*! Who's the daddy, Esther? Eh? Who's the daddy?' He pokes at her belly with his forefinger. 'Professor Plum in the map room with the laser-pointer? Colonel Mustard in the pantry with the turkey baster?'

Esther sucks on her tongue in such a way as to render a verbal response unnecessary.

'I wouldn't even mind' – Random smirks – 'but just as soon as you push the little buggers out you ship them straight back to Jamaica to live with your bloody mother!'

Esther snatches a clipboard from its temporary resting-place on top of a nearby towel rail and appraises it, frowning, struggling to maintain her composure. 'Don Hansard phone,' she informs him, indicating towards a yellow Post-it note glued to the top page.

Ransom pays her no heed. He is inspecting her bump with a look of morbid fascination on his face. '*Man!* That thing's incredible,' he exclaims (as if seeing it for the first time in all its magnitude). 'It's huge! It's multi-dimensional! Are you sure you got a kid in there and not a litter of bulldogs? It's mad! It's like three bumps all in one. It's like you're about to give birth to a giant, horizontal *turd* ...'

'Don Hansard phone,' she repeats, half an octave higher.

'Perhaps that wily, old piss-head didn't knock you up after all,' Ransom muses. 'Wanna know who I'm putting my money on?'

She stares at him, stony-faced.

'Mr fuckin' Whippy!' Ransom cackles, then commences whistling a child's nursery rhyme (to simulate the approach of an ice-cream van). Esther doesn't crack a smile. She peers down at her clipboard again, blinking.

'In fact d'you have any idea what a bloody *state* you look?' Ransom demands, stepping aside so she can appraise herself in the mirror. 'You're a mess! Your face is covered in acne. Your hair's just a mop. Your grooming's gone fuckin' haywire. I mean who the hell told you it was okay to combine fuchsia with apricot? *Eh?* You're Stuart Ransom's manager, woman! Start acting like it! Develop a bit of self-respect! Just look at your top! It's worn out. It's a fucking *rag*. The fabric's all thin and bobbly where it's been stretched over the –'

'He runnin' a Course Management seminar,' Esther butts in, reading from the board, 'an' he think you might –'

'*What?!*' Ransom scoffs, returning to his shave again. 'Hansard wants *me* to help run a seminar on Course Management?! Has he gone totally doo-lally? I couldn't Course Manage a piss-up in a fuckin' brewery!'

He pauses for a second, inspects his face in the mirror, does some final clearing up around his jawline, then adds, 'How much?'

'How much?' she echoes.

'The fee, Dumbo!'

'No fee.'

'Come again?' Ransom's incredulous. 'He expects me to do it f' *nowt*?!'

Esther shakes her head. 'He want you go as –'

'As his patsy? His mentor? His *bitch*?! To offer moral, fuckin' support?!' Ransom interrupts. '*Gratis*? Out of the goodness of my own heart?! With *my* fuckin' overdraft? Is he nuts?'

'As a student,' Esther finally finishes off.

Ransom's smile fades. He stares at her, blankly.

'A student,' she repeats. 'Don student. I said you probably wouldn't.'

'Probably?' Ransom's jaw drops. 'You told him I *probably* wouldn't ...?'

'It's four thousand for the week – dollar. No board. Then flight on top. We still in dispute with American Airline, remember? Don offerin' ten per cent reduction for some promotional DVD he been cookin' up. I tell him even with full complimentary we be stretchin' our budget –'

'Hang on a second ...' Ransom scowls. 'Please tell me you didn't actually let slip to that gobby, talentless little pip-squeak that Stuart Ransom is strapped for cash?'

'Strap?!' Esther echoes, astonished. 'We stony-broke, Stu! We mortgage to the hilt! We strugglin' to find cash for last night bar bill!'

'And you reckon that's okay, do you?' Ransom's almost hoarse with rage now. 'I mean you reckon it's perfectly acceptable, as Stuart Ransom's manager, as Stuart Ransom's *chief representative* on fuckin' *earth*, to go around cheerfully informing complete, friggin' strangers what he can and he can't afford?!'

'Keep your hair on, boy!' Esther exclaims. 'This Don Hansard we talkin' about ...'

'Holy *fuck*, Esther!'

Ransom grabs a towel from the nearby rail and pushes his face into it, horrified.

Esther sucks her tongue, bored. 'You went to Q School with Don Hansard,' she sighs, 'you bail him out in Finland over that dodgy score-card. He live in your house in Holland Park, rent-free, for eighteen month after he split from Shirley. That man *owe* you, Stu –'

She's interrupted by a gentle knock on the door. She inspects her watch. 'That'll be Toby. He schedule in for ten.'

Ransom's head remains sunk in the towel. His hands are shaking.

'An' we not even get to look at the itinerary,' she grumbles, observing the hands with a somewhat jaundiced eye. 'You want him come back in the morning? You got Terence Nimrod at nine ...'

Ransom makes no effort to respond.

'We ain't got nobody for the bag,' she persists. 'The course got three caddie, but they all book up an' *I* sure as hell not humpin' that thing around again ...'

She places an anxious hand on her stomach. 'I hear James Ray twiddlin' his thumb in Dublin while Tim Pagel recovering from back surgery ...'

Still nothing from Ransom.

'Look, me not wanna freak you out, Stu,' she murmurs, her tone suddenly gentle, almost caressing, 'but you been talkin' about yourself in the third person again ...'

Pause.

'The shrink said ...'

'Bollocks!' Ransom's face emerges from the towel, puce and indignant.

'You done it three time in as many minute.' Esther is typically unyielding. 'You said, "as Stuart Ransom manager"; "as Stuart Ransom chief repre—"'

'It was a figure of speech!' Ransom hisses.

'Everything that come out your mouth is a figure of speech.' Esther shrugs. 'Everything that come out *my* mouth is a figure of speech, come to that.'

'I don't think you grasp the meaning of a "figure of speech",' Ransom rejoins.

'I understand perfectly well, thank you very much,' Esther demurs. 'I also remember all what the shrink say about it. He say referrin' to yourself in the third person was an early warning sign that you was becoming "detached from reality" and it must be strongly discourage under *all* possible circumstances.'

'I can't believe you're bringing this up!' Ransom's childishly defensive, bleating, almost stamping his foot. 'And at such a critical moment, Esther! The start of the week's play!'

'There never gonna be a good time, Stu,' Esther maintains.

'At the *start of a week's play*, Esther!' Ransom reiterates. 'It's completely counter-productive!'

A second knock on the door.

'The pro-am not till Friday,' Esther informs him, checking the itinerary.

'And it was a *virus*,' Ransom persists, slinging the towel on to the floor. 'A *virus*. Yeah? I was *ill*. My face was like a balloon. My balls were covered in scabs. It was *glandular*. I only saw the shrink because the insurance people –'

'It a *yeast* infection, Stu!' Esther snaps. 'If a woman get a yeast infection she go to the chemist an' buy herself some bicarbonate, then it done and dusted. When you get yourself a yeast infection it glandular fever! It "Stop the world! Hold the front page! Stuart Ransom got him some tiny little scab on his testicle!"'

'How many times do I have to repeat myself?' Ransom's bored and exasperated. 'The yeast infection was just a tiny symptom of the larger *malaise* ...'

'As God is my witness' – Esther raises an impatient hand to ward him off – 'Jimmie tell me you was discussing the Course Management idea just a couple of day since ...'

'Oh yeah, I discussed it with him all right.' Ransom's face is glowing. 'I discussed it with him directly before I *sacked* his scraggy arse!'

'Course Management always come in handy,' Esther persists. 'Remember Royal Birkdale? *Huh?* Micky fall down on his knee an' he *beg* you not to use that wood on the twelfth ...'

'The bloody wood!' Ransom throws up his hands. 'One shot! One, stupid, bloody shot! When will I ever hear the end of it?'

Esther stares at him, darkly.

'Well if you not listen to your coach, an' you not listen to your caddie, then maybe ...'

'Maybe what? I should listen to *you*?' Ransom smirks, contemptuously.

A third knock at the door. Esther hands him the clipboard, then bends down, with a grunt, to pick up the dropped towel. 'Could do worse,' she murmurs, straightening up again.

'See this?'

Ransom points to the small cut on his cheek. 'This is what happens when I give you free rein with my career, Esther. I end up meeting a deranged, drug-addled, bottle-toting kid whose mother I put into a coma at the hotel she formerly worked in as a *publicity* stunt.'

'No point cryin' over spilt milk.' Esther shrugs. ''Specially when it get ya page twelve in the *Mail* ...' she snorts, mirthlessly. 'Man, that as close as you been to the sport section in some while ...'

'This is precisely why my life is falling apart!' Ransom gurgles.

131

'This is precisely why you *got* a career right now,' Esther corrects him.

'I have a career because I'm a world-class golfer,' Ransom corrects her.

'You got a career because you could handle a club an' had good hair – good, thick hair – fifteen, long year ago,' Esther retorts, sharply. 'Ya got lucky, Stu. But your luck finally run out. Now you gotta buckle down an' work, same as the rest of us.'

Ransom's hand moves to his hairline, then down to the cut on his cheek again.

A fourth knock sounds on the door.

'Some likkle-ickle, baby cut on your cheek!' Esther guffaws, heading off to answer it. 'I took a bigger blow to my dignity this afternoon gettin' your room upgraded.'

'Great. Terrific. *Thanks*.' Ransom turns to face the mirror again, wincing. 'The gloves are finally off, eh?'

'Gloves?' Esther chuckles, wryly. 'I wa' dragged up in Trenchtown, Stu. We never had us no gloves in the ghetto.'

'*Jeez*. Cue the friggin' violins!' Ransom mutters, palpably outmanoeuvred.

'Listen up,' Esther volunteers, fingers gripping the door handle. 'If you want me *treat* you "world class", then you better start *behavin'* world class: play a round in under four over par, dally more than twenty minute on the range, phone your wife so's I don't spend half my born day fieldin' her call, quit them muscle relaxant an' ditch the belly putter. Deal?' Esther spits on her palm and proffers him her hand.

Ransom doesn't respond. He's staring down at his itinerary, scowling. After several seconds he pulls the yellow Post-it from the front and screws it into a ball. 'Don fucking Hansard offering *the* Stuart Ransom pathetic, little hand-outs on a Course Management seminar?!' he scoffs. 'That's pure, unadulterated bullshit! It's an outrage! I mean a whole ten per cent off for a tragic DVD appearance?!'

'Third person, Stu,' Esther warns him, sharply.

Ransom drops the Post-it into the toilet and flushes. 'That sucks, man,' he mutters, watching its frenetic progress around the bowl with a distinctly martyred air. 'That stinks. That just really fuckin' ...'

He yanks, aimlessly, at the sagging belt on his robe as the offending, yellow scrap finally disappears from view. '... that *smarts*.'

4

'Why fret?' she demands. 'Why all this pointless fretting? You can entertain who you like in here. It's not the men's toilet *per se* – it's your own, private room. It's your cubby. It's your special little watchtower ...'

Jen pulls out a stool, sits down on it, tosses a blonde pigtail over her shoulder, bends forward, pushes her two thumbs into the diamanté-lined elasticated tops of her pink knee-high socks and yanks them both up by a couple of extra centimetres.

'My "watchtower"?' Gene echoes, bemused.

'It's kinda weird, though, don't you reckon?' Jen peers around her, frowning. 'I mean having an office with a large window looking straight out on to the latrines?'

She twists sideways, presses her hands on to the wide shelf that runs below the window and gazes through it. At this precise moment the door into the toilet opens, a man enters, sees Jen at the window, does a rapid 180-degree turn and leaves.

'God. I bet you see some extraordinary sights in here,' she sighs.

'Strange as this may seem, Jen' – Gene struggles to control the edge of sarcasm in his voice – 'I'm in the toilets to work' – he motions towards the mop – 'not to perve on the poor clients all day.'

'But why else would there be a window if you weren't meant to look out of it?' Jen demands.

'So people can look *in?*' Gene hazards a guess. 'Ask for help, maybe?'

'But why would they want to do that?'

'I've no idea ...' Gene shrugs. 'For reassurance. Or if there's a blockage in one of the toilets, or if they've run out of –'

'Hi there!'

Jen waves through the window at a teenage boy who has just entered. He blushes, apologizes, and leaves.

'Bless him!' Jen coos. 'He thinks he came into the Ladies by mistake!'

'Perhaps you could move back a little?' Gene suggests.

'I see you've won three awards!' Jen jumps up and goes to inspect a series of certificates on the wall. 'You're such a clever boy! Such a powerhouse! Is there *anything* you're not brilliant at, Eugene?'

She turns and bats her lashes at him.

'Oh, I can think of a few things,' Gene murmurs, scowling.

'I love this place!' Jen skips around the office, baby-clapping. 'It's just wonderful! I'm perfectly at home! Are you hiring at the moment?'

'No.'

'Aw.'

Jen sticks out her lower lip and pretends to look traumatized.

An elderly man enters the toilet, spots Jen, exclaims loudly, then dashes for a cubicle. He slams his way inside and shoots the bolt.

'Oh dear.' Jen presses her nose against the window and peers out (leaving a large smudge of make-up in her stead). 'I think we might've given that old boy a bit of a turn ...'

The toilet door swings open again. Before she can instigate any further chaos, Gene grabs Jen by the arm and frog-marches her into an extensive broom cupboard to the rear of the room.

'Gene, you old devil!' Jen squeals as he gently prods her inside.

He holds the door ajar with his body, maintaining a careful gap of at least two feet between them.

'So what exactly can I do for you, Jen?' he asks. He sounds careworn.

'Ooh! Now *there's* a question!' Jen camps it up for all she's worth.

'I'm serious.' (He's having none of it.)

Jen leans her elbow against the wall, curls a pigtail around her finger and assesses him, coolly. 'Was Sheila really pissed off yesterday?' she wonders. Gene takes a moment to consider his answer, but before he can respond: 'Because she's quite *scary* when she's angry, don't you reckon?' Jen runs on. 'She actually quite *scared* me when I rang. Does she scare you too, sometimes?'

She blinks up at him, tremulously.

'No. Sheila doesn't scare me.' Gene almost smiles in spite of himself.

'Then why didn't you tell her about Stan half-inching the jeep?' Jen enquires, with killer precision.

'Why?' Gene echoes, unnerved (and not a little indignant). 'That's none of your business, quite frankly.'

He delivers her what he imagines is a reproving look. Jen appears signally unmoved by it. He quickly relents. 'I was just biding my time if you must know,' he backtracks. 'I planned to tell her after dinner, but then you rang and beat me to it …'

His attention is momentarily diverted by a brief commotion in the toilets (the rattling of a plastic toilet roll holder as it jumps clear of its metal supports and clatters down on to the stone tiles below). Gene scowls over towards the stalls, then returns his focus back to Jen again. 'Peerless timing, by the way,' he adds.

'I aim to please!' Jen bats her lashes, unrepentant. 'So did Ransom get back in contact?' she wonders, almost as an afterthought.

'Ransom?' Gene reaches up and pulls the tiniest remnant of a spider's web from the corner of the doorframe. 'When?'

'Last night.'

'Nope.' Gene shakes his head. 'Why would he?'

'Why?' Jen's astonished. 'To apologize, you idiot! For ditching poor Stan like that.'

'Oh. Uh, no.' Gene wipes the remnant of web on to a clean piece of shammy which protrudes from one of several pockets in the front of his uniform (a baggy, synthetic jumpsuit with questionable design attributes). 'He didn't, as it happens.'

'What a worm!' Jen's appalled. 'Well it's extra lucky I turned up when I did, then, eh?'

She beams at him, proudly, ruthlessly pressing home her advantage.

'You saved the day,' Gene affirms, somewhat mechanically, 'like I said in my message –'

'Stan was shitting himself,' she interrupts, 'he begged me not to ring you – *pleaded* with me. Did he mention that?'

'Uh ...' Gene pushes an uneasy hand through his auburn hair. 'He said Ransom wanted him to head back to the rectory and pretend like a gang of local hoodies had 'jacked the vehicle. I swear to God he was seriously considering it! He thought you'd cancel his trip. He was going frantic about it. Then the nausea kicked in, obviously ...'

'We were just happy to get him home in one piece ...' Gene does his best to head her off.

'I guess this means you kinda *owe* me.' Jen sighs, inspecting her nails then glancing up, coquettishly. Gene meets her gaze, somewhat guardedly. Jen promptly misreads his expression. 'Are you cross with me because I had to run off before you could make it home yourself?' she demands.

'Not at all.' Gene's shocked. 'You were late for your shift. You'd already gone way beyond the call of duty ...'

Jen inspects the split-ends at the tip of her pigtail for a while, mollified. 'I can't believe he never rang to apologize.'

She grimaces. 'What a spineless little shit! I'm gonna give him a piece of my mind the next time we meet up.'

Pause.

'You think there'll be a next time?'

Gene's understandably quizzical.

'Sure. Why not?' Jen shrugs. 'We need to seek retribution. I mean it's not personal or anything,' she smirks. 'Heaven forbid! It's just karmic.'

It takes a full second for Gene to digest this information, then another to muster his response to it.

'Have you given any thought to going public?' Jen wonders, meanwhile.

'Sorry?' Gene's still five paces behind.

'It'd be a fab story for the tabs, don't you reckon?' she muses. 'Bad-boy golfer feeds under-age kid muscle relaxants then takes him for "joyride" in stolen military jeep?'

'Bloody hell!' Gene's horrified.

'We'd naturally do our best to keep Stan's personal details out of the mix,' she concedes, 'but if the Tuckers can make a mint out of this stuff ...'

'The Tuckers?'

Gene stares at her, blankly, then suddenly – unexpectedly – everything just falls into place.

'The Tuckers!' he exclaims, knocking the side of his head with his palm, infuriated by his own idiocy. '*Ann* Tucker – *Noel* Tucker. I *knew* the face was familiar!'

Jen raises a single, inquisitive brow.

'I bumped into him again yesterday on my rounds,' Gene explains. 'Stratton Street. There's a girl with red hair ...'

'That'll be Vee,' Jen affirms. 'Really pretty. Party organizer. Into all the forties stuff. I never met the mum. She worked as a housekeeper at the Thistle. Before our time, I guess. A real sweetheart by all accounts – bred cats – wouldn't say boo to a goose. Patty Marsh from the laundry was her best bud ...'

'Hang on a second' – Gene's frowning – 'I'm certain the name was Wickers on the electoral roll. I checked it against my details before I made the visit.'

'Tucker was Reggie's business name,' Jen elucidates, 'the name he tattooed under: Reggie T. You must remember Tucker's tattoo parlour on Kildare Road?'

'Of course.' Gene nods. 'Next to the old Bingo Hall.'

'Well he always went by Tucker, but his real name was Wickers. Tucker was his mother's maiden name. The dad buggered off when he was a kid. I'm not sure of all the whys and the wherefores, but while he always insisted on going by Tucker, the family went with Wickers, purely for legal reasons, I guess. Both his kids still go by it. Can't say I blame them, either' – she shrugs – 'given the dodgy nature of their dad's public persona – the Tucker legacy. All the BNP malarkey ...'

'And it was Stuart Ransom who put Ann Tucker into a coma with that stray ball of his ...'

'*Duh!*' Jen delivers him a pitying look. 'I found out all the gory details last night on Google,' she happily fills him in. 'Transpires that Mrs Tucker did a bit of fetching and carrying for an elderly neighbour – a widower – whose son'd bought him a couple of tickets for this big charity golf gala in Milton Keynes. The day of the actual tournament an ash tree falls on to his son's conservatory – it's chaos – and he can't actually make it, so Mrs Tucker kindly steps into the breach. Fast forward to a few hours later: Ransom's on the third hole teeing this massive shot. Mrs Tucker is sitting on a blanket enjoying a picnic – chowing down on a scotch egg or a sausage roll; history fails to record which it was, exactly – when, *whack!* Ransom's ball hits her square between the shoulders. She slams, face-forward, into the rough, a piece of pork meat jammed in her throat. Everyone thinks she's concussed from the blow – which she is – but they don't realize that there's a secondary problem till it's way too late.

140

She's starved of oxygen for about five minutes. Suffers serious brain damage.'

'It was just a fluke, though, an accident, surely?' Gene rallies to Ransom's defence. 'I mean not to diminish the obvious tragedy of the whole thing,' he qualifies.

'Oh yeah. Completely,' Jen concurs. 'But someone still had to take the rap for it. And like I said, her husband, Reggie Tucker, was Luton's premier local Nazi. He was madly litigious by all accounts. You might remember him as the public face of that long-running battle with the local Trades and Standards Commission – when the EU forced us to go metric a few years back? Reggie ran under the banner of "The Upholder of the Sanctity of the Great British Pint" ...'

Jen rolls her eyes. 'The pathetic old troglodyte.'

'Spoken with all the patriotic ardour of a girl who subsists entirely on root beer and Big Macs,' Gene mutters.

'The bottom line,' Jen continues (ignoring this cruel – if utterly accurate – assault), 'was that he was determined to get some kind of compensation for his family ...'

'I guess you can see his point,' Gene concedes.

'And naturally Ransom's the first person he tries to finger for it' – Jen nods – 'but it turns out Ransom isn't insured. Worse still, he's stony broke. In fact he's recently declared himself bankrupt after the collapse of his clothing line – although rumour had it at the time that he'd secretly squirrelled most of his cash abroad, to one of the Caribbean Islands. Barbados? Bermuda?'

Gene shrugs.

'So next he tries to finger the course itself – who it turns out are actually part of this massive, American-based conglomerate – and it doesn't take him long to realize that with the meagre resources at his disposal he hasn't a hope in hell of beating them in court. He even chances his arm with the St John's ambulance people ...'

Gene winces.

'Not a good look,' Jen agrees.

'But what about his wife, meanwhile?' Gene interjects. 'Ann, was it?'

'Well Ann is now out of the coma and slowly recovering in hospital under the tender ministrations of a Haitian nurse. Takes almost a year before she's ready to sit up, another three months before she can be fed orally, another six till she can start talking again, and then, when she finally does, it's in pidgin French! Won't utter a single syllable of English! Refuses to! It's Mr Tucker's worst nightmare: he finds himself married to the enemy!'

'A rich irony.' Gene grins, tickled by the idea.

'And then some!' Jen concurs. 'He promptly starts legal proceedings against the hospital ...'

'Oh dear.'

'... and then six, short months later, he kicks the bucket.'

'Ouch.' Gene winces.

'Heart attack brought on by all the stress.' Jen shrugs. 'Noel promptly takes over where his dad left off. But Noel's a total flake – has a dope addict girlfriend who's up the duff. The whole thing implodes, basically. Gets really nasty. Really complicated. Really personal.'

'Is the mother fully recovered now?' Gene wonders.

'Not sure.' Jen pulls her T-shirt askew and shows Gene a small star on her collar bone.

'The collar bone,' she informs him, 'is one of the most painful places to get a tattoo ...'

She shows him a second star on the other side. 'So muggins here gets two.'

'And that's Reggie's work?' (Gene tries not to inspect the stars too closely.)

'Nope. They're Vee's. She worked as her dad's Saturday girl for a while – trained as his apprentice. Did these babies illegally, obviously.' Jen curtseys, proudly. 'She was pretty good even back then. Although after he died she got into all this weird, ultra-realist stuff ...'

Jen grimaces.

'Hang on ...' Gene's confused. 'I thought you said she was a party organizer?'

'Yeah. Yeah, she was. And she didn't just organize, either – she was a *real* party girl' – Jen gives him a significant look – 'but after the accident she became her mum's main carer. Needs must. They'd sold the dad's business premises to settle their legal fees, so she set up this little studio at home, quit partying and started concentrating on the tattooing side of things again.'

'Is she any good?' Gene wonders.

'Oh yeah. She's a genius at it' – Jen nods, emphatically – 'turns down way more commissions than she accepts. Her dad was a real traditionalist – roses, swallows, pin-ups, that kinda stuff, but Vee's completely left that scene behind her, now. She's like ultra-ultra real. Some people love what she does, others think she's completely whacko. I dunno – I guess it just depends on what you're into ...'

Jen shrugs. 'I mean I'm more in the traditional camp myself ...'

'Traditional?!' Gene snorts. 'You?!'

'Yeah.' Jen frowns. 'Like I'd much rather have a cartoon on my arm than something more literal ...'

She pauses again, thoughtfully. 'Although you'd be surprised how uptight people get about the whole thing. There's this massive division in the tattooing world – this chasm – between the artists who do the traditional stuff and the ultra-realists. Floating around in the middle you've got the "mech" bunch – the nerds – who do all the nasty, sinewy, machine-based work ...'

Gene scratches his head, bemusedly, struggling to follow. 'My crass, half-baked take on it,' Jen volunteers, 'if you're interested,' she adds (with a rare flash of modesty), 'is that

Vee jumped on to the ultra-realist bandwagon to shake off the shadow of her dad. It was a pretty long shadow – pretty *dark* ...'

She pauses for a moment, glancing around her, speculatively (as if finally becoming aware of her immediate surroundings): 'This is the cleanest, tidiest, most ridiculously anal broom cupboard I've ever had the privilege of spending time in,' she ruminates. 'It's absolutely spotless. It's psychotic! You could eat off the floors ...'

She inspects Gene, quizzically. 'Don't take this the wrong way or anything, but d'you honestly think this job offers a sufficient level of challenge for a man of your obvious dynamism?'

Gene just smiles, distractedly. He's still pondering the Tuckers.

Jen's eyes narrow a fraction. 'So you're interested in our little Miss Vee, are you?' she wonders.

'Interested?' Gene echoes, his cheeks reddening.

'Considering a nice sleeve or a back piece, maybe?' she teases.

'Absolutely not!' Gene's horrified.

'I guess there are worse people you could go to,' Jen maintains. 'I mean did you check out the detail on Noel's chest piece? That weird kind of wicker effect? It was stunning. Just like the real thing. And did you notice the snake?'

'I caught a brief glimpse of it.' Gene nods.

'Well that was her early stuff. She's got way better since. Although I think it's only fair to warn you' – she grins up at him, mischievously – 'word on the street is she's addicted to quims these days.'

'Quims?' Gene echoes, frowning.

'Yeah, quims. She specializes in merkins. And nipples – post-surgical. That's where the real money is.'

'I'm sorry ...?' Gene shakes his head, confused.

'Vagina wigs – merkins,' Jen smirks. 'She simulates hair on baldy vaginas. It's an Eastern thing. In the West we can't wait to get rid of it. In the East there's this craze for tattooing it on.'

Gene laughs, incredulous, but then his mind rapidly turns back to the previous morning: the cream room; the padded table; the mirror; the torch.

'I'm serious!' Jen insists. 'There's this huge market for it over in Japan. A certain percentage of Japanese girls never develop genital hair – the Japanese aren't a particularly hairy race – and they feel completely self-conscious about it –'

'But I thought Japan was the original home of the tattoo,' Gene interrupts, suspicious. 'Why travel halfway across the planet?'

'Because the practice is so closely associated with the underworld over there that it's still considered really disreputable to get tattoo work done,' Jen explains. 'Vee's a serious artist and very discreet. Her reputation's spread chiefly through word of mouth. The stuff she does looks totally real. She's the best. Go to her site on the internet. It's just amazing. I'll give you the address if you like ...' She pauses for a second as if summoning it up from memory: 'www. baldytwinkle.com'.

'Hilarious.' Gene smiles.

'It's true!' Jen squeals, slapping his arm. Gene winces. She draws back her hand and quickly checks her watch. '*Balls*. I'm rota'd on at ten. It's five past.'

She bends down and pulls up her socks again.

'Dodgy elastic?' Gene speculates.

'My kid sister said my knees are looking bony,' Jen grumbles. 'D'you think my knees are looking bony?' She hitches up her short skirt. 'Am I too thin? Be honest. My mum says it's all the stress of the exams ...'

'You're not serious about going to the papers?' Gene firmly sidesteps the contentious subject of Jen's knees.

'Give me a break!' Jen drops her skirt, insulted. 'Although feeding muscle relaxants to a minor? That's fucked up! It's heinous! The poor kid was flopping around like some kind of crazy rag doll when I found him.'

'You didn't mention that to Sheila, did you?' Gene anxiously interjects.

'Mention what? That he was all floppy?'

Jen flops forward, to illustrate.

'The muscle relaxants.'

'How d'you mean?' Jen straightens up, frowning.

'You didn't happen to mention to Sheila that he'd taken –'

'Of course I did!' Jen's horrified. 'She's his *mother* for heaven's sake! She has every right to know what sick kinds of mischief the little twit is getting up to behind her back!'

Gene's face falls.

Pause.

'Aw come *on*, Gene!' Jen guffaws, tenderly cuffing his cheek. 'D'you think I was born yesterday?'

'Well you blabbed about the dope.' Gene jerks his head to one side, irritated. 'You told her the house was "wall-to-wall vomit" ...'

'Did I?'

Jen ponders this for a moment. 'Oh. Yeah. I suppose I did ...' She shrugs. 'Well I sincerely apologize if I inadvertently violated your precious wall of silence.'

She pulls an apologetic face.

'There isn't any wall,' Gene snaps.

'Then I'm sorry if I unwittingly served a tiny ball of truth over the sagging but dependable net of lies that is your marriage,' she neatly modifies.

'I always intended to tell her,' Gene murmurs, palpably wrong-sided. 'It was simply a question of finding the right –'

'It's entirely up to you what you choose to keep from your wife,' Jen announces, blithely.

'She takes things so much to heart.' Gene's suddenly almost emotional. 'She always blames herself ...'

'*Aw*. She's very sensitive.'

Jen sticks out her lower lip.

'Yeah. She is.' Gene falters, feeling inexplicably stupid.

'If I can change the subject for just one second,' Jen rapidly interjects, stepping back and appraising him, appreciatively, from top to toe, 'd'you have any idea how incredibly *hot* you look in that uniform?'

Gene's initially surprised, then embarrassed, then nonplussed by this declaration.

'I mean Raylon's such an awful, non-breathable fabric, don't you reckon?' she twinkles, tweaking his collar as she saunters past him. Then, as she exits his office, 'Is it only me,' she sighs, glancing winsomely over her shoulder, fanning her face with her hand and winking, saucily, 'or has your central heating just gone haywire?'

'*Spice?*'

Stuart Ransom cocks a mildly jaundiced eyebrow. He and two other men are sitting at a table in the golf club's second-best restaurant (caps off, no tie) having just shared a sumptuous breakfast together. It is almost ten o'clock.

'Yeah, spice,' the first man – gawky, skinny, bespectacled, pale yet heavily freckled, wearing baggy, brown cords and a lightly checked, brushed cotton shirt with the buttons fastened right up to the collar – tentatively expands, 'it's an anagram. S.P.I.C.E. Each letter represents a different concept.'

'Not an anagram, you fool!' Esther brusquely interjects from a nearby table (speaking through a mouthful of her third *pain au chocolat*). 'It an acronym. You never done a crossword before? Lord! What they teaching you people at school these days?'

At Esther's intervention, the skinny man – who is twenty-five years old and whose name is Toby Whittaker – blushes right down to the roots of his hair.

'Fuck me, Esther,' Ransom snaps, exasperated, 'either join us or butt out, will ya?'

Esther promptly returns to her puzzle book.

The second man – older, heavy-set, blond, charming, expansive, slightly degenerate – chuckles under his breath. 'Don't you just love her?' he murmurs, eyeing Esther, appreciatively.

'Love her? Oh yeah. Like a dose of the bloody clap,' Ransom rejoins.

'S stands for simplicity,' Toby continues, somewhat haltingly.

'Well ya certainly know *all* about that ...' Esther grumbles (*sotto voce*, but still clear as a bell over the clatter of cutlery and the ceiling fans). She places down her puzzle book and commences checking the messages on her phone. 'James Ray just message me,' she calls over. 'He want forty-four per cent an' a first-class flight from Dublin on top ...'

'*Forty-four per cent?!*' Ransom's agog. 'Just for humping my bag around like some glorified friggin' *hod* carrier? Has the world finally gone mad?!'

'You got a better idea?' Esther demands (rotating her head – with the full complement of Jamaican sass – like some kind of enraged cobra).

'I do, as a matter of fact.' Ransom glowers back.

'Yeah?'

A difficult silence follows.

'Are we talking mind-control techniques, here?' The blond man – a journalist called Terence Nimrod – tries to jolly things along.

'Uh, no. More like methods of persuasion,' Toby explains (still pink from Esther's earlier insult), '*tools* of persuasion.'

'Gotcha.' Terence Nimrod picks up his coffee cup, notices that it's empty, then puts it down again, slightly deflated.

'Sorry, Tobe old boy' – Ransom inspects his own cup (still half full) – 'but whose bullshit idea did you say this was again?'

'There you've got me.' Toby looks abashed. 'I heard him on the radio while I was driving down, but I didn't quite catch –'

'You passed your test! Hallelujah!' Ransom proffers a high-five.

'I got a lift.' Toby pulls his collar away from his throat with a nervous finger. 'My mother drove me. She has an old college pal in Dunstable ...'

'Don't you find brushed cotton a little warm during the summer months?' Nimrod queries.

'I love brushed cotton.' Ransom lowers his hand, his expression wistful. 'My grandmother always had brushed cotton sheets on the beds when I was a kid ...'

'S for sincerity, was it?' Nimrod rapidly changes tack (keen to forestall one of the golfer's interminable childhood reminiscences).

'Simplicity,' Toby gently corrects him. 'In order to persuade people in an effective way, your ideas need to be really simple, straightforward and easy to grasp ...'

'No one ever bothered asking Attila the Hun for his exam certificates,' Ransom smirks.

Toby opens his mouth and then closes it again.

'Yeah. I hear old Attila could be *very* persuasive on his day,' Terence Nimrod deadpans.

'A phenomenal diarist, by all accounts,' Toby chips in.

'Diaries?' Ransom idly fingers the cover of the copy of Bruce Lee's *Artist of Life* (which is sitting on the table alongside his placemat). 'I bet those babies'd be worth a quick squizz ...'

He reaches for the pencil resting on top of Nimrod's trusty notebook, grabs it, scribbles something on to a paper serviette, folds it up and places it into the top pocket of his shirt.

'S for simplicity, then,' Toby quickly reiterates (a somewhat stricken expression on his face – although the note on Ransom's napkin merely says 'Lamisil Once'), 'followed by P which stands for perceived self-interest ...'

'Not *actual* self-interest?' Nimrod's momentarily engaged.

'Uh, no.' Toby shakes his head. 'I don't suppose it really matters *why* you're persuading someone – what your motivation is – so long as you're doing it effectively. There's nothing explicitly moral about this technique ...'

'Nobody ever made a million from selling people anything they actually *need*,' Ransom muses (ever the cynic).

'Aspirin,' Esther pipes up from her adjacent table (a line of cappuccino foam on her upper lip).

'Ballpoint pen,' Nimrod expands.

'Peer pressure plays an important role,' Toby steps in. 'I mean you're more likely to be able to persuade people of something if they see that their peers have already been convinced.'

'Think the Rwandan genocide,' Nimrod solemnly opines (trying to raise the conversational bar).

'Think Diet Coke,' Ransom counters (automatically lowering it).

'The I is quite an interesting one ...' Toby struggles manfully on.

'Is that a new edition?' Nimrod jabs a plump finger at Ransom's copy of *Artist of Life*. 'I read it years ago. From what I can recollect, the poetry's pretty torrid ...'

'I've a signed first edition at my house in LA,' Ransom promptly fibs. 'Lee's thoughts on "plasticity" struck a real chord with me. This industry's always been chock-a-block with cock-suckers and phonies ...'

Nimrod grabs the book and quickly flips through it. 'Just promise me you're not embarking on another of your interminable Eastern phases,' he pleads, 'the raw fish diet, the atrocious headbands, the enigmatic press releases ...' He rolls his eyes. 'How's a hardworking hack ever meant to scrape together any decent copy from that?'

'Now I come to think about it,' Ransom ruminates (apparently oblivious to Nimrod's pleas), 'I suppose martial arts might easily fall into the "Individual Sports" category ...' He glances up, visibly jarred by the notion. 'D'you reckon martial arts are selfish, Tel?'

'Selfish?' Toby echoes, bemused.

'*All* arts are selfish.' Nimrod throws the book back down again. 'Isn't it obvious? Jesus was a humanitarian, not a watercolourist.'

'Be that as it may,' Ransom persists, 'I read something pretty deep in there last night – pretty amazing – along the lines of' – he clears his throat and simulates a reverential mien – '"Without the black sky there would be no stars, and without the little stars we would have nothing to compare the big ones by ..."'

Nimrod listens to Ransom's cod philosophizing with a measure of forbearance, then turns towards Toby with a conspiratorial wink. 'It's all downhill from here, Tobe,' he murmurs. 'Next thing we know he'll be quoting gnomic chunks of unintelligible bullshit at us from *The Art of War* – like Paul Robinson on *Neighbours*.'

Ransom grabs the book back, infuriated (his flush truly busted). 'I was given it by a fan if you must know,' he growls, 'just some stupid kid. I was telling him about my brief correspondence with Linda Lee Cadwell –'

'Correspondence?' Esther glances up from her novel with a snort. 'You was legally oblige to send the poor woman a letter of apology after you get chuck out of a book-signing, drunk.' Ransom glares at her, darkly.

'I studied Wing Chun for almost fifteen years,' Nimrod shares.

'Fifteen years?!' Toby rocks back in his chair. 'Are you serious?!'

'Why wouldn't I be?' Nimrod asks (*faux*-offended).

'No reason,' Toby flounders. 'I just ...' He clears his throat. 'I just didn't have you down as a big martial arts fan, that's all.'

'So what *did* you have me down as?' Nimrod wonders.

'A big fat old lard-arse, that's what!' Ransom sniggers, nudging Nimrod in the ribs and then picking up his coffee cup to take a sip.

'I *am* generously proportioned' – Nimrod fondly pats his significant girth – 'principally because I wrecked my knee in competition. But I was a force to be reckoned with in my day. Spent eighteen months in Japan on a scholarship studying with the best: a former pupil of the Yip Man, no less.'

On the word 'yip', Ransom's hand suddenly goes into spasm, spilling coffee on to the tablecloth. He curses under his breath.

'The Yip Man?' Toby echoes, intrigued, helping to blot up the spill with a couple of stray napkins.

'*Professor* Yip Man to the likes of you,' Nimrod teases him. 'Bruce Lee's old Master ...' He reaches towards the book. 'There's probably a photograph ...'

Ransom struggles to return his cup to its saucer as Nimrod opens the book and starts paging through it.

'Talking of the yips ...' Toby observes, directing a significant look towards Ransom's cack-handed manoeuvrings.

'It's a trapped nerve,' Ransom quickly brushes him off, rotating his shoulder. 'I fucked it up yesterday jump-starting this old Hummer ...'

'Here we go.' Nimrod finds what he's looking for. 'Page fifteen.'

The caption under the photo reads: '*Bruce Lee (right) and his only formal martial arts instructor, Yip Man.*'

Both men inspect the photo for a second, impressed by Yip Man's look of serene austerity.

'Bruce Lee.' Nimrod chuckles, pointing.

'Some random nine-hole fan I was chatting to online the other day was telling me how there's this entire site dedicated to the condition on the net,' Toby volunteers. 'It's got a warning sign that flashes up discouraging people from reading the contents unless they're already a sufferer. Apparently the human mind is so suggestible, so fragile – so ... well, *persuadable* – that if you even try and engage with the yips on a purely intellectual level then you're much more likely to fall victim to it.'

'It's a trapped nerve, Tobe,' Ransom repeats.

'You're still using the belly putter, though?' Toby persists.

'So what if I am?' Ransom's starting to bridle. 'If it's good enough for Sergio ...'

Esther glances up from her puzzle book.

'An old Hummer, eh?' Nimrod neatly interjects, with a grin. 'Takes me back to the glory days ...'

'Yeah. *Yeah.*' Toby finally detects the sudden atmosphere. 'Well, I guess it's just a question of mind over matter ...'

Ransom grimaces. His hand is hidden from view, shoved firmly into his pocket under the table.

'... and now that you've finally managed to put that nasty case of shingles behind you –' Toby expands.

'Glandular fever,' Ransom curtly corrects him.

'My youngest daughter had it,' Nimrod sighs. 'Completely destroyed her GCSE year ...'

'I met this guy the other day who survived terminal cancer.' Ransom's keen to change the subject. 'Not just once or twice, but on *seven* separate occasions.'

'But if the condition was terminal ...' Toby's frowning. 'I mean isn't that a contradiction in terms?'

'Seven times?' Nimrod's intrigued. 'How the hell'd he manage that?'

'Uh ...' Ransom's stuck for an answer. 'Force of will,' he eventually suggests.

'That's phenomenal.' Nimrod's visibly moved. 'What type of cancer?'

'I dunno. Every type. All types. Take your pick.' Ransom shrugs. 'He came from a family of fortune-tellers ...'

'Witches?' Nimrod's reaching for his notebook. 'Was there a black magic element to the story?'

'Not that I'm aware of. They were palm-readers. He's related to some famous palm-reader – Cheerie ... Charley ... I don't remember the name, off-hand ...'

'Cheiro,' Toby suggests.

'Got it in one!' Ransom's impressed.

'Cheiro's a legend.' Toby shrugs.

'Well this guy was apparently born without a lifeline.' Ransom struggles to remember the basic details. 'The cards were totally stacked against him. I mean it was pretty much predestined that he would die from the outset. Everybody thought so. But he didn't. He conquered it and he survived it – time and time again. He blew a huge, wet raspberry in the face of Destiny.'

'*Lord give me strength!*' Esther snorts (she's put aside the puzzle book). 'The man taken you for a damn fool, Stu!' Ransom considers his response for a second. 'Nah' – he shakes his head – 'it wasn't like that. He had a kind of ...' He frowns, plainly conflicted (as if battling with the prospect of even pronouncing the word out loud). '... a kind of quiet *integrity*. Very modest and unassuming. Looks a little like Tom Watson ...'

'How old?' Nimrod demands.

'Mid-thirties, but very old-fashioned. Has this ... this timeless quality about him. Remember those kids at school who were raised by their grandparents? Clean tank top? Lightly greased-back hair? Nicely polished shoes?'

'Does he still read palms?' Toby interrupts.

'Not sure. Yeah. Maybe.'

'D'you think he'd consider doing it professionally?' Nimrod follows up. 'For a tabloid?'

'But the cancer's not even the half of it.' Ransom returns to the story (which is coming back to him, now, in neat, bite-size chunks). 'After it went into remission for a while – and he finally thought the whole, shitty ordeal was over with – he was involved in a serious car smash. Not his fault – his aunt or someone was driving. Everybody died except him. Oh, and his niece, Mallory, who he adopted. Her whole face was torn apart – her jaw shattered, her tongue bitten half off. His legs were totally mashed. He had to have them pinned back together again. He was stuck in a wheelchair. It was years before he could walk. But now he competes in all these triathlons to raise money so's he can take the kid to America for groundbreaking plastic surgery ...'

'Where'd you find this guy?' Toby's awestruck. 'Does he write a blog?'

'What's his name?' Nimrod adds. 'D'you have his number?'

'We got chatting in a bar.' Ransom shrugs. 'I stayed over at his house the other night. He's a massive fan. Said he'd taken huge amounts of inspiration from my career over the years ...'

'*There* we are!' Esther snorts.

'Sorry?' Ransom glares over at her.

'If the man takin' inspiration from *your* career, he plainly delusional!'

'Or just his email address ...' Nimrod persists.

'Delusional?' Ransom echoes. 'Fuck you!'

'I'm fascinated by palm-reading,' Toby muses. 'I'd love to get my palm read by a real professional. Find out if nine-hole's got a future – whether Turbo Golf's actually a goer. God knows I could do with the encouragement as things stand ...'

'If he got him no lifeline and he *still* survive,' Esther reasons, 'just think about it: a lifeline don't mean shit! Either way, the man a sure-fire liar.'

Toby scowls, confused.

'By your way of thinking, Esther,' Nimrod interjects, 'if I always drive at fifty on a road with a thirty limit, then *ergo*, the road doesn't actually exist.'

'Crazy logic!' Esther snorts.

Nimrod turns to Ransom. 'Is this guy local by any chance?'

'What's with you and the fucking attitude?!' Ransom suddenly confronts Esther across the tables. 'You're Stuart Ransom's manager for Christsakes! Start acting like it!'

'Watch your mouth!' Esther is trenchant.

'I'd blame it on the hormones if you weren't always such a friggin' bitch,' Ransom mutters.

'You want hormones ...?' Esther growls.

Ransom turns to Toby. 'I call her the Black Widow,' he confides.

Toby smiles, agonized, not daring to respond.

'This is her third bub on my watch an' I've never yet shaken hands with a dad.' Ransom shrugs. 'I think she kills the poor bastards and eats 'em.'

'Go to hell!' Esther hisses.

Toby looks mortified.

'Here's an interesting fact for you.' Ransom seems enlivened – even cheered – by the horribly strained atmosphere he's engineered. 'Did you know that we inherited our aggressive impulses from our spider ancestors?'

'Spider ancestors?'

Toby blanches. He's mildly arachnophobic.

'Yeah, spiders,' Ransom reiterates. 'We share a genetic background. Why else d'you reckon Nimrod's got such hairy shoulders?'

Nimrod smiles wanly as Ransom slaps him, jovially, on the back.

'Spiders are naturally aggressive,' Ransom expands, 'same as we humans are ...'

He tips his head, disparagingly, towards Esther (who is sending an SMS on her phone, jabbing away at the keypad with a face like thunder).

'But most other animals in the world seek to actively *avoid* conflict,' Ransom continues, 'by resorting to various strategies. A pecking order, for instance ...'

'Like hens?' Toby's quick to catch on.

'Yeah, like hens. And take the piranha, for example. Piranhas are completely lethal. They're these *bona fide* little killing machines, but because they're so dangerous – and they're fully keyed into this fact about themselves – they choose to fight each other with their tails, not their teeth.'

'They slap each other around?' Toby grins.

'Like Laurel and Hardy' – Ransom chuckles – 'but with fins!'

Esther's looking up from her phone now, gazing at Ransom through slitted eyes.

Nimrod grabs his notebook and primes his pencil. 'So this fortune-telling guy ...' he starts off.

'Hold on a sec ...' Ransom focuses in on Toby with a sudden – almost bewildering – level of intensity. 'What was it you said the I stood for again?'

'Sorry?'

Toby's in a completely different head space.

'The I. In S.P.I.C.E.'

'Oh. *Right*. Yeah. The I. The I stands for incongruity.'

'Seven times, though?' Nimrod mutters, scribbling frantically. 'Surely that's gotta be a record of some kind?'

'Incongruity ...' Ransom echoes (apparently riveted).

'You're much more likely to be able to persuade someone of something if there's an unpredictable element to the set-up,' Toby expands. 'Something strange. Something out of the ordinary – like if there's a song written in a major key and then the composer sticks in a minor chord when you're least expecting it ...'

'Something unpredictable ...' Ransom repeats, a distant look in his eye.

'Like if you see a really beautiful woman but she has ... I dunno ...' Toby can't think of a suitable example.

'Stupid, blonde ponytails,' Ransom finishes off.

'A small gap between her front teeth,' Nimrod suggests, glancing over towards Esther, fondly. Esther peers down at her phone again, fighting back a smile.

'So we've got simplicity, perceived self-interest, incongruity ...' Ransom counts them off on to his fingers. 'Then C for confidence – which is pretty self-explanatory – and the E ...'

'Energy,' Ransom tries to pre-empt him, bouncing to his feet.

'Empathy,' Toby corrects him. 'People need to be able to "relate" at some level, to find you sympathetic ...'

'Right. Good. *Brilliant*. Well I'm off to the range.' Ransom grabs his baseball cap from the table and prepares to leave.

'Don't forget your book.'

Nimrod nudges *Artist of Life* towards him.

'Toby can have it.' Ransom checks for the phone in his pocket.

'Really?' Toby's touched. He reaches out for the paperback as Ransom applies his cap, touches the brim – by way of farewell – and casually saunters off.

'We not gone through the itinerary!' Esther yells after him. Ransom doesn't turn to answer, simply makes a little hand signal while he walks, as if to imply – much to his profound regret – that she is no longer fully audible.

'I'll be literally thirty seconds,' he pants, 'that's all, I promise.' Valentine stares at the proffered identification badge, almost disbelieving. She has a dozy, thumb-sucking Nessa on her hip. Her hair is swept back into a ponytail. Her fringe is drawn up into a single curler. She's wearing a wrap-around housecoat (red, covered with tiny, white dots) and a pair of fancy, white satin slippers with red bows, peep-toes and cute, wooden-look kitten heels. Her make-up is immaculate but her nail-polish – he immediately notices – is chipped.

'My brother said you work at the hotel,' she mutters, an edge of accusation in her voice.

Gene uses his sleeve to pat a light film of perspiration from his forehead. 'I do the odd shift there, yes,' he admits.

'Is that the uniform?'

He peers down at his green jumpsuit. 'No. This is ...'

For some reason he resists telling her about the Arndale.

'I work in a couple of places ...' He inspects his watch. 'In fact I'm currently on my lunch-break –'

'When Noel saw you here yesterday he thought Ransom might've sent you ...' she interrupts, looking over her shoulder, nervously (as if Noel could be hiding behind the door – possibly wielding a sledge-hammer). 'He got all stupid and paranoid about it.'

'But why would I be ...?' Gene finds this idea difficult to process.

'Your guess is as good as mine.' She shrugs. 'To spy on us, I suppose.'

She laughs, self-consciously.

'Well Ransom didn't send me,' Gene maintains.

'I already knew that.'

She gazes at him for a moment, her expression softening. 'Oh.'

His colour rises. 'Good.' He glances down at his clipboard. 'Thanks.'

'You want to read our meter again?'

She pushes back the door to reveal the hallway. 'Is there a problem? Didn't the numbers add up or something?'

'No, no, no. No problem ...' Gene clears his throat, self-consciously. 'I just didn't get around to reading it on my last visit. I must've got distracted ...'

'Can't imagine why.' She lifts her eyebrow, suggestively. Gene quickly shifts his focus from the immaculately raised brow to the lone curler in her fringe. It is large, white, plastic and filled with tan-coloured foam.

'You dig my retro-curler?' Valentine grins.

'Sorry?'

Gene drags his eyes away from the curler.

'My curler ...?'

She points. 'Of course it's not remotely functional,' she avers, drolly, 'just an accessory – part of my "forties housewife" look ...'

She performs a neat, little twirl, holding out the fabric of her housecoat. As she lifts the material she unwittingly reveals the span of soft, bare flesh inside her knee.

Gene's eyes shoot straight up to the curler again. They take refuge in the curler.

'You know how it is ...' she sighs, '"at home, doing the chores, still gorgeous, preparing to head out on a visit to the aerodrome ..."'

Gene's eyes remain glued to the curler. 'Well it looks real enough ...' he mutters.

She scans his face for a second, smiling but slightly perplexed. 'I'm just teasing.' She reaches up a tentative hand to touch the curler herself.

'Oh.' Gene nods. His stomach sinks. He adjusts his grip on his clipboard.

'I have a collection of housecoats,' she expands, pinching, dispassionately, at the spotted fabric. 'I buy them on the internet. There's still quite a market for them in France ...'

'My grandmother virtually lived in them,' he volunteers.

'Mine too.' She smiles. 'Although I prefer to wear them in the French way, like the French do: as a dress, with nothing underneath ...'

Gene's own eyebrows now rise, infinitesimally.

'What I mean to say is that the English like to wear them differently,' she flounders, her cheeks reddening, 'over the top of their clothes – like an apron ...'

Gene furtively inspects the housecoat as she speaks. It clings to her curves in a way he can't really believe a housecoat should. He remembers his grandmother's housecoats: nylon, blue gingham, loose, drab, lumpy ...

'The antique ones are nicer, though,' she runs on, embarrassed. 'Softer. Less synthetic. Better fabrics ...'

Gene nods. He can't really think of anything pertinent to add. Valentine bites her lip. Her lipstick, he notices, matches her housecoat perfectly, and there's a deep and immensely characterful dimple in her cheek.

'So when did you realize?' she wonders, eager to change the subject.

'Pardon?'

He glances up from her dimple.

'The meter. Our electricity meter ...?'

'Oh, that ...' He smiles, ruefully. 'I was about halfway home.'

'You must've kicked yourself!'

'Yeah ...' He nods. 'This isn't even my area. I'm usually based around Sundon Park – Limbury – Leagrave ... I'm just covering for a colleague who's been off sick all week.'

As he speaks she shifts Nessa on her hip and then adjusts her grip. He notices a tattoo on her arm – towards the top. It's a drawing of a cupcake with the words 'Daddy's Girl' written underneath. She catches him studying it. 'It's one of my dad's,' she explains. 'I had it made up from an original stencil of his after he died ...'

She smiles, self-deprecatingly. '... as a kind of two-fingered salute to the world, I suppose. He was a local tattoo artist – Reg Tucker. Reggie Tucker. You probably ...?'

'Sure.' Gene nods. 'He had a place over on Mill Street. A friend of mine owned the war games shop a couple of doors down.'

'Not Marek?'

Her face lights up. 'I haven't seen him in ages! How's he doing?'

'Great.' Gene grins. 'Still living the life of an international playboy with no visible means of support. Dividing his time between London and Warsaw – full of crazy schemes ...'

'Same old Marek, then.' She chuckles.

'He's actually ...'

Gene is going to say, '... my wife's ex,' but he doesn't. Instead he says, '... dumped his old Hummer on me. It's leaking dangerous quantities of brake fluid on to my back patio as we speak.'

'That piece of junk's still roadworthy?!' She laughs in sheer disbelief.

'Against all the odds.' He nods.

'Oh God ...' Valentine shakes her head as she remembers. 'We hired it to use as a centrepiece for this rave once and it broke down on the M1 – junction 12 – just after the turn-off for Toddington ...'

'Leak in the water tank,' Gene interjects, 'if I remember correctly.'

Valentine looks startled.

'Marek sent me to fix it,' he explains.

'Marek sent you ...?'

Valentine's confused.

'There was some lanky kid at the wheel with a thick Welsh accent,' Gene recalls, 'fancied himself as something of a mechanic.'

'That's Yorath.' Valentine nods. 'Really tall. Ruby on his front tooth ...'

'Then this huge girl in a tiny, leather minidress ...'

'Glenna Ross. Bright green eyes. Amazing singing voice ...'

'And a crazy woman dressed up as a cat.'

'*Tiger!*' Valentine yelps. 'Dressed up as a tiger! That was me! I was promoting this disgusting orange vodka drink ...'

'That was you?'

Now it's Gene's turn to look spooked. 'But you were completely ...'

He's going to say, '... deranged,' but stops himself, just in time, '... different,' he compromises, 'smaller.'

'I'd probably shrunk in the rain ...' She chuckles, wryly. 'It was such a filthy night – remember? I was out of my head on painkillers. I'd sprained my thumb, like a bloody idiot, falling off a bus ...'

Gene's still looking incredulous.

'I was going through this really clumsy phase,' she expands, 'kept tripping over – walking into stuff – dropping things. I'd bruised my coccyx, twisted my ankle ...' She shakes her head, forlornly. 'I'd just been dumped by my boyfriend, Mischa. He'd run away to become a monk' – she grimaces – 'which was kind of stupid *and* embarrassing. My dad had died. My brother and his girlfriend were struggling with all these chronic, addiction problems. We were pretty much broke. Mum was about to leave hospital after her accident ...'

She finally runs out of steam.

'I made you stick your head between your knees,' Gene recollects.

'And I puked on to my favourite shoes. A pair of killer stilettos covered in orange sequins. I was completely livid ...'

'Not the greatest of nights out,' Gene sympathizes.

'You looked different, though.' She inspects him, critically. 'Your hair was different, for starters – short. Like a skinhead.'

'I'd just finished a course of radiotherapy.'

Her eyes widen. 'Oh *God*. And there was me, hyperventilating, totally self-involved, jabbering on at you like a lunatic ...'

She's appalled.

'You'd wound your hair into these two, funny little buns ...'
He grins.

'Tiger ears,' she snorts. 'And you kept reciting that stupid
tiger poem at me –'

'William Blake,' Gene interrupts.

'Yeah. To try and shake me out of my blasted funk ...'

'It's the only poem I know by heart,' Gene confesses. 'I
learned it at school. If you'd been dressed as a squirrel I'd've
been screwed.'

'It was Fated, then,' Valentine declares.

They stare at each other for a second, both smiling,
delightedly. Then, 'My wife's a vicar,' Gene blurts out.

'Really?'

It takes Valentine a couple of seconds to process this
statement.

'I mean I know how weird it feels when someone you're in
love with suddenly becomes ...'

'Church of England?' she asks, her voice clipped, almost curt.
He nods.

She promptly lifts Nessa's dress to reveal a neat pair of
pants. 'We Tuckers aren't all complete reprobates, you know,'
she mutters, then turns and heads off down the hallway,
disappearing into a room on her left.

Gene remains where he stands for a moment, nonplussed,
uncertain whether to follow her or not. After thirty or so
seconds he decides that he should and enters the hallway
himself, instantly detecting – after a couple of steps – that
slight but pervasive smell of sandalwood incense. His eyes
alight on the large aspidistra and the black, Bakelite phone
which perches – like an old rook: head hung low, dull
plumage ruffled, wings slightly unfurled – on its handsome
walnut stand. He feels a sudden thrill of recognition at the
pattern of the antique floor tiles, a feeling – which instantly
confuses him – almost akin to coming home.

He remembers his grandparents' humble two-up-two-down on Charles Street: the highly buffed, red-painted concrete step which his grandmother burnished to a glassy finish every Friday, without fail; the brown door with its stiff, brass, horseshoe-style knocker and number twelve positioned directly above (notable for the absence of its second digit; the two represented – symbolically, at least – by a couple of tiny, black nail holes); the large, elephant's foot umbrella stand in the hall, stuffed with his grandfather's walking sticks (his childhood favourite with its finely carved bone handle fashioned into the shape of an albino otter); the air heavy with the smell of damp tea towels, boiled spring greens and bacon rind; a rich, olfactory maelstrom always gently underscored by the acrid, lemon scent of Jif scouring powder.

Gene pulls the door shut behind him. The natural light grows dimmer and is gently refracted through its stained glass into a dozy blur of burgundies, olives and ambers. Everything seems quieter and slower. He notices tiny fragments of dust floating in the air around him, buoyed up not so much by the air itself, it seems, but by ... by *sound*. By music.

Somewhere in the house a piano is being played – a brief refrain, repeated endlessly. Gene feels dull and soporific, like a heavy, crystal stylus stuck inside a groove; jumping forward, then back again, forward, then back again.

'It's my mother.' Valentine reappears beside him. 'She's learning the piano as part of her therapy. Erik Satie. She plays the same, few notes over and over ...'

As she speaks she leads him down the corridor, deposits him in front of the meter and then disappears upstairs. Gene opens the little cupboard, shines his torch on to the digits and is about to start taking a reading when he notices, with a scowl, that several of the screws that attach the main body of the meter to the surrounding brickwork have worked their way loose.

He focuses the light from his torch on to one of them and presses it with the soft pad of his finger. The entire box shifts under his touch, then a tightly folded wad of paper falls out from beneath it (where it has evidently been pushed to shore up the base).

Gene reaches down and grabs it, intending to push it back into its original position, but then something – he's not quite sure what, exactly – stays his hand. He glances around him – projecting a not-entirely-convincing veneer of studied casualness – before carefully unfolding the thing and giving its contents a cursory glance.

It's actually a letter – the top two-thirds of a letter, to be exact (and of a relatively recent vintage, at that). From what remains of the original, Gene is rapidly able to discern that it's a final warning from a large, High Street bank. The letter threatens the addressee of its imminent intention to foreclose on their home (he double-checks the address, grimacing – *yup*) for debts outstanding.

As he studies the letter, one of the screws (bottom left) works itself free from the brickwork and clatters down on to the tiles below. The meter (currently deprived of its paper support) tips forward slightly, with a mournful clank. Panicked, Gene quickly folds up the letter and shoves it back into its original place, then grabs the screw and replaces it, tightening it up with his thumbnail (he performs the same service to the other three).

Once this is done, he exhales, noisily (*Phew!* Close call!), then shines the torch back on to the digits to take his reading. He frowns. He draws closer to the meter, blinking. The six digits are now a neat row of zeros.

He closes his eyes for a second, then re-opens them ... *Still* all zeros! He rubs his chin, uncertain how to react. His face feels damp. He reaches into a back pocket, withdraws a white handkerchief and dabs it against his forehead as he ponders this conundrum. A cat silently glides down the hallway behind him, opting – when it reaches him – to slither, companionably, against his calves as it passes. Gene slams the cupboard door shut, with an ill-suppressed yelp, and turns, slightly panicked.

From where he's currently standing he can see into a small sitting room where the child now lies sleeping on an old-fashioned, brown sofa with heavy, dark wood trim. Each armrest is bookended by a further pair of large felines. The floor is covered by a series of ornate but threadbare oriental rugs of various sizes – at least six or seven of them – piled one on top of the other, in an exotic collage.

On one wall is a collection of round, antique, brass-coloured fish-eye mirrors. To the left of these, a handful of chipped and dented, metal, hand-painted signs lean up against the skirting, one advertising Bournville Drinking Chocolate, the others representing older brands he's not quite so familiar with.

A voluptuous wisp of smoke curls into his eye-line. Just as he's taking a tentative step forward to try and locate its source, his phone starts to ring. Both cats respond, in sync, leaping from their individual armrests and darting (with an almost choreographed precision) to opposite far corners of the room. Gene nearly drops his clipboard in his rush to respond (keen not to disturb the sleeping child) –
'Hello?' he whispers.
'Hello?'
'Hello?' he repeats, slightly louder (as the child sleeps on, unperturbed).

'Hello?' a voice says (a male voice, northern, marginally flustered). 'Is that ...? Uh ... *Bollocks*. Hang on a second ...' (Brief moment of indecision.)
'Christ Almighty – who the heck are *you* again?'

★ ★ ★

Although plainly in desperate need of practice (virtually every element of his game is currently in free-fall), Ransom has yet to actually make it out on to the driving range. Instead he may be located (by all but the most incompetent of Satellite Tracking Systems) standing plumb in the middle of a magnificent, giant, outdoor chessboard (the exquisitely wrought pieces of an abandoned game dotted all around him), enjoying a cigarette, his cap pulled down over his forehead, while he speaks, animatedly, into his mobile phone.

'... that antsy, little Muslim kid on reception,' he's muttering. 'Short-arse. Wonky teeth ... *You* know the one ...'

He kicks out his leg and idly prods at a nearby pawn with his toe. In the distance (approximately thirty or so yards away, due south) two men may be seen emerging from the residential segment of the hotel. After Ransom's third, desultory prod, the pawn rocks, topples and then rolls. Both men witness this act of low-level vandalism with what can only be described as looks of violent discomfiture and break – wordlessly – into a spontaneous trot.

One of them – shorter, heavier-set, in his shirtsleeves, possessed of a dramatic, dark blond comb-over which flaps up and down like a pedal-bin-lid as he runs – clutches a navy blue, gold-buttoned blazer in his hand. The second gentleman is taller, handsome – something of a dandy – wearing cream loafers, cream trousers, cream trilby (a maroon ribbon circling the brim), an expensive, lavender-coloured polo shirt and heavy, arty, dark grey Yves Saint Laurent-framed glasses. He moves with an exaggerated angularity (knees high, arms thrown out) like a stick figure in a poorly executed flicker-book animation.

'*Oi!*' the first man bellows, gesticulating, wildly. '*Oi! You! Stop! That game's still in progress!*'
Ransom gives no indication of having heard him. His ear remains firmly pressed into his phone.

'Apologize?!' he suddenly snorts, indignant. 'I'm not ringing to apologize – it was *his* weed for Christ's sake! He virtually foisted the stuff on me. Got it at bloody *Christian* camp! Nasty shit it was, too – almost blew my friggin' head off. Totally maxed me out ...'

He takes a final puff on his cigarette and then crushes the remainder beneath his heel as he listens. 'The analgesics are for a repetitive strain injury,' he says, with just a touch of hauteur. 'What the hell else was I expected to do? We were bouncing off the fucking ceiling! The situation was critical. He'd started thinking his fingers were edible – kept gnawing away at his thumb! Said it tasted like Wrigley's Juicy Fruit. It was a disaster! A bloody nightmare! I mean' – he gazes up at a neat, little bank of cumulus in the sky above him – 'I mean I'm not calling myself "the hero of the hour" or anything – far from it – but you should just count your lucky stars a sensible adult was on hand to try and keep a lid on things ...'

A brief silence follows, then, two seconds later, 'Jen? *Jen?!* The little minx with the ponytails? The chippy blonde? What the heck's *she* got to do with the price of fish?'

A sightly longer pause. 'Well Sheila's barking up the wrong tree. Stan's a good kid, a solid kid. Very discreet. Very mature. You've got absolutely no worries on that score ...'

As Ransom talks, the two men rapidly cover the thirty or so yards' distance between the hotel and the chessboard, drawing to a sharp halt on its outer margins, from whence they commence to address him, at volume.

'A game is still in progress!' the blue-blazered man honks. 'This board is fully booked until three!' Arty-glasses adds (officiously inspecting his watch – it's half past twelve).

'Well I guess we're just gonna have to agree to disagree ...' Ransom shrugs, blanking the two men completely. '*Comme ci comme ça*, as the French like to say. Did he get off to Krakow okay?'

'It's booked. This board is fully booked until three,' the blue-blazered man repeats (some of the aggression leaving his voice as the true identity – and eminent stature – of the personage he's currently addressing slowly starts to register), 'by Knott/Beevers Holdings plc – chief sponsors of this week's event. My name's Chris Padgett,' he adds (with a *soupçon* of swank), 'I'm the company MD.'

Ransom merely swishes a peremptory hand at him, indicates, self-importantly, towards his phone and turns away so that he might better concentrate. 'Well that's gotta be a good result by any calculation, eh?' he observes (with a generous – if profoundly unconvincing – measure of *faux*-jocularity).

He then listens intently for a second, scowling. 'The Hummer?'

He winces. 'I dunno. It's all a bit of a blur ... And if I can be completely honest with you, Gene' – he winces again – 'I don't actually have the luxury of dwelling on all this stuff right now. It's old history – kinda "surplus to requirements", if you know what I mean. The crud's really hitting the fan at this end. I'm up the proverbial gum tree. I've found myself short of a caddie. That's partly why I'm ringing. There's five per cent of my overall fee in the offing, five per cent of any prize money ... And let's not forget the work I'm hoping to do for local charities while I'm *in situ* – the oxygen of publicity and all that ...'

He pauses for a second, listening. 'No. No. I don't think you're quite grasping what I ...'

He listens again, frowning. 'I'm offering *you* the opportunity ...' he interrupts. Another pause. 'Aw, come *on*, Gino! It's not rocket science! It's just lugging a friggin' bag around ...'

The blue-blazered man gawps at the artily bespectacled man, as though perfectly astonished by Ransom's arrogance. The artily bespectacled man promptly strides to the other side of the chessboard to engage with Ransom himself.

'My name's Charles Del Renzio,' he starts off, 'Head of PR for this week's event. I'm afraid there seems to be some kind of confusion here ...'

'Then sort it out, will ya?' Ransom snaps, glancing up. 'Isn't it obvious I'm in the middle of something?'

The artily bespectacled man is momentarily flummoxed by Ransom's high-handed approach.

'You're in the middle of something all right!' the blue-blazered man harrumphs. 'You're in the middle of our game, you bloody imbecile!'

Ransom turns to appraise Blue-blazer, incensed. 'That's arrant, friggin' bullshit! The board was abandoned when I arrived here. The game was clearly over.'

'The board had been temporarily vacated,' Artily-bespectacled corrects him. 'A gull messed on Mr Padgett's jacket, so we were obliged to step back into the hotel for a second ...'

'A gull shat on your jacket?!' Ransom guffaws (his voice getting louder – and more northern – in a bid to attract the attention of a random couple of passers-by). 'It takes two, grown men to clean off ...' (he falls into insulting baby-talk), '... an 'ickle-wickle smudge of bird poop, now, does it?' He pouts out his lower lip. 'Aw, Diddums!'

'I actually popped up to my room to fetch a hat,' Artily-bespectacled explains, indicating (slightly embarrassed) towards his trilby. 'It was brighter outside than I'd anticipated ...'

'Good God!' Ransom expostulates (thrilled as his new audience – a father and son golfing combo – realize who he is and are thus compelled to draw closer). 'I got clawed on the neck by a broody gannet once, up at the Nairn Dunbar course – third hole, needed five stitches – and *still* I played on! Had a jab of penicillin on the ninth and managed to finish third – four under par – in a low friggin' gale! *That's* competitive edge for you.' He swings out his arm, dramatically. '*That's* sportsmanship in action. Call yourselves contenders? A little fleck of bird shit and you're running for the hills? It's a scandal! What are you, men or friggin' mice?!'

Ransom turns and poses for a photograph (the father snaps away, delightedly, the boy is beaming), then returns to his phone call, disgusted. 'Nah. Nothing important,' he mutters, 'just a couple of MOP's, arguing the toss. If I ignore them for long enough they might just ...'
He clicks his fingers. Nothing happens.

'Either you vacate the board now, Mr Ransom, or you'll leave us with no option but to call in Security,' Artily-bespectacled informs him, eyes darting back and forth, nervously, between the golfer and his new audience.

'Bring it on, Dick-weed!' Ransom tenses his muscles, exultant. 'Yeah! Bring it friggin' on! Make the call! Let's do this!'
'Yeah! Make the call!' the kid echoes.
'*Woo*-hoo!' The dad punches the air.

Artily-bespectacled loses his momentum, somewhat.

Ransom dutifully returns to his phone conversation. 'Experience isn't necessary,' he insists, 'in fact experience is actively *un*welcome. Experience is exactly what got me into this friggin' mess. Ignorance is bliss, Gene. I'm getting back to basics. I'm getting back to what's real; tuning into my "awareness continuum" ...'

'That's it! I've had a gut-ful of this idiot!' Blue-blazer turns to Artily-bespectacled, imperiously. 'Call Security!'

Artily-bespectacled takes his phone from his pocket, but hesitates.
'What're you waiting for?' Blue-blazer demands, irate. 'Make the call!'

'Well I'm very sorry you feel that way,' Ransom's muttering. 'It's a great opportunity. I mean it's ... Hang on a second ...'
Ransom removes the phone from his ear and starts inspecting the chessboard, critically.

'Who's white?' he asks, after a short pause.

'White?' Blue-blazer squawks, paranoid. 'What's it to you?'

'Oh-ho!' Ransom chuckles. 'On the defensive, now, are we?'
He turns and mugs at his small audience.

'I'll say he is!' the father promptly volunteers.

'Look at him! He's shitting his pants!' the boy crows (and
receives a sharp cuff around the ear for his trouble).

Ransom guffaws, delighted.

'Defensive? That's ridiculous – absolute rubbish! I'm not
remotely defensive!' Blue-blazer's huffing. 'The game's
patently still in the balance. You kicked over my pawn. I've
still got ...'

'Playing for cash?' Ransom turns to Artily-bespectacled,
brow cocked.

'A small pot,' Artily-bespectacled concedes. 'I mean just to
keep things interesting ...'

'What business is it of yours?' Blue-blazer brusquely interjects.

'So here's the deal.' Ransom's suddenly businesslike. 'I'll
quadruple whatever's currently in the pot if Pygmy boy there
hasn't got a stick of Touche Eclat tucked into his blazer
pocket which he nicked out of his secretary's handbag after
last night's obligatory, conference bunk-up ...'

'Touche Eclat?' Artily-bespectacled's completely at a loss.

'Pale make-up: foundation or powder or concealer,' Ransom
expands, 'something to simulate bird mess, basically, which he
smeared over the jacket, on the sly, when he realized he was
losing, so that he could disappear into the toilets and make
contact with a chess helpline on his BlackBerry ...'

'A chess helpline?!' Blue-blazer expostulates, agog. 'Are you
perfectly insane?!'

'The chalk was missing from the blackboard in the pool
room this morning,' the golfing father helpfully interjects. 'I
reported it to reception myself.'

'*Chalk!* A stub of chalk! The man's a genius!' Ransom
emits an ecstatic whoop, shoves his phone into his pocket and

makes a sudden beeline for Blue-blazer across the board. Father and son (after a tiny pause) join in the chase, approaching Blue-blazer – in a pincer movement – from the other side.

'But I don't ...' Artily-bespectacled is still mystified. Blue-blazer, meanwhile, has grabbed hold of a white knight to protect himself. Ransom scoops up a black queen. 'Checkmate!' he hollers. 'Game over! Throw down the jacket, my little friend, or suffer the consequences!'

'This is assault!' Blue-blazer hollers, as the child grabs at his jacket and attempts to run off with it. 'This is an utterly unprovoked assault! Del Renzio! Call Security!'
He batters clumsily at the child with the white knight and knocks him, backwards, into the small, privet hedge that has been planted a couple of yards beyond the board's outer perimeter. The top of the hedge has been cut to simulate the effect of castle battlements.

'Those chess pieces are custom made!' Artily-bespectacled runs towards them, horrified. 'They're individually crafted pieces of fibreglass. Each one costs in excess of seven hundred and eighty pounds ...'

The child lands at an ungainly angle, still clutching on to the blazer, his right arm twisted beneath his torso. His initial delight at having wrested the blazer away from his adversary is quickly overtaken by the cruel realization that all is not well with him, physically. He tries – and fails – to clamber to his feet again, inhales sharply, then starts to wail.

'What's wrong?' his father demands.
'My arm!' the boy keens, pawing at his shoulder, his cheeks flooding with tears. 'I can't lift my arm! I can't move my fingers!'

'D'you have any idea what you've done?!' The father rounds on Blue-blazer, jabbing at his chest, furiously, with his index finger. 'D'you have any idea who this *is?* This isn't just some insignificant, little nobody! This is the Wolf! *The Wolf,* d'you hear me?! This is Britain's number-one golfer in the under-twelve age range! The *Leamington Echo* called him "The Great White Hope of the British Game"!'

(As it so happens, the Wolf is actually ranked seventeenth in the UK under-twelve category.)

Ransom, meanwhile, has dropped the black queen, hurdled the hedge and is at the boy's side in a matter of mere seconds. He pulls the jacket out from under him, rifles through one of the pockets and unearths a packet of Polo mints. The boy is still clutching at his shoulder and whimpering as the father snatches the white knight from Blue-blazer's tight embrace and whacks him across the side of the head with it.

In the brief hiatus that follows (during which he has helped himself to a Polo mint and proffered one to the wailing child), Ransom is quickly able to assess the full extent of the boy's injuries. He promptly lifts him to his knees, positions himself to the rear, wraps his arms around his shoulder and chest, grips him firmly, tells him to take a deep breath, and then makes a sudden, sharp movement (which is followed by a small – yet deeply satisfying – clicking sound). He then releases the child.

'How's that feel?'

The boy sits quietly for a second, shell-shocked.

'How's that feel?' the dad echoes, dropping the white knight and hurdling the hedge himself.

'Disconnected his collar bone,' Ransom explains, proffering him a Polo mint (which is cordially refused), then delving back into the blazer's pockets again. 'There'll probably be a small amount of bruising. Just keep it rested for a day or so and he'll be right as rain.'

The boy has lifted his arm and is moving his fingers, gingerly, as the father watches on, in awe.

'You're a Godsend,' he murmurs. 'A genius!'

The Wolf (in accordance with his father's stupefied assessment of the situation) scrambles to his feet and commences an ear-splitting howl of victory (the howl is his trademark, his bugle call).

'How the hell do I go about thanking you?' the father demands, turning to Ransom, his eyes tearing up.

'Uh … I dunno …' Ransom winces (slightly unnerved by the baying child). He considers his response for a pico-second. 'A nice letter to the Official Website, maybe …?' He shrugs. 'A phone call to the local press …? I mean, whatever you feel comfortable with …'

As he speaks his attention is momentarily distracted by a second, mystery object in the blazer's pocket. He withdraws his hand and blinks down at it, quizzically. It is a small tube of a popular brand of spermicidal cream.

'*Wow*,' Ransom shakes his head as he inspects it, perfectly astonished. 'I thought you could only get this stuff as a foam – in those tiny, pump-action aerosols … *Man!*' he cackles. 'Are they seriously still manufacturing this shit in tubes? That's brilliant! It's hilarious!' He rocks back on his heels. 'Jesus, Joseph and Mary, I love this country! It's so friggin' *old* school!'

Valentine enters the room and discovers Gene standing in front of her tiny shrine, gazing – with some astonishment – at a large, black and white photograph of a vagina which hangs, lopsidedly, on the wall behind it.

'That's not what it looks like,' she says, bending down to blow out a tea-light (which still flickers away, doggedly, before the tiny, roaring, cartoonish image of Kali). 'I mean it's not pornography, it's art. It's a tattoo. The hair on the … the hair's not real. It's a tattoo.'

'But it's so incredibly lifelike,' Gene murmurs, squinting, then drawing in still closer, amazed.

'Yeah.'

She runs a nervous hand through her newly bobbed fringe. During her brief absence she's removed the curler and changed into a pair of high-waisted jeans: classic, dark denim, American-made; tight on the hip, baggy on the legs, with matching, beige, elasticated braces attached, and a snugly fitting gingham shirt underneath.

'It's not normally hung up there,' she adds, 'I was just showing it to a client.'

'The wicker was impressive,' Gene muses, 'but that's actually quite astonishing.'

'Wicker?' Valentine's slow to catch on.

'At the hotel. Your brother removed his shirt …'

'Really?' She scowls, irritated. 'Why'd he do that?'

'I'm not sure.' Gene turns to face her and immediately notices how the elastic of the braces curves around her breasts. He quickly turns away again. 'To show it off, I guess.'

'The wicker was an early piece,' she mutters.

'And now you've moved on to … uh …' Gene points, lamely.

'Merkins.'

She isn't afraid to say it out loud.

'Merkins,' Gene parrots, ruminatively.

'I got into it by accident,' she expands. 'I was offering a cosmetic tattoo service at my dad's parlour. He'd sent me on a course – learning how to do permanent eye-liner and lip-liner; that kind of stuff. I developed a really good technique for doing eyebrows – for tattooing hair, basically. I did some work on a woman with alopecia and she really loved it. She was quite a character; a performance artist. It was originally her idea for me to tattoo her … well … down there …'

She grimaces. 'Word quickly got around – especially on the internet. She helped me set up my website. Since then I've mainly concentrated on' – she clears her throat – 'on what you might call "specialist clients".'

'I suppose this gives true meaning to the phrase "a niche market",' Gene jokes, lamely.

She glances over at him.

'Niche,' he explains, instantly regretting this light-hearted foray, 'a shallow recess.'

'A niche?'

She returns her attention back to the photograph again, somewhat perplexed. 'I've never really thought of a vagina in that way before.'

'Me neither,' he mutters, humiliated.

'I've done my fair share of nipples – for women who've had reconstructive surgery on their breasts. I'm pretty good at them – matching the woman to the nipple; the right size, the right colour. It's really rewarding work. Bread and butter stuff. I've taken a lot of photographs. Some I'm really proud of. I mean I'm quite into scars in general. There's a specialist scar market – people who want scars' – she shrugs – 'and I can do that. I'm into all that ...'

'I had breast cancer myself,' Gene murmurs.

'Oh ... okay.' Valentine nods, distracted. 'It's not only about the body, though,' she continues. 'It started out that way, but now I'm mainly just obsessed by textures,' she confesses, 'abstract textures: wools, woven grasses, woodgrains, marble, even concrete. I've got this house-brick on my thigh ...'

'A brick?'

His brows rise.

'A couple of bricks.' She nods. 'I tattooed them there myself. I've got a photo in my portfolio ...'

She walks over to a large, black art folder which leans behind the door, unzips it and then pages through some photographic prints inside. Each piece is separated by a sheet of tracing paper. She eventually locates the one she's looking for and pulls it out.

'I'm completely obsessed by Louise Bourgeois,' she says, carrying it over, the tracing paper still in place. 'D'you know her work at all?'

He shakes his head.

'She's really old now, French, has this huge retrospective coming up at the Tate Modern ...' Valentine glances over, briefly, towards the slumbering Nessa. 'Not that I'll get a chance to see it.' She shrugs.

'Childcare a problem?' Gene speculates.

'Too scared to leave the house,' she murmurs, smiling.

'Too scared ...?' he echoes.

'I'm agoraphobic.'

As she speaks, she places the bottom edge of the print on to the rug, removes the tracing paper and reveals the image for his perusal.

'Her work deals mainly with issues surrounding women and domesticity,' she explains (focusing entirely on the photo now), 'women and the home, basically – women being defined, psychologically, by the actual fabric of their homes. That's my own, particular area of interest: ideas surrounding intimacy, privacy, anxiety; the textures of my immediate environment – the comfort I find in them and at the same time the feelings of disgust they sometimes evoke in me ...'

Gene stares at the photograph as she talks, struggling to process the glut of information she's feeding him. It is a beautifully taken picture of the left-hand side of her body – from knee to hip. On her thigh are two exquisitely well-tattooed bricks – house bricks, with a thick slick of cement oozing out from between them. Even as he marvels at the extraordinary artistry of her work, he is intensely conscious of the flesh that surrounds it – the quiet, soft canvas of her nudity.

'Did you take the photo yourself?' he asks.

'Yeah. My ex – the monk ...' – she grimaces self-deprecatingly – 'he was a professional photographer. He left me most of his equipment when he headed off to India. I enjoy dabbling. I use my bedroom as a darkroom. I mean they're not anything to write home about –'

'I don't agree,' Gene interrupts, 'I think they're really wonderful.'

'I heard this radio interview with her once,' Valentine continues, returning to her former subject (almost as if embarrassed by Gene's compliment, although – somewhat paradoxically – seemingly unperturbed by how exposing the photo is). 'The journalist asked her what her motivation was and she simply answered, "To survive."'

She shakes her head, fondly. 'You could hear in her voice – this cracked, dry, old, French voice – that she really, really meant it. She said her art was a way of creating order out of anxiety; making shapes out of this gnawing terror that burrowed away inside of her. I suppose that's basically what I'm aiming to do myself, but my medium has always been the skin – transforming the skin ...'

'Did it hurt much?' Gene wonders, seemingly transfixed by the image.

'It killed!' She laughs. 'I have a pathetically low pain threshold.'

'But you were pleased with the end result?'

She peers down at the photograph, frowning. 'I guess what most outsiders don't tend to understand is how little of tattooing – or body art in general – is about the design aspect; the formal decoration. From my perspective it's always been as much about the process as the end result ...'

'The pain of the needle?' he muses.

'Look at the Maoris.' Valentine nods. 'For them tattoos are a rite of passage. They're a marker of bravery, of maturity, of cultural acceptance. The tattoo represents not only a willingness to accept pain – to endure it – but a need to actively embrace it. Because life *is* painful – beautiful but painful ...'

180

She places the tracing paper back over the image and returns it to the folder. As she does so another print attracts her attention and she pulls it out.

'Here's a perfect case in point ...'

She carries the print over, places the bottom edge down and removes the tracing paper.

'This woman was forty-seven when I tattooed her vagina – a widow. D'you see the hundreds of shiny, white marks all over her skin?'

Gene studies the image, closely. 'What are they?' he asks. 'Stretch marks?'

'Nope. Little cuts. Self-inflicted. She used to slice herself with this special piece of shell ...'

Valentine lays the print down flat on to the floor, goes over to her shrine, kneels down in front of it and carefully removes something from behind the picture of Kali. She holds it out to him. He steps forward and takes it from her, gingerly.

'It's wonderful to the touch don't you think?'

'Is this the actual ...?'

He runs his finger over it, appalled.

'Incredibly cool and light and smooth, but still razor sharp ...'

He passes it back to her with a slight shudder.

'The client had these overwhelming feelings of inadequacy,' she explains. 'She'd been raised by an aunt. Her parents had gone to live in America when she was five or six. They'd taken her younger brother with them but they'd left her behind in Japan. She never really knew why. She felt ...'

She searches for the right word: '... gagged ... choked ... *smothered*. She had all these frustrations that she didn't feel it was socially acceptable for her to express. And crazy as it sounds, some of her deepest feelings of inadequacy were centred on her lack of pubic hair. The other girls at school used to tease her about it, and then, later on, after she was married, her husband did the same. She felt trapped – both physically and emotionally – in this pre-pubescent state ...'

Valentine returns the piece of shell to its original place, rises to her feet and picks up the print again.

'So when she found out about the work I was doing she spent virtually every penny she had to fund her trip over here. Aside from the cutting, she felt like the tattoo was her first, real act of self-determination. And once it was complete, she presented me with the shell as a thank you. She said the tattoo made her feel whole. And it wasn't the tattoo itself so much as submitting, voluntarily, to the pain of the needle. It was the *journey* of the tattoo, if you like, which is basically what this photo represents. I mean it's not beautiful or glamorous ...'

'Is it enjoyable?' Gene asks, sensing that he should contribute something, yet feeling unable to commit – wholeheartedly – to the stark image itself.

'Enjoyable?'

She bursts out laughing. 'How d'you mean? In a kinky, *Readers' Wives* kind of way?'

'No!' Gene's horrified. 'I mean the process – the actual tattooing ...'

'It's hard work' – she shrugs – 'a lot of bending over and craning. I get a certain amount of neck pain, twinges in my lower back, eye strain, cramping in the hand ...'

She tenses and un-tenses her right hand. As she does so he notices that three of her finger pads are an odd, purplish-blue colour.

'But you get used to it after a while ...'

She carefully covers the print with the tracing paper. 'And obviously it depends – to a large extent – on the attitude of the individual client. Most of my customers are from the Far East. They're generally really excited about the process – scared but excited ...' She grins, going over to place the print back into the folder. 'They've waited a long time for the work. It's a transformative act – the culmination of many years of stress and many months of planning –'

'How long would it take?' Gene interrupts. 'I mean a tattoo of this size …'

He points to the photo on the wall.

'Four or five hours. And I generally have to turn the tattoo around in one, long session, which can be fairly challenging …' – she grimaces – 'both for me *and* the client. There's no margin for error in this line of work. Then there's the weight of their expectation – which is huge …'

She walks over to the wall and straightens the painting on its hook. 'The work's compressed into this tiny, little area' – she points – 'but it's very, very detailed, and the needle needs to go in deep enough or the ink comes away with the scab …'

Gene winces.

'The skin over the pubic bone is especially delicate,' she continues. 'I mean it's always harder to tattoo over bone – the hands, the ribs, the foot … You have to be really, really careful or the ink can bleed and the overall effect is –'

'I wasn't snooping around,' Gene interrupts her, suddenly anxious. 'I saw a wisp of smoke through the open doorway, so I came in to investigate. But it was only …'

He points at the shrine where a stick of incense has recently burned out, leaving a powder-fine trail of grey ash in its wake.

'I chant,' she explains, adjusting one of her braces. 'Chanting with beads. Mischa taught me. He was really into Kali. It's his old shrine. I do it to relieve stress, sometimes.'

As she speaks her eyes travel from the sleeping child on the sofa to the crazy image of Kali, to the tattooed vagina above. 'I suppose this must all look a little … uh …' She bites her lip, self-consciously. '… nuts.'

'Not at all,' he insists, slightly too loudly, before frowning down at his clipboard, uncomfortably, as if preparing himself to say something, then not saying it and turning to inspect the azure-cloaked Virgin Mary that stands, close to his elbow, on the bookcase.

'My mother's a Catholic,' she explains. 'At least she *was* a Catholic,' she corrects herself, 'before the accident.'

In the brief, awkward silence that follows, they both listen out, instinctively, for the distant strains of the piano, but it is no longer audible. Neither of them has the slightest notion of when the playing actually stopped.

'Is she fully recovered now?' Gene asks.

'Hang on a second ...' Valentine cocks her head, still listening, 'D'you hear that?'

'What?'

'A crackling sound ... kind of like ...' She gestures with her hand.

'Uh ...'

Gene's eyes move from her face, to her hand, to her brace (which is now applying the lightest of pressures to her right breast), then over to the shrine, panicked.

'D'you have a phone?' she wonders.

Gene pats at his pocket, feeling for his phone, then pulls it out, looks down at it, aghast, and quickly shoves it to his ear.

'Hello?'

He listens for a moment.

'Yeah. No. Sorry. I didn't ... I must've ...'

As he speaks he winces at Valentine, apologetically. She shrugs.

He listens again.

'No. No. It's not ...'

He scratches his head, embarrassed. 'Could we talk about this later? I'm actually out on a ...'

He listens again, perplexed. 'Generous as the offer is, I really don't think Sheila would ... I mean she's still furious about ...'

He inhales, sharply.

'*Pussy*-whipped?' he echoes, affronted, then glances over towards Valentine (who is covering her sleeping niece with a crocheted, patchwork blanket). 'That's hardly fair ...' he murmurs, hurt.

A brief silence follows.

'Okay. *Okay*,' he finally concedes, his resolve palpably weakening. 'So where …?'
He removes a pencil from the front pocket of his overalls, bends over and scribbles something on to his clipboard, whilst balancing it, unsteadily, on his knee.
'I've a fair idea …' he mutters, '… just past the Lea Valley walk, then Someries Castle, and it's … Yeah. Fine. Six o'clock, sharp. But please don't …'

A long pause. Valentine stands by the sofa, watching him from behind. As he leans forward, the collar on his overalls moves back and is pulled askew. On the area of skin just below his neck she sees the upper region of a bruise. She stares at it, fascinated, then looks down at her hand.

'Well it's big of you to admit that.' Gene scratches his head again, suddenly disarmed. 'And I suppose no real lasting damage was …'
An extended pause.

'The Hummer?'
He straightens up again. 'I don't think …'
He gazes up at the ceiling.
'I mean the cost of petrol alone …'

He stares down at the floor, frowning. 'What kind of a uniform?'
He slowly shakes his head as he listens, 'No. The hat's too big and the jacket has this huge tear under the … *Hello?*'

He gazes at his phone for a second, confused, puts it to his ear again, removes it and stares at it, then shoves it, grimacing, into his pocket.

'Good. *Right*,' he says, turning back to face Valentine, a slight sheen of perspiration glowing on his forehead. 'Sorry about that.'

'Look,' Valentine says, taking a couple of steps towards him and reaching out her hand. He inspects the hand for a second, cautiously.

'The bruise,' she directs him, 'on the index finger. Circling the index finger ...'

She points to an angry bruise on her index finger.

'It's where I tried on your ring yesterday – Cheiro's ring. The whole area is bruised. And see here ...'

She turns over her hand and shows him her finger pads. Three of these are also bruised.

'Don't you think that's weird?' she asks, glancing up.

'I should probably have a quick word with you about the reading,' Gene answers, plainly unnerved by how close she's standing. 'One of the screws came loose ...'

As he speaks, upstairs – in the furthest reaches of the house – a loud crashing sound is audible.

'Piano lid!' Valentine clucks, turning to glance over at the sleeping child, suddenly anxious. The child shifts her position, with a gentle sigh, then settles.

'I should probably head back to work,' Gene mutters, losing his nerve. He glances down at his watch.

'Of course,' she answers, then reaches out her hand – the right hand, the bruised hand – and places it, softly, matter-of-factly, palm flat, fingers outstretched, over the area just below his right nipple. She rests it there for a second and then lifts it and places it at the base of his throat, just above his collar bone, then lifts it again and places it at his left shoulder, close to the armpit.

'What are you doing?' he asks, catching the hand, roughly, as it moves from its former position and down lower – towards his stomach.

'I have absolutely no idea,' she answers.

'So we're sitting on this bench together, just me and Sinclair, both kind of dumbstruck by what it's taken to get us there, basically; I mean all the crazy misunderstandings, the bad luck, the huge row with my mum, the spiked drink, the broken heel, the false alarm, the missed exam ...' Jen bites her lip, her eyes gently misting over as she recollects. 'And it's pretty much *the* most romantic moment of my entire life so far ...'

The boy nods, obligingly. He is sitting, alone and – he had somewhat naively presumed – inconspicuously, at a small, corner table in the bar at the Thistle. He is enjoying a solitary glass of Coke as he reads a thick, paperback copy of David Foster Wallace's *Infinite Jest* (which currently lies open, but face-down, at his elbow).

'I mean just try and picture how incredible this is – *uh* – what did you say your name was again?'

'Israel.'

Jen stares at him, incredulous, for a heartbeat.

'Okay. Well it's like something from a romantic comedy, Israel,' she continues (determined not to be thrown off her stride at this critical juncture in the story), 'just so absolutely perfect, so ridiculously beautiful and touching and ...' Words fail her. 'I'm like – I swear to God – I'm actually tearing up even thinking about it!'

Jen grabs the boy's napkin, dabs the corner of her eye, then passes it straight back to him.

'D'you think I'm incredibly sexy, by the way?' she wonders, throwing back her shoulders and pouting, provocatively.

'Sure.' He nods, non-committal.

'Thanks!' She giggles.

'By most European standards,' he qualifies.

Jen stops giggling (and is about to respond, tartly), then spots a tiny, sticky deposit on the otherwise pristine table top and commences scratching it off with her nail.

'So he's leaning in to kiss me,' she continues, buffing the table to a shine with her cuff, 'and I'm swooning. I'm holding my breath, waiting, *aching*, for the first, soft sensation of his lips against mine ...'

She glances over to her left, scowling. A customer is waiting to be served at the empty bar.

'Hold that thought ... okay?'

She dashes off to serve him. The boy returns to his book.

'So anyway' – Jen's back, in a flash, to complete her story – 'he's moving in to kiss me. My heart is just ... well it's just melting. It's pure liquid honey. But at the same time it's beating so fast, so *insanely* fast, it feels like it might actually explode out of my chest. It literally *is* exploding – *ka-boom! Ka-boom! Ka-boom!*'

The customer returns to the counter with a quibble over the order. Jen promptly dashes off, trilling her apologies. Israel returns to his book, with a sigh.

'Where were we?'

He's slower to put his book down this time, but does so, with an obliging smile, after completing his paragraph.

'Uh ... You were sitting on a park bench with your boyfriend in several inches of snow ...'

'Exactly! So he's moving in for our first ever real kiss and it's completely amazing, like this ridiculous Hallmark moment; something we'll be telling our grand-kids about, thirty years from now – and then totally out of the blue this ludicrous, little dog comes running towards us across the park. I say it's ludicrous because it's a really funny-looking, little thing – half pekinese, half chihuahua ...'

'A pee-huahua,' he volunteers.

'A chi-kinese,' she suggests.

'A chi-pee-huahua.' He grins, checking the knot on his tie then adjusting his heavy spectacles.

'The point is,' she interrupts, 'that it dashes towards us and then stops, abruptly, directly in front of the bench we're sitting on, before commencing this bizarre, little dance. Sort of crouching on its back legs and then turning in a circle, grunting. Kind of like a miniature jockey riding an invisible horse ...'

'Uh-oh!' the kid says.

'It's doing a poo' – Jen nods – 'but it's constipated. So it's just pushing and pushing. Twirling around. This really intense expression on its mashed-up little face ...'

'Not a scenario especially conducive to romance,' Israel sympathizes, portentously.

'I mean what are the odds, eh?!' Jen's indignant. 'The park's totally whited-out! Two inches of snow! It's all but deserted, and then this evil, little dog turns up and starts its agonized pirouetting.'

'A stray, perhaps?' Israel ruminates.

'I love animals,' Jen informs him, 'I *love* animals, but I really wanna jam my pointy, stiletto-ed heel up this constipated, little blighter's arse and kick him straight into the Wednesday afternoon of the following week.'

'Wednesday afternoons are always hideous,' Israel heartily concurs (back in Jamaica, from whence he hails, he enjoys extra maths tutoring after school on Wednesdays).

'And it's hardly like I'm the only one who's noticed,' Jen grumbles. 'Sinclair's forgotten all about the kiss and is gazing at the thing, bug-eyed, totally mesmerized ...'

'Ah, the irresistible allure of nature in the raw,' Israel opines, with a sardonic smirk.

'Anyhow,' she continues, shooting him a dark look, 'we're just sitting there – the moment completely ruined – gazing, in astonishment, at this hairy, little freak, when a woman turns up, out of breath, clutching on to its leash – just some dumpy, middle-aged woman; I've no idea who she is. But instead of grabbing the dog by the collar and hauling it off, full of apologies – much as you might expect – she stands a few feet away from it – completely ignoring us – and just observes its crazy antics in a reverential silence ...'

'What a breach!' Israel exclaims – almost sincerely.

'So now we're all just stuck there, like a bunch of idiots, waiting for this blasted dog to perform!' Jen's cheeks pinken at the memory. 'But it doesn't. So after a minute or two I begin to lose patience and say, "Excuse me, might it be possible to … *you* know …"

'I indicate towards the dog.

'"Pardon?" She stares at me, gormlessly. So I say, "Would it be possible to maybe … *you* know …" I make this sweeping gesture with my arm, i.e. "your runty, constipated, little dog is single-handedly destroying my mental, spiritual and emotional equilibrium right now." But *still* she doesn't follow me. She goes, "I'm sorry, is something bothering you?"

'So I go, "Yeah …" and I'm pretty, bloody incensed by this point, I go, "Don't you think it might be a nice idea to try and exercise some control over when and where your dog does his business?"

'The woman just looks at me like I'm insane. She says, "How can I be expected to control when he poops? Can *you* control when *you* poop?"

'My God!' Jen gawps. 'The cheek of it! I mean I'm in the middle of this romantic …' Words fail her.

'Tryst,' Israel fills in.

'Precisely, a tryst. I'm right in the middle of my first, romantic tryst with Sinclair and now I have this hare-brained, vindictive cow-bag trying to open a public forum on the intricacies of my bowel movements! I mean she doesn't even say "business", she says "poop"! Talk about a passion killer!'

Jen interrupts her narrative for a second and gazes at the boy, concerned. 'You do know that girls poo, don't you? Even extraordinarily beautiful ones like *moi?*'

'Sure.' He nods, wearily. 'I read Martin Amis's *Rachel Papers* in my final year at primary school …' He pauses. 'Not as part of the syllabus, obviously.'

'Good. Because I love dogs,' Jen continues (not really listening). 'I'm training to be a vet – well, I'm hoping to become a vet if I can salvage my A-levels. So I'm like: "Duh! I'm training to be a vet! Of *course* I know that!" Meanwhile the dog's just twirling away in front of us and now there's this thin string of dog poo suspended from his rear end with tiny chunks of poo hung on it – *strung* on it – like poo beads on a poo necklace ...'

Israel visibly recoils at the necklace image.

'Yeah!' Jen nods, vindicated. 'I know! Revolting! And naturally the dog is still squatting there, incapacitated, its arse jockeying around in the air, incapable of moving until the poo finally detaches itself.'

'A critical *impasse*,' Israel primly volunteers.

'Exactly.' Jen chuckles, pointing. 'One of those. So I go to the woman: "What's wrong with the poor creature? What the hell have you been feeding him?"

'The owner circles her dog a couple of times, inspecting him closely. "It's probably just hair," she says, finally. "He picks it up off the carpet. This happens to all dogs. It's nothing unusual."'

'My grandmother used to weave rag-rugs out of tattered strips of old clothing,' Israel volunteers; 'her dog would pilfer the scrap-box and then for literally weeks afterwards his back end would play host to its own, little fireworks party of crap and fabric ...' He smiles fondly at the memory. 'There was rarely ever a dull moment in Grandmother's house.'

'You have so much life experience!' Jen gushes.

'Thanks –' he shrugs – 'I don't have my own phone or personal computer, but I keep my eyes peeled and I read a ludicrous amount.'

'I like you,' Jen says. 'Let's be Besties.'

She offers him her pinkie.

'I'm not expecting to be in Luton for very long,' Israel cautions her.

'Gorgeous, attentive, sincere ...' Jen lists some of his many virtues on her hand, 'and your vocabulary's off the scale! Bags you're on my team for Scrabble!'

The boy inspects her, warily.

'Gosh! Isn't it close in here today?' Jen coyly fans her décolletage. 'Aren't you dreadfully itchy in that charming hand-knit?'

'I hail from the tropics.' The boy shrugs. 'In "Yard"' – he rolls his eyes, sardonically – 'if you're not sweating or itching then you're probably decomposing.'

'Great use of the vernacular!' Jen squawks. 'You're brilliant! You're a hoot! Did anyone ever tell you how hilarious you are?'

'Uh, yes.'

He nods. 'People tell me that all the time. Even when I'm being perfectly serious. I find it quite trying.'

She gazes at him, bewitched.

'How old are you?' she wonders.

'I'm almost fourteen.'

'D'you play a musical instrument?'

'No. You?'

'Trombone.'

She indicates a dry patch on her upper lip.

'I'm not musical,' Israel avows, 'but one of my great-great-great-uncles on my mother's side used to play brass with Francis Johnson. There's a strong, brass tradition in our family. My Great-Aunt Hulda was a famous teacher in Freetown –'

'Francis who?' Jen interrupts.

'He was one of the first really legendary black composers. I'm surprised you haven't heard of him. That's actually how my mum ended up meeting my dad. My dad originally played trumpet but he wanted to get into the keyed bugle. He took lessons from my great-aunt ...'

'I'm just *crazy* for Fela Kuti,' Jen exclaims, excited. 'I'm nutty about him – demented. Are you a fan?'

'Uh ... Like I say, I'm not very musical,' Israel demurs, 'I'm more of a literary bent.'

'I *love* Fela Kuti!' Jen gushes, undeterred. 'My brother converted me. You know: the hot brass section, the skin-tight trousers, the pidgin English, the trashy cover-art, the nudity, the stomping, the face-paint. I'm totally into all that radical, seventies, horn-based, semi-psychedelic African shit.'

'Good for you.'

Israel takes a sip of his Coke.

'I'm a chameleon,' Jen confesses, with a dramatic sigh. 'This …' – she describes her current, physical incarnation with a cursory swoop of her hand – 'this isn't who I am. This is merely a simulacrum, at best.'

'We don't have chameleons in Jamaica,' Israel muses, 'but we do have something called an Anole – a kind of lizard that changes colour when it's stressed.'

'Amazing. Did you ever think about getting contact lenses?' Jen wonders.

'I used them for a while,' Israel confirms, 'but I was very prone to eye infections.'

'Like a sticky, white goo all over the eye?'

He winces, remembering.

'You weren't cleaning them properly!' Jen's ecstatic. 'I had that problem myself! Now I use disposables – although they're criminally expensive …'

'I'm happy enough with my glasses.' Israel adjusts his glasses, self-consciously.

'I suppose there's always corrective eye surgery,' Jen suggests.

'I suppose there is,' he acknowledges.

'Although sometimes it makes people's eyes look all wonky.'

'I've heard that.' He nods.

'Your dad wears glasses,' Jen muses. 'I saw you at reception together. You must've inherited the bad gene from his side of the family.'

'He's not my father,' Israel mutters, glancing off sideways.

'Oh.'

Jen promptly removes Israel's glasses from his face and commences polishing them on her work blouse.

'My ma says my real dad had twenty-twenty vision.' Israel squints at her across the table. 'She says he needed it for his work: he was a professional arsehole.'

'I hear there's great money in that,' Jen wisecracks.

'I hate him.' Israel scowls.

'Why not divorce him, then?' Jen suggests, blithely.

'He's dead.' Israel's still scowling.

'Doesn't make any difference. You can always divorce his corpse.'

'Divorce a parent?' Israel's intrigued by the notion.

'Kids do it all the time nowadays. It's totally the rage.'

Israel continues to ponder this concept.

'We should research it on the net together after my shift,' Jen suggests. 'I have my own duplicate key to the office ...' She pulls a long, silver chain into view from under her blouse, on the end of which are two keys, a USB stick and a bottle-opener.

'Won't you need to get permission?' Israel asks, concerned.

'Hell no,' Jen snorts, 'I'm a law unto myself. I pop in there all the time to Google information about the guests.'

'Did you Google information on us?' Israel wonders, intrigued.

'Absolutely. I know your stepfather owns a company that manufactures cat litter. He ran for mayor in some hicksville town in Kentucky on an Independent ticket but lost his deposit. His mother was one of the first, successful, female orthopaedic surgeons in the South – she took up the vocation after her favourite uncle broke his back exercising a horse in the run-up to the Derby –'

'Completely off the mark.' Israel beams. 'My stepfather doesn't manufacture anything. He's allergic to cat hair. He's a lecturer at Berkeley where he's an acknowledged, worldwide authority on the works of Derek Walcott. He owns three, small sketches by Basquiat which he acquired – in exchange for a shirt and a coach ticket – after they got arrested doing graffiti together. He's fully ambidextrous – like me – and his non-identical twin brother is currently serving a punitive prison sentence in Indonesia for smuggling endangered birds' eggs.'

'How vile!'

Jen pops his glasses back on to his nose again and then carefully adjusts them to her satisfaction. 'So anyway, this evil little dog's just squatting there' – she hastily returns to her story (a couple of new customers have now entered the bar area) – 'with this filthy, poo-necklace-thingummy dangling out of its arse, and we're all just staring at it, waiting for it to drop, but nothing happens ...'

'Sounds like it might need some assistance,' Israel suggests, gently poking at the lone cube of ice in his Coke with a straw.

'Exactly!' Jen's impressed. 'You're so sharp! So intuitive! Oh God – you're not *gay*, are you?'

She grips the table in mock horror.

'If I wasn't before, then I probably will be by the end of this anecdote,' Israel sighs, camply.

'"He's going to need some assistance ..."' Jen relaxes her grip on the table (briefly mollified). 'That's precisely what his owner says. But after she's said it she just stands there, eyeballing Sinclair, all expectant. "Don't look at me!" Sinclair's totally freaked-out. "I'm not going anywhere near it!"

'"Well *I* can't do anything," the owner says, "I have a sensitive stomach."'

'*A sensitive stomach?!*' Israel clucks.

'The poor creature twirls and twirls,' Jen continues, 'until eventually I just can't bear it any more. "Okay," I say, "pass me a poo bag and I'll try and get rid of it."

'"You'll need to be extra-careful," – the woman's suddenly ultra-uptight and over-protective – "because long hairs can get twisted around the lower intestine and if you yank at them too violently you run the risk of disembowelling him through his anal cavity ...'"

As Jen speaks the couple who'd formerly entered the bar (and who'd been quietly reading the bar-food blackboard) make a rapid exit.

'I'm like: "Just give me a bloody poo bag!"' She rolls her eyes, petulantly. 'But of course she doesn't *have* a poo bag, so now I'm scrabbling around in my school rucksack looking for a tissue or a spare piece of plastic. Eventually Sinclair finds an old Wagon Wheel wrapper in his pocket and I'm obliged to resort to using that. I crouch down in the snow, trying to protect my fingers as best I can, and reach towards the back end of the dog ...

'"Oh, there's something you should probably know ..." the woman tells me, almost as an afterthought.

'"What's that?" I ask, still reaching.

'"He can sometimes be a little bit ..."

'The dog spins around and nips me! On the chin! I swear to God! The cheeky bastard turns and takes a lovely bite out of my chin! Draws blood! You can see the scar under my make-up ...'

She lifts her chin to demonstrate, but nothing is visible bar an impressive watermark where her foundation finishes on her jawline.

'Did you scream?' Israel wonders.

'Did I hell! I was in shock! And I was determined the little fucker wasn't going to get the best of me, so I quickly scrambled to my feet, grabbed his collar, spun him around, clamped his scraggy neck between my calves ...'

'Thereby cunningly disabling his front end ...' Israel interjects.

'Leaving both hands free to engage with the rear,' Jen confirms.

'Ah yes, the rear ...' Israel's visibly traumatized. 'How was it looking by this stage?'

'Dire. But I took my courage in my hands, rearranged the Wagon Wheel wrapper ...'

'We don't have Wagon Wheels in Jamaica,' Israel informs her.

'It's basically a large, round, slightly soggy chocolate biscuit with a marshmallow centre,' Jen explains, 'although that's a completely irrelevant detail at this super-charged point in the narrative ...'

'Sorry,' Israel apologizes.

'Apology accepted,' Jen graciously allows. 'So I rearrange the wrapper, and then I bend down and pinch on to the necklace at about its halfway point,' she explains. 'I guess it'd be around four inches long at this stage – which translates as approximately seven or eight centimetres ...' She pauses, drolly. 'Just in case you still feel like you're short on detail ...'

'Thanks,' Israel nods, submissive, now.

'Of course as soon as I start to yank, the dog's owner is hysterically cautioning me against exerting too much pressure, so I gently tug at it, then release, then tug, then release ...'

Jen performs a little pantomime of the process: 'Sort of like milking a cow; and the necklace gradually extends to about six or seven inches ...' She pauses. 'I inherited this doll off my mother when I was a kid. If you tugged on its blonde ponytail the hair would grow ...'

Israel receives this bonus piece of information without comment.

'Anyhow, after it reaches around the eight-inch stage the necklace stops coming,' Jen continues, 'it's plugged. The poor dog really starts straining. The owner's telling me to just "pinch it off ..."' She shudders. 'But I'm determined to dislodge the remaining clump of whatever it is that's causing the blockage, so I give it a final, sharp, little tug – the owner's pretty much hysterical by this stage – and then *Bingo!* Out it plops!'

'Thank the Lord!' Israel exclaims.

'I automatically release the pressure in my calves and the dog virtually explodes from between my legs and careers off across the park, the owner running after it in hot pursuit.

Naturally I try and gather up the necklace between my fingers so I can place it into a nearby rubbish bin ...'

'Brave, bold *and* public-spirited!' Israel commends her.

'... but it's then that I notice something hard and round through the mass of hair and poo in what was the final, plug-y, clump-y section. I press at it, gingerly, through the Wagon Wheel wrapper and realize that it's a piece of metal! As I do this, leaning forward, a drop of blood splashes into the snow from my chin, but I'm so intrigued that I barely even notice. I press at the clump more forcefully, detach the piece of metal and hold it up closer to my face to inspect it. Believe it or not, it's actually a Claddagh ring ...'

'A ...?'

'A special kind of traditional, Irish friendship ring. Two hands – one on each side – cradling a central heart. I hold it out to Sinclair – who's Irish. "You won't believe this," I say, suddenly almost tearful. "It's a Claddagh ring. The dog was corked up by a Claddagh ring! Looks like it's gold, too!"'

'Incredible!' Israel exclaims.

'Even as I'm talking, though, the dog and its owner are strolling back towards us, the dog on its lead again. "Should you tell her?" Sinclair asks. "No," I say, automatically, "that little fucker bit my chin. I'm owed."

'"What if it's a family heirloom?" Sinclair demands. '"Hard cheese," I scoff.'

'Finders keepers,' Israel confirms.

'But then before I can say anything else,' Jen continues, piqued, 'Sinclair is waving at the woman and beckoning her over. "Are you missing a Claddagh ring by any chance?" he asks. "A what?" The woman scowls. "A Claddagh ring." "What's that?" the woman demands. "A special kind of Irish friendship ring," Sinclair says. "Why d'you ask?" the woman wonders. "Because your dog just shat one out," I say and hold it up. She comes over to take a look, pinching her nose as a precaution against the smell. "Is it gold?" she wonders. "Strange as this may sound," I say, "I haven't had the opportunity to check the hallmark."

"'It isn't yours, then?'" Sinclair's straight to the heart of the matter.

"'I've never seen it before,'" she says, "'but I suppose it must be mine if my dog just shat it out.'"

'*Hmmn.* Interesting logic,' Israel ruminates, plucking at an imaginary beard.

'Yeah. Socrates' *Crito* has nothing on this,' Jen smirks.

'So what happened?'

'I held out the hairy, shitty Wagon Wheel wrapper with the ring in the middle of it and I said, "Well, if you want it, go ahead and take it."'

'Good call!' Israel grins. 'Did she?'

'Uh, nope,' Jen chuckles. 'She tried. She gagged. Then she demanded I clean the ring off in the snow.'

'And ...?'

'And naturally I refused.'

'You kept it?' Israel's impressed.

'Hell yeah!' Jen's cheerfully unrepentant.

'Where's it now?'

'I gave it to Sinclair. I had to: he's Irish. Although he's never actually worn it ...'

'Too fastidious?' Israel wonders.

'It's ridiculous!' Jen scowls. 'I told him about this brand of coffee in South America which is especially prized because the beans have been pre-digested by a civet cat ...'

'How'd he react?'

'He thought I was lying.'

'Were you?'

'Nope.'

The phone starts ringing behind the bar. Jen turns, lackadaisically, to apprehend it.

'Anyway, that's basically the story of how a constipated pooch almost ruined my love life,' she concludes, adjusting her bra-strap. She then pauses for a moment, frowning. 'How'd we get on to that whole subject in the first place?' she wonders, mystified.

'Uh ...' Israel struggles to remember. 'Didn't I ask for extra ice in my Coke at some point?'

'Oh. Yeah ... of course.' Jen nods, distractedly, then returns to the bar (honour fully satisfied) where she rapidly devours ten Rowntree's Tooty Frooties, half a Twix, a dried, reconstituted beef sausage snack and three out-of-date packets of prawn cocktail flavour crisps.

5

'*Awareness continuum?!* Are you serious?'
Sheila leans back against the sink with a loud snort of
derision.
'Afraid so.' Gene nods. 'And no experience is necessary. In
fact he said it'd be an active disadvantage ...'
  'Who needs experience?' Sheila throws up her hands,
dismissively. 'Experience is old hat! Boo shucks to experience!
I mean why bother hiring a professional when there's an
enthusiastic amateur up for grabs, eh?'
'Yours truly.' Gene bows, smiling crookedly. 'Although I'm a
little thin on the enthusiasm front.'
  'Sorry ...' – Sheila simply can't let this one go – 'but he
actually used the phrase, "*Awareness continuum*"?!'
'Fearlessly.' Gene chuckles (evidently delighted to have
captured her interest). 'And with no hint of irony.'
  'Incredible!'
'I think his exact words were, "I'm 'tuning in' to my
awareness continuum."'
He shakes his head, despairingly.
  'God forgive me for saying this,' Sheila mutters, 'but that
man truly is an intergalactic ass.'
As she speaks she turns and throws the dregs of her mug of
tea into the sink, then checks her watch (it's only ten minutes
until Evening Service), opens a nearby cupboard, removes a
large bottle of indigestion tablets, tips one out on to her hand,
tosses it into her mouth and chews, violently.

'He's certainly a little self-involved,' Gene concedes.

'A *little*?!' she expostulates, swallowing with some difficulty, then rinsing out her mug and slamming it down on to the draining-board. 'The man's a sociopath, Gene! An irresponsible egomaniac. You can't seriously be thinking about accepting his offer, surely?'

'Of course not. It's just ... I dunno ...' Gene looks hunted. 'Beneath all the arrogance and the bluster there's something ...' – he thinks hard for a second – '... an awkwardness, a feeling of ... it's like he's all at sea – completely rudderless. When we arrived at the Leaside the other night he just ... he fell to pieces. He was petrified.'

'He was drunk,' Sheila interrupts.

'He just seems incredibly lonely.'

'This man smoked drugs with our teenage son, remember?' she curtly reminds him. 'He encouraged Stan to steal the Hummer, then cheerfully abandoned him when the damn thing broke down ...'

'Ran out of petrol,' Gene corrects her.

'Oh, and let's not forget how he put that poor, local woman into a coma and then calmly refused to pay the family any kind of compensation. It was splashed all over the local papers again this morning ...'

'That was an accident.' Gene automatically rallies to Ransom's defence. 'He'd recently been declared bankrupt. His insurance had lapsed ...'

'You're a soft touch,' she grumbles.

'I just feel sorry for him, Sheila.'

'Here's a suggestion,' she volunteers, brightly. 'Why not conserve your sympathy for someone who actually deserves it? A Somalian refugee. A Prisoner of Conscience. The poor woman whose life he destroyed with that stupid, stray golf ball ...'

'Or her crazy daughter,' Gene muses, thoughtfully, then stiffens, involuntarily, once the words leave his mouth.

'Her crazy daughter?' Sheila frowns. 'She has a crazy daughter?'

'*No*. Not crazy exactly ...' Gene rapidly starts to backtrack.

'Then why call her crazy?' Sheila persists.

'It's just ...' Gene bites his lip. 'Remember that weird incident on my rounds the other day with the little girl and the trampoline?'

'Nope.' Sheila shakes her head.

'There was a little girl jumping on a trampoline without any pants on and the neighbour asked me to have a word with the mother about it. Well the mother's the crazy daughter. In fact she's the aunt. The real mother's in rehab. The child is the crazy daughter's niece. Although she isn't crazy. She's just –'

'Does this bizarre-sounding scenario have anything to do with your dear friend Jen, by any chance?' Sheila interrupts, her eyes slitting.

'Jen?' Gene appears puzzled by the mention of Jen. 'Uh. No. Although ...' He pauses. 'Although I was at the neighbour's house collecting the child when Jen rang me on my mobile ...'

Sheila stares at him for a moment, confused. 'So ... so you were running an *errand* for this woman?'

'Which woman?'

'The crazy daughter.'

'Yes. Although she isn't crazy. She's just ...' He thinks for a moment, and the only word to pop into his head is 'beautiful'.

'But you were actually at their house?' she interjects, alarmed. 'You were *in* their house?'

'Whose house?' Gene scowls, irritated at himself.

'The Tuckers? Isn't that their name?'

'Unofficially, yes. But they're actually down on the register as –'

'Yesterday,' Sheila interrupts, impatiently. 'This was yesterday, the day after the incident at the hotel?'

'Uh ...'

Gene nods, flushing slightly under the intensity of her gaze.

'Well you *definitely* didn't mention that before.'
Sheila's certain.
'Really?' Gene frowns, defensive. 'I'm pretty sure I did.'
'Nope. I'd have remembered. I mean it's such an odd
coincidence, don't you think? In a town this size? The
next *day*?! I would definitely have remembered something like
that.'

'You were somewhat preoccupied by the whole Stan
situation at the time,' Gene reminds her.
'And with good reason,' she insists.
'Absolutely.'

They stare at each other for a second, neither giving way,
and then, 'Lost!' she snorts. '*Lonely?!*'

'I'll drop Mallory off at speech therapy,' Gene promises
(refusing to get embroiled), 'but she'll need collecting just
after seven thirty …'

'You think by using loaded words like "lonely" and
"awkward" you'll tug on my Christian heartstrings and then
I'll miraculously relent, is that it?' she demands, her eyes
shining, combatively.
'Well what would Jesus do?' Gene asks, trying not to laugh.

'Lost!' she snorts again. 'Like some innocent, little lamb
strayed off the path of righteousness? You're unbelievable!'
He shrugs, self-deprecatingly.

'Unbelievable,' she repeats. 'But d'you know what the most
maddening part of it all is?'
The light in her eyes fades ever so slightly.
'What?' Gene's suddenly wary.
'You're completely right!'
'I am?'
'Of course you are. And I *know* it. Why else do you think my
stomach's perpetually cramping up into knots' – she rattles the
indigestion tablet bottle, vengefully – 'and I've no sodding
fingernails left to speak of?'

'Please don't think I'm just shifting the blame here,' Gene mutters, 'but from where I'm currently standing the PCC aren't helping matters much, either.'

'*Urgh*. The PCC,' she echoes, wincing. 'Why not throw in the threatened closure of the allotments while you're at it?'

'The Samuel Wright-Todd Memorial Window?' he suggests, grinning.

She closes her eyes for a second. 'I never thought it'd be a walk in the park, Gene,' she grumbles, her shoulders slumping forward, 'but the constant, niggling criticisms, the petty infighting, the complete lack of support from above ...' Words temporarily fail her.

'The woodworm problem in the vestry,' Gene cheerfully takes over from where she's left off, 'the loose tiles on the church roof, the persistent tagging on the back wall ...'

'That sneaky, little Humanist, William Tuttle, stealing all the funeral work right from under my nose!' Sheila fumes.

'Damn the man!' Gene grins. 'With his ridiculously low fees and his comprehensive service plan!'

'This infernal, sodding kitchen!' Sheila squawks, her eyes flying open. 'Not even room for a dishwasher or a decent-sized washing machine! The malfunctioning cooker! No proper freezer! And now they're seriously expecting me to help cater church events from over here?'

'The old reverend's wife used to manage it,' Gene gently fans the flames of her ire. 'I hear Mrs Noble's mini bacon quiches were second to none.'

'Francine bloody Noble!' Sheila slams down both her hands on to the yellow, laminated breakfast bar. 'The woman was a bloody saint!'

'Stalwart of the choir – unbelievable soprano voice – made all the kid's clothes herself, by hand ...' Gene provokes her still further.

'Fine! All right! Enough!'

Sheila laughingly concedes defeat, turning to place the indigestion tablets back into the cupboard, before – seconds later – withdrawing a stray pair of tweezers, sticky with dried cereal. 'How on earth ...?'

'I dread to think,' Gene mutters, his hand creeping around to the bruise on his shoulder.

'Will you make an appointment with the doctor?' she asks, not missing a beat.

'Nuh-uh.'

He shakes his head. 'I've got my six-monthly check-up in a couple of weeks. May as well sit it out.'

'Ah.'

She nods, her eyes briefly scanning his face, then she turns and peers through the tiny window above the sink and out into the back yard beyond.

'You're so bloody stoical,' she muses (as if commenting, dispassionately, on a tree or a cloud). 'It's amazing. It makes me want to hug you and slap you, all at once.'

'Thanks.'

He smiles, stiffly.

'Don't take it amiss.' She turns to face him again. 'It's a blessing, a kind of a ... a *gift*, almost. I've always found it truly enviable ...' She makes a half-cocked attempt to mollify him. 'And I know it's just your personality – your character – something you take entirely for granted – hardly even give a second thought to ...' She shrugs. 'I mean it's just *what it is*. It's just *who you are*. There's no support network – no faith – no gratitude ...'

Gene scowls. 'I hope I'm not ungrateful,' he murmurs, hurt.

'It's enviable,' she repeats, 'it's effortless. It's wonderful. And yet here I am, in my sanctimonious, little dog collar' – she tugs at her collar, balefully – 'supposedly representing everything that's good and just and decent, but actually consumed by bile and rage and frustration, finding everything so ridiculously bloody *hard* ...' Her mouth twists into a mordant smile. 'Then I look at you, all free and unencumbered, without care, without faith, and I see this ... this ... this easiness, this earnestness, this gentle acceptance of things ... this sense of infinite patience ... this ... this infuriating *piety* ...'

She throws up her hands. There are tears in her eyes.

'You feel things very deeply,' he insists, 'that's all.'

'And you don't?'

She delivers him a sharp look. He frowns, momentarily caught off guard.

'Bully for Sheila and all her misguided passion, eh?!' she scoffs. 'Angry, bitter, exhausted old Sheila! Bully for her!'

'You feel frustrated – unappreciated.' He moves towards her, instinctively, and touches her arm. 'That's inevitable. You're a woman in a male-dominated profession. It goes with the territory ...'

'No.'

She's not buying it. 'I'm judgemental. I'm opinionated. I'm short-tempered. And it's all rooted in ego. In pride.' She knocks his hand from her arm by adjusting her hair. 'I lack humility. I lack resignation. I'm too ... urgh ... *stressed* all the time. Like the other day, with the bishop –'

'That's just part and parcel of what you do,' he interrupts, possibly hoping to divert her, 'you're an arbitrator between the forces of good and evil.'

She ponders this for a second. 'Like Luke Skywalker?' she mutters, amused, in spite of herself.

'Or Miss Marple.' He grins.

'That'd be right.' She chuckles. 'Nothing too glamorous or high-tech – just the light perm, the pleated skirt, the nice, comfy pair of leather brogues ...'

'Down on the church allotments, spy-glass in hand ...'

Gene teases her.

'Not even Miss Marple could reason her way out of *that* particular hole.' She grimaces, plucking a stray hair off her sleeve.

'The decision's been made?' Gene suddenly looks serious. 'He's flogging them off?'

'Yup.'

She twists the stray hair around her index finger.

'You discussed the petition?'

'Of course.'

She looks up, defensive. 'I said we had over seven hundred signatures – two hundred more than we currently have ...'

'And how did he respond?' Gene demands.

'He didn't. He just shrugged.'

'He just shrugged?!'

'Pretty much.'

'Bloody hell!' Gene's incensed. 'How's that sanctimonious little prig manage to sleep at night?!'

'He sleeps like a baby,' Sheila sighs, removing the washing-up cloth from the washing-up bowl, wringing it out and then draping it over the tap. 'He doesn't really see it as a problem he can resolve. He says his hands are tied ...'

'That's bullshit! You *know* that's just bullshit!'

'Is it, though?' Sheila dries her damp fingers on a tea towel and then rubs her eyes with her knuckles, exhausted. 'It's easy to demonize him, Gene, but we both know – in our heart of hearts – that this was never so much a simple choice between right and wrong as a fluffed-up compromise between two lesser kinds of evil ...'

'Are you sure about that?' Gene's plainly not convinced.

'Uh. No,' Sheila admits, removing the tea towel from its small, plastic hook, shaking it out and then folding it in half, ready for use, 'which could well be a sign that I need to take a step back from the situation – distance myself from the campaign; try and focus my limited energies on something more positive, something more attainable ...'

'Nah. Not your style,' Gene maintains.

'My style?' she grumbles, grabbing a teacup and starting to dry it. 'What's my style, exactly? Three years of senseless rancour followed by a long and drawn-out nervous breakdown?'

'Why change the habits of a lifetime?' Gene teases her.

'Well maybe, just this once, I need to rise above – be the bigger person …'

Sheila's almost laughing as she says this.

'*Pshaw!*' Gene's incredulous.

'Thanks.' She shoots him a jaundiced look as she places the dried cup into a nearby cupboard.

'You don't need me to tell you that there's a massive principle at stake here,' he persists, 'which is that the church has a responsibility to the wider community, even if they don't happen to be members of the Christian faith *per se.*'

'You know, increasingly I'm coming to see the virtues in *your* philosophy,' Sheila muses, grabbing a saucer from the draining-board this time.

'Mine?' Gene frowns.

'Yeah' – she gives the saucer a cursory buff and then places it alongside the cup – 'taking the path of least resistance.'

'That's *my* philosophy?'

Gene's plainly irritated by this.

'I need to be more pragmatic' – she shrugs – 'compromise. Let things go.'

'Who *are* you,' Gene demands (only semi-joking now), 'and what the hell have you done with my wife?'

'I've placed her into an old box labelled "idealist",' she sighs, 'punctured the cardboard with a couple of air-holes, and then carefully taped over the lid.'

She gives the tea towel a cursory inspection. 'I don't think she'll be especially missed,' she adds.

'Well, for what it's worth,' Gene maintains, 'I've always really loved your reformist zeal.'

'*But one man loved the pilgrim soul in you,*' she quotes, '*And loved the sorrows of your changing face.*'

Gene looks at her, quizzically.

'W.B. Yeats. "When You are Old".'

She gazes around the kitchen, pensively. 'I *feel* old,' she mutters. 'I feel ancient. In fact I feel sort of ... sort of *desiccated.*'

'Like a religious coconut,' Gene suggests.

'Strung up on a high branch for all the blue tits to peck at.' She grimaces.

'I *do* love your pilgrim soul,' Gene avows, 'but not the sorrow. The sorrow part I can live without.'

'With idealism comes heartbreak. With stoicism comes ...' She thinks for a moment, scrunching up the tea towel in her hand. '... yet more stoicism.'

'Great! Bucket-loads of stoicism,' Gene grumbles, 'where the hell will we find the room to store it all?'

'We can rent a railway arch,' Sheila suggests.

'Yeah ...' Gene quickly warms to this idea. 'We can tie the bishop to a chair and chuck him in there, too.'

'Alongside my little box of idealism,' she muses.

'Not such a little box,' Gene snorts, 'how about an unwieldy, plywood crate with rusting, stainless-steel supports?'

Sheila refuses to take his bait. She turns and grabs a cereal bowl. 'Maybe my appointment to this post wasn't the start of something after all,' she ruminates, 'but the end of it.'

'How so?' Gene scowls.

'I just don't think they view me as a functioning part of the team ...' She finishes with the bowl and places it into the cupboard. 'And that's not only locally, but in the diocese as a whole ...' This time she grabs a dinner plate. 'I mean the bishop honestly seems to believe that my appointment was enough – that his involvement ends there.'

'The pace of change was always bound to be slow,' Gene interjects, 'you knew that when you accepted the post.'

'I basically just tick a box,' she continues, ignoring his interjection. 'I fill a quota. At best I'm a hollow symbol of change; the most shallow ... the most superficial ...' Words fail her, temporarily, and she polishes the plate with an especial vigour. 'It's his automatic, fall-back position every time I bring up any kind of problem I might be experiencing with the PCC or any kind of issue I might have with the church warden ...'

She places the plate down on to the worktop and quickly grabs another. 'He basically just peers at me over the top of his spectacles as if to say, "You're *there*, aren't you? I've done my bit. I've stuck my neck out. Now stop your infernal carping, woman, grit your teeth, and get on with it!"'

'He did stick his neck out,' Gene concedes.

'Yeah. I *know* that, Gene' – Sheila's starting to work up a real head of steam, now – 'but what's the point in making a controversial appointment if – once the appointment's finally secured – you just back off, holding your hands up, basically refusing all further involvement?'

She finishes drying the second plate and slides it on top of the first. 'I mean I'm virtually disabled by the PCC, the church warden's from the Dark Ages, every remotely interesting initiative I try and undertake is either blocked outright or dies a slow and painful death due to a universal lack of interest ...'

'Is this a crisis of faith?' Gene asks, mock-seriously, peering down at his watch. 'Because Evening Service starts in approximately two minutes.'

Sheila frowns but says nothing. She reaches out and grabs a third plate.

'What's that thing you're always quoting at Mallory?' He tries his best to pep-talk her. 'You know – that weirdly sadistic thing about God always testing the people he loves best the hardest?'

After a long pause in which she dries the third plate with a spectacular level of thoroughness, Sheila finally rouses herself to answer him: '*For he maketh His sun to rise on the evil and the good, and sendeth rain on the just and the unjust,*' she suggests.

'Uh, no,' Gene demurs.

'*The inestimable treasure of tribulation,*' she second guesses.

'There you have it.' He nods, gratified.

'So I suppose – by my own warped logic – that I must be incredibly blessed right now ...'

She smiles over at him, brightly, then places the third plate on top of the other two. 'I must be *tremendously* blessed, *stupendously* blessed.'

'Is that a roundabout way of saying you're depressed?' Gene wonders, concerned.

'Uh ...' She ponders this for a while. 'Let's change the subject, shall we?'

He stares at her, uncertain whether to do as she asks. Her mouth is slowly turning down at its corners. Her jaw is tightening. Her nostrils begin to flare.

'Let me finish off the drying,' he murmurs, reaching out his hand for the cloth.

'It's almost done, now,' she sniffs, glancing up at the ceiling as if to preclude any unwanted accumulation of excess moisture in her eyes.

'D'you know anything about agoraphobia?' he promptly demands (keen not to precipitate a total breakdown directly before Evening Service). 'Is it a curable condition? Didn't you counsel a parishioner with it at one stage?'

'Agoraphobia?'

She struggles to focus. 'Uh ...'

'I met this young woman today –'

'Fear of the marketplace,' Sheila butts in (pulling herself together with what appears to be a mammoth amount of effort).

'Sorry?'

'*Agora* ...' She grabs another cereal bowl. 'It's the Greek for marketplace. Agora-phobia: a fear of the marketplace.'

'I see.' Gene is nonplussed.

'There was a woman I visited while I was in training up in Sheffield. Her name was ...' She thinks hard for a second as she looks down at the cereal bowl then notices a small food remnant still gracing its rim. 'Nina. Late thirties, early forties, unhappily married. Her husband was incredibly overbearing. Didn't take the condition seriously – just thought it was yet more evidence of a basic lack of moral fibre ...' She places the bowl back into the sink, and then stares, glumly, through the window. 'I think it was him who got the church involved, although it wasn't an especially successful manoeuvre. She just really seemed to resent it.'

Sheila raises a hand to her face but Gene cannot tell – from the rear – if she's moving aside a strand of hair or wiping away a tear with it. 'Not my greatest piece of Community Outreach work, as I recollect.'

Her voice starts to shake a little.

'This woman I met today – this agoraphobic ...' Gene is about to confide in her about the meeting with Valentine (the broken meter, the strange bruise), but then – in the light of the whole Stan farrago – he suddenly thinks better of it and falls silent.

'This woman you met today ...' Sheila prompts him.

'Uh ... Yeah. She'd done something really strange to herself,' Gene improvises.

'Really?'

Sheila glances over her shoulder at him, her powerful, dark eyes dulled with a profound indifference.

'She'd tattooed a brick on to her leg,' Gene expands. 'Several bricks. Incredibly lifelike ...'

'Bricks?' Sheila echoes, blankly.

'She's an artist. It was some kind of an art statement, I suppose. She showed me this photograph. It was really beautifully taken ...'

'Ah ...'

Her eyes suddenly glimmer with a momentary show of engagement. '*Women Who Marry Houses*,' she muses.

'Women who ...?'

Sheila returns the tea towel to its hook.

'It's the title of a book I salvaged from the church jumble a couple of years back. Looked intriguing. There was a quote on the title page by Anne Sexton – one of the women poets I wrote my dissertation on at Oxford ...' She picks up the four, dry plates and places them into a cupboard. 'It went something along the lines of ...' She frowns as she struggles to recall it: '*Women marry houses. It's another kind of skin.*'

She shrugs. 'An odd concept, really, but it's always stuck with me for some reason.'

Gene gazes at her as she speaks – slowly drinking in her ragged fringe, her deep frown lines, an area of inflammation in the centre of her right cheek, a suggestion of staining on one of her front teeth – and suddenly feels an incredibly powerful rush of emotion towards her.

'You're amazing,' he says, his voice low and unexpectedly guttural. 'So bloody wise.'

She turns to look at him, shocked.

'Don't be ridiculous!' she snaps, then pats him on the shoulder, straight after, almost as an afterthought, before heading off, morosely, to Evening Service.

'I'm sorry ...' Valentine stares at her brother, her cheeks flushing, her expression one of complete bewilderment. 'What kind of therapist did you say he was, exactly?'

Noel turns to the small, rotund, beetle-browed Asian man currently perched on their sofa and says, 'What kind of therapist did you say you were?'

'What kind? *Hmmn*. Well, I suppose – in the current vernacular – you might call me "a jack of all trades",' he says, amiably.

'Karim was recommended by Salvatore at the daycare centre,' Noel fills in. 'He works with three – was it three?' He looks to Karim for confirmation and Karim nods. 'Three, yes.' 'Three of the other patients. Salvatore says he works magic, that he's a genius.'

Karim merely flaps his hand, modestly, at Noel's compliments. He is wearing a pair of thin, white cotton trousers which finish some distance above his beige socks and brown sandals, a long, white cotton smock, with a light, grey cotton waistcoat over the top (its small, front pockets bulging with various paraphernalia). His hair curls behind his ears and he has a short, neat, prematurely greying beard but no moustache.

'The Arabic translation of Karim,' he volunteers, 'is "the generous one".'

He raises his eyes heavenward. 'I believe that I have been given my many gifts by Almighty God, and that it is God's will for me to share them generously. So here I am, today' – he shrugs – 'sharing them with you and your charming family.'

As he finishes speaking his gaze moves from the statue of the Virgin Mary to the picture of Kali on the shrine. The large, framed photograph on the wall of the genital tattoo has now been removed, but his gaze rests on the spot where it was formerly hung, as if – by some paranormal mechanism – it might actually still be visible to him.

'Could I get you a drink?' Vee wonders, finally remembering her manners. 'A cup of tea, perhaps?'

'No, not for me. I can't stay long.' Karim grimaces. 'My stupid wife is in the car.'

'Then you must invite her in!' Valentine insists, horrified. 'She'd be very welcome ...'

'Please don't take this the wrong way' – Karim leans forward and pulls up a sock – 'but I'm actually relishing this brief interlude apart.'

As he speaks, Valentine glances towards her brother (who is busily tapping out a text on his phone), then leans over and peers through the front bay window. Between a couple of the slats in the blinds she sees what appears to be a magnificent, old Citroën (pale blue, with exquisite chrome-work). Sitting in the back seat, somewhat incongruously, is a lone woman in the full veil.

'Don't be shocked,' Karim counsels, gauging her expression (that foggy, insect-ridden no-man's-land between surprise and alarm). 'It's just a silly phase. A kind of social revolt against what she perceives as the corrupt and corrupting mores of Western society' – he snorts, mirthlessly – 'chiefly represented by yours truly, of course!'

He performs a little bow, palms pressed together, then adds, 'Perhaps a Sprite, or a Diet Pepsi?'

Noel promptly heads off to the kitchen, still texting. Valentine continues to inspect Karim's wife. It's a warm evening. She is fanning her face (the tiny part of it that's still visible) through a tiny slit in the dense mass of heavy-seeming, black fabric.

'She looks hot,' Vee observes.

'It's like a portable bread oven inside that thing,' Karim clucks. 'Crazy! My current philosophy is that if I give her enough rope ...'

He simulates sudden asphyxiation (hands at his throat, eyes popping, tongue out), then removes a handkerchief from the pocket of his waistcoat and vigorously blows his nose on it.

'I tell her it's a form of cultural hysteria' – he dabs at his nostrils, fastidiously – 'an emotional anorexia. Not about faith! *Ha!* Not remotely. God is Love! God is Wisdom! God is Truth! God is Generosity – *Ya Karim*, eh?'

Valentine smiles, obligingly (although she's not entirely sure what she's smiling at).

'God isn't just dotted here or there, boxed into a series of little, sacred spaces,' Karim expands, scowling, 'hidden under that piece of black fabric – swirling around like a tiny whirlwind inside the cool shadows of the mosque – trapped within the vowels of a prayer … Heavens, no! He's everywhere, inside every created thing …' He throws out his hand, expressively (the white handkerchief waving its fleeting surrender between his fingers). 'God is the invasive gaze of an arrogant stranger!' he exclaims. 'God is the modest curl of a pretty lip into a welcoming smile. God is the warmth of the sun on a beautiful girl's bronzed shoulder. God is the exquisite brush of cool silk against a tautening nipple. God is *life*, eh?' He grins. 'He enlivens us! He stimulates! He titillates! God opens us up, he doesn't shut us down. He didn't give us the whole, wide world so that we should wrinkle up our noses and turn away from it, full of haughty condemnation, riddled with disgust …'

Valentine nods, intimidated (her arms folded, defensively, across her chest), then glances over towards his wife again.

'She's just acting out,' Karim grumbles. 'It's a pointless charade – a farce! Forget modesty or reserve or decency or restraint – it's sheer bloody-mindedness. It's all about control …'

Karim pats the handkerchief over his forehead and then shoves it back into his pocket. 'Of course she won't listen,' he mutters, 'so what can I do? It's embarrassing. People think I'm a monster. She loves it. She absolutely loves it. She's my second wife. Only twenty-one years of age. Attended Catholic school. Grew up in Barking. *Is* barking, to my way of thinking ...'

'What happened to your first wife?' Valentine wonders.

'Nothing happened to her.' Karim's indignant. 'She's perfectly fine! She lives in Delhi. She nurses my ailing mother.'

'I see.' Valentine chews on her lower lip, somewhat apprehensively. 'D'you have children?'

'Yes I do.' He nods. 'Three. Two by my first wife – both sons – and one daughter by Aamilah.' He thumbs, contemptuously, towards the window. 'Milah's an awful mother. The child – Badriya – is very fat. Milah just feeds her and feeds her. We share our home with Milah's sister, Farhana. She loves to cook. All they do is feed each other and watch DVDs. And sometimes they watch daytime TV – awful TV – and pass haughty pronouncements on it. "Oh that woman is so ugly! Oh that man is so degenerate!" I tell them, "Nobody is forcing you to watch it!" but they don't pay me the slightest heed. I might as well be invisible for all they care. The house is a terrible mess. A pigsty! They're completely useless. The child is huge. Like a balloon. It's ridiculous. I mean the woman has an A-level in politics and economics, but she lives like an imbecile.'

Noel returns holding a tray with a lone can of Coke on it. He proffers it to their guest.

'Couldn't you find a glass?' Valentine murmurs, embarrassed.

'I'm fine with a can, just so long as it's good and cold,' Karim insists. He takes the can, cracks the ring-pull and takes a long, deep draught.

'I'll fetch Mum,' Noel volunteers, then promptly heads out of the room again, still clutching the tray, before Valentine has a chance to react.

She stares after him, scowling. Karim looks around for somewhere to place his can.

'Sorry ... here ... please ...' Valentine unfolds a small, occasional table in front of their guest so that he can put his drink down on it.

'Don't be sorry.' Karim smiles up at her. 'An attractive girl need never be sorry.'

'And a plain girl?' she counters.

'A plain girl should be constantly apologizing!' he exclaims. 'What else?!'

She gazes at him for a moment, shocked, her eyes widening.

'Yes, yes, I'm incorrigible!' He chuckles. 'I was an incorrigible baby – so my mother always tells me – who grew into an incorrigible boy, then into an incorrigible teenager. And now I am an incorrigible man. My life is packed full of incorrigibility. There's nothing to be done about it. Nothing at all.'

'It's just ...' Valentine yanks on her fringe, unsettled. 'Please don't take this the wrong way, but I'm still not ... I mean Noel didn't get around to telling me what it is that you actually ...'

'Because he doesn't know himself!' Karim expostulates, delighted.

'... what it is that you *do*, exactly,' Valentine finishes off, confused.

'Let me lay my cards on to the table.' Karim leans forward and spreads his hands across the small, drinks table in a symbolic gesture. 'It's never what people think, okay? The service varies from client to client. It's basically tailor-made – I believe the fashionable lingo is "boutique" ...'

He emits a snuffling laugh.

'It certainly isn't just wham-bam-thank-you-mam,' he expands, 'if that's what you're imagining! It's much deeper, much more profound than that. It's about *intimacy*. Enjoying something *intimate*. A special bond. A closeness. Sometimes we sing spiritual songs or I recite to them from learned texts during a hand or foot or head massage. Sometimes they play with my finger' – he holds up his index finger – 'or gently stroke my belly' – he pats his rotund stomach, beatifically. 'I teach a special kind of pelvic bouncing. It's extraordinarily effective, if I say so myself! A person's sexuality can take myriad forms. I can make a woman come by clapping my hands together ...'

He claps his hands. 'Or by making them laugh, or with simple eye contact ...'

He gazes at her, owlishly. Valentine blinks, then shudders.

'That's right,' Karim repeats, holding her gaze, 'just by simple eye contact. Although I'm not afraid to get my hands dirty ...' He lifts a plump, graceful hand, to illustrate. 'It's a tailor-made service, but it's a complete service. Satisfaction is guaranteed ...' He pauses for a moment, mid-sentence, inspecting his raised hand, fastidiously. 'My hands *are* actually dirty. I do apologize. I polished my car after breakfast. I'd booked the morning off, then your brother phoned ...'

'It's a lovely car,' Valentine interjects, peering over towards the window again (happy for the distraction). 'Is it an old Citroën?'

'A *Citroën*? Heavens, no!' Karim scoffs. 'It's a Tatra. It's Czechoslovakian. Very rare. There's only a couple of them in the country as we speak.'

Valentine moves still closer to the window and inspects the car more thoroughly.

'The engine is in the boot,' he informs her.

'I've never seen anything like it,' she muses. 'Is that a third headlight in the middle of the bonnet?'

'Yes,' Karim confirms, proudly, 'and there's a bonus fin on the back.'

'It's like something from an old film or a cartoon,' she marvels. '*Batman* or *The Jetsons* ...'

'*The Wizard of Oz*,' he volunteers.

'Why not?' She grins. 'Careering along the yellow brick road, horn blaring, a couple of Munchkins behind the wheel ...'

'Bags I be a Munchkin and you be Dorothy!' he cackles, suddenly wildly over-excited. 'Milah can be "It"!' he adds, guffawing.

Valentine's grin falters.

'You remind me a lot of Dorothy.' He chuckles, still running with the idea. 'A sweet, little farm girl. The quaint way you dress – your funny, bobbed fringe ...'

Valentine touches her fringe again, uncertain how to react.

'But I'm getting carried away with myself again!' he chastises himself, taking another quick sip of his Coke, placing down the can, lacing his fingers together and then leaning back into the cushions. 'Do please feel free to ask any questions about the service I provide. Don't be shy! Be as specific as you like. I won't be offended. I'm impossible to offend.'

Valentine thinks hard for a few seconds. 'So you're actually ...' – she clears her throat, embarrassed – ' you're actually more of a ... a *sexual* therapist?'

'People sometimes call me that' – Karim nods, wincing slightly – 'although there are other words and phrases that describe what I do more effectively. Of course I have no formal, therapeutic training – if that's what's troubling you – no documentation I can show you. No degree from the university of heaven knows where. No GCSE or NVQ. All I have is this ...'

Karim straightens up and indicates, respectfully, towards his head. 'And this ...'

He indicates, respectfully, towards his heart. 'And this ...'

He indicates, respectfully, towards his penis.

'Bloody hell!' Valentine bites her lip, uncertain quite where to rest her eyes.

'Serious brain injury can sometimes result in a dramatic increase in sexual appetite,' Karim continues, suddenly more businesslike. 'It's nothing to get embarrassed about. It's not shameful or wrong. It's just a very basic, very natural animal instinct. There's no point in fighting it or getting upset about it. We need to be calm, focused and pragmatic.'

'I'm not fighting it,' Valentine insists (perhaps a fraction too hotly), 'it's just ...' She frowns. 'So you've already spoken to Noel about all of this? I mean ...' She shakes her head, confused. 'Noel's perfectly happy with the idea of ...?' She can't quite bring herself to say it.

'Heavens, no!' Karim throws up his hands, shocked. 'I haven't breathed a word of it! And Salvatore will have been very discreet – the last thing he wants to do is risk alienating his loyal client base.'

'Because I'm not really sure if he'd entirely *like* the idea of you and our mum ...' – Valentine gestures, limply – '... you know.'

'In the act of coitus,' Karim interjects, mildly.

She winces. 'He's just very ... uh ... *protective*.'

'Of course.' Karim shrugs. 'He's a loving son. He believes he's protecting her, but all he's really protecting are his own fragile sensibilities. He finds it difficult to perceive his mother as a fully functioning sexual animal. And that's absolutely fine' – he shrugs again – 'although profoundly detrimental to her basic physical and mental well-being.'

He delivers her a beaming smile. 'Luckily, what Noel doesn't know about can't hurt him, eh?'

Valentine is quiet for a while (perhaps struggling to come to terms with what's just been said).

'Is it expensive?' she eventually enquires. 'The ... the ...'

'Service,' he fills in, cordially.

She nods.

'Well I'm not a charity' – Karim chuckles – 'but I *am* Karim. I *am* Generosity. I have charitable instincts. I won't bleed you dry, in other words. My requirements are almost criminally modest.'

'And it's not … it's not illegal or anything?'

'Illegal?!' Karim scoffs. 'Not remotely!'

'And you would visit us approximately …?'

'Twice a week.' Karim removes a small diary from his waistcoat pocket and checks his schedule. 'I have a regular, Monday afternoon slot up for grabs from early August – between two and three thirty – and a regular, Thursday morning slot to start immediately – between ten and eleven forty-five.' He pauses, speculatively. 'The initial three or four sessions consist of basic, trust-building exercises and last only half an hour – the client tends to get tired quite quickly to begin with, so the fee will vary accordingly … And of course it goes without saying that before I can wholly commit to your mother's treatment I will need to be formally introduced to her and to feel assured of a certain … I don't know … *chemistry*: a spiritual and emotional rapport …' He pauses again. 'I think it only fair to warn you that I generally turn down more clients than I accept. This isn't just a job for me, you see. It's a mission. It's a divine gift. Some people call me an "Angel of Love", a cherubim. I'm a conjurer' – he waggles his fingers at her – 'I make magic. I conjure miracles. And as such I need to feel completely at ease in my working environment.'

As he speaks he turns to apprehend Valentine's shrine, a slight frown denting his forehead. 'May I deduce from your shrine that you are a devotee of the goddess, Kali?'

'Um …'

Valentine's eyes also turn towards the shrine.

'Because while I respect your enquiring spirit – I sincerely do' – he smiles at her, ingratiatingly – 'I happen to know, from intense, personal experience …' – his hand flies back to his heart and his eyes briefly flutter towards the ceiling – 'that there is only one God, and the best way to draw close to him is through combating the ego. There really is no other path. Kali is a digression, a deviation, an exotic fancy, a macabre, physical projection of your destructive inner God-instinct, a charming but invidious pipe-dream –'

'I only use the shrine for chanting,' Valentine interrupts him, slightly panicked.

'Let me put it this way,' Karim persists. 'When Dorothy wanted to speak to the Wizard, what did she do?'

'Do?' Valentine echoes, mystified.

'Yes. What did Dorothy do?' he repeats.

'Uh …' Valentine thinks for a few seconds. 'Well she took a trip to Oz, I guess.'

'Exactly!' Karim slaps his diary on to his knee, delighted. 'She headed straight for Oz! She didn't waste her precious time deifying the red shoes or becoming a loyal devotee of the Wicked Witch – what earthly good would that have done her?! Dorothy sensed – and quite correctly – that the shoes and the Witch were just a colourful distraction, a part of the sideshow …'

'I take your point,' Valentine murmurs, somewhat piqued (and not a little beleaguered), turning to face the door through which she can just about discern her brother gradually descending the stairs (her grumbling mother in tow).

'Well I'm very glad we've sorted that out,' Karim mutters, tucking away his diary and turning towards the door himself, his round face breaking into the broadest of smiles. 'Now for the fun part, eh?!' He chuckles, rubbing his soft, plump hands together in gleeful anticipation of their imminent arrival.

'If there's one thing I've learned about this business,' Ransom hypothesizes, airily, 'it's that nobody will take you seriously unless *you* take yourself seriously. That's the chief piece of wisdom I offer any dumb kid who's honestly thinking about entering this rat-race: I say, "Take yourself seriously. Take yourself *really* fuckin' seriously. Because if *you* don't take yourself seriously, then – trust me – no other fucker will, either."'

'I suppose talent will out, eventually,' Gene concedes, somewhat distractedly, as he peruses the drinks menu.

'Fuck talent!' Ransom scoffs. 'Talent-schmalent! I mean look at Mourinho. Look at what *he* did. He called himself "The Special One". The *Special* One! He gave *himself* that name! It's like …' Ransom throws up his hands exasperated. 'It's like … why the hell wait for someone else to realize how special you are? Life's too fucking short! *Make* yourself special! Immortalize yourself! Book your *own* place in friggin' history!'

Gene waits a couple of seconds for the rousing conclusion of Ransom's diatribe to fully resonate into the surrounding atmosphere, then places down the menu. 'Uh … in reply to your earlier question,' he mutters, 'a glass of lemonade would be great.'

'A lemonade?' Ransom's visibly underwhelmed. 'They do freshly prepared smoothies here. Have a strawberry smoothie. Have a blueberry and banana smoothie.'

'A lemonade's absolutely fine,' Gene avers.

'Or a fruit mocktail. They do this ginger and lavender mocktail with loads of freshly squeezed lemon in it. What's that thing called again?'

Ransom turns to the long-suffering waitress, enquiringly.

'A Ginger Mule,' she answers, her hand hovering over her pad.

'A Ginger Mule. Can you make that with extra Spirulina?' Ransom enquires. 'And a shot of vodka? Maybe a teaspoon or two of powdered kale?'

'That would be two mocktails combined,' the waitress informs him, grabbing the menu and scrutinizing it for a second. 'A Ginger Mule and a Sea Breeze, so it would cost twice as much …' She places the menu back down on to the table. 'Then there'd obviously be the price of the shot on top.'

'The cost is irrelevant,' Ransom informs her, haughtily, then turns to Gene. 'D'you like Spirulina?'

'And I can't promise how good it would taste,' she interjects.

'I don't know what Spirulina is,' Gene confesses.

'It's plankton,' Ransom tells him, ignoring her interjection, 'the stuff whales feed on. It's great. It's a super-food. It makes your shit come out smelling like Play-Doh.'

'Really?' Gene looks mildly nauseated. 'And that's supposed to be its chief selling point?'

'Why not?' Ransom demands. 'D'you *like* the smell of shit? Are you especially *attached* to the smell of shit? Is this some weird, little picadillo you've developed during those long, hard years manning the front lines, perchance?'

Ransom grabs Gene's military cap as he speaks (which sits – with the torn jacket – on the plush banquette beside him) and plops it, unceremoniously, on to his head.

'Uh ...'

Gene scowls.

'I mean who *likes* the smell of shit?' Ransom declaims, outraged. 'It's shit! That's why it's called shit! It stinks like shit! It's *shit!*'

'I may be totally off the mark, here' – Gene slightly adjusts the angle of the cap on his head – 'but I think the word you're after is "peccadillo". The original, Latin root is *peccare*, or "to sin".'

Ransom gapes at him, astonished.

'I helped my wife cram for her Latin exam at Divinity School' – he shrugs, his colour rising – 'and a couple of things just seemed to stick ...'

'Spirulina's a type of algae produced by water and sunlight,' the waitress volunteers (plainly eager to move on). 'It's meant to "refresh the colon", and that's why your ...'

She twizzles her hand, expressively, keen not to enter into any further detail.

'It makes your shit float,' Ransom enthuses. 'It's like four, friggin' flushes before those torpedos will quit the bowl!'
The waitress winces.

'Sorry,' Gene apologizes.

'She'd better get used to it!' Ransom snorts. 'This is a *golf* club for Christ's sake! Pretty much all pro-golfers ever *do* is witter on about their friggin' bowel movements! Why else d'you think they flog date brownies in the lounge? An' huge slabs of friggin' banana cake? Bran and raisin muffins for breakfast? If you're backed up and you've got eighteen holes in prospect it's a minor, fuckin' catastrophe! Golfers need to be kept regular. It's critical – a top priority – one of the ten Golfing Commandments ...'

'Thou shalt not be constipated,' Gene murmurs.

'Is it fresh ginger in that mule of yours?' Ransom turns back to the waitress. 'Or is it that filthy, condensed sugar-syrupy crap?'

'I think it'll be fresh, but I'm not one hundred per cent sure,' the waitress confesses.

'Well if you don't know, then how about you toddle off and ask someone who does?' Ransom suggests.

'The smoothies sound delicious,' Gene steps in, diplomatically. 'Why not try a smoothie?'

'I don't want a smoothie,' Ransom informs him, indignant. 'I'm having a double Scotch. The mule's for you.'

'But I already ordered a lemonade ...'

'Great – a lemonade and a double Scotch.' The waitress quickly scribbles down the order and then scoots off, expertly sidestepping Toby Whittaker as she goes.

Toby is holding a half-pint of brown ale as he approaches. 'You won't believe this ...' he exclaims, carefully steadying the glass in the wake of the speedy waitress.

'Try me,' Ransom harrumphs, already bored.

Toby places his glass on to the table, pulls out a chair and sits down, uninvited (much to Ransom's evident irritation).

'So I asked for a half of brown at lunch and the barman says they don't stock it. I'm consequently obliged to neck a glass of draught Guinness instead ...'

Ransom yawns, majestically.

'Anyway, I head to the bar this evening, ask for a bottle of lager and the barman – *different* barman – says, "We're also offering brown ale, sir," and suggests two varieties, *both* organic!'

'Incredible!' Ransom expostulates, sarcastically.

'This place is amazing!' Toby continues, seemingly undaunted. 'Beautifully designed, state-of-the-art facilities, stupidly luxurious, attentive staff – nothing's too much trouble. They even have a twenty-four-hour concierge service. I mean we're on the outskirts of *Luton*, for heaven's sake!'

'I hate to bust your bubble,' Gene gently informs him, 'but I think you'll probably find that you can order a half of brown in most reputable establishments around here without too much trouble – and a few *not* so reputable, come to that. We're only forty-five minutes from London, after all.'

'Who drinks brown ale anyway?' Ransom snorts. 'Old men and dick-heads, that's who.'

'Your regiment's stationed locally?' Toby surmises, his eyes resting, somewhat quizzically, on Gene's casual clothes and military cap.

'Lesbians and cyber-punks,' Ransom mutters, darkly, 'and people at sheep dog trials. And scientists. And Morris Men. And student friggin' engineers ...'

'Uh, no,' Gene puts his hand to his head, embarrassed.

'This is Gino,' Ransom interjects, 'my new caddie.'

'Gene,' Gene corrects him, removing the cap and placing it down on to the table, 'and I haven't formally –'

'Toby's my "ideas man",' Ransom interrupts again.

'I'm a Sports Strategist,' Toby expands. 'I'm into futures. You should visit my blog.'

'Toby's the guy behind Turbo Golf.' Ransom grins. 'He's campaigning to reduce the standard game to nine holes.'

'It's simply a question of convincing the professionals,' Toby explains. 'Ransom's fairly progressive by golfing standards, but the rest are a depressingly traditional bunch.'

'If it ain't broke why fix it?' Ransom shrugs.

'I mean who really has the time for an eighteen-hole game in this day and age?' Toby persists. 'If your average game was nine holes it'd totally transform the sport on countless levels. It'd democratize it for a start. It'd dramatically reduce the average age of the golfing demographic. It'd halve waiting times on popular courses. And think of the environmental benefits! I'm basically re-thinking golf for a new, techno-savvy generation. I've invented several variations on the game: Punk Golf, Target Golf … They basically turn the traditional game inside out. You can play Target Golf by downloading a special program on to your phone. It sounds really high-tech, but it's actually –'

'Let's not bore Gino to death with all of that,' Ransom groans.

'I'm not remotely bored,' Gene maintains.

'Well I am,' Ransom grumbles, 'so if it's … oh *bollocks!*' He suddenly slips down in his chair.

Toby automatically snaps to attention. He scans the bar and rapidly locates the problem: 'Twenty to four and approaching,' he mutters. 'Pushy Dad with kid in tow.' Ransom turns to Gene, panicked. 'Start talking about something important,' he hisses, 'quick!'

'Uh …' Gene's caught on the hop.

'Go on,' he prompts him, 'tell Toby about your preacher wife – or your car accident – or your cancer.'

'What?' Gene's disconcerted.

'Gino here had terminal cancer over seven times but he cured himself with crystals,' Ransom helpfully informs Toby.

'I had terminal cancer once,' Gene corrects him, irritated, 'and I've never knowingly used –'

'Only the once?!' Ransom's appalled. 'But that skanky little blonde barmaid at the Thistle –'

'I've had cancer eight times, in total, but only once was it terminal. The other times it was just …' – Gene shrugs, determined to underplay it – 'just your standard small lumps and inflamed moles and stuff.'

'Hang on a sec!' Toby suddenly pipes up, excited. 'So you're the man with no lifeline? The son of Cheiro? But that's incredible! Why the hell didn't you mention it in the first place?' He springs to his feet and proffers Gene his hand.

'I'm not Cheiro's son.' Gene shakes Toby's hand, somewhat overwhelmed. 'And Jen isn't skanky,' he adds, as an afterthought, glancing sideways at Ransom, 'just a little bit wayward, sometimes …'

As he speaks, the Wolf and his father draw closer to the table.

'So whereabouts in your body *was* this cancer?' Ransom butts in (ignoring the Jen reprimand). 'The brain? The foot? In one, main area or spread all over the shop?'

'Uh …' Gene pauses before he musters up an answer (patently startled – even disarmed – by the golfer's direct approach). 'Well it actually started off in the breast,' he confesses, his right hand automatically drifting to the area just below his left nipple, 'and then there was a problem with the throat …'

His hand moves to the base of his throat, near the collar bone. 'Then a tumour in one of the lymph glands under my left armpit – that was the really bad one …'

His hand moves to his armpit. 'It spread down to my stomach … uh …'

He briefly loses focus, glancing down at himself, frowning, before quickly retracing the short series of movements for a second time:

———

Breast, throat, armpit, stomach …

– then a third –

Breast, throat …

The Wolf and his father are now standing next to the table.

'I just wanted to take this opportunity to say another, quick thank you for helping us out this afternoon …'

The Wolf's father takes full advantage of the brief lull in their conversation.

'Don't be ridiculous!' Ransom pooh-poohs him, suddenly all smiles. 'You've got nothing to thank me for! What I did was pure instinct! A natural reflex! It wasn't remotely grand or brave or heroic …'

'What did you do?' Toby demands, intrigued.

'He saved our bacon, that's what!' the Wolf's father exclaims. 'He's a miracle worker! A Godsend! I'm Brendan Dick, by the way, and this is my very lucky, very grateful, very *gifted* son, Alfie, aka Little Dickie, aka the Dickster, aka the Wolf.'

The Wolf bays, to order (much to the evident dismay of the waitress, who is returning to the table with Ransom's drinks order).

'In fact while we're here I wondered whether we might just take this opportunity to bend your ear about the kids' comp. Alfie's not had the chance to play the course before –'

'That's a very tempting offer,' Ransom interrupts, gratefully snatching his Scotch from the waitress's tray and knocking back a quick mouthful, 'and under normal circumstances I'd like nothing better, but this gentleman here was just filling me in on some rather painful and sensitive details about his lifelong battle with cancer.'

'Oh.'

The Wolf's father's eyes turn to Gene, his expression an odd combination of irritation, pity and fear. The Wolf steps behind his father as if seeking shelter.

'Don't worry' – Gene smiles at the child – 'it's not contagious.'

'Not so far as we're aware.' Ransom shrugs, widening his eyes at the cowering Wolf, somewhat mischievously.

'Well maybe later, eh?' The Wolf's father turns to leave, somewhat deflated.

'Just by the by ...' Ransom stops him in his tracks. 'You didn't happen to see a big, blond bugger in the foyer on your way through to the bar? Burgundy waistcoat? Huge fat white hands? Sweating like a rapist? Crouched over a laptop?'

'Uh ...' The Wolf's father ponders this for a second. 'That description does ring a small bell, now you come to mention it.'

'Thought as much.' Ransom nods appreciatively, turning to Gene. 'Terence Nimrod,' he informs him, conversationally, 'the journalist. I was pretty sure I spotted him out there earlier.'

The Wolf's father prepares to leave again.

'Now I come to think of it ...' Ransom stops him for a second time. 'I don't suppose it could do you any harm to wander over and get yourself officially acquainted. Throw my name into the mix if you think it'll help. Offer to buy him a drink. Keep him up to speed on any recent developments in the kid's game.'

'That's not a half-bad idea!' The Wolf's father's suddenly beaming.

'Happy to be of service!' Ransom cheerfully rejoins, then turns straight back to Gene again. 'So this cancer of yours,' he mutters, grabbing a large cube of ice from his whisky glass, popping it into his mouth and crunching it – with a spine-tingling recklessness – between his molars. 'Did it fetch up in yer knackers, or what?'

★　★　★

There's no room in the garage for a car. It's full of bikes and filing cabinets and old tyres and rusty swing sets and stacks and stacks of over-filled boxes. Sheila has lifted several of these from the pile and is halfway through emptying out the first of them which has *The Rag, 1996* written on its side (circled, twice) in a heavy, black marker pen.

Sheila sits cross-legged on the dusty, concrete floor, relying on the last of the natural light – which filters in through the open garage door, tinged with a gentle, ethereal pink – as she squints down at an open poetry book:

*'Maybe I have plugged up my sockets
to keep the gods in?'* she reads.
*'Maybe, although my heart
is a kitten of butter,
I am blowing it up like a zeppelin.'*

She closes her eyes for a second, smiling, the skin on her arms goose-bumping, her nostrils flaring, revelling in the feeling of pure, undiluted pleasure these few, simple lines afford her. When she opens her eyes again, she unexpectedly catches her reflection in a nearby hubcap. Her face is joyous – illuminated. A rosy nimbus surrounds her head like a foggy halo of mustard gas.

She gazes at herself for a fleeting moment, shocked, then quickly turns away, slaps the book shut and tosses it (almost guiltily) back into the box. Three seconds pass before she is carefully retrieving it, straightening the dust jacket, lifting her black shirt and shoving it, furtively, into the waistband of her trousers (quickly yanking her priestly raiment back into place again).

She now pushes the first box aside and delves into the one that sits directly to its left (written across the lid – in heavy, blue marker this time – is *ODDS AND SODS*). From the top of it she withdraws an old altar cloth (partially destroyed by moths) and a folded-up child's duvet cover with matching pillow in the design of a racing car. Under these are four cuddly toys: a bear without a head, a felt elephant with its ears partially chewed off, a somersaulting dog with the springs dangling from its battery compartment and a duck.

Under the toys are two plastic bags, one containing Stickle Bricks, the other, Lego and part of a small train track. Next she withdraws three books. The first two (one is Gaskell's *Life of Charlotte Brontë*, the other an old, obtuse-seeming hardback called *Synonyms Discriminated*) she hurriedly puts to one side, the third she inspects the cover of and then clucks her satisfaction at the title before resting her back against a large, empty Calor Gas bottle and starting to page through it.

She pauses at the beginning of Chapter Three, her eye momentarily distracted by something: a tiny silver sequin, squeezed by the urgent push of alternating pages into the book's yellowing spine. She pulls it out, inspects it for a second, then drops it, carelessly, into her lap.

Her eye focuses on the chapter's opening paragraph: '*Behind the layers of ambiguity and dissonance the agoraphobic longs for meaningful and rewarding involvement in the outside world. This may mean that there were lapses and breaches in her early feminine training that make it difficult for her to accept the renunciations usually accepted by women ...*'

As she reads, she slowly becomes aware of a slight commotion outside. She lifts her head and listens, scowling, gradually discerning the soft purr of an engine idling in neutral, the occasional clank of metal against railings interspersed by snatches of conversation and the jarring blurt of music from a phone.

She flares her nostrils, irritated, and returns to her book again, turning back a few pages, her eye settling on a paragraph that has been underlined in soft, dark pencil by the book's previous owner: '*Although she did succeed in masking it, underneath she was seething with rage at the injustice done to her.*

It was the emergence of these feelings that she feared in subsequent
social situations, as well as the fear of more injury, that turned her
into a recluse ...'

The engine – having idled temporarily – now roars back
into life, brakes squeal and then the engine idles once again to
accompanying laughter.

'The most dangerous place for women,' she reads, *'is in their own*
homes. One cannot read a newspaper without realizing the
dangers of the street, yet social scientists have known for years
what the public resists: the greatest danger is from "loved ones"
and others whom we know ...'

More engine noise, high-pitched female giggling, then (and
this is the deal-breaker) the sound of breaking glass. Sheila
springs to her feet and charges outside. She belts across the
back garden, jinks through a specially engineered tear in the
fence, expertly sidesteps a hodge-podge of small graves and
ends up hard against the black, wrought-iron fence that
shelters the churchyard from the road beyond.

As she draws to a sharp halt, the poetry book – currently
having slipped down to thigh-level – travels still further down
her trouser leg, resting, momentarily, at her knee.

Three Asian boys and one girl appraise her, quizzically.
'Sorry to be a party-pooper,' Sheila huffs, observing a broken
cider bottle on the pavement while bending down and feeling
for the book, 'but I'm afraid the fun stops here.'

The quizzical appraisal continues, then one of the boys –
the one standing on the pavement with the girl (the other two
are in the car; an old, brown Honda with gold hubcaps and
darkened windows) – smirks, dismissively, 'We weren't having
no fun, missus ...'

He turns to the girl. 'Was you havin' any fun?' he enquires,
cordially.

'Nope,' the girl says, shrugging.

'You sure about that?' the boy in the passenger seat asks.

235

'Yeah,' she confirms. 'It's been total crap. One of the crappiest *ever*, in actual fact.'

'*That* bad?!' The first boy looks slightly put out.

'On my mother's life!' She nods.

'Her mother's a zombie!' the kid in the passenger seat guffaws.

'No she ain't!' the girl squeals, shrilly.

'Her mother's Freddie Kruger!' the passenger kid rejoins, then a series of baroque, Freddie Kruger impressions are enacted while the lone girl bleats her protest.

Sheila has a momentary inkling that she might be in imminent danger of losing her moral authority (if, indeed, she had any to begin with), so she does the first thing that enters her head – she starts singing.

'*Once in Royal David's city*
Stood a lowly cattle shed,
Where a mother laid her baby
In a cradle for its bed ...'

Sheila does not have an especially good singing voice, but it is strong – some might even call it 'strident'. The kids stop their zombie impressions and turn to appraise her again, surprised.

'*Mary was that mother, mild,*' Sheila sings, undaunted, '*Jesus Christ her little child.*'

As she quickly inhales between verses, the kids exchange glances.

'That definitely ain't no recording voice,' the first boy mutters.

'Are yous a nun?' the girl asks.

'A nun?' Sheila echoes. 'No.' She shakes her head. 'I'm actually ...' She falters for a second, then smiles. 'I'm a guard dog.'

She points to the church: 'My kennel.' She grins.

'You're weird,' the kid in the passenger seat mutters.

'Woof!' Sheila says, nodding.

'What's wrong with your leg?' the first boy demands (Sheila keeps reaching her hand down towards her knee to try and dislodge the book).

'Woof!' Sheila answers, shaking her leg so that the book falls out from the bottom of her trousers. She bends over to pick it up then holds it out to her audience. 'Woof! Woof! Woof-woof woof, Woof woof!' she explains ('It's a poetry book, stupid!' in canine-lingo).

As she barks, the boy in the passenger seat receives an SMS on his phone. 'Musa's at the Galaxy!' he yells. The kids on the pavement dive into the back of the car.

'Woof woof!' Sheila barks, waving jauntily as the car U-turns and roars off.

From the corner of her eye she sees an elderly neighbour walking down the opposite pavement towards her.

'Bye bye!' she effortlessly translates into English, still waving. 'God bless! Have fun at the Galaxy!'

She beams at the neighbour. 'Good evening, Mrs Malmouth!' she trills. 'Beautiful weather! Incredibly balmy!' Then she turns and scuttles off, eyes rolling, horrified, poetry book clutched – like a piece of defensive armour – against her breast.

Valentine is carefully transporting a glass of warm, malted-chocolate milk along the softly lit, blue and brown-tiled hallway to her niece, upstairs. She is wearing a pair of men's silk boxer shorts (in mint green) and a tight, black, cotton vest with a tiny, black and green silk kimono thrown over the top. On her feet are a pair of black flip-flops with strange, three-inch-thick rubber soles. Her hair is swept up into a ponytail and the fringe into a quiff. Virtually her entire face (excluding eyes, lips and nostrils) is smothered in a smooth, gently browning paste of crushed avocado.

As she passes the electricity meter her eyes flick, distractedly, towards it. She walks on, then pauses, then walks back again, nudging the tip of her nose with the back of her free hand before pulling the door open and peering inside. She squints up at the dial, then scowls and withdraws, noticing, as she does so, a fleck of the avocado face-mask smudged on to her hand. She licks it off and heads upstairs.

Two minutes later and she is back again, *sans* milk, but with her tiny, green torch clutched expertly between her fingers. She peers into the little cupboard, stands on her tippy-toes and directs the light from the torch towards the dial. On it she sees a clean and unapologetically homogenous line of zeros.

She blinks and looks again. Still the zeros. She frowns. She gently pats the meter with her spare hand (in much the same way a hard-pressed Victorian husband might gently pat the cheek of a swooning wife following a monumental loss at the racetrack).

The zeros doggedly persist, but the meter itself shifts under her touch. Valentine takes a quick step back as a small quantity of red brick dust cascades down on to her bare toes. She scratches her head, confused, then shakes the dust from her feet, leans down and peers underneath the body of the meter, shining her torch up into what appears to be a small crevice below it.

'*Valentine!*'

A call from upstairs.

Valentine jumps, startled, then quickly composes herself. 'Just a minute, Mum ...'

She continues her inspection, eventually spotting a folded-up piece of paper which she carefully removes and then drops (without much thought), on to the tiles below. Next she kneels down and shines her torch into the small gap between the meter and the wall. After a brief, speculative hiatus she shoves in a couple of exploratory fingers.

'Valentine!'

This time Valentine ignores her mother's call.

Beyond the gap she feels a deep crevice of approximately seven or so inches wide by (at the very least) three or more inches deep, which has – to all intents and purposes – been gouged out, by hand.

Valentine's confidence – and sense of intrigue – grows, exponentially. She gently starts to lift up the body of the meter and is easily able (with the billowing extrusion of a little extra dust) to lift the bottom section of it several inches clear of the wall, revealing, hidden behind it, a neatly made storage space, a secret shelf; a small safe, of sorts.

Neatly piled inside this compact area are approximately twenty small boxes of varying dimensions – the kind you might store rare coins in – some are plastic, some are wooden, some are tin, some are sheathed in worn, plush velvet. Each is wrapped in clear polythene with a white, sticky label attached to the top.

In one corner of the shelf is a small file for storing papers. Just above it is something (approximately the size of a sandwich) wrapped up in tissue. To the side of it, another object, also wrapped in tissue, the size of a large wand.

Valentine quietly inspects the contents of the shelf, initially with a look of complete bewilderment, then, with an overwhelming sense of dismay. Her mind turns to Gene and his earlier meter reading.

'VALENTINE!'

She drops the meter (like she's been delivered a sharp shock) and it clanks back – somewhat wonkily – into its original position. She rubs her eye with her free hand, appalled, then withdraws the hand, with a gasp, revolted by the slimy layer of goo on her cheek.

The stupid face-mask …

'VALENTINE! VALENTINE! *MERDE!*'

'IN A MINUTE, MUM!' she yells, frustrated, bending down to retrieve the dropped wad of paper and starting to unfold it (perhaps half-intending to wipe her avocado-besmirched fingers on it).

'*VALENTIIIIINE!!!!*'

She curses under her breath, quickly re-folds the thing and shoves it back under the meter, grimacing.

'Damn you, Noel,' she hisses, clenching her fists, incensed. 'Damn you, damn you, *damn* you!'

Then she slams the door shut, her eyes prickling with angry tears, her expression defiant, her fingers leaving an incriminating, greasy, brown-green slick on the paintwork.

'I'd be very happy to pay you,' Toby Whittaker insists, 'I mean whatever rate you normally charge. We could book an appointment ...'

'I don't think you quite understand,' Gene repeats, exasperated, feeling in his pocket for his car keys. 'I've not read palms professionally since I was a kid. It just isn't something I feel comfortable with ...'

They are standing together in the car park. It's almost dark. 'I thought you drove a Hummer,' Toby murmurs, inspecting Sheila's beat-up old Renault Megane with an air of vague disappointment.

'I do drive a Hummer,' Gene maintains, squinting down at his watch. 'I mean I *own* a Hummer, but filling the tank these days costs something like the annual average income of a third world state ...'

'Is there a special line for the career?' Toby persists, holding out his hand. 'It's all very hush-hush' – he lowers his voice, conspiratorially – 'but I've recently been made an offer by this crazy, Chilean entrepreneur.'

'Uh ... there's a Line of Head and a Line of Life.' Gene takes the proffered hand and gives the palm a cursory inspection. 'I suppose both could be interpreted as having some basic relevance in career matters.'

He peers down at Toby's palm in the semi-darkness. It's virtually impossible for him to delineate one line from another in such poor light.

'Although the plain truth is' – he drops the hand – 'some idiot reading your palm isn't going to have the slightest impact on how your career pans out. To succeed at work – or in any field of endeavour: your health, your relationships – all that's really required is plenty of stamina, a level head, a thick skin, the occasional burst of inspiration and, if all else fails, a ridiculously – even stupidly – positive outlook.'

'You think it's all just mumbo-jumbo, then?' Toby grimaces, gazing down at his own palm, deflated.

'I think people are the masters of their own destiny,' Gene responds, then falters, loathing how trite this sounds. 'I mean we're all constrained by the hands we're dealt,' he continues, 'by the straitjackets of biology and gender and geography – but above and beyond that ...'

He shrugs.

'You beat the cancer, though,' Toby interjects, hopefully. 'No lifeline, the cards completely stacked against you, but you beat the bloody cancer.'

'I'm not ...' Gene scowls, confused, his train of thought momentarily disrupted by the sudden appearance of a heavily pregnant West Indian woman, wearing only a shower cap and a bathrobe. She's kicking up the gravel as she strides towards them in a pair of oversized moccasins.

'I simply made the best of it.' He focuses in on Toby again (almost rueful at what he perceives as his own signal lack of insight). 'That's pretty much the most any of us can do, surely? Just go to bed at night thinking, I screwed stuff up, but I tried. Things may've gone haywire, but I did the best I possibly could.'

He locates the car key on his ring and pushes it, clumsily, into the lock. The bathrobed woman is now shouting distance away from them.

'Me want sleep, but some pesky badger diggin' around in an overturn bin out back!' she yells over. 'Had a word with Security and the man jus' shrug at me: "Screw you!" basically. So I say, "Ain't them thing full of TB?" He just shrug another time. So I go, "You speak English? *Eng-lish?*" An' he say, "Sure, I speak English." The man a Pole – some big, ugly, flat-face Pole. Head like a damn steam-iron! I say, "You even know what a badger is?" "Sure I do," he say. Nasty look in his eye! "Well *tell* me then," I say. An' he jus' shrug again, like I some nasty smell under his nose. Make as if to turn away. Me go, "They got no badger in Poland or something?" He just flap his hand and start to walk. I swear I hear him say: "I know what we *don't* got in Poland ...'

She grimaces, enraged. 'Got him a *real* attitude. A real, *nasty* attitude.'

As she finishes speaking she draws to a halt in front of them. She is out of breath. She supports her massively low and distended stomach with her free hand. The other hand holds a mobile phone.

'Perhaps you frightened him,' Toby ventures, slightly nervous.

'How so?' She glowers.

'With your ... in your ...' He gestures, lamely, towards the bathrobe.

'You think he ain't seen no woman in a robe before?' she snorts, incredulous.

'Possibly not wandering around the car park ...'

'Wanderin' around the car park?' Esther squawks, livid. 'Me not wanderin' around the car park!'

All three of them are silent for a second as they jointly mull over the patent illogicality of this statement.

'Me not "*wander*",' Esther grumbles, quickly honing in on Toby's sloppy choice of verb as the root of the problem. 'Me not "*wanderin*'" around.'

'Rampaging, then,' Toby volunteers, unhelpfully.

'Did you try ringing reception?' Gene quickly interjects.

'Say *what*?!' Esther turns to appraise him, haughtily.

'About the badgers,' Gene persists. 'Did you try and ring ...?'

'Good God!' Esther expostulates. 'What wrong with you people? Of course me rang reception! *Three* time, no less! Of *course* me rang reception! You think me *want* to be out here in me bathrobe? I nine month pregnant! Eight and a half month ...' she quickly corrects herself, glancing towards Toby. 'Hair in a shower-cap! You think me *want* to be "wanderin'" around the car park this hour?!'

'Of course you don't.' Toby places a calming hand on her arm. She promptly shakes it off.

'The man jus' plain rude!' she mutters, pursing her lips. 'Me done nothin' to deserve that attitude.'

'Perhaps his English wasn't too great.' Gene tries to mollify her.

'Who you work for?' Esther snorts, her eyes focusing in on Gene's military headwear. 'International Peace Corps?'

'This is Gene,' Toby promptly steps in to oversee formal introductions. 'Nephew of Cheiro, remember? Stu's new caddie?'

Esther just scowls into the distance, ignoring Gene's proffered hand.

'Gene, this is Esther, Ransom's manager,' Toby continues, 'and just for the record,' he adds, somewhat punctiliously, 'the International Peace Corps are generally to be found sporting a rather fetching pale blue helmet.'

He nudges Gene, surreptitiously. 'After a couple of days around Ransom you may consider upgrading to something bulletproof,' he murmurs.

'Red helmet, blue helmet,' Esther mutters, 'me work in this industry long enough to know what that look of his all about.'

'You could always lodge an official complaint,' Gene suggests, dropping his hand and returning it to the Megane's door handle.

'I'll come with you if you like' – Toby nods – 'for moral support. Or, better still,' he adds, 'we could go and deal with those pesky badgers ourselves.'

He looks to Gene for back-up.

'You serious?' Esther's suddenly wreathed in smiles. 'Me try earlier but the bin way too heavy ...' She puts a hand to her hip. 'My back killin' me now ...'

'No trouble!' Toby nods. 'Gene?' he repeats.

'Sure.' Gene lets go of the handle, somewhat regretfully.

'Jus' there ...' Esther all but coos, broadly indicating in the approximate direction with her phone, 'side of the main kitchen block.'

'It's as good as done.'

Toby promptly starts off and Gene turns to follow, but Esther grabs a hold of his arm before he's two steps away from her. Toby glances over his shoulder, disgruntled.

'No problem, Tobe.' She genially waves him on. 'Me jus' borrow him for one minute.'

Her grip (Gene immediately discerns, alarmed) has a surprisingly tenacious and implacable feel to it.

'Sorry – just hold on a second ...' Sheila swaps the phone from one ear to the other. 'This number is for "V", you say, and "V" is one of Gene's ...?'

She listens again, frowning. She is dressed for bed in an old, oversized pair of men's paisley, silk-mix pyjamas which have been darned on the front and are frayed at the heel.

'A problem with her meter ...'

She pushes up her sleeve, quickly scribbling down 'V' and a number on to the pad next to the phone with a heavily chewed, two-inch-long pencil stub.

'A tattooist?'

She pauses for a moment, her eyes focusing, blankly, on a damp-stained patch of Artexed ceiling just to the left of the dusty, seventies-era wicker light shade.

'Uh … that does ring a vague bell,' she concedes. 'He mentioned something about a tattooist while we were chatting this afternoon …'

Sheila glances down at the pad again, perplexed, trying to meld things together in her mind.

'But how would she have known to contact the hotel …' she wonders, 'unless …?'

Something odd suddenly strikes her.

'Hang on … this … this "V" person – this tattooist – she wouldn't also happen to be the Turner girl, would she?'

A short pause.

'Wickers?'

A longer pause followed by a mirthless snort.

'Incredible as this may seem, Jen, the stars on your collar bones weren't *entirely* at the forefront of our conversation …'

A further pause.

'Sorry?'

A look of vague alarm.

'You *broke* into the office?'

Another pause.

'Oh. Okay. So you have a duplicate key …'

Sheila shakes her head, grimacing, then continues to listen, somewhat long-sufferingly.

'Well that's very … yes … that's … that's … that's …'

Nodding. Bored.

'… I *fully* understand how important this is. You've made that point *very* clearly. I …'

Another pause.

'I promise to tell him just as soon as he gets ...'

Sheila checks her watch (it's a quarter to eleven), '... yes ... right ... *fine*. Well if I've gone up to bed by then, everything's written down on the pad by the phone.'
Short pause.

'I'm afraid I have no control over whether he chooses to answer his mobile or not.'
Look of slight irritation.
'I've no idea. He's at a business meeting.'
Pause. Exasperated eye-rolling.

'... with Stuart Ransom, if you must know, at some exclusive new golf club over towards ... *Sorry?*'
Blinks. Taken aback.

'But how ...?'
Listens, head slightly cocked, plainly annoyed.

'Yes, I'm perfectly well-acquainted with the layout of the men's toilets, Jen ...'
Infuriated grimace.

'Well nothing's set in stone ... I mean there was talk ...'
Sheila holds the phone away from her ear for a couple of seconds, rolls her eyes then returns the phone to her ear again, wincing.

'... there was talk of him caddying for a few days, but I don't seriously imagine ...'
Two haughtily raised eyebrows.

'D'you think you might manage to hold on until morning?'
(*Delivered with an almost saccharine sweetness.*)
'Oh. You *don't*. Okay ...'
Dangerously polite.

'Well I'll be certain to tell him that.'
Still dangerously polite.

'I'm not being scary.'
Sheila inspects the ceiling again, her nostrils flaring.

'I'm *not* being scary, Jen!'

Mutters silent incantation.

'Loafers?'

Look of utter bemusement.

'Uh … no …'

Sheila slowly shakes her head. 'No, he didn't …'

Dismissive.

'But I hardly think a few drops of coffee will prove fatal to the …'

Sheila hears the front door opening, turns and lifts a quick hand to forestall Gene from speaking as he appears in the hallway.

'Yes. Well that's lovely. Oh dear, I think …'

Unconvincing.

'… I think Mallory might be calling me from upstairs. I should probably …'

Angry grimace at Gene, followed by a brusque 'winding-up' gesture with her free hand.

'Thank you, Jennifer. I'm sure it'll be very much appreciated. Lovely …'

Icily professional.

'You be sure to enjoy the rest of your evening, now …'

Pause.

'Goodnight. Yes. Goodnight. Yes I will. I've written down the number. Yes, he knows how to reach you. Thank you. Take care, Jennifer. Goodnight.'

Sheila places down the receiver, closes her eyes for a moment, draws a deep breath, and manages (with considerable effort) to suppress the worst of her feelings of irritation. When she opens her eyes again Gene is standing before her. He has the military jacket slung over his arm but is still wearing the cap.

'What on earth do you look like?' she enquires, shooting a withering glance towards his headgear.

'One of Ransom's crazy brainwaves …'

He snatches the cap off, embarrassed. 'Please tell me that wasn't Jen,' he mutters, following her through to the living room (where he carefully slides the cap on to the sideboard).

'You said you'd be back by nine ...' Sheila grumbles.

'I left a message on your phone ...'

'Saying you'd be home well before ten.'

Sheila throws herself down on to the sofa.

'I got waylaid by Ransom's manager as I was getting into the car,' he explains. 'There were these badgers running amok in the rubbish bins near her room. One had jammed his head inside this thick off-cut of crenellated, silver tubing ...'

'It appears that Jen's feelings have been *deeply* injured,' Sheila enunciates, drolly, plumping up the cushions and then shoving them behind her and leaning back, imperiously, 'by your omitting to tell her about your caddying plans during the cosy, little chat you had in the broom cupboard this morning.'

'What?' Gene's astonished. 'But that's ridiculous! The idea hadn't even been mooted at that stage.'

He pulls his phone from his pocket. 'And after the stiff dressing-down his manager just gave me ...'

He turns it on and registers a prodigious number of voice mails and SMSs.

'The girl's a pest,' he mutters. 'She's developing this mad vendetta against Ransom. It's like she's obsessed.'

'Is she ringing his mobile, too,' Sheila wonders, tartly, 'or just yours?'

'I had it switched to message-bank ...'

Gene glances up, observing Sheila's expression (on the chilly side of glacial).

'And we weren't "together" in the broom cupboard,' he rapidly backtracks. 'I made her hide in there because she was upsetting all the customers. I stood – in full, public view – on the other side of the door.'

'"Customers"?' Sheila snorts (suddenly bored and exhausted by the whole affair). 'Is that their official designation, now?'

As she speaks she picks up the TV remote, turns the television on, tunes it to *Newsnight* and presses 'mute'.

On the arm of the sofa is an open copy of *Women Who Marry Houses*.

'You found it, then,' Gene says, pointing (eager to change the subject).

'Did you know that Jen has a duplicate key to the office,' Sheila wonders, 'and that she sneaks in there after work to mess around on the computers?'

'Uh ...' Gene frowns.

'You *do* know?'

Sheila's shocked.

'I know she doesn't have a computer at home' – he shrugs – 'so she sometimes uses the hotel's one to type up her essays for college.'

'Well, Jen was messing around in there tonight when the phone rang. It turned out to be a woman desperate to get in contact with you following a reading you did on her electricity meter ...'

'Right.' Gene nods, trying not to appear too alarmed by this piece of news. 'Did she happen to leave a home phone number?'

'A mobile number. On the pad,' Sheila confirms. 'Jen said it was a woman called "V", a tattooist –'

'That'll be the one I was telling you about this afternoon,' Gene interrupts, going to fetch it.

'She said this "V" was very distressed,' Sheila calls after him.

Gene picks up the pad and frowns down at Sheila's message, uncertain how to react. He opts to say nothing, just tears off the top page and pushes it into his pocket.

'And that she's actually one of the Tuckers,' Sheila continues, 'the "crazy" daughter, no less.'

Gene nods, flushing slightly, as he strolls back through to the living room. 'There was the incident with the trampoline, remember?'

'Vaguely,' she concedes, 'but I'm not sure if you made it clear that those two stories were connected: the trampoline and the tattooist ...'

'Really?' Gene scratches his head, glancing over towards the TV. 'Well I guess I just presumed –'

'So you actually went back to the house again?' she interrupts, frowning. 'Was this Ransom's bright idea?'

'Ransom?' Gene's confused.

'Why not? He could be employing you as a kind of go-between,' Sheila gamely improvises, 'a peacemaker.'

'In my little turquoise helmet,' Gene mutters, darkly.

'Pardon?'

'It had nothing to do with Ransom,' he maintains. 'I just forgot to take the reading the first time around, that's all.'

'You went to take a reading and then you forgot to take a reading ...' Sheila's not entirely buying it.

'There was a rat in the bath,' Gene explains. 'It's a long story, but basically I fished it out and was carrying it around by the tail, not quite sure how to dispose of it, when I managed to barge in on this woman having a genital tattoo ...'

Sheila is staring at him, wide-eyed.

'So I forgot to take the reading – it slipped my mind – and returned today, on my lunch-break, but when I tried to take it this time ...'

'Sorry. Back up there for a second. You *barged in* on a woman ...?'

'... it looked like there was evidence of tampering with the meter,' Gene continues. 'I didn't really know what to do – what to say – so I just made my excuses and got out of there.'

Sheila frowns, momentarily diverted by this final detail. 'You think she's been defrauding the electricity board?'

'God no, not ...'

Valentine's name hangs in the air before him, dances in front of his lips, beckons to him – like the warm froth of milky foam on top of a steaming cup of cappuccino. Just uttering this name out loud (how much he longs to feel it fizz and bubble on his tongue!) seems like a strange kind of breach – a sworn secret idly shared – almost a betrayal.

He turns away for a second, slightly puzzled, using the jacket slung over his arm as a temporary diversion. He shakes it out and then hangs it over the door handle.

'At least I don't think so,' he finally mutters. 'It looked just fine to start off with, but then I noticed a couple of the screws were loose and tightened them with my thumbnail ...' He turns back to face her again. 'The whole structure was very unstable. It was being propped up from below by a wad of paper – a letter. When I pulled it out ...'

'A letter?'

Sheila's struggling to keep up.

'Yes. From their bank, threatening to foreclose on the house. And when I pulled it out to take a quick look, the digits on the meter all miraculously turned to nought.'

Sheila stares at him, saying nothing.

'I felt a little responsible, obviously,' he runs on, 'and there's no real evidence of foul play, but I'll definitely need to mention it in my report ...'

He rubs his eyes, tiredly. 'Although if there *is* foul play, then I seriously doubt that she's involved. She seems a nice enough kid. Genuine. Straightforward.'

Gene uses the word 'kid' with a measure of care. He glances over at Sheila to see how she receives it. Sheila is deep in thought.

'But what'll happen to the mother if they lose their home?' she wonders.

'God only knows' – he shrugs – 'maybe the council will step in.'

'Doesn't the son work?'

'I've no idea. His girlfriend's in rehab. He's a bit of a mess. Then there's his daughter and several dozen cats ...'

'And you say this ... this "V" is agoraphobic?'

'Apparently so.' Gene nods.

'Poor kid!'

Gene feels a slight sense of satisfaction, then a corresponding sense of shame, at the apparent efficacy of his little linguistic scam.

'Maybe it's a sign,' Sheila muses, 'an opportunity for Ransom to finally set things right. I mean his arriving in the area like this – apparently at random – then the argument in the hotel, then your meeting with this "V" girl, his employing you as his caddie, the discovery of the letter ...'

'All part of God's great plan?' Gene snorts, mirthlessly.

'Maybe you're to be an "agent" of some kind?' She smiles, mischievously. 'A mediator, an arbitrator, a modern-day Pandarus ...'

'Pandarus?'

'From Homer's *Iliad*. He breaks the fragile truce between the Trojans and the Greeks by an act of despicable treachery ...'

'Strange kind of arbitrator,' Gene mutters, uneasily.

'But he reappears as a go-between in Shakespeare's *Troilus and Cressida*,' she adds, 'brings together the two lovers.'

'Does it end well?' Gene's suspicious.

'Nope. Not especially,' she admits, still smiling, 'but then meddling so rarely does. That's partly what makes it so seductive.'

'I know you're only joking,' Gene says, suddenly nervous, 'but there's a worrying look in your eye.'

'*Perhaps God is only a deep voice,*' she sighs, half under her breath,

'*heard by the deaf ...*'

'Pardon?'

'Anne Sexton.'

'Anne ...? The woman you were quoting this afternoon?'

'The poet. Yes.'

She grabs the book from the arm of the chair, turns to the dedication page and passes it to him.

'*Women marry houses*,' Gene reads. '*It's another kind of skin.*'

'Your "V" has married a house,' Sheila observes, almost smugly.

'She's built herself into a kind of fortress,' Gene partially concedes, 'with all the make-up and the period clothing and the brick tattoo ...'

'It's actually quite a fascinating book.' Sheila grabs it back again. 'The basic premise of the thing is that agoraphobics aren't so much victims as unyielding feminists, women refusing to comply to the rules of gender, the rules of society. It's like they're unable to compromise. They're passive at one level ...' She frowns. 'If a refusal can *ever* be considered passive, which, quite frankly, I doubt ...'

'It seems they often have an overbearing father-figure,' Gene volunteers.

'I marked out some interesting paragraphs. There's a chapter called ...' She starts paging through the book. 'Here it is: *A Most Unlikely Radical Feminist and an Artist* ... page sixty-nine, and I quote: *She became a daddy's girl and was frequently the only one in the family that could talk back to him, but only about inconsequential matters. She was solicitous of her brother and sought to protect him from the wrath of their father on his infrequent occasions of rebelliousness. Towards her mother she was similarly solicitous, but felt neither awe nor affection ...*' She turns the page. 'And see here ...'

She points: '*Her neurosis, developing as it did, was her rebellion.*'

She looks up at him, her eyes glinting, then glances down again. '*There are many kinds of death*,' she proclaims, portentously, '*the biological is but one.*'

'So you think ...' Gene starts off.

'And listen to this ...' Sheila turns on a few extra pages. '*Those who want to organize or even reorganize knowledge or beauty must do so alone.*'

She shakes her head, fascinated. 'I'd never really thought about art in that way before, as a reorganization of knowledge or beauty ... *Those who want to organize or even reorganize knowledge or beauty ...*' she slowly re-reads, 'true artists, in other words, great innovators, *must do so alone.*' She ponders this for a second. 'Genius, inspiration, art ... they're rarely communal. They're intrinsically solitary.'

Gene watches her intently as she talks.

'You're really enjoying this,' he says, surprised – even alarmed – by the extent to which this is true.

'Sorry?'

She frowns up at him.

'It's the first time I've seen you looking so excited – so engaged by something – in ages ...'

Months, *years*, he thinks.

'It just reminded me ...' she starts off, then stops, abruptly.

'How everything was before,' he says, 'before ...' – he indicates around him, loosely – '... all this.'

'Before God,' she interjects, baldly, just in case he thinks she hasn't fully understood.

'You were Called.' He shrugs, resigned (if not exactly enthusiastic).

'I brokered a deal,' she mutters (not even allowing herself the grandeur of a Calling).

'You were Called,' he reiterates, firmly, 'and you answered. You knew it was never going to be easy.'

'If it were easy ...' she starts off, then can't be bothered to complete her thought.

'*Perhaps God is only a harsh voice,*
Heard by the deaf ...' he quotes, inanely.

'*A deep voice*,' she corrects him, scowling, then puts down the book and turns off the television. 'Time for bed,' she sighs, false-yawning, 'the alarm's set for five.'
She clambers to her feet.

'Thanks for waiting up,' he murmurs, 'it's much appreciated.'
He reaches out a hand and touches her shoulder. She glances down at his hand and softly, briefly, covers it with her own. They stand there for a moment, at peace, then Gene's phone begins to ring.

'Bloody hell!' Gene expostulates, with a start.
'Bloody *Jen*, more like!' Sheila mutters, snatching back her hand and heading for the door, her gait slightly bow-legged and beleaguered in her oversized pyjamas, like a cowboy after a long, hard ride, or a tragic toddler, gamely waddling to the bathroom after a small yet catastrophic bed-wetting incident.

Jen's legs are up and resting, lackadaisically, on the desk (both feet neatly crossed at the heel). She has carefully taken off her work skirt (perhaps to avoid creasing it) and is leaning back on the chair in just her shirt, some salmon-pink-coloured low-rise pants, and a pair of tan-coloured pop-socks.

'I'm still at work ...'
She's chatting away on her mobile, twiddling a ponytail with her spare hand. 'I've been messing around on the computers, and guess what I just found ...?'
She scowls.

'Who already rang you?'
She continues scowling.

'I *did* give her your number, but it's way after eleven. I didn't think ...'
Eyes rolled.

'But that's different, Gene, we're *pals* ...'
Sticks out lower lip.

'Has Sheila been kicking your butt again?'
Mischievous snigger.

'She's a *beast*, Gene! I swear! She's terrifying! When I spoke
to her earlier she made all the hairs on my arms stand on
end ...'
Jen drops the ponytail and gently strokes her phone arm,
gazing down at it, tenderly, like it's a dwarf rabbit at a
petting zoo.

'It's that scary voice of hers ...'
Pause.

'Does she use that scary voice in bed at all?'
Nano-pause.

'Don't hang up!'
Pause.

'There's stuff we need to discuss. Not about Vee. It's
Ransom. I've been doing a bit of detective work ...'
Jen glances towards the computer screen.

'Turns out that Ransom's manager – a woman called ...'
She leans forward, squinting at the screen ...

'Esther! Exactly. Esther Wilson. Well this manager has a
sister, a well-known Jamaican politico. A hot-head. A
troublemaker-cum-disgraced MP-cum-writer-cum-poet-cum-
all-round-social protester called Victoria. Victoria Wilson. I've
downloaded all this stuff about her. She was in the papers
recently talking about the use of petro-chemicals in the Costa
Rican pineapple farming industry. Anyhow this sister's staying
in the hotel with her arty-farty four-eyed boyfriend. Turns out
she has a kid ...'

Pause. Scowls.

'I *am* getting to the point ...'
Grimaces, irritated.

'Why are you so out of breath?'
Pause.

'Then let's meet up in the morning for a ...'
Raises hand, limply.

'But I've ... You're really gonna ...'
Takes the phone away from her ear. Inspects the phone. Scowls at the phone. Points at the phone, accusingly.
'Dickweed!'

Ransom is sitting on the bed, stark naked, except for a single, pristine, white leather golfing glove.

'Will ya cover that damn ting up?' Esther asks, indicating, vaguely, towards his genital region (unable to bring herself to maintain eye contact).

'It's nothing you haven't seen a million times before,' Ransom grumbles, half-heartedly plucking at the counterpane (but to no perceptible good effect).

'Me can't discuss business when ya ... ya ...' She waggles her hand, visibly oppressed.

'Then let's not talk business!' Ransom exclaims. 'My corns are killing me! I'm gagging for a foot massage.'

'The bub set on makin' him an early appearance.' Esther delivers this momentous piece of news (with all due ceremony) to the digital alarm clock on Ransom's bedside table. 'Me back was strain earlier, now it end up in contraction. Them comin' hard – every twelve minute or so.'

'It's way too soon!' Ransom protests, quickly reaching over to grab a pillow and pressing it, firmly, into his groin area (as if to shelter his genitalia from the harsher truths of the reproductive process). 'Are you sure it's not just wind again?'

'This ain't jus' wind, Stu,' Esther snaps, 'trust me.'

'*Bollocks*,' Ransom curses. He wiggles his fingers inside the glove and scowls. The new leather's still a fraction stiff. He forms a fist.

'So is everything good to go?' he wonders.

'Me rang the local hospital.' She nods. 'My bag already pack. Me call a cab –'

'I mean the tournament,' Ransom interrupts, pulling the glove off and throwing it down, disgruntled. 'What time's the photographer arriving tomorrow?'

'Ten.' Esther inspects her clipboard.

'Will anyone be doing make-up?'

'Some girl from the spa. I roped in Toby to lend a hand. You got him number, an' ya got mine for an emergency.'

'So how long are you planning to go AWOL?' Ransom glares at her, balefully.

'Twenty-four hour, max.'

'Oh.' Ransom is secretly awed by Esther's bewildering work ethic (and this inevitably contrives to irritate him still further). 'Well what about your mother?' he demands. 'Have you rung the mardy old bitch yet?'

Esther suddenly leans forward, clutching on to her stomach, gasping. It's another contraction. She checks her watch. Ten minutes. Ransom surveys her violent discomfiture with the haughty, dispassionate gaze of a beach-dwelling iguana watching a suffocating sprat gyrating wildly in the final, liquid millimetres of a rapidly evaporating rock-pool.

'That quick bunk-up with old Jimbo's not looking like such a great idea now, eh?' he quips.

The contraction lasts a full two minutes. Once it's passed, Esther slowly straightens up again.

'Me mother not comin' ...' She's still slightly out of breath. 'Her brother contract pneumonia. She nursin' him at home. Joah an' Ephie are stuck wid her neighbour ...'

'Hang on ...' Ransom's confused. 'So who the hell's gonna haul the bub back to Jamaica?'

'Uh ...'

Esther carefully considers the likely impact of her answer. Eventually she murmurs, 'I manage to persuade Vicki.' She's virtually inaudible.

Ransom stares at her, blankly.

'Her lover doin' some research at the British ...'

On 'British', Ransom throws down the pillow, leaps to his feet, runs to the bathroom, slams the door and shoots the bolt.

'Come on, Stu!' Esther groans. 'Me cab here any minute now ...'

'If she's within a two friggin' mile radius of this room, Esther, I swear to God ...'

Ransom gurgles, hysterical.

'She not coming here,' Esther insists. 'She stayin' in town.'

'Does she know where we are, though?' Ransom refuses to be pacified. 'Does she have the address?'

'She not give a toss, Stu. Trust me ...'

Esther crosses her fingers behind her back. '... you name never even come up.'

Nano-second pause.

'What?!'

Incredulous.

'Not at *all*?'

Ransom unshoots the bolt, opens the door by an inch and peeks through the gap. 'You seriously expect me to believe that?'

'Believe what you want ...' Esther shrugs, standing her ground. 'It a fact.'

'I thought you weren't on speaking terms,' he snivels.

'We not.'

'Oh.'

Ransom considers this for a while.

'She come wid her lover,' Esther repeats. 'He's doin' research at the British Library. They visitin' all the museum an' such wid her boy ...'

On 'boy', Esther starts, then quickly turns her face away. 'Vicki's dating men again?' Ransom's astonished. 'I thought she'd sworn off dick for good ...'

Nano-pause.

'Vicki has a *kid*?!'

Ransom opens the door still further and pokes out his head. He's now dressed in a bathrobe.

'Yeah ...' Esther nods, determinedly off-hand. 'Some college professor. Some hot-shot from America. They meet up at a conference. The boy from his first marriage.'

'What's his name?' Ransom enquires.

'Dr Hilary somethin' ...' She shrugs. 'Dr Hilary Wild. Dr Hilary Mane. Dr Hilary Horse ...'

She shrugs again.

'Is he wedged?' Ransom demands.

'Sorry?'

'Is he pelfed?'

Ransom rubs his thumb and his forefinger together.

'A college professor?!' Esther chuckles. 'You serious?' She quickly checks her watch again. 'Now before me run off ...'

'*Man.* I can't believe you've just sprung it on me like this!' Ransom comes out of the bathroom and throws himself down on to the bed again. 'My nerves are completely fuckin' *shot* ...'

He holds both hands out in front of him. They're shaking uncontrollably.

'First it's the friggin' Tucker kid,' he mutters, appalled, 'next it's the West Indies' answer to Lorena friggin' *Bobbitt*!' He shakes his head, uncomprehending. 'Michael bloody Moore with a tan an' a fanny ...'

Ransom's hand disappears inside his robe for a second. 'I swear to God,' he gasps, 'my balls have disappeared inside my body cavity!'

'You gotta listen, now, Stu.' Esther's gazing down at her clipboard. 'Nimrod tell me there gonna be a big piece runnin' in the *Daily Sport* tomorrow ...'

'Right here in Luton of all places!' Ransom jabbers on, regardless. 'What the heck did *Luton* ever do to deserve this?'

'... some crazy bullcrap sayin' ya had a bust-up on the club outdoor chessboard with this week tournament event sponsor ...'

'Sorry?'

Ransom withdraws his hand and looks up, sharply.

'Full mark for imagination!' she concedes, smiling to herself, wryly.

'An article in the *Sport*?' he echoes.

'Don't worry,' Esther promptly reassures him. 'You was practisin' on the range when it all happen ...'

'Ah.'

Ransom gently cups the back of his head with his hand in a classic gesture of self-comfort.

'I already phone the lawyer ...' Esther continues.

'The outdoor chessboard ...' Ransom softly reiterates (as if struggling to call this architectural landmark to mind). 'There was a bit of playful rough-housin' with some fans at one point – on my way over to the range this'd be ... A young fan ...' He frowns. 'I guess you could say it was in the general *vicinity* of the chessboard ...'

'No mention of a kid.' Esther reappraises her notes. 'They sayin' you assault the event sponsor after he thrash you in a game ...' She turns over the page. 'Mr Chris Padgett, MD for Knott/Beevers Holdings plc,' she reads.

'Thrashed me?! Are you havin' a laugh or what?!' Ransom's outraged. 'That's friggin' libellous! I wasn't even playing! I was just having a quick ...'

'Of course ya not playin'!' Esther snorts. 'How ya gonna play chess? Game of Kings! Domino more your style – quick hand of rummy ...'

'I resent that!' Ransom's riled.

Esther shrugs, indifferent.

'I resent that!' Ransom repeats – for want of anything more fruitful to contribute (aside from pure – and patently groundless – indignation).

'Then a couple hour later,' Esther continues, returning to her former subject, 'followin' "a long, liquid lunch",' she reads, diligently, 'you was spotted in the club bar ...' – she clears her throat – '"offerin' a grovelin' apology to Mr Padgett after he threaten to press assault charges an' pull you from the tournament."'

She gazes up at him, one brow slightly raised.

'Complete bloody hokum!' Ransom squeaks. He crosses his legs, then uncrosses them again. 'Is there a photo by any chance?'

'Photo?!' Esther demands, her eyes slitting. 'Photo of what?'

'I don't know.' Ransom's jumpy. 'An artist's impression – something hashed-up on a computer ...'

'A cartoon, maybe ...' Esther gamely hypothesizes. '*Alice in Wonderland* theme ...' She rubs her chin, thoughtfully. 'Stuart Ransom playin' Alice, wid his long, blond hair an' his frilly, blue-checker dress. Mr Padgett playin' a fat Cheshire Cat, guardin' him a nice sack of cash ... Big, banner headline: "No Cheque, Mate!" an' a small puff underneath sayin' ...' She holds up her clipboard and reads directly from it: '"Yet more humiliation for troubled ex-golden boy of British golf ..."'

It takes a few seconds before Ransom gets wise to the fact that this neatly posited scenario isn't just a baroque flight of fancy on Esther's part.

'*Call that panty-waist Del Renzio!*' he yells, springing to his feet, incensed. '*We gotta tear the little bitch a new arsehole!*'

'Call him?' she snaps, withering. 'Why me do that when he already phone this afternoon an' tell me all about it?'

Pause.

'*Huh?!*' Esther juts out her chin, combatively.

'The slimy, little grass!' Ransom mutters, somewhat cowed.

'ME LEAVE YOU FOR *HALF* ONE HOUR, STU,' Esther bellows, 'AN' *NOW* LOOK WHA' HAPPEN!!'

'YOU'RE HAVIN' A BABY, ESTHER!' Ransom bellows right back. 'I DIDN'T WANNA STRESS YOU OUT!'

'BULLSHIT!' Esther yells.

Nano-pause.

'What the hell ya *thinkin'*?!' she groans, dismayed, hand pressing her brow. 'The event *sponsor*, Stu! The event sponsor of all people!'

'You reckon that vindictive, little dwarf Padgett leaked the story?' Ransom wonders.

'HOW YOU EXPECT ME TO KNOW?!' Esther explodes again. 'WHEN YA NEVER TELL ME NOTHIN' WHAT'S GOIN' ON?!'

'Fuck *off!*' Ransom squawks, his voice fluting, schoolboyishly.

'YOU MAKE ME LOOK A DAMN FOOL, STU!'

Esther squares up to him, steaming, brandishing her clipboard.

'*THINK ABOUT THE BLOODY BABY!*'

Ransom takes a quick step back, hits the bed, sits down and curls his top half into a defensive ball (using both arms to shield his head) while Esther repeatedly smacks his upper back with the clipboard, her hugely distended belly banging into his face from down below.

Although patently tempted, Ransom neglects to register any further comment at this stage.

Esther finally pauses for breath. 'Me *know* you does foolish thing, Stu,' she reasons (as much for her own benefit as the golfer's). 'It your *nature* to do foolish thing. You *are* a damn fool! And God knows, me well *accustom'* to chargin' about the place cleanin' up all your ignorant mess. But the event *sponsor*, Stu? The *sponsor*?!'

'I didn't lay a finger on him, Est.' Ransom lifts his head slightly, wincing.

Esther clouts him in the face with the clipboard and then drops it on to the bed, leaning over him, still breathing heavily, her hand resting on his shoulder for support.

'Me suppose to be ya manager, Stu,' she pants, 'for God's sake jus' let a girl *manage*, will you?'

Ransom slowly lifts his hand to feel his nose for any evidence of permanent damage (the hand – as a matter of pure, scientific interest – is no longer shaking).

'"A grovellin' apology in the bar"?!' he grumbles, while she shifts her weight from his shoulder and slowly straightens up (grimacing as she does so and massaging her hip). 'I'd eat my own *liver* first. Wait till the next time I see the little twerp. I'm gonna screw his head off like it's the lid on a kid's-size bottle of friggin' ketchup!'

'Unbelievable!' Esther steps back with a derisory snort. 'An' ya wonder why Poulter warmin' himself up for the British Open in Illinois – John Deere Classic; seven hundred grand up for the takin' – an' where Stuart Ransom? *Huh?* Right here! *Luton!* Stony broke! Wid his precious swing, an' him stinkin' feet an' him *belly* putter!'

'Lighten up, will you?' Ransom's indignant. 'What happened to your infernal, bloody mantra of "all publicity's good publicity", eh?!'

He stares at her suspiciously. 'Had a sudden change of heart, have we? Or maybe ...' – a sly look enters his eye – 'maybe you're just a teensy-weensy bit miffed because you didn't get to painstakingly stage-manage every detail of this sordid, little scenario for yourself?'

'*Stage-manage?*' Esther's almost lost for words. 'You think me *want* this kind of coverage?'

'Of course you do!' Ransom snorts. 'You moved my meeting with Noel Tucker to the Thistle for Christ's sake!'

'How many times I have to tell you?!' (Now it's Esther's turn to be indignant.) 'Noel *aks* me to move it there!'

She's sweating, heavily, and as she speaks (Ransom coolly notes) two expansive, damp patches are bleeding outwards from under the armpits of her shirt.

'Sorry, Est, but I'm not buyin' it,' he mutters, 'and the fact that I'm not buyin' it sets off a whole series of alarm bells in my head.'

'Alarm bell?' Esther echoes, dumbfounded.

'Such as why I needed to stay in town that night,' Ransom continues. 'I mean why couldn't I just turn up at the club a day early like we originally scheduled?'

'We already discuss this, Stu.' Esther's exasperated. 'The club had some last-minute fire licence issue.'

'Okay. Then why didn't you come and join me at the Leaside?' he persists.

'We not *afford* it, Stu.' Esther's growing increasingly frustrated. 'Me stuck in a crummy B&B, other side of the ring-road, wid no transport.'

'Nah' – Ransom's still not satisfied – 'there are definitely some unresolved issues here ...' (He's patently incapable of coming up with any, just off the cuff.) '... fundamental issues, Est, *critical* issues, connected to trust.'

He glares at her, balefully. 'Bottom line is, I'm vulnerable right now. You *know* that – better than anybody. I need people around me I can depend on. People I can trust. People I can take at face value. I need reliable back-up, Est. I don't wanna just feel exploited. I need to be cosseted – nurtured – *cherished*, even – to feel like I'm the captain of my troops again. I need a proper team – a *real* team – with an unshakeable faith. A unity of purpose. A coherent –'

'*Bullshit!*' Esther's had enough. 'An army only as good as its leader, Stu. Face it: your game gone to shit. Your *life* gone to shit. An' I's the only troop you got left standin' right now. Jus' *own* it, boy, then deal with it!'

A short silence.

'My game's a little unpredictable,' Ransom finally concedes (struggling to remain calm in the face of this sudden onslaught), 'I'm the first to admit that ...'

'Me gone.' Esther suddenly grabs a hold of her distended belly and wheels towards the door (like she's planning to use it to ram her way out of there; which – on a symbolic level, at least – isn't too far from the truth).

'Did you remember my Lamisil?' he calls after her. Esther's fingers are clutching on to the door handle.

'Bathroom cabinet ...' she grunts. 'Oh yeah, an' me got Del Renzio to call in a favour ...' She blinks a couple of times (sweat is dripping from her brows and down into her eyes). '... some local kid to carry your bag, *gratis*. He come at breakfast ...'

'But there's no need ...' Ransom's irritated.

'How so?' Esther glances over her shoulder, with a grimace.

'Because I've already got someone lined up.'

'This *exactly* the problem, Stu!' Esther spins back around again, steaming. 'Communication! Ya know?!'

'I was just about to tell you ...' Ransom starts off.

'You think me born yesterday?' Esther scoffs. 'I seen your man in the car park, dressed up like some gay rookie soldier-boy from *Platoon*.'

'Totally wrong era,' Ransom interjects.

'Sorry?'

Esther doesn't appreciate the interruption.

'Wrong era. The cap and the jacket ...'

'ME DON'T *CARE*, STU!' Esther yells.

Ransom gazes at her, hurt. '*Wow!*' he eventually mutters. 'You're always the one bangin' on about how the devil's in the details ...'

'Well here a lickle detail for ya,' Esther hisses. 'Me tore him off a strip, then sent him packin'. He not comin' back here any time soon.'

Ransom doesn't immediately react. He fiddles with the cord on his bathrobe for a moment, then looks up, coldly.

'You *do* gotta go,' he says.

Esther checks her watch, prepares to say something, then bends over, gasping. Ransom turns and glances at the bedside clock.

'Seven minutes,' he murmurs.

There's a sharp rap at the door.

'Cab's here!' Toby yells, trying the handle. 'I've thrown your suitcase ...'

He enters the room, espies Esther, and quickly leaps forward to offer support.

'Is she okay?'

He looks to Ransom, shocked.

'She'll be fine.' Ransom waves his hand, serenely. 'She's just hamming it up because I sacked her.'

Nano-pause.

'You did ...

'You say ...

WHAT?!

Esther and Toby each enunciate their own, uniquely individual three short syllables in a perfectly timed – almost farcical – conjunction.

An attractive, well-presented middle-aged woman answers the door. Gene starts (somewhat taken aback), then formally introduces himself, apologizing, sincerely, for the lateness of the hour. She puts a finger to her lips and says (alternating between English and French, but with the former language spoken in a heavy, almost theatrical French accent), 'Hush! *Faites attention!* The child sleeps! Welcome! I'm Frédérique,' then cordially invites him in.

Everything about Frédérique seems perfectly normal, except for her dressing gown which she appears to be wearing the wrong way around (her arms pushed uncomfortably forward, her shoulders slightly hunched: like a surgeon bewilderingly disabled by his surgical scrubs).

She leads him through to the sitting room where she indicates towards the sofa and offers him refreshment. He politely declines. He repeats (for the third time) that he is eager to see Valentine. She nods but does nothing, just stands there, openly devouring him with her eyes, her entire face illuminated – transfigured, even – by a wide, slightly intimidating, sixty-watt smile.

To break the impasse, Gene changes his mind and asks for a glass of water. She nods again, then carefully bends down and starts laboriously removing something from beneath her nightdress. It is a nappy.

'I don't know why they persist in putting these things on me,' she says, pulling it off, 'it's so strange *n'est-ce pas? Si honteuse!* So unnecessary!'

She holds it out to him, indignant. 'Look!' she says. 'A nappy!'

'Yes. Yes, I see ...' Gene murmurs, nodding, and then (for want of anything more pertinent to add), 'I'm sorry.'

'My dear, dear friend,' she sighs, eyes raised, melodramatic, 'this is not the life I was intended for!'

'No,' Gene concedes, with a wry grimace, 'I feel that way myself, sometimes ...'

She drops the nappy to the floor.

'What life *were* you intended for?' she asks, undermining this question – while she speaks – with a flutter of extraordinary hand movements that seem to relate on no discernible level to the enquiry she's just made.

Gene ponders his answer for a while.

'I always wanted to be a cricketer,' he eventually confesses, 'or a pilot, maybe, with the RAF –'

'I always wanted to be a dancer,' she interrupts, 'a beautiful ballerina.'

She commences twirling around the room, her balance shot, her arms still chronically restricted by the dressing gown.

Gene takes out his phone and rings Valentine's mobile. She answers immediately.

'Where are you?' he asks, at a whisper.

'Where are you?' she asks, also at a whisper.

'In your house,' he says. 'The sitting room. I'm with your mother. She's dancing.'

'*Shit ...*'

He hears the gentle creak of bed springs. 'You got here sooner than I thought. I'm upstairs with Nessa. She had a stomach-ache. She couldn't sleep. Just hold on a second ...'

She hangs up.

Valentine's mother stops dancing, slightly out of breath, then squats down on the carpet and prepares to urinate.

'Your mother's urinating on the rugs,' Gene mutters (still into his phone – although he knows she won't hear him). 'What should I do?'

As he speaks he hears the sound of footsteps clattering down the stairs. He stands up (wincing, half-indicating, almost apologetic) as Valentine staggers into the room, yanking on a pair of red, tracksuit bottoms. She grinds to a sudden halt on apprehending her crouching parent, then draws a deep breath, pushes back her shoulders and sets her expression.

'Gene!' she announces, breezily, walking towards him, smiling, holding out her hand. 'How good of you to come!'

Gene takes her hand – her small, soft hand with its inexplicably bruised finger pads – and politely shakes it. He immediately notices that her face is clean of make-up. It's plain and flushed. There are freckles on her nose. Her brows are thin and pale red in colour. Her eyes are pink-rimmed. She looks beautiful – natural as a rabbit – but entirely different.

'Your mother was good enough to let me in,' he murmurs, doing his best to play along. She doesn't automatically release his hand. He feels a tickling sensation in his chest, like his lungs are a fledgling sparrow which she's gently compressing in her grip.

'I've been working on the design for your tattoo,' she continues, brightly, as though reading from a bad script. 'I do hope you'll be pleased with the work I've done.'

'Great!'

Gene nods, bemused. 'Fantastic!'

'So if you'll just head through to the studio for me ...'

Valentine indicates the way and finally releases him.

'Absolutely ...'

He totters towards the door, strangely light-headed (when did he last eat?), anxious – in this sudden explosion of liberty – that he might lose his bearings completely and fly into a window pane.

Valentine turns to her mother, now.

'Time for bed, I think,' she murmurs, bending down to retrieve the abandoned nappy.

Her mother stands up.

'I couldn't go,' she mutters, piqued. 'I pushed and pushed, but nothing! *Pas une goutte d'urine!*'

'You already went, remember? Ten minutes ago? Upstairs. In the bathroom.'

Gene hears their conversation as he walks down the corridor. He reaches the door of the studio and tries the handle. It doesn't give. The door is locked. He tries it again. It remains locked.

'I was dancing!'

Valentine's mother performs a small pirouette.

'That's lovely.' Valentine nods. 'I see you've got your dressing gown on back to front ...'

'Have I?'

Her mother peers down at herself.

'Yes. Shall we take it off and then head up to bed?'

Her mother neglects to answer. She's just caught her own, distorted reflection in one of the room's several, antique, fish-eye-lens mirrors.

'Your father collected those.' She points, grimacing. '*Si vilains!* I always hated the damn things. So unflattering!'

Valentine's tired, bare face breaks into an unexpected smile. 'The mirrors!' she coos. 'Well done! We should write that down in your book ...' She grabs her mother's arm and pats it, delighted. 'First thing in the morning, just as soon as you wake up, we'll write it down together.'

'What?'

Her mother frowns, snatching her arm away, confused. 'Dad's mirrors,' Valentine persists. 'He collected round mirrors. You never liked them – you thought they were unflattering. We should write it down in your Memory book.'

Her mother says nothing for a few seconds, just gazes at her, aghast, and then, 'Poor creature!' she murmurs. 'You poor, deluded, *foolish* creature with your ... your Memory books and your ugly mirrors and your hairy cats and your remote controls!'

She shakes her head, appalled. 'Always living in the past! *Si tendue! C'est une plaisanterie!* Always harking back! This terrible prison of ... of *regret.*'

She throws up her hands, despairing. 'How long must I live in this place? *Eh?* Gnawing on the hollow husk of this other woman's life? Stuck in her shabby home with her ignorant family, wearing her ugly, stupid, shapeless clothes?'

She plucks, irritably, at her dressing gown. 'Constantly guarded and spied on! Never free or happy or at ease! *C'est tellement cruelle!* It's all so pointless! I despise you! No! Worse! I *pity* you!'

She grabs the nappy, hurls it to the floor, then turns on her heel and storms upstairs.

After a five-second pause, Gene reappears in the doorway. Valentine doesn't look up. She's staring down at the carpet.

'The door was locked,' he murmurs.

Her lips are moving.

'I hate her!' she's whispering. 'I hate her! I *hate* her! I hate her so much – *so* much – and then I hate myself for hating her. Oh God, she's right! It *is* a terrible life! I hate it, too: the house – the drudgery – the cat hair – the filth! She's right. She's *right*! It *is* a prison. It *is* ugly! It *is* stupid! These rugs. The sofa ...'

Long pause.

Valentine focuses in on her legs. She grimaces at the red, tracksuit bottoms.

'This terrible tracksuit,' she mutters.

Short pause.

Gene soberly inspects the tracksuit bottoms.

'It's a little baggy on the knee,' he concedes.

She looks up, surprised, then looks down, then looks up again, irritably.

'Just a little baggy,' he repeats, with a gentle, teasing smile, 'around the knee area.'

She looks down again. She looks up again.

'They're Noel's.' She scowls, embarrassed. 'I yanked them on in the dark. You got here sooner than I expected.'

'I ran.' He shrugs.

'Really?' She's momentarily diverted, even flattered.

'How far?'

'Not far. Less than a mile.'

Valentine inspects the tracksuit bottoms again, forlornly.

'A bold match with the green kimono,' Gene volunteers.

'Screw you!'

She starts to smile, in spite of herself, then shakes her head and scowls.

'I hate this!' she groans. 'I miss my mum. I miss her *so* much! I'd do anything to get her back.'

She shakes her head, appalled. 'All those things that irritated me before ... The cats, the Catholicism ... everything too close, too stifling, too familiar. She drove me mad! We weren't even especially close – I just took her for granted. Yet here I am, trying everything I can to scrape her back together again. Gathering up all these stupid, tiny little fragments … She's *right*! I *am* a hypocrite. It *is* sad. It *is* deluded.'

'It was always bound to take a period of adjustment.' He struggles to defend her.

'Oh *God*. I can't breathe. I'm short of breath.' She covers her face with her hands. 'She does it every time. She takes my breath away. Everything's fine. Everything's okay, and then suddenly …'

She tries to fill her chest with air, but just gulps.

'Whenever my daughter gets really stressed,' Gene confides, stepping forward, 'there's always one, completely foolproof way of snapping her out of it.'

Valentine drops her hands and stares at him, her eyes panicked and unfocused.

'A piggy-back,' Gene concludes, somewhat flatly.

'Sorry?'

Valentine frowns.

'A piggy-back. It's the world's greatest stress-buster. It never fails.'

'Hang on a second.' Valentine still isn't quite sure what he's getting at. 'You're not seriously suggesting …?'

Gene thinks for a moment, and then, 'Sure.' He shrugs. 'Why not?'

He takes off his jacket and throws it on to the sofa. Her turns his back to her and holds out his arms, glancing over his shoulder.

'Jump on.'

Valentine just stands there.

Gene drops his arms. 'I mean if you think you're too *old* for a piggy-back …'

His tone is fond, but teasing. 'Or too serious, or too important …'

'Fine.'

Valentine yanks up the tracksuit bottoms, moves in close behind him, lightly rests her hands on his shoulders and prepares to jump. The first attempt is a disaster. Her jump is too low and he grabs the fabric of the tracksuit on one leg while missing the other altogether. It's as much as she can muster not to crash, spread-eagled, to the floor.

'Useless!' Gene gently mocks her.

'My tracksuit's too baggy!' she grumbles.

'Really?' Gene muses. 'And there was me always thinking tracksuits were designed to *improve* flexibility.'

'Fuck you!'

Valentine pulls off the tracksuit bottoms and throws them on to the sofa alongside his jacket. She straightens her boxer shorts to maintain levels of propriety.

'Ready?' she barks.

'As I'll ever be.' He nods, bracing himself.

Valentine leaps. This time it's a good jump. He deftly grabs her legs and bounces her, effortlessly, up on to his hips. He shoves his forearms under her knees. She tenses her thighs and throws her arms around his shoulders. Her hot cheek presses against his ear.

'Giddy-up!' she puffs, sarcastic, spurring him on with a bare foot.

Gene starts off with a few, brief circuits around the room, then veers into the hallway, turns a sharp left, heads towards the studio, performs a rapid about-turn, canters towards the front door and then back again. They repeat this trajectory several times. On their third circuit, as they draw close to the front door, Valentine kicks out a leg and points.

'It's so bright,' she mutters, intrigued, 'is it a full moon out there tonight?'

'Uh … Yeah,' he pants, pausing, 'or as good as.'

'Are you sure?'

'Yeah,' he repeats, nodding. 'Pretty much.'

'Then we should go moon chasing!' She laughs.

'Moon ...?'

'Didn't you ever do it as a kid?' She angles her head to stare at his face. 'Get shit-faced on mushrooms or cider or skunk, then jump in a car and go moon chasing?'

'No,' Gene confesses, 'can't say that I did.'

'Then let's go!'

She bounces up and down, excitedly. 'You don't know what you've been missing!'

She spurs him on, impatiently, with her foot.

'Really? Outside?' Gene's anxious. 'Are you sure ...?'

'Why not? It's late. There'll be no one about.'

She reaches forward and unfastens the latch – her breath on his cheek – and in that brief instant she is transformed from a simple weight – a general load, a casual burden – into a complete physical entity. He feels the intimacy of his hands beneath her knees. He feels her breasts against his back. The silk of her kimono brushes his arms.

He bites his lip, stricken, wondering how on earth he has contrived to arrive at this place.

'*Mooon* chasing!' she croons, laughing.

'What about your mother?' he asks, daunted.

'Just for a minute,' she begs him. 'It's been so long ...'

'How long?'

'Ten months. A year? Please. *Please.*'

'But I thought ...?'

'*Please* ...' she wheedles, hugging him more tightly, angling her toes towards each other, 'I feel fine when I'm with you. I can do it. I know I can. Just for a minute ... *one* minute ...'

He ducks down his head and they charge outside.

'*Mooon* chasing!' She laughs, pointing to the sky, ecstatic.

'Which way?' he wonders, half-registering the regretful creak of the gate behind him, then the mournful crunch of the tarmac beneath his feet. The moon hangs in front of them –

huge, smug and unassailable – behind the opposite terrace of houses.

'Number seventy-three' – she points – 'there's an entryway ... the place is derelict. It's been empty for years. As kids we all thought it was haunted. There's a gap in the fence out the back, then a line of garages ...'

He follows her directions, feeling less and less confident – less distinctively himself – with every advancing step he takes. '*Mooon* chasing!' she whoops.

They enter the passageway and are immediately immersed in a thick, cool dankness, their heightened senses cruelly assaulted by the fuzzy squeak of ripe urine, the grumbling snarl of burned plastic, the poignant whisper of mildew ...

He feels her inhale, sharply, then hold her breath, her eyes squeezed shut, her arms tightening around his neck, her nose pushing – puppy-soft – against the skin behind his ear. He thrills to feel her burrow into him. He burgeons in the face of her helplessness – inflates, expands – feels effortlessly bold and brave and powerful. His skin glows and prickles with a sudden, jolting – utterly ludicrous – significance.

Five ... six ... seven ... *eight* thudding seconds later and they emerge back into the light again. Gene blinks, peering around him, momentarily disorientated. They're in a long wild garden, high-walled on either side.

The moon shines down, its gaze bold and frank and unremitting, its industrious rays carefully highlighting every edge and leaf and angle, every gland and hair and pore with delicate splashes of luminous, yellow ink. Gene feels the gentle swipe of its brush against his throat, tastes its mellow lustre against his lips.

He apprehends – with a slight shudder – that the world is at once cloaked by this exotic radiance (feathered, sheathed, obfuscated), yet also tenderly picked clean by its glinting beak. This is not a searchlight or a spotlight – not a light with which to intimidate or interrogate – and yet, in spite of that (or perhaps, even, because of it) he sees that it is a light where all that is hidden must somehow, inexorably, be revealed. He knows, in that instant (his heart singing and howling and lurching), that he will envelop Valentine in that lemon glow, and that he, in turn, will be enveloped.

Gene starts wading through the garden – like a doughty, lard-smattered, cross-Channel swimmer entering the choppy surf – his feet far less sure now, sometimes stumbling, forging a chaotic route through a seemingly impenetrable mess of biting nettles, old bricks, broken furniture and brambles. He feels the skin on his arms being torn and stung, feels Valentine tensing her knees and feet, but she does not release her grip on him or urge him to turn back again. Her head is angled to the sky, her pale throat arching, a luminescent hummingbird thirstily imbibing the abundant lunar nectar.

He follows a thin, cracked, concrete path. They pass a ruined pond, then a large, lopsided Christmas tree strangled by honeysuckle, then, just beyond that, an improbable heap – a giant mound – of fresh grass clippings. The back fence lies ahead of them. His arms are smarting and aching. The moon suddenly dips behind a cloud.

'I can't see the gap ...'

He blinks into the darkness, panicked.

'Set me down. I'll find it ...'

He unhooks his hands from behind her knees, but – and this is the thing that will haunt him later; an unforgivable detail; a terrible omission – he neglects to disconnect his warm, flat palms from the gleaming shellac of her skin as her feet slither to the ground. His hands – almost as if now creatures of their own agency – run up the side of her legs to her hips as she lightly descends, concluding in the delicate silk of her shorts as she lands.

She remains where she is for a moment, her arms slung loosely about his neck, her forehead pressed softly into the middle of his back.

He worries that she might cut her bare feet on a remnant of broken glass. He remembers, in passing, that Mallory wanted him to check her geography homework, that he needs to ring the tax office, that there's a problem with the liquid soap delivery at work, and the overwhelming nature of these worries – their dull particularity, their utter inexorability – spurs him into inhabiting the moment more absolutely, as if a scale has been tipped, or a heavy weight has been dropped on to the opposite side of a seesaw, a weight so thudding and absolute that he has been thrown into the air, jettisoned, like a cannonball, and while he knows – he *knows* – that everything must crash and splat and splinter once gravity finally takes its toll, just to *be* there, to feel the glistening immediacy of that moment, the freedom of it, the heat of it, the cloying warmth of its stickiness …

Valentine's hands, meanwhile – those mysterious hands, those artistic hands – are moving over his shoulders, then swooping down to his ribs. She feels each rib, individually, plays them like the slight, multicoloured, metal keys of a child's xylophone. His body sings to her touch – not a grand composition of different movements and complex parts (something you might require a full orchestra to produce), but a tiny, reedy, little tune, an inconsequential ditty written for a four-stringed banjo, a battered kick-drum and dented harmonica.

'There isn't a gap,' he mumbles, again, as the moon re-emerges from behind its cloud spitting out joyous cheekfuls of lemon curd. They stand still, barely breathing, drenched – almost submerged – in the sweet intoxication of its dripping yolk.

'Someone must've sealed it up,' she murmurs.

He lifts his hands from her hips and she pushes herself harder against the back of him.

'If you let go of me, I'll drown,' she whispers.

'If I don't …' he replies –

But the tongue in his mouth is no longer his instrument. It is heavy with longing; unwieldy; a damp, feather eiderdown of desire. It is too late, he tells himself (never more cynical and adept than in this instant): the trigger has been squeezed, the deathly mechanism has been enabled, the fatal course of a bullet has now been set. No amount of bleating or praying or willing or cajoling can halt it or stall it or call it back.

6

Sheila has an extremely furtive air about her. She is dressed in her standard, drab black and dog collar, but her hair is down and unkempt, falling over her face – one large segment hastily pinned back with an oversized paper-clip. She is in Stanislav's room, sitting at his small desk, hunched over his computer, completing an email.

Pressed under her elbow are three editions of a magazine (hailing from some time in the early nineties), poorly printed on low-quality paper, which she has recently dug out of a box in the garage. The magazine is called *OnTheRag*. The cover of the top copy features a photograph of a bulldog with a tampon dangling from between its lips wearing a Union Jack bikini stuffed with screwed-up pages from the *Sun*.

Another edition is opened to the contents page where there are four contributors' mug shots, one of which is of Sheila herself as a student journalist, spitting out her tongue, fists clenched, combatively, at her chin (on the knuckles the words 'riot' and 'grrl' scribbled in Biro, a lit roll-up clutched between the 'g' and the first 'r'). She wears heavy, black eye make-up and her brutally hennaed hair is carelessly sculpted into a jaunty mohican.

Elsewhere in the house, two phones are ringing.
After an extended period of frenzied typing Sheila re-reads her email, grimaces, re-reads it again, adds a couple of tiny alterations, then presses 'send'. One of the phones stops ringing. She glances down at her contributor's photo with a

wan smile. The second phone stops ringing. She rises to her feet and goes to stand in the doorway.

'Bugger off, school governors!' she mutters, peeking around the doorframe like a naughty child, then checking her watch, guiltily, her shoulders slumping forward slightly.

The second phone starts up again. Its insistent beep appears to be emanating from the general direction of her bedroom. Sheila plods off to answer it, removing an elastic band from around her wrist (which the post had come tied up in that very morning) and arranging her hair into a scruffy ponytail.

Arriving at her dressing table (where the phone currently sits), she swipes an impatient hand over her new hairstyle, encounters the paper-clip, scowls, pulls it out and inspects it, bemused.

Her phone rings on as she drops the clip into a tiny, cracked ceramic bowl (containing a vial of anti-nail-biting solution, a pair of cheap stud earrings and an acorn) which perches to the rear of the table's protective, glass top. She finally picks up the phone. It falls silent the instant she places it to her ear. She opens her mouth to speak, then closes it again, shrugs, throws down the phone and leans forward to look at herself in the mirror.

She seems neither depressed nor delighted by the weatherworn sight that greets her there, just rubs a tiny crust of sleep from the corner of her left eye and roughly shoves her fringe behind her ear. The natural curl in her hair refuses to be gainsaid, however, tossing the doughty lock (like a persistent drunk being repeatedly ejected from a nightclub) straight back out on to her cheek again.

Sheila tuts, yanks open a drawer, removes a pair of nail scissors, unties her hair, pulls the fringe over her eyes, grips it between her fingers and hacks off several inches. She stares at herself and then hacks off a further inch for good measure (carefully wrapping the cut hair inside a tissue which she

---

pushes into her pocket to dispose of later). The remaining hair she ties back into a ponytail, then nods at her reflection, satisfied.

She returns to the desk in Stan's room, perches on the edge of his chair and shuts down the Outlook Express, but hesitates before closing down the entire computer. Instead she opts to access her My Pictures file and goes to her five most recent downloads, one after the other.

'Astonishing!' she mutters, her face pressed up close to the screen, her fingers delicately guiding the mouse. 'It's all there – fully realized ... just needs the odd, tiny ... a little bit of ... the minutest *tweak* ...'

As she speaks she raises her free hand to her cheek to tuck her unruly fringe behind her ear, but there is no fringe. The fringe is reduced. Yet still, the hand tucks, then tucks again, then tucks for a third time before resting, finally, on her throat. Her throat seems unusually warm to the touch, the tips of her fingers incalculably more sensitive.

'Just needs someone to step in and shift things around,' she mumbles, gazing at the screen. 'Set things into context. A fixer. A visionary. A *mediator* ...'
The downstairs phone starts ringing again.
'Christ was a mediator,' she muses, hoarsely, finally looking up.

Somewhat haggard and bleary-eyed after a long and spectacularly unproductive night at the hospital, Toby Whittaker is trying (and failing) to referee an argument between two quarrelsome beauticians in the cramped passageway outside Ransom's hotel room.

The first beautician (a short, dark-haired Cockney woman with the muscular physique of a serious masseur and an impeccably neat uniform) is haranguing the second beautician (a gangly, impossibly skinny blonde with improbably long lashes, three, thick stripes of white war-paint on each cheek, an eye-wateringly tight white catsuit, silver wedges and the kind of frilly, white apron you might sometimes find – under the label nurse/chambermaid – in an Ann Summers dress-up box).

'I was booked in on Tuesday,' insists the brunette. 'Miss Wilson, his manager, came in and spoke to me herself as a matter of fact.'

'Well I was booked in yesterday,' the blonde effortlessly one-ups her, 'at the very last minute, so I can only guess that she must've been harbouring some really serious misgivings about the tin-pot beauty concession you're running in this joint.'

Joint?

The brunette beautician's jaw drops.

'You say you were booked in by Esther?' Toby interjects, inspecting the itinerary (keen – at the very least – to prevent an all-out fist-fight).

'Of course by Esther!' the blonde snorts. 'Who else?!'

'But this is a special promotion for the Hotel's Additional Leisure and Pampering Facilities,' the first beautician's smarting, 'it makes no earthly sense to book someone from outside to do the make-up.'

'What kind of nutty, half-baked organization books Stuart Ransom to promote their new venture in the first place?' the blonde retorts (drifting away, somewhat, from the issue at hand). 'It's like booking Jack the Ripper to promote a women's refuge! It's totally nonsensical!'

The brunette turns to Toby for a snap reaction. The blonde also turns to Toby (before he's had a proper chance to amass his – no doubt perfectly coherent – thoughts on the matter). 'It's crazy!' she persists. 'It's peculiar!'

'S.P.I.C.E.,' Toby answers (robot-like).

'Sorry?' The blonde blinks.

'S.P.I.C.E.,' Toby repeats. 'It's an anagram. Each letter represents a word and each word represents an idea about the psychology of persuasion. The I in S.P.I.C.E. stands for incongruity. Things don't always need to make sense in business. In fact sometimes things work out better if they don't.'

The blonde ponders this for a second.

'Okay, so you're saying that by inviting Britain's most dysfunctional golfer as a celebrity guest in their opening week this club's barmy management somehow believe they're persuading people into thinking that they're bullet-proof? They're projecting "confident but quirky"? They're projecting cocksure *and* "knowing"?'

Even as she implicitly derides this idea the blonde is slowly being seduced by its inherent logic. She starts appraising Toby with a renewed level of interest.

'It's an acronym, by the way,' the brunette beautician gently interjects.

They completely ignore her.

'S.P.I.C.E. It's an acronym,' she repeats.

'And it can't just be a total coincidence that every other seasoned British pro-golfer of any repute is off playing on the America Tour right now ...' the blonde blithely continues. 'I mean beggars can't be choosers, eh?'

'That's an interesting take on it,' Toby concedes (plainly preferring to try and keep his powder dry on this issue). 'Although I think I favour "legendary" over "dysfunctional" ...'

'Let's settle on "notorious".' The blonde spits on her palm, then cordially offers him her hand.

'And another thing ...' Toby continues, grasping the hand (with a girlish wince), then promptly forgetting what he's about to say (perhaps being momentarily stricken with conscience over what the handshake actually represents).

'Where's your bag?' The squat brunette takes full advantage of this hiatus. 'And why are you dressed in that ridiculous outfit?'

'Where's your manners?' the blonde promptly snarls. 'And why is your uniform the colour of cat vomit?'

'Given your extremely low opinion of the client,' (Toby finally remembers his second point), 'why are you so eager to do his make-up?'

'Because I'm a true professional, stupid!' the blonde exclaims, rolling her eyes. '*Duh!*'

'Well there's no mention of the booking on Esther's itinerary.' Toby glances down at Esther's clipboard, smarting.

'I flew in on the red-eye from Glasgow.' The blonde raises the stakes a level. 'I've been doing some intensive restyling work on ...' – she pauses, struggling to conjure up the correct calibre of celebrity – '... Lulu,' she eventually volunteers. 'It was incredible – totally life-affirming. We finally waved bye-bye to her safe but boring trademark faded-ginger thatch.'

'What shade is she now?' the other stylist can't resist asking. 'I call it "balsamic vinegar",' the blonde explains. 'It's a very unusual, very rich, very *radical* black/burgundy tone of my own devising.'

'On a redhead?' the brunette clucks. 'Doesn't that just really bleach her out?'

'Lulu?!' Toby chuckles. 'What on earth is the old girl doing with herself nowadays?'

'How odd!' the blonde retorts, sarcastically. 'That's *exactly* what Lulu said when I mentioned *your* name! She said, "What on earth is ..."' – she leans forward to read his badge – '"... what on earth is Toby Whittaker doing with himself nowadays?" But with her trademark cute, geriatric Scottish accent, obviously.'

'And what did you tell her?' Toby wonders (sensibly paranoid).

'I said, "I'm not entirely sure ..."' the blonde sighs.
'"Probably sticking his tongue half a mile up Stuart Ransom's arse, same as always."'

A difficult silence follows.

'I always thought Lulu lived in the Home Counties,' the Cockney eventually pipes up, 'near Elton.'

'Eltham? Isn't that in south-east London?' The blonde scowls. 'Sorry?'

'Eltham Palace ...?'

'No, *no*, not Elt*ham* – Elt*on*. As in John, the singer.'

'You have this tendency to really swallow your words when you speak,' the blonde informs her, bluntly, 'it's quite off-putting.'

The brunette stares at her, perplexed.

'I actually run a Sports Strategy website,' Toby pipes up (plainly still wounded by the 'Ransom's arse' quip).

'I know' – the blonde nods – 'and it's not half bad, either. Straightforward layout, good colour palette, not too much copy, snappy graphics ...'

'You like the graphics?'

Toby's embarrassingly grateful.

'I researched you online. Last night. And for the record' – she fluffs out the frill on her apron – 'I think nine-hole's a great idea, in principle. But you'll definitely need to rethink the name – "Turbo's" just way too petrol-heady for the Green Brigade ...'

While she continues to hold forth, emphatically, on this subject, the door to Ransom's hotel room is gently eased open. The golfer (still in his bathrobe and brandishing a toothbrush) stands and blearily appraises the three of them, his tired, bloodshot eyes finally resting (somewhat quizzically, even fearfully) on the loquacious blonde.

'By the way' – the blonde focuses in on her rival beautician – 'I fibbed about Lulu. The hair's still bleached-out ginger – the colour your pee goes after a chronic bladder infection ...'

She turns to Toby Whittaker: 'And she has no idea who you are. Not the slightest clue. She has no idea who Stuart Ransom is, either ...' The blonde tips her head towards the golfer. 'Sport just isn't her bag. Although she's passionate about yoga – likes to keep her hand in at netball –'

'*You* ...' Ransom brusquely interrupts (after swallowing a mouthful of spit and foam). 'Inside.'
He thumbs over his shoulder (completely ignoring the other two). The blonde promptly sashays past him and into the room, still talking, nineteen to the dozen.
'Fact is, I think she just really enjoys showing off her pins in her dinky little netball outfit. The legs are apparently always the last thing to go. She has this special, funky, tartan bib ...'

As the door slams shut again, Toby hears Ransom muttering, indignant, 'You do know I was standing behind the door for that entire conversation?'
'That's handy,' the blonde rejoins, unabashed, 'it'll save me from having to repeat myself. My throat feels a little strained.'

'What've you come dressed as?' the golfer demands (piqued). 'An extra from the Cirque du Soleil? A maggot? Adam friggin' Ant?'
'What've *you* come dressed as?' the blonde retorts. 'An old has-been? A sore loser? The unholy dick-head who sacks his manager of fourteen years' standing in the final stages of a near-fatal labour?'

Whittaker cringes as he hears this, his free hand moving down, guiltily, to the phone in his pocket.

'How'd you find out about that?' Ransom snaps, somewhat taken aback.
'The web, stupid!' the blonde retorts.
'And you believe everything you read?'
(Ransom tries to sound withering.)
'Everything about you? God, yes – and worse.' The blonde chortles.
'Well that's very reassuring.' (Ransom is poignant.)

A brief silence follows. Toby Whittaker turns to the brunette beautician and prepares to speak (first clearing his throat).

'What's that racket?' the blonde mutters (before Toby can follow through).

'Nothing. I left the shower running.'

'Why?'

'Why else? Because I'm waiting for it to heat up!' Ransom answers, defensive.

'Shockingly un-environmental!' the blonde grumbles. 'Bloody typical!'

'I'll turn it off, then ...' he mutters, his voice fading, temporarily. 'In fact the sight of you in that dreadful catsuit's just reminded me ...' he yells, over the squeak of new taps turning, '... I'm nearly out of toothpaste.'

'Has your hairline receded even further since Monday,' the blonde calls after him, 'or is it just the criminally unflattering light in this hotel room?'

'We've just come from the dentist,' Karim explains, somewhat flustered, 'the appointment overran. She's feeling a little woozy. She had some root-canal work done. All she needs is a cup of sweet tea and a seat in the corner. She won't be any trouble ...'

The woman in the *burqa* wobbles slightly on her feet. Karim grabs her arm and mutters something, gruffly, in what sounds like Arabic. The woman doesn't answer just glares down at the floor, sullenly.

'Of course! Come inside!' Valentine exclaims, concerned. She turns and leads the way down the corridor. 'Through here – she can stretch out on the sofa. I'll put on the fan ...'

They follow her into the sitting room where Karim gently assists his wife to sit down. She props herself, stiffly, on the very edge of the seat, then hisses, sharply, when a cat pads towards her.

Valentine apologizes, shoos the cat through the door and then moves a large, free-standing Art Deco fan across the room, plugs it in and turns it on.

'It's such a hot day again,' she murmurs, angling it towards the woman. 'Stuffy ...'

The woman – Aamilah – pointedly turns her face away from the breeze of the fan, then fastidiously picks a cat hair from the knee of her black robe.

'Like I say,' Karim repeats, irritated, 'just get her a cup of sweet tea – maybe a biscuit ...'

He addresses Milah again in his own guttural tongue. She doesn't answer, just shakes her head.

'No biscuit,' he qualifies.

Valentine nods. She is immaculately attired in a full-skirted red gingham dress with built-in petticoats and a pair of red, strappy, gladiator-style sandals with a little inch-high heel. Her wrists clack with heavy, plastic bracelets. Her fringe is curled. Her hair falls in ringlets over her shoulders. Her make-up is immaculate. She seems completely at her ease; beatific – even joyous – the epitome of effortless femininity (although the overall effect is somewhat compromised by a large, blotchy stress rash which stands out, starkly, across her breastbone).

'Should I turn the fan down slightly?' she fusses, heading over to adjust the dial. As she reaches out her arm, she senses Milah's eyes fixing, disapprovingly, on her cupcake tattoo. Milah mutters something under her breath. Karim responds to it, sharply. Milah lowers her eyes again, submissively.

'A sweet tea,' Valentine announces brightly, straightening up. 'Would she like milk?'

She addresses this question directly to Karim.

'Black is fine,' Karim insists.

Milah murmurs something.

'Just a splash, then,' Karim rapidly modifies.

'And you?' Valentine asks. 'Should I make a pot?'

'No, I'm good.' Karim shakes his head. 'Too many stimulants play havoc with my libido. Diminish my sense of focus.'

Valentine's eyes dart towards Milah. Milah stares at the floor. Her expression is unreadable.

'I mean we could always cancel today's session if ...' She bites her lip, her eyes moving anxiously back and forth between the two of them.

'Absolutely not!' Karim's horrified. 'I wouldn't dream of it. It's only a short, twenty-minute session, but building up trust is imperative. It's critical. We need to establish a routine. Regularity is essential for people in your mother's condition. They experience love not through words but through actions. We need to let the patient know that we can be depended upon.'

'Of course.' Valentine nods, intimidated.

Karim removes his handkerchief from his waistcoat pocket and pats his face with it. 'I'll head upstairs directly if that's acceptable?'

'Absolutely. Would you like me to ...?'

Valentine starts towards the door.

'No. It's fine.' He shoves the handkerchief away again. 'I prefer to find my own way – to arrive under my own steam – strictly on my own terms, in other words. I can't get caught up in family politics. That would be fatal. I come as a friend – freely – not as a gift or as a favour. I must strive to be independent.'

Karim performs a formal little bow to each of the two women and then promptly leaves them. They both listen, in silence, as his gentle tread recedes up the stairs.

'Tea,' Valentine mutters, then dips (almost a small curtsey) and leaves the room herself.

When she returns, several minutes later, holding a small, round copper tea-tray, she is astonished to find Milah sitting on the floor (like an infant), the rugs around her strewn with photographs that have been removed (without leave) from her art portfolio.

Milah glances up at her.

'I did art at school,' she announces, in perfect English, 'but I quit halfway through my A-level. The Prophet – peace be upon him – cursed the image-makers. In our religion tattooing is *haram*.'

'*Haram?*' Valentine echoes.

'Forbidden. Allah curses the person who does tattoos and the person who has tattoos done.'

'I see.'

Valentine frowns, uncertain what to say.

'Although you can become a Muslim with a tattoo,' Milah concedes. 'Even if you've applied tattoos. Islam erases all the sins you have committed before becoming a Muslim. Allah is Oft-Forgiving and Most Merciful. You can still pray, do *wudhu* and perform all your Islamic duties with a tattoo. Look ...'

Milah scrambles to her knees and lifts the black robe to waist level. Underneath the robe she is stick-thin and wears a vest and a pair of fashionably baggy jeans. She yanks down the waistband and shows Valentine a neat, blue 'tramp-stamp' depicting a couple of small dolphins (standing, tail to tail) on her lower back.

'I love dolphins,' she explains, mournfully, 'but I regret having it done now. I try and keep it hidden from my daughter. It's important for a mother to set a good example ...'

Valentine places the tray down on the sofa, then unfolds the small, occasional table and transfers the tray on to it. She is angry about the photos but struggles not to show it.

Milah drops her robe and clambers to her feet. She heads back to the sofa, leaving the photos on the floor, moving through them without much care.

Valentine immediately crouches down and gathers them together.

'I had a portfolio once,' Milah sighs, plumping herself down again. 'I loved art. But when I think about how much I loved it now – how passionate I was – it just seems so strange; almost unbelievable. When you love something that much – with such a high level of intensity – it can almost become a kind of burden, a worldly attachment, a distraction from what's truly important.'

She pauses for a second, thoughtfully. 'I suppose Karim feels that way about his healing work with the disabled. He thinks it's charitable. He thinks it's a gift from God.'

'He was amazing with Mum,' Valentine concurs. 'As soon as they met he had her eating out of his hand. I've never seen her so completely at ease with a total stranger. It was incredible.'

'He's enormously wealthy,' Milah continues, ignoring Valentine's interjection. 'Independently wealthy, but he inherited all these strange ideas about service from his mother.'

She glances over towards the door, then lowers her voice, furtively. 'His mother ran a chain of brothels in Calcutta,' she confides, with a shudder.

'It must be a little tricky ...' Valentine starts off.

'I mean if you decided you wanted to dispense with his services for any reason,' Milah continues, pointedly, 'it wouldn't be a problem for him, financially.'

'So how did the two of you meet up, originally?' Valentine tries to change the subject.

'My boyfriend's grandmother had a stroke ...' Milah starts off, then puts a hand up to her cheek. '*Ow*. My jaw's really hurting,' she groans. 'My lip's still completely numb. I refused any anaesthetic until halfway through, but then the pain got so bad ...'

Valentine straightens up from her portfolio, shocked. 'You refused anaesthetic for root-canal work?'

Milah shrugs. 'I'm one of those people who likes to know exactly what's happening to them. No sugar-coating. I like to feel what's going on – be totally aware. My family all think I'm hyper-controlling ...' – she flaps her hand, dismissively – 'but it's really just hyper-sensitivity. I'm an empath.'

She glances over at Valentine. 'D'you know what that means?'

Valentine nods. 'I have a fair idea.'

'I'm just amazingly sensitive,' Milah continues. 'Like my ears are very sensitive, for example.'

She points to her ears (which lie concealed beneath a shiny layer of black cloth). 'Sudden noises can really spook me. I'm like a wild zebra, or a deer ... Sometimes the sun dips behind a cloud and I get this massive shock. Like a real jolt. And the wind really freaks me out. I'm just mega-mega-sensitive.'

She ponders what she's just said for a minute, then adds, almost as an afterthought, 'In fact I find the *burqa* really helps with that. The *burqa* is like Allah's love embracing me, it's like I'm folded up in his love. Everything just bounces off it. I'm totally safe in here, totally focused and at peace.'

Valentine has stopped packing up her photos and is now listening intently.

'I suppose it's the same for you with your clothes and your make-up,' Milah suggests, sensing this interest, 'even the tattoos. It's like they're a shield. And the real, vulnerable you is just hiding behind them.'

Valentine ponders this hypothesis for a second, slightly unnerved.

'I guess I tend to see the hair-dye and the tattoos and the antique fabrics *as* me,' she eventually responds, 'the best part of me. The perfect part.'

'The bit you can control.' Milah nods.

'Exactly. And the rest is just ... just ...' She struggles to find the right word.

'A mess,' Milah helpfully contributes.

'... just ... just *slime*.' Valentine goes one step further, her earlier veneer of joyous ease and calm suddenly shattering. 'Just a big pile of nasty, stinking –'

'Like in *Doctor Who*,' Milah interjects, enthused, 'when they open up a Dalek and you peek inside and there's just this big, ugly pile of pathetic, throbbing *goo* ...'

'That's it!' Valentine's both shocked and delighted by this comparison.

'I used to feel that way too,' Milah confides. 'It was horrible. I felt so vulnerable. Everything flooding in. Nothing to stop it. No centre, no *core*.'

'Just this big, black, angry hole ...'

'A bottomless pit.'

'Which you could fall into at any minute.'

'And that hard, angry voice just barking away at you, telling you how stupid you are, how ugly and ungrateful, how everyone despises you, how you *deserve* to be despised ...'

'You had the voice too?' Valentine's astonished.

'Oh yeah.' Milah nods. 'All the time. I couldn't look at myself in the mirror. Couldn't meet my own eyes. I felt so ugly and tired and used-up and *fat* ... I just thank Allah – every minute of every day – that I reverted back.'

'You ...?' Valentine frowns.

'I reverted back to Islam.'

'You were raised a Muslim?'

'Nope.' Milah shakes her head. 'It's like a figure of speech. My parents are both atheists. They grew up in Pakistan but they were raised as Christians. I went to a Catholic school in Portsmouth. With Islam you don't "convert" you "revert back".'

'I don't understand ...' Valentine's confused.

'You revert back to an original, natural belief,' Milah explains, 'back to your original nature – who you always were underneath. You start again. The slate is wiped clean. Allah is the original Old Testament God. Ours is the original, Abrahamic faith.'

'But wearing that thing isn't ...' Valentine points to the *burqa*.

'The full *burqa* isn't a requirement, no. A woman should be modestly attired and her head always covered. The *burqa* is a preference. It's my choice. It's like my way of showing Allah – and my husband, my family, the wider community – how much he means to me. It's like I'm at once obliterated by my love for him and also embraced in his love – protected by him.'

'I'd love to ...'

Valentine is about to say 'obliterate the bad bits'.

'Try it on?' Milah completes her sentence for her.

'Uh ...' Valentine blinks, anxiously. 'Isn't it very hot?' she asks (by way of sidestepping the issue).

'Not really.' Milah is already pulling off her *burqa* – first the *niqab* that hangs over her head and shoulders. 'Obviously you have to move around really carefully because you lose a big chunk of your peripheral vision. And it can be difficult not to trip over on the fabric until you're fully accustomed to walking in it.'

Next Milah removes her *abaya* – the lower, robe part of her outfit – and offers it to Valentine. Valentine's gut instinct is to refuse – point-blank – to put it on, but she is momentarily disarmed – and distracted – by the extraordinary sight of Milah now completely exposed: her extreme youthfulness comes as a shock, for one thing; her natural grace, her lovely neck (her dark hair drawn back into a neat bun), her gappy teeth, her boyishly lean figure ...

In person she is an entirely different creature from the crabbed and sullen individual Valentine had previously envisioned – she's light as a feather; a little, modern sylph; a wide-eyed, coffee-skinned Edie Sedgwick.

While Valentine digests this jumble of sense-impressions, Milah is carefully pulling the *abaya* over her head, and before she knows it she has been engulfed – devoured, consumed – by its heavy, sepulchral folds. Her initial sensation is one of weight and heat, then of airlessness (a sudden spasm of panic, then one of equally sudden – and unexpected – calm). She briefly revels in the scent of the thing – it smells of the road, the street, the town, of dust and detergent, of spice and otherness. Her scrabbling hands eventually locate the armholes and her head the neck hole. As soon as her head pops out Milah is pulling on the *niqab* which is slightly elasticated around the forehead and made of a silkier, lighter fabric. Milah expertly adjusts the thin, divided grille over her eyes, centring it on her nose, then steps back – this newly hatched praying-mantis of a girl – gazing at her, concerned (like a kindly warden checking up on the mental well-being of a favoured inmate).

'How is it?'

'I don't know. Fine. Airless. Stuffy.'

As Valentine speaks, the light fabric of the *niqab* gets drawn into her mouth. She blows it out.

'Walk around a bit.'

Valentine starts to walk. It's difficult, especially in the shoes she's wearing.

'It's like a coffin,' she puffs, kicking off the shoes.

'A shroud.' Milah nods (apparently not remotely offended by the notion).

'That doesn't worry you?'

'Nope.'

She grins. 'Just imagine' – she chuckles – 'if you went outside now and walked up and down the street, nobody would have the slightest clue who you were. In fact they'd think you were me.'

'Sorry?' Valentine stiffens.

'Nobody would know it was you.'

'Outside? On my own?' Valentine's throat contracts.

'You'd be anonymous – completely free. Imagine!'

'You reckon?' Valentine slowly turns towards the door, tantalized.

'Be quick, though,' Milah urges her, grabbing the crocheted blanket from the arm of the sofa and lightly draping it over her head and shoulders. 'I'll wait here.'

She sits down and reaches for her mug of tea.

'Okay, then ... Sure. Why not?' Valentine readjusts the grille over her eyes and nose, then heads, unsteadily, towards the door. Her heart starts to beat faster as she walks down the hallway. Every footstep feels weighted and momentous. Her body is unusually clumsy and lumpen – yet humming with an unexpected sense of significance.

It's difficult to negotiate space. Her hip bumps into the phone table. She steadies herself, straightens the phone, grazes the aspidistra with her sleeve, and reaches for the door latch. Her hand is clammy and shaking a little.

As she twists the lock, her mind turns – inexorably – to the previous night: the cold metal of the latch between her finger and thumb; the touch of Gene's ear against her cheek; the push of her breasts against his back; that feeling of carelessness – of insolence – of ... of *ease* ... a sensation she hasn't felt since Mischa left ... and – she grimaces, plainly pained by the thought – since Dad died.

She shudders, twisting the little handle still harder and yanking the door wide, tensing up, involuntarily, as if waiting for the whole world to fall in on her – like an overstuffed suitcase tumbling down, without warning, from the top of a cupboard; its contents a petrifying jumble of light, air and sound.

She waits to stall, to freeze, inhaling sharply in preparation (as if, at some level, she thinks she deserves such a bombardment:

Adulterer!

Coward!
Parasite!).
But nothing.

Instead she finds herself neatly one-step-removed, preserved like a pickle, or a quail's egg in aspic, peeking out, tentatively, at the world through her grille. She feels like an inquisitive projectionist gazing into the cinema. The film plays on in the auditorium (the sound a muffled echo) but she isn't really watching it or following the plot. Her involvement is just mechanical. The reel spins, unassisted. The pressure is lifted.

Valentine is overwhelmed by an intense feeling of gratitude and relief. She almost laughs out loud as she steps down into the front garden.

I am Aamilah, she thinks, another girl with a different life, a better girl. She glances down the road with the eyes of a stranger. She is free of herself.

Passing through the gate, her robe briefly catches on the intricate ironwork. She pauses to free the fabric (does so without much effort) and is about to step out on to the pavement when she sees someone walking towards her – a woman with a pram. She steps back and lowers her eyes, her cheeks flushing, humiliated (like a child caught with its fingers in the biscuit barrel). The woman walks by without a second glance.

I am the dead Valentine, she thinks, a sweet darkness stirring within her, a strange ghost of Valentine haunting my former life ...

She goes to inspect Karim's car. Karim's car is framed in black – like an invite to a funeral. The dead Valentine marvels at the shine of the chrome-work. The dead Valentine runs her hand along the side panels. But she is dead and feels only the vaguest notion of solidity. Everything is something but nothing in particular; just stuff, just a series of random atoms held momentarily in position – for the briefest of interludes –

by a complex concatenation of time and space and human willpower. Everything is whole. Everything is unstrung.

Dead Valentine gazes up the road. She is no longer fearful, she is blank as an unaddressed letter. She is dead. She is empty. She is *un*.

Without fear there is no gravitational pull from the world around her. Without fear there is no climax, no shattering *dénouement*, no live wire, no earth wire, just a calm, cool, blue neutral.

She suddenly frowns, quickly glances down, and focuses in, closely, on her feet. Her frown deepens. She gingerly lifts her right foot from the pavement ... *Fine*. She gingerly lifts the left ...

Urgh! *Urgh!* Chewing gum! Melted into a vile, satanic glue on the warm concrete slab!

You clumsy idiot! A large bead of sweat runs down her cheek. It hangs, precariously, on her jawbone ...

Hot. Hot. *Hot!*

She curses under her breath, turns, and hobbles back to the house, flops down on the front step, lifts the robe, and commences picking the sticky mess from her heel.

'Bloody typical!' she huffs, as it sticks to her picking fingers. 'Disgusting!'

In the sitting room, several minutes later, Milah helps her to remove the *niqab* and *abaya*.

'How was it?' she asks.

'Sticky,' Valentine murmurs, catching hold of the *abaya* with her hand and inspecting the hem. 'I stood on a pile of chewing gum. It was all over my foot.'

Her face is glowing with perspiration. She feels drained and exhausted.

Milah isn't entirely satisfied by this response.

'Okay – I felt ...' Valentine tries to think, to analyse. 'I felt like a little girl playing hide and seek ... but there was nobody – nothing – coming to find me ...'

Milah nods.

'I felt free. Then I felt kind of ... well ... embarrassed – fake. Then I felt ...'

She can't find adequate words to describe her brief experience (even to herself). She frowns, finally settling for, 'Incredibly bloody hot.'

Milah grins. She pulls on the *abaya*, then rapidly adds the *niqab*, adjusting it down over her shoulders until she once again resembles a dowdy, portable, Victorian bathing hut.

Valentine goes over to check her hair and make-up in one of the several, circular wall mirrors. She looks hubcap-ugly. She winces. As she does so she hears the clank of the front gate. Milah hears it too and turns towards her, tensing.

'That'll be my brother.' Valentine gestures, distractedly, towards the sofa and the tea-tray. 'I should probably ...'

She darts into the hallway as her brother comes falling – almost headfirst – through the door.

'Where've you been?' she stage-whispers, grabbing his arm, expertly, with one hand, while shielding the jardinière with her other. 'I had to send Nessa to daycare in a cab.'

'Keep your hair on!' Noel mumbles, straightening himself up, snatching his arm away, then inspecting his dishevelled sister with an unapologetic smirk (plainly drunk – or stoned – or both).

Valentine grabs him by the arm again and escorts him (past the sitting room) into the relative privacy of the studio.

'I found the whip,' she rounds on him as soon as the door is shut, 'and the wallet.' She shudders. 'You *swore* you'd got rid of them.'

Noel appraises her, dopily.

'You *swore* you'd got rid of them!' Valentine persists. 'The guy who read the meter ...'

'Ransom's little sneak!' Noel snorts, infuriated. 'I thought you said it was all sorted?'

'It was,' she insists, 'but then he came back again later and the stupid thing just went haywire ... I was upstairs with Mum. I swear to God I had *no idea* ...'

Noel just shrugs.

'Why the hell didn't you tell me about it the other day?' she demands, incredulous. 'Warn me, at the very least?'

'You said it was all sorted!' Noel repeats, almost indignant.

'Well it wasn't. And now it's just this great, big, ugly *mess* ...'

Valentine looks to Noel for some kind of useful response, but Noel just shrugs again, drunkenly.

'D'you *want* us to get sued by the electricity board?' she exclaims, astonished by his apparent indifference. 'Or worse? Prosecuted by the police?'

'That was Dad's special, little hidey-hole,' Noel grumbles. 'I had nothing to do with it. Why's it *my* problem all of a sudden?'

'Because you're the man of the house now' – Valentine's utterly exasperated – 'and because you swore you'd get rid of the bloody stuff! I trusted you! I thought you'd dumped it or buried it – you promised me, Noel!'

'I've had other shit to deal with!' Noel growls.

'Oh yeah?' Valentine's not buying it.

'*Yeah!*' Noel insists.

'But this is *really important.*' Valentine tries her best to reason with him. 'And you promised me,' she repeats, limply.

Noel appears signally unmoved by this more measured approach.

'And I was dumb enough to *trust* you!' Valentine rapidly loses her cool again. 'God, what a bloody *idiot* I've been! Now we're in *all* kinds of trouble.'

She puts a hand up to her throat. Her lower lip starts to wobble.

'I said I'll deal with it and I will!' Noel stolidly maintains, observing the warning signs (even through the bleary filter of dope and booze). 'But this shit takes time, Vee.' He burps, loudly, mid-sentence. 'It's a delicate transaction.'

'You said you'd trash it. Destroy it all.'

Valentine's shocked to discover that her brother has other plans.

'Changed my mind.' Noel shrugs.

'What's that supposed to mean?'

'It means I changed my mind,' Noel snorts, 'what else?'

'Well if *you* won't take care of it then I'll handle it myself!' Valentine turns, abruptly, towards the door.

'No you fucking won't!' Noel roughly grabs her arm.

'I can't speak to you when you're like this!' Valentine shakes him off. 'I can't believe that stuff's still in the house! It makes me sick to my stomach even thinking about it!'

'I said I'd sort it out, okay?'

Noel's patience is starting to wear thin.

'What if he gets in contact with the police?' she demands.

'Who?'

'Gene.'

'*Who?*'

'The meter guy.'

'We've not done anything illegal.' Noel shrugs. 'The stuff was Dad's ...'

'But the meter's the property of the electricity board.'

'Big fucking deal! We just plead ignorance ...'

'And what about the business?' Valentine persists. 'I've only just started getting things back on track. What'll happen if this gets out? Everything'll be ruined!'

'I'll move the stuff!' Noel's exasperated. 'Stop freaking out! It'll be *fine*.'

'I've got an appointment at twelve, Noel.' Valentine's almost in tears. Her nerve rash is flaring up. 'How the hell am I expected to concentrate when I'm feeling so stressed?'

'Uh ... Oh yeah – the appointment.' Noel looks shifty. 'I think he might've cancelled. His kid's got flu or something ... pneumonia ... measles ...'

Noel takes out his phone and starts scrolling through his texts.

'Cancelled?' Valentine's aggrieved. 'When did this happen?'

'I dunno ... Yesterday ... Tuesday ... He sent an email, then he confirmed by ...'

'Did he reschedule?'

Noel continues searching.

Valentine goes over to an old Apple Mac and printer which are perched on a white, plastic table in the corner of the room (alongside a photocopying machine and a large, metal cabinet full of inks, paper towels, salves, gloves and disinfectants). 'I've been up since four this morning finalizing the bloody artwork.'

She turns on the computer and accesses her messages, searching for the relevant contact details. As she does so, the computer chimes to indicate the arrival of new mail.

'Next month,' Noel finally pipes up, reading from his phone. 'He can do the last two weekends in August, or – failing that – it'll have to be Christmas. He says he can't book any more time off work till then.'

Valentine doesn't respond. She's reading the new email wearing a look of confusion – bordering on panic.

'What's wrong?' Noel demands.

Valentine turns. 'Nothing.' She obstructs the screen with her body. 'I'm just pissed off you didn't bother telling me, that's all.'

'Isn't Kafir coming this morning?' Noel rapidly changes the subject.

'Karim. He's upstairs with Mum. His wife's in the sitting room. She was feeling dodgy after some heavy dental work.'

'Good-good.'

Noel nods. He looks down at his phone.

'She's in all her robes and what-not.'

Noel doesn't respond.

'In fact I'm not sure how happy she is about –' Valentine starts off.

'*Fuck* ...' Noel interrupts, glancing up, then back down. 'Gotta dash, kiddo.' He shoves his phone into his pocket and strides over to the sink in the corner of the room.

'Please don't mess up the sink!' Valentine's irritated. 'It's meant to be kept sterile.'

Noel ignores her, bending over the basin, turning on the cold tap and splashing water over his face and neck.

'So you're definitely going to move the stuff?' Valentine simply can't let it lie.

'Yup.'

'When? Soon?'

'Soon as.'

He grabs a white towel (from a nearby rack), dries himself with it, tosses it, carelessly, behind the taps, dashes over to Valentine, gives her a noisy kiss on the cheek, then leaves the room. She wipes away the kiss with her palm as she listens to him ransacking the kitchen cupboards for crisps and biscuits before going for a quick pee in the downstairs toilet and dashing straight back out again.

Once the front door slams, she goes to a full-length mirror on the wall and inspects her reflection in it. 'Slime,' she murmurs, focusing in on her nerve rash, touching it, grimacing, then returning her full attention to the email on her computer and re-reading it once, twice, three times.

'This is crazy!' she whispers, standing stock-still for a couple of minutes, staring up at the ceiling, before turning and walking over to her black, padded tattooing bench, climbing on to it and lying there, face-down, silently, for what feels like an age, feet together, arms pinned to her sides, face crushed into the synthetic fabric.

7

'There are two kinds of women,' Ransom informs her, posing, raffishly, on the state-of-the-art driving range while she carefully applies a touch of concealer to a large, red spot which is erupting – like a brave, little sunrise – from between the clefts of his chin.

'There's the women who *will* have sex with you, and the women who *won't* have sex with you because they think that if they *do* have sex with you then you won't respect them afterwards. This second kind are the worst, because they actually think that by *not* having sex with you they represent more of "a challenge", so when they *do* finally have sex with you (and – let's face it – it's only a matter of time), it will somehow be more "meaningful" ...'

Ransom enunciates the word 'meaningful' in much the same way a normal person might enunciate the word 'diarrhoea'.

'Gracious!' Jen steps back and appraises the golfer, awed. 'Golfer/businessman, golfer/role model, golfer/philosopher, golfer/*psychologist* ...' She winks at Toby Whittaker who stands nearby holding a large, white, light reflector, several changes of clothes and a furled umbrella. 'Is there really no end to your talents?'

'Golfer/chauvinist,' Israel mutters from his nearby perch – a small, portable sports-stool – where he is diligently ploughing his way through the final chapter of his book.

Ransom inspects the sullen teen (as he poses) from the corner of his eye.

'Where'd the kid come from?' he demands. 'What's his function? Spear-carrier? Messenger boy? Eunuch?'

'He's my *protégé*,' Jen clucks (as Israel delivers Ransom a look of searing condescension, then returns, with an eye-roll, to his reading matter).

'Haughty!' Ransom avows.

'Into the light, please!' the photographer yells.

'Strange how that'll happen sometimes,' Jen muses, 'when you blithely cast aspersions on someone's racial, emotional and sexual integrity ...'

'What the hell does he look like?' Ransom wonders, inspecting Israel's pink tie and mauve shirt combo with a slightly curled lip.

'That's his style,' Jen sighs. 'He's sensitive – artistic ...'

'Toby?' the photographer yells. 'Toby, is it? A couple of inches higher with the ...'

'What's he reading?' Ransom demands, swatting at his cheek. 'I think you'll find it's ...' – Jen lowers her voice as she moves in closer to pick off the remains of a tiny gnat (which has just been embedded into his foundation) – '*a proper book.*' She pats him on the shoulder, reassuringly. 'Not anything you need to worry your pretty little head about.'

'Looks weighty,' Toby amiably interjects as Jen rapidly retreats and Ransom quietly admires her slim but jaunty rump.

'Into the light!' the photographer yells, again. 'And raise the club just a fraction ...'

'It's no *Ulysses*,' Israel avers (with a nicely judged measure of condescension), 'but still fun for all of that.'

'Where'd you nab the stool from?' Ransom grumbles, jealous.

'The light!' The photographer's voice gives slightly under pressure.

'It's mine. I brought it with me.' Israel's suitably smug.

'How old did you say he was?' Ransom turns to Jen again.

'To the front, *please!*' the photographer yells.

'Thirteen.'

'A fraction higher with the reflector!' the photographer persists.

'You're thirteen years old and you carry a *fold-up stool* about the place?' Ransom's appalled.

'It packs down into a very convenient size,' Israel maintains, 'which fits neatly into my briefcase.'

'Fuck me!' Ransom's astonished. 'Who's he think he is?' He turns to Jen, indignant. 'The black Quentin Crisp?!'

'His parents are guests at the hotel.' Jen scowls. 'They're caught up in some big family crisis, so I'm baby-sitting. I promised them I'd take him to the Hat Factory, but he wasn't especially sold on the idea –'

'No need to go to a factory – we've got plenty of hats here!' Ransom interrupts. 'Toby, throw the kid a hat.'

'The Hat Factory is an *arts* centre,' – Jen's withering – 'they hold drumming and dance classes ...'

'Chuck the kid a hat, Tobe,' Ransom repeats. Toby hesitates (he's struggling to hold up the light reflector).

Ransom grabs a couple and throws them himself. One hits Israel square in the face, the other lands on his lap. Israel adjusts his glasses, lifts his book, clears his throat and continues to read.

'Put one on,' Ransom suggests.

Israel ignores him.

'What's his friggin' problem?'

Ransom turns to Jen again, exasperated.

'It's a very general rule of thumb,' Jen confides, 'but hats don't always tend to combine well with glasses.'

'Spike Lee seems to manage okay,' Ransom snits.

'And anyway,' Jen runs on, 'his mother probably wouldn't approve.'

'His mother? What's she got to do with the price of beef?'

'She's one of those intellectual types. Dogmatic. A real stickler. Hates sports. Especially *gol-ol-ol-olf*. Thinks it's ...'

'Oh here we go,' Ransom mutters, promptly returning to his posing.

'What?'

Jen looks *faux*-insulted.

Ransom just smiles, cheesily, for the camera.

'Fine!' Jen *faux*-huffs, going to stand next to Toby. Toby continues to hold the light reflector aloft.

'*Gol-ol-lluf?*' Jen quietly intones.

Toby glances over at her.

'*Gol-ulf?*'

Jen *faux*-retches.

'It's a funny word,' Toby agrees, slightly uneasy, 'there's no fixed etymology –'

'Etty-botty-whatty?' Ransom butts in, scowling.

'Word origin. The history of the word. Where the word originally comes from ... like ...' Toby thinks for a second. 'Like rugby, for example – the word and the game have a fairly precise historical origin ...'

'You don't say?!' Jen gazes up at him, lashes fluttering.

'Yeah ... The word comes from the name of a school – Rugby School in Warwickshire ...'

'Maybe just leaning on the club, now,' the photographer suggests, 'taking a break, peering out into the deep, blue yonder, hand shading your eyes ...'

Ransom obliges.

'There was a pupil at the school, a boy called William Webb Ellis, and he was out on the sports field playing a football match when he suddenly felt an overwhelming urge to just pick up the ball and run with it. This was circa 1820-something ...'

'But why did the school have that name in the first place?' Ransom demands.

'Sorry?'

'Why was the *school* called Rugby?'

'*Duh!*' Jen responds, with a derisory tooth-kiss. 'Because it was destined to become the name of an internationally renowned team sport, *obviously.*'

'Uh ... I've no idea,' Toby admits (slightly thrown off-kilter by Jen's interjection), 'it was probably named after a wealthy, local benefactor ...'

'Pah!'

Ransom returns to his posing.

'*Gol-ol-olfff,*' Jen belches.

'From what I've read,' Toby continues, 'it's generally held that the word "golf" is a derivation of two medieval words that were used to describe various stick and ball games current at around that time ... I can't remember them both, off-hand, but one was definitely "*kolf*" which relates to the Germanic "*kolbe*" or "club", and is probably also related to the Dutch game "*kolven*" ...'

'When's Gene planning to turn up?' Ransom grumbles (still posing).

'Cricket's another quite interesting one,' Toby notes (pleased to see Israel listening, intently, to his brief explication). 'It's thought the Old French for "stick" is "*criquet*", although they aren't really sure whether the term refers to the actual bat or the wickets.'

The photographer strolls over (as he deftly changes the reel of film in his camera). 'We should probably move on to a new location while the weather's still holding up,' he suggests.

'I've got someone bringing a Hummer,' Ransom tells him. 'I'm very keen to project this certain "look".'

'Great – a theme!' the photographer notes, dourly.

'Kind of pared down. Uncompromising. Mean. Mysterious,' the golfer persists. 'Me in black. Very enigmatic – I might swap the cap for a bandanna at some point ...'

(Jen snorts.)

'My caddie's in military gear. Antique. Then there's this old Hummer – like I said – which we'll definitely use as part of the backdrop.'

'Of course you're free to do what you like,' the photographer concedes (plainly riled), 'but it's probably worth bearing in mind that in the general brief the client was *very* specific about needing a certain amount of ...'

'Post-apocalyptic. *Mad Max* meets *The Matrix* meets something they haven't even invented yet,' Ransom continues, describing it with his hands. 'I'll be holding my club like a weapon – a crazy fusion of old-fashioned sporting hero and futuristic Ninja ...'

'The all-black gear does tend to gobble up the light,' the photographer interjects, 'and Mr Del Renzio –'

'Screw Del Renzio!' Ransom snorts. 'What's Del Renzio know about anything? He isn't even here! Del Renzio can go suck eggs for all I care.'

As Ransom holds forth, Toby is taking the opportunity to check his texts.

'Anything from Gene?' Ransom demands, mid-flow.

'Uh, no. I'm actually just getting an update from the hospital.'

'Did you ever meet Gene's wife?' Ransom automatically turns to Jen.

'Why?'

'She rang me this morning. I was still half-asleep. Got my number off the kid's phone, apparently. Started bangin' on at me about getting myself a tattoo.'

'Sheila?'

Jen's immediately suspicious. 'Are you sure about that?'

'Absolutely. The stroppy priest. What's she called again – Sandra, Sylvia ...?'

'Sheila,' Jen repeats.

'That's the one.'

Ransom practises his swing a couple of times. 'Sheila. Yeah. The priest wants to get me inked.'

'But why would Sheila ...?' Jen's befuddled.
'Because of the Tucker girl. There's a daughter. She's a tattooist. Sheila thinks it could be an act of "public reconciliation" with benefits on either side. Said she was "just putting it out there".'

'But how ...?'
Jen's still struggling to make sense of this.
'Dunno.' Ransom shrugs. 'Bottom line is, I'm terrified of friggin' needles.'
'What's Gene think?'

As Jen asks this question, she's grabbing Israel by the arm, pulling him to his feet, frog-marching him over to Ransom and positioning him by his side. She then removes her camera phone from her pocket, steps back and takes a quick photograph of the two of them with it.

'No idea.' Ransom shrugs. 'Wouldn't have a clue. I'll happily ask him if he ever bothers turning up ...' He pauses. 'What're you doing?'

Jen takes another photo. In this one Israel is pulling an especially unenthusiastic expression.

'Say "prunes",' Jen tells them, and takes a third shot. She then inspects the battery count – it's low – grimaces, and slips her phone back into her apron pocket.

'Well from what I know of Vee' – she escorts Israel back to his stool – 'she normally tattoos twinkles.'

'Vee?'
Ransom's picking, surreptitiously, at his chin spot. Israel returns, sullenly, to his book.

'Vee. *Vee*. The Tucker girl. She specializes in twinkles.' Jen points down at her own twinkle to illustrate. 'You know, twinkles ... minnies ... Lady Gardens.'
Ransom's jaw drops.

'She's kind of all arty and abstract. Dresses like a forties pin-up. Really girly. Does this ultra-ultra realist stuff – remember Noel's wicker? On his chest? And the snake?'

'The baby's absolutely fine!' Toby suddenly interjects, delighted, 'and they've finally got Esther's haemorrhaging under control ...'

Israel looks up from his novel, frowning.

'They've called her Prudence.'

'Baby Prudence!' Jen coos. 'So cute! So retro!' She turns to Israel. 'I guess that makes you an uncle for the ...' She squints up into the sky. 'What'll it be, Izzie? The third time?'

'Aunt Esther was haemorrhaging?!' Israel mutters, glowering. 'Why's nobody ever tell me anything?!'

Toby looks to Ransom (clearly anticipating a response of some kind), but Ransom simply practises his swing again, very cleanly, very precisely, then shoves his club into his bag, pulls down the brim of his cap and walks off, at speed, whistling maniacally.

Gene is leaning on the wall outside the rectory, talking on his phone.

'Just ... just ... just back up a second ...'

He looks pale and exhausted. His shirt is knotted, carelessly, around his hips, his T-shirt is soaked in sweat. A lock of his hair hangs over his forehead. There's a new, blue tinge in the taut skin of his eye sockets.

'You're with ...? But *how* ...?'

He stares down at his free hand as he speaks, abstractly registering a couple of bloodied bramble scratches across his knuckle, and then – completely without warning – suddenly falls prey to an astonishingly intense recollection (a cinematic still, writ bold, but with the back-up of an additional tactile reel – a sensual 3D effect – which tinkles along his spine like a soft, yellow dusting cloth sliding across the cool, black and ivory keys of a baby grand piano). He vividly remembers that hand – that same, scratched and bloodied knuckle – shoving Valentine's naked hips down on to his own naked hips – midst a tangle of grass cuttings and ivy fronds and wrenched-aside clothing – pushing those keen hips wide, peeling them open – greedily, mercilessly – like a deliciously ripe pomegranate, manipulating them, feeling them hike and splurge and resist and buckle, feeling his fingers clenching and controlling the soft flesh on her thighs, grinding himself into her, pulsing and throbbing, utterly ruthless, utterly brutal ...

He blinks, horrified, his nipples tautening.

'Sorry?'

He blinks again.

'Sorry – I didn't ...'

He struggles to refocus.

'Which kid? Where ...? At the club? But ...?'

He shakes his head.

'In hospital?'

Pause.

'Last night?'

Pause.

'But she said ...'

Pause.

'I don't know, Jen. I'm not sure. Things are a little ...'

He winces, scratching at the slight auburn stubble of overnight growth on his neck.

'*What?*'

Hand drops. Look of gaping astonishment.

'Would you ... Could you just repeat that?'

Listens, incredulous.

'*My* Sheila? Are you serious?'

Listens intently.

'But ... But *why* ...?'

Slowly shakes his head. Mouth tightens.

'Are you sure this isn't just a wind-up, Jen?'

Anxious pause.

'Okay. Okay ... Fine.'

Rubs his eyes.

'No. No I haven't, actually. Not today ... I've been ...'
Gene peers down, mournfully, at his running shoes. 'I've been charging around the place all morning ...'

He glances back over towards the house, almost fearful now.

'Well I'll definitely have a word with her ... I just can't ...'
Pushes back fringe, irritated.
'I mean I'll speak to her about it ...'
Shakes head.
'But this is definitely news to me.'
Pause.
'Okay. Yeah ... Fine ... As soon as I've ... Okay. Bye.'

Gene snatches the phone from his ear – grim-faced – and quickly accesses his contacts file. He runs down the names until he reaches Valentine's. His thumb twitches over 'dial' and then freezes as his mind is overrun by the extraordinary memory of the tangling silk of her hair strung between his fingers. She is below him – gasping – on her back. He is thrusting into her. The force of his hips is pushing her away, so he tightens his fingers into fists (his hands resting either side of her head, just behind her ears, his knuckles up close against her scalp) and he yanks her back towards him by her hair.

Her eyes spring open and she gazes up at him, shocked. His heart somersaults, but then she smiles – a slow, lazy smile, a delirious smile – emits a groan – her irises starting to roll, her lashes fluttering – so he pulls still harder, still tighter, and finds himself the master – the tyrannical despot – the helmless helmsman – of a pounding, elephant stampede of bellowing, trumpeting, galloping pleasure.

His ecstasy is blind and fierce and thundering – limitless – coarse – savage – volatile. He is pumped full of air – is an infinite inhalation – and yet is asphyxiated; throttled; smothered by a billowing cloud of red African dust. His pleasure is all-hearing (could detect a pin drop) and yet is deafened – blasted, rent – by the all-consuming blare. He is at once utterly joined-up, immersed and connected, yet impeccably isolated and alone. He is a still centre, hidden, like a tiny, happy ant, inside an immense, scorching grassland of pure, clean, unadulterated fear.

As suddenly as this vision comes, it goes.

Oh God!

Gene turns off his phone, with a silent groan –

What the fuck have I done?

He is possessed by the violent urge to flee – to run. He shoves his phone into his pocket and turns, but before he's taken half a dozen steps he hears the front door slam and Sheila calling.

'Gene!' she yells, then, '*Eugene!*'

He stops. He turns. He can feel his knees creaking.

'Where are you going?'

She's smiling, trotting gamely towards him. She seems unusually exuberant. Almost – he blinks – *radiant.*

'Nowhere!' Gene unties the shirt from around his waist (simply for something to do with his hands). 'I wasn't going anywhere … I was just …'

He pauses.

'I mean I was running. I was going for a run. I've been for a run. I was … I was … cooling down. I was getting a cramp. I was winding down.'

'Where've you been?' Sheila interrupts. 'I haven't seen you all morning. Did you come up to bed last night?'

Gene is staring at her hair, confused. 'Has something happened to your fringe?' he asks.

'We missed you at breakfast.' Sheila ignores his question. 'Mallory wanted you to help her with that biology assignment.'

'Geography,' Gene corrects her.

'Exactly.'

Sheila nods.

'Sorry ...' Gene pulls on his shirt and begins doing up the buttons, although just matching each button to its individual hole, honing in on them with his clumsy fingers, manipulating them appropriately – opening and pushing – seems almost beyond him.

'I've been ... I've been running – training,' he mutters.

'In jeans and a good shirt?'

Sheila's consternated.

'Uh ... No ... Yeah ... I ... I must've nodded off on the sofa. Then I didn't want to wake you by barging into the bedroom.'

'Oh.'

Sheila nods (a 'well that's obviously just stupid' kind of a nod).

'So why'd you decide to take your phone?' she idly follows up.

'Uh ...' Gene's stumped. 'I don't honestly remember,' he answers, flatly.

'I saw you through the window, leaning against the wall, having this long, intense conversation ...' Sheila glances up at the church roof as she speaks. 'D'you think it might rain later?'

'It wasn't especially long.' Gene scowls. 'A minute? Two minutes at most.'

'Well why didn't you just come inside?' she demands, her eyes still following the roof-line.

'I was catching my breath.' He shrugs.

'So who were you talking to?'

Sheila focuses in on his face again.

'Nobody.' Gene's jumpy. 'I mean nobody important. Just Jen. She rang from the golf club. She's over there with Ransom and some kid she picked up at the hotel ...'

'Jen again?' Sheila grimaces.

'I know,' Gene acknowledges. 'It's insane.'

'She has the hugest crush on you,' Sheila sighs, world-weary.

'*Jen?*' Gene almost laughs out loud at the notion. 'No. Not Jen
– she's like that with everyone.'
'It's like she feels she has some special claim on your time,'
Sheila muses.
'I think she sees me as a father-figure' – Gene's eager to turn
back the tide of Sheila's rising paranoia – 'or a trusty, older
brother.'
  'Are you having an affair with her?'
Sheila asks this in the sweetest of tones, almost
sympathetically.
'What?!' Gene's astonished.
'Are you having an affair with Jen?' Sheila cheerfully repeats
(although not quite so sympathetic the second time around).
  'D'you *think* I'm having an affair with Jen?'
Gene looks disgusted. He *is* disgusted. He's outraged (and the
sense of his own rank hypocrisy only serves to exacerbate it).
Sheila squints up at him. 'Nope. Not really,' she eventually
decides, 'although I guess I wouldn't have asked if I didn't
have my doubts.'
  '*Jen?!*' Gene almost bursts out laughing again. 'She's still in
school – a kid. How could you possibly think ...?'
'An atmosphere.' Sheila shrugs. 'An instinct. Call it female
intuition. And she's so obviously infatuated ...'
'That's just ridiculous!' Gene mutters, embarrassed.
'Don't pretend you haven't noticed,' Sheila snorts, wryly.
  'It's not just me,' Gene insists, 'she's like that with
everyone. She has this ... this hyperactive personality – this
crazy energy. She's a born flirt. In fact the more she flirts the
clearer it becomes that she's just taking the piss.'
  'Ha!' Sheila laughs.
'What's so funny?' Gene's offended.
'Your total naivety about women.' Sheila shakes her head.
'You're an emotional caveman!' she teases, slapping his arm,
delighted. 'It's actually quite hilarious.'

Gene scowls, wounded. 'You almost make me wish I *was* having an affair with her,' he mutters, 'to prove that I'm not just some insensitive lunk.'

'*Hmmn*. Acting against character,' Sheila smirks, 'not a recommended course. Could prove a little dangerous.'

'And if I had been?' he wonders, still more piqued (principally at himself). 'Then what?'

'Good heavens,' she snorts, suddenly finding the whole discussion a source of unbridled merriment, 'I'd be crushed! My whole world would explode into a million tiny pieces! I'd be torn apart! I'd be devastated!'

She's joking, but not entirely.

'But then I'd pick myself up,' she continues, somewhat more thoughtfully, 'shake myself down, dust myself off, and be free to reinvent myself all over again, from scratch.'

As Gene struggles to process the wider implications of this statement, Sheila leans forward and plucks something from his ear. It's a tiny blade of grass. She plucks another from his fringe, then a third from his sideburn. She holds them out to him on her palm, quizzically. He focuses in on them, his throat constricting, his mind temporarily overwhelmed by the sense-memory of the pungent smell of a compost heap; that heady, green dampness; that clammy moistness; that rich, mulchy steaminess.

He suddenly finds himself supine – lying flat on his back – a careless Puck – cushioned – buoyed-up – by a billion tiny, green blades, and he is kissing Valentine – loose, wet kisses, dog kisses. Their faces are covered in grass cuttings, their tongues, their lips. They are play-fighting in a messy, grassy blancmange. She is grabbing handfuls and pummelling him with them, laughing. She is spreading them over his chest. Her hands are green – her obliging thighs, the delirious fissure between her breasts – made tactile with the stickiness of sweat and cum.

He feels the energy of that grass – its pungent vitality – seeping into his skin. He feels a kaleidoscope of verdant emotions: innocence, freshness, newness, sourness, jealousy, immaturity, virility. He embraces everything green – everything it represents – all in one go; bolts it back, swallows it like a tequila shot, devours it like an oyster. He places his hand behind her neck and pulls her throat to his lips. He sucks, he licks. He knows that her blood, if she should bleed, would be flavoured with spearmint.

Down below he feels her green hands hard at work. Those careful, competent, horticultural fingers are finding his hardening cock, manipulating it, squeezing it, angling it, and then planting it, greedily, deep back inside of her.

'Oh bloody hell!' he exclaims, returning to himself, with a shudder.

'What?'

Sheila's nonplussed.

'Sorry?' he blinks, his cheeks reddening.

'Oh bloody hell!' Sheila mimics.

'I ... I ... I think I might've lost my keys.'

Gene starts slapping at his pockets. He quickly locates them. 'Panic over!' he announces, holding them up, victorious, and then striding, decisively, towards the house. Sheila follows him, frowning. He keeps one step ahead of her until they're through the door.

'Jen said you'd been in contact with Ransom,' he says, trying his best to sound unflustered, directing his words up into the stairwell. 'Early this morning. She said you suggested he get himself a tattoo.'

'Yeah ...' Sheila disappears into the kitchen. 'It came to me this morning, in a flash.'

Gene continues to gaze up into the stairwell.

'A moment of divine inspiration!' he mutters, his stomach churning.

'I guess you could call it that,' Sheila calls back.

Gene scratches his head (yet more grass cuttings).

'Although turns out he's terrified of needles,' she adds.

He hears her clearing cups and plates from the kitchen table.

'Are you still there?' she calls through, after thirty or so seconds.

'Yes.'

He feels glued to the spot.

'I thought you might have a private word with him about it, later,' she tentatively suggests, 'see if you can persuade him.'

'I wasn't really planning on going back,' Gene confesses.

Sheila pops her head into the hallway. 'But I thought you'd made up your mind to help him out?'

She looks disappointed.

'Seems his manager wasn't too keen on the idea.' Gene shrugs.

'Lucky for you he just sacked her.' Sheila grins. 'Didn't Jen mention it earlier?'

'How'd you find out about that?'

Gene neatly sidesteps the question.

'Online. Anyway, it's Ransom's call, surely?'

'Uh. Yeah.' Gene grimaces. 'I dunno. I suppose so.'

'Then what's the problem?' Sheila demands.

Gene walks past her and into the kitchen. He goes to the sink and pours himself a glass of water.

'Then what's the problem?'

Sheila follows him. Gene takes several, large mouthfuls from the glass as she stands behind him, waiting.

'The whole place just felt …' He places the glass down on to the work surface. 'I dunno. Everything was just so …'

'What?'

Sheila sounds impatient. She glances at her watch.

'Expensive. Luxurious. I mean the way people *live* in those places …' Gene shakes his head, appalled. 'The way they behave. The casual extravagance. The waste. The sense of entitlement ...'

'It's a *golf* club, you big idiot!' Sheila snorts.

'It felt uncomfortable ...' Gene persists. 'Stupidly decadent. The plush upholstery, the over-attentive service, the raked gravel, the landscaped gardens ... I suppose I just don't feel especially at ease in that kind of an environment.'

Sheila is silent for a minute, then, 'Decadent?'

Gene says nothing.

'Decadent? *Seriously?!*'

Gene picks up the glass again.

'Maybe you were right about Ransom,' he forges on, determinedly, 'I mean all the bad publicity and the endless bullshit and the dressing up ...'

'Of course I was right about Ransom!' Sheila exclaims.

'Then there's the situation with the Tuckers,' Gene continues. 'It's combustible. The girl's plainly unstable. The brother's a loose cannon. I'm just not in any hurry to get more involved in all of that.'

Sheila pulls out a chair and sits down.

'The girl has an incredible talent,' she says, her brown eyes glowing with an almost evangelical zeal. 'I mean she *really* has an incredible talent. I went to her website this morning – just thought I'd have a quick look around out of idle interest – and I was absolutely blown away. I was just *completely* overwhelmed. It's conceptual dynamite, Gene. A fraction sloppy and incoherent as things stand – in need of a little tidying up – but the basic building-blocks are all in place.'

Gene says nothing, just stares at her, appalled.

'I don't think she has the slightest clue how universal some of her ideas actually are,' Sheila runs on, 'how well they'd travel into the realm of High Art. It's incredibly exciting. I mean it's all *there*. Just needs to be re-jigged a little. Which is where I come in, obviously.'

Gene slowly places down his water glass with an almost inordinate level of care.

'I dashed her off an email. She got back to me within the hour. Then I sent one to Pammy Sullivan ...'

Gene turns to face the window. He suddenly feels overwhelmed by the urge to burst out laughing – or burst into tears – or both.

'Pammy's that girl from college I co-founded the magazine with,' Sheila explains. 'Remember? She runs this huge gallery space in Spitalfields. She was on the Turner Prize panel a couple of years back.'

Sheila quickly inspects her watch again.

'I sent her a little teaser. Didn't give too much away. It's just a question of organizing things – you know: presenting them coherently. And on a purely psychological level – in terms of her agoraphobia and other emotional issues – if we can somehow connive to get Ransom on board it'll bring in the added bonus of a whole extra element of healing ...'

'You didn't mention Ransom in the email?'

Gene turns back to face her, horrified.

'Good heavens, no! That's something we'll need to discuss face-to-face.'

She stands up and goes to fetch her bag.

'I'm heading over there now as a matter of fact.'

Gene turns towards the window again. He feels physically sick.

'D'you mind if I take the Megane?'

Gene doesn't answer. His mind is reeling.

'D'you mind if I take the Megane?'

She comes up close behind him and gently slides her hand around his waist.

He stiffens, imperceptibly, as she rests the side of her cheek against his shoulder, then quickly withdraws again with a snort.

'Don't mind me for saying this,' she mutters, all cruelly apologetic, 'but you're in desperate need of a shower, my love.'

8

Valentine draws a deep breath, steadies herself and yanks open the door to find a slight, strong-faced, brown-eyed woman standing there, damp from the rain and clutching at her hair.

'I don't quite know what's happened,' the woman exclaims, evidently perplexed, 'but on my way over here my fringe just seemed to ... to disappear ...'

'Pardon?'

Valentine focuses in on the woman's fringe, confused and slightly alarmed.

'Sorry – hi, I'm Sheila.' The woman smiles – her nut-brown eyes shining – holding out her hand and grasping Valentine's fingers, warmly.

'It's certainly very short ...' Valentine acknowledges, disarmed, awkward, and almost apologetic, as she inspects the tiny, frizzy tuft which juts – like a cruel bowl-cut or a monk's tonsure – from the top of Sheila's forehead.

'The mystery of the disappearing fringe!' Sheila rolls her eyes, self-deprecatingly.

'Where d'you think it's got to?' Valentine wonders, laughing – somewhat nervously – while resting her fingers at her nape (which blotches redder by the second).

'I'm not entirely sure ...' Sheila shrugs. 'I parked down at the bottom of the road ...' She runs through all her recent movements, in forensic detail, 'Then I got drenched in a sudden downpour – no bloody umbrella! Typical! – and once it was over I caught a brief glimpse of my reflection in the side-mirror of a car, and the fringe ... *Poof!*

She makes an extravagant, 'hey presto'-style movement with her hands.

Valentine beckons her inside, nodding distractedly.

'What an abysmal first impression!' Sheila chuckles, striding past her, and then, 'Oh I love this!' She gestures around her, enthused. 'The original fixtures all still *in situ*. The tiles, the glass in the door ...'

She points to the aspidistra.

'Gene's grandmother always kept an aspidistra in the hallway. They're so wonderfully evocative of that whole post-war era.'

Valentine walks on ahead of her (evidently somewhat overwhelmed by this first mention of Gene, by name) and shows her into the sitting room where a small child sits playing with an old doll on the rugs.

'So who do we have here?' Sheila demands, striding over. The child gazes up at her, shyly.

'This is Nessa, my niece,' Valentine awkwardly performs the introductions, 'and I'm Valentine, obviously.'

She bites her lip, her cheeks flushing.

Sheila leans down and grasps Nessa's hand.

'How d'you do? My name is Sheila ...' She smiles, mischievously. 'You may have noticed that I've lost my fringe. It's completely disappeared. Would you like to help me search for it?'

Nessa nods, gingerly.

'Good! Well let's start off with the easy places ... uh ...' Sheila lifts up the doll's dress. 'Not under there ...' She peers into one of Nessa's ears. 'And it's not in your ear ... *hmmn* ...' She gazes around her, speculatively. 'Shall we check under the sofa cushions?'

Nessa jumps to her feet and goes to look under the sofa cushions. Here she unearths a shiny, fifty pence piece and

holds it out to Sheila in the palm of her hand with a delighted
squeak.

'Fifty pence!' Sheila exclaims (as Valentine quickly trots over
to relieve her of it). 'What a find!'

As she speaks Sheila spots her reflection in one of the small
collection of brass-eyed mirrors.

'Oh bloody hell!'

She inspects herself in it, chuckling forlornly. 'This'll
frighten the living daylights out of all the poor old dears at
Evensong!' She takes a tiny step closer. 'What on earth have I
done to myself? I only snipped off a couple of inches.'

'It's probably just the rain and the muggy heat,' Valentine
hypothesizes, a small line of moisture glowing on her upper
lip, 'and maybe a touch of natural curl.'

'Good theory!' Sheila applauds this hypothesis. 'But enough
about my stupid hair.' She turns, decisively, from the mirror.
'I'm here to talk about you and your amazing work, Valentine.
It's completely astonishing. So beautiful. So gritty. So *odd*.
I've never seen anything like it before – not ever. In fact I've
been on this ridiculous high all morning since I first visited
your website ...'

As Sheila enthusiastically holds forth, Valentine finds it
virtually impossible to maintain any kind of eye contact. She
feels sick. Her shoulders and arms ache with repressed
tension. Her hands are clenched. She initially struggles to take
Sheila's compliments at anything approaching face value, and
then – the horror! – when she finally realizes that Sheila *is* in
fact being sincere, feels an alarming combination of panic and
self-loathing. As a direct consequence of this, instead of
responding verbally (a polite denial, a gracious 'thank you',
even just a small, modest shrug) she immediately seeks refuge
in the ongoing drama of Sheila's catastrophic fringe (gazing at
it while she speaks, analysing it, running through all the
feasible options in her head).

'The work itself is exquisite – that goes without saying,' Sheila continues to enthuse. 'I mean that almost *medieval* level of attention to detail, all the strange, psycho-sexual connotations, the fascinating cultural implications, all those amazing, *amazing* nipples! And then the weird, Oriental angle! There are just so many *layers*, so much to feed the mind upon; such bounty – such abundance – such … such incredible *richness*, both in form *and* in content –' Sheila suddenly breaks off, panicked. 'You look upset – overwhelmed. Am I coming on too strong?'

'It's just …' Valentine gnaws at her lip. 'I could always try and even it out a bit. I took a hairdressing option at college.'

'Pardon?' Sheila's initially confused. 'Sorry?' then nonplussed. 'Oh – you're still worrying about my *hair*?!' She puts a wary hand to her head again. 'But it's nothing!' she insists. 'Don't give it a second thought. It was only the initial shock. It doesn't matter in the slightest. I'll just …'

'I always do my own,' Valentine runs on, 'and my mum's and Nessa's. I'm perfectly handy with a pair of scissors.'

'Is it really all that bad?' Sheila turns back to the mirror again, embarrassed.

'No!' Valentine insists. 'It's absolutely fine. I just thought … I mean if you've got a spare ten minutes I could easily …'

Sheila continues to inspect herself.

'I suppose it *does* look rather dreadful,' she sighs, 'but the fringe is so short now I can't really see how …'

Valentine quickly moves to her side. 'It's a radical solution, I know, but what if we just took it all off? I mean all the rest …'

She takes hold of the side sections of Sheila's hair and draws them away from her face.

'Do a Mia Farrow. You've got the perfect shaped face for a shorter cut. Good cheekbones. Strong jaw. If we just …'

'Take it *all* off?'

Sheila's eyes widen.

Valentine drops the hair and takes a hasty step back. 'I mean not if you're –'

'Why the hell not?' Sheila interrupts, with a grin.

'It's a big decision.' Valentine's cheeks redden again.

'Blow it!' Sheila chuckles. 'Let's live dangerously. It's only *hair*. Let's take it all off! What do I care?!'

'Maybe think about it for a while,' Valentine cautions (alarmed by how readily Sheila is now embracing the idea). 'I could put the kettle on ...'

'Nope. The decision's made.' Sheila won't be gainsaid. 'Go grab your scissors. Let's do this! It'll be fun!'

She pauses. 'I mean so long as it isn't too much trouble ...'

'Not at all!'

Valentine takes hold of Sheila's hair again. 'We'll need to be quite brutal. I may have to get Dad's clippers out to add some definition around the nape and the ear ...'

'It'll always grow.' Sheila shrugs, gung-ho.

'Okay.' Valentine drops the hair, her mind racing. 'Okay ...' she repeats, blankly. 'Good. Right. Well you'd better follow me through to the kitchen, then.'

She grabs Nessa's hand and they walk down the hallway together, past the studio and into the rear section of the house.

The kitchen is a cheerful, well-lit room with a wooden, enamel-topped kitchen table standing square in the middle of a worn but period-appropriate linoleum floor.

'Wow!' Sheila appraises the beige and green cabinets, impressed. 'I've not laid eyes on anything like these in a while. What are they? Painted tin or painted enamel?'

'Uh ... I'm not really sure – enamel, I should imagine.'

Valentine is lifting a cat off a red rocking chair and then placing Nessa on to it, with her doll for company and a picture book. Nessa hunkers down, obligingly.

Sheila touches the curtains, wistfully (they're in an old, white cotton, printed with little red apples). 'Isn't it funny how something as insignificant as a piece of old curtain material can call back so many memories? Be so redolent of another period?'

'Dad loved this kitchen,' Valentine murmurs, opening a drawer in a slightly battered red and white dresser in search of her dad's clippers. 'Poor Mum wasn't quite so taken with it, though.'

'Is your mum at home today?' Sheila wonders.

'You just missed her.' Valentine locates the clippers and places them on the table. 'She's popped into town with one of her old friends from … from before …' Valentine falters, unsure how much Sheila knows of her personal history.

'Before the accident.' Sheila nods, unabashed.

'Yeah. A couple of her old pals still help out sometimes. Take her on day trips and stuff. They're very good with her – very patient.'

Valentine unwinds the black, electric cord from around the body of the clippers and then pushes the plug into a socket located low in the wall. She straightens up. 'We'll need to wet your hair before the cut. I'll grab a couple of spare towels from the airing cupboard.'

She disappears for a brief interlude.

Sheila, meanwhile, has a fond chuckle at the red and white bread box and matching sugar, salt, tea and coffee canisters. She runs her fingers over the small, glass knobs on the cabinets then inspects the wide collection of period enamelware on the rack above the dresser.

'You tend to forget how incredibly satisfying really good design can be,' she volunteers as Valentine returns to the room clutching a couple of clean towels, 'how enriching to the soul it is just being surrounded by lovely things – seeing them and using them, *touching* them …'

'Mum and Noel think it's like living in a museum' – Valentine places the towels on to the draining-board and plugs up the sink – 'but I've always loved it.' She pauses, smiling dreamily. 'I guess it's a hangover from my dad.' She shrugs, the smile fading. 'We definitely had our issues, but a passion for forties design was one of the few things we really shared. We'd spend half our lives at loggerheads and the other half hunting for special pieces together at car-booters and jumble sales.'

'That's good, though, surely?' Sheila avers. 'Healthy.'

'I suppose so,' Valentine muses, turning on the taps, 'although sometimes I feel kind of smothered by them – you know, all these ... these *things* – by the need to protect them, preserve them, against Mum and Nessa and Noel. Then I feel guilty, like I'm being really selfish.'

'Must be quite confusing,' Sheila sympathizes.

Valentine gazes at Sheila, frowning. 'Yeah ...' She nods, tucking some hair behind her ear and then lightly touching the same hand to her throat (where the blotching has now faded a little). 'They just don't seem to understand that it's the only positive way I have of engaging with Dad now he's gone. There's so much other stuff left over, so much bad stuff, all these feelings of ... well ... I dunno ...' she trails off.

'Abandonment,' Sheila contributes.

'I can hardly blame him for dying of a heart attack!' Valentine grins, lopsidedly. 'It's weird, though,' she continues, frowning, suddenly thoughtful, 'because I was always the one who argued with him – about pretty much anything and everything – but now it's like I've taken over the dad role. I'm constantly getting it in the neck for trying to preserve ... for being the only real grown-up ...' She scowls. 'It's like I hate him and I've *become* him – the controlling one, the bully. I dunno. It's really, really strange.'

'There's always the tattooing,' Sheila volunteers, 'that's his real legacy to you, surely?'

'Yeah' – Valentine nods – 'although I was hardly the world's most enthusiastic apprentice. And he always really hated my experimental work.'

'You'd be appalled if you saw the state of the rectory.'
Sheila shakes her head, forlornly. 'It's just a horrible mess – a
celebration of all the worst kinds of design. An awful mish-
mash of the seventies and the eighties. Full of old, inherited
pieces nobody else'd give house-room to … All these heavy,
dark sideboards and grim, collapsing bookshelves.'

Valentine beckons her over to the kitchen sink which has
slowly filled up with warm water, then drapes one of the
towels around her shoulders. 'Hold this in place to protect
your clothes.'

She grabs an apron from a peg on the back of the door and
covers her dress with it, tying it into a neat bow at the back.

'It's life's subtle, little niceties – these fine, almost *honest*
aesthetic details …' – Sheila sweeps out her arm, majestically
– 'which are so easy to lose touch with when you're drawn to
a so-called "higher calling".'

She breaks off, slightly embarrassed. 'I know it sounds
pretentious, but it's so easy to become brutalized by the
all-consuming make-do-and-mend world of the C of E …'
She scowls. 'It's recently started to dawn on me what a great
pity it is – what a waste, how *dangerous* it is, even – to close
down that side of yourself. To turn away from external beauty
as a kind of necessary function of self-realization. It shouldn't
ever need to be a question of either/or.'

'Although maybe it's quite nice – quite refreshing – to just
ditch all the trivial stuff,' Valentine muses, her mind turning
to Milah, 'and focus solely on the renunciation part.'

Sheila bends forward over the sink.
'But *is* it just trivial?' she argues. 'Don't people create art,
celebrate beauty – in whatever medium: words, sounds,
clothes or images – as a way of describing the indescribable, a
way of engaging with a higher realm, a spiritual realm, even?
There are some paintings – some poems – which seem to
speak directly to the soul.'

'Yeah. Maybe ...' Valentine shrugs. She grabs a small, cream enamel jug and commences pouring water over Sheila's hair, careful to protect her face while she does so.

'How about you, then?' Sheila persists. 'Why do you create art?'

'One of my biggest inspirations has always been Louise Bourgeois,' Valentine automatically harks back to her conversation with Gene from the previous day.

'I love her!' Sheila exclaims, lifting her head and clanking it into the enamel jug in her excitement. 'I did a phone interview with her in the eighties for the magazine. She was just ... just so incredibly awe-inspiring! So articulate! So mischievous! And believe it or not I actually *sensed* there might've been an influence – very subtle, totally implicit. I think that's partly what I was responding to so positively this morning.'

'Well you'll probably already know that Bourgeois always said she created art "to survive",' Valentine doggedly continues. 'That's kind of how I feel about it. When I pick up the tattoo gun or I draw a perfect eyebrow on to my face with an exquisitely sharp kohl pencil, I sort of feel my focus shift. I feel a pressure lift. I'm released from the need to think about all this other stuff, this bad stuff, the negative thoughts, the anxieties ...'

'Art's like a kind of prayer,' Sheila suggests.

'Yeah.' Valentine's quizzical. 'I never really thought about it that way before ... I guess I tend to forget my emotions when I'm doing a tattoo,' she struggles to explain. 'I stop asking questions. I stop panicking. I'm so focused, so intent.'

'*Exactly* like a prayer, then.' Sheila grins, vindicated.

'Although art's all about ego' – Valentine frowns – 'and isn't prayer meant to be the polar opposite of that?'

'It's just a question of intent,' Sheila argues, 'if the art expresses something sublime then how can it help expressing God?'

'Yeah ...' Valentine doesn't sound entirely convinced.

'Was your dad much of an artist?' Sheila wonders (tactfully moving to less esoteric ground). 'Did he have a good reputation in the world of tattooing?'

'He was always very traditional – very old-fashioned. Hated the ultra-realist stuff.'

Valentine chuckles to herself, wryly. 'It's actually quite scary to think that I'm continuing his legacy at some level … that I'm the dutiful daughter carefully following in his footsteps; you know, just by maintaining the house, the way I dress, the tattooing. I always thought I was so defiant, such a rebel …'

She trails off, anxiously.

'You can enjoy things in common with a person without needing to identify with them completely,' Sheila opines.

'I was always so embarrassed by him, though,' Valentine confesses, 'the things he did and said in public – the political stuff.'

'But when everything's said and done, he was still your dad.'

Sheila baldly states the obvious.

'I'm marked for life!' Valentine concedes, almost joking, but not entirely.

She applies a small dab of shampoo to Sheila's hair and gently rubs it in, then performs a brief head massage with her fingertips. The skin on Sheila's arms forms into appreciative goose-bumps.

'That's lovely,' she sighs. Valentine's fingers instantly stiffen.

'So you have a formal background in art?' she asks, quickly picking up the jug and starting to rinse.

'Nope.' Sheila shakes her head (miraculously avoiding getting water in her eyes). 'I studied English at Oxford – did a PhD – but in my free time I helped set up this radical arts magazine called *OnTheRag*. It caused quite a stir at the time – was considered ground-breaking in terms of graphics and content. We had a strong art agenda. A lot of the people I brought through ended up becoming big figures in the international art establishment.'

'That woman you mentioned in your email?' Valentine suggests.

'Exactly. I've been off the radar for quite a few years now, but I like to think I still have pretty good instincts.'

Valentine finishes rinsing, then wrings the excess water from Sheila's hair and uses the spare towel from the draining-board to rub it dry.

'Okay' – she forms the towel into a little turban – 'I think we're pretty much done here.'

Sheila straightens up, carefully holding the turban in place with her hand, then follows Valentine to a nearby chair and sits down on it.

'So you …' – Valentine opens the dresser to find a comb and some scissors – 'you met your husband at university?' She remains turned away from Sheila as she asks this question, her voice purposely casual.

'Heavens, no!' Sheila snorts. 'Gene's not remotely academic!'

She pauses, guiltily. 'Although that's through no fault of his own, obviously,' she quickly modifies, 'his education was so heavily disrupted as a kid by cancer therapy.'

'So how many times …?' Valentine locates the comb and scissors in their special, leather pouch.

'Seven, all told. Then a major car accident a few years back which killed his sister, severely injured his niece and shattered his leg.'

Valentine's shocked. She immediately recalls the crazy-paving of scars on Gene's belly and his chest. Her skin tingles as she visualizes that body so beautiful and strong and lean, yet so clumsily sewn together – carelessly hacked together, like a badly made rag doll – with reams of wild, shiny white stitching. Her pupils expand. Her nostrils flare. Her throat contracts.

'We actually met while my dad was having minor surgery on his gall bladder,' Sheila explains, oblivious. 'I grew up in Suffolk, but my parents moved to Luton when I was nineteen. Dad had a job in air-traffic control. I was in the middle of a divorce at the time, stuck at home with Stan …'

'Stan?' Valentine echoes, hoarsely.

'My son. Gene's stepson.'

Valentine nods.

'Anyhow,' Sheila continues, 'I met a few people while visiting Dad on the ward – some of the local volunteers. They persuaded me into doing a couple of shifts on the hospital radio station. There was a Christian-led group in charge of the rota. Gene was constantly in and out of the place having bouts of chemo. His cancer had been declared terminal at that stage, but he was such a positive person, really inspirational.'

'You were married previously?' Valentine double-checks the bow on her apron, places the open pouch on to the table, then moves to the back of Sheila and carefully unwinds her turban.

'Yeah. I'd got hitched to this Polish guy at college.' Sheila grimaces. 'I guess you could call it a marriage of convenience. He was the brother of a dear friend of mine who needed to secure residency in the UK. We'd liked each other from the off … It was kind of calculated and completely un-calculated at the same time …'

'Spontaneous,' Valentine interjects, fluffing out her wet hair and then grabbing the comb.

'Exactly.' Sheila nods. 'He'd run this Polish film cooperative – pre the '89 revolution. It was all very "underground" and exciting as I recall. Either way' – she shrugs, as Valentine commences combing – 'it was a huge mistake. I fell pregnant with Stanislav and he ran a mile. I dropped out of college, had this huge crisis of confidence …'

'That's pretty difficult to imagine!' Valentine grins, almost disbelieving.

'You don't know the half of it!' Sheila retorts. 'I'd always been very ambitious, very centred, very driven – wanted to grab the world by its lapels and really shake it up. Then suddenly all that certainty, all that focus seemed to fall away from me.'

'But you kept the baby,' Valentine observes (oddly protective of the student Sheila).

'Yeah. I was into my thirteenth week when I found out about it – pretty late. I stayed at college until the end of my third trimester then moved back home for the birth. My mother was very supportive. She's one of those really lovely, wholesome, nurturing types. She offered to take care of Stan, full-time, when I returned to university. I was eager to finish my education – attended for one term, enjoyed the holidays; everything seemed hunky-dory – and then on the train journey back up to Oxford after the Easter break I had a kind of ... well, I guess you'd call it an epiphany.'

Valentine has combed out Sheila's hair and is now slowly walking around her, assessing the work to be done. She stops in front of her.

'An epiphany?' She reaches over and grabs the scissors from the pouch.

'Yeah. I mean it sounds so ridiculous when I describe it in actual words and sentences – it was more of a *feeling* than an event as such.'

'An epiphany,' Valentine repeats, savouring the four, sharp syllables on her tongue, and then: 'What kind of a feeling, exactly?'

'Well, I was sitting on the train' – Sheila adjusts the towel around her shoulders – 'it was fairly empty, not peak hour or anything, and I had my back to the engine. The countryside was flowing by backwards – I remember that very clearly for some reason. I'd been enjoying a book. It was part of the reading list for a course I was attending on the Colonial Novel: *An Area of Darkness* by V.S. Naipaul?'

Valentine just shrugs, apologetically.

'I'd reached this section – about seventy-odd pages in – when Naipaul spends almost an entire chapter describing the Indian attitude to defecation. It was kind of funny and disgusting. I was eating an apple. I put the book down on to the seat beside me and just sat there for a moment trying to dislodge a piece of apple skin from between my teeth with my tongue.

'I sort of de-focused. Then the door at the far end of the carriage opened and a woman – a British Rail employee – came trundling into the compartment with a drinks trolley. The trolley made that loud, jiggling-clinking-clanking sound as she shoved it along. She pushed it down the middle of the carriage towards me. I was still holding my half-eaten apple. And as she approached I just ...' Sheila's voice breaks slightly. 'I *saw* God. I just *saw* God – moving towards me in a kind of heatwave with the woman and the drinks trolley ...'

'Crazy!' Valentine's amused and startled.

'I know. Completely weird. Completely random and nonsensical. It was just this ... this overwhelming sensation. Like the world was suddenly turned inside out. The hairs on my arms stood on end. I just *felt* God inhabiting the train, filling the train, filling me. I was *touched* by God. It was completely out of the blue. Came from totally left field' – she shrugs (almost regretfully) – 'and that was that. My old life was over.'

'You were born again.'

'Yes.'

Valentine moves to the back of Sheila and pulls her hair into a ponytail with her hand.

'Speak now or forever hold your peace!' she intones, mock-warningly.

'My peace is held,' Sheila maintains with comic sobriety.

Valentine cuts the hair above her fist then flashes Sheila the disembodied ponytail.

'Toodle-oo!' Sheila waves, grinning, as Valentine shows it to Nessa (who strokes it, with a coo) then places it into a nearby pedal bin.

'You've got loads of cats,' Sheila idly volunteers (as four saunter into the kitchen in quick succession).

'Eight. Mum used to breed them. Now she hates them.'

'I quite like cats,' Sheila muses.

'God turning up with the drinks trolley!' Valentine chuckles, returning, with renewed vigour, to the task at hand. 'Who'd've thunk it?'

'Depressingly prosaic,' Sheila snorts, 'I'm hardly giving St Paul much of a run for his money.'

Valentine chuckles and commences the cut, proper. Sheila closes her eyes and relaxes for a while as Valentine snips and fluffs and fusses.

'Is Gene very religious?' Valentine suddenly asks.

'*Gene?!* Heavens, no!' Sheila exclaims. 'Not remotely! Although ...' She pauses for a second. 'Credit where credit's due – it was basically down to Gene that I became a vicar in the first place.'

'Really?' Valentine's intrigued.

'Yup. It was being around Gene, experiencing his patience and his quiet optimism and his ... well, his *goodness* in the face of such terrible adversity that finally developed what'd been a pretty random, religious experience into something way more coherent.'

'But if Gene isn't religious himself' – Valentine's confused – 'then how can you –'

'I struck a kind of ... well, I suppose you'd call it a *deal* with God,' Sheila hastily interrupts. 'I hadn't known Gene very long at that stage, but late one night – after we'd been chatting for hours over mugs of watery drinking chocolate in the hospital cafeteria – I went home, knelt down at the foot of my bed and said to God: "If you're powerful enough to turn me inside out like this – and for no apparent reason – then you're powerful enough to heal that lovely, good, patient man at the hospital.""'

Valentine stops the cut for a moment, surprised.

'I mean I was very green back then, very silly, very pushy, slightly *scared*, even,' Sheila confesses, 'and – in all truthfulness – I think I was secretly hoping to be disappointed at some level, looking for a way out.'

Sheila blows an especially ticklish chunk of cut hair from the end of her nose. Valentine recommences the cut, frowning.

'It was also a subtle way of consciously engaging with the feelings I'd started to develop for Gene,' Sheila expands, 'feelings which'd gradually evolved – over a series of days and weeks and months – from pity to compassion to love. And of course there was an element of pragmatism to the whole thing, too,' she confesses, wryly. 'I just sensed – *knew* – right up front, that Gene was to be a vital part of my journey; a necessary part, an essential part. I honestly don't think I would've had the mental and emotional strength to go on and pursue a career in the Church without Gene's example – his constant guidance and good counsel and support.'

'You think your prayer cured Gene?' Valentine demands, almost indignant.

Sheila winces. '*A man's steps are of the Lord*,' she promptly quotes – almost ironically, '*How then can a man understand his own way?*'

'But you *do* think that you saved him?' Valentine persists. 'That he owes his life to you?'

'Nope. I think he owes his life to God. I think God saved him. I was just a lucky filter. An adjunct.'

'But how does it … how does it all *work*, exactly?' Valentine wonders, still inexplicably irritated. 'I mean if Gene isn't religious. If you've never actually shared the same, core beliefs? Doesn't it make him feel almost …'

She's going to say 'used', but then stops herself at the last moment.

'How does it work?' Sheila echoes, closing her eyes and smiling, blithely. 'How does it work? With endless amounts of compromise, of course! And self-denial. And frustration. And confusion. And bitter recrimination. And constant resentment. And utter boredom ...' She pauses, briefly, to draw breath. 'And bouts of incandescent rage,' she continues, opening her eyes again, 'gales of hysterical laughter. Perhaps even the *tiniest* sprinkling of Divine Providence ...' She glances up at Valentine, shrugging, resignedly. 'Pretty much like any marriage, I suppose.'

'Thank God you're finally here!' Toby yanks open the Hummer's door, his face flushed, his glasses slightly awry, visibly stressed. 'Ransom's gone to ground. There's a photographer halfway through a shoot, a publicist having a meltdown and a weirdly argumentative, freelance beautician in war-paint and a skin-tight, white jumpsuit ...'

Gene opens his mouth to answer. He's barely had a chance to unfasten his seat belt.

'Oh, and Esther's had the baby,' Toby runs on, oblivious, 'a girl – ten pounds, green eyes – but she haemorrhaged during the delivery and has this ridiculously rare blood type ...'

'AB negative?' Gene jerks to attention (both hands instinctively returning to the wheel).

'Uh. No ... Yeah ... I'm not sure ...' Toby blinks. 'She'll be fine. They texted earlier to say she's stable.'

Gene reaches for his phone and starts scanning through his contact details. 'I'm actually O negative,' he confides, 'which means my blood is compatible for transfusion to all other blood types.'

'Promiscuous blood, eh?' Toby grins, intrigued.

'I have a close relationship with the local blood donor group,' Gene murmurs, somewhat stiffly. 'You start to feel a certain responsibility ...'

'Stonking wheels, by the way.' Toby takes an appreciative step back, straightens his glasses and inspects the jeep.
'Yeah. I've got it on a kind of permanent loan.' Gene finds the number he's searching for and presses 'dial'. 'It belonged to my son's dad – my wife's ex. He bought it to promote his war games shop.'

'Esther's called the new baby Prudence – Prue ...' Toby flattens his palms against his cheeks, frowning. 'That was my grandmother's name. She died last year ...' His frown deepens. 'My face feels really hot. D'you think I might've contracted something on the ward?'

'You said Ransom'd gone to ground?'
(Gene niftily changes the subject.)
'He's locked in a toilet cubicle,' Toby elucidates. 'Been in there almost an hour, now. He's refusing to speak to anyone but you.'
'Me?' Gene starts (as his call is finally connected).

'Yeah. Every time I try and whisper something encouraging through the door he activates the flush to drown me out.' Toby pauses, embarrassed. 'I'm just the stupid Joe Bloggs who manages his website,' he adds, 'I'm not really equipped to deal with this kind of stuff.'

'Hello? Lillian?' Gene promptly leaves a message for his blood donation contact: 'It's Gene – hope you're well. Uh ... a little bird tells me there's been a sudden run on AB negative. It's only a couple of months since my last donation, but you've got my number if you need it. Give me a ring or text or whatever ... Thanks.'
He hangs up.

'Esther'd know how to handle it,' Toby mutters, kicking one of the front wheels, speculatively. 'That woman's a bloody marvel – has the patience of a saint.'

'Sounds like Esther has her hands pretty full right now …'
Gene pockets his phone and jumps down from the jeep. His
knee creaks as he lands.

'D'you hear he's given her the old heave-ho?' Toby asks,
indignant.

'Is it true?' Gene suppresses a wince as he slams the jeep's
door and then locks it.

'Yup. Although I doubt it'll stick. Never does. The more I
hang around them, the more I'm starting to see this as one of
the all-time great sporting romances …'
Toby's expression is one of inexplicable wistfulness as he
delivers this pronouncement.

'You reckon?' Gene doesn't appear entirely convinced as he
pockets his keys and they start off across the gravel together.

'They're like golf's Taylor and Burton,' Toby expands.

'Not the most functional of role models,' Gene avers.

'She has all the strategy, he has all the spunk.' Toby shrugs.
They walk on in silence for a while.

'Although if it actually comes down to taking sides,' Toby
mutters (with uncharacteristic militance as they stride into the
foyer), 'then I'm definitely batting for Esther. I'm on Esther's
team. Ransom might be a genius, but Esther's the glue that
holds his career together' – he scowls – 'and he's a bloody fool
if he thinks otherwise.'

'So what's the SP on today's drama?'
(Gene seamlessly shifts their conversational focus from the
general to the particular as they draw up outside the Men's.)

'Wouldn't have a clue,' Toby snorts. 'He was happy as Larry
one minute, then the next: Armageddon. Par for the course,
really …' – he winces – 'if you can forgive the chronically
cheesy golfing metaphor.'

Gene grants him immediate absolution (a kindly pat on the
shoulder) and leaves him standing a nervous guard at the
toilet entrance. Five seconds later, he is dutifully stationed
outside the pertinent cubicle –

'Hello? Ransom?'

(*Gentle knuckle-rap.*)

'It's Gene, here.'

No answer.

Gene peers around him, taking a brief moment of respite from the blaring sirens of anxiety sounding inside his head to enjoy the state-of-the-art porcelain and plumbing.

'This place is pristine,' he murmurs, awed, 'Italian marble. Foot pumps for the sinks – even the soap dispensers are like pieces of –'

The toilet door is thrown open. Ransom grabs Gene by the arm, yanks him into the cubicle, slams the door shut and then rapidly shoots the bolt again.

'Why no uniform?' he demands, giving him the once-over, with a scowl. His eyes are red-rimmed. His hands are shaking. His breath smells of cigarette smoke.

'Uh ...' Gene peers down at himself. 'I'm in khaki. The jacket was slightly constricting in the heat. The cap's in the back of the Hummer.'

'So have a little punt on who just turned up,' Ransom interrupts, flattening both palms against the cubicle wall, straightening his back and his arms, transferring his body-weight to his heels, relaxing his neck and dropping his head between his elbows (a latter-day James Dean but with male-pattern-balding issues). His voice sounds hoarse.

'Sorry?'

Gene tries (and rapidly fails) to re-establish his own, inviolable sense of personal space. A black baseball cap is hung on the peg behind the door. His shoulder nudges against it. There are four cigarette stubs floating in the bowl.

'Friggin' Jen!' Ransom's head pops back up. 'Jen's here! Skanky Jen! Done up like some kind of weird Albino Cherokee! Moonlighting as a beautician!'

'Jen?'

Gene tries to sound surprised and fails.

'I mean what *is* it with that girl?' Ransom drops his arms. 'What's the deal? Huh? Is she off her hinges? Has she some kind of fucked-up agenda? Is she a genius? A maniac?'

'I don't think she's –' Gene starts off.

'What's she *want*?' Ransom interrupts. 'You're closer to the kid than anybody ...'

'I'd hardly ...' Gene demurs.

'I mean she's plainly besotted with you.'

'Don't be ridiculous!' Gene's horrified.

'The way she follows you around making goo-goo eyes like some sad, little, blonde puppy ... *"Oh I love Gene! He's so brave! So wise! So emotionally friggin' intelligent!"*'

'Are we talking about the same Jen, here?' Gene snorts, amused.

'What does she *want*? Eh?' Ransom scowls, plainly bewildered. 'Is this some kind of a set-up? Is she being hired by the tabloids? Are the two of you in cahoots?'

He slowly starts working himself up into a lather. 'Is this whole thing some kind of sick joke being played out at my expense? *Huh?* Is friggin' *Esther* behind it? Or Jimmie Mack? Or that buck-toothed, big-eared retard, Micky Dwight?'

He rubs his forehead with his palm. 'Or is it one of the big boys? Portman Enterprises? The Omar Consortium? Lincoln friggin' Insurance? Has their fixer gone feral? Tandy? Tandy Lane? Has Tandy decided to start playing by her own, fucked-up rules again? Has Tandy started getting greedy? Eyes bigger than her friggin' belly?'

Ransom pauses, gazing deep into Gene's eyes, the colour draining from his face. 'Who *are* you? You look different – something's changed. What's changed? Did you even *have* cancer? Is your wife a priest? Why'd a priest want me to get a friggin' *tattoo*? It doesn't make any sense! That tiny, pink room ... The photo of the girl with her head between her ankles ... the Shredded Wheat ... Is it all just a lie? *Tell* me!' He grabs Gene by the shoulders. 'D'you even work at the

hotel? Was it just some elaborate stage set with you playing a barman and me playing myself, but not playing myself because I never really play myself because I'm always too busy playing Stuart Ransom playing the friggin' super-hero, playing golf, playing … Aw *fuck*, man!'
Ransom drops his hands.

'Did you have any breakfast yet?' Gene wonders.
Ransom gazes at him, blankly.
'Did you have any breakfast?' Gene repeats.
'What is this?' Ransom demands. 'Some kind of low-level psychological device to throw me off track?'

'I'm concerned about your blood-sugar levels.' Gene lowers his voice as he hears a third party entering the toilets and using the latrine. 'You seem very stressed out. The whites of your eyes are bright red.'
Pause.
'Have you eaten anything today, yet?'

Ransom flips over the toilet lid and sits down on it.
'I can never fully relax on these things when they stick out from the wall,' he grumbles. 'No proper base, no foundations, no *root.*'
'Hygienic though' – Gene rallies to the porcelain's defence – 'and from a purely practical perspective, really easy to keep clean.'

'A man needs something to press his heels against!' Ransom bleats. 'Is that too much to friggin' ask for nowadays?!'

'How about we go and get a muffin?' Gene whispers, placing a cautionary finger to his lips as the user of the urinal draws yet closer, washes his hands at a sink and then places them under the dryer. 'Or a sandwich? A glass of orange juice? You look exhausted.'

'*Exhausted?!*' Ransom bellows (much to Gene's evident disquiet – even though the dryer still gamely blows). 'You don't even know the *half* of it! I live out of a friggin' suitcase, Gino! My swing's gone to shit! My hands won't stop shaking!

I'm using a belly putter! A *belly* putter! That's like announcing to the world that you can't get a hard-on! A *belly* putter for Christ's sake! It's humiliating!'

Gene listens, intently, as footsteps echo across the tiles in the general direction of the exit.

'And on top of that, I'm friggin' broke!' Ransom whimpers (Gene is profoundly relieved – and grateful – to hear the door slam). 'I'm lonely! I'm permanently constipated! I never see my kid! I'm surrounded by haters! My dad's mouldering away in a care home! Bloody *Fleur* has rheumatoid friggin' arthritis! I'm up to here with it, Gino ...' He measures halfway up his forehead with a flattened hand. 'Up to friggin' *here* ...'

Ransom's voice suddenly breaks, he covers his eyes with his palms, rests his elbows on his knees and breaks down in tears.

'Fleur?' Gene's totally at sea.

'Fleur. *Fleur!*' the golfer snaps, glancing up (the tip of his nose playing host to a majestic string of snot). 'Stuart Ransom's *wife*, you friggin' *idiot!*'

'God, yes. Of course.'

Gene's suitably apologetic.

'It affects her joints – knees, elbows, hips, fingers ...' Ransom forms dramatic claws out of his own hands to illustrate. 'I mean it's pretty bad ...'

'But isn't it a condition they can medicate quite successfully?' Gene leans over to pluck a couple of tissues from the square, toilet-tissue dispenser on the wall and passes them across. 'People can live perfectly normal lives ...'

'Yeah. *Yeah.* I know that.' Ransom grabs the tissues, irritably. 'It's just that ever since she was diagnosed I haven't felt ... you know ...'

He blows his nose, noisily, then puts his head in his hands again, traumatized.

'Your feelings have changed?' Gene takes a shot in the dark.

'I can't bear to be around her.'

'Okay' – Gene nods – 'well that's a perfectly normal ... I mean it always takes a while to adjust ...'

'It *scares* me. It *disgusts* me. It's just this bloody great ...'

'Challenge,' Gene prompts.

'Downer,' Ransom corrects him.

'D'you still love her?' Gene cuts to the chase.

'Nope.'

Ransom's dead-eyed.

'Not at all?' Gene's surprised.

'Nope. She bores the fuck out of me.'

'Not even ...?'

'And on top of that I find her repulsive,' Ransom adds. 'She gained weight since the kid. She's a dim-wit. Thick as shit. The sound of her whining, American voice turns my blood to ice.'

'Oh.'

Gene pushes back his fringe. His forehead is peppered with tiny specks of perspiration.

'And she likes a drink,' Ransom continues, really getting into the swing of things. 'She's pure poison when she drinks. She's deadly friggin' nightshade when she drinks. An ugly, overweight, witch-fingered troll with a stupid voice and a filthy, friggin' attitude.'

Pause.

'White trash. Beautiful vagina, though – credit where credit's due. She got it tightened after the birth.'

Further pause.

'Could do with the same friggin' procedure on her fat friggin' *mouth* ...'

Further pause.

'I hate her.'

Further pause.

'I friggin' *hate* her.'

Gene grimaces. He is unsure what more he can helpfully contribute to the discussion at this stage.

'The kid's fine,' Ransom generously concedes. 'Cute.
I don't have a problem with the kid.'
'Have you considered –'
'Divorce?' Ransom butts in.
'Counselling?' Gene modifies. 'For the sake of ...'
   'That bitch will fleece me for every penny I've got,'
Ransom growls. 'Where's the incentive to do well – to win – if
that ignorant bitch is gonna fleece me for every penny
I make?'
Gene opens his mouth and then closes it again.
'Where's the psychological incentive? I mean every time I pick
up a club, the friggin' ... the friggin' *pressure* ...' Ransom
shakes his head, inarticulate with frustration.
   'Doesn't sound like much fun,' Gene admits.
'You know what it's like?' Ransom hisses. 'It's like getting a
daily friggin' enema – getting your back-end sluiced out – in
front of the general public.'
'No fun at all,' Gene concedes.
'It's like being violated – brain-fucked. It's like you're heading
off on a lovely, family picnic – everyone's all happy and
excited – but before you leave the house you catch a sudden,
sidelong glimpse of Dad, holed up in the bathroom, peeing
into the lemonade bottle.'
   A short silence follows as both men take a moment to
digest the weird implications of this stark, familial simile.
Then, 'So you sacked your manager ...'
'Esther. Yeah.' Ransom nods.
'D'you not think – under the circumstances – that might've
been a little bit ... well ... rash?'
   'Esther's lost the faith.' Ransom shrugs. 'I was just keeping
her on for old times' sake. And that's me to a T, Gino! That's
me all over: golf's Mr Nice. Golf's Mr Approachable. Golf's
Mr Total friggin' Push-over ...'
   'But wasn't she –'

'Feeding the papers information behind my back?' Ransom
interrupts. 'Yeah. Making me look ridiculous? Absolutely.
Diminishing my brand? Yup. One hundred friggin' per cent
she was.'

'Are you sure about that?' Gene's evidently not convinced.
'Because when we chatted last night she seemed very
protective of your –'

'Did she warn you off?' Ransom grins, delighted.

'I honestly believe she has your best interests at heart,' Gene
persists.

'Oh she can put on an impressive front all right,' Ransom
interrupts, with a snort, 'but underneath all that cack – below
the glossy exterior – lies a mangy, flea-bitten old Den Mother;
a lactating she-wolf defending her territory. I'm an asset to
Esther, remember, so she guards me very carefully. Keeps
people at a distance. Undermines my confidence. Poisons my
relationships. Controls every, little detail of my life. It's like
she's running a cult. The Cult of Stuart Ransom. But I'm just
the figurehead, the puppet. Esther's pulling all the strings.
She's brutal. I'm simply an object to her – fodder – a
commodity.' Ransom shakes his head, disgusted. 'Esther has
no confidence in my playing ability so she feeds the press
stories about me, sets up little "scenarios" to get me into all
kinds of trouble, then feeds off the notoriety.'

Gene takes a while to grapple with this notion,
intellectually.

'Like the situation with the hotel and the Tucker kid,'
Ransom kindly elucidates. 'A perfect case in point. We were
due to meet at the Leaside – at Noel Tucker's behest. And
I'm hunky-dory. I'm good with that. Then I get a last-minute
text from Esther saying the kid's demanding a sudden change
of venue. I'm like, fine – whatever. So I turn up at the Thistle
– like a friggin' lamb to slaughter – with absolutely no idea
that it was the hotel the kid's mother worked in before her
head injury …

Fuuuuck!'

Ransom gesticulates, wildly. 'I'm left wide open, Gino! I'm hog-tied, *gelded*. The Tucker kid insists that the venue change was *my* idea. I know for a fact that it friggin' wasn't. An argument develops. Someone – naming no names: *Esther* – has helpfully alerted the press. There's this huge, plate-glass window ...' He mimes the giant dimensions of the window. 'And the rest, as they say, is history.'

He sighs, forlornly. 'But that's Esther for you. That's how she operates. That's what she does. Esther's the power behind the throne, the Kingmaker. She made that bad shit happen. She set that situation up, then swore *black is blue* she didn't. But her grubby little prints were all over it, man.'

'Hasn't she been with you for years, though?'

'Oh yeah.' Ransom nods. 'Started off as my caddie, way back in "Yard". She's like family. Closer than family. I love her to friggin' pieces. I'd die for that manipulative bitch. *Seriously,*' he emphasizes (perhaps detecting a small measure of incredulity in Gene's expression). 'But just because you're close to someone doesn't mean they aren't extremely capable of being a twat,' he persists. 'The general rule is: the closer they get, the more they end up taking you for friggin' granted. They grow arrogant – complacent. Somewhere along the line you lose your mystique. They start thinking they're indispensable.'

Ransom snorts, humourlessly, at the sheer idiocy and wrongheadedness of this concept. 'Bottom line: the only *truly* indispensable person in this set-up is Stuart Ransom. End of. Everything rests on these two, broad shoulders ...' Ransom pats his own shoulder. 'It's a huge, friggin' responsibility, Gino, believe me. A massive strain. And the last thing I need – the last thing these two, broad shoulders need – is haters in my troupe. I don't need people on *my* journey worrying about *their* journey. The truth about Esther is that she's only really interested in one person: Esther. It's like Stuart Ransom is a big fish surrounded by swarms of tiny, little parasites; little sprats with rows of nasty, little teeth nibbling away at his flanks, devouring his living flesh as he glides about in the ocean of life. And he can sustain that pressure in times of plenty – *natch!* Ransom swipes his hand through the air, dismissively. 'But when times are lean, these mangy little critters don't let up – if anything they get worse. They grow bold and start taking proper bites, yeah? They're like: "just trim the tip off his tail!", "just nab a couple of his scales!" ... They think he won't notice, but he notices every, tiny friggin' detail. He's *wired* to notice, see? He's ultra-aware. He's like ... He's like ...' – Ransom's eyes start to de-focus – 'like this majestic antelope at a dried-up watering hole. He's tensed and ready to run. He's *ultra*-ultra aware. He feels the tick on his rump burrowing its filthy head into his skin. He feels the flea skipping around like a little bastard behind his ear. He feels the cattle egret gently landing on his shoulder ... He feels it all. He feels everything. He sees everything –'

'Until this gigantic crocodile suddenly erupts from its hidey-hole in the mud, grabs his leg and yanks him into a filthy oblivion,' Gene interrupts, with a grin (perhaps not taking Ransom's vainglorious panegyric quite as seriously as he ought).

'A crocodile?' Ransom's confused. 'What's the friggin' crocodile meant to represent?'
'Nothing.' Gene shrugs. 'It's an actual crocodile. It's real life.'
'It represents "real life"?' Ransom's still confused.
'No. It just *is*. It's random.'
'Then it represents the "randomness" of "real life"?'
'No. *No*. It was a joke – a bad joke,' Gene qualifies, flatly.

'Oh ...' Ransom ponders this for a while, patently unsettled. 'What you plainly haven't grasped,' he gently confides, 'is that I was actually using the antelope as symbol of something else – as a metaphor.'

'A simile,' Ransom automatically corrects him, 'and I did realize.' He shrugs, apologetically.

'I generally find it helps if I re-imagine myself as an animal,' Ransom elucidates, 'something wild, uncompromised, powerful, living on its wits, driven purely by its gut instincts.'

'Have you ever considered re-imagining yourself as a human being?' Gene wonders (unable to resist playing devil's advocate). 'I mean someone with a different psychological outlook, perhaps? Someone less competitive, someone more … more open, more vulnerable?'

'No' – Ransom is signally unimpressed with this idea – 'why the fuck would I want to do that?'

'Because it might prove beneficial,' Gene persists. 'It might actually –'

'Bottom line: the life of a professional sportsman is all about the spiel,' Ransom explains. 'It's about talking yourself into the right head-space, yeah? On an average day I don't take more than thirty per cent of what I say seriously.'

'Thirty per cent?' Gene's shocked. 'So seventy per cent –'

'… of what I say is bullshit. Exactly!' Ransom concludes, proudly, then ponders this admission for a second. 'Yeah. Roughly seventy per cent is pure bullshit.'

'Seventy per cent?' Gene repeats, incredulous. 'Seventy per cent of *everything* you say …'

'It's like self-hypnosis. CBT. Call it what you will.'

'But *seventy* per cent?' Gene's appalled.

'Okay, maybe fifty,' Ransom concedes.

'And the rest?'

'Hustle. Hype. Pep-talks. Mind games.'

Brief pause.

'Bloody hell!' Gene's profoundly moved by this revelation. 'But that must just be really … I dunno … *exhausting* …' He struggles to get his head around it. 'Not to mention demoralizing.'

'Nah.' Ransom shrugs. 'It's easy – it's like second nature to me now. It's the daily diddle, the bunco, the racket – the thing that gets your arse out of the clubhouse and on to the green. It's just the spiel.'

'Okay,' Gene interjects, 'so that's all well and good for Stuart Ransom "the sportsman". But what about Stuart Ransom the person – the living entity – the *soul*? What about the individual *inside* all the spiel? How's he feel? What's he thinking?'

'Uh ...' Ransom tries – momentarily – to enter this foreign person's headspace. 'My feet stink. My shirt's too tight. I need a crap. The air-con's on too low ... Wow – that pretty masseur's got amazing jugs, will she jack me off if I give her a big enough tip?'

'Good. Great. I get the picture ...' Gene lifts a hand, sickened.

'Some guys go in for all the humility stuff.' Ransom shrugs. 'Beckham's made a friggin' *career* out of it. You know, the whole: "I'm so lucky to be here right now"; the whole: "I don't actually have an ego"; the whole: "Tiger Woods is golf's greatest ambassador – he's brought the game to a whole new friggin' fanbase" malarkey; but the way I see it, that's just another kind of spiel – part of the Big Sporting Lie. An' I'm too friggin' real for that, man – got way too much self-respect.'

'So you don't believe those people are being honest when they say that stuff?'

'Hell no!' Ransom chuckles. 'Are you crazy?! They're professional arse-lickers! It's totally agenda-driven – just a different kind of bullshit.'

'Maybe they've realized that it's actually better for them,' Gene volunteers, 'I mean psychologically, emotionally – to look out at the world with ... without cynicism? Without the spiel? With humility? With an open heart?'

Ransom stares up at Gene, appalled. 'Please assure me that you didn't just use the phrase "with an open heart"?'

'I know it sounds a bit corny – a bit lame, even,' Gene concedes, 'but I do generally like to try and find the positives in any given situation.'

'And that's *your* spiel,' Ransom allows.

'But I don't think it is a spiel.' Gene's duly niggled. 'It's not rehearsed or calculated. It's more of a ... a life philosophy – a general outlook – an instinct.'

(The word 'faith' almost tips his tongue but he easily shuns it.)

'Philosophy?!' Ransom splutters. 'Philosophy-*shmilosophy*! Philosophy's just spiel with A-levels!'

'It's way bigger than that,' Gene persists. 'It's about who you are. It's about what's inside. It's about this strong feeling of ...'

He puts a hand to his ribs and then suddenly – unexpectedly – loses all momentum. The word 'well-being' dies on his lips.

'Of what?' Ransom gazes up at him, quizzically.

Gene frowns, confused. The saliva in his mouth has turned to sawdust. He feels a burning sensation in his chest – a sudden, lurching indigestion – and while he's all too familiar with the lesser gradations of this feeling (embarrassment, unease, discomfiture), this goes way beyond all those. It's a fiery worm burrowing through his gut. It's a carousel ride after a bucket of toffee-coated Butterkist. It's a ripe cheese, confined within its sheath of claustrophobic plastic, left way too long on a sunny countertop. It is strong and mean and queasy. It consumes him entirely. He finally apprehends – his heart sounding with a deadening thud from deep within him – that this extraordinary feeling is nothing more – and nothing less – than a crippling, paralysing, asphyxiating sense of *shame*.

And it is biblical in its proportions. It is a plague of locusts devouring every, living thing – every stray shoot of grass, every flower, every leaf – with their ferociously active and merciless mandibles. It is the incapacitating roar of the Tower of Babel (the aural incomprehensibility of the jet engine in take-off). But it is quiet, too – it is intimate: it is St Peter, steadfastly denying Jesus before the third cock starts to crow.

Shame. An emotional caustic soda that is systematically gnawing into everything that's good and calm and true within him. A poison that – he realizes, to his profound horror – may only be expelled by the telling. A boil – a sickening pustule – that can only be cured by the lancing.

'Well, whatever works for you,' Ransom blithely opines (moving on, with typical efficiency). 'Although from where I'm standing that sounds dangerously like the kind of shit people come up with when they've lost all remaining shreds of self-respect and ambition. It's the philosophy of a loser – someone who's run out of options.'

'Pragmatic rather than idealistic,' Gene murmurs (still – even as he's cruelly pole-axed by this whirling, emotional maelstrom – unable to resist the urge to classify).

'Think about it this way,' Ransom volunteers, 'the piranha chooses to fight other, hostile piranha with its tail, not its teeth. It's Darwinian – any other approach would be counter-productive for the species as a whole. It's a basic survival mechanism, yeah? You just do what works in your particular circumstances. Some people are perfectly happy to eat shit. These are the people who work in electricity sub-stations, on the buses, in IT, in catering – your Regular Joes. Other people like to kick against the pricks, stand out from the crowd, reject second-best, despise compromise ...'

'And a piranha ...?'

(Gene's struggling to keep up. His hand presses against his ribs. He still looks stricken.)

'The piranha's a realist. It knows that if it fights another piranha with its teeth then it'll probably end up screwed, so it does what it needs to do.'

'Piranhas are pragmatists, at root.' Gene nods, not really sure whose argument this furthers (in fact he's not sure of much as things currently stand).

'I was in the dentist's the other week getting my veneers bleached,' Ransom recalls. 'I picked up this magazine – science magazine – and there was an article in it all about how the brain is just a machine which works by staging a series of "neuro-battles" ...'

'Neuro-battles?' Gene echoes.

'Yeah. Different parts of the brain compete with each other to control the body. They stage these little neuro-battles and the strongest part of the brain wins. It's like a permanent, ongoing competition – a game. Which means it really doesn't matter a toss how you like to package it: "Oooh, I don't have an ego", "I'm all spiritual and shit", "I'm really modest and humble" ... It doesn't friggin' *matter*, because – bottom line – conflict is natural. It's written into our DNA. We *are* conflict. Just like the spider is ...'

'The ...?'

(Gene finds himself utterly incapable of fully encompassing this latest – and perhaps most startling – of Ransom's many hypotheses.)

'And d'you know what *really* freaks me out about the whole thing?' Ransom demands, irate.

Gene shakes his head. He honestly hasn't got a clue.

'These so-called "boffins" are planning to use this piece of knowledge to build a whole new generation of robots. Can you believe that?'

(Ransom doesn't actually wait for Gene to respond.)

'They're gonna build a whole, new generation of robots with two-tiered brains, yeah? The conscious brain and the unconscious brain. They're gonna establish this same level of competition within the robot's mechanical bonce, and when they do, trust me, those evil metal fuckers are gonna take over

the world. They're gonna take over the friggin' *world*.
Simple as.'

'But surely ...?' Gene's starts off.

'Did your schizo-grandad happen to play the trumpet?'
Ransom wonders.

'Sorry? My ...? Uh ...' Gene's all at sea. 'My schizo ...?'

'The trumpet?' Ransom repeats, miming a trumpet.

Gene finally catches up. 'Not the trumpet, no.'

'Oh.' Ransom looks vaguely disappointed.

'If I remember correctly it was actually ...'

'A fife?' Ransom prompts, his red eyes suddenly very focused.

'Not a fife, no, more of a ...'

Gene battles to describe the instrument's special curves with
his hands.

'A horn?' Ransom interrupts, struggling to contain his
excitement.

'No, no, not a horn, but something very ...'

'A bugle?' Ransom springs to his feet (as if having been
physically jolted forward by an unexpected parp from exactly
such an instrument).

'Yeah,' Gene confirms, 'a bugle, but with ...'

Gene twiddles his fingers.

'A *keyed* bugle?' Ransom grabs Gene's twiddling hand and
grips on to it, emphatically.

'I've still got it somewhere, up in the attic.' Gene tries –
within the boundaries of polite behaviour – to free himself
(and fails).

A peculiarly uncomfortable five-second hiatus follows before
Ransom says, 'Well that's exactly what we need to finish off
the outfit.'

'Oh. Okay.' Gene shrugs.

'You know, now I actually come to think about it' –
Ransom releases his grip and leans over to grab his hat from
its hook – 'maybe a Club Sandwich wouldn't be too far off
the mark: granary bread, extra bacon, extra avocado. Mango

power shake. Packet of parsnip crisps. Banana. Nectarine. Handful of cashews ...'

He pushes the cap down on to his head, un-shoots the latch, saunters out of the cubicle and appraises himself for a second in the mirror.

'Bloody hell!' he murmurs, applying a moistened thumb to each of his eyebrows. 'Beware the heavy-handed blonde with the foundation bottle!'

'Sorry' – Gene pops his head around the door, confused – 'are you actually expecting me to go and fetch that for you?'

Sheila gazes at herself in the mirror, draws a sharp breath and bursts into wild peals of maniacal laughter. She then stops – just as abruptly – steps in closer to her reflection, scowls, blinks, raises a tentative hand to her head, then reaches out – with the same hand – to touch her image (like an incredulous primate on first encountering its reflection in a clear, mountain pool).

Valentine stands at her shoulder, saying nothing.

Finally: 'It's just that I hadn't actually realized ...' Sheila whispers (unusually emotional – feminine – *girlish*, almost), 'I mean the transformation – it's extraordinary! It's like ... it's like I just ...'

She gestures, ineffectually.

'Like you just hatched,' Valentine fills in, nodding. 'Like you're fresh out of the egg. Like you're brand-new.'

Sheila closes her eyes and shakes her head (as if this profound feeling of joy she's experiencing must be deeply inappropriate at some level – transgressing a fundamental Commandment, at the very least). When she opens them again she glances down, surprised. Nessa is clinging to her legs, her pink cheek pushed into the fabric of Sheila's trouser, her blonde halo of curls bobbing against Sheila's priestly uniform's ineffable black like a spume of heavenly foam.

The child cuddles with an unexpected intensity. Sheila finds it impossible (in her heightened state) not to be moved. She turns her head to make direct eye contact with Valentine, her hand indicating, her brows raised. She mouths the word '*Ow!*' and grins.

'You like it, though?' Valentine steps forward and fluffs Sheila's tiny fringe. 'I mean it's quite radical, but you can definitely carry it.'

'Not much left to hide behind.' Sheila stares at herself again, in wonder.

'Will Gene approve?' Valentine murmurs, suddenly anxious.

'Gene?' Sheila seems confused – almost startled – by this question. '*Hmmn* … Will Gene like it?' she ponders, gazing at her reflection for a second, then shrugging. 'Yeah, of course – I'm sure he will.'

'Well, for what it's worth, I think you look amazing.' Valentine bends down and gently prises Nessa's arms away. 'It's taken years off you. The strong eyebrows work a treat – that powerful jawline – those wonderful, angular cheekbones …'

'Look at me!' Sheila marvels, twirling around, buoyed up by all the compliments. 'Dowdy old Sheila Phillips sporting a Valentine Wickers Original!'

She beams at her, delighted. 'I'm just so incredibly grateful.'

'It was nothing,' Valentine insists – almost ashamed – removing a tissue from her pocket and wiping Nessa's nose with it.

'It was extremely kind of you,' Sheila persists, 'and bloody brave, come to that. The effortless way you handled those scissors! You really must have nerves of steel.'

'Brave?' Valentine scoffs.

'Although I guess once you've etched a deep line of permanent ink into a total stranger's skin,' Sheila reasons, admiring, 'everything else must feel like a walk in the park by comparison.'

'Walks in the park aren't really my *forte*,' Valentine avows, grimacing.

'Gene did mention something about that.' Sheila nods, sympathetic. 'How long since you last ventured out?'

Valentine gazes, anxiously, into Sheila's shining face, looking for any evidence of aside. There is none.

'This morning,' she finally murmurs. 'Mum's new therapist brought his wife over to the house. She was wearing a full-length black robe. I tried it on and stepped outside in it, just to see how it would feel.'

'Really?' Sheila's fascinated. 'A *burqa*?'

'If I'm with someone I trust – I mean if they make me feel safe and I'm in the right kind of mood ...' She pauses. 'But that's incredibly rare. It hardly ever happens. And even then sometimes this sudden feeling of panic ... I mean the thought of being in wide open spaces or – worse still – in crowds ...' She puts a hand up to her throat. 'So much for the nerves of steel, eh?' she mutters.

Sheila thinks hard for a moment. 'Did you ever stop and think that your problem with the outside world might be completely rational?' she asks.

'My agoraphobia?' Valentine lifts up Nessa and slings her over her hip.

'Well your mother went for "a walk in a park",' Sheila logically expands, 'and she ended up in a coma.'

'But the odds on that happening again ...' Valentine's plainly wary of this approach. 'I mean it was just a random accident.'

'So there's no ill-feeling on your part?' Sheila persists.

'Ill-feeling?' Valentine echoes.

'Towards Ransom? Your brother? Your mother, even?'

'My mother?' Valentine's confused.

'For clipping your wings. For imposing this huge duty – this awful burden – of care. For stifling your independence.'

'How d'you figure that one out?' Valentine's still befuddled.

'I read somewhere once how women often develop agoraphobia as a kind of unconscious protest ...'

Valentine shakes her head, instantly resistant.

'... a way of striking out against the social and sexual straitjackets that society imposes on them,' Sheila persists, 'and most of those pressures tend to originate in the home, with the family.'

'Trust me, I've never needed any extra help in screwing up my life.' Valentine smiles, darkly. 'I generally seem to manage that all by myself.'

'I find that hard to believe.' Sheila tuts.

'And anyway,' Valentine continues (embarrassed by Sheila's quick show of loyalty), 'Dad and Noel's grief only really turned to anger – I mean so far as I can remember – once money entered the equation; all the hassle with the insurance people – the fight for compensation – the good publicity, the bad publicity.' She grimaces. 'As if the sum total of Mum's former life had a specific *figure* you could attach to it ...' she sighs, frustrated. 'I never had much time for that approach. "Happiness is the path of least resistance" – at least that's what I keep trying to tell myself.'

'I was sitting at my computer this morning' – Sheila nods, encouraged – 'and I suddenly thought: She should tattoo him! She should tattoo Stuart Ransom! Put this whole thing – this awful feud – to bed, once and for all. Start a fresh chapter! It came to me in a flash.'

'Like a divine intervention,' Valentine deadpans.

'I just thought: She needs to define herself as an individual in the world. Strike out! Take a stand! Do what she does best! Reclaim her life ...' Sheila pauses, conscience-stricken. 'Does that sound crazy to you?'

Valentine gazes at her for a while, perplexed.

'A little,' she confesses, keen not to offend. 'I mean what could I possibly hope to gain by ...?'

'The publicity for one thing,' Sheila quickly steps in. 'From what I can tell, Ransom's very smart at using the media – good *and* bad – to his own advantage, so why not play him at his own game? I mean if you can't beat him –'

'That sounds dangerously like my brother Noel's philosophy,' Valentine interrupts, 'and it's ended in nothing but misery. Stuart Ransom has this clever way of twisting things.'

'But it's also a grand gesture, don't you see?' Sheila persists. 'An act of public reconciliation. A rising above. A shaking free.'

'Sounds fine when you put it that way,' Valentine concedes, 'but the logistical problems alone ...'

'Well he's staying in the local area, for starters' – Sheila tries to look at the positives – 'so travel wouldn't be too much of an issue. And while Gene's working as his caddie ...'

'Sorry?'

Valentine frowns.

'Gene's caddying for him this week,' Sheila blithely repeats.

The temperature in the room suddenly drops by several degrees.

'He didn't mention that,' Valentine murmurs.

'Oh. Okay ...' Sheila rapidly reassesses the situation, slightly panicked, trying to think on her feet. She draws a deep breath. 'Gene told me about the problem with the electricity meter,' she confesses.

Valentine's face stiffens.

'And not just the meter ...' Sheila haltingly continues.

'What else did he tell you?' The colour drains from Valentine's cheeks.

'The letter,' Sheila murmurs, apologetic, 'from the bank. He read it by accident.'

'Letter?' Valentine scowls (this isn't quite what she was expecting).

'The letter threatening to foreclose on the house,' Sheila explains. 'I just thought ...'

'Foreclose on the house?' Valentine repeats. 'Whose house?'

'He said it was propping the thing up – the meter – all the screws had come loose. It fell out while he was doing the reading. He thought it was just a random scrap of ...'

'A letter from the bank?' Valentine mumbles. 'But why would ...?'

Her grip on the child becomes so tight that Nessa squeals a sharp complaint. Valentine places her down, gently, on to the floor, then slowly straightens up again.

'He honestly didn't realize ...' Sheila backtracks.

'You're starting to scare me, now,' Valentine warns her, her jaw tensing, fists clenching, as if readying herself for sudden combat. 'You say he's working for Ransom – there's a problem with the meter – you want me to do a tattoo – there's some ... some *letter*?'

'I just thought: She needs a quick injection of cash – and how better?' Sheila runs on, alarmed. 'I mean it'd be an amazing way of generating interest in your work – of creating a spectacle. Because art's all about the gesture – the moment – the event ... You know: the buzz – the chatter – the conversation ...'

Valentine gazes at Sheila for a few seconds without responding, then turns and hastens from the room. Sheila gazes after her, flummoxed. She smiles down, brightly, at the child. After a moment or two she turns and follows. She finds Valentine in the hallway, reaching inside the small cupboard that houses the meter, her fingers scrabbling, clumsily, at the screws. Brick dust cascades on to the tiles below.

'Will he go to the authorities?' she demands, her voice much tighter and harder now.

'I can't ... I'm not really in a position to answer that.'

Sheila quickly reaches forward to support the body of the meter as it clanks sideways, now barely still attached to the wall. 'Careful!' she warns her.

The folded-up letter drops into Valentine's hand. She opens it and scans it.

'They're going to foreclose on the house,' she murmurs, glancing up, horrified, holding it out towards Sheila for a second and then snatching it back again to double-check. 'They sent this thing … God … *weeks* ago!'

'You really had no idea?' Sheila's suitably appalled by the apparent magnitude of this revelation.

Valentine slowly shakes her head, her eyes glued to the text. 'Noel has legal control over all of Mum's assets. He hasn't …' She shakes her head again, her voice breaking. 'That stupid, sneaky, double-crossing little …'

'I'm incredibly sorry! I honestly thought …'

'We're all screwed!' Valentine covers her face with her hands.

Sheila wants to embrace her – to comfort her – but she's still supporting the meter. She tries to let go of it and it tilts dramatically to one side revealing the small, secret dug-out that's hidden behind. She gazes at the neat rows of tiny boxes, astonished.

'If they take away the house I'll die,' Valentine murmurs, half to herself, 'I'll just shrivel up and I'll die. I'll just …' She drops a hand to her throat.

'You won't die,' Sheila assures her, 'you'll be *fine* – you've still got plenty of options.'

'What about Mum?' Valentine gasps, the true horror of the situation gradually unfolding in her mind. 'And Nessa? What will they do? Where will they go?'

'I'm sure – if it comes down to the wire – then the council will provide temporary shelter.'

'Temporary shelter?' Valentine echoes, as if these two words are the most awful, the most chilling conjunction in the entire human lexicon.

'You probably need to get in contact with the bank,' Sheila counsels, 'keep the lines of communication open. Give them a quick call. Set up a meeting and explain your circumstances. There may still be some wiggle-room ...'

Sheila pauses for a second. She can't quite believe she just used the phrase 'wiggle-room'.

'Am I being punished?' Valentine covers her face again with a shudder. 'Is God punishing me? Is it my fault? Is it bad karma? Have I been so evil, so disgusting, so *bad*?'

'Of course not!' Sheila insists.

'How can you say that?!' Valentine drops her hands, tortured. 'I've done so many terrible things – *despicable* things. Thought things – wished things ...' She gazes at Sheila, her pretty face crumpling. 'Oh God,' she groans, 'you've *no* idea.'

She turns on her heel, the letter clutched to her chest, and charges upstairs with it.

Sheila is left standing, alone, with the meter in her hand. She stares at the collection of tiny packages. She adjusts the meter and a fresh cascade of brick dust descends from above. She curses, then senses a slight movement behind her. She glances over her shoulder. It is Nessa, the child.

'What an awful mess!' she exclaims, with a forced joviality. 'I think we probably need a dustpan and brush, don't you?' Nessa nods.

'D'you know where Valentine keeps them? In the kitchen, perhaps?'

The child nods, then promptly trots over, squats down and reaches her fingers into the dust.

'Although a Hoover might be better,' Sheila muses, half to herself, idly noticing that a thin layer of brick dust has settled on to a couple of the – formerly pristine – boxes. She instinctively leans forward to blow it off, and the next instant the meter comes away from the wall completely, crashing down, scarcely supported now, its wires ripping loose as it descends.

Sheila's first priority is to shield the crouching child from its impact, so she doesn't jump back – as is her initial instinct –

but interposes her body between them, taking the bulk of the
meter's weight on the front of her shin, then somehow
conniving to catch it again before it smashes into the floor
tiles below. Several tiny packages and boxes also cascade
down in the ensuing chaos and scatter on to the floor
around them.

The pain in her leg is quick and sharp. She squeezes her
eyes tight shut, places the meter on to the tiles and remains,
bent double, gasping, applying a steady pressure to the painful
area with the palms of both hands.

Her head starts to swim.

'Balls, balls, *balls*,' she mutters. 'Balls, balls, balls, balls,
balls!'

She sits down, heavily, in the dust.

'That really hurt,' she says. '*Balls*,' she adds. She continues to
apply pressure to the throbbing area.

'Maybe I've chipped my shin,' she muses, tiny fireworks
exploding in the black at the back of her eyes. Her mouth
suddenly feels dry. She wants to pull up her trouser to inspect
the area but is fearful of what she might find. Blood? A jutting
shard of bone? A lump the size of a duck egg? She
commences to rock back and forth, muttering *ow, ow, ow*
under her breath.

Behind her the child is playing with the fallen boxes. Inside
one she has found a signet ring, inside another, a medal. She
picks up a third, slightly larger package wrapped in a layer of
brown paper and a layer of greaseproof. She pulls them off,
squeaking excitedly, like she's unwrapping a birthday present.

Sheila turns – still clutching at her leg – and opens her eyes
just in time to see the child producing a plain but well-made
pigskin wallet from the greaseproof layer.

'*Nessa! Drop that!*'

Sheila starts. It's Valentine, who has returned – *sans* letter –
and stands apprehending the chaotic scene before her in a
state of advanced agitation. She leans forward and snatches

the wallet from the child's grasp, then exclaims, in disgust, and lets it fall to the floor again. It lands in a thin layer of brick dust.

'*Screw it!*' she exclaims, then promptly bursts into tears, grabs the stray sheet of greaseproof and picks it up again, clumsily – fastidiously – like it's the corpse of a poisoned mouse or a dog turd.

Sheila watches on, confused, her eyes returning to the child's other booty which she immediately notices is decorated with Nazi regalia.

'Bloody hell – is this stuff real?' she wonders (her voice – to her own ears – sounding like its original source is the distant aspidistra).

'Are you hurt?' Valentine sniffs, through a startling Rorschach test of cascading mascara.

'My shin got a bit of a bash, but I'm sure it'll be fine,' the aspidistra responds, calmly. Sheila is impressed by how serene and dispassionate the aspidistra seems.

'Should I take a look?'

Valentine is promptly on her knees beside her. She is still holding the wallet, gingerly, in her palm, where it sits – blonde and innocuous – in its little square of greaseproof as a child's portion of chips at a country fair.

Sheila inspects it, quizzically, as Valentine carefully places it down on to the tiles again – well clear of the brick dust. She then rolls up Sheila's trouser leg to inspect the dented shin. Sheila gingerly un-peels her hands from the painful area. She can't bring herself to look.

'Is it bad?' she wonders.

A short pause follows.

'Perhaps I should take a quick look at the other one, for comparison …'

Sheila's eyes widen.

Valentine rolls up Sheila's other trouser leg and compares the two shins in close conjunction.

Then: 'It's pretty nasty. There's a lump, a kind of graze standing up all bluey-white, and this big, black blood blister all the way along ...'

'Any bone?'

'Nope.' Valentine shakes her head. 'Does it hurt?'

'Like hell. It throbs; sharp throbs – like I'm being repeatedly stabbed by a little dagger.'

'We need some antiseptic and a packet of peas to bring down the swelling. Wait here.'

Valentine springs up and charges off down the hallway.

Nessa, meanwhile – in the wake of Valentine's sudden absence – takes the opportunity to shunt herself across the tiles to take another look at the wallet. She prods it with her finger.

'Soft,' she says, then tries to pick it up.

'No, no – I don't think you should touch that, Nessa,' Sheila cautions her, 'we don't want it to get all dusty from your hands, do we? It's very precious ...'

The child ignores her. She continues to grapple with it.

'Here' – Sheila reaches out and takes the wallet from her – 'let me have a look ...'

She also grabs the greaseproof paper. 'Valentine keeps it all wrapped up, like this, see?'

She starts folding the greaseproof around it, the child standing at her shoulder, watching on, fascinated.

'There's some dust on it already ...'

Sheila blows on the wallet to try and shift some of the dust, then lightly polishes it with her shirtsleeve. She blows on it again. As she blows for the second time – front and back – her eye catches a slight imperfection in the hide. She scowls down at it, worriedly, then prods at it with her index finger, grimaces, draws it in still closer to her face, and is surprised to be able to delineate several digits of a number.

'Leave it! Give it here!'

Valentine – who has just arrived back with the requisite bundle of medical provisions – swoops down and snatches the wallet from her.

'It's dirty!' she pants. 'You mustn't ...'

'It's just a bit of dust,' Sheila explains, mildly defensive.

'No, *no*, I mean it's a dirty thing – a filthy thing ... Part of my dad's collection of war memorabilia.'

Sheila's still none the wiser.

'It's made from human skin.'

Three-second pause.

'Bloody hell!' Sheila flinches, startled. Her face creases up with disgust.

'I thought Gene had ...' Valentine's confused. 'When you said earlier ...'

'Gene definitely didn't mention this.'

Sheila's shaken. Her voice is shaking. She feels extraordinarily distressed by the mere fact of this object – the sheer, moral offence of its physical existence; by its dangerous proximity; its spiritual toxicity ...

Valentine assesses her reaction, almost coldly.

'The ones with numbers are obviously more valuable,' she explains.

'That's revolting!'

Sheila instinctively wipes both hands on the front of her shirt.

'There's a whip, too,' Valentine adds.

'Whip?' Sheila echoes.

'From one of the camps – I forget which.' She shrugs. 'Auschwitz, Treblinka ... He'd bring it out on special occasions when we were kids. Tell us stories. Show it off.'

Sheila says nothing. She's momentarily lost for words. Flaccid. Sickened.

'This is his *real* inheritance.' Valentine smiles, her eyes hard as flint. 'These are the things we took pleasure in together. His ... his legacy? Isn't that the word you used earlier?'

Sheila just shakes her head, appalled.

'His legacy,' Valentine repeats. 'The skin. The ink. The tattoo. The gift. The pain. The artistry ... Doesn't seem quite so wonderful now, does it?'

'This was your father's collection,' Sheila stolidly maintains. Valentine concedes this point with a small tip of the head.

'But I do love the skin,' she muses, 'just like he did. And the paler the skin, the stronger the mark – the brighter – the more indelible ...'

'It's different.' Sheila winces. 'God – how can you bear to *hold* that thing?!' she explodes. 'How can you bear to *sleep* at night knowing that it's just lying there, hidden, inside your home?'

'I can't.' Valentine shrugs. 'But I do.' She slowly shakes her head. 'It's like you love something' – she turns the wallet over in her hand, tracing the number with her finger, mesmerized – 'and then you're punished for loving it. I love tattooing but I'm my dad's apprentice. I love the skin – I'm obsessed by it – it's so magical and strong yet so unbelievably sensitive – it's the thing that holds all the feelings in – the thing that touches the world; the mask, the source, the base, the surface ...'

Sheila looks down at her watch. Even as she does so she can't quite believe she's doing it. She looks up again.

'I have to go,' she says, scrambling to her feet.

'Of course.'

Valentine steps back, resigned. She half-smiles. Her eyes are dead.

'No, I mean I really *do* have to go. I really do. I have a baptism at two ...'

'Of course,' Valentine repeats. Still, the dead eyes.

Sheila tests her bad leg – tries to rest her weight on it. It takes her weight easily but then burns so much as the fabric of her trouser falls down across the shin again that a spurt of pure bile jets into her mouth. She peers over at Nessa, who is quietly watching everything as it unfolds before her, mouth agape, wearing a look of childlike wonder.

'Very nice to meet you, Nessa,' she mutters, ruffling the white curls on the child's head. She takes two steps towards the door, then retches, then a further few steps and retches again, her eyes focused, with a maniacal energy, on those wise, green leaves of the aspidistra.

9

'Did you know that the word – the actual *word* – for "individual" didn't even exist in Japan until 1884?' Jen asks, casually fishing the seam of her white catsuit out of the crack in her bottom as she speaks. 'It first came into regular use following an early translation of Rousseau's *Social Contract*.'
Brief pause.
'Actually, yes – I think I may have stumbled across that particular idea before …' Terence Nimrod nods.
'It's not "an idea",' Jen corrects him, sternly, 'it's "a fact".'

They are standing on the green by the fourteenth hole (Ransom is hiding here, determined to avoid the start of the Children's Tournament at the first), crowded – like a flock of human vultures – around a large packet of Gummy Bears which Israel has recently produced from his briefcase.

'Nimrod spent part of his misspent youth training in Japan,' Toby helpfully interjects, politely pressing flat a nearby divot (recently generated by Jen's unsuitable footwear) with the trusty heel of his Hush-Puppy.
'Really?' Jen's naturally intrigued. 'I hear the drop-out rate among junior *Rikishi* is really high. They treat those fat kids like little slaves. How long did you stay at the *Heya* for, altogether? Time to grow a top-knot?'

Another brief pause follows, punctuated by the laborious champing of several jaws.
'Do they really force-feed the kids at Sumo Stables?' Jen persists. 'Or is that just another of those sick Western myths?'

Ransom – ear-wigging in on their conversation from a few feet away (where he's just inadvertently hooked a practice shot with a 'lucky ball') – almost chokes on a mouthful of Vitamin Water.

'The force-feeding I didn't have a problem with' – Nimrod smiles, blithely – 'it was the constant chafing from my *mawashi* which really got my goat.'

Another brief silence.

'Nimrod at *Sumo* School?!' Ransom simply can't contain himself a moment longer. 'Just because he's the size of a friggin' whale?! *Seriously?!* Is this a wind-up or what?!'

'I generally find that great satire, like fresh Battenberg,' Jen reasons, airily (to no one in particular), 'always benefits from being broken down into its constituent parts.'

'Marzipan, thin layer of jam, two types of sponge …' Nimrod muses, fondly.

'Battenberg?' Israel's confused. 'Cake or man?'

'Both, I imagine,' Nimrod surmises. 'Toby?'

'A cake, a man and a location,' Toby promptly confirms. 'It was created in honour of the nuptials of Queen Victoria's granddaughter to Prince Louis of Battenberg in the mid-1880s. Prince Louis had four brothers, which is what the four sponge squares dressed in marzipan were intended to represent.'

Israel inspects Toby with a renewed level of respect. Ransom scowls.

'The Japanese have this very powerful conception of shame' – Jen quickly returns to her former subject – 'but guilt's not nearly such a big deal there. Shame is social, see? Guilt is individual. *Ergo*, guilt is an intrinsically selfish emotion, *ergo*, I shouldn't feel guilty for eating too many Gummy Bears, at least not in the abstract – but it would be shameful if I deprived the charming Mr Whittaker here of his rightful portion.'

'Intriguing hypothesis.' Nimrod takes another bear.

Ransom rolls his eyes, exaggeratedly.

'It's the same in many African cultures,' Israel volunteers, 'if you commit a crime and it isn't discovered then you don't feel guilt. It's all good. Only the *discovery* of a crime makes it a problem.'

'That's just weird.' Toby shakes his head.

'Heard it on the World Service.' Israel shrugs as Toby reaches for yet another bear, then mutters, 'I'm frazzled – didn't get much sleep last night,' by way of an explanation.

'Guilt is a very Catholic emotion.' Nimrod nods, gnomically. 'Repentance, guilt, self-loathing … all very Catholic emotions.'

Gene arrives – *sans* 'lucky ball' – to hear the tail-end of this conversation.

'No sign of it in the bushes,' he puffs, 'how lucky was it?'

'Irreplaceable.'

'Oh.'

Israel offers him a Gummy Bear. Gene takes one and pops it into his mouth, unthinkingly.

'Like, "the-ball-Tony-Jacklin-won-the-US-Open-with" lucky?' Nimrod wonders, taking out his notebook.

'It's an autographed Arnold Palmer ball.' Ransom scowls. 'The King gave it to me himself.'

'Why did you have it among your practice balls?' Gene looks irritated. 'I had no idea when I handed it to you that it was anything special.'

'It's a *lucky* ball,' Ransom snaps. 'Where the fuck else am I gonna keep a lucky ball other than with my practice balls? How the fuck is the luck meant to rub off on the other balls if it's locked away in a glass-fronted friggin' cabinet?'

'Did you know that it can take a golf ball anywhere up to a thousand years to decompose naturally?' Jen asks, followed, after a short pause, by, 'The *King*?! For real?!'

'Arnold Palmer is the greatest golfer in history.' Ransom shrugs. 'Arnold Palmer is the greatest golfer of all time. Ever.'

'If I'd only known it was there ...' Gene grumbles.

Israel passes Toby the Gummy Bear packet, and turns to Gene. 'Why don't I come and help you look?' he suggests. 'That's very kind of you.' Gene smiles down at the kid. 'How about if I scour this section again' – he points – 'and you take the other side?'

Israel folds up his portable stool, slides it into his briefcase and then hands it to Jen for safekeeping.

'If a black man had been playing professional golf since the genesis of the game then a black man would be the greatest golfer of all time,' he opines. 'Fact is, they were only ever allowed to lug old whitey's clubs around.'

Ransom squints at him, baffled, eyes slit against the sun, then turns and stares at Jen, with a look best described as 'ominous'.

'I've heard that point made before.' Nimrod nods. 'And if Woods is any indicator ...' Toby concedes, popping another Gummy Bear into his mouth.

Israel and Gene head off into the scrub again.

'Where the hell did that photographer get to?' Jen mutters, unnerved.

Nimrod is gazing after Gene, intrigued. 'You'd never know there was anything different about him,' he murmurs. 'I mean aside from the slight limp and the military get-up, he's just your average Joe; a normal, friendly bloke. Straightforward. Good-looking. Unpretentious ...'

'Really modest.' Toby nods. 'Doesn't act like he thinks he's anything special.'

'It always amazes me how some people have this inbuilt capacity to just shake off their pasts,' Nimrod muses. 'No scar tissue. No baggage. They just step free of it all, easy as.'

'He's a one-off,' Jen sighs. 'Strong, but with this really soft, really sensitive side.'

'It's like, how the hell do you get your head around it?' Nimrod wonders. 'Being so unlucky and then so lucky? How d'you find a balance? Where d'you end up, psychologically? It's fascinating.'

'I've had the best of luck and the worst of luck during my career,' Ransom sighs. 'I've been up, floating in the clouds, then down, grubbing around in the dirt –'

'The gutter,' Jen helpfully interjects.

'And I've often found the good times way harder to handle than the bad,' he continues, 'which is pretty fascinating, psychologically speaking.'

'But you say his wife's a minister?' Nimrod's straight back to Gene again. 'C of E?'

'He only has one nut,' Ransom volunteers, 'they inserted a little, silicon bag. Apparently it feels totally normal to the touch.'

Short silence.

'Although there's some reduced sensitivity.'

'Well thanks so much for sharing.' Jen acid-smiles.

'And while we're on the subject …' (Ransom promptly changes the subject), 'don't you just friggin' *hate* it when people think they can re-write history like that?' (He's plainly still smarting from Israel's earlier comment.) 'I mean how the fuck are you expected to engage with that kind of backward logic?'

'You can't respond to it.' Jen shrugs. 'It's unanswerable.'

Ransom nods, mollified.

'Let's face it,' Jen continues, 'black people are always gonna be way better at sport than we are, and they're always gonna be way better at music and they're always gonna be way better at religion. They're better dancers, better lovers … Case closed. End of.'

'That's so fuckin' *racist!*' Ransom howls, outraged.

'DWI.' Jen chuckles.

'Turn it around,' Nimrod suggests, sagely, 'and see how it sounds.'

'Eh?' Jen's slow on the uptake.

'Well if I said, "White people are better at ... uh ..."' – he struggles to find suitable examples – 'okay, if I say, "They're better at science and they're better at poetry and they're better at needlepoint–"'

'Hip-hop,' Jen interrupts, 'black people are way better at poetry than us.'

She ponders for a second: 'And the Indians are geniuses at sewing and shit.'

Short pause.

'And the Chinese invented fireworks,' she adds.

'Fireworks?!' Ransom snorts.

'Fireworks – *gooood*,' Nimrod essays, sagely, 'gunpowder – *baaad*.'

'*Hmmn*.' Jen considers this for a second. 'Okay ... So the Chinese are great at haikus, gardening and calligraphy. And they invented Buddhism, which is really cool.'

'You think one thing counters the other?' Toby snorts.

'Great news!' Nimrod grins. 'The invention of penicillin cancels out the evils of colonialism!'

'Hallelujah!' Toby declaims. 'Jesus Christ cancels out the Arab-Israeli conflict!'

'Thai green curry shits briquettes on the tsunami!' Ransom chortles.

Toby and Nimrod exchange nervous glances.

'Shits briquettes?' Jen echoes, frowning. 'You mean like charcoal briquettes?'

'Huh?' Ransom's instantly defensive.

'Shits *briquettes*?!' Jen cackles. 'That's so fucking *gay*!'

'If he doesn't end up finding the ball, maybe I can build a little something out of it.' Nimrod turns and glances back over towards the distant figure of Gene again. 'Mention Gene by name. Talk about the cancer ... Psychic caddie loses precious ball but wins eight-round battle against terminal cancer ...'

'Shits *briquettes*?!' Jen's crossing her legs and bending over with ill-suppressed hilarity. 'I swear I'm gonna pee myself!'

'Mention the silicone testicle' – Ransom pointedly ignores Jen – 'for a bit of colour.'

'You think he'd be comfortable with that?' Toby's alarmed.

'Of course! He lectures about it in *schools* for Christsakes. It's a badge of friggin' honour.'

'Shits *briquettes!*' Jen gurgles.

'Take this.' Ransom passes his mineral water to Toby, grabs Jen by the arm and escorts her (still knock-kneed) several paces away from the group.

'Oh God, I really, *really* need a bush!' she pants.

Ransom stares at her, scowling, until the panting abates a fraction.

'You play a wind instrument,' he murmurs, inspecting her upper lip.

'Sure do.'

'Clarinet?'

'Fuck off!' Jen squawks. 'Trombone.'

'How d'you manage to blow with that stupid thing stuck through your tongue?'

'I take it out.'

Jen opens her mouth to reveal the stud, then curls the tip of her tongue around to jiggle it from underneath. Ransom watches this, appalled.

'You do know what people think when they see a girl with a stud in her tongue?' he asks, trying – but failing – to adopt a concerned, paternal tone.

Jen gazes up at him, quizzically, still jiggling.

'They think, That girl loves giving head. She's a slut – one level up from a prostitute.'

Jen snaps her mouth shut but continues to gaze up at him.

'Give head – fellatio – blow-jobs,' he elucidates.

'Really?'

Her face falls.

Ransom starts to look uncomfortable, and then, 'Of course it's a sex aid!' Jen grins, her expression joyous, illuminated. 'Why the hell else would I bother getting it done?'

'For fashion!' Ransom's suddenly almost indignant on her behalf.

'*Aw*, wise up, Grandad!' Jen pokes him, fondly, in the belly (which he immediately tightens). 'And it's worth bearing in mind,' she adds, as an afterthought, slightly more serious now, 'that we're *all* little better than prostitutes in the West. Capitalism is our pimp, the banking system our client, consumerism the clap, celebrities our crabs ... God – I'm dying for a *waz* ...'

She commences walking (knock-kneed, grabbing clumsily at her catsuit), towards a nearby patch of rough, containing, she notes, delighted, an abundance of willows: the impressively sculptural *Salix Viminalis* to the centre, banked (on either side), by the startling black, native *Salix Nigricans* and daringly fronted by the low, purple skirts of *Salix Purpurea*.

'Impressive planting!' Jen yells over her shoulder, pointing. 'Native species! Very good! Very *sensitive* ...'

Ransom just scowls after her, in silence, critically out-manoeuvred, still holding in his stomach, both eyes red and prickling.

Valentine is standing in the hallway, the heavy receiver to the black Bakelite phone pressed against her ear. She is on hold, waiting to speak to someone at the bank. Nessa is lying prone on the tiles nearby, knickerless, wearing only a vest.

'I'm swimming!' she calls, kicking out her feet and paddling with her arms. 'Look! Swimming!'

'Where did you put your pants, Nessa?' Valentine asks, irritated.

'Swimming!' Nessa gurgles, making fish faces as she breaststrokes.

'You need to put on your pants, Nessa!' Valentine snaps.
'*Now!* D'you hear me?'

Nessa is offended by her sharp tone. She immediately sits up,
pulling her feet into her body, linking her arms around her
legs, making herself small, compressing herself.

'Do you remember where you were when you took
them off?'

Valentine instantly feels guilty.

Nessa shakes her head. She rests her chin on her knees and
stares straight ahead, sullenly.

'Answer the bloody phone, will you?' Valentine mutters,
slapping at her hip, impatiently. '*Please!* Before I lose my
nerve completely.'

She hears the front gate squeal and turns her head, alarmed.

Noel?

Mum?

A cheerful trill of female voices – the creak of a faulty pram
wheel. A child laughs. Two dark shadows appear on the front
step, speaking in lightly accented English.

'You take it all *way* too literally, Aamilah,' one of the voices
says as the door knocker is gently rapped.

'She won't hear that, Hana – way too soft. Knock again.'

'She *will* hear it.'

'She won't hear it. I barely heard it myself. Let Riya have a
go. Riya, lift the knocker and give it a good ...'

The door knocker raps again, just once, hollowly.

'Oh dear, oh dear. *Very* disappointing, Riya!'

'Don't be so *mean*, Hana – she did her best!'

'You need to teach her to knock several times in a row. You
can't just knock something once. That isn't a proper knock.'

'It's a sharp rap.'

'No it isn't. A sharp rap is like *rat-a-tat-tat!*'

Brief silence.

'We should probably knock again.'

'If we knock it again she'll think we're a bunch of lunatics. *Bang-bang-bang! Bang-bang-bang!* She'll think we've come to arrest her or something.'
Pause.
'Well she's obviously not in.'
'Of course she's in! She's agoraphobic, you idiot! She can't go out. She's *always* in.'

Valentine listens to this ongoing conversation standing – glued to the spot – by the aspidistra. She slowly puts down the phone receiver and winces as it produces a deafening *ding*.

'*Yaha!* What was that?!'
'What?'
'A ringing sound!'
'I didn't hear anything.'
'Seriously?!'
'It's probably just in your head.'
'A ringing in my head?!'
'Yes.'
'No. I don't think so, Hana.'
'It's hard to hear anything through all this bloody fabric.'
Brief pause.

'Shall I take a little peek through the letterbox?'
'No Aamilah!'
'Why not?'
'Oh do let's make banana sago pudding when we get home! I really fancy some banana sago! Or sweet, stuffed plantain … Aamilah! *Don't!*'

Valentine sees the letterbox being slowly pushed open and a pair of lively brown eyes being affixed to the gap.
'Hana – there's four hairy cats all staring straight at me and a little girl sitting on the cold tiles without any pants on!'
'Get away from there, Aamilah. Stop snooping!'

Valentine flattens herself against the wall, hoping she'll be obscured by the aspidistra, but then cringes with

embarrassment as the eyes peer towards her, widen, then
quickly withdraw again. The letterbox snaps shut.
  'What?'
Silence.
'What's wrong, Milah?'
'Nothing!'
'Then why are you pulling that ridiculous face?'
'I'm not ...'(*something mumbled*).
'Speak up, Milah! Stop mumbling!'
'I'm *not* pulling a face, Hana, all right?!'
'Yes you are! You're rolling your eyes like some kind of mad
woman!'
'I'm not!'
'Look at Riya! She thinks you're a freak! Is your Amma
behaving like some kind of crazy nutter, Riya?'
Short pause.
'Ha! See?! She's nodding!'
  Valentine quickly steps forward and yanks the door open.
Two women in *burqas* and a small, plump child dressed
entirely in pink are crowded together on the doorstep.
'I'm so sorry!' Valentine and one of the women both chorus in
conjunction.
  'I was phoning my bank when you started to knock,'
Valentine explains, 'I was actually stuck on hold so I
couldn't ...'
'My sister is incredibly nosey,' the second woman pipes up.
'Please let me apologize on her behalf.'
She holds out her hand.
'I don't need you to apologize on my behalf!' the first woman
exclaims. 'I already apologized myself thank you very much!'
  'It's just that there was only one caller remaining – I'd
almost got through – then you knocked on the door and I
didn't want to jeopardize ...'
  She reaches out and grasps the second woman's hand.
'Hello, I'm Valentine, very pleased to ...'

'Farhana,' the woman introduces herself, her pretty, mischievous eyes crinkling warmly at their corners, 'Aamilah's sister – but please don't hold that against me.'

'Farhana!' Aamilah is scandalized.

'Valentine's such a pretty name!' Farhana pointedly ignores her.

'Thank you.' Valentine nods.

'Were you born on Valentine's Day?'

'No. I was actually conceived on Valentine's Day. My birthday's in November. The 14th.'

'Oh.'

'This is my daughter, Badriya,' Aamilah pipes up. 'We were taking her to the People's Park for a picnic and I suddenly thought, Valentine's just around the corner ...'

'Hello there,' Valentine greets the small child, evidently slightly ill at ease, then covers her confusion by calling Nessa to the door.

'Nessa, come and meet Badra ...' she stutters.

'Badriya,' Aamilah repeats.

'It means "Resembling the full moon",' Farhana explains.

'How lovely!' Valentine exclaims, smiling down at the round-faced child who stares back at her, stolidly.

'She's not confident with other children,' Farhana murmurs as Nessa clambers past Valentine to apprehend their visitor and Riya (in response) retreats, horrified, into her mother's skirts, gazing at the genial Nessa with a disapproving scowl. She yanks her mother's robe and mutters something into its folds.

'Yes. We can all see that she's not wearing any pants, Riya,' Aamilah responds, sharply.

'Which is why we suddenly thought – or at least Aamilah here thought – it might be nice if we could take the two of them over there together so that they could run around and play for a while ...' Farhana battles on, uneasily. 'We've brought a small picnic ...' She indicates towards a large, Tupperware container and a Thermos in the storage space underneath the pram.

'Well that's extremely kind of you ...' Valentine starts off.

'Of course I told her it was a silly idea!' Farhana genially rounds on her sister. 'I said, "She'll probably be busy – it's all very last minute." Then I said, "And why on earth would she entrust two complete strangers – one of whom is plainly a maniac – with the care of her precious niece?" Eh?' Her eyes sparkle.

'You're always undermining me, Hana!' Aamilah hisses, furious. 'Especially in front of strangers!'

'I'm not undermining you, Milah,' Hana snorts, 'I'm merely stating the obvious!'

'If something is obvious then it doesn't need stating, does it?!' Aamilah snaps.

'You've placed Valentine on the spot,' Farhana clucks. 'Look at her! She doesn't know where to put herself!'

'No. Not at all. I'm absolutely fine,' Valentine insists.

'See? She's fine!' Milah grumbles. 'She's only embarrassed because you've drawn attention to how embarrassed she is!'

'Listen to what you're saying!' Farhana flaps a dismissive hand. '*How embarrassed she is!* She was *already* embarrassed when I pointed it out. Her cheeks are flushed.'

'Her cheeks are fine! It's only too much make-up, you idiot!' Aamilah rounds on her sister. Valentine lifts a tentative hand to her cheek.

'So what about the huge nerve rash on her neck?' Farhana demands.

'Farhana! You don't know how to behave!' Aamilah's mortified. 'I'm so sorry about my sister!' she gushes.

'*Urgh!* Tit for tat!' Farhana shrugs, amused.

Valentine can't help smiling herself.

'Her name means "Good deeds",' Farhana continues, encouraged, thumbing towards her sister. 'She selected it herself, and I'm afraid she takes it all rather too literally ...'

'Shut up!' Aamilah's furious.

'But you do!' Farhana laughs. 'You're a terrible busy-body! A bull in a china shop!'

'I'm not a bull! How can you say that?' Aamilah turns to Valentine, hurt. 'D'you think I'm a bull?' she demands.

'A bull?' Valentine echoes, barely keeping track of their conversation.

'*Ho!* That's definitely a yes, then!' Farhana interrupts, chuckling.

'No it isn't!' Aamilah stamps her foot, livid.

'Anything other than a decisive no in that particular context is definitely a yes,' Farhana persists.

Aamilah eyeballs Valentine, piteously.

'Of course you're not a ... a bull,' Valentine quickly assures her, 'I was just ... you know ... on the phone ... and Nessa was about to ... to have a bath ...' she continues, awkwardly, staring down at her niece, who, true to form, is now wearing her vest over the back of her head as a hood, the flesh over her bare nipples bulging – compressed by the garment's skew hem.

'Good gracious me!' Aamilah exclaims, pointing, disapprovingly, to the child's bare genitals. 'Everyone can see your Nu-nu, child! Where's your modesty?'

'Aamilah!' Farhana exclaims. '*Hush!*' as Valentine leans down and removes Nessa's vest from the back of her head.

'Don't hush me!' Aamilah snaps. 'I'm just telling the poor child that it's wrong to show your Nu-nu to a bunch of complete strangers.'

'It's a mother's job to tell a child such things,' Farhana cautions her.

'Her mother's a drug addict,' Aamilah scoffs, 'her grandmother's two slices short of a loaf, her father's a hoodlum and her aunt's too scared to leave the house ... Just look at the poor thing – she plainly needs guidance!'

Valentine's jaw drops, in pure astonishment, at Aamilah's outrageous impudence.

'Aamilah!' her sister whispers, horrified.

'*What?!*' Aamilah looks from one woman to the other, indignant. 'It's only the truth!'

A brief silence follows as all parties rapidly reassess the situation.

'Uh ... Perhaps that trip to the park ...' Farhana starts off, doubtfully.

'Rain-check.' Valentine nods, pulling Nessa, protectively, against her legs.

'Did I go too far?' Aamilah asks, eyes widening.

'Several miles.' Farhana nods.

Aamilah lifts her *niqab*. 'I do this kind of thing all the time,' she confides, barely apologetic.

'Never thinks before she speaks.' Farhana also lifts her *niqab*. 'Total idiot. Completely tactless.'

'Please forgive me!' Aamilah pleads, grinning, in spite of herself.

'Not wanting to leave the house is hardly a crime,' Farhana concedes, 'in some cultures that kind of behaviour is actively encouraged.'

'I already apologized, Hana!' Aamilah clucks. 'You're always five steps behind me!'

'Dustpan and brush at the ready,' Farhana sighs, long-suffering, 'sweeping up all the mess.'

Valentine opens her mouth and then closes it again.

'Can we have a quick word somewhere private, maybe?' Aamilah suddenly asks, pushing her daughter over to the care of her sister and then threading past Valentine and into the house. Valentine gazes after her, uncertainly (as Aamilah introduces two, random cats to her neatly slippered toe), then apologizes to Farhana (for what exactly she is unsure) before turning to follow her.

Aamilah is comfortably ensconced on the sofa in the sitting room, *niqab* completely removed, when Valentine arrives there. She pats the cushion beside her.

'Okay, so I screwed up,' she says, 'I just got over-excited, but I actually have something really important to share with you.'

Valentine does not feel inclined to sit down. She remains where she stands, frowning slightly.

'Nessa,' Aamilah addresses the child in a gentle, almost keening voice, 'I see your panties are on the rug over there. Will you pick them up and put them back on again, please? There's a good girl. Your auntie and I need to have an important conversation, and we can't do that if we're all too preoccupied by your Nu-nu, can we, now?'

She pats the cushion again as Nessa heads off, perfectly obligingly, to retrieve her pants. This time Valentine sits down.

'I just wanted to say …' Aamilah starts off, then, 'That's two legs in one hole, Nessa! Have the sense you were born with, child! Put your other leg in the other hole …'

She observes Nessa's progress for a few moments. 'Good job! Well done! And I want you to keep those *on* now, please, like a proper, grown-up girl, all right?'

Nessa nods.

'Thank you.' Aamilah smiles. 'Now go and play with your dolly. Make sure your dolly is wearing her pants, too, please. And all your other toys as well.'

'I don't think her teddies …' Valentine starts off.

Aamilah flaps an impatient hand to silence her. 'Teddies too,' she persists. 'All good girls and all good toys need to be kept decent at all times.'

Nessa toddles over towards some crayons and paper in the corner of the room.

'Draw a picture of yourself looking all pretty and decent in your lovely pants,' Aamilah suggests as Valentine exclaims under her breath – a combination of amazed and amused – at Aamilah's dogged persistence over this issue.

Nessa picks up her crayons and starts to draw, finally allowing Aamilah to relax and focus her full attention back on Valentine again. 'Karim told me about the agoraphobia on our drive home this morning,' she tells her, confidentially. 'Salvatore told him about it at daycare. I just wanted to let you know that I honestly had no idea – none whatsoever – when I suggested you put on the robe and head outside in it earlier ...'

'Of course.' Valentine nods, bearing her no ill will whatsoever.

'Good,' Aamilah sighs, relieved. 'I mean I've never even considered asking an English girl to try on my robes before. My robe is a sacred thing to me. Not the garment itself, obviously, but what it represents.'

'I completely get that,' Valentine concurs.

'Afterwards – I mean after I left here – I just thought, That girl is so oddly attached to the way she looks, the external part of herself, the superficial part of herself, and she dresses herself up but she never leaves the house. I just thought, That's really weird. And then I thought, Allah has made her agoraphobic for a reason, of course. As a test. And Allah always tests the people he loves the most. "*Wherever tears fall, divine Mercy is shown* ..." She really needs to know that.'

Aamilah's sharp brown eyes suddenly soften. She reaches out and pats Valentine's arm. 'Allah really loves you,' she whispers, 'he really, really loves you. I can feel it when I'm near you. This special atmosphere. This lightness. This sense of closeness. I feel your need. You remind me so much of myself. The Prophet – peace be upon him – once said, "The Faithful are like mirrors to each other" ...'

'Thank you,' Valentine mutters, somewhat uneasily (unsure how much of a compliment she considers this to be).

'Allah is compassionate and all-forgiving,' Aamilah continues. 'I know in my heart that he sent me here today for a reason.

One of our Seven Articles of Faith is that good and bad is predestined by Allah. Like I say, everything happens for a reason, and I think – in fact I'm certain – that Allah wants you to love him. He wants you to stop hating yourself and to dedicate your life to loving him instead.'

'That's very –' Valentine starts off, haltingly.

'You don't even have to think about it,' Aamilah interrupts, 'you just need to do it. This minute. Right now. Make that decision in your heart to turn towards Allah.'

'It's just …' Valentine frowns, her eyes lingering on Nessa.

'*Understand that all shall be well*,' Aamilah quotes, serenely.

'Right.' Valentine nods.

'I mean just give it some thought.' She inspects Valentine's face, intently. 'You're a beautiful girl. Imagine how amazing it would be if you focused all that loveliness on Allah instead of on the world. Imagine what a great gift you would be bringing him. If you stopped the tattoos and gave up the clothes and the make-up – all these barriers which stand between you and complete happiness.'

'So you … you think I need to give *everything* up?' Valentine's somewhat taken aback (even rendered slightly resentful) by this stark prospect. 'Doesn't God – Allah – love me as I am?'

'Are you happy?' Aamilah demands.

'Uh …' Valentine thinks for a second. 'No. Not especially. But there are things in my life that make me feel worthwhile – which give me a strong sense of …'

'As Karim always likes to tell me,' Aamilah quickly butts in: '*Paradise is encompassed by the things we dislike to do, while the fires of Hell are encircled by our desires.*'

Valentine stares at her, perplexed.

'Sometimes it's the very things we like the best – the things that fuel our egos – that make us unhappy. We just don't realize it. We think the pain inside – the fear inside – is something that threatens the happiness those things bring us –

but in fact it's those very things – which we hold on to so desperately – that are the very *source* of our misery! When you let go of those things you let go of fear.'

Valentine ponders this for a while. She briefly remembers the dead Valentine of that morning – the *un*-Valentine – peeking blankly through her grille at the fine chrome-work on Karim's car. She shudders, involuntarily.

'Of course I'm running ahead of myself, here.' Aamilah picks a stray cat hair from the knee of her robe, simulating nonchalance. 'It's just that I'm so excited by the idea of what it would mean to you and to Allah if you gave yourself back to him again.'

Valentine nods, mutely. She doesn't really know what else to contribute.

'There's this brilliant website which I found very helpful when I was first thinking of reverting back to the one true faith myself.' Aamilah reaches into a pocket inside her robe and removes a small piece of paper with a phone number and an address neatly printed on to it. She passes it over.

'The phone number is my mobile. I want you to ring me on it whenever you feel like you need to. The internet address is for *HowToBeAGoodMoslemGirl.com*. It's very basic but really useful. Sets everything out way better than I ever could.'

'Thanks.'

Valentine takes the slip of paper and puts it down on the arm of the sofa.

A short silence follows. Outside, on the front step, Farhana is softly singing an indecipherable nursery rhyme to Badriya. Nessa listens from her spot on the floor, head cocked, intrigued.

'So what about this little picnic of ours?' Aamilah wonders, grinning.

'Oh … uh …' Valentine's eyes turn towards Nessa.

'We brought along a spare robe, just in case,' she wheedles. 'Farhana and I will walk either side of you. We'll protect you.

Nothing bad will happen. We'll be your bodyguards. You'll be completely safe with us, I swear.'

'It's not … I'm just not sure …'

Valentine slowly shakes her head. Her throat starts to contract. 'Mum will be home in an hour or so. And I need to contact the bank …' She starts to try and clamber to her feet. 'In fact I should probably …'

'We'll be forty minutes, tops,' Aamilah doggedly persists, grabbing the fabric of Valentine's skirt to stop her from getting up. 'We'll just stroll down there in the sun, have a quick snack on the grass – feed the pigeons, maybe – then head straight back home again.'

'It's nothing personal, I just don't think … I just really couldn't …' Valentine struggles to explain herself.

'Don't think. Just act!' Aamilah exclaims. 'Be our cousin for an hour. Be one of us. Stop being Valentine, full of doubt, always over-analysing everything. Be … be beautiful, happy, laughing Hamra, our retarded niece from Leicester.'

'You have a retarded niece in Leicester?' Valentine's slightly perplexed.

'Yes. Well, no,' Aamilah modifies, 'he's retarded but he's our nephew and he isn't actually called Hamra. Hamra's a girl's name. It means "red" in Arabic. Red' – she grins – 'like a Valentine.'

'Hamra,' Valentine echoes, amused, softly touching her hair.

'Red for love,' Aamilah nods, encouraged. 'Red for a rose. Red for …'

She casts around for further examples.

'Red for blood,' Valentine murmurs, anxiously, 'red for danger.'

'Red for sacrifice.' Aamilah nods, her brown eyes igniting, enthused. 'And for strawberries,' she then quickly adds, with a shrug and a grin, 'and cherries, of course, and post-boxes and … and red for a robin's breast …' – she jumps to her feet –

'and fire engines' – she heads for the door – 'and poppies and ladybirds and ...' She pauses for a moment. 'While I think of it,' she muses, pulling on her *niqab*, 'we made *pakoras* for lunch ...' She pops her head out into the hallway. 'Hana!' she yells. 'Hana! *Hana!* Did you remember to bring the ketchup?'

'Here he is!' Jen exclaims, emerging from behind a bush, her white, Lycra catsuit still loosely dangling – like a giant used condom – from around her hips. 'It's everybody's favourite cancer-victim!'

Gene stands frozen, like a statue, sweat cascading down his cheeks, staring at his phone. He is re-reading a text from Sheila which says simply, 'We rlly nd to spk about V. URGENT!'

'Hello?'

He finally glances up. Jen stands before him, the upper half of her torso encased in only a skimpy, gold bikini top.

'Bloody hell, Jen!'

He shoves the phone away and rapidly averts his gaze, his offended eyeballs seeking temporary respite in the cool green spears of a clump of ornamental grass. He looks pale and distracted. It suddenly occurs to Jen that the moisture on his cheeks might not be sweat after all, but something infinitely more perturbing.

'Are you all right?' she asks, scowling. 'You've been behaving really weirdly ever since you got here.'

Gene bends forward and retrieves a rusty, old padlock from the grassy knoll. He inspects it, with interest, then murmurs, 'Antique ...' and drops it again. He peers up into the sky where a low-flying plane leaves a curling vapour trail in the heavens' gently beaten Turkish-blue enamelwork. The contours of his face seem oddly sharp – as though freshly etched in a new – less kind, less congenial – shade of chalk.

'What's wrong?' Jen repeats, almost panicked, now. 'You look really pale.'

'Nothing. Nothing's wrong.'

Gene drags his eyes back down from the heavens, reeling them in like two errant kites on unreliable strings. But his pupils will not be curtailed. They jump and start like hatching frogspawn in a murky pond.

'Are you ill?' Jen's aghast.

Gene doesn't answer. He feels temporarily disconnected from his usual, brash familiarity with vowels and consonants.

'Dehydrated?' Jen demands. 'Did you have a row with Sheila? D'you need to sit down?'

Gene remains very still, as if stillness alone can forestall the things he has done and the things he must soon be compelled to do.

'I've really messed up,' he eventually murmurs, half to himself, his lips barely moving. The eyes remain unfocused.

'Messed up? How?' Jen takes a small step closer.

'I can't tell you' – he smiles, wanly – 'but it's bad.'

'Why can't you tell me?' Another small step.

'Because it's …' he slowly shakes his head.

'You don't think I can be trusted?' Jen's deeply offended.

Gene shakes his head again, laughing to himself, hoarsely. Then:

'Yes.'

'*Gene!*' She cuffs him – possibly a fraction harder than just playfully – on the shoulder. He takes the blow, still laughing, his eyes moistening with tears. His insides feel all sharp and tense and tightly packed, like the compressed coils in an old-fashioned sprung mattress.

'Okay, you're officially freaking me out, now!' Jen snaps. 'Just tell me what's wrong!'

'Nothing.' Gene closes his eyes. 'I'll be fine in a minute. I'm just having a little … a little moment, that's all.'

'Why? About what? Is it the ball?'

'Ball?' He opens his eyes again.

'The lost ball?'

He turns and glances around him, fuzzily, as if only just getting his bearings. He's at the golf course – he's inside his own body – it's a fine day – there's a kid in the rough a short distance away searching for something, valiantly poking around in the undergrowth with a specially fashioned twig.

'Is the boy taking part in the Children's Tournament?' he asks.

'No. He's here with me. I brought him. You seriously don't think I can be trusted?' Jen persists, hurt.

'That outfit …' Gene sighs, appraising her, almost mournfully, 'not really your average golf club attire.'

'It's my African-Warrior-Queen-Space-Bandit look.'

Jen puts her hands on her hips, thrusts out her chest and poses.

'I see.' Gene's none the wiser.

'I'm Shaka Zulu's Martian wife.'

She puts her hands behind her head, messes up her hair and angles her hips.

'Very fetching.' Gene smiles, wanly.

Jen stops posing. 'You think I can't be discreet?' she challenges him, growing increasingly irritated by his dislocated air. 'Well how d'you fancy *this* for discretion?' She draws a deep breath. 'See the kid?'

She thumbs over her shoulder towards the distant Israel. Gene nods. He sees the kid.

'Ransom's secret love-child!'

Gene's eyes widen.

'And he doesn't have the first clue about it!'

'Who doesn't?' Gene demands. 'The kid?'

Jen nods.

'And Ransom?'

'Not really sure …' She shrugs, tying the arms of her catsuit into a knot around her waist. 'Plays a close game, that one.'

'Have you said anything?'

'Nope. But I kind of hinted. The kid's mother's Jamaican – his manager's sister, and the dates definitely add up.'

'So – hang on – his mother's Esther's sister?'

'Yup.' Jen nods. 'I tried to tell you last night on the phone. She's over here for the birth. She's this strident environmentalist. Wages a one-woman campaign against the Jamaican tourist industry. Calls it "parasitic" – the New Colonialism. Very sharp. Very scary. But the kid's a complete sweetheart.'

Gene scratches his head, trying to take this all in. 'So what exactly are you hoping to achieve by ...?'

'Not sure.' Jen shrugs. 'I'm just playing it by ear. Having a bit of fun. Generating chaos. I'm visualizing myself as some kind of toxic, intergalactic super-being who's been dropped on to the earth from another galaxy by a mischievous deity. We have a completely different moral outlook in my part of the stratosphere. More arbitrary, more stringent, more sophisticated. Am I the bad girl?' she ponders, tip of her right index finger pressing into her chin, eyes raised in a semblance of deep thought. 'A skinny, blonde scourge? A dark mistress of anarchy, artifice and contrivance? Or am I' – she swaps to her left index finger and raises her eyes to an adjacent angle – 'the complete opposite? An inspirational, Lycra-clad angel-sprite, single-handedly fighting the forces of disinformation with my trusty, golden bazookas, straw wedgies and deadly mascara wand?'

Jen produces her mascara wand from what seems like thin air.

'So this isn't still all about Stan ...?' Gene hazards a guess.

'It's like he brings out my Gaia energy,' Jen sighs, gazing over towards Ransom (who is obsessively inspecting his hairline in a couple of the photographer's sample shots). 'I've not really got a handle on it myself yet. It's very strong, very instinctual ... And like I say, I'm not even entirely sure if it's to the power of good or evil.'

'Well maybe you need to try and work that out before you –' Gene immediately starts to caution her.

'It's like being on fire!' Jen interrupts, enthused. 'It's amazing! It's like I just woke up. It's like … it's like Jen's finally coming into focus. She's arrived! She's *here*.'

'You were always here,' Gene assures her. 'You're generally very present, by and large.'

'Really?' Jen looks bored. 'I'm not so sure.'

'If you want my advice …' Gene starts off.

'Oh God, no. Don't spoil it with your sensible advice,' Jen clucks. 'Good advice is the last thing I feel like hearing right now. *Pshaw* to good advice! Good advice is like, *urgh*, yawnsville, foot-tap, eye-roll.'

'Well maybe there's a useful message in that,' Gene counsels.

Jen stares at him for a few seconds, ruminatively, then her focus shifts slightly, and after another, shorter, somewhat more speculative pause:

'Holy *fuck*, Gene! You little scamp!'

He glances over his shoulder, spooked.

'Do my eyes deceive me,' Jen demands, with a pantomimic gawp, as he turns back around to face her again (still none the wiser), 'or are those a bunch of filthy love bites on your neck?'

There are no empty tables in the crowded hospital canteen. Sheila scans the room, her eyelids weighted by an excess of painkillers. She is precariously balanced on one crutch, her handbag swinging on her shoulder, her free hand clutching on to a packet of egg mayonnaise sandwiches and a piping-hot cappuccino in a sealed, plastic cup. She eventually fights her way over to a spare chair in the corner, smiles at the table's glowering occupant and asks if she might occupy the seat.

The woman she addresses is slight, of colour, and wears a heavy pair of square, tortoiseshell reading glasses which have slipped halfway down the bridge of her nose. Her small face is framed by a mass of wild, curly black hair. Her full lips shine with Vaseline. She has dark rings under her eyes.

'Sure,' she says, after a long, five-second pause, 'feel free.' She twitches her nose then returns to her book. It's entitled *The Diary of Frida Kahlo – An Intimate Self-Portrait*. The cover is an arrestingly amateurish daub by the artist of herself in the guise of a scary, witch-like wild-woman. This cartoon is – by sheer coincidence (and in the loosest possible sense) – a fairly accurate depiction of the general overall demeanour of the person currently in possession of it.

Sheila sits down, with a grunt. Her lone crutch falls to the floor. She curses under her breath. The glowering woman gazes up at her, laconically – a further five seconds pass, another nose twitch follows – then she sucks on her tongue and bends over to retrieve it.

'You fall?' she demands, in her husky but nicely modulated Jamaican accent. 'Or something fall on you?'

'Something fell on me.' Sheila takes back the crutch, with a nod of thanks. 'An electricity meter. I tried to block it with my shin …'

The woman bursts out laughing. Her laugh is like the warning bark of a hyena. Several people turn to peer at them, alarmed.

'I'm waiting for an x-ray,' Sheila continues (somewhat discomforted by the laugh herself). 'I blacked out mid-way through a baptism – just for a couple of seconds, tops – and my parishioners insisted on dragging me down here. The doctor thinks the bone might be chipped.'

She pauses (embarrassed by this high level of unburdening). 'They only have one free crutch in casualty. Somebody stole the other.'

'Shins can be dicey,' the woman muses. 'I crushed both my shins one time during an anti-logging demonstration in south-eastern Venezuela – Bolivar State. Been there?'

Sheila shakes her head.

'Well site security "accidentally" rolled a twenty-ton pile of timber on to our small group of protesters. One man was killed outright – decapitated – a local indigenous tribesman, a chief. Father of twelve girls. Another lost both his legs. I broke both feet. Shins were crushed. The nearest hospital was twenty-nine hours away. Dirt roads. Mountain passes. They called for a helicopter but it never came. We did the journey in an open-backed Land-Rover. We had one bottle of water between five of us and nothing to eat. The pain was incredible. I had two blood transfusions. Contracted a rare form of hepatitis as an added bonus.'

She grimaces at the memory, twitches her nose, and then returns to her book, a slight sneer playing at the corner of her lips.

Sheila gazes at the woman for several seconds, uncertain how to react (Awe? Sympathy? Incredulity?), then unwraps her sandwiches, takes a bite and carefully eases the lid from her coffee cup. She watches the woman read.

'I really enjoyed the Heyden Herrera,' she eventually murmurs.

The woman ignores her.

'His biography of Frida Kahlo,' Sheila adds, almost to herself.

'Never read it.' The woman glances back up again, takes a sip from her glass of orange juice and snaps a small chunk from the end of her unappetizing-looking organic flapjack.

'It's very good.' Sheila shrugs.

The woman pops the flapjack into her mouth then appraises Sheila from under heavily weighted lids as she chews.

'Why?' she eventually wonders.

'Well it's very detailed … uh … nicely anecdotal, cleverly structured, beautifully illustrated … Oh, and he pulls no punches about the serious artistic and emotional ramifications of her tram accident.'

'Tram accident?'

The woman twitches her nose.

Sheila nods.

'There was a tram accident?'

'The handrail went straight through her womb,' Sheila expands. 'She was eighteen. The bus was criminally overcrowded. It's what defined Kahlo as an artist – as a woman. She could never have children. She spent her entire adult life in unendurable pain. That's basically what her paintings are all about.'

'*Hmmn ...*' The woman continues to appraise Sheila, eyes still half-closed, then eventually murmurs, 'You remind me of ... What they call that old girl again? Sister Mary Beckett? The art critic?'

'Sister Wendy Beckett,' Sheila corrects her (uncertain whether to be pleased or offended). 'Well I'm very flattered ...' (she opts to settle for the former), 'although I'm not actually a nun, I'm a minister.'

'Well you got hair like a nun,' the woman counters.

'You think so?' Sheila raises her hand to her head. 'I only just had it cut.'

'It's gay hair,' the woman opines, with a mischievous snort. 'Gay nun's hair and that's a fact.'

'Thanks.' Sheila smiles back, brusquely. 'Ever considered a career in the diplomatic corps?'

'It's funny you should ask that ...' the woman snorts again, not remotely offended.

'It is?' Sheila's nonplussed.

'It is,' the woman confirms, gnomically.

'How so?' Sheila persists.

'I work in the field of human and environmental rights,' the woman explains, 'I spend my whole life rubbing up against arseholes and diplomats.'

'A lawyer?' Sheila asks. 'Or a journalist?'

'Lawyer, blogger, activist. Although I've been disbarred from practising in half the West Indies and most of both the Americas. I stir up shit, basically,' she continues, taking another sip of her juice. 'They call me a bitch-kitty, a rabble-rouser, a ball-breaker ...'

'You're the anti-diplomat,' Sheila opines.

'Just like your good friend Jesus Christ,' the woman smirks, then twitches her nose, then peers down at her book, then blinks, then twitches her nose again, then looks up. Sheila is anxiously combing her fingers through her hair.

'The hair's cute,' the woman clucks. 'I'm a big fan of those butch gay girls. I lived with two gay nuns in Barbados for six months one time. We was protesting against a two hundred million dollar landfill site.'

'Any injuries?' Sheila wonders, drolly.

The woman opens her mouth and loosens one of her front teeth. She then pushes it back in again, adjusts her glasses and returns to her book. As she reads the glasses slip back down her nose.

'Are you prone to headaches at all?' Sheila wonders.

'Pardon me?'

The woman glances up, irritated.

'Headaches?'

'Why d'you ask?'

'I notice how your glasses keep slipping down your nose. Mine used to do that all the time. I suffered from these really terrible headaches and I didn't know why. Thought it might be an allergy or something. Turns out it was caused by reading through out-of-focus eyeglasses. When the glasses slip down your nose they automatically go out of focus. You're straining your eyes without even realizing.'

Several seconds pass in quizzical silence and then: 'A very lot of words come out your mouth,' the woman observes, staring at Sheila's lips, fixedly, as if they alone might be at fault.

'In the end I bought these things called Wedgees ...' Sheila reaches into her handbag (refusing to be intimidated) and withdraws her glasses case. She opens it and removes her glasses. She shows the Wedgees to the woman. 'They're small and padded ... I got them by mail order. They fit snugly on to the end of each arm. Stop the glasses from slipping. I swear I haven't had a single headache since I first bought them.'

'A miracle!' the woman exclaims, dourly.

'Well they've certainly worked for me.' Sheila shrugs.

The woman – clearly against her better judgement – takes the proffered glasses and inspects the Wedgees. She squeezes them, somewhat aggressively.

'I do get headaches,' she finally admits, passing them back, 'and my son, Israel, gets them worse. He also wears glasses – reads a lot.'

Sheila carefully removes the Wedgees from the arms of her glasses, then indicates towards the woman to pass her pair over. The woman hesitates, grimaces, then takes hers off. Sheila grabs them and gently pushes the Wedgees on to the end of either arm.

'Give them a try.' She passes the glasses back to the woman. The woman takes them and puts them on.

'Shake your head as much as you like,' Sheila suggests, 'they'll stay in place.'

The woman shakes her head.

'What you call these things again?' she demands, finally fully engaged.

'Wedgees. But I'm sure there are other brands ...'

The woman shakes her head for a second time.

'They won't shift,' Sheila insists.

'They ain't shifting,' the woman confirms.

'Told you.'

'I do suffer from headaches,' the woman reiterates. 'I read a lot of contracts, lot of legal papers, letters, newspaper clippings on the computer, that kind of stuff.'

'So Frida's more along the lines of light relief, eh?' Sheila smiles.

'I been asked to write a book – part autobiography, part self-help bible for bolshy radicals. Publishers want an activist's version of P.J. O'Rourke's *Holidays in Hell*. You ever read that thing?'

'Yup.' Sheila nods, enthused.

'*Huh* …' the woman mutters (plainly unimpressed by the positivity of Sheila's response). 'Piece of supercilious right-wing balderdash.'

'Pretty funny, though.' Sheila shrugs.

'People think I'm funny, but I never really see it myself,' the woman mutters. 'They say my son is funny, but I never found him funny, neither. He's weird – real weird – but funny? *Nuh*-uh.'

'Perhaps it's simply your natural candour?' Sheila suggests. 'Thing is I'm struggling to get started' – the woman pointedly ignores Sheila's insight – 'can't tell what to put in and what to leave out. My lover give me this thing for inspiration' – she holds up the Kahlo book – 'but it's all over the place …'

She violently shakes her head again. The glasses stay *in situ*.

'Well what kinds of autobiographies *do* you like?' Sheila wonders.

'Never actually read one cover to cover.'

'Oh.'

'Never had the luxury,' the woman confides, 'always had something way more profitable to do with my time.'

'*Hmmn*. Could seem a little arrogant,' Sheila gently chides her. 'I mean to try and write something which you expect other people to read without doing any of the basic groundwork yourself …'

'Who you calling arrogant?!' the woman hisses, furious (several diners turn around again).

Sheila bounces back in her seat, her tongue stumbling over an apology, as the woman commences to cackle (evidently delighted by the extremity of Sheila's reaction).

'Of course I'm arrogant, Wendy!' She claps her hands together, gleefully. 'How else I gonna survive out there? Eh?' She then shakes her head, perhaps a little more forcefully than is required.

'You can keep those if you like' – Sheila indicates towards the Wedgees (refusing to be provoked) – 'I have a spare pair at home.'

'I don't want to keep them.' The woman scowls, starting to remove her glasses, offended. 'I can buy my own. I was just trying them out.'

'I have a second pair at home,' Sheila persists. 'I bought them for my mother but she had laser treatment and gave them back.'

'Well if you put it like that ...' The woman grudgingly accepts the offer, then, after a second's thought, 'You can have this in exchange.'

She removes some loose, printed papers from between the pages of her book, closes it and pushes it across the table towards her. 'It's a review copy. Not even in the stores yet.'

'But wasn't it a gift?' Sheila automatically resists.

'Who cares? I'm not even reading the damn thing,' the woman confesses. 'Look – I had some work-related papers hidden inside.' She grins.

'Why are you hiding them?' Sheila wonders, intrigued.

'I'm on a six-month break. A holiday from trouble. I promised faithfully not to get involved in anything.'

'Promised who?'

'My man.' She shrugs. 'My son.'

'So what are the papers about?'

'They're a "spirited defence" of Responsible Tourism.' The woman rolls her eyes, drolly.

'You mean like eco-tourism?'

'Lord have mercy!' The woman shudders, theatrically.

'There's a problem with eco-tourism?' Sheila's bemused.

'A problem?' The woman looks astonished at Sheila's evident naivety on the issue. 'Okay, in brief' – she knits her fingers together and leans forward on the table, fixing Sheila with her steely gaze – 'I think we all accept that global tourism is one of the major threats to cultural and biological diversity in the "third world" right now, if not on the planet as a whole,' (she doesn't wait for Sheila to respond), 'and that transnational organizations are only the tip of a giant iceberg – corrupt governments, airline monopolies, Bretton Woods, a Western culture that hinges on notions of entitlement and excess – they all play their part. But the way I see it, the eco-tourists are just as bad – worse, even. Their dogged pursuit of paradise on earth? Pure hokum! These folk are way more complacent, more dangerous, more downright despicable than the "real" shit-heads by a mile! Why? Because they're even more deluded. At least the shit-heads know what they want – cold, hard cash, at any price. The eco-tourists think they can fly and gawp and consume with perfectly clean consciences for a few extra dollars and some bogus assurances. But let's face it … uh …' The woman grasps for Sheila's name and then realizes that she doesn't know it.

'Sheila,' Sheila interjects, holding out her hand.

'Let's face it, Wendy, they're just another cog in the same, corrupt system. They're not helping anyone or changing anything. It's superficial, not systemic.'

Sheila nods, still holding out her hand.

'I'm a Deep Ecologist,' the woman continues, ignoring the hand. 'You ever hear of Deep Ecology, before, Wendy?'

'It rings a vague bell,' Sheila avers.

'Left Biocentrism? Environmental ethics blended with left-wing causes?'

'Absolutely …' Sheila nods.

'We oppose economic growth, capitalism and consumerism,' the woman brusquely continues. 'I'm Victoria,' she finishes off, 'Victoria Wilson. Vicki Wilson to my friends.'

'So how'd you get involved in all this stuff?'

Sheila uses the rejected hand to pick up her coffee cup and take a sip.

'I just opened my eyes and took a good look around me.'

Victoria shrugs.

Sheila puts down her coffee, picks up her sandwich and takes another bite.

'I grew up in Jamaica,' Victoria expands. 'When I was sixteen I began working, part-time, in this Anglo-American-owned holiday resort – part of a big franchise. Couldn't get a job anywhere else … Didn't take long till I started to notice the glass ceiling for local employees. Everybody in management positions was shipped in from abroad. Same deal with all the items sold in resort stores – even the food served in the restaurants was shipped in from Florida or someplace. It was basically just a new, more subtle kind of colonialism in which our "paradise" culture was superficially celebrated – patronized, boiled down into a series of offensive, easily digestible clichés – and profoundly degraded: local people were banned from the beaches, paid pitiable wages and forced to live in makeshift "service" villages while all the profit they made – and I mean *all* the profit, every cent – was filtered clean away from the "host" island, straight back to the multinational mothership.'

'Almost like a modern apartheid,' Sheila muses, through further mouthfuls of her sandwich.

'"Almost"?!' Victoria clucks, outraged. 'They exploited our resources – because that's all we were; all our country was – all our country *is*: a series of "resources" to be pitilessly consumed. They paid no heed to local people, our well-being, our culture or our environment. They're just cancers, devouring everything that's good and pumping out filth and disease by way of exchange – poisoning our seas, our rivers, our soils, poisoning our people's minds, creating a deep sense of disenfranchisement, nurturing feelings of inadequacy and frustration and hopelessness and envy. They're carcinogenic. They're the devil incarnate. They sicken me.'

A short silence follows.

'It must feel good to make a difference,' Sheila finally volunteers. 'I always dreamed of making a difference. But it's so much harder than you think – I mean to break through all the red tape, the petty interests –'

'It's not hard,' Victoria interrupts, flapping her hand, dismissively, 'it's only hard if you play by their rules, if you think you can change things, piecemeal, from within. That's a fool's approach – pissing in the wind – a criminal waste of valuable energy.'

Victoria takes another bite of her flapjack.

'In the Church we tend to value the virtue of obedience,' Sheila explains, 'to encourage a state of humility …'

'You think Jesus Christ was obedient, Sister,' Victoria snorts, 'or humble? Hah! Shows how much you understand theology!'

Sheila shifts in her seat, uncomfortably. 'I hear what you're saying, and I respect your opinion, but I can also see the virtue in compromise. It's often a harder, more flawed, more frustrating route – I mean there's this aggressive streak in me which really needs confining …'

'So don't confine it!' Victoria's exasperated. 'Act on gut instinct!'

'That's what my husband's always saying' – Sheila shakes her head – 'but it's part of my journey to confine it – a test of my faith.'

'So nuns can get themselves hitched in this country?' Victoria exclaims, mugging astonishment.

'You've never felt the urge to improve yourself?' Sheila asks, scowling.

'Why tie yourself up in knots?' Victoria demands, contemptuous. 'Why over-think everything? That's definitely a privilege of the West – life's so easy you need to be *inventing* problems!'

'You're absolutely right, of course,' Sheila immediately concedes (taking this one square on the chin). She shakes her head, almost forlornly, and smiles. Victoria suddenly – unexpectedly – returns the smile, almost as if she's seeing Sheila – her essence, her sense of inner conflict, her humanity – for the very first time. The encroaching storm clouds lift from her face. Her eyes glow like two silky dollops of heated molasses. Sheila finds herself reddening slightly under the unexpectedly intense spotlight of this odd woman's approbation. She takes another bite of her sandwich to disguise her confusion, eventually murmuring, 'Although if I can offer a small word of warning: I'm not sure if absolute certainty always makes for the greatest autobiography ...'

'*Huh?*' Victoria's smile instantly sets. The long shadows return. 'How so?'

'Because people need to empathize. I mean if you want this book to be inspirational – a kind of political call to arms – there needs to be the odd chink in the armour ...'

Victoria ponders this for a moment.

'I suppose we might call it the "handrail through the womb" moment,' Sheila adds, as an afterthought.

'*Urgh* – the handrail!' Victoria grimaces. 'Trust me, I had plenty of those in my time. But definitely nothing I feel the need to share. That's the bit I *don't* want to think about. That's the bit I *never* want to think about.'

'And that's precisely why you're blocked' – Sheila shrugs – 'because the handrail moments provide relief – and meaning – and contrast. They make everything else – the stuff you *can* control – more vivid, more coherent.'

Victoria pushes her flapjack away (as if the flapjack is the harsh truth she doesn't want to acknowledge). She remains silent for a while.

'Perhaps you're worried that if you commit some of these things – these handrail moments, these perceived "weaknesses" – to paper' – Sheila pushes her luck still further – 'that if you face up to them, in print – in public – then not only will you risk showing vulnerability – a dangerous quality in your line of work – but you may even start questioning your whole *raison d'être*, seeing your protests – your campaigning – in an entirely new light, as part of something more internal, a different kind of struggle ...'

'Nuh-*uh*.' Victoria shakes her head. 'Vicki Wilson was always bolshy – always stepping outside the boundaries, always slightly off-key – ask anybody. I was born breech, on Halloween. They had to cut me out from my mother's belly. They heard me screaming before the doctor could finish his incision. Like the wail of a banshee my ma always tells me. Poor old boy was so scared he almost dropped his scalpel!'

'Is that possible?' Sheila's incredulous. 'I mean for a foetus to actually ...?'

'Nope.' Victoria shrugs, laughing.

A brief silence follows. Victoria pulls her plate back towards her and prods at her flapjack with her index finger. Sheila finishes off the first half of her sandwich in one large mouthful.

'I always dreamed of being a writer,' she starts off, once she's swallowed.

'You dreamed of being a lot of things,' Victoria grumbles, 'why'd you end up as none of them?'

'Good point,' Sheila acquiesces, with a woeful chuckle, wiping her mouth with a paper napkin.

Another short silence and then, 'I was fifteen,' Victoria starts off, haltingly, eyes lowered, pushing her flapjack around the plate, 'just dropped out of school, spending the hours drinking, smoking ganja, dating the son of a local gangsta, not a sensible thought in my head, and my big sister – not me – is working at the local resort, finding lost balls, caddying on their golf course ...' Victoria grimaces. 'She's real ambitious, though, funding her own way through university – Applied Sciences; wants to become an engineer. That girl was always clever with her hands, always fixing shit, always making shit ... Anyhow, one day she meets this white boy – English boy – pretty handy with a putter – earning a few dollars giving golf lessons at the resort. Beach bum. Long, bleach hair. Musical – keen brass player. Finds out our family is related – my mother's side – to Francis Johnson, the famous band leader. In fact Aunt Hulda still teaches the keyed bugle in Freetown. He begs an introduction. Starts taking a few lessons. And somewhere along the line we bump into each other – don't ask me how – I barely remember – and it's crazy: fireworks! Three months down the line, I'm pregnant. The day I find out, this boy is off on the other side of the island playing in some big-money tournament. The next day he wins the damn thing. The day after that he ups and flies home. No letter, no phone call ... And best of all, my big sister leaves with him. They been together ever since.'

'As a couple?'

Victoria shrugs.

'But he knew about ...?'

'She told him. Apparently he just laughed. Brushed it off. Didn't believe it was his. Gave me two hundred dollars for an abortion. Left it in an envelope with the folk on reception.'

'How awful!' Sheila's appalled. 'Did you actually follow through with it?'

Victoria shakes her head. 'I'm waiting for my appointment at a local clinic and the doctor is running late for some reason. There's a pretty, beige girl sitting three chairs along with a septic wound on her finger. She's a Borrincano –'

'Bori ...?' Sheila interrupts.

'From Puerto Rico. Turns out she injured her finger releasing a hawksbill.'

'Is that a kind of bird?'

'No, a turtle. It was trapped in a fishing net. She's a marine biologist, an ecologist. Anyhow, to cut a very long story short, we started to chat and ...' She shrugs. 'Marisol picked me up, brushed me down, read me the riot act and completely turned my life around.'

'You kept the baby?'

Sheila's eyes are suddenly prickling (this tale is – to all intents and purposes – her tale).

Vicki nods. 'Marisol was a strict Catholic – ten years older, well educated, politically savvy. She was in on the ground floor with the WAGM – spoke at one of their first, international conferences –'

'The WA ...?'

'World Anti-Golf Movement. This huge course had been built on a string of coral islands just adjacent to one of her main research posts. The impact of the thing – water depletion, toxic contamination of the reef with pesticides, fungicides and weedicides, the adoption of landscaped, foreign eco-systems and plants, the raft of new diseases this brought to the indigenous surrounds –'

'You bonded over your hatred of a common enemy!' Sheila interrupts, grinning.

Victoria scowls, irritated. 'Marisol opened my eyes – taught me to look at the world from a completely fresh perspective – became my mentor – encouraged me back into part-time education – helped organize a USAID scholarship – supported me all the way through law school. It wasn't just a matter of –'

'But if it hadn't been for that golfer ...' Sheila persists.

'You think I should be grateful?!' Victoria snaps.

'No. *No* ...' Sheila realizes that she needs to tread carefully, here, 'but you should always be honest – especially with yourself, and with your reader, by extension.'

Victoria sucks on her tongue, annoyed. 'Why? So it can look like everything I am, everything I believe in, everything

I've achieved in the Deep Green movement, against all the odds – as a poor, young, black woman and a single mother – was just part of some … some petty, little teenage vendetta? Nah-*ah*. No way. Because – trust me – this man doesn't deserve the credit – *none* of it – nor the publicity for that matter.'

'Okay … okay …' Sheila gently concedes the point, then carefully considers her response for a second, her eyes soft and unfocused. 'Okay, so how about – purely on pragmatic grounds, for the sake of the book, and your blood-pressure – you try and put a slightly different, slightly less defensive spin on it …' She pushes her sandwich aside, decisively (as if thereby creating an open arena for free, intellectual exchange). 'Stop seeing that particular phase of your life as a private humiliation, a personal disaster, a critical mis-judgement on your part and start seeing it as … as a message, a kind of fable; something with universal relevance; a metaphor, a sort of … of *paradigm*, almost. You were the island that he conquered and then exploited. Your baby was the waste to be casually disposed of … Yes, he was a pig – of *course* he was, it's patently obvious – it goes without saying, and because it goes without saying there's really no need to say it, or to think it, or to feel it, even. So rise above. Take the higher path. Be magnanimous. Maybe go one step further, and admit that the experience actually *taught* you something. It was a hard lesson, sure, but it was a true beginning. He was the piece of grit in the mouth of an oyster that turned – with Marisol's guidance and your raw determination – into a pearl.'

Victoria opens her mouth, scowling, and starts to say something.

'Don't worry that you're giving him too much credit, either,' Sheila interrupts, hand raised, 'because what happened with him was just a starting point, nothing more; a seed was planted but it took the soil and the rain and the light and the sun to create a flower. Approached from that angle, with that attitude – you know, benign dispassion; cheerful indifference – all ideas of vengeance, of a long-term vendetta or of petty revenge just seem absolutely irrelevant. They simply don't figure. They aren't even on the radar.'

Victoria – lips pressed back together again (with some considerable effort on her part) – ponders what's been said in a quizzical silence, one brow slightly raised, her skinny index finger drawing a looping hem into the condensation along the top of her glass.

'How does Marisol feel about the book?' Sheila wonders, her eyes following Victoria's finger as it gracefully loops. 'What's her advice been?'

Victoria's finger stops looping, slowly drops, then rests quietly on the table, a thin coating of moisture on the pad briefly conjoining her soft flesh to the lacquered surface.

'Marisol ...' she starts off, then her voice wavers. She closes her eyes for a moment, draws a deep breath, clears her throat (as if irritated by this unexpected show of vulnerability) and tries once again: 'Marisol died in 2003, from non-Hodgkin's lymphoma ...' Her voice sounds clipped this time around, almost dispassionate. 'It's a disease often associated with pesticides – kills golf managers and farm workers. She was diagnosed in the July and died five weeks later.'

'My God, I'm so sorry,' Sheila interjects, horrified. Victoria shrugs. 'I was heavily involved in the anti-globalization protests that year – spent several months working at Vandana Shiva's Research Foundation for Science, Technology and Natural Resource Policy at the foot of the Himalayas. It was an incredibly productive time for me – an amazing time – an activist's dream come true ...' She pauses, pressing her lips together again, her nostrils flaring. 'Of course I knew there were some problems with Marisol's health ...' she murmurs, her voice softer, now, 'there'd been a number of scares since the RAMSAR wetlands campaign – all that contact with raw sewage – but I never thought ...'

'Were you still together?'

Victoria shakes her head. 'We were never a "real" couple, not in any formal sense – we both moved around so much, were so caught up in Deep Green issues, mine chiefly developmental, hers much more marine based – but we were definitely soul mates. Her parents never knew she was bi – still don't. They're very traditional people, very respectable. They'd be crushed to find out.'

Sheila ponders this for a while. 'So in terms of the book ...'

'My boy has no clue who his father is' – Victoria grimaces – 'and I have no intention of telling him, either.'

'You don't think he has a right to know?' Sheila's surprised.

'He thinks he's dead.' Victoria shrugs.

'You told him that?' Sheila's shocked.

'Yup.' Victoria nods, unrepentant.

'And he doesn't ... he doesn't suspect?'

'Nope.'

'How about the father? I mean if he's still in a relationship with ...?'

'Esther told him I had the abortion. It just seemed easier. We made an uneasy truce: I help keep an eye on her kids back in Jamaica and she keeps her mouth firmly shut.'

'Esther?' Sheila echoes, then her cheeks suddenly flush.

'You got a problem?' Victoria demands, instantly on guard.

'No. No. Not at all.' Sheila breaks eye contact and reaches down for her lone crutch. 'It's ... uh ... it's just that I hadn't ... I mean I didn't actually realize ...' She grinds to a slow halt.

'Realize what?' Victoria glowers.

'Uh ...' Sheila releases the crutch, sniffs, lightly touches her nose, and then calmly re-establishes eye contact. 'I had no idea how much of a drain golf actually is on the world's ecology,' she offers, somewhat limply. 'I mean I'd never really considered ...'

'In the US alone it contributes around 50 billion dollars per annum to the national economy.' Victoria happily clambers back up on to her soapbox. 'It's huge business – represents powerful vested interests. They have around 18,000 courses covering 1.7 million acres, guzzling 4 billion gallons of fresh water, daily. On that basis alone it represents an ecological holocaust. Four *billion* gallons. That's equivalent to the entire US population's residential water use each day. One in eight people on this planet have no access to safe drinking water. The UN estimates that by 2025 over 2.8 billion people will be experiencing severe water scarcity ...'

'Terrible.' Sheila nods. She glances down at her watch. 'Nearly time for your x-ray?' Victoria hazards a guess. Sheila weakly smiles in the affirmative.

'On the positive side,' Victoria adds, as a cavil, 'we're starting to see the bottom fall out of the market in places like Japan and Thailand following the economic downturn in the East. A lot of the smaller companies have gone bust, player numbers have significantly declined, although the Chinese and Indian markets are obviously going to prove –'

'I just really, *really* want to say,' Sheila rudely interrupts her (her brown eyes grave, her voice deeply emphatic), 'that I think you've got a great story to tell – an inspirational story – a story that could entertain, enlighten, educate ... I mean it's ... it's *all* there! I can just see it in my mind's eye: a tragedy, a tale of hope in the face of terrible adversity, a love story, a real girl's adventure; at once beautiful and moving and dangerous and exciting and sad and ... and *brave*. You just really need to tell it as honestly as you can – as straightforwardly as you can – in your own words, in your own way. It truly deserves that. Marisol deserves that – and your son. Just forget about the O'Rourke. Forget about the publishers. Sing your own song and sing it truthfully. It won't matter what kind of a voice you have, because it's *your* song. It's who you are. And when you sing a song like that there's simply no room for … for bluff or pretence or fudging or humbuggery, because you've done *nothing* to be ashamed of – nothing. Just speak your truth. Just … I dunno … just open your heart and let the whole, damn thing slip out of you – *tumble* out of you – *gush* out of you like a newborn – all dark and quick and hot and bloody …'

Victoria stares at her, astonished.

'I mean that's … that's just …' Sheila falters, 'that's just my humble opinion, obviously.'

She shrugs, self-consciously.

A short silence follows in which Victoria stares down at her flapjack, deep in thought. Sheila takes a small sip of her coffee. She notices that the front of her hand is glowing but can't quite work out if it's with perspiration or just steam from the hot liquid in her cup.

'Okay …' Victoria finally looks up, carefully adjusts her spectacles (although they haven't shifted down her nose by so much as a millimetre) and leans over the table towards her, snaking out her lean but surprisingly strong hand and grabbing Sheila's fingers with it.

'If you care so much about the damn thing, then do it with me!' She grins, squeezing Sheila's fingers until she almost squeals. 'C'mon! Do it *with* me! Take a sabbatical. Come to Jamaica. Work with me for six months. I'll give you free accommodation, basic living expenses and fifteen – no, scratch that – *twenty* per cent of the 40,000 dollar advance.'

Three seconds pass as Sheila's eyes shift, anxiously, from Victoria's emphatic smile to the slightly pinkening tips of her fingers.

'C'mon, Sister Wendy!' Victoria squeezes still harder, impatient – almost exasperated. 'Put your money where your mouth is for once!'

'Are you crazy?!' Sheila flutes, trying – and failing – to withdraw her hand, her heart clattering against her ribs like a clockwork mouse, her eyes strangely hopeful, almost fearful.

'You *betcha*! Crazy as a three-legged cat with a firecracker tied to its tail!' Victoria affirms, proudly, nostrils flaring, her brown eyes hard and cold as a dead eel's.

'But Hamra's such a *heavy* kind of name, Aamilah,' Farhana whines, plaintively, 'so boring, so harsh.'
'How d'you *mean*, "boring"?!' Aamilah grinds to a sudden halt, outraged by the impudence of this statement (and Valentine – whose hand she's holding, stops too, as does Nessa, whose hand Valentine holds). 'Have some imagination! Hamra means "red" so it's absolutely perfect!'
  'Red?' Farhana echoes, stopping herself now (she's pushing Badriya in her pushchair slightly ahead of the other group). 'Yes!' Aamilah exclaims, exasperated. 'Like her hair! Like a heart! Like a *Valentine*, you idiot!'
'Oh.'
They all commence walking again.
  'For some, strange reason I had it fixed in my head that Hamra was the name of the wife of Adam,' Hana calls over her shoulder.
'The wife of Adam?! No way!' Aamilah is contemptuous. 'It definitely means "red". Adam's wife had a totally different name. It doesn't even *sound* like Hamra.'
  'Well I do think it was Hamra, actually,' Farhana persists.
'It *wasn't* Hamra, Farhana!' Aamilah's enraged. 'I'm completely positive that it wasn't, okay?'
'But I'm sure I remember –'
  '*Hawwa!*' Aamilah interrupts, exuberant. 'It was Hawwa! Adam's wife! Hawwa!'
Silence.
'Well Hawwa sounds extremely similar to Hamra. They both start with an H and end with an A and both have two syllables.'
'*And?!*'

'You said they sounded totally different!'

'*Ha!*'

This time Farhana stops in her tracks, startled by her sister's unladylike expostulation (and the rest of the group almost pile straight into her). '*Ha?* Ha what?!' she demands.

'*Ha!*' Aamilah repeats, jinking past and marching ahead, smugly.

'You are *so* childish sometimes!' Farhana calls after her. 'And remember: "*He who has no manners has no knowledge*"!'

'Admit that you were wrong, Hana!' Milah trills.

'Fine! *Fine!*' Hana grumbles, walking on again. 'And now the endless gloating, I suppose!'

'Go on! Admit it!' Milah's free hand jousts the air, victoriously. 'Admit that you were wrong, Hana! *Say* it!'

'I'm happy to admit it!' Hana insists. 'It doesn't bother me one bit! But it still doesn't change the fact that Hamra is an ugly, heavy kind of name …'

As the three women make their stately (if voluble) progress down the road together, Valentine (the putative subject of the two sisters' intense discussion) has only half an ear on their conversation (which, through the close fabric of her slightly musty, undersized *hijab*, feels like it's taking place in another room). The other half of her consciousness focuses on the beat of her own heart, which echoes in her head – resounding, fuzzily, between her ears – like a tiny but strenuous game of tennis being played by two wasps using gongs for rackets.

She feels hot and disorientated. The robe is over-long and keeps catching underfoot. In her mind she is struggling to visualize Gene's face – his strong hands tucked beneath her knees, the slim bones of his hips, the scent of his hair, his ear against her cheek – trying to recreate the effortless confidence and ease she felt the previous night, but every time she visualizes these things with anything amounting to success (and a brief feeling of mildly distracted euphoria descends) another image promptly pops into her head – of Sheila (Sheila twirling in front of the mirror – Sheila's face wreathed in delighted smiles – Sheila remarking, jauntily, on the kitchen curtains) and her throat contracts and her heart duly plummets. I deserve this! she thinks. Every second of this torture! The world closing in! The sky up so high! *God!* Throat so tight! Heartbeat-heartbeat-heartbeat-heartbeat … Her vision begins to blur and her head starts to spin.

'I knew a Hamra at school' – Farhana is still considering the various ramifications of Valentine's new name – 'and she laughed like a pig. She wore braces. Her ears stuck out like jug handles.'

'At school?' Milah scowls. 'Are you sure? I definitely don't remember a Hamra at school.'

'It's a miracle you remember anything about school!' Hana snorts.

'How d'you mean?' Milah demands.

'Because you were always off playing hooky!' Hana kindly elucidates.

'Playing *hooky*?!' Milah repeats, sarcastic.

'Yes! Playing hooky!' Hana's eyes widen, indignantly. 'What's wrong with that?!'

'I was "bunking off", Hana.' She briefly raises her eyes, heavenward. '*Astaghfirulla!* May Allah forgive me! I wasn't "playing *hooky*"! I mean, *seriously*?!'

'Yes, "seriously"!' Hana grumbles. 'Who elected *you* head of the Word Police, Milah?'

She turns to Valentine. 'Playing hooky, Valentine. What do *you* think?' she demands.

'Hamra,' Milah interjects, punctiliously.

'Sorry?' Valentine glances over her shoulder, her heart pounding and pounding. The little wasps with their gongs playing faster and still faster.

'"Playing hooky". Are you familiar with that saying at all?'

'Uh …'

'It sounds American,' Milah interjects, contemptuously.

'Playing hooky?' Valentine echoes, distractedly, trying not to get the fabric of the *hijab* caught in her mouth while simultaneously shifting herself and Nessa to one side as a woman tries to walk past them along the pavement in the opposite direction. She fails to negotiate this transition rapidly enough, though (Aamilah doesn't bother giving way at all) and the woman – who has just turned a corner – ends up being crushed into a hedge as they sail past, *en masse*.

Valentine mutters an apology – gagged by the *hijab* – and the woman shoots their group a lethal look. They turn right and head out on to a busier road.

'Well how about "Jehaan"?'
Valentine has been focusing on the cracks in the pavement. Her face is drenched in sweat. She has no idea how much time has passed since she first started focusing on the cracks. It could be seconds, it could be minutes. Time has condensed and then expanded inside a screaming wave of panic. Or was that blaring commotion just a bus roaring past? Was the sensation outside or within? She suddenly can't tell. She becomes confused about which response is real and which is simulated, then – in a brief moment of existential crisis – wonders how her feelings *can* be simulated. Aren't feelings always true?

Nessa's hand in my hand, she thinks, Nessa's hand in my hand.
She glances up – *mouth dry, can't swallow* – just in time to see a man in the passenger seat of a slow-moving silver car grinning at her while calmly and deliberately showing her the finger. Her eyes widen. She is jolted. She holds tighter on to Nessa's hand and turns to look at Milah who chunters on, apparently oblivious.

'Jehaan?' she's saying. 'Why Jehaan?'
'Because it means ...'
'I *know* perfectly well what it means thank you very much! It means "intelligent one" if I'm not mistaken.'

'You *are* mistaken, Milah!' Hana chuckles, delighted.

'Pardon?'

'It doesn't mean intelligent one! You're wrong!'

'Yes it does!'

'No, it doesn't. It means ...'

'Yes it *does*, Hana! The Prophet – peace be upon him – had a niece called by that name.'

'I don't think the Prophet – peace be upon him – *did*, Milah.'

'He did. You know that I have a photographic memory for such details ...'

'Pardon me?! I don't know anything of the kind!'

Their conversation is briefly interrupted by a phone ringing. The ringtone (which causes the over-stimulated Valentine to start and almost trip) features a haunting, echoey male vocal singing *Ya Allah Ho Ya Alah! Ya Allah Ho Ya Alah! Ya Allah Ho Ya ...*

Milah stops, reaches inside a pocket in her *abaya*, pulls out the phone and places it to the spot on her *hijab* where her ear should be.

'Hello?' she barks, releasing Valentine's hand and turning, 'What ...? What?'

The silver car, meanwhile, is slowly reversing back up the road again. The man in the passenger seat is simulating the act of masturbation through his window while pulling a series of obscene faces, spurred on, it would seem, by the driver (the harsh echoes of his laughter are audible through the glass).

Valentine grabs Nessa's shoulder and turns her face into her skirts, her cheeks reddening under the *hijab*. She glances over towards Farhana who is casually leaning into the pram to adjust the angle of Badriya's sun-hat, and then to Aamilah who's still struggling – apparently oblivious to the dumb-show – with the conversation on her phone.

Her breath comes in gasps. She suddenly realizes that the robe deprives her of most – possibly even all – of her traditional modes of social response: to gesture back, to shout something, to swear. Not only do these stifling acres of heavy black fabric render her blankly inarticulate, but – somewhat paradoxically – easier to objectify and more vulnerable to attack. She turns towards Farhana again, her eyes pleading for guidance. Farhana – ignoring the macabre pantomime playing out beside her – merely smiles and murmurs, '*Rahimullah!* May Allah have mercy on him!' before adding, 'Do you like spicy food, Hamra?'

Hamra? Valentine blinks. She struggles to focus. 'Do I like spicy food? Uh ...'

Does Hamra like spicy food she wonders. Does Hamra ...?

Valentine nods. 'Yes. Yes. Yes she does ...' she stutters, 'Although she's not –'

'And little Nessa?' Farhana interrupts. 'Does Nessa like it, too?'

Valentine frowns. 'Nessa?' She glances down. 'I'm not sure.' She shrugs. 'I mean she's quite an adventurous eater at home – loves all kinds of fruit and vegetables. Even olives. They give them tacos at daycare, sometimes. She enjoys those ...'

Aamilah finally completes her conversation, shoves the phone into her pocket and joins them again. She grabs Valentine's hand and they continue walking. Farhana is talking about the first time she tried olive tapenade (hated it). Milah passionately holds forth on the subject of avocados. 'I love tomato salsa, but that slimy, pale green paste? *Urgh!*'

'Guacamole,' Valentine murmurs, struggling to keep her eyes focused steadfastly ahead, icy trickles of sweat cascading down her spine.

All the while the silver car slowly trails them. Bored now of hand gestures, the man on the passenger side is unbuckling his belt and yanking down his jeans (intending to moon them, perhaps).

Valentine is seething with rage. It's as much as she can do not to fly at the car – kick in the passenger door – pull the

man out by his hair – head-butt him in the face – respond like
any true Tucker would. She is incandescent. Her fury is
white-hot and scalding. The little wasps between her ears are
suddenly silent; they've been incinerated and replaced by a
giant, copper kettle – perched, somewhat precariously, on a
fiery hob – which billows steam and whistles.

'I hate it! It looks like snot!' Aamilah's back on the subject
of avocados again (after a brief diversion into the virtues of
hummus). 'Tastes like it, too! Revolting!'

'Perhaps if you added a little more salt and lemon,'
Valentine suggests, 'a dash of paprika ...'

'No! It's the texture! Disgusting!'

They eventually arrive – and not a moment too soon – at
the outer reaches of the park. Farhana turns the pushchair on
to the grass and sets off across the green. Aamilah and
Valentine follow. The car sounds its horn.

'Don't look back!' Aamilah warns her. She peeks sideways
into Valentine's face, then performs a quick double-take.
'*Subhaanalla!*' she exclaims, raising her hands. 'Praise be to
God! A little miracle! Your *eyes*, Hamra! The fear has
completely gone – evaporated – *pouf!*'

'Because I'm angry!' Valentine hisses, astonished. 'That was
so horrible! Degrading! How can you bear it?'

'*Bear* it?' Aamilah repeats, equally astonished. 'But it's a
gift, don't you see?' She lightly touches her hand to her
diaphragm. 'Righteous anger – degradation – humility – pity –
they're our fuel! Feel them burning deep inside of you!
Here ...' – she taps her chest – 'in your heart.'

Valentine grimaces beneath the *hijab*, bemused. She tries to
search her heart, but the map is old and the compass is faulty.

'*Now* you start to understand, eh?' Aamilah persists. 'This
is precisely why we do it, Hamra. This is the fight! This is the
very essence of what we are! This is for him: for Allah. This is
the love ...' She pauses for a second (her eyes briefly fixing
on the ever-more-distant Farhana), then scowls, tuts and

suddenly yells, 'Hana! *Hana!* Under the tree!' She gesticulates, wildly. 'Hana! Over there! The tree! Under the ... The *tree*, Hana! Not ... No! *No!* Not next to the *dog* toilet, you idiot!'

'I was having the rise out of you, Gene, *seriously!*' Jen coos, as he raises an anxious hand to his neck (for the umpteenth time) while she tenderly swipes a touch of pressed powder over his glistening i-zone. He and Ransom are posing by the Hummer, as a duo. Gene (at his own insistence) is in profile, part obscured by shadow, hat pulled down low, golf bag hitched on to his back, military manoeuvres-style.

Ransom has two white stripes painted across either cheek (Jen's idea) and a skinny black tie (belonging to a wine waiter) tied like a bandanna around his head. He swings his club a couple of times, grimaces (half a canny eye on Jen and Gene), swings again, miscalculates his angles and kicks up a spray of gravel. This hail of stones narrowly avoids hitting Terence Nimrod (who has annexed Israel's stool – the bored teen having only recently wandered off to watch the closing stages of the Kids' Comp.) and Del Renzio (who is talking away, emphatically, on his mobile phone).

'There's something missing from this set-up,' Ransom murmurs, dissatisfied (perhaps finally half-registering Esther's absence).

'A bugle,' Jen suggests.

Ransom stiffens. A vague look of surprise, quickly surmounted by a vague look of recognition (imbued with a slight tinge of amorousness), quickly surmounted by a tiny glimmer of fear flits across his face.

'Or a suppurating tattoo.' Jen grins.

The golfer reaches over and pushes his hand into Gene's jacket pocket. He withdraws the old, red bugle tassel and gazes at it, watery-eyed.

'Are we ready yet?' the photographer boredly chivvies them along. Gene snatches back the tassel (message duly received) and they each return to their former places.

'So you don't think this tattoo thing has legs, then?' Ransom finds his light and strikes a pose as Jen rapidly retreats.

'Hold that!' the photographer calls.

'The tattoo thing? Nah. Not even stumps.' Jen goes to stand alongside a jittery-seeming Del Renzio. 'I mean no offence to the lovely Sheila, Gene,' she modifies, 'but this idiot nearly kills the girl's mother' – she thumbs, dismissively, towards the golfer (much to his evident disgruntlement) – 'neglects to pay his insurance premiums which *does* kill the dad, plays a cruel game of tabloid ping-pong with the brother for several years – sending him into a tragic, narcotic funk – then some hare-brained C of E minister with too much time on her hands comes up with the crazy notion that the exchange of a tattoo – a *tattoo* of all things – will finally – miraculously! – set things straight between them; become some grand symbol of redemption, a Band-Aid to all their problems; so they'll finally make their peace and live happily ever after ...' she snorts, disgusted. 'It's delusional – deranged, even.'

'Bloody hell!' Terence Nimrod exclaims (having listened to Jen's snarky diatribe, completely agog). 'Your wife's a genius, Gene!' He quickly reaches for his notepad. 'This idea's dynamite! Pure tabloid gold! Is the Tucker girl much of a looker by any chance?'

'I mean what kind of tragic, screwed-up, half-cocked morality is that?!' Jen sneers (including Nimrod's recent contribution in her general, critical overview).

'Great – keep holding it!' the photographer repeats.

'In Sheila's defence ...' Gene suddenly starts off (straightening up and thereby inadvertently ruining the shot). The photographer curses (he's using an old box camera with an especially slow shutter speed).

'Oh dear. Very sorry.'

Gene returns to his pose, chastened.

'There *is* no defending it, Gene,' Jen persists. 'It's just crass, and weird, and wrong, and kind of ... well ... *creepy.*'

'And conceptually brilliant!' Nimrod adds (his former enthusiasm evidently undimmed).

This time it's the golfer's turn to straighten up, perplexed. The photographer curses again, exasperated.

'Are you still managing to feature the main body of the hotel in the background?' Del Renzio (for reasons unknown – except to himself) decides to choose this awkward moment to make his organizational presence felt.

'The far end of the portico,' the photographer confirms, scowling.

'And we've not even started to factor in your embarrassingly girlish fear of needles,' Jen adds.

'Brilliant!' Nimrod grins, pen blazing like a plastic meteor across the page.

'It's just that when we initially brainstormed this shoot at HQ,' Del Renzio confesses (to nobody in particular), 'we didn't really envisage the tank in the shot, or the whole "post-apocalyptic" angle for that matter –'

'It's a friggin' *Hummer,* you imbecile!' Ransom interrupts (hitting the fastidious PR man with all the suppressed wrath and hostility he's plainly harbouring for his skinny neighbour in Lycra). 'And for your information,' he adds, flicking a couple of stray thunder-flies from the pristine, white hide of his golfing glove, 'there's no "angle" with Stuart Ransom, okay? This isn't simply "an angle". It's who I am. It's not a question of "degrees", yeah? You can't measure it with a friggin'... a friggin' *set*-square. It's real. It's *all* real ...' He gesticulates, grandly. 'This is *real life* not some phony piece of cooked-up, two-bit PR bull-crap.'

Brief silence.

Ransom recommences posing. Jen burps, then apologizes.

'I'm a *sportsman*' – Ransom straightens up again, unable to let this thing pass – 'I'm an *artist*, not some grinning, little monkey who'll just dance around to order. When you hire Stuart Ransom you hire a Master Spirit, yeah? A Social Lion, a legend – a tiny piece of folklore ...'

'*Master Spirit?!*' Jen echoes, incredulous.

'You hire a *giant*, yeah?' Ransom barges on, oblivious. 'A friggin' monster, a *Tyrannosaurus Rex ...*'

'A dinosaur!' Jen sniggers.

'You can't house-train Stuart Ransom!' the golfer snaps. 'He's not tamed and neutered, jumping around to order like some cuddly, little spaniel, he's a savage, friggin' *beast*, yeah? A big, fat, black grizzly tearing through your trash ...'

Ransom holds up his bear paws. 'You get hair on the friggin' walls with me!' he growls. 'Eight, giant, yellow claws impacted with filth tearing up your bed-sheets! You get a huge pile of stinking dung on your manicured lawn! Because Stuart Ransom always brings the shit, yeah? He brings *fear*! He brings *excitement*! He brings *integrity*! He brings the Game – the *heart*! – the Full Sporting Legacy!'

Another brief silence.

The golfer strikes a pose. The photographer readies himself to take the shot.

'Eight claws? Can that be right?' Jen idly muses, turning to Toby.

'My gut instinct is ten,' Toby Whittaker answers, apologetically (from his customary – and suitably anonymous – position behind the light reflector), 'five on each of the front paws, another ten on the back. Twenty, all told – but you certainly shouldn't quote me on that.'

'I *will* quote you, Tobe,' Jen insists gazing over at him, adoringly. Toby blushes.

Ransom straightens up, with a sneer, ruining yet another shot.

'Do bears build nests or dig holes?' Jen wonders.

'They live in dens' – Toby nods – 'they scratch them into hillsides or under the root systems of large trees. Sometimes they inhabit caves ... In fact by a weird coincidence I was actually discussing the strange reproductive life of bears with Esther only yesterday.'

He surreptitiously glances over towards Ransom to gauge his reaction (there is none).

'That *is* odd,' Jen concurs.

'I'd bought her a little toy bear for the baby,' Toby continues (another glance. *Still* no reaction).

'How sweet!' Jen interjects.

'... and she mentioned how she'd had this chat with an obstetrician the other week who told her that when female bears mate they go through a process called "delayed implantation" which basically means that the female's fertilized egg floats around in her uterus for a period of anything up to six months. Then, when she goes into hibernation, the foetuses – usually a couple of them – attach to the wall of the uterus and the cubs arrive approximately eight weeks later while the mother's still asleep.'

'A pain-free delivery!' Jen gasps. 'You gotta love it!'

'Exactly.' Toby chuckles. 'Another really fascinating detail is that if the female isn't physically heavy enough to survive the winter while simultaneously providing milk for her young, the body automatically terminates the pregnancy and the embryo is simply reabsorbed back into her body again as a form of nutrition.'

'Can you hold that thing a little higher, please?' the photographer demands (Toby has let the reflector slip during the course of this conversation).

'Yeah, Whittaker' – Ransom glowers – 'we're not just standing here for fun, you *dick*.'

'So okay ... uh ... maybe just a couple more of these' – Del Renzio quickly steps forward (desperate to take control of their wayward schedule) – 'a few relaxing at the spa, a handful standing by the front desk wearing the club shirt and tie and … *uh* … yes … I think we can probably call it a day after that.'

'Time to head on up to your room and chop us out some sweet, fat lines!' Nimrod gleefully quavers, making 'street-style' gun gestures with both hands.

'You're not seriously considering undertaking this procedure on club premises?' Del Renzio interrupts, horrified. 'Because we'd definitely need to pass the idea by management, first.'

'Just imagine the health and safety implications!' Jen clucks.

'Give me a friggin' break!' The golfer straightens up, indignant (yet another shot ruined). 'Pass it by management my friggin' arse!'

'I'm just not sure if it's the kind of image we're keen to project.' Del Renzio doggedly stands his ground (Nimrod still mugging away, theatrically, to the rear).

'I mean it's hardly what you'd call "five star" behaviour,' Jen eye-rolls.

'I've already had to contend with a deluge of complaints about your blonde friend here.' Del Renzio tips his head, disparagingly, towards his staunchest supporter.

'She's no friend of mine!' Ransom snorts.

'Sorry? Complaints about *moi?*' Jen's astonished.

'Yes,' Del Renzio confirms.

'Is it the shoes?'

Jen points to her wedges: 'Do they breach the dress code?'

'How about the shoes, the transparent leotard, the gold bra and the fact that you were sighted by several of our younger players earlier openly urinating in the rough.'

'Oh that's classic!' Ransom is richly entertained by this detail. 'That's friggin' hilarious!'

'Are you completely positive that was me?' Jen's sceptical.

'Sure he is!' Ransom scoffs.

'From the detailed descriptions we received, I think we're fairly certain.' Del Renzio nods.

Ransom strikes another pose, enlivened.

Del Renzio inspects his watch again. 'The Kids' Comp. is due to finish in an hour or so,' he informs the golfer, 'and you're officially scheduled to –'

'"The club shirt and tie?!"' Ransom suddenly expostulates, haughtily. 'Just what kind of brain-dead, castrated, cheese-ball d'you think you're dealing with, here?'

Del Renzio opens his mouth to answer.

'Did Esther sanction that?' Ransom interjects (before he has a chance to), then, 'Fuck it! *Bollocks* to it! You and your friggin' schedule can go hang for all I care!'

Del Renzio closes his mouth again.

'Screw you!' Ransom persists (in case Del Renzio hasn't quite got the message yet). 'And screw your management committee! And screw the friggin' sponsor, and screw the Kids' Comp., come to that ...' He pauses, thoughtfully. 'Although I may opt to check out the spa a little later on if I feel so inclined,' he concedes.

'Maybe we can make an exception for the Kids' Comp.,' Toby nervously pipes up. 'It's always nice to spare a bit of time for the kiddies, eh?'

'Stipulated in the contract?' Ransom enquires, jaundiced.

'Yup,' Toby confirms.

'Fine – whatever,' Ransom snaps.

'I'm sorry to be a pain' – Gene pushes back his cap – 'but I'm actually meant to be collecting Mallory from ballet in just over half an hour.'

He raises his hand to his neck again.

'Remember,' Jen cautions, 'we're talking about a woman with serious mental problems, a grudge and a tattoo gun, here.'

Ransom blanches. He turns to Gene for confirmation.

'She's slightly agoraphobic,' Gene admits, 'or so I'm led to believe,' he quickly adds.

'And even if you *do* manage to get her on board with the whole idea,' Jen continues, 'she'll want complete creative control. Then there's still the psycho brother to contend with ...'

'Whadda you think?' Ransom turns to Gene.

'I dunno.' Gene shakes his head, somewhat torn.

'You got any ink yourself, Gene?' Nimrod wonders.

'None. You?'

'Big back piece. Kuniyoshi tribute – "Hatsuhana Prays under Waterfall". Got it done in Brighton about seven years ago. Took over sixty hours.'

'You've got a big tattoo?' Toby's fascinated. 'I had no idea you were into all that.'

'Big back, big tattoo,' Nimrod confirms, smugly. 'Fortieth birthday gift from my wife. Never regretted it,' he adds.

'Although I do think that when a man reaches a certain *age* ...' – Jen winces – 'what with the loose texture of the skin – the tags – the sun spots – the moles ...'

'So this Tucker girl's a bit of a looker, then?' Nimrod persists.

'Utterly gorgeous' – Jen nods – 'but barmy. Mad as a box of frogs – think Kelloggs Fruit Loops with extra nuts.'

'Perhaps you need to sleep on it,' Gene volunteers, darting Jen a warning look.

'Good idea,' Toby agrees.

'Yeah. Take your time – think it over.' Jen nods. 'Be careful. This is a big decision. Tattoos are permanent, remember? The very last thing you want is to come over looking like some sad, old publicity hound desperately trying to recapture their long-distant youth.'

'Why change the habits of a lifetime?!' Nimrod murmurs, with a husky chortle, then stops chortling, in an instant, as Ransom shoots him a killer scowl.

'Before this goes any further' – Del Renzio tries to instil yet a further note of caution – 'I'm definitely going to need to have a quick word with our lawyers about the various legal ramifications of –'

'Fuck it!' Ransom yanks off his bandanna and slams it to the ground. 'Let's do this! Let's make this shit happen! Right here! Right now! Before I change my friggin' mind! Ring the mad bitch!'

He throws Gene his club, then drags the paint down his cheeks with both palms.

'Don't say I didn't warn you!' Jen trills.

'Best decision you ever made!' Nimrod counters.

'Sorry – who exactly are you expecting me to call?' Gene's bemused.

'C'mon! Let's do this!' Ransom repeats, clapping his hands together, trying to get enthused. 'This shit is *fated*, yeah? History in the making! It's Destiny! *Woo-hoo!*' he hollers, pumping the air with his fist. 'Let's embrace the Power of Now! Let's jump into the abyss!'

Terence Nimrod springs to his feet. Gene dumps the golf bag, scowling, and rips off his cap. Toby Whittaker reaches for his phone. Jen pops a stick of gum into her mouth, with a smirk, then casually proffers a dumbstruck Del Renzio the rest of the pack.

10

Sheila is standing on the small landing at the top of the stairs
peering up at the hatch that leads into the rectory's attic
space. She is wearing a towel (having recently indulged in a
quick – but extremely necessary – flannel wash at the
bathroom sink), has a light bandage around her bad leg and
an old pair of leather Clarks sandals (buckles loosely jangling,
unfastened) on her feet.

After a few seconds' indecision she sighs, mutters
something indecipherable under her breath and hobbles into
Stan's room to fetch the chair from behind his desk. While
she's there, she turns on the computer – simply out of habit –
waits for it to power up and then accesses the inbox. A
selection of emails appears. Some are for Stan. Several are
from various church bodies. One is from Valentine, sent (she
checks the time) not long after her hasty exit. She grits her
teeth and opens it.

'i don't know what to do to make this all better,' it says (no
capitals, no formal introduction to speak of), 'just tell me what
to do and i'll do it. anything you want. i'll tattoo r. if you like.
i'm sitting here, researching some images. i have some ideas –
good ideas (grass – images of). did you hear back from your
friend with the gallery yet? i'm so sorry about what happened
to your leg, sheila. i'm so sorry about, well, *everything*. I mean
that from the very bottom of my idiotic heart. you're a good

person. i'm sorry I got so stroppy before (very ignorant –
weak). just tell me what you need me to do and i'll do it,
xx
valentine (wickers).
ps. please forgive my spelling. i can't get the spellcheck to
work for some reason.
x'

Sheila bites her lip. Her hand shifts the mouse to the 'reply'
box and she clicks it:

'Dear Valentine,' she writes, 'I've still not heard back from my
friend with the gallery or from Ransom, yet – for that matter
– but it's early days and Gene's on the case with Ransom
even as we speak. Love the grass idea! Brings to mind (bit
random – forgive me – a quote from Isaiah: *All flesh is grass
And all its loveliness is like the flower of the field* ...
(Seems very appropriate under the circs.)
    By the way – I'm *so* sorry I rushed off like that, earlier. I
honestly *did* have a baptism at two (The hair was a sensation!
They all absolutely loved it)!
    re. the other problem: have you considered calling the
police? Entrust them with your father's collection for
'safekeeping'. Say that you had no idea about the meter or the
private store (Kill two birds with one stone).
    Of course it goes without saying that I'll back up your story
if needs be ... I just had *oh sod it sod it sod it the strangest
hospital bleugh brainstupidcauliflower* ...'

Sheila stops typing, draws a deep breath, and re-reads her
response. She grimaces and deletes the last sentence. She
re-reads it again, and when she reaches the sentence starting
'Of course it goes without saying', she repeats the phrase, out
loud, in a light, posh, mocking voice, then tuts with

frustration, straightens up, grabs the chair and drags it, unsteadily, into the hallway.

Once she's positioned it to her satisfaction she clambers on to it, wincing, and pushes up the hatch into the attic (blinking rapidly as a small army of tiny, dead black beetles and spiders' webs fall into her upturned face). She feels around inside the hatch for the metal ladder which she carefully unfolds, then clambers off the chair – using the ladder for support – tests that it's secure and begins climbing the rungs, very slowly, one at a time, muttering *ow ow ow ow* under her breath with every successive step she takes.

Halfway up, her towel starts to fall off. She snatches at it but then finds herself unable to retie it with only one free arm (and the weight gingerly held off her injured leg), so grimaces, drops it, and continues her ascent, naked.

'Ridiculous!' she mutters, as her head accesses the dark of the roof-space. 'Completely ridiculous!'

She waits patiently for her eyes to adjust to the light. 'Where are you, old buddy?' she murmurs glancing around, squinting slightly. She then continues to climb until she's able to press her palms flat on to the floor, transfer her weight on to them, twizzle around and sit down.

She catches her breath for a minute, then pulls her legs through the hatch, centres herself and stands up. On the wall to her right is a light switch. She flicks it. Nothing.

'Typical!' she grumbles, then peers down at the floor (to make sure she's walking on solid boards) and inches her way forward, reaching out, blindly, for the cluster of objects that quickly crowd into the void of space around her.

Soon her eager fingers are grappling with the unsympathetic corners and edges of a series of crates and boxes, then pushing (even worse) into the doughy, dusty plastic of sacks and bin-bags full of clothes and fabric. Eventually (a gasp of recognition!) she finds what she's looking for: a large, old leather suitcase from her Oxford days (a gift from her grandparents).

She grabs the handle, and – grunting loudly – lifts it free of the surrounding clutter then staggers over to the open hatch with it. She puts it down for a minute and rubs her sweating forehead with the back of her arm (briefly assessing how best to proceed). She picks it up again and tries to push it through the hatch but it will not fit. She curses (then promptly reprimands herself), bends over and retrieves it, slams it down, opens it and commences emptying out its contents, carelessly at first (a gown, some rolled-up posters, several bottles of exotic hair dye, three knitted hats, a college scarf, an old pair of oxblood-red nineteen-hole DMs with steel toe-caps …).

She holds the boots up close to her face, chuckling, then sits down – temporarily seduced – her legs poking out through the hatch again, to assess the remainder of the case's contents in a more leisurely manner.

Next – with a delighted gasp – she pulls out an old, red and black striped mohair jumper with overlong arms. The neck has gone and it's full of holes, but she sniffs it, kisses it, her eyes filling with tears, holding it up, shuddering, against her cheek. She then digs into the case again and withdraws an old bottle of perfume (White Musk from the Body Shop), unstoppers it and sprays some on to her neck, then winces (it's gone off). Finally she pulls out a roughly made, hand-sewn banner (four feet by three feet), torn down one side, proclaiming the legend: O.U.S.U.:

FIGHT THE TAX!

She smirks her recognition, runs her fingers over the scruffy stitching, then gently re-folds it and places it to one side with the remainder of the case's other contents.

'Okay …' She closes the case, zips it up and tries to fit it through the hatch again. This time it almost squeezes through, but not quite. The ladder gets in the way but it's the handle that actually lodges it. She scratches her head. 'How the hell'd he get the damn thing up here in the first place,' she mutters, 'if it can't …?'

She ponders this conundrum for a minute then attempts to resolve it with a hefty kick. The case hardly shifts and her sandal comes flying off, dropping down to the landing below.

'Oh for heaven's sake!' she exclaims, kneeling down (the leg apparently no longer troubling her) and trying to yank it free with her hands. It won't budge.

'Oh come *on*!'

She tries again but makes no progress. She then loses her temper and punches it, repeatedly with her fists, almost losing her balance and toppling down on top of it, head first.

She draws back, alarmed, her leg starting to ache again, feeling light-headed and nauseous. She rests her forehead inside the crook of her arm, panting gently, and tries to think her way around the problem. After a minute or two she drops her arm and throws back her head, exasperated.

'Am I stuck up here?' she asks the rafters, her fists clenching, her face defiant. The rafters hold their lofty counsel.

'Seriously. *Seriously!* Am I actually *stuck* up here?!' she repeats, furious.

Still, no audible response from the wise beams above.

Valentine perches at her computer in her red and white dress, her head still completely covered by Aamilah's spare *niqab*. Her mother is standing in the doorway, watching her closely as she prints out a series of photographs depicting different types and textures of grass (some fine, some dense, some long, some rough, some carefully manicured).

After a couple of minutes Valentine senses a presence behind her. She turns.

'D'you want something, Mum?' she asks, slightly irritated. 'I thought you were having a quiet lie down for an hour?'

'Why are you wearing that mask?' her mother demands (with an expansive gesture of the hands).

'It's not a mask,' Valentine explains. 'It's a *niqab.*'

'*Hmmn.*' Her mother grimaces, not entirely satisfied with this response.

Valentine returns to her print-outs.

'Are you hiding something again?' her mother persists.

'No.' Valentine shakes her head. She pauses. 'Again?'

'You were always the most awful, sullen child,' her mother sighs (yet more expansive gestures). 'Full of pointless secrets. I'd say, "Tell me the problem, Valentine, confide in your mama," and you'd say …'(her mother adopts the most ridiculous, keening voice), '"There's a flickering, little light inside of me, *ma mère.* I need to shelter it with my hands so's the wind can't blow it out. I need to keep it secret. I need to keep it safe …" *Ah oui!*' her mother sighs. 'You were completely *loco* – a loony-tune! – even back then.'

Valentine has fully turned from the computer and is now staring at her mother, intrigued.

'I actually said that?' she asks, touched (against all her instincts). 'About the little, flickering light?'

'Yes.' Her mother nods, then pauses, thoughtfully, pushing some hair behind her ears. 'Or maybe that was Noel?' She frowns. 'Or maybe that was Frédérique? Frédérique was always an incredibly clever and poetic child.'

'But I thought …' Valentine scowls, confused.

'Yes' – her mother nods – 'yes. *Merci.* That was me. I was Frédérique. I was she.'

She curtseys, holding out her skirt.

Valentine stares at her, suspiciously. 'What's that you're wearing on your hands?' she asks.

'*Pardon moi?*'

Her mother fans her face, coquettishly.

Valentine stands up. 'Those rings – where did you get them from?'

'These?' Her mother inspects her fingers. 'Karim gave them to me, as a token. *Après nous avons fait l'amour.*'
She giggles, coyly.

'I don't think he did.'
Valentine walks towards her and grabs her wrist. Each finger is decorated with a ring – some with two or even three – from her father's collection.

'*Ow!*' her mother exclaims, snatching back her hand. 'Let me go! *Salope!* Always so rough! Such a bully!'
She turns and scampers off.

'You can't have those!' Valentine pursues her down the hallway, cornering her at the bottom of the stairs, holding her against the wall and yanking the rings – one by one – from her fingers. 'You had no business taking them, Mum!'
'They're *my* rings!' her mother bellows. '*Touts les miens! My* house! *My* hands! *My* life! *My* rings!'

Valentine wrenches the final ring from her fingers and carries them away with her, her mother now in hot pursuit. 'Give them back!' her mother yells.
'No!' Valentine charges into the kitchen where a cardboard box (in which she'd earlier stored her father's collection – and then carefully hidden it, under the sink) now sits, open, recently pilfered, on the kitchen table. She throws the rings inside and starts closing the lid. Her mother flies at her, determined to get them back.

'You don't know what you're doing!' Valentine pushes her away – more violently, perhaps, than she'd intended – shoving her back, flailing, into the hall. 'These aren't for you to wear. They're Dad's!'
'They're mine, *salaud!*' her mother yells.

Valentine picks up the box and holds it in front of her, walking around to the other side of the table to try and maintain a solid, passive space between them both. Her mother prowls around the table after her. On the third circuit her mother starts to pick up speed. Soon they are both running.

All will be well, Valentine is thinking, all will be well. She wonders what Hamra would do. Empty Hamra, uncompromised Hamra, red Hamra, free Hamra, dead Hamra, fearless Hamra. Then it dawns on her.

'I should've done this years ago,' she mutters, heading for the back door.

'What are you doing?' her mother demands, grinding to a halt, shocked.

'I'm getting rid of them.' Valentine removes the key from the lock, wrenches the door open, steps outside, slams it shut again, drops the box and locks it before her mother can elbow her way through.

'You can't go out there!' Her mother presses herself up against the window, outraged.

Valentine grabs the box and charges down the garden. There is a small, slightly rusty portable waste incinerator standing close to the shed. She places the box next to it and goes into the shed to find charcoal, an old lighter, some kindling and a can of petrol, then returns outside clutching them.

Her mother is banging against the back door and yelling. 'All will be well,' Valentine murmurs, her hands shaking, uncontrollably, 'all will be well.'

She carefully places the charcoal, the kindling, the boxed and un-boxed rings – not forgetting the purse and the whip – inside the incinerator, then douses them with petrol. She tears the box itself into workable segments, presses it down on top, adds more petrol and then replaces the lid. She steps back, appraising her work, the lighter in her hand. She tries to draw a deep breath but can't inhale.

'All will be well,' she murmurs, striking the lighter, kneeling down and holding it to one of several holes cut into the lower section of the metal bin. The flame flares, touches the kindling, then instantly goes out. She strikes it a second time, then a third. The fourth time the kindling takes. No sooner has she started to celebrate its finally catching than she's toppling back, alarmed, as the entire incinerator is engulfed in flames. A huge tongue of fire snakes from the metal chimney in its lid, reaching several feet into the air and setting light to the lower branches of an ash tree that hangs into the garden over the fence from next door.

'Oh God!' Valentine scrambles a few feet away then rises to her knees, her hands covering her mouth. When the sight gets too distressing she closes her eyes. She feels the heat on her face. She feels the hard ground pressing into her shins.

'All will be well,' she tells herself, then sinks back on to her heels, her fingers splayed into the grass. She feels it under her fingers. She starts to delineate individual strands. She opens her eyes and gazes at it, bringing her veiled face forward, drawing closer – inch by gradual inch – to the ground. Soon her nose is pressed into it, her forehead. She is completely bent over, suppliant, bowed down.

'Take me,' she murmurs, hearing the whoosh and crackle of the flames through her veil, hearing the individual leaves sizzle, the metal knock, the creak of wood – every sound so neatly contained, so strictly partitioned, so singular, and yet so thoroughly consumed and subsumed by the fire's hungry roar.

She feels a sense of quietness deep within herself, of space, of peace. I am a void, she thinks. I am done. I am beyond care – beyond fear.

How long does she lie there? She cannot tell. But when she finally lifts her head the flames have gone; the metal bin no longer belches fire, only smoke. The fence is singed, and part of the shed's grey roof. The air around her plays host to a thousand tiny black flakes of dark confetti – originating from some mysterious source – which float downwards then seem to evaporate, like tokens in celebration not of an earthly union, but of a curious *un*doing – a gradual unravelling – which is at once the start of something and the glorious beginning of another ending.

Valentine stands up and walks, mechanically – almost zombie-like – to the back door. She turns the key in the lock and twists the handle. The door stays shut. The bolt has been shot. She barely reacts, just walks over to a nearby rockery, picks up a half-brick, carries it back with her and smashes the window with it. She does a thorough job: knocking out any sharp or jagged fragments, dropping the brick, then shoving her arm through the gap and un-shooting the bolt.

Inside the kitchen all is chaos. Her mother has tipped over the dresser and turned the table on to its side. Enamelware lies chipped and dented in every corner. The kitchen cabinets have been kicked and gouged and scratched. Even the curtains have been ripped down from the window.

Valentine walks through the chaos, into the hallway and pauses, briefly, in the doorway to her studio. This room has also been trashed – perhaps a fraction less thoroughly – her inks cabinet has been pulled open but only a half-dozen bottles smashed. Towels cover the floor. The taps are on (Valentine goes to turn them off). The printer lies in pieces, although the computer gives every appearance of still being functional.

A phone starts to ring. Valentine turns and is drawn – trance-like – towards its sound. On her way to answering it she passes by the sitting room where she espies her mother, face-down on the sofa, arms and legs thrown out, replete; exhausted. On the floor around her lie several photos from Valentine's portfolio (ripped in half) and her shrine, upended, the photo of Kali crushed into a ball, the string of Japa Mala beads snapped and the beads themselves scattered.

She walks on, past the staircase where Nessa sits, halfway down, in her vest and pants, freshly awoken, red-cheeked, bemused, sucking on her half-filled baby beaker.

Valentine holds out her hand and the child bumps her way down to join her. The base of the stairs is covered in broken pot and soil. The aspidistra has been divided into two large chunks and lies, roots up, tangled with the wire of the black Bakelite phone. The ringing sound comes from Valentine's mobile which lies half-hidden under a pile of compost. She picks it up, blows away the worst of the dirt, pulls off her *niqab* and answers.

'Hello?'

Her cheeks are streaked with mascara. She listens for a second, frowning.

'It *is* me – it's Valentine.'

She looks confused.

'Sorry … When?'

She shakes her head, then glances down at the child (now clinging on to her leg) and distractedly tousles her hair.

'Fine. But I'll need someone to look after Mum and Nessa. Noel's not around.'

Brief pause.

'You'll drive me?'

Vague look of hope.

'Okay …' She nods, then frowns, then looks confused again. 'Thanks.'

She hangs up, sighs, and slowly walks back to the kitchen where she gently places Nessa on to the rocking chair, grabs a nearby cat and plops it on to her lap.

'Stroke him,' she says. 'Love him. Make him feel happy again.'

She then ties back her hair, turns on the tap, leans forward and scrubs her face in the sink – violently, fastidiously – for several minutes, dries it on a tea towel, pulls on her apron and starts cleaning up the mess.

★　★　★

'What did she say?' Toby walks up beside him. 'Will she do it?'

'Yeah' – Gene nods, his cheeks slightly flushed – 'but she needs someone to baby-sit her mother and her niece.'

'Got anyone in mind?'

Gene blinks a couple of times. He seems to be finding it difficult to focus.

'What about the brother?'

'Uh … He's not very reliable.'

'How about – you know?'

Toby tips his head towards Jen who currently sits, alongside Israel, in the back of the Hummer waiting for a lift back into town.

Gene grimaces. 'I'm not sure if that's such a good idea.'

'What isn't?'

Jen pops her head through the open door on the passenger side.

'Are you rostered on at work tonight?' Gene asks, hoping to avoid the issue.

'Why?' Jen demands.

'The tattooist needs someone to baby-sit,' Toby helpfully interjects.

'Oh. Sure.' Jen shrugs. 'Fine. What time?'

Gene scowls. 'I thought you were dead set against the whole tattoo thing,' he mutters.

'You did?' Jen looks surprised. 'Whatever gave you that impression?'

'Maybe the fact that you tried everything within your power to *dis*suade him.'

'I was using reverse psychology.' Jen grins.

'So you do want him to get the tattoo?' Gene's perplexed, almost impatient.

'Of course I do, you numbskull!' Jen snorts. 'I'm the Harbinger of Chaos, remember?'

'Is that your official title?' Toby wonders.

'Yup.' Jen nods. 'I've got little tags sewed inside all my clothes.'

'Must be *very* small tags,' Israel avers, from the back seat.

'Nano,' Jen affirms.

'I thought you were the Angel of Peace,' Gene grumbles.

'Exactly.' Jen nods again (apparently quite content with the contradiction). 'Are we ready to head off yet? Bubs here was due back at the hotel over an hour ago.'

Israel snorts at Jen's impudent use of the word 'bubs'.

Gene checks his watch. 'I can only take you as far as Crawley Green Road ...'

'Right-o.'

'D'you mind if I tag along too?' Toby wonders. 'I need to find myself a B&B in town. And I was hoping to pop in and see Esther at the hospital.'

'Fine. Climb in.'

Gene walks around to the driver's side, jumps on board, throws off his hat, belts up and starts the engine. When he unexpectedly catches a brief glimpse of his own reflection in the side mirror, he notices a worn, almost beleaguered set to his face.

The next quarter of an hour is spent gradually adjusting to the considerable bump and roll of the antique vehicle, not to mention the earth-shattering volume of engine noise. Jen and Israel soon cut their losses during a small build-up of traffic by the Windmill Trading Estate and jump ship, opting to head back to the Arndale on foot, via St Mary's Road.

Gene waits – idling in neutral – for several minutes, then finally concedes defeat and turns the engine off. He checks his watch then peers over at Toby who still appears happily ensconced.

'If you're thinking of heading to the hospital,' he suggests, 'then you could do worse than follow them into the town centre and get a bus. The X31 should get you there, or the 7 or the 8 –'

'D'you mind if I ask you something?' Toby interrupts.

'Nope.' Gene shrugs.

'You've seen Ransom and I working together – in pretty close proximity – over the last couple of days or so ...'

Gene nods.

'And from what you've observed, d'you think ...' He pauses, losing confidence.

'Think what?' Gene prompts.

'D'you think he respects me at all?'

'Respects you?' Gene repeats, surprised.

'Esther says – I mean she seems to think – that he doesn't. That he doesn't respect me.'

Gene considers his response for a second. 'Well, he sacked Esther,' he finally offers, 'and he hasn't sacked you yet.'

'Maybe he only sacks the people he actually respects,' Toby suggests, 'the people who offer some kind of a direct challenge to his authority or his blinkered world-view. I'm the first to admit that I've never really done that ...' He smiles, somewhat sheepishly. 'Wouldn't really dare.'

'You're not confrontational by nature,' Gene observes, 'nor am I. But that's often a useful quality in business – and an invaluable quality in life, for that matter. So long as you respect yourself – know what your perimeters are – I can't really see a problem with the softly-softly approach.'

He pauses for a second. 'Instead of wondering whether Ransom respects you, why not spend a little more time considering whether you respect him – whether you share the same goals, whether you like him as a person, as a boss, even.'

'I had this great opportunity come my way recently.' Toby frowns. 'Esther thought –'

'You're kind of like a family,' Gene interrupts, 'everyone playing different roles.'

'That's *exactly* what Esther said.' Toby grins.

'Really? What did she think your role was?' Gene can't resist asking.

'Idiot child.'

'Oh.' Gene digests this for a second. 'That seems a little harsh, perhaps.'

'I did an engineering degree at university – specialized in biochemistry.' Toby fiddles, uneasily, with the top button on his collar. 'Esther thinks my talents are being wasted where I am.'

'Not much of a fan of nine-hole, eh?' Gene chuckles, tiredly. 'She's quite a traditionalist at heart.'

'You seem to care an awful lot about what Esther thinks,' Gene notes.

'I like Esther,' Toby confesses, almost shame-faced. 'I respect her enormously. I just wish ...'

'I hardly know Esther,' Gene admits, 'but she strikes me as being pretty ...'– he clears his throat, keen not to offend – '... hard-nosed,' he eventually finishes off.

'We have a mutual interest in engineering.' Toby cheerfully sidesteps the 'hard-nosed' comment. 'She's very practical. We both have this weird kind of, I dunno, "spatial" side. We're very different people, but we *see* stuff in exactly the same way – process information in the same way. I mean she doesn't have that many opportunities to showcase those skills in her current line of work ...'

'So you think Esther's talents are being wasted, too.' Gene cranes his neck to try and see if the traffic is moving at the roundabout. It isn't.

'Absolutely.' Toby nods. 'I've been banging on about it for a while, now – not that she ever listens to anything I say.'

'Well that's something else you have in common, I guess,' Gene states the obvious. 'You each want the other to break free from Ransom, but you still don't seem quite able to make that same transition yourselves.'

'She appears strong – almost invulnerable. Aggressive. Hard-nosed,' Toby concedes, 'but there's a fragile core. It's all just a big front with Esther. She's one of those "bark worse than their bite", people. When you spend a bit of time with her, once her guard finally comes down – you know, late at night, after a quiet meal and a couple of drinks ...'

'When she finally allows herself to relax.'

'Exactly. When she finally "allows" herself,' Toby repeats, 'because she so rarely allows herself anything. And even if she does happen to let you weasel your way inside that prickly, barbed-wire fence she surrounds her heart with, if she does let you inside then you'll definitely pay a price for it afterwards. She can be really ruthless. Makes all these catty comments. Ignores you. Undermines you in groups. But the way I see it she's just running scared. Doesn't want to show weakness – doesn't dare to.'

'In case the whole edifice collapses.' Gene nods.

'She's just so bound up in what Ransom wants, what Ransom needs.'

'Have you ever considered that maybe she sees another side to Ransom? A side that you don't actually get to see?' Gene suggests. 'A more human, more vulnerable side?'

'She feels sorry for him.'

'That's not exactly what I meant.' Gene frowns.

'Yeah ...' Toby doesn't seem especially keen to consider this idea in any depth.

'Like I say,' he runs on, 'I had this opportunity to move into a completely different sphere, and Esther was all for it. But then I thought ...'

'Have you ever considered the possibility that Esther might be rivalrous with you at some level?' Gene suddenly volunteers (too tired to bother tip-tocing around the issue any longer). 'That she might perceive you as some kind of a threat, even? She certainly warned me off pretty ferociously the other night.'

'She's territorial.' Toby nods, mournfully.

'She's been with him for an awfully long time,' Gene observes. 'The bond between them must be very powerful.'

'How d'you mean?' Toby scowls.

'They're a real partnership.' Gene shrugs. 'She must've given up an awful lot to be with him – family, home-life, her financial security. It can't have been easy all these years.'

'She has two kids living with her mum in Jamaica,' Toby affirms. 'She hardly ever gets to see them.'

'Which naturally leads one to think that her feelings might be a little bit more … dunno … more *complicated* than those that are habitual between a manager and a client.'

Toby looks alarmed. 'You think she's in love with him?'

'Well you said yourself that you thought it was "one of the great sporting romances".'

'Did I?' Toby now seems shocked by his earlier pronouncement.

'She's made sacrifices' – Gene shrugs – 'and people don't generally do that for no good reason.'

'Unless they're in some kind of a rut,' Toby avers.

'Or lack confidence,' Gene hypothesizes.

'Can't envisage any alternative,' Toby adds.

'Or maybe if they think they've burned all their bridges …'

'I'm gonna be completely honest with you, here …'

For the first time during their conversation, Toby half-turns to face him. 'I don't respect Ransom any more, Gene,' he confesses. 'In fact I'm not sure I ever did. And I know it's shocking – disloyal, even – but I just really need to get it out there, in the open.'

'Everybody needs to let off a little steam sometimes,' Gene murmurs, uneasy.

'I think I was just blinded by the big spiel, by all the hoopla and the celebrity,' Toby runs on, emboldened. 'The truth is that I think he's just a bully and a sneak. And a fat-head – incredibly selfish. And that he uses people –'

'People use him, too,' Gene interrupts.

'It's the culture,' Toby concedes.

———

451

'He's a performer.' Gene makes a feeble attempt to defend the golfer. 'It's all swagger for the most part – just a front.'

'A front for what, though?' Toby smiles, somewhat cynical.

'Who knows? Feelings of inadequacy – impotence – humiliation – loneliness – wounded pride ...'

'I really want out of the whole thing,' Toby mutters, 'I just wish I had some kind of ...' – he shakes his head, frustrated – 'an incentive – some kind of ... of encouragement – a *sign* ...'

'I thought you said there was this other opportunity,' Gene reminds him. 'Maybe it's time you looked into that in more detail.'

'I'm just *racked* by uncertainty, Gene!' Toby slaps his hands on to his thighs, frustrated. 'I'm a mess. I lack the confidence. I just need ...'

He shakes his head again.

Long silence.

'D'you want me to look at your palm?' Gene finally asks, exhausted.

'No!' Toby exclaims, almost offended. 'I couldn't possibly ask you to do that!'

He stares straight ahead of him, stiff with desire, silently counting the dead flies on the windscreen.

'Just a very quick look,' Gene sighs, 'while we're stuck in ...'

Quick as a flash Toby is holding out his left palm, then his right, unsure which of them Gene will want to inspect. Gene straightens up in his seat, pushes back his shoulders, smiles the most keen, most professional, palmist's smile he can possibly muster, then reaches out his own hands and gently takes them both.

11

Vicki Wilson is transporting bulging bagfuls of baby provisions from the boot of her hire car to a temporary berth by the reception desk when Israel and Jen turn up, sweating heavily and slightly out of breath. She peers down at her watch.

'You're over an hour late,' she grumbles. 'What happened?'

'We're so sorry, Mrs Wilson,' Jen gushes. 'The class overran. There was an impromptu performance at the end. Some of the parents came along. Israel didn't want to back out – let the other kids down ... I swear.' She gazes over at him, beaming. 'Your son was quite the star of the show!'

'Congratulations.' Vicki delivers him a wan smile. 'You took to the drumming, then? Or were you dancing?'

'Drumming,' Israel responds.

'Dancing,' Jen also responds, at exactly the same time.

'Both,' Jen then rapidly elucidates (as Israel gazes down, fixedly, at the floor). 'It was wild. Unstructured. Totally free-form. We all tried a bit of everything – myself included ...' She performs a winsome little twirl.

'Wonderful.' Vicki smiles, indulgently. 'Now here's the thing,' she continues, 'I spent all my spare cash at Mothercare in the Arndale so I'll need to run upstairs and get a few extra notes to pay you, but I left the hire car unlocked in the multi-storey ...' She proffers Jen the keys. 'It's a red Kia, second floor, just next to the lift. You can't miss it. Would you mind heading up there and keeping an eye on it for a couple of minutes?'

'Second floor?'

Jen takes the keys.

'That'd really help me out.' Vicki nods. 'The girl's a Godsend!' she turns and informs the receptionist behind the desk who hands them their room key as Jen happily scampers off.

'Will ya help wid these baby ting here, Israel?' Vicki drops the posh accent, points to the pile of bags, takes his briefcase by way of exchange, then goes to call the lift. Israel does as he's asked – slightly nervous – and once they're both inside and comfortably ensconced, she turns to inspect her reflection in the mirrored back wall, checking her nostrils and pushing back her hair. 'Now you want tell me where you *really* been all day?' she asks, her manner easy, her voice still casual.

'*Wha'?*' Israel instantly looks panicked.

'I was early an' I drove myself down to the class. You not there. Man say you not been there all day.' She turns to face him. 'So where was you exactly, son? Eh?'

'Me not want dance,' Israel starts off, terrified.

'*Where?*' his mother repeats.

'Nowhere. We just hung out at a golf course all day.'

His mother freezes.

'You never tell me Aunt Esther haemorrhage,' he adds, indignant (possibly hoping to gain some kind of moral advantage).

'What happen there?' she demands, her voice low now, and ominous.

'Nothing happen! I just read my book is all! There was some kids playin' a tournament ...'

The lift arrives at the correct floor and the doors automatically open. Israel steps out. His mother places his briefcase in the hallway beside him but stays put herself. 'What else?' she asks.

'Nothing.' He shrugs. 'It was boring. I read my book.'

'What *else*?' she persists.

'There was a golfer – being photograph. Jen help him with his make-up.'

'You speak with him at all?' his mother demands.

'No.'

Israel shakes his head.

'He speak with you?'

'No.'

His mother lifts one, profoundly suspicious brow.

'No!' he insists.

'You got anything else you need to tell me?' she asks.

'No.' He shakes his head, then quickly reconsiders. 'Only I'm sorry.'

'That it?'

'Uh. Yes.' He frowns. 'Me think so.'

'Fine.'

She releases the doors-open button and prods the ground floor one.

'Go pack your bag,' she tells him, refusing all eye contact.

'We leavin' here tonight.'

'Tonight?' he echoes, then, 'It not Jen fault!' he squeaks. 'Me hate the drum! You know me got no rhythm!'

The doors close.

'Ma!' he yells.

The doors open again. She stares out at him, her eyes glowing like embers.

'You forget ya money.'

She doesn't move, just continues to stare, unblinking.

The doors close again.

'Holy shit,' he mutters.

*   *   *

'Say that again,' Noel prompts her.

'I'm tattooing Stuart Ransom.'

Noel sits down on the bottom stair, stunned.

'Tonight,' Valentine adds. 'I've got a baby-sitter.'

'You're going *out*?' Noel is incredulous.

'He didn't want to come to the house.'

'I wouldn't *let* him in the house!' Noel snorts.

Valentine is just about to offer a tart rejoinder about there not *being* a house for much longer when their mother emerges from the sitting room eating a bowlful of cold Ambrosia Creamed Rice.

'Fuck *off*, Mum,' Noel hisses. He gestures, dismissively.

She just stands and gazes at him, balefully, as she eats.

'FUCK *OFF*, MUM!' he yells, springing to his feet.

His mother shows him the finger and stalks away.

'Don't take it out on her!' Valentine automatically leaps to her mother's defence.

'So all that bullshit about not being able to leave the house ...' Noel starts off.

'I've been approached by a woman who thinks my work might be ready to exhibit,' Valentine explains.

'I'm always telling you that!' Noel's outraged.

'She has contacts with this powerful London agent ...'

'Bully for you!' Noel snaps. 'But what the fuck does Stuart fucking *Ransom* have to do with all of this?'

'She thinks it'd be good publicity.'

Noel just gawps at her.

'I know it hasn't worked out that way before ...' Valentine murmurs, almost ashamed.

'Have you lost your mind?' Noel whispers, awed. 'After everything he's put us through, Vee?'

Valentine just shakes her head.

'She shakes her head!' Noel laughs, playing to an imaginary crowd.

'You *both* made that stupid deal with the insurance people, remember?' Valentine admonishes him. 'To keep it in the public eye – play on the original grudge – earn yourself kickbacks. You actively *courted* the publicity after Dad died. And it was all just pretend – a lie! You made a farce out of what happened!'

'*He* did that!' Noel exclaims.

'But you *knew* it was all just baloney – that it was high stakes – and you didn't give a hoot. He just happened to play a better *game* than you did and that pissed you off. You began to forget what it was all really about – Mum – me – our family ...'

'He blackened my fucking name!' Noel's furious. 'He twisted things! He made me look a twat! *I* was the victim, and he made me look a twat!'

'*Mum* was the victim!' Valentine's outraged. 'Not you, not Dad ...'

'And now you're going to tattoo him?' Noel holds up his hands, incredulous.

'I just want ...' Valentine starts off.

'You're gonna regret this.' Noel shoves past her and heads down the hallway. He slams into the kitchen and tries to turn on the light. It won't turn on. He swears and strides back out into the hallway again. He tries another light switch – still nothing.

'When did the electricity go off?' He pushes past Valentine and yanks open the little cupboard that houses the meter. The meter – which is now leaning, at an unsteady angle, half inside the small safe it once obscured – threatens to tip out. He grabs it, expostulating.

'What the fuck happened here? Where's all Dad's stuff gone?'

'The meter fell off,' Valentine explains, uneasy now, 'so I took the stuff out and I ...'

He slams the cupboard door shut.

'Where is it?' he asks.

'Burned.'

Noel just gazes at her.

'I burned it,' Valentine repeats, 'outside. In the incinerator.'

'You burned Dad's collection?'

Noel leans back against the wall, stunned.

'After I found the letter,' Valentine adds.

'Letter?' Noel mumbles.

'From the bank. Saying they're going to sell the house. This house,' she adds, 'our *home*.'

'I can't believe you burned them.' Noel stares at her, mesmerized.

'We should've done it years ago,' Valentine maintains. 'It was stupid to try and sell them. If the wrong person got wind of it the publicity would destroy everything I've ...' – she falters – '... we've worked so hard to ...'

'You think you're some kind of a saint!' Noel laughs. 'I swear to God you think you're some kind of a fucking –'

'The meter fell out of the wall!' Valentine yells. 'It nearly broke this woman's leg! She saw all the boxes! She was holding the wallet *in her hand*!'

'You're insane.' Noel shakes his head, disgusted.

'If you'd sold them ...' Valentine persists.

'I wasn't *going* to sell them!' Noel slaps his palm against the wall, barely controlling his anger. 'I was *never* going to sell them, you fucking idiot!'

'Then why keep them hidden here all this time?' Valentine demands. 'And lie about it on top?'

Noel sits down on the stairs again, lounges back on to his elbow and smilingly appraises his sister.

'Why are you looking at me like that?' she asks, spooked.

'You don't think very much of me, do you?' Noel grins.

'Same as Dad. You're *exactly* the same as he was. You think I'm a fucking retard – a failure, a loser.'

'That's rubbish!' Valentine's outraged.

'Oh yeah, but Valentine's the good one – the arty one, the clever one. Valentine's Daddy's little angel – the great, fucking tattoo artist. The big, fucking *party* girl who suddenly decides – when everyone needs her the most – to just lock herself away! So vulnerable! So sensitive! Poor, little Valentine – playing the victim, same as always. And me? *Eh?* Who am I? Just the fuck-up, the block-head, the flunky, the errand boy who can't ever do anything fucking *right!*'

'You said you'd get rid of them!' Valentine's still indignant. 'I've just spent the best part of two years – two *years!* – negotiating a deal with a holocaust museum.'

'Straight after he died,' she continues, ignoring him, 'you promised!'

'I just *negotiated a deal*,' Noel repeats, losing his temper again, 'to donate them to a fucking *museum*, you fucking *half-wit!*'

Valentine just stares at him.

'Did you hear me?' he asks, quieter now.

'I heard you.' Valentine nods.

'I can't believe you fucking *burned* them!' Noel exclaims.

'Which museum?' Valentine demands.

'What does it matter *which* museum?! You fucking *burned* them!'

'You should've told me,' Valentine murmurs. 'How was I expected to know?'

'This was *my* way of making things right,' Noel hisses. 'This was *my* moment – *my* way of making things sit better. But now you've gone and stuck your fucking *oar* in and you've ruined it, same as you always do!'

He stands up and quickly darts forwards (she instinctively flinches) then just politely sidesteps her, with a tired, dry laugh.

'If I wasn't bumping I'd've fucking *killed* you for this,' he whispers, then offers her a limp-fingered, bittersweet salute and quietly leaves the house.

⋆　⋆　⋆

Vicki is standing with Jen by the boot of the Kia. Vicki is handing her some money. Jen is looking confused.

'But this is double the amount we agreed,' she murmurs, mystified.

'I know' – Vicki nods – 'because I'm hoping to take up a little more of your time.'

'Oh. Okay,' Jen promptly agrees. 'Although I'm meant to be baby-sitting at eight ...'

Vicki opens the Kia's compact boot. 'Would you mind checking to see if anything's left in there?' she asks.

Jen turns and leans into the boot. She closely scans inside it. There's nothing in there. She's about to say, 'There's nothing in here,' but before she can open her mouth, Vicki has delivered her a hefty shove from the rear, half up-ended her into the boot, grabbed her legs, tossed them in and deftly slammed it shut.

'I know who you're working for,' she announces, coldly, then walks to the driver's side, climbs in, starts the engine, fastens her seat belt and calmly pushes the gears into reverse.

Gene guides Mallory ahead of him into the house – like a little human shield – his hands resting lightly on either shoulder. Once inside he removes her school blazer, hangs it on a hook alongside his military jacket, then looks around – somewhat anxiously – for Sheila.

'Is that you, Gene?'

A muffled voice.

'Sheila?'

He turns on the spot.

'*Help!* I'm stuck in the bloody attic!'

He walks to the bottom of the stairs and peers up. From this vantage point he can see the hatch into the loft which is blocked by ... he squints ... a suitcase?

'The case got lodged,' Sheila yells (as he mounts the stairs, two at a time), '… and I've managed to hurt my leg.'

'Is it bad?' Gene grabs the fallen towel and passes it to Mallory who obligingly heads off to the bathroom – ever fastidious – to hang it over the heated rail. He kicks away the single sandal, climbs a few rungs of the ladder and begins wiggling the case to try and release it.

'I don't know how you got the damn thing up here in the first place!' Sheila tries helping from her side.

'Have you been trapped for long?' Gene enquires.

'Forty minutes – an hour?'

'If you'd only just waited till I got back …' he reprimands her as the case is gradually un-lodged and starts to inch through the gap.

'Thank God for that!'

No sooner is the case in motion than Sheila is tossing down her other sandal – it bounces off Gene's shoulder – and following it down herself. Gene drops the case and quickly straightens up to try and guide her.

'I'm fine!' she snaps. 'Step back – don't touch the leg!'

She emerges, naked, but for a bandage and an ill-fitting mohair jumper (one nipple hangs through a hole. It barely skims her buttocks).

'What on earth …?' He is about to enquire about her nudity (then her injury), but is startled into silence by her new haircut. Mallory has now returned and is standing beside him, equally astonished – it would seem – by Sheila's ungainly emergence.

'Mummy! Your *hair*!' she gasps, followed by, 'What *are* you wearing?!'

'Perhaps you should go and put the kettle on,' Gene suggests, guiding her (his little shield again) towards the stairs. Mallory is less keen to oblige him this time around. She goes down backwards, one step at a time – clinging on to the banister – eyeing the transformed Sheila (horror-struck) all the while.

Sheila limps into their bedroom.

'I forgot how *itchy* this thing always was against the skin,' she grumbles, pulling it off over her head and grabbing her dressing gown from behind the door (virtually slamming it into Gene's face as he tries to follow her). He waits for a second and then cautiously enters.

Sheila is inspecting her filthy hands.

'What happened to your leg?' he asks.

'Uh ...' She looks up, vaguely. 'The electricity meter.'

Gene waits for more information, his eyes moving, anxiously, between the bandage and her shorn hair.

'It fell off,' she adds, 'and thwacked me' – she points – 'right there.'

'Is it bad?'

'I passed out – only very briefly – during a baptism.' She shrugs. 'They initially thought the bone might be cracked, but turns out it's only chipped. There's a big blood blister ...'

Gene inspects the slight swelling on her foot. 'Shouldn't you be resting it?'

Sheila doesn't answer. She is gazing off, unfocused, into the middle distance.

'Is something ... is something up? Wrong?' Gene wonders – suddenly curiously inarticulate – finding himself parched and alone in a linguistic desert – verbally dry – barely capable of placing one, exhausted syllable in front of the other.

'Something wrong?' Sheila echoes, gazing at him, owlishly. 'It just feels like something's ... something's happened, maybe?'

'It actually dawned on me while I was stuck up in the attic,' Sheila muses. 'It was ridiculously hot up there – stuffy – and I was completely naked ... uh ...'

She looks momentarily distracted.

'You were saying?' Gene prompts her.

'Yes.' She nods. 'I was sat up there and I was thinking that either something amazing was happening to me – *is* happening – connected to faith, I guess – to God; either that or I'm completely losing my marbles.'
She grins.

'And you think that's funny?' Gene murmurs, visibly alarmed.

'I've taken a pile of painkillers, so I reasoned that it was just …'

She fades out again, then refocuses, without any prompting. 'I actually *barked* at these kids the other day!' she snorts.

'Barked?' Gene echoes.

'Yes. I barked at them. Asian kids – messing around out back. I woofed. Then I sang a hymn: "Once in Royal David's City", which – as you probably know – has always been a hymn I've found especially dreary.'

'You didn't mention that before.' Gene frowns.

'About the hymn?'

'About the barking.'

'Maybe that's why they call it "barking mad",' she quips, flatly.

'Were you up in the attic for any particular reason?' Gene wonders.

'Yeah …' She looks around her, distracted again.

'You brought down your old suitcase.'

'I did.' She nods. 'In fact …'

She sits down on the bed. 'It's been a very odd day. Almost like a dream.'

She puts a hand to her hair then leans forward and tries to inspect herself in the dressing table mirror.

'That's a pretty radical haircut,' Gene murmurs. 'Quite a departure. I mean it's … I … I *like* it. It's very …'

'Radical?!' Sheila chuckles, amused (almost indifferent), teasing it with her fingers. 'Valentine cut it for me. The fringe was all …' She flaps her hands (like it's too much effort to

explain in full). 'In fact while we're on the subject of
Valentine' – she gazes up at him, accusingly – 'I just can't
believe you didn't tell me about ...'

'Kettle's boiled!'
Mallory pops her head around the door.
Gene is frozen to the spot.
'Did you heat the pot?' Sheila asks.
Mallory nods.
'Good. Well I fancy half and half – one Earl Grey, one
Breakfast Tea. Just two bags if that's okay ...'
Mallory nods again.
'And I've bought us a McVitie's Jamaican Ginger Cake as a
treat – it's very soft so you should be able to manage a little
bit of it. I've put it in the bread bin. Take it out and cut a few
slices – not too many. Be very, *very* careful with the knife.
We'll both be down in a minute.'

Mallory nods then half-turns as the land-line in the hallway
starts to ring.
'Ignore that,' Sheila instructs her, 'it'll only be work. Oh, and
while you're still here' – she grins – 'I should probably warn
you that I have a big piece of news to share with you over tea
– exciting news.'
'*Yipeee!*' Mallory claps her hands and skips off, delighted.
'We're going to Eurodisney!' she sings, all the way down
the stairs.

'Eurodisney!' Sheila snorts. 'Good try, kiddo!' she shouts.
'Better luck next time, eh?!'

Gene hasn't moved. He is in a state of profound mental
and emotional turmoil. His mouth is dry. His eyes are
burning. He parts his lips to speak at exactly the same instant
as Mallory trills: 'I *love* your new hair, Mummy!' from the
bottom of the stairs.

'Thank you, Mallory,' Sheila shouts back, then turns to
Gene with a fond smile. 'Aw! Bless her!'
'Big news?' Gene creaks.

'Did you get my text?' Sheila asks (determined not to be diverted from her original course). He nods, grimly, expecting the worst – almost willing her to know everything simply to save him from the trouble of saying it out loud; composing it into tawdry sentences. So many words available ... he muses (moving from his former state of verbal paucity to one of verbal superfluity in the course of a mere instant), feeling himself floating – without hope or sense or mass – in an alien constellation of possible nouns, verbs and pronouns.

'It was just so uncomfortable – embarrassing,' she clucks, 'I mean she had no idea that you were working with Ransom, for starters –'

'I didn't think ...' Gene tries to interject.

'And she didn't have a *clue* about the letter.'

'The letter?' Gene echoes.

'From the bank. The one you said you'd found. She had no idea – not an inkling. So when I mentioned it – thinking she already knew – she had this awful kind of ... of mini-meltdown. Then the bloody meter fell out of the cupboard. Nessa was sitting on the floor just behind me so I took the weight of it on my leg.' She points to her bandage. 'Valentine had run upstairs, in floods of tears, meanwhile ...'

Gene winces.

'And that's when I find the little safe – the collection. It was all just so ...' – she draws a deep breath – 'so completely overwhelming.'

'Hold on a second.' He frowns, shaking his head, confused. 'The meter fell out and you found ...'

'Her dad's collection,' Sheila repeats, 'behind the meter. The whip, the medals, the rings, the wallet.'

She blanches. 'I actually picked the thing up. I held it in my hand. There was the registration number ...'

She shudders. 'Valentine went mad when she found me holding it – I honestly had no idea at that stage. She came over all dark and full of self-loathing, talking about how bad she was, how she deserved to be unhappy, how she hated herself, how she was just like her father, all this stuff about his "legacy" and her love of the skin and how the paler the skin was the stronger the mark ...'

Sheila shakes her head, exhausted. 'I just wish you'd told me in the first place,' she rounds off.

'There was a wallet?' Gene's still all at sea.

'The pride of his collection, apparently. A skin wallet. From a concentration camp.'

Gene stares at her for a few seconds, uncomprehending.

'And this stuff was actually being stored ...?' he finally murmurs.

'Behind the meter. In a little safe. Like a dusty, brick larder. You're telling me you didn't know?' It's now Sheila's turn to look disbelieving.

'Nope.' Gene shakes his head.

She stares at him for a minute.

'You look awful. Pale. D'you feel okay?'

He nods. Then he shakes his head again, his shoulders slumping forward.

'I've done something terrible –' he starts off.

'Tea's ready!' Mallory yells up the stairs.

'We're on our way down!' Sheila calls back.

'Sorry.' She stands up and moves towards him, frowning, concerned. 'I've been so busy banging on about myself ...'

She reaches up and softly touches his cheek then his forehead with the back of her hand. Gene's mobile starts ringing from his jacket pocket in the hallway.

'Warm,' she murmurs.

He tries to tear his eyes away from hers but he can't. He tries to swallow but he can't. He feels his guilt leaking from every orifice. He is drenched in self-loathing.

'Tell me!' She gazes up at him, her eyes full of a sudden tenderness. 'It can't be all that bad, surely?'

'Come on!' Mallory calls. 'Before it goes cold!'

Sheila doesn't move.

'I ... I ... I ... I did a reading,' Gene stutters, nauseous, 'for Ransom's assistant, and I ended up lying about what I saw.'

'You mean a palm reading?'

Sheila withdraws slightly, shocked. Gene nods. *Coward!* he's thinking. *Quitter! Gutless ninny!*

These insults whirlpool around him, every harsh consonant dressed – as though for combat – in jingling spurs.

'But I thought ...' – she's confused – 'I thought you didn't do that kind of thing any more – simply as a matter of principle.'

'I don't.' Gene winces, listening to his phone ringing, the spurs jangling, half there, half absent, his tongue in ribbons. 'But he begged me. We were stuck in traffic.'

'Well I can't pretend I'm not a little disappointed.' Sheila limps over to a nearby chest of drawers, takes out some pants and a pair of tracksuit bottoms and starts to gingerly pull them on under her dressing gown. 'I mean to do a reading in the first place, but then to lie about the results ...'

'There were just so many bad things about the hand' – Gene struggles to focus, to defend himself – 'a weak Line of Head, an interrupted Line of Life, his Line of Fate ascending to the Mount of Saturn – which is a really tragic sign at the best of times ...'

'So you lied.' Sheila has her back to him. She's taken off her dressing gown and is now putting on a bra. Gene idly watches her reflection in the dressing table mirror. Her nipples are the colour of drinking chocolate – beautiful – a pale, creamy, malted brown. He blinks.

'So you lied,' she repeats.

'It reminded me of when I was a kid and I got presented with a tragic hand,' he murmurs, 'I'd always try and accentuate the positive no matter what.'

'By lying,' Sheila persists.

'By improvising,' he modifies.

'Improvising?' Sheila's incredulous. 'How, exactly?'

'Well,' Gene struggles to remember, 'there was a car overheating nearby and the driver was pouring a bottle of water into the tank ... I suddenly found myself telling him that there was a strong connection with travel and water on his hand – there was a tiny square near the Line of Life which made me think of ...'

'Travel and *water*?!' Sheila snorts.

'... of a lake, or some kind of ... an enclosed expanse of ...'

'Hardly the world's most imaginative scenario!' Sheila pertly derides him.

'But that was the awful thing!' Gene confesses. 'He lapped it up! He was ecstatic! It was exactly what he'd been hoping for! He told me how he'd recently become obsessed by this Mexican tycoon, an engineer who's developed this system, this state-of-the-art treatment system for creating giant, crystal-clear lagoons.'

'Lagoons?' Sheila's becoming a little overwhelmed by all this information.

'He'd reached out to this man and he'd been offered some kind of work experience in Chile or Peru – I forget which – but he can't drive and he was naturally nervous about such a radical change in direction at this stage in his career.'

He looks to Sheila for some kind of input but she's momentarily preoccupied with adjusting her hair in the mirror.

'Then he asked me if there was any prospect of ... of romance.'

'Romance?!' Sheila echoes, amused by Gene's use of the old-fashioned term.

'His Line of Heart curved down from the base of the Mount of Jupiter,' Gene explains, 'which generally indicates a lack of perception – no judge of character – naivety – the prospect of great disappointment in love – so I said I thought he *would* find love, but in a completely unexpected way, in a completely unexpected time and place.'

'Suitably vague and enigmatic,' Sheila commends him.

'Then not content with that, he asked me if he would ever marry or have a child.'

'Please tell me you didn't ...' Sheila's wincing.

'I just told him what the hand said.'

'What did the hand say?'

'There were no clear signs either way about marriage, but the hand definitely implied that he would have one child.'

'Boy or girl?' Sheila wonders, jaded.

'The line was very faded so I guessed a girl.'

'Was he happy with that?'

'He went very quiet for a minute or so and then he said that he thought that the child Esther – Ransom's manager – had just had, baby Prudence, was *his* child.'

'*What?!*' Sheila's eyes widen. 'They slept together?'

'Once.' Gene nods, turning slightly as his mobile phone starts ringing again from inside his jacket pocket in the hall.

'Wow!' Sheila's still coming to terms with this revelation.

'I know.' Gene sighs.

'No wonder you look ill.' She laughs.

Gene doesn't laugh.

'That's not why I look ill,' he starts off, haltingly.

'I've just accepted a job in the Caribbean,' Sheila interrupts.

Gene stares at her, dumbstruck.

12

Esther is propped up in bed, chatting away on her phone, looking worn but happy (and considerably less bulky), a newborn baby snuggled into the crook of her arm.

'Girl!' she's saying proudly. 'All a' ten pound!'

This brief look of womanly contentment falters for a second when she espies her younger sister, Victoria, striding across the ward towards her, her face like thunder.

'Me better go ...' she murmurs.

'What a' *hell* possess you, Esther?!' Victoria demands, slamming to a halt at the base of the bed, pointing at the phone, accusingly. 'That him there?'

'What up wid you all a sudden, Vicki?' Esther hastily terminates the call.

'Him happy now?' Vicki follows up, still glowering. 'Him gonna take you back? *Huh?* Now you done all his dirty work?' She snatches Esther's phone and inspects the tiny screen, holding it close to her face, trying to make sense of it.

'Calm yourself!' Esther hisses, glancing around the ward, embarrassed. Vicki tosses the phone on to the coverlet, disgusted, then proceeds to draw the curtain around the bed.

'Me can't believe you blabbed!' she yells, once the rest of the ward has been neatly obliterated by a pale swathe of stiff fabric. 'Me own sister!'

'Blabbed where?'

Esther places a finger to her lips, scowling, to warn her sister from disturbing the baby.

'Stuart Ransom! Where else?!' Vicki bellows.

The baby opens its eyes, with a milky hiccup.

'Blabbed how?' Esther stutters, using her nightdress to pat the corner of the child's mouth.

'Me need a' go!' Vicki starts pacing, manically. 'Me want a' go, *now* …'

She leans over and tries to grab the baby.

'*Victoria!*' Esther exclaims, pushing her away. 'You crazy?!'

'You not hearin' me, Esther!' Vicki exclaims. 'The man *know* about Israel! He find out about him son!'

Esther gazes at her, in stunned silence, then: 'Na-ah.' She shakes her head. 'Na-ah.' She shakes it again.

'You ever met a girl call Jen in your travel?' Vicki demands.

'Jen?' Esther's bemused.

'Blonde girl. Skinny. Work at the hotel?'

Esther's uncomprehending. She frowns down at the baby as if – by some miracle – this tiny, newborn scrap might contain some of the answers.

'Well she been minding Israel for the day,' Vicki runs on, 'took him to some drum class – some dance class – or so me thought. Turn out she took him to the golf course instead.'

Esther's chin shoots up. Her eyes widen. 'Wha' happen?' she asks, hoarsely.

Vicki shrugs. 'Something and nothing.'

Esther leans over, wincing, and gently places baby Prudence into the crib by her bed.

'Please tell me this some *bad* joke,' she whispers.

Vicki shakes her head.

'What Israel say?'

Vicki shrugs.

'Who this girl?' Esther demands. 'Where she now?'

'Boot a' my car.' Vicki crosses her arms, defensively.

Esther stares at her, brows raised. 'What she doin' there, Vicki?'

Vicki shrugs again.

'You kidnap her?'

'A' push her in me boot, an' a' drove her here.'

'You hurt her?'

'*Wha?!*' Vicki sucks her tongue.

Esther stares at her, warily, trying to make some loose semblance of sense out of the situation.

'Him want custody, now?' Vicki demands. 'After *fourteen* long year? Tell me, Esther!'

'Oh Lord!' Esther leans forward on the bed, clutching on to her stomach like her belly is aching. 'It all over – a' screwed!' she mutters. 'A' screwed now, for sure!'

The baby starts to wail, plaintively. Vicki goes to inspect it. 'This him pickney, an' all?' she asks, pointing, wrinkling up her nose.

Esther shakes her head.

'Then who this poor baby's father?' Vicki demands.

'Nobody,' Esther growls, 'just some random fool.'

'You got a fool for your baby-father?!' Vicki sucks her tongue again.

'Come down here a minute.'

Esther points to a chair by the bed, her expression grave.

Vicki doesn't move.

'PARK YOURSELF!' Esther yells, slapping the seat.

Vicki sits, glowering.

'Me got something me need to get off me chest,' Esther starts off.

'Me already know what you done!' Vicki springs up again, with a glare.

'You not know it all' – Esther shakes her head, speaking softly, mournfully – 'trust me.'

Vicki scowls and grudgingly returns to her seat.

'All right ...' Esther prepares herself. 'All right. So ...' She raises her eyes.

'Everything okay in here, ladies?'

A cheerful, Irish nurse pops her head through the curtain. Both sisters turn and glower at her, in unison.

'I'll take that as a yes, shall I?'

She rapidly withdraws again.

'All right …' Esther starts off, then falters, then laboriously clears her throat.

'Spit it out!' Vicki grumbles, instantly impatient. 'Me not got all day, here!'

'All right …' Esther shields her eyes with her hand as she speaks. 'Me never tell Ransom you was pregnant, Vicki,' she murmurs.

Vicki frowns at her, not quite following.

'Me never tell him. Ransom never knew.'

'*What?!* Of course you tell him!' Vicki springs to her feet again, sneering. 'Of course you tell him! Him left money for the clinic!'

'Them dollar was mine. Me never tell him. He never knew.'

Short silence.

'Why?' Vicki finally demands, still not fully comprehending.

'We had plans – him and me – we two – then you happen along …'

She shrugs.

'Plans?' Vicki echoes.

'Me had a *bond* wid him, Vicki, a relationship, a partnership. It was bigger than just …' She shrugs again.

'You hook up?' Vicki's breathless, winded, trapped in a foreign landscape between fury and heartbreak. 'Gi bun wid him?'

'Never!' Esther shakes her head.

'But you want to, though?'

Esther shrugs.

'So how you scare him off?'

'A' tell him you was back with Jerrick Bailey,' Esther smirks, 'on the sly.'

'One time!' Vicki's indignant.

'*Ha!*' Esther snorts, vindicated. 'How come you so sure the pickney not his?'

'Me get him to wear boots is how,' Vicki clucks (appalled at her sister's naivety).

'You not got Ransom to wear 'em?'

'He wear 'em.' Vicki nods.

Esther slits her eyes. 'You meddle with 'em?'

Vicki sucks her tongue, neglecting to answer. Instead she walks to the end of the bed and stares up at the ceiling.

'Fifteen long *year*, Esther,' she eventually murmurs, full of wonderment at the magnitude of her sister's betrayal, 'and not even a *word*?'

'*A*' was wrong,' Esther concedes, 'but what him and me had was *bigger*, Vicki –'

'Bigger than what?! His own pickney?!' Vicki interrupts, patently astonished by her sister's casual impertinence. 'This how you apologize? Call it *wrong*?! That all?'

'Him got a real talent, Vicki,' Esther tries to explain, 'we was a team. We stuck together through it *all*. Fifteen *year*. And who was it support the whole family, meantime? Who buy Mamma house? Who pay for Israel go to school? Huh? Was me, Vicki! Him and me!'

'Hear yourself!' Vicki squawks.

'If a hadn't been him it would a been somebody else, Vicki,' Esther gently remonstrates. 'You was bad news – no motivation – spoil everything for everybody. Bring shame on the family. You need to learn yourself a hard lesson. An' ya *did* learn it. Because a' what me done. Look there!' Esther points, proudly. 'See you now! See what you become!'

'See *me*?!' Vicki exclaims, amazed, then, 'See *yourself*, sista! See what *you* become! *Hear* yourself, sista!'

Esther says nothing.

Vicki paces up and down for a few seconds, then pulls up, sharply. 'You tell Mamma?'

Esther shakes her head.

'An' him *never* know?' Vicki repeats, still trying but failing to comprehend the full implications of this revelation.

Esther shakes her head.

'Good Lord!' Vicki's thoroughly befuddled. 'Now what the hell me suppose to do with *that*, huh?'

Esther shrugs.

'Ransom never know him got a son,' Vicki repeats, as much to herself as to her sister, 'Israel never know him got a daddy. All because a' what *you* done.'

'True,' Esther acknowledges (still no word of an apology).

'Well, somebody sure gone and told him now,' Vicki reasons, almost with a grim kind of satisfaction. 'You must a let it slip somewhere, somehow.'

'It all over, then,' Esther murmurs, bleakly, still not willing to accept this possibility.

'Best thing all round!' Vicki remonstrates, softly.

Esther finally starts crying.

Vicki stands up and walks to the end of the bed, trying to get her thoughts in order. As she stands there, in confusion, a pair of hands start grappling with the curtains, trying – and failing – to find the gap. After thirty or so seconds the hands move lower, the curtain is lifted – from its base – and a bunch of flowers appears from under it, then a small, open box with a ring standing proud in it, then finally, a head.

'Sorry – it's me, it's Toby, hi,' Toby finally announces himself, still on his knees, patently surprised – and somewhat flustered – to see Esther's sister glaring down at him. 'This isn't exactly ...' His eyes move from one devastated sibling to the other, then: 'Marry me, Esther!' he flutes, proffering the ring. 'Let's run away together! I know it's my baby!'

Silence.

(S.P.I.C.E.! he's thinking, his cheeks flushing a deep and unforgiving red, S.P.I.C.E.!)

'Marry me, Esther!' he repeats. 'I think I'm in love with you. In fact ...' – he shuffles forward on his knees (the curtain still affixed to his shoulders like some kind of bizarre, chivalric cape) – 'in fact I *know* I am, I'm *sure* I am.'

Vicki bursts into gales of hysterical laughter. 'I *know* I am! I'm *sure* I am!' she parrots, cruelly.

Esther gazes at Toby, astonished, for a full fifteen seconds then, 'Stand up you damn fool!' she sharply expostulates.

Terence Nimrod is leaning against a pillar in the grand entrance to the hotel foyer, passing some time with an irascible Ransom (who is nervously smoking – tapping ash into his cigarette packet) as he impatiently waits for the housekeeper to release the spare key to Esther's room on the (patently false) proviso that he wants to gather together some extra personal effects for her elongated stay in hospital.

'I mean he's not a big guy,' Nimrod amiably chunters, 'but he's solid, emanates a kind of … yeah … *solidity*. And very burnished, very … very "buff" – to use my daughters' favourite adjective. Anyway, we were stuck in there for the best part of an hour, just hanging around. It's a nice room but a small room – wooden floor, heavy drapes, the classic box seat in the window – all fairly uninspiring, except for this amazing, red leather *chaise longue* sitting in one corner which is very dramatic, very over the top, very camp …'

Nimrod takes Ransom's cigarette, steals a puff, then returns it. 'So our photographer – Kenny, the guy who's turning up to take some shots tonight – was just fixating on this *chaise longue* and saying, "We gotta get Fiddy to lie on the *chaise longue*! We gotta make him do that!"'

'Fiddy?' Ransom glances over at Nimrod, frowning.

'Fiddy – Fifty Cent – the rapper. It was one of those maddening situations where time constraints oblige you to conduct the interview while they're taking the photographs – a real pain in the arse. Anyhow, Kenny was just desperate to get

Fiddy on to that *chaise longue*. We'd all been gassing about his latest book ...'

'Autobiography?' Ransom speculates, taking a deep pull on his cigarette.

'Business-cum-self-help-manual. He was in early negotiations with Robert Greene at the time – you know: *The 48 Laws of Power*, *The Art of Seduction*?'

'Yeah.' Ransom nods (plainly all too familiar with these works).

'Anyway, we're standing around together in this cramped, little space and Fiddy's PR is telling us about Fiddy's favourite theory which he calls "The Lion in the Room" ...'

'The Lion?' Ransom scowls.

'It's hilarious. Apparently Fiddy thinks the best way to dominate a business meeting – *any* business meeting – is by the simple expedient of refusing to nod.'

'What?' Ransom scratches his head, distractedly.

'Not to nod. To refuse to nod. Basically you've just got to attract the attention of the speaker with strong eye contact but then keep perfectly still. Don't nod.'

'But why *would* you nod?' Ransom's confused. He peeks around the pillar to check if there's any progress being made on the key front. There isn't.

'Because that's what people instinctively do in meetings,' Nimrod explains, 'they automatically nod when the speaker is making his presentation. It's unconscious.'

'I never knew that,' Ransom confesses.

'Well, Fiddy's theory is that if you hold the speaker's attention but *don't* nod, it undermines the speaker's confidence so that they increasingly start to direct the entire presentation towards you – the non-nodder – to try and win you over. Naturally everyone in the meeting starts to notice that the speaker is directing his presentation entirely to you – one person – so they all start directing their attention towards you, too, just to try and work out why, thereby transforming you into the Alpha Male – the "Lion in the Room".'

'So if you don't nod ...' Ransom's finally catching on. 'You become the Alpha Male. It's just basic dominance behaviour.'

'I like it!' Ransom's impressed.

'There's always been a close relationship between rap music and business,' Nimrod expands, airily. 'It's a street music. It's all about the hustle. I mean Fiddy was a drug dealer way before he ever laid down a beat. Business is very much "his thing".'

'The Lion in the Room,' Ransom muses, nodding approvingly.

'So anyway,' Nimrod gets back to his story, 'it's in the context of all these hard-boiled, no-nonsense, Alpha-style business theories that we suddenly start thinking: Wouldn't it be funny to get the Lion – Fiddy – to lie down on this red *chaise longue*?'

'Why?' Ransom demands.

'Why?' Nimrod seems slightly irritated by this question. 'Because we just didn't see how he would agree to do it, obviously.'

'You wanted to humiliate him?' Ransom speculates.

'We just wanted to have a little pull on the Lion's tail, that's all.' Nimrod grins. 'Make him growl – see how he'd react.'

'Fair enough,' Ransom concedes. 'Did he do it?'

'Kenny and his PR actually had a bet on it. The PR said there's absolutely no way on God's good earth that Fiddy will agree to lie down on the *chaise longue* – he's a rapper, been shot nine times – it'd be *way* too compromising, too emasculating to stretch out on that thing ...'

'Emasculating,' Ransom echoes, half under his breath. 'But then Kenny says, "Well if I can even get him to *sit* on it – let alone *lie* on it – just to *sit* on it and have his picture taken, then I win ... *uh* ..."' Nimrod waves his hand, imperiously. 'I forget the precise amount – a tenner – whatever ...'

'Did he sit on it?' Ransom asks.

'Well that's the weird thing.' Nimrod chuckles. 'Fiddy finally comes into the room – very gracious, very polite, very ...'

'Buff,' Ransom fills in, throwing the last segment of his cigarette to the ground and crushing it underfoot.

'Exactly – buff – and Kenny takes a few photos in the window-seat, a couple standing against the drapes, then he turns and looks over at the red *chaise longue* ... As you can imagine, we're all in an advanced state of hysteria by this stage ...'

Ransom peers around the pillar again. The desk clerk is talking to the housekeeper.

'... and he says, "How about a couple of shots lying down on that *chaise longue*?" He points to it. Then Fiddy – ever the gentleman, really polite – clocks the *chaise longue*, registers the issues, raises one brow, then just shrugs his shoulders and goes, "Sure." He walks over to the *chaise longue* – prowls over there all smooth-jointed, like a panther – and he throws himself down on it! No bother!'

'Fiddy lay down on the *chaise longue*?' Ransom's fully engaged now.

'He lay down on it!' Nimrod confirms. 'And I swear to God, he was a fucking *Lion* when he lay down on that thing! He lay down on it like a fucking *Lion*! Almost like he *knew*! Like he sensed we all had this secret, little bet going on, and he wasn't in the slightest bit bothered or intimidated by it, because he *was* the Lion. Fiddy *was* the Lion! He just didn't give a shit! He pretty much Alpha-ed us all out of the building!' Nimrod grins, remembering. 'Amazing! Absolutely bloody amazing!'

'I was chatting to Andy Helmsley the other week' – Ransom (not to be outdone – by Nimrod *or* Fiddy, for that matter) snatches up the Lion mantle and promptly runs with it – 'he's one of South Africa's most promising up-and-coming faces on the golfing scene …' He peeks around the pillar (the desk clerk has – much to Ransom's satisfaction – dispatched an assistant desk clerk to bring Ransom Esther's spare key). 'And he's telling me about this bush-walk he did in one of the big African game reserves recently. They were heading home through the veld at sunset, about four miles from base camp, just the three of them with a ranger – who's armed with a small rifle – and while they're walking they can hear this constant groaning sound …'

'Groaning?' Nimrod echoes.

'A weird groaning' – Ransom nods – 'fairly close by. Follows them wherever they go. So after a while Andy turns to the ranger and says, "What's making that strange groaning noise?" The ranger says, "It's a lion. It's a dominant male. He's escorting us through his territory." Well as soon as they hear this they're all just cacking themselves – can't walk fast enough – can't get close enough to the ranger and his rifle, basically …'

The assistant clerk arrives with the spare key and the two of them duly plod after him around the side of the main building to a less flashy area just between the bins and the car park.

'So after the best part of an hour of hiking and groaning,' Ransom continues his story while they walk, 'Andy finally asks the question that's weighing on everyone's minds. He says, "If the lion attacks, what are the chances of you killing it with the first shot of your rifle?" The ranger shrugs and says …' – Ransom adopts a generic, 'African' accent – '"None, sir. We'd be screwed. The rifle's only good for making a commotion, aside from that it's of no practical use at all. He's way too big and too fast and too powerful – a trained assassin, a killer …" So they all walk on, literally *shitting* themselves, for a few minutes longer, then the ranger adds, "But don't stress out about it, man. It's fine – it's all good. If this guy wanted to kill you he would've done so over an hour ago."'

'Bloody hell!' Nimrod's shaken.

'Yup.' Ransom chuckles (pleased with this response) as they draw to a halt in front of the door to Esther's room. The clerk proceeds to shove the key into the lock, twist it and push the door wide. Both men pause for a moment on the threshold, surprised by the warm, slightly unhealthy, Vicks Vapour Rub-tinged fug that greets them as they prepare to enter. They immediately apprehend that this part of the hotel complex is far less well finished and maintained than the areas they've grown accustomed to.

Ransom steps inside, frowning. It's a small, cramped room. There are no proper curtains at the lone window which faces out on to a series of large, metal bins, brightly illuminated by an external light which floods, unremittingly, into the room. Esther has hung a large petticoat – blotched with stains and ripped down one side – from one of the plastic window fitments, to try and block it out.

The bed is small and has no proper linen. Hanging over the back of a broken chair are several pieces of Esther's underwear – a bra, two huge pairs of pants – which have been hung up to dry. There is no shade covering the bulb on the bedside light and no light-fitment whatsoever up above, just a series of wires dangling from the pelmet.

Ransom turns to look at the assistant clerk.

'This is a shit-hole,' he mutters. 'Why's she staying here?'

'Staff accommodation.' The clerk shrugs.

Nimrod scratches his head and gazes around him. 'Does she normally stay in rooms like this?' he asks.

'Dunno,' Ransom admits, 'I've never been to her room before.'

'Never?' Nimrod's surprised. 'In fifteen years?'

'Nope.'

Ransom walks to the bedside table and inspects the three, cheaply framed photos on display there. One is of Esther's mother sitting on her porch in Trenchtown, cradling Esther's daughter in her arms. A second features Esther's son and a boy who Ransom now knows to be Israel posing proudly in new school uniforms. The third is of Esther and Ransom, taken many years ago. Ransom picks it up, surprised. In it a long-haired Ransom celebrates winning second place at the Spanish Open while a thinner, younger, grinning Esther stands behind him – in her caddie's uniform – holding aloft the winning ball.

Ransom shudders and places the photo down, his eye returning, nervously, to Israel in his uniform. He grimaces and reaches out to pick it up, but his hand starts shaking so violently that he rapidly withdraws it again.

To cover his confusion he steps forward to open a door into what he presumes will be the bathroom. Instead he discovers a tiny cupboard. Inside it are two shirts, two dresses and – folded up on the floor – a jumper and a single pair of trousers. Underwear aside, these appear to be the sum total of Esther's clothes. Another shirt lies neatly folded on the bed where Esther has been sewing on a mis-matching replacement button.

'Where's the bathroom?' he asks.

'Down the corridor,' the clerk answers. 'It's shared.'

Ransom nods. He is gazing down at an old, worn-out pair of carpet slippers.

'Can you find what you're looking for?' Nimrod asks.

Ransom shakes his head. He doesn't really know what he's looking for, but whatever it is, he's certain that he won't find it here, in this shabby room. He walks over to a battered suitcase that leans up against the wall, opens it and exclaims as a pile of sugar and coffee sachets, tiny soaps, bags of tea and mini packets of biscuits fall out. Nimrod comes over to take a look.

'In all the time I've known Esther,' he murmurs, 'we've never shared a proper meal together. She never seems to *eat* …'

He bends down and starts gathering the supplies together. Also inside the case are an old Bible (the paper cover worn almost to nothing from overuse) and a grey box file. Ransom opens the box file. It's crammed with newspaper cuttings from the entire length of his career, each one carefully folded, dated and preserved in plastic.

'She scoffed those three *pains au chocolat* the other day,' he volunteers.

'She scavenged them from me and Tobe,' Nimrod admits, then scowls. 'I mean I don't want you to take this the wrong way, it's just ...' He peers around him, shaking his head, depressed. 'How long since her last pay cheque?'

'Wouldn't have a clue,' Ransom admits (possibly not as ashamed by this admission as he might be). 'She pays herself.' He straightens up and reappraises the room.

'This is like ...' He pulls on his chin, mystified by the alien scene he surveys. 'I saw a documentary on TV the other night about this Indian guy who had a huge stomach tumour. Had it for years – since he was a kid, but he was always too poor to do anything about it. It just kept growing bigger and bigger. Eventually it grows so massive that it's endangering his life – pressing down on his vital organs. He gets referred by some charity to a specialist who agrees to get his team to operate. When they do, they realize that it isn't a tumour at all, it's a lost twin.'

'A twin?' Nimrod echoes.

'Yeah. Somehow or other this guy's twin brother had ended up forming inside of him – inside his own stomach.'

'*What?!* Is that a true story?' Nimrod clutches his own capacious gut, horrified.

'Yeah. They had an interview with the actual surgeon and everything. For some reason the twin had been trapped inside this guy's belly but – get this – it was *still alive*! Had no brain, but it was alive. And when they cut open his stomach a nasty little hand shot out.'

'*Fuck!*' Nimrod exclaims. Even the waiting clerk looks appalled.

'Disgusting!' Ransom nods, peering around him. 'And that's what this reminds me of. Can't quite put my finger on it ...' He frowns. 'It's almost like Esther is that little trapped twin, that messed-up little twin living a sordid, closed-off life, feeding on ...'

He doesn't utter the word 'me', but it's clear that this is how his mind is working.

'Sordid,' he repeats. 'And just ...' he sighs, 'a real, friggin' downer, basically.'

Nimrod doesn't seem quite able to amass an immediate response to this theory. He just closes the suitcase and straightens up, with a grunt.

'Let's get the hell out of this shit-hole,' Ransom murmurs, 'before I get angry.'

She looks so beautiful when she answers the door to him that it almost feels like an ambush: a kidnap attempt – a sudden punch to the stomach – a sack over the head. He is winded by her – incapacitated. She is all in red: a tight-fitting red satin dress, red gloves stretching way beyond her elbows, high, red heels, her red fringe hanging straight over her eyes (catching in her delirious lashes), her hair in several, ornate plaits which are twisted into a neat, little bun and covered with a flat, red bow at the back.

Her eyes are black-lined. Her lips are like cherries. He just gazes at her for a few seconds, astonished, then the next thing he knows they are pressed up against the sitting room wall having sex.

He knows her body now, even tightly sheathed and slippery as it is; a ripe, red plum, its yellow flesh pressing out against the smooth arc of its cool, fragrant skin. He understands the basic groundwork, has visited the orchard like a hungry finch, has gorged on the fruit and rejected the pips, has explored the geography.

She smells of almonds, like a plump Bakewell pudding; and he is the spoon, the whipped cream, the helpless dollop of warm custard. She steams. He applauds, his tongue hanging out (like a bloodhound espying a raw chop in a cartoon).

She is topped with melted apricot jam. It makes her shine. Beneath that: the spongy gold, the give, the softness. Then still further down, the firmer butteriness of a thin-baked layer of crumbling shortcrust.

'Pardon?'

'The leg – Sheila's leg – was it as bad as it looked?'

She closes the front door behind him and leads him through to the kitchen. He stands facing the window, hands braced against the sink. He is staring at the red glimmer of her reflection – red and white – a squirt of chili sauce in a dish of thick, Greek yoghurt. It's not yet dark, but there are candles flickering away on the table, which confuse him.

'Jamaica?' she mutters. 'But why?'

He turns. A cat slithers around his legs. His mouth is dry. 'There was a chance meeting at the hospital with …' He scowls. 'It's complicated.'

He glances down at his watch. Jen is late. He takes out his phone and tries to ring her. His call goes straight to message bank.

'How complicated?' she asks. She is standing right in front of him, reaching out her hand and touching his fringe. He stops breathing. Minutes advance then retreat. Somebody is speaking. It is him. What is he saying? He doesn't know. He doesn't care. He is a stuck second hand on a railway station clock ticking forward, then back, forward, then back.

'And you're just going to let her go?' she asks, frowning, lounging against the table – her hip jinking like a bright lozenge of cough candy. 'Let her leave? Just like that?'

He inhales. He tries to phone Jen again.

'What do the children think?'

They are standing by the little, hallway cupboard, inspecting the broken meter.

'Almost set fire to the fence,' she's saying, 'but I burned them all. Noel went mad – said he was negotiating a deal with a museum. I don't know if I even believe him. Will you tell her for me, though? Please?'

He nods. His phone rings.

'Jen?'

'Gene?'

'Toby? Where are you?'

'In a cab, heading back to the hotel. Ransom just phoned. Seems Del Renzio's on the warpath. Management's dead set against the tattoo happening on the premises.'

'So what now?'

'Well you know Ransom – he's so pig-headed that if anything it's made him *more* determined. Del Renzio's hiked up Security, but the photographer's already on site. Nimrod's worked out a cunning back route into the room. I've given him your number. You'll need to convene in the car park ...'

'We're still at the house. Jen's a no-show. The electricity's off. We can't leave until ...'

'D'you need a hand? I'm a trained engineer. Want me to turn the cab around and head on over?'

'Are you sure you don't mind?'

'It's early days,' Toby confides (a smile in his voice), 'but if I'm hoping to win over Esther then I suppose I could do worse than getting some baby-sitting practice under my belt.'

She's sitting on the stairs, her ankles apart, her thighs pressed together, her elbows on her knees, her chin in her hands. He stands before her like a humble penitent waiting anxiously before an altar – the glorious altar-cloth – the holy scent – her voice a prayer.

He feels so angry – so disappointed – so betrayed – that he could tear himself apart with his own hands – rip himself to pieces. He feels at once potent and worthless – he is a spoiled meal – an unwanted gift – a river that has overrun its bank.

'... halfway through lunch, just relaxing under the tree when these three boys turn up with a ball ...'
He tries Jen again.
'... And I swear they did it on purpose! There was juice everywhere – all over the blanket, the food. I was just so ... so *angry*! I grabbed the ball and I *threw* it at him but I couldn't ... I mean because of the *hijab* I wasn't able to ...'
He tries Jen again.
'... just spat. Didn't say a word, just spat. I felt sick. I honestly couldn't believe ...'
He tries Jen again.
'... And I suddenly thought: Here I am, nothing to be afraid of, nothing to defend, but so terrified of everything, so ashamed inside, so compromised, and here they are, so much to defend, so unafraid. I was just ... I was in *awe*. And like Aamilah said ...'
He starts counting backwards, from a hundred, in his head ...
38, 37, 36 ...
'... I focused on the grass. Felt it under my fingers. I thought, There's a message here – in the detail, if only I could ...'
He places a tiny, smooth pebble into the shallow basin of her belly-button, then runs his finger in a lazy ring around it.
'I never felt afraid,' he confesses, 'I always dreamed of being a soldier – like my grandad. I wasn't ever afraid to die. I wanted to live, but I was never afraid to die. I don't deserve any credit for it. It's just what I am. I don't know why I've always felt that way. It wasn't resignation, more like ... I can't even think ...'
'When I talk to you it's like' – she frowns – 'like my words aren't just sounds. It's like they're tiny pieces of my soul which you hold in your palm and you stroke.'

Even as she speaks, a gong sounds in his head. Its
vibrations set his teeth on edge. Is it the gong they sound just
moments before they pull a performer from the stage? Is it a
saucepan in the face? Is it the gentle resonation of an eternal
truth? The tinny howl of a mystic singing bowl?

Toby finally arrives, borrows Valentine's torch, fiddles
around for five minutes, reconnects the electricity, and is then
settled down on the sofa, beaming – quite the hero – with a
bottle of cola, a sandwich and the TV remote. They head
outside to the car. The moon is hidden behind a cloud. Gene
stores her equipment in the boot.

'Not the Hummer, then?' she asks, placing her lean, neat
feet in her fine, red heels where Sheila usually stores a clutch
of empty water bottles, two, old prayer books and her
favourite string shopping bag.

How much for a double room at the Leaside? Sorry,
how much?

She slips down in the seat, slightly curled up, knees pressed
together – just millimetres away from the gearstick – a perfect,
terrified, scarlet mouse, and gazes at him, unblinking, like a
child hypnotized by the wonders of Christmas, for the entire
duration of the drive.

Sheila is sitting on a chair in Stan's bedroom, her forehead
resting on the desk. An email has just been downloaded on to
the computer.

Oh my God, Sheila! How long has it been? Twelve years?
Thirteen? How the heck *are* you? What on earth are you
doing with yourself nowadays? Okay – so I managed to glean
from your email that you're still with the Church (the phrase
'one of my parishioners' was a bit of a give-away ...) but aside
from that? How's the gorgeous Marek? Are you still in

contact? And the baby? Oh Lordy! All grown up by now, I suppose.

Are you well? We missed you at the big Keble reunion last year. Do you still receive the college magazine? I've been loosely involved with it over the past decade or so (although increasingly less since the girls arrived). If you've fallen off the mailing list then forward me your contact details and I'll pop you back on again.

Yes, I'm fine. The arthritis is still a problem but I manage to keep it at bay with a special diet (No caffeine! No red meat! No fruit! No booze!) and a strenuous, daily Pilates workout. Hard yakka (as my Australian nanny might often be heard to mutinously intone), but mustn't grumble!

Luella just turned four (on Tuesday – thanks for asking) and Phemie is a terrible two, but almost, *almost* three. Afraid I can't agree with you re. the *Telegraph* article. The journalist was a bit of a shit, but I'm notoriously cagey about my private life (what tattered vestiges currently remain of it!).

We must meet up. Contact Vania (my benighted PR) with some dates and we'll sort something out (might not be poss. till late October, my end – post Toronto International Art Fair where I'm meant to be delivering a series of lectures which I haven't even started to get my head around yet).

Re. your artist/photographer. I had a quick peek at the website and the work certainly looks interesting – although I'm not sure what the wider, legal ramifications might be (you should probably have a quick word with her about this). A friend of mine (Gillie Maar – you may have heard of her) tried to exhibit some of the Win Delvoye Art-farm pieces recently and ended up in all kinds of hot water.

The work is very fresh, very visceral, very 'real' (as you say), although I'm not sure if it needs to be 'worked into some kind of complete theoretical framework' (?!). I do tend to feel that it's generally best not to over-think these things (the way we did in the nineties, eh?) but to approach them holistically, enjoy their gradual development in a more tentative, more honest and organic way.

I'm definitely thinking Kat von D/Michael Hussar (which *can't* be bad).
Off to Boston for a few days, but leave this with me and I'll give it another ponder on the plane.

Do take care of yourself –
XX Pam
PS No more coffee, darling! *Way* too acidic!
PPS Vania thought your email was completely hilarious! Wonderful! Same old Sheila, I thought: breathless, volcanic, zealous, grandiloquent. All knees and elbows. Do or die. No half measures …
Bless you!
X
PPPS Remember *OnTheRag*, Sheila?! Oh *God* – what were we like?!
X

Sheila lifts her head and then bangs it back down again. She lifts it and then bangs it. She lifts it and then bangs it.

'This is why,' she murmurs, 'this is why I dropped out. This is why I fell pregnant. Because of smug idiots like *you*, Pammy Sullivan. With your spoilt, self-satisfied, fat-headed, lecture-giving, coffee-avoiding … *Urgh!*'

As she speaks, the vehemence of her words and the angle of her face cause a silken thread of drool to drip from the corner of her mouth and down on to the carpet. She straightens up, alarmed, patting her lips with the collar of her dressing gown.

Her eyes fix on the screen.

'What on earth are you doing with yourself nowadays?' she parrots, in withering tones.

'How's the gorgeous Marek?'

'Do you still receive the college magazine?'

'*Urgh!*' she exclaims, reading on.

'... more tentative, more honest and *organic* way!' she witters. 'Vania thought your email was completely hilarious!'

'Oh ha! ha! ha!' she trills, then, 'Breathless? *Volcanic?!* I'll give you volcanic!'

She grabs a mini-baseball sitting, innocuously, on Stan's desk and throws it – with a strangled yell – on to the nearby bed.

She closes her eyes and inhales.

'Okay, okay ... She *likes* the work,' she murmurs, 'she thinks it's "interesting". This is actually very positive. This is actually *good* news.'

She opens her eyes.

'*Is* this a nervous breakdown?' she wonders, startled, trying to encompass what that might consist of in her mind.

'I don't feel nervous,' she eventually surmises, 'and I don't feel broken.'

She tips her head, speculatively. 'A little chipped, maybe.'

She turns and inspects the ladder which still hangs, unfolded, in the hallway. She considers Mallory and her copious tears over dinner.

'But I don't *want* you to go to Jamaica, Mummy!'

Her mind turns to Gene – how quiet he'd been at tea, how wan and hollow-seeming and compliant, then to her earlier conversation with Valentine.

'I mean if Gene isn't religious. If you've never actually shared the same, core beliefs, doesn't it make him feel almost ...'

Sheila scowls.

'Almost what?' she wonders, spooked. She promptly recalls their pre-tea chat about the illicit palm reading – his feelings of guilt. Was there something odd in the way ...?

Something ...?

'No wonder you look ill!' She re-enacts their conversation, remembering herself laughing, on edge, just wishing she could tell him, yes … her mind packed full of other stuff – her big escape – her sacrifice – her … Gene just standing there, same as always, at the edges of the page – Gene, the white surround – the frame – the margin.

She recalls the odd look on his face.

'That's not why I look ill.'

Is that what he'd …? Or was it …?

'That's not why I …'

Her heart momentarily freezes.

Is there something else? Something wrong? Was he about to …?

She stands up, panicked.

'No.'

She sits down again.

The phone starts ringing.

She stands up again, turns, and limps out of Stan's room, heading towards the sound. In the hallway is her old suitcase, pressed up against the wall. She pulls it out, places it down and opens it. She stares at it, frowning.

'Really must check those messages,' she sighs, but doesn't move. Instead she kicks off her sandals and steps inside it. She sits down, then lies on one side, curling up, reaching out her arm to grab the lid.

'Breathless! Volcanic! Zealous! Grandiloquent!' she announces (perhaps somewhat grandiloquently), then lets it fall.

Five seconds later: 'Just a little chipped,' she mutters.

Ten seconds later: 'For heaven's sake, Sheila! This is completely ridiculous!'

Much to Gene's evident discomfort, Valentine insists on clutching on to his hand from the moment they leave the car, throughout their clandestine journey to Ransom's room, during the brief but detailed consultation (in dramatic whispers) between she and Ransom about the nature of the tattoo itself, on a short trip to the bathroom (where she stares into the mirror and emphatically whispers, 'All *will* be well,' then turns, with a gulp, 'I'm doing this for Sheila. It's for her. To make amends. You'll tell her that, won't you?'), right up until she finally commences unfolding her portable tattooing bench and unpacking various, exotic items of tattooing paraphernalia (and some less so – the rubber gloves, the sterile wipes) from a large and battered holdall.

In fact she barely shifts her eyes from his face, even (and this is a source of some confusion and embarrassment) during a series of formal introductions. There's a thoroughly bedazzled Terence Nimrod, for starters (who flits around the room like an earthbound, media Tinkerbell, a trusty Bic his magic wand), a photographer called Kenny (a small, fine-boned, shaven-headed Spaniard – with cold, thick-black-lashed green eyes and an improbably perfect smile – to whom Gene takes an immediate dislike) and Kenny's downtrodden assistant, Duke (a tall, powerful-looking, ginger-haired Glaswegian – with a surprisingly effete voice – who seems to have no real function except as the silent repository of intermittent abuse).

Kenny has a tiny, digital camera and he snaps away with it from the moment they enter, interspersing savage assaults on Duke (delivered in a whispered, rasping, guttural Spanish, which Duke doesn't appear to understand) with a series of keening instructions and compliments ('Chin up – God you're *so* beautiful. I love it! I love you! You're amazing! You're dynamite! Now just … good … good … give me *just* a little bit more of the … Perfect! You're a genius! You're a natural! This is *so* easy! You're making this *so* easy for me! I love it!').

Ransom seems subdued. He admits to having taken a fistful of benzodiazepines and has a bottomless glass of whisky virtually glued to his right hand. He and Valentine circle each other, warily (like two, tired dogs eyeing the same padded basket), but all exchanges – while cool – are profoundly courteous. Gene almost detects a quiet kind of bond there; an immediate, almost instinctual shorthand operating between them, like they're members of two very different tribes (one disports itself, wildly, in rough hides and feathers, the other simply glistens, mysteriously, in hi-tech, silver fabrics) who have fought and been wounded in the same awful war.

Ransom appears to love the grass idea ('So stupid!' he raves. 'So random! So obvious!'), and seems still more delighted when Valentine goes on to describe how she'd like to tattoo a 'hole' right in the middle of it. 'Imagine ...' she whispers, eyes shining excitedly, 'the messy, geometric textures of the grass, then that harsh, dark, cut into the compacted soil beneath; the man-made juxtaposing the arbitrary – the formal juxtaposing the natural – the surface juxtaposing the subterranean ...'

Ransom wonders (with typical, golfing homo-centricity) whether there might even be the suggestion of a ball inside this posited 'cup' of hers. Valentine's enthusiasm immediately diminishes. She shakes her head. 'The tattoo is all about desire,' she tells him (eyes still intermittently darting towards Gene's), 'not deliverance. Possibility is everything – the bud, the green shoot. Fulfilment – the flower – is death.'

'Good point,' Ransom concedes, doing an excellent job (Gene thinks) of looking like he knows what the hell she's banging on about.

Del Renzio phones the room (on a series of spurious provisos) three times during the ten minutes subsequent to their arrival. Nimrod – in a state of acute paranoia – takes the precaution of putting on some music (finally settling – after a period of heated debate among the assembled parties – on Willie Nelson's charming covers album *Across the Borderline*; the one CD from the small selection kindly provided by the hotel that nobody actively hates).

He tries to adjust the volume according to how much noise Valentine's tattoo gun produces. She obligingly plugs it in and hits the foot pump while Gene dashes outside to check how audible it is from the hallway. After several trips in and out, it's decided that the volume necessary to disguise the resultant buzz will be so loud as to engender complaints from nearby residents. Nimrod – still thinking on his feet – dashes off to his room and returns – minutes later – holding an electric razor.

'So here's the deal,' he explains. 'We'll keep playing the music at a reasonable volume for the duration of the tattoo. Meanwhile, someone needs to stand guard in the hallway. If Del Renzio – or one of his punks – approaches the room then this person needs to rap on the door – as if they're waiting to gain access – at which point Ransom will wrap himself up in a towel and come to the door with this razor buzzing at his chin as a diversion while the rest of us make ourselves scarce – I dunno – maybe hide in the bathroom.'

'But what about the bench,' Gene wonders, 'and the inks, and the gun?'

'Ransom only needs to open the door by a few inches,' Nimrod suggests, 'be belligerent. Act like he's pissed. Then the guard needs to lead the way – come up with some kind of urgent message to serve as a distraction – like – *uh* – Esther's taken a turn for the worse in hospital … God forbid,' he adds, with a wince, 'or there's been a call from American Nike about a sponsorship deal.' He grins. 'We'll just befuddle them – distract them – blind them with science – then the next thing they know – after a measure of kerfuffle – the door will've slammed shut again. End of.'

Everybody nods.

'So who stands guard?' Ransom wonders, removing his shirt and rotating his shoulders (gingerly preparing his back for an imminent, physical assault).

'Well I'm writing the piece so I'll definitely need to hang about.' Nimrod glances around him. 'And Kenny's taking the shots …' His eyes fall on Duke. 'Can we spare Duke for the job?'

'Not possible.' Kenny shakes his head. 'Duke is my assistant. He's on fifteen quid an hour. He really needs to assist me for that kind of money.'

A short, somewhat quizzical silence follows.

'Well how about Gene?' Nimrod suggests.

'I'm easy.' Gene shrugs. He glances over at Valentine who immediately looks panicked.

'I'll just be on the other side of the door,' he tries to console her.

She continues to look anxious. Her hand rises to her throat.

'How about I pop out there now, while you finish setting up, so you can grow accustomed to the idea?' Gene suggests. 'And if at any time you start to feel like you're losing control or getting too stressed then just yell and I'll dash straight back inside again.'

Valentine finally relents, nods, and recommences unpacking and arranging her inks. Gene disappears into the corridor, breathing a deep sigh of relief. Ransom promptly follows.

'So what's that all about?' he demands, as soon as the door's been yanked shut behind him.

'Sorry?'

'This weird power you have over these girls. It's kind of creepy. What is it? What's your technique?'

'There's no technique,' Gene demurs.

'No technique? *That's* your technique. Good call.' Ransom nods. He suddenly starts running on the spot, the ice and whisky sloshing around in his glass.

'You feel okay about the tattoo?' Gene promptly relieves him of it for the sake of the carpet.

'Nope. Scared stupid. Shitting myself.'

Ransom continues to jog.

'Shaking like a friggin' leaf.'

Gene gazes down the corridor.

'I dug out the cornet,' he volunteers.

'Really?' Ransom stops jogging.

'It's in the car.'

Ransom starts jogging again.

'Valentine was telling me earlier how a lot of her clients actually get tattooed *for* the pain not in spite of it,' Gene volunteers.

'Friggin' masochists!' Ransom snorts.

'They see it as a kind of rite of passage,' Gene persists. 'I mean look at Maori culture – there's almost a spiritual aspect to it. Their tattoos are a symbol of endurance, of strength, representing a journey into manhood.'

'Fuck pain,' Ransom pants, 'I mean *fuck* pain. Seriously. Fuck it. It's over-rated. I friggin' hate it. I hate pain.'

'No point resisting,' Gene counsels. 'If there's one thing I've learned about pain during my various bad health experiences, it's that you've got to try and work with it. I'm not saying embrace it, but don't resist it. Just let it be what it is. Accept it. And keep loose. Don't tense the muscles. Always try and breathe through it.'

'Fuck pain.'

Ransom stops jogging, snatches his glass, swallows the remainder of his drink in a single gulp and then gasps.

'You'll need to keep up your blood-sugar levels,' Gene warns him.

'Don't people ever get bored of all the cancer shit?' Ransom wonders, handing back the glass and then leaning forward, hands pressed on to his knees, trying to catch his breath. 'Just the constant harping on about it the whole time? I mean it's gotta wear a bit thin, hasn't it? I bet your wife's sick to the back teeth of it. I bet she's like, "Fuck it, Gino, can we just talk about the friggin' *weather* for once?"'

'Sheila's incredibly tolerant.' Gene smiles, wryly.

'I wonder where Jen's got to,' Ransom muses, peering down the corridor, wiping his mouth with the back of his hand. 'You'd think she'd be here with bells on, man, if only to friggin' gloat.'

'Jen's gone AWOL,' Gene murmurs, 'which is probably no bad thing under the circumstances.'

'You better believe it!' Ransom harrumphs, hand pressing down on the door handle. 'The girl's nothing but a friggin' pest. She's toxic.'

'She could certainly be considered an acquired taste,' Gene concurs.

'*Acquired?!* That's a polite way of putting it!' Ransom snorts, pulling wide the door. 'She's like that fucked-up Italian cheese with maggots running through it.'

'*Casu Marzu*,' Gene volunteers. 'It's Sardinian.'

'Yeah *yeah* – whatever.'

The golfer steps into the hotel room and slams the door shut behind him.

Gene leans back against the wall with a wan smile. He inspects Ransom's empty glass, then jiggles the ice around in it. He closes his eyes for a second. He feels exhausted. He opens his eyes again, places the glass next to the skirting and takes out his phone. He starts going through his messages. There's one from the blood donation people, two from work, five from Jen (consisting of a series of vague, squawking sounds, but with no actual message attached) and most recently (ten past eight to be precise), there's a missed call from Sheila.

'*Gene – you need to ring me as soon as you get this. It's ten past eight. Something very odd has happened. It might be really serious. You need to ring me – ring my mobile, not the house. Just as soon as you get this …*'

(brief pause)

'*It's not Mallory. Mallory's fine. I'm fine. Just ring me.*'

Gene scratches his head, scowling, then quickly connects his phone to Sheila's mobile. After two rings she answers it.

———

'Gene? Thank God it's finally you! What took you so long? I've been staring at the phone just *willing* it to ring! I'm a nervous wreck!'

'I'm sorry. I've only just –'

'Did you hear from Jen?' Sheila interrupts.

'Jen?'

'I thought you mentioned something earlier about getting Jen to ...'

'She didn't show up,' Gene mutters.

'Okay. *Okay.* Well did she get in contact? Make her excuses?'

Gene frowns. 'There were a couple of messages but they weren't really ...'

'What did she say?'

'Nothing. They were mainly just interference.'

'Fine. Okay. Okay. Okay ...' Sheila's plainly very agitated.

'Just calm down,' Gene cautions her, concerned, 'take a deep breath.'

'Okay. So there's no simple way of putting this,' Sheila runs on, oblivious, 'and it may sound really weird to you because it *is* really weird, but I think Jen's been kidnapped.'

Brief pause.

'Kidnapped?'

'Yes. There was a garbled message on our answer-phone. She rang this afternoon, shortly after you came home with Mallory. It was really difficult to decipher. She sounded extremely distressed. She said something about "Israel's mother – Vicki". Putting two and two together I'm guessing that she might've been referring to Vicki Wilson – Ransom's manager's activist sister – the woman who wants me to help her with the book.'

'Hang on, just ...' Gene turns to face the wall. 'The woman who wants you to help her with the book is ...?'

'Ransom's manager's sister.'

Gene's brows shoot up. 'And you didn't think to mention that little piece of information earlier?'

'There are a series of … *uh* …' – Sheila's plainly discomforted – 'let's just say "special circumstances".'

'Yeah, I know.' Gene nods.

'Sorry?'

'I know about …' Gene glances towards the door. 'Jen told me.'

'I just didn't want to over-complicate matters. It was all getting a bit …'

'Convoluted.'

'Exactly.'

'So you're telling me that Jen left a message on our answerphone, earlier this afternoon, actually stating that she'd been …?'

'Like I say, it's quite hard to decipher. I've listened to it about a hundred times. I should probably just play it to you – that's why I got you to ring me on my mobile. I'll hold the phone up close to the machine. Hang on a minute …'

A brief scrabbling sound is followed by a mechanical *click*, then the message commences to play.

'Gene – *bmuff* me – *please* limun – my ph*mumn* is nearly *numf* of … Vick *wuffon* Israel's *mun* ther just shoved me *nefoo* the … I don't *knuff* where … iff you *numf* this … *please* …'

The line falls dead.

'Did you get that?' Sheila demands. 'Shall I play it again?'

'What makes you think …?' Gene starts off, bemused.

'She sounds scared – *really* scared – and her voice is strangely muffled – like she's in a tunnel or some kind of confined space.'

'It could just be a bad line,' Gene argues.

'But she *does* sound scared.'

'That doesn't mean she's been kidnapped. She simply said that someone called Vicki shoved her' – Gene grimaces – 'and to be perfectly honest, Sheila, knowing Jen as I do …'

'Okay, so you're going to have to suspend your … *uh* …' Sheila struggles to find the right word.

'D'you feel all right?' Gene interjects. 'How's the leg?'

'Of course I don't feel all right!' Sheila exclaims, exasperated. 'I'm in a complete, bloody state! What's that word? ... Credulity? Cynicism? It's a "c" word – it's definitely a "c" word.'

'Whatever it is, I'll suspend it,' Gene promises.

'It's just that ...' – Sheila clears her throat – '... this is going to sound a bit strange, okay, but I climbed inside my suitcase earlier.'

'Your suitcase?' Gene echoes.

'Yes. I climbed inside my suitcase. The phone was ringing. I was on the computer. I walked out on to the upstairs landing and I found myself gazing down at my suitcase – being really ... really *drawn* to it. I opened it up and then the next thing I know I'm climbing into it – climbing inside my suitcase and closing the lid. I know it sounds odd. It *is* odd. And even as I was doing it I was thinking, What the hell are you playing at, Sheila? This is completely ridiculous!'

'What *were* you playing at?' Gene cordially enquires.

'I don't know. But it was like ... I can't explain it. It was like this powerful *urge* to be in a confined space. Kind of the same, basic impulse that made me go up into the attic, earlier.'

'But I thought you went into the attic to fetch your case?'

A brief silence follows.

'It's kind of like I'm having a ... a sort of *melt*down,' Sheila continues, 'like there's this new, slightly uncontrolled me who keeps doing all this really arbitrary stuff ... But I'm *not* – obviously,' she rapidly assures him, 'not melting. I basically feel okay. A little tired, maybe – over-wrought – drained – cynical – empty – directionless – frustrated – exhausted, but not melted. Definitely not melted.'

'Well that's ... that's very reassuring.' Gene suddenly has the curious sensation that his head might be about to explode.

'I just feel like it's the *culmination* of something,' Sheila continues, 'something ... I ... I don't *know* what it is. You joked the other day about it being a crisis of faith but I still have faith – in abundance! I mean my faith is one of the few things I remain completely certain of – although I'm not sure quite how ... how *sustaining* it is at this particular point in time.'

She pauses, speculatively. Gene glances down at his watch. Even as he does so he realizes that the time is irrelevant. What was that poem ... (he finds himself idly pondering), or was it just a trashy song lyric? '*All we have is time until the end of time*'?

'So then I started to speculate,' (Sheila is talking again), 'that it might be about a journey, about my leaving – you know, this ... this "culmination" – that it might be about my doing something utterly ego-driven and selfish for once, but at the same time something utterly elevated and generous and philanthropic – like going to Jamaica to work on the book. But the more I've sat here thinking about it, the more convinced I feel that this isn't about me at all. It's not *about* me, Gene! I've been so focused on myself – so self-absorbed – and what I really needed was to be ...'

'So you think God might be a guiding presence in this ... this "culmination" of yours?' Gene asks, barely keeping the exhaustion out of his voice.

'It's like my almost turning away has actually been a turning towards ...' Sheila runs on, amazed. 'It's like ... I'm sorry, Gene,' she groans, 'but I simply can't explain this to you – a cynic, a non-believer – in human words.'

'Human words?' Gene echoes.

'That sounds crazy – I *know* it does, but the life of faith, the sense of grace or no grace, the relationship a person establishes with God doesn't always tally with rational ideas and language. *That's* been my mistake. *That's* why when I came across the kitten poem by Anne Sexton in the garage the other day ...'

'Kitten?' Gene murmurs (growing more disheartened by the second).

'"*Maybe I have plugged up my sockets
to keep the gods in?*"' she quotes,
'"*Maybe, although my heart
is a kitten of butter* ..."' I forget the last line ... hang on ...
'"*Maybe, although my heart
is a kitten of butter* ...'" she repeats, haltingly,
'"*I am blowing it up like a zeppelin.*"'

Short pause.

'Blowing up. The kitten of butter. Nothing making sense.'

'I don't remember you mentioning this poem before –' Gene starts off.

'It's like I've been trying to fill in a crossword, you know – with *letters*,' she interrupts, 'when I *should've* been doing a jigsaw puzzle. Making sense out of images. Because it's not linguistic, it's visual. I've finally realized that my intellectual life and my religious life are completely at odds with each other. I think I may have a kind of ... of *visual* faith – *heart* faith, *gut* faith – and I've been making the stupid mistake of ...'

Gene glances up at the ceiling then closes his eyes. He struggles to gather together his depleted resources.

'And that's fine,' Sheila continues. 'It's not a problem. It's *absolutely* fine. In fact it's actually a huge weight off my mind at some, strange level.'

'So if I can finally summarize,' he interjects, 'you're ringing me because you honestly think ...' – he struggles to bite back the powerful feeling of irritation that grips him – 'you seriously believe that my work colleague, Jen, might've been kidnapped by Esther's sister, Vicki Wilson. Ransom's ex,' he adds.

'Ah. So you *do* know about that connection.' Sheila's relieved. 'That's good. That's a relief. I've been struggling with the idea of breaking a confidence.'

'Jen brought him – the boy, I mean.' Gene lowers his voice. 'Vicki's son, Israel – she brought him to the club this afternoon.'

'What happened?' Sheila's outraged.

'Not much so far as I can tell.'

'This certainly gives Vicki motive,' Sheila muses.

'Yes. I suppose it does to some extent,' Gene concedes.

'Well, to answer your previous question,' Sheila rapidly follows on, 'I *am* completely convinced. It's a leap of faith – of course it is, at one level – but I just … I just *know* – have this powerful gut instinct – that Jen is in a confined space, like an attic, or a suitcase. And after I listened to the tape about a hundred times I decided that the strong likelihood is that she's stuck in the boot of a car. I know it sounds insane …'

'So you're presuming that this Vicki has a car – maybe a rental.'

'A hire car. And at the start of the tape there's something that sounds a tiny bit like a siren. This wailing sound – did you notice it?'

'No.' Gene shakes his head.

'Well I have a hunch that it's a siren, which leads me to think that Jen might be stuck in the boot of a hire car parked in or around the hospital grounds.'

'I see.' Gene nods.

'It's funny,' Sheila murmurs, somewhat bitter-sweetly, 'but when I thought this was all about me – *my* journey – I actually started to wonder whether I'd hurt my leg simply to facilitate the weird, chance meeting with Vicki so that I could finally fulfil my long-held literary ambitions. Like this was to be God's gift to me. A thank you. A big pay-off. I mean the canteen was packed, and it was *way* after lunchtime – only one spare seat, at *her* table. I honestly thought it was all about me and writing – that I would finally write a book – return to writing.'

'I had no idea,' Gene mutters, jaundiced.

'Because I locked it all away,' Sheila sighs, portentously, 'I packed it all up and stored it in the attic – after Stan came. But it was *always* there.'

'I see,' Gene repeats (through gritted teeth).

'Be that as it may,' Sheila barrels on, oblivious, 'it's all irrelevant, really, because I've now realized that I was barking up completely the wrong tree – this whole thing wasn't about me after all. None of it was. I'm just a quiet observer – a dispassionate pair of eyes. I'm a tool. My ego got in the way a bit for a while back there – that's partly why I'd been thinking all this crazy stuff about you and Jen – questioning the true nature of your relationship. It was ludicrous – laughable – I can see that now.'

'Right.' Gene nods, uncomfortable.

'Anyway, the long and the short of it is that I need you to drive over to the hospital and see if you can find her.'

Gene draws a deep breath. 'But I'm stuck here, Sheila,' he explains, 'I'm helping with the tattoo. *Your* tattoo. I'm looking after ...'

He can't say her name. He opens his mouth and then closes it again.

'I fully appreciate that,' Sheila concedes, 'but this is important – a crisis.'

'As I'm sure you can imagine,' Gene persists, 'she's incredibly stressed and anxious. I'm her entire support network. I can't just up and leave. She's depending on me.'

'Are you with her now?' Sheila wonders.

'No. I'm standing guard in the hallway.'

'Standing guard?'

'The club's management are kicking up a stink about the tattoo.'

'Then just nip off,' Sheila suggests.

'Just "nip off"?!' Gene's appalled. 'I don't think you quite understand ...'

How important I am, he thinks.

'Just pop your head into the room, let her know that you're still out there, then quickly nip off. She'll be busy with the tattoo – preoccupied. It's not going to take you very long. Forty minutes, tops.'

'The hospital's a good twenty-minute drive from here!' Gene's outraged.

'That's a wild exaggeration!'

'No it isn't!'

'Look – I'd go myself but you've got the Megane. I'm looking after Mallory, and above and beyond all that I can hardly *walk* let alone drive. My head's completely fugged up from too many painkillers.'

'Under any other circumstances –' Gene starts off.

'You *have* to go, Gene,' Sheila interrupts, 'or I'll go crazy. I'll explode. I mean I *really* will lose the plot.'

'Well perhaps you should try and get a grip on yourself!' Gene snaps.

'Gene, I *know* that Jen is trapped!' Sheila howls. 'This is serious! Think about it from *her* perspective! She'll be completely and utterly petrified!'

'Okay.' Gene's finally had enough. 'I'm not for a minute suggesting that what you've experienced isn't of great significance, but from where I'm standing you've had a bit of a scare, you're completely exhausted and over-wrought, you've taken a shit-load of prescription drugs ...'

'Don't do this to me, Gene!' Sheila warns him.

'Earlier this afternoon you were cheerfully deserting us – your entire family, not to mention your congregation – apparently on a whim, to go and spend six months halfway across the world with this Vicki Wilson woman. Now you suddenly think she's a dangerous felon – a kidnapper.'

'She's not dangerous!' Sheila scoffs. 'She just might end up doing something … something extreme – unexpected – if push comes to shove. No pun intended. She's an activist – a live-wire – a bit of a lunatic.'

'Now she's a lunatic!' Gene exclaims, exasperated.

'Yes. *Yes*. She's a lunatic! And that's precisely what I *like* about her. She's brave but slightly deranged. She's very loyal, very driven, possibly slightly paranoid, very protective, very passionate …'

'More words,' Gene murmurs, dryly (before he can stop himself), 'I thought it was all about the visuals from here on in.'

'Ow,' Sheila mutters.

'Sorry,' Gene promptly apologizes.

'I don't know why, but you just seem really … I don't know … *angry* today,' Sheila muses.

'Great.' Gene rolls his eyes.

'Defensive. Preoccupied. And maybe you have good reason to be. That's fine. I *accept* that. But this isn't about you or me. This is about Jen and Vicki. They need our help.'

Gene starts walking down the corridor.

'What if I phone Jen's dad and tell him what you've told me?'

'He'll think you've taken leave of your senses!'

'*Exactly!* There's your answer!'

'Gene' – Sheila's voice is suddenly as dark and smooth as a bar of Swiss chocolate made from seventy per cent cocoa mass – 'I don't have the time or the energy to play games with you right now. I want you to drive to the hospital. I don't know how much more adamant – more emphatic – I can be about this. You need to get in your car and drive to the hospital. I *mean* it. If you don't do it … actually, no. I'm not going to make threats. I'm just telling you. I'm saying to you that if our marriage or my faith or our life together stand for anything then you need to do as I've asked. I can't add anything to that. In fact I'm going to ring off. And if – or

when – you ring me back, I want you to have Jen with you. I
need to know that she's okay. Right. I'm going to hang
up now.'
Slight pause.
'But before I do, please understand that I am in a state of
acute, emotional turmoil and your job, your *responsibility* is to
make it stop.'
Another slight pause.
'That's all I have to say. Good luck. God bless you.'
Sheila hangs up.

Gene stands in the hallway, immobile, for several minutes,
then he turns, walks back to Ransom's hotel room and opens
the door. Inside he finds the golfer – now lying prone on the
tattoo bench – chatting away, amiably (Nimrod writing, the
camera flashing) while Valentine carefully applies a large,
purple stencil between the centre of his shoulders. She seems
calm, he notes, perfectly at her ease and completely engrossed.

Esther finds her sister sitting on an empty bench by the large,
push-button snack-dispensing machine. The helpful Irish
nurse (who has been kind enough to push her there in the
ward's only wheelchair) tactfully retreats, although not without
first indicating, warningly, towards her watch.
'Five minutes, all right Esther? Then straight back to baby!'
Esther readily acquiesces.

The sisters sit in silence for four minutes, at least, then
Vicki finally rouses herself – blinking, stretching, yawning – as
if from a light slumber.

'Say yes?' she eventually wonders, with a smirk.
'Say what?' Esther scowls.
'To your fool?'

Esther sucks her tongue.
'Tell me!'
'Me not say yes, me not say no.' She shrugs.

'He the poor pickney father?'

Esther merely grimaces, then, 'Gonna let that girl out from the boot of your car?'

'Soon enough!'

'Vicki!' Esther reprimands. 'You get put away for that!'

Vicki sucks her tongue, in response. 'Me don't care!'

'Your son – he'll care!' Esther reminds her.

They both stare – with a measure of interest and indifference – at an elderly man struggling to operate the snack machine. After several, clumsy attempts he manages to acquire himself a small packet of biscuits. He removes them from the slot and then inspects them, astonished.

'Me could never come back home an' not feel like shit,' Esther confides. 'Every time I see your boy I feel a wrench in my belly. Hurt so bad,' she clucks, watching on, idly, as the old man tries, and fails – all fingers and thumbs – to gain access to the biscuit packet.

'You want me to lie?' Vicki asks. 'Say me know all along? Even if Izzy never forgive me for it?'

Esther scowls, unsure quite how to respond to this generous offer.

''Cause I will' – Vicki shrugs – 'for my one an' only sister.'

Esther shakes her head, her eyes suddenly filling with tears. 'Me got nothing here, Vicki, I swear!' she sniffs. 'No life, no man, no work – me own pickneys don't even know who their mammy is.'

'Boo-hoo!'

Vicki cordially offers her condolences.

'Me deserve worse.' Esther grimaces.

'Well none of us been angels,' Vicki concedes.

'You gonna let Israel see his daddy now?' Esther wonders.

'You gonna let baby Prue see hers?' Vicki snorts.

'Me got a whole lot of things to ponder on,' Esther ruminates, then, '*Here!*'

She reaches over and snatches the biscuits from the old man's hands, deftly tears the packet open and passes them back again.

'Now get away with you!' she harangues him. 'Go on! Enjoy!'

The man takes the biscuits and slowly shuffles off, plainly terrified.

'You a long time gone,' Vicki observes, watching his gradual progress, almost sympathetic.

''Specially if you *starve* to death!' Esther concurs.

A thirty-second silence follows, then Vicki starts to chuckle, disproportionately, almost hysterically, her hands clasped together, her thin shoulders jerking up and down like a mass-produced cardboard skeleton cut-out at Halloween.

'What you got to laugh about?' Esther demands, smiling herself.

'Not a thing!'

Vicki commences upon another, violent paroxysm. 'Not a damn thing!'

'Me neither!' Esther cackles, clutching on to her belly and laughing till her round cheeks are soaked with tears, half in sheer delight, half in complete agony.

The three of them are sitting – like the three wise monkeys – squashed together on the sitting room sofa. There's a party atmosphere. A video of *Chitty Chitty Bang Bang* plays on the TV. They're drinking tea (milk in Nessa's case) and sharing a packet of lemon puff biscuits.

'I prefer to pull off the top layer first, dip the side without cream on it into my mug,' Toby explains, 'eat it, then follow up with the crunchy, creamy bottom layer.'

He proceeds to illustrate this technique, somehow conniving to over-dip the biscuit so that the soggy end breaks off as he tries to withdraw it.

'*Mon Dieu! Tu es vraiment enfant,*' Frédérique exclaims, observing the soggy biscuit floating like a pastry raft in his tea mug, enchanted. 'Such a baby! See! Even Nessa has more sense than this!'

Toby tries to retrieve the soggy wedge with his fingers but it promptly breaks into several, smaller pieces. Nessa, meanwhile, has split her biscuit in half (following Toby's example) and is delicately lapping off the lemon filling – a tiny remnant of it decorating the tip of her nose.

Frédérique fastidiously dips her biscuit – whole – into her mug of tea, then places the soggy end between her lips and sucks.

'Oh that's good – that's clever.' Toby chuckles. 'Liquidizing the middle and then sucking it all out, *en masse*. Extremely creative!'

He's still remarking, in awe, on Frédérique's innovative biscuit-dipping techniques when a nearby cat decides to get in on the action – leaping up on to his lap, knocking his arm, and sloshing his mug of tea straight down his shirt front. He clambers to his feet, cursing, disgruntled, then quickly reaches up his spare hand to apply pressure to his temples (his head is suddenly throbbing – perhaps jolted by the sudden movement).

On screen, the famous, green car is driving along a hilly pass and – if the swelling music is anything to go by – is just about to grow mechanical wings and take flight.

'You've got to rewind if I miss the song!' he exclaims, piqued. 'It's not fair! I don't want to miss the song!'
He dashes off down the hallway towards the kitchen, still clutching his temples, holding his mug aloft, and arrives at the sink just in time to hear the others commence yelling and cooing as the car leaves the road and takes to the air.

'*I don't believe this!*' he yells, slamming his mug down on to the draining-board, pushing in the plug and turning on the tap. '*Press pause! Press pause!*'

In the other room he can hear laughter and sporadic applause. He reaches towards a cleaning cloth then stiffens, inhales sharply, takes several, rolling steps to the side (still grinning his dismay at missing the flying car), half-turns, sees the rocking chair directly behind him, feels himself collapsing, and somehow, miraculously, throws himself into it.

The chair nearly rocks over at the swift violence of his descent. It hurtles backwards, then forwards, but is quickly stopped by the dead weight of his legs (stretched out, knees locked) and by his heels, which press firmly – like two, trusty, leather brakes – into the antique linoleum.

It's on his third circuit (he's yelling her name, furiously – a feeling in his gut that goes way beyond embarrassment/exasperation/frustration/disbelief giving his voice a strange, extra quality of unrestraint) that Gene finally thinks he might detect a response. He grinds to a sudden halt and turns – head down, shoulders hunched, scowling – furtive as a city fox.

There's a car parked on its own – slightly removed from all the others – adjacent to the fence in the far reaches of the lot. He trots towards it, ears pricked, not sure if it's just random, peripheral noises he's hearing or a more regular but muffled banging sound originating from somewhere closer to hand. The car – he immediately notes as he draws abreast of it – has been left unlocked. The banging continues. He walks to the back end and deftly presses the lock. The boot springs open. Jen unfurls like a jack-in-a-box.

'I've shat myself!' She grins, holding out her arms so he can help to lift her out.

'Are you okay?' he asks, astonished.

'Fine.' She nods. 'I knew you'd come in the end!'

She delivers him a giant, wet kiss on the cheek. '*I wuv vu!*' she baby-talks. 'You're my hero, Geney-boo!'

Her legs wobble a little and he quickly tightens his grip to support her.

'How long have you been trapped in there?' he asks.

'Dunno.' She shrugs, shivering, peering around her, blearily. 'Few hours, I guess. Is this the hospital car park?'

'Couldn't you hear the sirens?' Gene pulls off his jacket and hangs it over her skinny shoulders.

'Yeah ...'

She glances down at herself, slightly dazed. 'Look!' She gingerly lifts up a leg. 'I got lickle brown testicles!'

'This is Vicki Wilson's car?' Gene demands, the anger rising within him.

'Hire car' – Jen nods – 'and I could tell when she got out that she'd left it unlocked – probably thought I'd have the basic nous to escape under my own steam. But could I? Could I heck! It's been like a bad episode of *The* bloody *Krypton Factor*! Feels like I've been picking at that sodding mechanism for ever.'

She holds out her hands. The nails are all bleeding.

'Bloody hell, Jen!' Gene's appalled. 'You must've been terrified!'

He starts gently leading her towards his own car, which is parked fifty or so yards away.

'As luck would have it I happen to feel very comfortable in confined spaces.' Jen hikes up her leotard and waddles. 'As a kid I spent all my free time under tables and in boxes. You know, sometimes it's great to be able to shut everything out and just ... just *focus*. My head feels all light and clear and un-mangled.'

'Shall we ring the police?' Gene wonders.

'Nah! I just want to get home and have a wash – change my clothes ...' She waddles on, breathing heavily. 'Pinch your nose if you need to – I won't be offended. The burn in my regions is incredible – the squelch and the itch! I mean I

waited a couple of hours, but then I just thought: *Screw it –*
what's to lose?'

'D'you have any idea why she did this?' Gene shakes his
head, horrified.

'Oh yeah' – Jen chuckles – 'my enforced period of reflection
has been very fruitful in that regard …' She grins up at him.
'She was probably just pissed off. In fact I probably kind of
deserved it.'

'That's still no excuse for what she's put you through,'
Gene snaps.

'But if she hadn't locked me up then you wouldn't have got to
play the hero!' Jen teases. 'And you do it with such vim!
Such gusto!'

She play-punches him in the ribs.

'Sheila actually deserves most of the credit.' Gene recoils,
confused by this fond assault. 'She deciphered the answer-
phone message.'

'Then high-fives to Sheila!' Jen grins, still shivering but
patently enjoying his confusion.

They draw up to the car and Gene takes out his keys.

'Well I can't sit in the front,' Jen murmurs, peering down at
herself, concerned. 'I'd hate to leave a permanent record of
this embarrassing little interlude on your clean upholstery.'

'It doesn't matter,' Gene insists, unlocking the front door and
pulling it wide then trotting around to the boot in search of
a blanket.

Jen peers through the back window where she espies an old
newspaper and something with a passing resemblance to a
bugle case.

'Is that an old newspaper on the seat, there?'

She opens the back door and leans inside. It's a recent edition
of the local paper (featuring a leading article on the threatened
closure of the allotments). She quickly unfurls it, spreads it
out and then hops in, lying down on her belly, legs kicked up.
Gene returns without the blanket.

'Are you sure you'll be okay like that?'

He's understandably quizzical.

'I'm jolly!' she insists, waving over her shoulder. 'I'm joyous! Beatific!'

Gene gently closes the door and walks around to the driver's side. He climbs in, putting on his seat belt and adjusting the rear-view mirror before reaching for the ignition. As he re-angles it he sees Jen (thinking she's out of eye-shot) irritably batting away a tear from her cheek.

'She's not going to get away with this,' he murmurs, 'even if you do refuse to get the police involved.'

'Revenge is a dish best served with chips,' Jen mutters, 'in newspaper. No cutlery. Generous sprinkling of salt.'

Gene doesn't respond. He starts up the car, indicates and pulls off.

Three minutes later:

'How on earth will you go about explaining the state you're in to your parents?' he demands, pulling on to the Dunstable road (following a series of complex, logistical manoeuvres to bypass the M1).

'I won't explain it. I'll try and sneak in through my bedroom window.'

She pauses. 'Although I should probably come up with a story just in case,' she muses, 'like I got locked in the big storeroom at work and the batteries died on my phone ...'

'This isn't right, Jen,' Gene mutters. 'They deserve to know the truth. What she did to you tonight was really wrong.'

'I know that!' Jen clucks. 'But fair do's to the woman,' she persists, her jovial tone returning. 'Shaka Zulu's Martian wife snatched her son and took him to see his dad without asking her say-so. It was provocative. She was pissed. This was pure tit for tat. A symbolic act of revenge.'

'Symbolic at what level?' Gene scoffs. 'The woman locked you in her trunk!'

'The boot was unlocked,' Jen persists. 'Could you wind down your window? The smell back here is making me want to puke.'

Gene does as she asks. They are quiet again for a few minutes, then, 'Can I ask you something, Gene?' Jen wonders, 'It's kind of personal.'

'Of course.' Gene nods.

'Are you happy?'

'Happy?' he echoes, slightly shocked.

'Yeah. Would you say that you were basically content, overall, with your lot in life?'

Gene considers his answer for a few seconds.

'For the record, a long pause before answering isn't traditionally an especially positive indicator,' Jen gently chides him.

'I guess I'm just a little bit suspicious of the word "happy",' Gene responds.

'You think the CIA are behind it?' Jen grins.

'It's a very simple, very uncomplicated word but life isn't generally either simple or uncomplicated.' Gene shrugs.

'You know sometimes I'm sitting on the sofa at home watching a film, cuddled up with Sinclair, and I'll suddenly think, Am I happy? and I won't be able to answer. It's like my heart just freezes. I get all panicky. Or I'll be pissed and doing a mad conga on the dance-floor with a few of my friends – having a wild, old time – and then the same thing – same question – not even a fully-formed question – one word – pops into my head: "Happy?" And it's like – *ka-pow!* – all the joy just melts away – completely evaporates. It's really weird.'

'Some people say that true happiness is all about giving, never about receiving.' Gene nods. 'That as soon as you try and hold on to something – to define it or grasp it too tightly – it automatically disappears. But when you give, on the other hand –'

'It's like I always used to drink tea with sugar in it as a kid,' Jen interrupts, 'three, heaped spoonfuls. Then one day I thought: I should give up sugar! Be more grown up! Protect my teeth! So I stopped taking sugar – wham! – just like that. And for the next couple of weeks every time I had a cup of tea it was absolutely, bloody disgusting. Eventually I got fed up with it – couldn't take it any more. I was like: I'll just bang in a couple of spoonfuls, you know, on the sly ...'

'I know exactly where this is heading!' Gene grins.

'It was revolting!' Jen exclaims. 'And I remember thinking: You gave up something you enjoyed and you suffered for it. Then you showed weakness and you suffered some more. This is fucked! Life is shit!'

'But now you enjoy it without sugar?' Gene checks.

'Yeah. Now I don't notice.' Jen shrugs.

'I don't like to harp on about it,' Gene volunteers, 'but an awful tragedy or an illness tends to make you change your perspective on what happiness actually is. It's a cliché, but bad experiences tend to make you grateful for small mercies, make you reappraise your priorities.'

'So you think it's all relative?'

'To some extent.'

'Maybe you've just lowered your expectations,' Jen muses, 'not given up so much as ... I dunno ... given in.'

'That's precisely what Ransom thinks.' Gene laughs.

'Then it *must* be true, Gene!' Jen trills.

'It's more like ...' – he frowns – 'sometimes to *not* want something is the greatest kind of happiness.' His frown deepens as he struggles to explain. 'To do without. To break a need. To accept rejection. Just to appreciate what you already have. To find joy in the really small, really insignificant things.'

'Christ, that sounds tedious!' Jen exclaims.

'I suppose it depends on the nature of the person involved,' Gene concedes, his mind turning to Sheila.

'Like if God hands you the shitty end of the stick,' Jen ruminates, 'say – for argument's sake – you're stuck in the boot of a car for an extended duration, your theory is that the best way to survive it is to be thankful that you can still twiddle your toes, even if you've just shat your pants, can't manipulate the lock and have an excruciating cramp in your neck?'

'Ah, pearls of wisdom from the black annals of the boot,' Gene teases. 'I suppose it was only ever a matter of time ...'

'I'm going to write a self-help book,' Jen jokes. 'I'll call it *Boot Up.*'

'Or *Get Booted!*' Gene suggests.

'*Trunk Calls!*' Jen cackles.

'Be sure and put me down for a copy.' Gene smiles.

'It'll all be very free-form ...' Jen expands.

'A series of random, little Jen-style thoughts and aphorisms.' Gene nods.

'Like a very long Hallmark card but with more swearing.'

'Great concept.'

'Nothing too serious – mainly filler and make-up advice, very short on good sense, absolutely no rules.'

'Just a light buffet of Jen wisdom.' Gene chuckles.

'Yeah. Something nice and easily digestible – finger-food for the internet generation. Maybe a little toy hidden away inside somewhere ...'

'Like a Christmas cracker or a self-help Kinder Egg.'

'Exactly!' Jen's enthusiastic.

'And the basic philosophy?'

'No philosophy. No guidance. No structure. No pay-off. No real consequences. Just stuff and then more stuff.'

'Stuff?' Gene double-checks that he's heard her correctly.

'Yeah, stuff. Like, here's some stuff, here's some other stuff, here's some more stuff. Just stuff – more and more stuff, different kinds of stuff which is really only the same stuff but in different colours and with different names; stuff stacked up on top of itself in these huge, messy piles ...'

'Sounds a little unstable.' Gene frowns, concerned.
'Oh yeah' – Jen chuckles – 'it's all very precarious. That's part of the fun. It's constantly threatening to topple over – to crash.'
'And when it does?'
'Then it does! It topples! It crashes! The shit hits the fan for a while, then the fallen stuff just re-configures itself and everything pretty much goes back to normal.'

'So this "stuff" is purely physical or ...?'

'It's both. It's hard and soft. Most of it's just ideas, just chatter. This big, stupid, inane conversation blaring in your ear which is determined to draw you in. And either you despise it or you embrace it. That's entirely up to you, of course.'

'And which do you recommend?'
Gene jinks on to the Leagrave Road.
'Oh I don't know,' Jen sighs. 'Neither – either. Although you may as well join in because it'll go on anyway, even if you don't, so what the heck, eh?'

'If you can't beat 'em ...'
'You got it!' Jen makes a brave attempt at a perky American accent.
They are both silent again for a while.

'I mean I *know* it's stupid and kind of fatuous,' Jen sighs, 'but what's wrong with just wanting to be a part of the glow – the energy – the buzz?'
'The glow?'
'Yeah. The stupid conversation – the hysteria – the bullshit. The big inside the small – the small inside the big – the riot – the party – that chemical they fill balloons with ...'

'Helium,' Gene suggests.
'Inhale the helium! Breathe it in! Hold on to the rose of delusion – yeah! – grip on to it as tightly as you can! Cling on to it, even as the blood trickles down your wrists!'

Gene pulls into Jen's road. 'Perhaps I should come in with you,' he murmurs, slightly disturbed.

'Nope. It'll be fine. It'll be great. I'm all good.'

He reverses the car into a space a couple of doors down from Jen's house.

'The lights are off,' he observes.

'Fab.'

Jen doesn't move.

'How about …' Gene half turns in his seat. 'I mean just for the sake of argument, say, you consider abandoning the prickly rose of delusion concept – the whole Shaka Zulu's Martian wife angle – re-sit your A-levels, go to university, become a vet, join a reputable practice, gain some valuable experience, raise some funds, travel, maybe volunteer at an animal refuge somewhere exotic … the kind of "stuff" – *real* stuff – you always dreamed of as a girl?'

'Be good and kind' – Jen beams – 'cultivate my caring side.'

'You'll need a strong trowel and some secateurs.' Gene chuckles (running with the gardening metaphor).

'More like a rotovator and three tons of chemical fertilizer!' Jen snorts.

'But it'd be worth all the effort in the end,' Gene assures her.

'Well I'll certainly take that on board.' Jen opens the door – before Gene even has a chance to unfasten his seat belt – and clambers out of the car, unaided. She straightens up, slightly creaky, and pops her head through the front window. He notices that one of her false eyelashes is coming loose from her eyelid.

'You really *are* my hero,' she repeats, yanking off the lash then patting him tenderly on the shoulder. 'Massive thanks, Batman. Big hugs to Sheila.'

She pauses. He thinks she's going to add something – something heartfelt and meaningful, perhaps, relating to their former conversation. Instead she just points at his arm and squeals, '*Wah! Huge spider!*'

He starts, glances down at his sleeve (almost panicked), then realizes – a fraction of a second later – that it's just the false eyelash and grimaces.

'*Gotcha!*'

She slams the back door, beaming, baby-waves and off she trots.

Gene peers after her, fondly, as she retreats, then plucks the lash from his arm, shakes his head, places it into the ashtray, sighs, rubs his cheek, checks his watch and curses.

13

Sheila has been struggling to pray. She has tried several
locations: her bedroom (where she keeps half-opening her
eyes and peering at her new haircut in the dressing table
mirror), Stan's bedroom (oh, the maddening lure of the
computer!), the kitchen (that infernal buzz of the fridge!), the
living room ...

In the living room, she's asking God to guide her – to fill
her with gentle light instead of rage – to allow her to become
more patient, more open, more humble like his only son, Jesus
Christ, her saviour – when she suddenly finds that her eyes
are open and she's staring, blankly, at the bookshelves. She
closes her eyes: 'Dear Father, please help me to be still, to be
more focused ...'

Her eyes are open again. The bookshelves again. She
frowns. She shuffles forward on her knees, wincing. She
reaches out her hand and removes a copy of *Cheiro's
Palmistry For All* from the shelves.

Her eyes scan the line of books. She shuffles to the right a
little – more wincing – and is replacing the book back in its
usual position when the doorbell rings. She scowls, looks
down at her watch, stands up (with some difficulty), winces,
tightens the belt on her dressing gown and hobbles off to
answer it.

Two people are standing on the front porch: a man and a
woman. The woman is slight and young and wearing the full
veil. The man is short and rotund with curly hair and a

cheerful face. 'Good evening,' he says, 'I do apologize for calling at your home at such a late hour, but I'm afraid we have something of a crisis on our hands.'

'Is this church business?' Sheila enquires, slightly stiff.
'It's very …' He frowns. 'I hate to be indelicate … It's a personal matter. Is your husband at home? Perhaps I might have a quiet word with him?'

'My husband is out,' Sheila all but snaps (irritated).
'Then maybe my sister-in-law, Farhana …' He indicates towards the woman. The woman – Farhana – steps forward. She holds out her hand. She has smiling eyes.
'May we talk in private?' she asks. 'It's about Valentine – Valentine Tucker.'
'Valentine Wickers,' Sheila corrects her.

The woman turns and indicates towards the road. There is a beautiful car parked just the other side of the driveway. Inside the car are three figures: another woman dressed entirely in black, a small child, dozing on her lap, and a second figure, hunched over, covered by what looks like a towel or a blanket, their head in their hands, sobbing.

'Beautiful car,' Sheila says, slightly spooked.
'It's a Tatra. It's Czechoslovakian. Very rare.' The man nods. The woman rolls her eyes, sardonically.

'I've never seen one before.' Sheila can't help smiling. 'Are you local?'
'Yes we are.' The man nods again, then indicates towards his female companion, his expression almost pained, and politely withdraws. He goes to stand over by the wall. He removes a string of prayer beads from his waistcoat pocket and proceeds to run them, distractedly, through his fingers.

Sheila peers down at the woman.
'Perhaps we could go inside for a moment, Sheila?' the woman suggests.
'Okay.'

Sheila steps back and lets the woman walk past her, into the hallway. She then closes the door and guides her into the kitchen. The woman perches herself on a kitchen stool and draws a deep breath. Sheila stands before her.

'I have momentous news,' the woman starts off, her eyes still smiling, 'wonderful, exciting news: Valentine has just testified her faith!'

Sheila frowns, struggling to understand. She takes the weight off her bad leg.

'Valentine is reverting back to Islam,' the woman further elucidates.

'She's ...' Sheila's confused. 'Reverting back ...?'

'And an important stage in this process is that she repents all her sins and performs good deeds,' the woman sweeps on.

'She's reverting back ...?' Sheila repeats, still not making any sense of it.

'Which means asking third parties for forgiveness.'

'Is this about the leg?' Sheila asks, vaguely indicating.

'The leg?' The woman tips her head slightly.

'When I was visiting her at home earlier ...'

'She has something she needs to get off her chest. She wants to speak with you in private, but she's very afraid, and the last thing on earth she wants to do is hurt your feelings.'

'Of course' – Sheila frowns – 'but I thought Valentine was ...'

'I just want to prepare you,' the woman continues, 'to ask you to be gentle with her. She's had a terrible evening. She's in a very vulnerable state but she's extremely determined. She insisted we come over here. She longs to make amends so that she can offer her first prayer with a clear conscience and an open heart.'

'Sorry – so that's ... that's actually *her*? Outside? In the car?'

Sheila finally makes sense of the situation. The woman nods, gravely.

'But I thought …?'
Sheila limps over to the front window, her heart beating faster. 'Bloody hell. Who *are* you people?'
She turns, her face draining of colour.
'All will be well, *Inshallah*,' the woman murmurs.

Gene checks his phone. He has ten missed calls. He can't bear to hear them, just shakes his head, shoves the phone into his trouser pocket and peers over on to the back seat. He grabs his jacket, frowns, cranes his neck, removes his keys from the ignition, jumps out of the car, pulls open the back door and peers inside again. No bugle case. No bugle.

He scratches his head. He sniffs his jacket. He pulls on his jacket, mystified, slams both doors shut, secures the car and heads off.

He takes the back route to Ransom's room. When he arrives at the door he tries the handle and finds it locked. He frowns. He knocks. Nothing. He knocks again. After several seconds Ransom pulls the door open. He is shirtless, holding a glass of whisky – no ice this time – and seems drunk and belligerent.

'Where the fuck've *you* been?' he demands. Gene looks past him, into the room. The tattoo bench is still set up. The gun lies on the bed, and a small tray holding dozens of little plastic thimbles full of ink.

'Where is everyone?' he asks.
'Gone.'
Ransom staggers over to the bed – a trail of blood dripping down his back – and collapses on to it. 'All buggered off.'

'Everyone?'
Gene shuts the door.
'Let's see …' Ransom tries to shape his thoughts into some kind of order.
'Terry – twinky little photo dude – went out for a fag. Never came back. Then his assistant goes – forget his name – same

thing. Nimrod gets a call from the front desk. Seems they've been appre –' Ransom hiccups; 'hendy –' he hiccups again; 'hendy – appre –' He blinks.

'Apprehended.'

'By Security.' Ransom nods. 'So Nimrod goes on a mission to try and get 'em back again. Valentine – tattoo girl – is in the bathroom –'

'What's she doing in the bathroom?' Gene interrupts.

'Having a friggin' meltdown because poor old Tobe is ...'

He turns his face away and inhales, sharply.

'Tobe?' Gene echoes. 'Toby?'

'Crow-bait,' Ransom squeaks.

'Crow ...?'

'Kicked in,' he groans. 'Checked out. Popped off. Belly-up. *Crow*-bait.'

Gene stands where he is, momentarily incapable of movement or speech. Then:

'Toby's *dead*?'

'I mean this was *my* moment!' Ransom protests. 'I was being so, friggin' *brave*. I was sucking it all up, man! I was *growing*! I was learning all this shit about myself – all this profound, fucking shit about myself. I was confronting my fear, Gino! It was like ... it was friggin' *magical*. Friggin' *magical*, man! I was so strong. So *alive*. Then all of a sudden ...' Ransom gestures. 'Phone rings. Tobe's dead. Toby's friggin' *dead*. The friggin' ... the stupid, friggin' *prick*! The *idiot*!'

He shakes his head, disbelieving. Gene opens his mouth to speak.

'I mean there *you* are,' Ransom gestures, dismissively, struggling to hold back the tears, 'ten times with cancer. All that friggin' *fuss*, all that friggin' *drama*. All the ladies lapping it up. Wearing the badge – selling the friggin' *T*-shirt. And there's old Tobe ...' – he shakes his head – 'stupid, boring, dusty old Tobe who can't even friggin' *drive* ...'

He falls backwards on the bed, drink held aloft, upsetting several of the little pots of ink. Most tip on to the tray, but a couple fall clear. Gene watches, horrified, as their contents slowly spread across the counterpane.

'... and he just gently ups and pops his little clogs.'

'But I was with him only a couple of hours ago ...' Gene murmurs, still not quite believing it.

'You think your presence is enough to shield him from *death*?!' Ransom sneers, struggling to pull himself straight again. Gene goes over to give him a hand.

'I saw him a couple of hours ago and he was fine,' Gene insists. 'He fixed the electricity meter. He seemed really ...' Gene frowns. 'He seemed really fine, really cheerful.'

'Well he wasn't fine,' Ransom corrects him, drolly, 'he was dying. We are *all* dying, Gino. We are *all* slowly dying. But Tobe did it quicker. Tobe cut to the chase. He got in there first. Tobe beat me and he beat you – beat *you*, Gino,' Ransom emphasizes. 'How d'you feel about that, eh?' He grins. 'Tobe did it first. He paid a debt we all must pay. He beat *you*. Came first. Won the death trophy. Held it high. *Attaboy*, Tobe!'

Ransom clumsily applauds an invisible, triumphant Toby, his drink sloshing everywhere, then slowly shakes his head (plainly deeply moved by his own gripping summation).

'How did you find out?'

Gene gathers up the spilt ink pots (as if keeping his hands busy will preclude a sudden descent into jabbering insanity). 'Tattoo girl got a call from her brother ...' Ransom sighs. 'Noel rang her. Said he got home and the whole friggin' kitchen was full of water. He left the tap on – Tobe. Getting himself a drink. I dunno ...' Ransom waves his arm. 'Washing up. I dunno. Anyway, he was sitting in a chair – rocker – dead as a dodo. Dead as a doornail.'

'But what about ...?' Gene starts off – a thousand questions springing to mind.

'He called the police,' Ransom continues, oblivious. 'They were on their way over. His mum was curled up on the sofa with the kid. Happy as Larry they were! TV blaring. Hadn't noticed a thing. Fucking amazing! Didn't even know there was a corpse in the kitchen. Fucking amazing!'

Ransom salutes this astonishing fact with his glass.

'So Valentine went straight home?' Gene asks. 'Did she get a cab?'

'Nope. She locked herself in the bathroom. She was already in the bathroom – that's why I took the call.'

'Sorry?' Gene interrupts his frenzied tidying. 'You took the call?'

'From Noel.' Ransom nods. 'She was locked in the bathroom.'

'But when did …?'

'Uh … after photo-twink went outside. Saw you weren't there. She did her nut, pretty much.'

Ransom shakes his head, mournfully. 'Not good. Definitely not a good look, Gino – leaving that poor mental-case in the lurch like that. You let us down badly, there, Gino. You fucked up, man. You let down the tattoo girl. You let *me* down. I mean fuck only knows what I've got on my back right now …'

He tries to peer over his shoulder then gives up. 'Hurts like friggin' hell, I know that much.'

'So she got a cab home?'

Gene starts to pack up the tattoo bench, realizes that his fingers are all inky and goes to pull a couple of tissues from a box on the bedside table.

'Nope. No cab. She called in the Gestapo.'

'Sorry?'

'Friggin' …' Ransom gesticulates, inarticulately. 'Said she was giving up tattooing. Said it was a sign. All wrapped up in a towel, she was. Nuts! Mascara down her cheeks. Zombie eyes. *Burning!* Demented! Comes barrelling out of the bathroom, snatches her phone, makes a call. Next thing I know there's two women banging on the door like the secret police. Cover her up in a shroud and carry her off. Kidnap her. Can't see their faces. They won't meet my eyes – 's like I'm friggin' *invisible* or something! Completely shat me up! I mean I'm still in a state of *grief*! I've got blood and shit running down my back! This isn't finished! I'm a work in progress!'

'Did she seem frightened of these women?' Gene demands, heart thumping. 'Did they introduce themselves?'

'Kept calling her "Hammer! Hammer!"'

'Hammer?'

'Yeah. She's going, "I can't go home! I can't go back there! My sanctuary was my prison! My mother was my jailor!" Crazy, dramatic shit like in a really bad film. *Craaazy* shit! And they're wrapped around her like two jackdaws, squawking. He just looks at me, like, "This is fucked." I'm like, "You're telling me, mate! This is some crazy, screwed-up shit, man."'

'He?' Gene interrupts.

'Eh?'

Ransom momentarily loses his flow.

'He? There was a man?'

'Yeah, with the kid – looking after the kid. It's like a family outing! He goes, "What can I do?" Shrugs. Seemed a nice enough bloke. I'm like, "Can't you control your women? You got 'em wrapped up like friggin' … friggin' … black … Like friggin'" …'

Words fail him. He knocks back the rest of his glass.

Gene quickly finishes folding up the bench. He throws everything else into Valentine's holdall, closes it and straightens up.

'What are you doing?' Ransom wonders, watching him, blearily.

'I should probably head over to the house. Take this equipment back. See what's going on. See if everyone's all right.'

'What about me?' Ransom demands. 'What do *I* do now? There's no one here! I'm in grief! Tobe's dead! I've not had any dinner! I got blood all down my friggin' back!'

Gene re-opens the holdall and removes a plastic roll of sterilized wipes.

'I'll clean it up. Just turn around.'

Ransom turns, like an obliging child, arms raised.

'*Fuuuck!*' he gasps. 'Hurts like hell when I move my arms. *Fuuuck*. That stings, man.'

Gene removes a handful of wipes from the container and gently dabs away at the streaks of blood. The purple felt-tip doesn't shift too readily. There is a measure of swelling. After a minute or so the tattoo-work becomes more visible. There's a little ring of exquisitely drawn grass, a fairy-ring, a *wreath*, almost. Gene shudders.

'How's it look?' Ransom demands.

'Uh ... Good. It's like a perfect, little ring of grass. It looks great. Considering she'd only just started, it looks surprisingly finished – complete, almost.'

He reaches down to look inside Valentine's holdall for some kind of cream or lubricant. He finds something he deems appropriate, opens the jar and dabs some on.

'You should probably have a couple of glasses of water, order a sandwich from room-service then go to bed. Lie on your front. Try and keep the wound as clean as you possibly can ... in fact ...'

He is about to close the holdall and notices some large, plastic bandages.

'I could put on one of these bandages if you like, just until the thing stops bleeding.'

'It's still bleeding?' Ransom looks terrified.

'Just slightly. Only because I cleaned it ...'

Gene pulls out a bandage and inspects it, trying to work out how it should be applied. This simple task suddenly seems way beyond his reach. Ransom, meanwhile, collapses sideways, on to the bed and immediately starts to drift off. After thirty seconds he emits a gentle snore. Gene grimaces, abandons the bandage and clambers to his feet.

'Get Esther to order me a big, meat pasty.' Ransom's eyes flicker open as the mattress shifts. 'This was *my* night! *My* friggin' night!' He waggles a censorious finger. 'Lazy, useless, good-for-nothin' friggin' … friggin' *slut*!'

Sheila climbs into the back of the car. A woman – entirely veiled, who refuses all eye contact – softly introduces herself as Aamilah. She sits between the two of them – a young girl sleeping on her lap – representing a slight but indomitable human buffer. Valentine is dressed in a voluminous black robe. Her head is wrapped in a colourful shawl. She is gripping on to a grey towel.

'Are you all right?' Sheila asks in hushed tones, eager not to disturb the child, leaning over, trying to touch her hand. 'I thought you were over at the golf club tonight?'

'There's so much …' Valentine makes a tiny, frantic gesture, pulling her hand away. 'I can't.'
She covers her face and breaks down into sobs.

'*Hush! Hush!*' the woman cautions her. 'Calm yourself! Remember your dignity! You'll wake Badriya!'
'Sorry!'
Valentine shakes her head.

'She's very confused,' the other woman interprets. 'It's been an extremcly stressful and upsetting night for her – but an *important* night, huh?'
She nudges Valentine's arm. Valentine nods. 'Yes. Yes,' biting her lip.

'And now there's something she needs to get off her chest,' the woman continues.

'What is it?' Sheila leans further forward. 'Valentine?'

'*Please!*' The woman lifts a warning hand, making it clear that her space has been encroached upon. Sheila draws back again, riled.

'I've given up tattooing,' Valentine whispers, then, 'Don't say anything! It's the only thing to do. It's necessary. It's ...' She looks to the veiled woman.

'*Haram,*' the woman fills in, gently rocking the child.

'I don't ...' Sheila frowns. 'Look, we can't talk properly like this. Why don't you just come inside for a minute? I can make you a cup of tea.'

'It was all leading here,' Valentine doggedly persists. 'To this place. To this sacrifice. Like you were saying this morning. About the train – what happened. That promise you made. It's the only way I can feel right – shake the guilt – the fear – by giving up everything I care about.'

'You're obviously very tired.' Sheila leans forward and tries to comfort her. 'It's been a long day ...'

'I burned the wallet and the other stuff. I ... I ... Noel said he was going to give it to a museum,' Valentine stutters, overwhelmed.

'Hamra,' the second woman interrupts her, 'you're avoiding the issue. Come *on*, now. We haven't got all night! Just tell her!'

'I slept with Gene,' Valentine continues, almost without pausing, gently rocking. 'Last night. And I'm so sorry – *so* sorry. I know you must hate me and I don't blame you. I hate myself. I just want to beg your forgiveness so that ...'

'She's throwing herself on your mercy,' the veiled woman interprets.

Sheila is silent for a minute, then, 'There's really no need for all of this,' she murmurs (unsure whether she's actually addressing herself or Valentine). 'No need for all of this ...

this *drama*. It's absolutely fine. You're just scared. You're just confused. It's going to be absolutely –'

'Do you forgive her?' the veiled woman demands.

Sheila gazes at her for a moment, stunned by her insensitivity. 'Of course I'll forgive her!' she hisses. 'Of *course* I will, but on my own terms thank you very much!'

'Don't forgive me, Sheila!' Valentine whispers. 'Make it harder for me! *Please!*'

She clenches the towel with her fingers, rocking frenetically. The child stirs.

'It's time to get Badriya back to bed,' the woman cordially informs them both.

Sheila sits in silence for a minute.

'Don't do anything rash because of me,' she gently appeals, 'let's just …'

'I'm not. I'm not.' Valentine shakes her head, tears trickling down her cheeks.

Sheila leans forward again.

'Remember, I'm here for you. I can support you. Nothing's set in stone. This is all just a terrible mistake. I'm sure things will look better in the morning.'

'Please try and calm yourself,' the woman firmly counsels, raising a warning hand again.

'I *am* calm.' Sheila scowls.

'There's a child present,' the woman adds.

'I'm *perfectly* calm,' Sheila repeats, through gritted teeth.

'Good' – the woman nods – 'because you're not the only person on earth whose husband has ever been unfaithful. Try and remember that. You're not alone in all of this.'

Sheila glares at the woman.

'I'm not sure how helpful your contribution is at this stage,' she says.

'You're upset,' the woman sighs, 'you feel the need to lash out, *BarakAllahu feekum* – may Allah bless you.'

Sheila is seething with rage now.

'How old are you?' she asks.

'Valentine knows what she's doing.' The woman ignores her question. 'She's made her decision. She's done the right thing. She has repented. She feels a great peace. She knows that she is among friends.'

'I'm so sorry, Sheila,' Valentine murmurs.

'You've apologized,' the woman counsels her. 'You've been very brave. You can't do anything more than that. Remember, Allah willed this. It was pre-determined. Everything happens for a reason. I'm really, *really* proud of you, Hamra. Congratulations.'

She pats Valentine's knee.

'Well done.'

The woman finishes speaking and indicates towards the second, veiled woman – Farhana – through the car window.

Valentine puts her face in her hands and starts crying again. Sheila can't tell whether these are now tears of fear, of guilt or of relief. The door on her side of the car is pulled open.

'Can I help you out?' Farhana asks, indicating towards Sheila's injured leg, concerned. She offers Sheila her hand. Sheila doesn't take it for a few seconds then finally relents. 'Thank you.'

Farhana helps her from the car, then slowly leads her back to the house.

'I can tell that there is a great need in you to do good, Sheila,' she murmurs, 'a powerful need. It's so strong, so beautiful – it shines out of you. It surrounds everything you do. Remember: God loves you and blesses you with all your interior struggles. *JazakAllah!* May God reward you for all your kindness and understanding.'

She lifts Sheila's hand to her lips and kisses it through her veil.

'I hope your leg gets better soon. *Fi Amanullah!* May God love and protect you.'

'She places Sheila on the doormat inside the hallway, gently closes the door and silently retreats. Sheila stands there for several minutes, before, 'He *slept* with her?'
She remains exactly where she is for another couple of minutes then performs a rapid, 180-degree turn.
'He *slept* with her?' she demands, scowling (of the opposite wall, now), perhaps hoping – somewhat naively – for a different response.

14

Jen happens across Nimrod in the car park having a crafty fag. He looks up, scowling, as she approaches. She is heavily burdened by luggage – a hefty travel-bag slung over one shoulder and an instrument case in either hand.

'D'you hear about Toby?' he asks.

'Nope.' Jen shakes her head. 'What about him?'

'He was doing your baby-sitting gig last night and suffered a massive aneurysm – brain haemorrhage – or that's what they're saying.'

'Toby's dead?!' Jen's jaw drops. She promptly dumps her luggage.

'Yup.' Nimrod nods.

'Bloody hell!' She gazes at him, amazed. 'How's Ransom doing?'

She reaches for Nimrod's cigarette.

'He's great. Got up at sunrise – sheet glued to his back. Spewed his guts out. Had a shower. Ate a huge breakfast. Went over to the driving range. Tried a few shots. Realized that his back was all tight and scabbed up. Modified his swing. Headed out on to the course and hit three eagles in a row. Burst into tears. Is still out there, celebrating. Keeps saying, "Pain is the answer! Need more pain! Pain is the solution! Life is pain! Pain is life!" Crap like that.'

'Wow.' Jen takes a quick puff of Nimrod's smoke.

'Business as usual,' Nimrod grins, weakly.

'Wow.' Jen takes a second puff. 'That's so fucked up.'

'I was very fond of old Tobe,' he sighs.

'He still had so much to give.' Jen nods. 'What future nine-hole?'

'Turbo Golf?' Nimrod shrugs.

'Tragic.'

'The economic arguments for it were certainly always fairly persuasive,' Nimrod loyally opines.

'Not to mention the environmental ones. I said as much to him myself.'

'I mean just on logistical grounds alone, his position was virtually unassailable.'

'Maybe Ransom should really get behind the idea,' Jen suggests. 'Build a nine-hole foundation – use his celebrity to create a proper legacy, as a tribute.'

'Yeah.' Nimrod nods, reaching out for his cigarette. 'Sweet thought.'

Jen surveys the car park.

'Gene here yet?'

'Nope.'

'I saw the piece you did …' Jen winces.

'Like it?'

'It was very well-constructed,' Jen concedes. 'Nicely punctuated. Great use of the semi-colon in the second paragraph. Interesting mixture of nouns and adjectives.'

'Aw, thanks, Jen,' Nimrod mugs.

'Although I'm not sure how happy Gene'll be with it.'

'I've had about thirty texts already.' Nimrod pulls out his phone. 'People are loving the whole cancer/palmist angle. *Chat* want a two page spread. *Take-a-Break* have me on redial.'

'This is your Woodward and Bernstein moment!' Jen baby-claps.

'Yeah. So proud!' Nimrod gushes.

'Nothing so strange as the truth, I guess,' Jen muses.

'You reckon?' Nimrod doesn't look convinced.

'I mean he lost the ball, he lost his balls … great hook.' She pauses. '*Did* he lose his balls, though?'

'I believe one still remains intact, the other is silicone.'

'Really? He told you that?'

'No, I think you told me that.'

'Wow.' Jen takes back the cigarette. 'I swear to God the man's my hero. He's my rock. I just … I just completely and utterly adore him.'

She blinks back *faux*-tears, then inhales.

'One of the good guys.' Nimrod nods, slightly confused.

'Like Tobe,' she exhales.

'Yeah. Like Tobe.'

'Good old Tobe.'

'Yeah. Good old Tobe. God bless him.'

Nimrod reaches out for his cigarette. Jen passes it over and picks up her bags. 'We move on!' she trills, tripping off in her heels.

Nimrod nods, grimacing, fag dangling from the corner of his lip, already distracted, his finger jabbing out a text.

Sheila is completing last night's washing-up as Gene enters the kitchen. Mallory is sitting at the breakfast bar, hunched over a bowl of burned porridge.

'Mum burned the porridge,' she groans, '*again*.'

'Yum!' Gene smiles.

'Enjoy your shower?' Sheila glances over her shoulder, smiling.

'Uh … Yes. Thanks.'

Gene pulls out a stool and sits down. He notices that Sheila is wearing her old, college-era red and black mohair jumper over her standard religious garb and that her hair has been washed and … Was that actually *gel*? In the fringe?

He removes an orange from a nearby fruit bowl and tosses it, slightly anxious, from hand to hand.

'She's changed her mind about going away,' Mallory tells him with an exaggerated eye-roll.

'Has she, indeed?'

Gene looks over at his wife –

A hint of lightly tinted lip salve?

Sheila is wiping down the draining-board.

'I'm leaving the pan in to soak,' she says.

'Then I suppose I should lug the case back up into the loft again,' he tells Mallory.

'Good!' Mallory's obviously still smarting from the whole Jamaica interlude. 'Before some idiot breaks their neck on it.'

'Right. If you've eaten all you want then you'd better finish off getting ready for school,' Sheila tells her, reaching for the bowl. Mallory happily submits. She stomps out of the kitchen.

'She's delighted, really.' Gene smiles.

'I know.' Sheila nods.

Gene digs his fingers into the orange and starts to peel it. He feels stuck for words.

'I *know*,' Sheila repeats, more emphatically. Gene continues peeling. Sheila returns to the sink.

'And I'm actually fine about it,' she adds.

'How's the leg?' Gene changes the subject (although he isn't entirely sure what the subject currently is).

'I retied the bandage. It came loose overnight.'

Sheila carefully lifts up her trouser to demonstrate what a great job she's done.

Gene tries to focus on the bandage, but he suddenly finds it hard to look at her, as if she's bathed in a bright light or standing above him, looking down, the sun at her back, smiling, in a park, on a picnic, like in the old days.

'It actually feels a lot better this morning than I thought it would.'

She rolls the trouser down again. 'So what time did you finally get in last night?'

'I can't look at you,' he says.

She doesn't respond. He *can't* look at her. He wonders if he's about to burst into tears. Scream. Fall off his chair as though hit by a sudden burst of mortar fire.

'Just after four,' he eventually grinds out. 'I must've fallen asleep over the steering wheel for an hour or so.'

'Yes.' Sheila nods. 'I saw you through the window – dead to the world.'

He finishes peeling the orange and stares at it, helplessly. He supposes that he is now obliged to eat the damn thing.

'You were still up?' he asks, pulling off a segment.

She nods again.

'Is there something …?' he asks, then finds it impossible to finish his sentence so pops the segment into his mouth and chews.

'Valentine's converting to Islam,' Sheila informs him, her tone studiedly casual. 'She came over last night with a couple of friends. I was completely …' She struggles to find the right word. 'Banjaxed. It really was extraordinary – completely extraordinary –'

'I found Jen,' Gene interrupts her, after swallowing.

'Yes. I got your text. What a relief!'

Mallory wanders into the kitchen to try and locate a lost hairband.

'Will the police need to speak with you again?' Sheila wonders.

'Uh … I'm not sure. I shouldn't think so. I suppose it depends on what they discover in the autopsy.'

'So sad.' Sheila shakes her head.

'He seemed like a very sweet man.'

Mallory leaves the room again.

Sheila looks at her watch. Gene pulls off another segment of the orange and places it into his mouth where it sits on his tongue like a small, indigestible missile. The effort of working his jaw seems almost beyond him.

'Just for the record,' Sheila murmurs, her eyes focused on his lips, 'I'm not angry about what happened – I mean I was upset at first – more astonished than anything – disappointed. And I'm not standing here and suggesting that I'm entirely blameless – I mean I'm hardly perfect – I suppose I must've deserved this at some level –'

'Please don't say that!' Gene interrupts her, horrified, the lone segment blocking up his tongue, falling into his cheek, making him lisp. He stares at the orange in his hand. He hates the stupid orange. So bright. So tart. So complete.

'I don't want to apportion blame, Gene,' Sheila sighs, 'and I don't want to pass judgement – in fact I don't actually want to *talk* about it. I just want to ...'
She throws up her hands. 'To forgive you, I suppose. To draw this act of generosity from deep within myself and pass it over to you, like a gift. Sidestep all the rancour and the unpleasantness and just ...'
She shakes her head. 'Carry on. Battle on. Try and survive it.'

Gene laboriously chews and swallows the orange segment as she speaks. The act of doing so seems like the most awful – the most crass and monstrous – offence against her dignity.

'That's very big of you,' he mutters after swallowing. His voice sounds tighter – less humble and obsequious – than he'd expected it to.

'I'm actually grateful,' Sheila confesses, with a rueful laugh, 'to get this rare opportunity to be the bigger person. After the initial shock there was just this ... this immense – this overriding feeling of ... I suppose I can only call it relief. Just ...' – she shakes her head – 'this sense of calm, of certainty, that we'd be fine – that *I'd* be fine. In fact this act of betrayal – this horrendous show of weakness on your part – might actually be a kind of ... a *test* – a way of drawing me still further into my faith – of bringing me still closer to God.'

Gene continues to stare at the orange. He imagines repeatedly stabbing at it with a fork.

'Obviously to lose her to "the other side" ...' Sheila concedes, her smile faltering, 'and I know it's childish of me – pathetic, even. But to ... *Urgh!*'

She smashes her fist on to the laminate in front of him. Gene almost jumps out of his skin.

'Oh dear. How embarrassing!'

She withdraws her fist and stares at it, slightly confused.

'I'm really sorry, Sheila,' he mutters, 'I just feel so ...'

'That was a difficult pill for me to swallow,' she runs on, oblivious. 'And it's crazy because it's the same God – you know – the same God – *my* God – *our* God – just viewed through a slightly different pair of spectacles.'

Gene puts down the remains of the orange. They both stare at it.

'I still trust you,' she adds, 'weird as that may seem. I still have confidence in you. I still *believe* in you. And I want you to be happy.'

'I love you too,' Gene responds, automatically, then realizes that she hasn't actually said that she loves him and feels ridiculous. Sheila stares at him, frowning slightly.

'This feels odd,' he confides, 'to be having this conversation. Unreal. Like we're not really ... like we're ...'

'But on the positive side,' she calmly talks through him, 'it's like the boil has finally been lanced. This has been a major wake-up call. I've had to weigh up my priorities – move out of my comfort zone – no more faffing around. And it's actually come as something of a relief ...

'*Phew!*' She physically demonstrates her relief, grinning.

Gene reaches out his hand and starts carefully separating the orange segments, as if the orange alone represents something actual – something tangible.

'I mean I always thought you were so perfect – so good – so honourable. And now I've finally realized that you're just a normal, flawed human being like the rest of us I ... I don't know … It's as though this awful burden has been lifted. I feel like I can …' She inhales deeply.

Mallory wanders into the kitchen again. She's looking for her lunch box. Sheila removes it from the fridge and passes it to her. She wanders out again.

'Maybe you're still a little angry,' Gene suggests.
'You want me to be?' Sheila asks, almost pitying.
Gene withdraws his hand from the orange.
What if I said yes? he thinks. What then?

'You look tired,' Sheila observes, 'pale.'
'I feel exhausted,' he confesses, rubbing his eyes with his hand. A second or so later he realizes that his fingers still have citric acid on their tips. His eyes start to sting.

Sheila checks her watch again. 'Go back to bed. I'll prepare you a quick tray. Sweet tea. Cornflakes. Bring it up before we leave.'

Gene feels the straightness gradually leaving his spine. Something is being extracted. Something is being exacted. He's just not sure how or why or what, precisely, just that it must be and that it is.

'Killing me with kindness,' he murmurs, trying to look up at her, but still, the light, and now, the sting. Sheila leans forward and picks up the orange peel, presses the pedal on the bin with a quick pump of her foot and tosses it away.

'We should probably …'
Gene is going to say, 'compost that,' but then – for reasons he can't quite entirely fathom – decides against it.

'So Tiger Woods has just won the British Open.' Ransom lowers the bugle and wipes the spit away from his top lip with the palm of his hand. 'He's wending his way down the Galway coast to the Irish Open in this stunning 3 Series 325Ci Rwd BMW Convertible –'

'Hang on a second,' Jen interrupts, lowering her trombone, 'why would Tiger be in a car?'

'Sorry?' Ransom turns and glowers at her.

'Tiger Woods would just fly into the Irish Open on his private jet.'

'Anyway,' the golfer staunchly continues, using the flap of his shirt to polish the bugle's mouthpiece (no evidence of a tremor in either hand), 'he arrives at this tiny, little service station in the middle of nowhere and this thick-as-shit Irishman comes toddling outside to fill up his tank ...'

Jen cringes. Ransom pretends not to notice.

'So he jumps out of the car to go get himself a bottle of water from the shop ...'

'A shop?' Jen snorts. 'I thought this was meant to be some tiny, primitive little service station in the middle of nowhere?'

'... and as he clambers out, a couple of golf tees fall from his pocket ...' Ransom persists, then pauses (although there's actually no interruption from Jen at this juncture), '... so the little Irish ...'

'Yeah, yeah,' Jen makes a 'let's just skip the racist bullshit, already,' gesture.

'... jumps forward and scoops them up off the forecourt. He holds them out to Tiger and says ...' (Ransom adopts a dreadful, Irish accent), '"Sure, what are those tings, there, Tiger?"'

'Ha!' Jen laughs.

'That's not the punchline,' Ransom curtly informs her.

'So we're seriously meant to believe,' Jen scoffs, 'that this service-station attendant knows the identity of Tiger Woods – a golfer – but is still incapable of identifying one of the world's most basic pieces of golfing equipment, the tee?'

'... and Tiger says ...'

'That's ridiculous!'

'... and Tiger says ...'

'Completely ridiculous – and not in a funny way, either.'

'And Tiger says, "They're for balancing your balls on when you're driving!"'

Jen gazes at him, blankly.

'Then the little Irish … anyway' – Ransom waves his own hand (mirroring Jen's earlier gesture) – 'he says, "My God, those clever people at BMW tink of everyting, don't they?!"'

No reaction from Jen.

'"Those clever people at BMW tink of everyting, don't they?!"' Ransom repeats.

'I get it,' Jen assures him, 'I just think the joke would be funnier if it wasn't so obviously the work of a puffed-up BMW marketing department somewhere.'

'It's not about BMW,' Ransom objects.

'It would be way better if the car was an Irish make.'

'Irish?!' Ransom scoffs. 'What? Like the DeLorean DMC-12?'

'Why not?' Jen shrugs.

'Because that'd be an altogether different kind of joke, you friggin' idiot!' Ransom protests.

'We should go surfing,' Jen suddenly suggests, catching sight of a distant – plainly frazzled – Del Renzio on the skyline, heading towards them, Terence Nimrod in hot pursuit.

'Surfing?' Ransom scowls.

'Yeah. You and me. Take the brass. Pack up the motor. Buy a litre bottle of white rum. Head down to Cornwall.'

She starts to deconstruct her trombone and return it to its case.

'We don't have a motor,' Ransom demurs.

'We'll get Nimrod to drive us in his car.'

'I'm broke,' he confesses.

'There's always my savings from the hotel.'

'But I've just got my swing back!' Ransom protests.

'Exactly.' Jen nods.

'How d'you mean, "exactly"?' Ransom demands, putting the bugle away, somewhat regretfully.

'Delayed gratification,' Jen opines, gnomically, 'it's the new black.'

'What?'

'Ever heard of the theory that walking away from something is actually the best way of walking towards it?'

Ransom thinks for a moment.

'Nope.'

Jen fastens the clasp on her trombone case and picks it up. She's ready to go.

'You never told me what you did to your hands.' Ransom is staring at her mangled fingertips, intrigued.

'Let's save that for the journey.' Jen grins, then winks, then starts off. Ransom gazes after her, perplexed.

'But I just got my swing back!' he murmurs, hurt.

'I'm certain the Irish have produced other cars,' Jen yells over her shoulder, leaving the green and entering the rough, '*way* better than the DeLorean.'

'Bollocks!' Ransom yells. 'Unless you're thinking of the friggin' Shamrock!'

He curls his lip, derisively.

'How about the TMC Costin?' Jen demands (full volume).

'It went bankrupt in the friggin' eighties, you twit!' Ransom bellows.

'They sold the chassis rights to an American auto developer,' Jen bellows back, her voice getting lost in the gentle wind, 'by the name of Daniel Panoz. The Panoz Roadster remains in production to the present day and is still based on the Costin design!'

Ransom struggles to process this information.

'We'll need a photographer!' Jen adds (full volume). 'For the holiday.'

'What?!' Ransom scowls (barely audible).

'Bloody BMW!' Jen cackles, gesturing obscenely. 'You're such an old, corporate whore! WHORE!' she repeats (another gesture – in case he can't quite hear her). 'It's so embarrassing! EMBARRASSING!'

Ransom remains where he is for a few seconds longer (deeply offended), then swears under his breath, shakes his head, picks up the bugle case (wincing slightly as he straightens up), inhales deeply, winces again, embraces the pain (C'mon! Embrace the pain you old fool! Embrace it!) and rapidly strikes out after her.